A TIME OI

COME EVIL DAYS

From Across the World Torsten Fredriksson, 26 September 1941 – For immediate release:

Hitler stands poised on the cutting edge of victory, just as did Napoleon at Borodino 129 years ago. His string of victories is unbroken in the east but autumn weather is bearing down and the rains will start soon. And in mid-October, winter.

Still, Smolensk has fallen, the last great fortress before the capital. Hitler's military genius has not yet failed, nor that of the German army.

Russia and Great Britain reel in uneasy alliance, battered by and separated by two thousand kilometres of victorious German Army, Navy and Air Force. September, October, November, December. Are these the final four months of Western European civilisation as it is now constituted?

Also by Joe Poyer in Sphere Books:

THE CHINESE AGENDA
THE CONTRACT
THE DAY OF RECKONING
OPERATION MALACCA
THE BALKAN ASSIGNMENT
NORTH CAPE
VENGEANCE 10
TUNNEL WAR
DEVOTED FRIENDS
A TIME OF WAR: THE TRANSGRESSORS

A Time of War
Volume II
Come Evil Days

JOE POYER

SPHERE BOOKS LIMITED
London and Sydney

First published in Great Britain by
Sphere Books Ltd
30–32 Gray's Inn Road, London WC1X 8JL

TRADE
MARK

Set in Plantin

Printed and bound in Great Britain by
Cox & Wyman Ltd, Reading

For those who sacrificed,
from one who benefited.

To every thing there is a season, and a time to every
purpose under heaven:
A time to be born, and a time to die; a time to plant,
and a time to pluck up that which is planted;
A time to kill, and a time to heal; a time to mourn
and a time to dance;
A time to cast away stones, and a time to gather stones
together; a time to embrace and a time to refrain from
embracing;
A time to get, and a time to lose; a time to keep, and a
time to cast away;
A time to rend, and a time to sew; a time to keep silence,
and a time to speak;
A time to love, and a time to hate; a time of war, and a
time of peace.
Ecclesiastes 3:1

MAIN AND SECONDARY CHARACTERS

Torsten Fredriksson	Swedish journalist and narrator
Jeanette Rodale	French artist, heiress and his lover
Rolle Taubmann	Gestapo, Paris
Keith Thorne	American pilot
Jacob Yitzak	Polish musician
David Yitzak	Polish army officer
Deborah Yitzak	Wife of David and then Keith
Shirley Case	Keith's fiancée
Keith Thorne, Senior	His father
Charlotte Simpson	His lover
Friedrich Prager	German Panzer officer
Sonja Vishenka	His wife
Joachim Brenner	Army officer and boyhood friend
Erwin Rommel	Commands Seventh Panzer Division in France
Klaus Mahr	Commands Security Company at Slavets
Charles Atkins	British attaché and tank officer
Johan Erko	Finnish staff assistant to Marshall Carl von Mannerheim
Erika Brotherus	*Lotta Svard* volunteer
Lers Radikko	Finnish army officer
Timothy O'Brien	Sergeant-Major, Royal New Zealand Army
Wendy Hiller	Yorkshire librarian
Rand Dobson	Officer, Royal Australian Navy
John Peters	Commander, HMS *Adelaide*, Royal Navy
Sir Martin Dunbar-Naismith	Admiral Commanding, Western Approaches
Leon Tarkington	Captain, HMS *Hara*, Royal Navy
Walter James	Surgeon, HMS *Sanda*, Royal Navy
David Fletcher	Surgeon, HMS *Sanda*, Royal Navy
Alfredo Marchetti	Officer, Italian Army
Guilo Maroni	Captain, Italian Army

Vincente Osano	Colonel, Italian Army
Hans Jurgensen	Obersturmfuehrer, Norwegian SS Viking Regiment, Sixth SS Division
Mikhail Gregor Dogorov	Officer, Red Army
Olga Semonova Dogorova	His mother
Alexander Prokovitch Braun	Sergeant, Red Army
Alexander Ivanovitch Siderov	Second in Command, Battery A, Third Regiment, Fourth Army
Vera Andropova Shatnikova	Childhood friend and lover in Moscow
André Smirnovitch Sinhovsky	Commands Battery A, Forty-Second Artillery Regiment, Tula
Lev Raiken	Commissar, Forty-Second Artillery Regiment, Tula
Valenka - Valentina Orlova Shemenkova	Mess Attendant, Forty-Second Artillery Regiment, and Dogorov's lover
Saburo Takeda	Officer, Sixth Sasebo Special Naval Landing Force
Ryuko Takeda	Younger sister
Michitaka Takeda	Younger brother
Mariko Sumata	Announcer, Radio Tokyo
Gohay Ueda	Senior Warrant officer
Jacob Suranyo	Japanese interpreter

FOREWORD

Come Evil Days is the second book of a multi-volume novel, *A Time of War*, which deals with people involved in the greatest human catastrophe in recorded history. The effects of this obscene conflict are felt today and will probably shape events for a thousand years to come. While it was begun by politicians and jingoists manipulating historical imperatives, it was fought by ordinary men and women. Beyond patriotism, political naïveté or fear of the consequences should they refuse, each person who participated had his or her own reasons for doing so, else the war could not have been fought.

I have chosen seven warriors – American, Australian, British, German, Italian, Japanese, Russian – and one neutral Swedish journalist, from which to distil the horror of World War II. None of these eight men are heroes or cowards, fools or geniuses and none have a measurable effect on great events. They live and die as no more than they are, like the millions who did so in actuality, and when they have finished, perhaps we will have gained a bit more insight into the reasons why human beings dedicate more energy and treasure to the business of killing one another in organised warfare than in any other endeavour.

As in the first volume, *The Transgressors*, I must caution the reader that I have made every effort to eliminate forty-plus years of hindsight and prejudice and to present the incidents of war as the characters involved would have viewed them. If a character's perceptions seem less than yours, please remember the years that have passed – also that the combat soldier knows less about what is going on than anyone else. Also remember that while his prejudices may not be yours, yours might seem equally bizarre to him.

The reader will find no 'good-guy versus bad-guy' treatment in *A Time of War*. Such simplistic concepts exist only in the minds of propagandists and rarely in the perceptions of the man at the 'sharp end'. Victors write history but never a balanced picture.

All characters, except historical personages, are entirely fictitious and any resemblance to persons living or dead is purely coincidental. All military unit designations, with very few exceptions, below Army level are also fictitious.

I have taken every care to make certain that information presented in *A Time of War* is correct but I beg the reader's indulgence for any errors encountered. The various manuscripts have been in preparation for six years and more than four hundred interviews and research notes were compiled during the past twenty years. Many, many people have helped me with information, diaries, photographs and personal stories and many have volunteered to read the final manuscripts for accuracy. But when all is said and done, I must and do take full responsibility for any errors of fact or omission.

My special thanks and a great debt of gratitude are due to Robert Gillon, USMC Retired; Joseph Poyer III, USMC; Alan York, RN Retired; Alex Watt, RAF Retired and Hiro Wantanabe, IJN Retired, for their advice, corrections and support. Also to my editor, Colin Murray, and agent, Giles Gordon, who have done as much as anyone to make this book possible.

Joe Poyer
California, 1984

Thou hast chosen war and
That will happen which
will happen,
and what is to be we know not.
God alone knows.

Genghis Khan

Operation Barbarossa June - July 1941

The intense pre-dawn silence along the Russian border reminded him of the other times he had waited for H-hour on the borders of Poland, Norway, Belgium. Even the smell of the forest was the same as a year ago in the Ardennes. Major Friedrich Prager, commanding the First Battalion, First Panzer Regiment, First Panzer Division, Army Group South, was satisfied because Operation Barbarossa had released him from a limbo of rumours and uncertainty.

They were about to begin the final step in the restoration of Germany to a pre-eminent position in the world, a process that had started with the appointment of Adolph Hitler to the Chancellorship in January, 1933. Since then, Hitler had done what the Kaiser and his Imperial Army had failed to accomplish in 1914–1918 and conquered nearly all of Western Europe. Now the final march, to defeat the Bolshevik threat to the entire world, was about to get underway.

The sound of engines in the growing dawn startled him from his reverie. The familiar ripple of excitement coursed along the line of Panzer IV tanks as they were enveloped in petrol fumes. Morale was high and his own eagerness was reflected throughout the battalion, throughout the entire Group in fact.

At 0333, a signal rocket arced against the red-gold sky and a drum-roll of cannon fire swept the horizon. Prager turned to the river as exploding shells wove a sudden curtain of earth and steel shrapnel on the far bank. The guns were three minutes early in this sector.

A second rocket flared and early or not Prager shouted, 'Go!' into the microphone. A line of squat, grey tanks swarmed into the River Bug and churned the calm waters to mud as they were swallowed in mist. Prager felt the droplets on his face and could not restrain a grin. The Mark IV lurched under him and the engine bellowed as the treads clawed up the muddy bank onto the territory of the Union of Soviet Socialist Republics. As far as he could see in any direction a line of tanks stretched, and behind them came lorries filled with soldiers, vague and insubstantial-seeming in the sunlit mist; and behind them, endless columns of marching infantrymen.

These lines reached from the Baltic Sea in the north to the Black Sea in the south, a distance of three thousand kilometres. Three and a half million German soldiers and their allies moved against four and a half million ill-prepared and, he hoped, surprised Russians in the largest military assault the world had ever seen.

Prager called the first halt within sight of the border post they had been watching for days. He deployed several tanks from his headquarters company to either side of the road. He had been assured the evening before in the final briefing that the Russians would put up little or no resistance but neither he nor any other field officer present had believed it. For two weeks, German troops and equipment had been moving up to the jump-off line within sight of Russian border positions. In this sector, the terrain was flat farmland and scattered forest. They could scarcely have concealed their preparations from a blind man.

Even so, and in spite of the artillery barrage, he saw a Russian border guard running towards them, rifle slung, waving them back, as if they were merely lost. In the flat morning light, Prager saw clearly that the man was more puzzled than frightened. Before he could signal to the others to hold fire, a machine gun chattered and the man collapsed like a bundle of rags. Prager had seen that boneless fall often enough to know that the man had died instantly.

In a sudden, inexplicable burst of anger at the dead Russian guard, Prager shouted at his gunner to destroy the post. The gunner, an eager young sergeant, had anticipated the command. The tank bucked immediately as the 75 millimetre gun fired and the border post exploded in flame and splinters. As the smoke cleared, he saw several more border guards running across the fields and he realised at that moment that the Russians had not even laid minefields!

Prager ordered the column to resume speed, puzzled and not a little shocked at himself. Was that irrational surge of temper an indication that he had been away from combat too long and had lost self-control? But something told him that it was merely a precursor to this phase of the war which would be unlike any ever witnessed to date. Supposed allies for nearly two years, the inevitable breakdown was clearly the result of communist cynicism and duplicity. Germany would have much for which to exact revenge.

Uneasily, he avoided thinking about his Russian wife at home in Hamburg.

Captain Mikhail Gregorvitch Dogorov stood smoking in the early dawn as his artillery battery began their morning routine. A thin mist rose from the meadow as the sun, already hot, blazed out of a coppery sky. A haze of dust from yesterday's exercise hung in the still air, giving it a peculiar metallic taste. It was unseasonably warm for early summer and already his wool uniform hung on him like a damp blanket.

His command, Battery A of the 3rd Artillery Regiment, was encamped some fifty kilometres east of Brest-Litovsk and had been for nearly a week. They were taking part in the Soviet Fourth Army's summer manoeuvres.

Tomorrow they would be back in the garrison and in spite of the heat, dirt and general discomfort of field conditions, Dogorov knew he would regret the return to the boring routine and the strict discipline of the fort. He had been forced to take his leave in late winter and so the relatively relaxed atmosphere that enveloped Battery A's camp in the last week of manoeuvres had seemed almost like a summer holiday.

Dogorov knew that his regiment had done well – his battery in particular. They had gained the highest marks in the regiment and had been allowed an extra field day to practise for the Divisional finals in July. Only a single field problem scheduled for early afternoon remained – a live firing exercise with high-explosive shells – and he had granted the men free time until then. Some had chosen to sleep late but others were already sun-bathing or washing clothes. As he finished the cigarette, he heard the dull rumble of artillery to the west.

Curious, he listened. There were no training sessions scheduled for the morning that he could remember. Dogorov snorted at himself. Rumours! They had been making the rounds of the mess for more than two months, all claiming a massive German build-up behind the border until everyone was seeing German soldiers behind every tree.

But there is no reason for Germany to attack, he thought. In fact, it would be damnably foolish of them, involved as they are with the British in North Africa. That was not only his assessment but that of the army command and the government in Moscow, as well. Why just the day before manoeuvres had begun, *Pravda* had stated bluntly that there was no substance to such tales.

The overflights of German aircraft were simply the result of mistakes in navigation, a government spokesman had explained. The Nazi-Soviet pact and the extensive trade between the two countries was cited as clear evidence of mutual friendliness. Rumours to the contrary of overt provocations were the work of British spies attempting to embroil Russia in their war with Germany.

Dogorov glanced at his watch – nearly 05.30. The sound of aircraft penetrated the early calm. He shaded his eyes against the morning sun to see four aircraft cruising at high altitude from the northwest. As he watched, they changed direction in a long curve until they seemed to be heading directly for him.

An uneasy feeling gripped him and he started irresolutely towards the communications tent. All aircraft looked so much alike, he thought as he struggled to recall the identification silhouettes seen months before.

The leading aircraft was almost above them now. He shielded his eyes against the glare of the summer bright sky just as it began to lose altitude.

Dogorov shouted a warning and began to run. Soldiers gaped at his odd behaviour, then discipline asserted itself and they followed. All four aircraft were diving at the camp which the engineers had sited in a level, open field. The roar of the engines drowned the rumbling of distant artillery.

Machine gun fire tore through the camp and one man screamed and tumbled headlong. Bombs fell and the meadow erupted in plumes of earth and grass and showers of steel. The inane thought ran through his mind that he had never been bombed before – the Finns had few aircraft remaining by the time he was transferred to Karelia.

As suddenly as it began, it was over and the aircraft disappeared into the summer sky.

Major Friedrich Prager's panzer squadron raced through a nameless village while its stunned inhabitants peered from doorways or stood beside the road, clutching one another in fear. Children screamed and women stared after them fearfully. In the fields men watched, shocked into silence as their world turned upside down.

No resistance had yet been offered, but as they left the village Prager spotted a group of motor vehicles fleeing ahead along the main road and ordered four tanks to deploy. He couldn't be certain but they looked like military vehicles – then he laughed at himself. There were no private motor cars or lorries in Russia! Everything belonged to the State. He shouted the command to open fire into the microphone.

One motor car exploded immediately and three lorries within moments. The remaining vehicles turned off the road towards a distant stand of trees. As they bumped across the fields, they began to string out and his gunners whooped and shouted catcalls. Prager ordered a barrage just ahead of the lead vehicle and was elated when the panicked Russians ran full-tilt into the curtain of exploding steel. Only four made it through to the trees.

Watching his laughing crews, Prager was suddenly conscious of a great flood of affection for his men. In the year since his return from France and active front-line duty, he had forgotten how strong were the emotional ties that welded soldiers together in wartime.

The column resumed speed and a few minutes later ran past the burning hulks. From the number of mutilated bodies, the lorries had obviously been carrying troops. Several more burned furiously in the fields but there was no time to investigate. The rifle companies following behind would take care of them.

By mid-afternoon, they had penetrated thirty kilometres into Russian-held Poland without serious resistance. It was obvious the Russians had been taken by surprise, as intelligence had predicted. For more than two weeks German forces had been moving into position, often in plain view of Russian border posts, yet there was no sign that they had taken even the most rudimentary precautions. There were no artillery concentrations, no forward ammunition dumps, no troops dug in, no fortified positions; nothing at all to indicate that the Red Army was expecting an attack.

They laagered that night in the middle of a vast, empty plain that stretched in shimmering green waves as far as the eye could see. Standing on the turret of his Mark IV, Prager was infused with a distant feeling of unease. The vast plains seemed endless and filled with menace. Just what lay out there, he wondered. Had the Russians tricked them after all? Had they left only the thinnest of screens along the border, intending to suck them into the depths of Russia before striking?

He sat down on the turret and lit a cigarette. The battalion had acquitted themselves well today. If he could just rid himself of this uneasy feeling that had as much to do with the campaign in general as it did with this mysterious emptiness so unlike anything to be found in Western Europe.

During the autumn and winter of 1940–41, Prager had been assigned to Army General Headquarters, *Oberkommando des Heeres*, where he worked as one of a number of staff assistants to Lieutenant General Friedrich von Paulus, Deputy Chief of the General Staff charged with planning the *Barbarossa* campaign. Prager had played an intimate role in the initial stages, at first marvelling at the Fuehrer's strategic conception, but becoming increasingly uneasy over the assumptions underlying the detailed planning that emanated daily from the Chancellory.

Ten panzer divisions containing thirty-five battalions had defeated the combined armies of France, Belgium and England. Therefore, it was calculated twenty-one panzer divisions of seventy-three battalions would be required to defeat the larger but quite primitive Red Army – particularly after their poor showing in Finland. Unfortunately, only twenty-two new battalions had yet been formed, and those mostly by reducing the average strength of existing panzer divisions from 258 to 196 tanks.

Germany's infantry had totalled 129 divisions in June 1940 – including mountain troops. In the intervening year, that strength had only increased by thirty-three new divisions distributed among forty-seven corps. And although many of the new divisions were mechanised, they were equipped only with captured French, Belgian and Czechoslovak vehicles for which few spare parts were available.

Worst of all, German industry under that fatuous fool Goering had not yet been reorganised to support an extended war. The party, it appeared, was fearful of provoking resistance from the German folk if life became too harsh.

In the autumn of 1940, Prager had requested a line command. But it was late the following May before his transfer to command a tank battalion in von Kliest's First Panzer Group, headquartered east of Lublin a few tens of kilometres from Russian-occupied Poland, came through. He had hoped for a position with his former commander, General Erwin Rommel, now in North Africa, because he liked and admired Rommel. But because of his wife's nationality, he had not dared make such a request for fear of provoking questions. He knew there were already two black marks in his record, the first for helping that American, Thorne, escape an SS firing squad in Poland – and in the process disgracing an SS General – and the second for marrying Sonja Vishenka, a Russian citizen and former member of the Communist Party.

To compound his troubles, the orders for his transfer had come through so quickly that there had been no time for him to move Sonja to Berlin. So she had remained behind in Hamburg, in his parents' old house by the Wansee River, exposed to the certain hostility of the neighbours as his French mother had been in the previous war. In all, they had spent less than a week together since their marriage and God only knew when he would see her again.

It took Dogorov an hour to regroup his stunned battery, care for the wounded and bury the twelve dead. Afterwards, he ordered the battery to strike camp and ruthlessly supervised the elimination of any unnecessary equipment that could not be replaced at the fort. Each man carried a field pack with two days rations, a rifle with a standard combat issue of 150 rounds, a waterproof and blanket. The supply wagons were stripped down to essentials – ammunition and the wounded. His own tent and all his personal effects had been destroyed by a bomb, including his side arm.

Dogorov was certain that he had seen black iron crosses on the attacking aircraft. And the gunfire was constant in the west; so there had been no mistake – the *swollich* huns had attacked Russia. If they marched hard, Dogorov calculated, they could rejoin the Brest garrison before sunset.

The sun roasted the marching men and a dust-plume trailed the column as Dogorov pushed them hard. To spare the horses, only the wounded rode. They had left the forest behind and flat, empty fields with little shade lay on either side.

At mid-morning, an American Ford driven probably by a high party official with his family, appeared. The auto swerved off the road to avoid the horse-drawn caissons and ignoring orders to halt, bumped along the verge and disappeared east to the jeers and curses of the battery. An hour later, they encountered the first refugees who grew so rapidly in number that they were forced to a halt still ten kilometres short of the fort. Grimly, Dogorov ordered bayonets fixed and forced a way through the press, ignoring warnings and demands for assistance.

The intense heat was taking its toll. The sky was unmarred by cloud and the sun diabolical. Elderly and young alike were strewn along the roadsides gasping for breath. Twice, he saw family members mourning over a body. No one had a clear idea what was happening. No one had actually seen German troops; mass panic had simply swept people out of the city and suburbs.

Aircraft materialised without warning and fell on the packed refugees. Machine gun bullets ripped the road, killing people in swathes. Six aircraft in echelon played follow-the-leader. Three times, they strafed the road while Dogorov's drivers whipped the horses into a frenzy dragging the heavy cannon into the fields. One gun received a direct hit scattering broken men, horses and cannon among the refugees. In less than five hours, Dogorov had lost one gun and a quarter of the men in his battery. Stunned, he could only walk the roadside, staring.

The dead and dying were everywhere; young and old, grandfathers and little children, mothers and strong men; the slaughter was heartless. Two little girls with pigtails and ribbons were crumpled beside the lifeless body of a woman without a head. Next to them lay a grandmother in black – black dress, black shoes, black shawl – except where blood had splashed the fabric. Beside her, a young boy was staring at the blood pulsing from the ragged stump that was all that remained of his leg. The screams of wounded humans mingled with those of wounded horses; Dogorov had the horses shot, but there was nothing he could do for the people and in any event, his responsibility was not to these relatively few individuals, but to the mass of the Russian people and the Soviet nation.

The attack of the Nazi dive bombers did have a salutary, if grim, effect. It drove all but the most panic-stricken refugees off the road and his attenuated battery was able to make better time. The endless afternoon wore on. Heat drifted across the landscape and the air was thick with dust. For ever afterwards the metallic smell of summer heat and country dust would invoke this terrible day for Dogorov.

They were within two kilometres of the city when they came under machine gun and rifle fire. Motorcyclists appeared near a clump of trees. Dogorov first thought they were being fired on by their own troops but through the field glasses borrowed from his second-in-command, Lieutenant Alexander Ivanovitch Siderov, he saw the peculiar coal-scuttle helmets and grey-green uniforms he had last seen a year and a half before in a nameless Polish village on the east bank of the Bug.

Drivers whipped horses around and gun crews unchained and unlimbered the two remaining guns. A tank clattered out of the trees and stopped in the middle of the road. Its turret revolved and the stubby gun depressed. Smoke whipped from the muzzle and Dogorov felt the screaming rush of molten air as the shell tore over their heads to explode well to the rear.

He sensed rather than heard a breech being slammed shut and twirled to look. Siderov himself was peering along the barrel, intending to fire point blank. He jumped back, jerking the lanyard, and the cannon roared. The shell burst ahead of the tank, spraying it with gravel and pieces of steel casing. While the crew loaded another shell, Siderov spun the elevation wheel. The tank fired again and its shell struck the caisson of the second cannon and exploded. Bits of steel and flesh whined in all directions. Shrapnel sang overhead as Dogorov buried his head in his arms. Somehow, Siderov escaped the shrapnel that scythed through the gun crew, killing them to a man.

Amid the screaming of wounded horses and men and the rapid crackling of small arms fire, Siderov coolly checked his aim and fired again. The tank lurched. Dogorov scrambled to the gun and grabbed up a shell as Siderov spun the breech open. He dodged the red-hot casing that flicked out and shoved the new one in, burning his hand on the hot chamber. Siderov shouldered him aside and spun the breech closed. Off-balance, Dogorov sat down abruptly and the cannon fired a third time. And again the tank lurched. For just an instant, a reddish patch glowed at the base of the turret and then a fireball blew the turret hatch off and a crown of black smoke roiled into the still air.

A fierce wave of exultation swept Dogorov and he sprang up screaming curses and thrust another shell into the open breech. Siderov shifted his point of aim and the warhead exploded just short of the trees. They had only been issued high-explosive shell for the exercise; HE was effective against fortifications or tanks but not infantry as the warheads contained no shrapnel.

The German soldiers, suddenly bereft of their chief protection opened up with a second machine gun hidden in the trees.

'There!' Dogorov shouted, but Siderov was already training the cannon around. Someone pushed him out of the way and crammed a shell into the open breech. Siderov fired and, without waiting to see the effect, fired again as soon as another shell was loaded. Machine gun fire swept over them and the man who had superseded him as loader, collapsed with a neat hole under his right eye.

If only they had shrapnel, Dogorov thought wildly. Swearing, he gave the order to break off action and retreat.

Just at dusk, Stukas found them again. Dogorov had learned a hard lesson earlier and so had spread the column well out along the road. The attenuated battery scattered into the fields on either side, and gathering dusk made it difficult for the German pilots. Yet they killed eight horses and destroyed two wagons before breaking off. Dogorov saw a single flash of sunlight, bright as the evening star as the aircraft disappeared in the west.

They camped that night in the same semi-forested area from which they had started fourteen hours before. In all, he calculated as he watched the weary men care for the remaining horses and gear before throwing themselves down on the bare ground to sleep, he had lost twenty-three men killed and fourteen wounded, twelve horses, three supply waggons and two guns. But what was worse, he had not once seen a single Russian soldier other than those under his command. Nor a single Russian aircraft. And they had come under fire on the eastern outskirts of Brest which could only mean that a key fort in the border defences had been eliminated.

Siderov dropped down beside him. Dogorov could not see his face in the darkness, but supposed it was as tired and worried as his own. The lieutenant was older by about ten years – his lack of party membership partly responsible for that. Dogorov found him an excellent field officer, unlike so many he had encountered since the purges. The war would certainly provide ample opportunity for Siderov's worth to be noticed. They discussed what had happened, neither of them wanting to broach the problems of tomorrow. And neither wanted to suggest that Nazi forces had managed to advance so far over the border in one day.

'A fluke,' Siderov sighed after a long silence.

Dogorov grunted. 'Does it matter?'

'I don't know. Perhaps if the regiment had not been on manoeuvres, we might have made the difference at Brest. I cannot believe this is anything other than a local success, possibly even a German response to British provocations, as *Pravda* and those party workers warned last week.'

'If that's the case, then where are our aircraft? Have you seen one all day?' Dogorov shook his head. 'No, Alex, I think this is part of a major attack along the entire Fourth Army Front. We've known for a long time that it was in the making.'

There was nothing more to be said. Sleep was more important now if they were to survive tomorrow. Calling upon the iron self-discipline engrained in him by years in the service, he rolled up in the ill-smelling horse-blanket a gunner had found for him. There was one consolation, he thought; the ammoniac smell of the blanket might keep fleas away.

Marauding German aircraft appeared at first light to harass them and German motorcycle patrols, armoured scout cars and tanks swarmed along the roads. Dogorov decided by the end of the third day to give up the attempt to find a way to Brest and ordered the battery to fall back on Zabinka, fifty kilometres west, which had been designated a rear area staging base during the past winter's reorganisation. They began to move that night across country to avoid the German armoured spearheads.

They reached the outskirts of Zabinka on 29 June – far too late. Studying the town from the edge of the forest, they could see German tanks and soldiers patrolling the rail yards. The fact that no apparent precautions had been taken against air raids told Dogorov a great deal. Not once in seven days had they seen a Russian aircraft.

That night Dogorov sat by himself, watched by the exhausted and hungry survivors of his battery. Surrender? Food, rest, fresh clothing. Care for the wounded? Two more had died today, one of gas gangrene. They had been unable to raise on their field radio before it ceased to function any but units like theirs, also trapped, under fire, running, surrounded, dying. There was no answer from Fourth Army Headquarters, from divisional or regimental HQ. And Brest was ominously silent. Their pleas for air cover went unacknowledged, as if the Red Army had ceased to exist.

How could it have happened? Dogorov asked himself over and over. They had been assured time and time again by the Party and by Moscow – by Stalin himself – that the Germans would not attack – 'all rumours to that effect are British provocations, comrades. No, you are not allowed to take precautionary measures as these might be interpreted as hostile acts by Germany.'

They had been abandoned by Moscow; nothing else explained the mysterious silence, the lack of orders, the lack of air support, the Nazis swarming everywhere. Grimly, he made his decision. They would move south into the Pripet Marshes – a vast, sparsely-inhabited area encompassing the southern points of Belorussia and the northern part of the Ukraine, filled with swamps, thick forests and few roads.

It seemed at times as if they were the last survivors of the Red Army in existence as they retreated deeper into the Pripet, harried by German aircraft and motorcycle patrols. What few inhabitants they encountered were hostile. This part of the Ukraine had been held illegally by Poland before September 1939 and the people considered themselves Polish rather than citizens of the Soviet Union. Dogorov therefore had no compunction about confiscating what food and clothing had not been hidden and burning fields and buildings wherever he thought they might assist the Nazis.

The Fourth Army, of which his artillery battalion had been part, was stationed in the West Special Military District and was responsible for the sector between the edge of the Pripet on the north and Brest-Kobrin on the south. Dogorov had chosen to move southeast as the Kiev Special Military District was held in great strength by the Fifth, Sixth, Twenty-Sixth, Twelfth and Thirty-Seventh Soviet Armies. Kiev was not only the centre of the Ukraine, but controlled the approaches to the great industrial area between the Dnieper and Don Rivers, as well as the oil-rich Caucasus. Few military districts in the Soviet Union were as strongly fortified.

Stukas materialised from the sun's unendurable glare, the only warning the horrible whistle and the stutter of machine guns. Dogorov had never before encountered, never dreamed of, anything so demoralising as these killer aircraft. His battery, diminished by half in the first week of attacks, dwindled further and three had even deserted.

The desertions angered him deeply. He was torn between delaying to find and execute the cowards, and continuing the march. As a compromise, he assembled the survivors that evening. Less than sixty remained and all were shadowed and gaunt from fear, hunger and exhaustion. And despair. Most of the men in his battery had been conscripted from Baranovichi and city bred as they were, had looked on summer manoeuvres as hard duty. So it was understandable that the silence of the endless marsh, the heat, the humidity and the constant fear combined to produce in them a sense of defeat.

To hold them together, Dogorov had to invoke a greater fear. 'Three men have deserted,' he snapped. 'By now they will have surrendered or been captured by the Nazis... and shot. Good riddance! They were cowards who betrayed Russia.' At the last moment, something urged him to avoid the modifier 'Soviet'.

'The Nazis know who has killed their soldiers from ambush and who has stolen their food and equipment. They will torture and execute any man of us they take. If they do not, I, as the representative of the Soviet State, will!'

Their sullenness was like a pall, but he saw the new fear in their eyes.

At the end of the second week of July, they left what had once been Polish territory. Tiny villages, many of them no more than a few farms clustered together, became more numerous. And it was soon obvious that in this remote corner of the Union, the Soviet government's writ was barely heeded.

As Red Army men they were greeted with suspicion and ill-concealed hatred. But if supplies were given grudgingly, information was plentiful; in fact the villagers seemed to delight in passing on bad news.

'Brest fell on the first day but the fortress held out until the end of the month. Then all were killed.' This last with a long face.

'Kovel was razed to the ground. All Jews and Communists were shot,' a middle-aged woman told them, trying hard to conceal a smile.

'The Red Army is being surrounded and cut to pieces. They say that over six hundred thousand prisoners have been taken,' an old man wearing a smelly sheepskin coat, in spite of the heat, cackled.

'Defeatist talk,' Dogorov replied in a conversational tone, 'in time of war is punishable by death.' He slapped the man hard enough to knock him down and his old wife rushed in, screaming imprecations, and slapped the peasant's face also. Dogorov added a kick for good measure.

*

On the 19 July, they entered a village to find it deserted. An elderly peasant in bast shoes and a homespun blouse belted with a thin cord appeared and announced furtively that he was the village mayor and a good Communist. He asked permission to travel with them.

'It's like this, Excellency,' he muttered, reverting to the old form of address. 'The Nazis are burning the villages of those who help the Red Army. And they are hanging all Communists and officials. There are a number of people who would gladly betray me . . .' His voice quavered and his knees buckled at the thought of the rope. 'Our people all ran away to the forest when they heard you were coming.'

The old man was able to provide only sketchy details regarding German troop movements and Dogorov had little faith in their accuracy. But he claimed that elements of two Nazi divisions had moved into the area to root out the last Red Army survivors – which explained the sound of heavy guns on their flanks during the past two days.

The mayor led him to his office and cautioning him to be quiet, quite unnecessarily as the building was deserted, unlocked a closet and proudly showed Dogorov a telephone which, when he picked it up, emitted the harsh singing of an operational line.

Dogorov laughed for the first time in weeks and tapped the hook until an operator answered. It took twenty minutes to get through to the Kiev Special Military District headquarters where he was shuffled from office to office before a clerk, who refused to even hear his name, ordered him to hang up.

'I don't care who or where you are,' the unknown clerk shouted, 'this telephone line is reserved for important military communications only.' The instrument went dead.

Angrily, Dogorov tapped the hook again until the exasperated operator returned. 'Listen, comrade,' he said, overriding her protests, 'I want you to put a call through to STAVKA, General Headquarters, in Moscow. I want you to announce that it is Captain Mikhail Dogorov, Third Artillery Regiment, Fourth Army, calling from behind German lines. Do you understand that?'

The operator protested that she was not allowed to telephone as far as Moscow but Dogorov shouted down her objections. 'This is a military emergency,' he roared.

Dogorov listened to the whistling and snapping of the telephone line and the operator's determined voice as she browbeat and begged her way across the country to the Moscow exchange. A Moscow switchboard defeated her, however. The military operator refused to accept the call and cut her off in mid-sentence.

Dogorov was too angry even to swear. The operator waited a moment for further information. 'Captain Dogorov, please, I have further calls waiting.'

Dogorov roused himself then. 'One more, only,' he promised. 'Connect me to the Food and Nutrition Ministry in Lenigrad, Madame Olga Semonova Dogorova.'

'But comrade Captain, I don't even know if the lines are up. The Nazis...'

'One more call,' he commanded. It was a long shot, but as he had the use of the telephone...

He heard the switchboard operator in Leningrad answer and the call was put through directly to the Food and Nutrition Ministry. His mother's business-brisk voice answered and his throat constricted suddenly with emotion so that he was unable to speak for a moment. The operator guessed at his reaction and said quickly, 'Madame Dogorova? I have your son on the line.'

'Mikhail!'

His name roused him. 'Mother... are you all right?'

'Of course. Never mind about me, where are you?'

Suddenly conscious that he was speaking over an open line, Dogorov told her only that he was safe enough and begged for news.

Astonished at the miracle of the telephone call, Madame Dogorova still had the presence of mind to understand her son's predicament. She quickly described the advances made by the German forces and their allies – the Finns, Hungarians and Rumanians – along the three thousand kilometre front. 'German and Rumanian troops have reached the Black Sea. Minsk has fallen and Smolensk is threatened. Our losses have been very high. The Finns have attacked us in Karelia, Pskov has fallen and the Baltic States are being invaded...'

An accented male voice broke in. 'Captain Dogorov, you will report your exact location, the number of troops under your command and the number and type of weapons...'

The line developed a strident buzzing that made further conversation impossible and Dogorov stared at the telephone, then, as if it had burned him, dropped the handset. Shaking, he tore the cord from the connection box on the wall.

The old man wailed, but Dogorov ignored him and hurried out. In minutes, he had roused the sleeping men and formed them up in marching order. Gaunt horses were harnessed to the guns and they left the village quickly, the old man shouting at them to wait while he ran to his house for his belongings. Dogorov never saw him again.

Shortly before dawn, he allowed them to rest beside a quiet lake shimmering in the fading moonlight. Dogorov lit a cigarette and gave the carton of Belmors that he had found in the village to Siderov to pass out – a welcome change from the poor quality makhorka tobacco and a twist of newspaper which were all they were able to find on rare occasions.

Dogorov took a deep breath. 'The Nazis are very close,' he began without preamble. 'I found a working telephone in the village and got through to Leningrad, but a German, speaking Russian, broke in. So, we will abandon our guns.'

The men stirred in surprise, but no one protested. From the corner of his eye, Dogorov could see that Siderov was relieved.

'We will bury the breechblocks and push the cannon into the lake. The horses will be used for food as necessary.' Dogorov hesitated, suddenly unsure. Perhaps it was better they knew the truth, he thought. So far they had stuck by him with little complaint. He recalled his mother's stories about the Revolution and the Civil War and the father he had never known. There were no officers in those days. Every man had known his duty and done it and their guide had been the Marxist Dialectic and the exhortations of Lenin. The true spirit of the Russian soldier had been evident then – as he hoped it would be again. He searched their faces in the dying moonlight.

He told them what he had learned from his mother. The news that Smolensk – Smolensk, the gateway to Moscow – was under siege shocked them badly. 'So,' he concluded, 'unless we reach Kiev, we can expect only quick death in battle or slow death in prison camp. You've all heard the tales the villagers tell.'

No one demurred, and by dawn the guns had been tipped into the lake to lie among the lily pads and cattails like discarded toys after a summer holiday.

The atrocity stories began.

Jews and Communists were being shot out of hand and harsh reprisals against the civilian population for infractions of German rules or law had become common. Whole villages in what had once been the Pale, the area in which Jews had been confined under Tsarist law, were being systematically destroyed and the inhabitants executed or sent away to special prison camps, or so the rumours maintained.

Dogorov had seen in Finland how rumours could grow out of all proportion and wreak havoc on morale. But there was a consistency now that made these rumours believable. He had no doubt that Jews and Communists were being singled out. Jews because the Germans had even less use for such parasites than did the Russians and the Communists because they were mortal enemies of the Nazis.

The gloating peasants had told them only a small part of the Brest garrison story. In the third week of July, a sergeant stumbled into their camp. The man was half-starved and almost out of his mind with shock and exhaustion, but by the following night the tenuous security offered by armed Russian soldiers and two good meals had restored him and that evening he was coaxed into telling his story.

'We were surrounded the very first day,' he said in a toneless voice that Dogorov found disconcerting. 'The Nazis threw everything at us. Their artillery fired continuously and they had a huge mortar they called Karl, which fired two thousand kilogram bombs. They broadcast all the details on loudspeakers to terrorise us into surrender.' After a moment, he went on. 'My signals company was part of the Sixth Orlov Red Banner Division. Most of our division was on summer manoeuvres. We broadcast what was happening over and over again but there was never any answer.'

The sergeant, whose name was Chizov, shivered at the memory. 'The Nazis captured most of the Kobrinsk Fort, the central portion of the Terespol Fort and the Volinsk Hospital. But that didn't make any difference to us. We had plenty of ammunition for our guns and we expected help at any moment.' His voice faltered. 'We had no idea that the... Nazis had driven...' He took a deep breath, '... driven as far as they had. We thought that...'

Dogorov was conscious of firelit faces pressing close, hoping that the man's story was not true. He tried to read their expressions. Were they feeling as he did, Dogorov wondered? Were they angered by Chizov's story, or depressed?

'But no one came to relieve us,' Chizov continued. 'No orders were received, nothing. We became a band of brothers, those of us who stood at Brest. There were no officers then, no more commanders or sergeants or privates. We were all Red Army men, the way it used to be.

'We fought on and were pushed back further and further into the cellars of the fort until we were living like rats. All of our leaders were killed; Captain Zubachev, Commissar Fomin and all the rest. I myself saw Major Garilov's position overrun. We fought until we ran out of ammunition and food.' Chizov looked at him and Dogorov saw in the narrow crinkling of his eyes and the shadows that turned his face to a death mask, the pride in their accomplishment.

'It was that,' he hissed, 'the lack of ammunition that finished us, not their damned soldiers, or their guns and mortars. We had no more ammunition. Nothing more to fight with but our hands and our bayonets.'

The spark of pride died and tears ran down his cheeks. 'There was nothing left to do but die or run away. I ran. My comrades died, but I ran,' he finished in a whisper.

An embarrassed silence prevailed for some time after Chizov finished. Then, as the fire died down and no one moved to replenish it, the whispered conversations began. Dogorov overheard bits and pieces but did nothing to stop them.

Several argued that they would be better off surrendering to the Germans than dying in the swamps. Another soldier, his confidence increasing as Dogorov remained silent, said loudly enough for all to hear, 'The State has deprived us and our families for twenty-seven years so that the Red Army and the defence industry could have priority. And for what? It's all been for nothing! The Nazis rolled over us as if we did not exist. They are killing our families and friends by the thousands, perhaps by the millions!'

Siderov glanced at Dogorov and touched his holster. Dogorov shook his head. Instead, he cleared his throat. 'We are not children. We all know what has happened. We know that a disaster such as none of us dreamed possible has struck Mother Russia. But what is the alternative? Do you wish to die on a Nazi bayonet or starve to death in a Nazi prison camp? What has changed? Moscow exists and the Soviet Union continues. Each and every one of us will do our duty because we must. Remember the heroes of the Revolution? They stood against the entire world and triumphed. Shall we do less?'

After a moment, he stood up and scuffed out the campfire.

Long after the camp had quieted, Dogorov lay wondering how it had all happened. The government's fear of foreign attack had always verged on paranoia. Hadn't they been taught from earliest childhood that Russia was surrounded by enemies who desired nothing more than her destruction? Hadn't every school child been taught to shoot a rifle and throw a handgrenade to defend the Soviet State? Hadn't he given up his first love, astronomy, because the State had required his services in the Red Army? Dogorov groaned. What had happened?

I am not blind, he told himself. I can see the aberrations in the system, I can understand why the government enforces harsh discipline and the forced collectivisation of farms. We Russians need a strong hand to drive us to do what our natures deny. But haven't we gone beyond that need? What sense is there in Stalin creating about himself an aura of omnipotence? What need had he to destroy the Army command with his purges except to secure his own position? Why does he continue to oppress the people with a monstrous bureaucracy which reserves all the privileges for itself? Only the most ignorant, or the most fanatical, could justify such excesses.

That night, Dogorov was in despair. They had thrown away the nation in Moscow, he concluded, because they preferred to play their deadly political games and thus did not perceive the growing threat to the State. They pacified alarm with talk of foreign provocations and showy trials and lurid accounts of British defeats in the West.

But after a while he came to the conclusion that, no matter what happened, he would continue to fight for Russia. Russia was more than dust and stone and grass and trees. Russia was his home, his land, and no matter the government, Russia and the Communist ideal, would endure.

*

The level plains of the Ukraine opened and they left the damnable frustration of swamp and marsh behind. The First Panzer Division of Army Group South had driven hard into the hinge between the Soviet Fifth Army at Kovel and the Sixth at Lwow and the heavy resistance was at last beginning to give way.

Major Friedrich Prager signalled his squadron to halt and dismounted stiffly. They had been pursuing a Russian armoured unit for two hard days and in all that time they had hardly been out of their tanks. He limped about the Mark IV inspecting visible, and gauging invisible, damage. The engine was running rough and the driver in desperation had wedged the choke mechanism to keep the engine revs up. Another few dozen kilometres, Prager thought, before the engine packed it in. It must be caked solid with carbon from poor quality petrol and it was unlikely that the battalion maintenance company would have located a new engine - or even be able to find them by tonight.

The Russian tanks somehow managed to move at a pace that was ruining his equipment. Those ancient T-28 medium tanks had a top speed on roads of only thirty-seven kilometres per hour, while his Mark IV Panzerkampfwagens, which mounted a heavier 75 millimetre gun, could do forty-two. But they had been moving across the nearly treeless steppe and the Soviet tanks had begun in better repair.

The Soviet Fifth Army was the first to mount serious opposition as they retreated to the southeast and Kiev. But only two days ago, the latest batch of prisoners had claimed to be part of the Sixth Army and they were utterly demoralised. The Soviets were surrendering en masse now, often without even the pretence of fighting. When they did stand, their efforts were half-hearted at best and it reminded him of spring 1940 and the race across France.

Twice, Prager had flown back to divisional headquarters for briefings and the last time the Fiesler Storch had passed for twenty minutes above a column of Russian prisoners marching four and five abreast to the rear. During the briefing, they had been told that similar columns were retreating towards Kiev, no more anxious for a fight than those taken prisoner. Intelligence speculated that the Russians were under orders to fall back and regroup in the vicinity of Uman, a small town between the Bug and Dnieper rivers.

His radio operator handed him a scribbled note. A concentration of Russian tanks had been spotted by reconnaissance aircraft a kilometre ahead, arrayed on either side of the road. His weariness vanished. At last, he thought, they have run out of fuel!

Except for the Russian tanks, nothing stood in their way but scattered infantry units as far as a Ukrainian village fifteen kilometres southeast. If they reached it tonight, he meant to do everything in his power to stop long enough for a thorough field overhaul of the battalion's vehicles.

Prager detached three tanks and sent them to attack from the flank. Minutes later, a covering Stuka squadron radioed that they had the Soviet tanks in view. Prager led the six remaining panzers across the fields in extended order, breasting the steppe grass like hunting destroyers he had once seen in the Baltic. They topped a rise just as the Stukas appeared, three of them in echelon. The Russian tanks were just inside a lonely copse of trees, the only cover as far as the eye could see. The radio operator handed up the key and earphones and slid the plug into the turret jack. Code stuttered down from the Stuka.

'Three tanks stationary in trees, five in semicircle at two hundred metres.' Prager translated the dots and dashes in his head. 'Presume tanks northwest belong you. Birds in net. Instructions?'

Prager was nettled by the man's flippant attitude. Damned air force, he thought. A few hours flying, shooting up the countryside at little risk, then home to a hot bath, hot meal and a hot woman – if the stories were true.

He swallowed his resentment and instructed the Stukas to strike at the Russian tanks in the semicircle. He could see through his glasses that they were hull down from his own position and would be difficult to dislodge. The flight leader acknowledged.

A moment later the Stukas winged over one after another and dove. He heard the distant clatter of machine gun fire and thought he saw a tracer glint as the Russian tanks defended themselves. Satisfied that the Stukas would keep them distracted, at least until his flanking column closed to firing distance, he gave the order to open fire.

Explosions raced the rim of the steppe, but Prager could only spare a quick glance at the Stukas' handiwork. Shells from his tanks tore into the thicket of trees and he was astonished when people ran out; men, women and children in ragged civilian clothing. A machine gun fired and running figures fell. He reached for the R/T microphone, but replaced it immediately, remembering the tank they had lost two weeks before when he had allowed civilians to leave the line of fire before attacking an infantry position.

A woman had suddenly veered towards them and had thrown a flaming bottle of petrol into the open turret of the nearest Mark IV. He had seen the tank commander throw himself out to die writhing in flames as the tank exploded, killing the other four crew members.

Many civilians welcomed them as liberators – even as others sabotaged their equipment, knifed their sentries and took to the woods as guerrilla fighters. The Russian woman had died under a storm of machine gun fire and as his own tank had ground past her body, he had seen that her long hair was exactly the same colour as Sonja's. In that moment, he had realised that there were no civilians in this war.

Two Russian shells exploded nearby in quick succession and a third smashed into the tank immediately behind. A red-yellow pillar of flame soared straight up from the turret and the entire vehicle shuddered, slewed sideways and stopped, burning furiously. Blobs of molten steel had spattered his turret, one of which burned a hole in the canvas padding within a centimetre of his arm.

The Stukas flickered in for a second pass and the flanking column opened fire at the same moment. Dust and smoke clouds rose about the copse, obscuring his view. Then the Stukas, having expended their bombs, made a final pass and used their machine guns. Prager could see two Russian tanks burning as his own jerked from the recoil of the 75 millimetre gun. Searing gases from the muzzle blast scorched his face and he crouched lower in the turret. The Russian fire had begun to slack off and Prager drove straight on, his tank leading the others in a ragged line abreast, the five survivors firing rapidly.

Now he saw through gaps in the smoke and dust a few Russian soldiers abandoning their vehicles. Machine-gun fire finished them quickly and he ordered a cease-fire. The other tanks formed up alongside him as they came round onto their original course. He sent a quick message to the Stuka leader thanking them for their assistance. The Stukas did a quick victory roll and streamed off to the northwest like a gang of disorderly boys spoiling for a fight.

They drove past the bodies scattered like mown grass. Prager stared down at elderly men, at women and the handful of children. Had they been with the Russian tanks or had they been hiding in the trees? Thank God Sonja was safe in Hamburg.

Karelia July 1941

Colonel Johan Erko stood in the centre of the clearing listening to the heavy artillery fire in the distance, and smiled. On either side of him, the men and officers of Finland's Second Jaeger Brigade, Group O, held their horses and listened with him. A copper sun glared from the burnished sky and they might have been participating in just one more of the endless manoeuvres that had occupied them all spring.

But far to the south the Germans were striding through the Baltic States, the Ukraine and Central Russia as the Red Army ran before them like frightened children. With the memory of the Winter War of 1939–40 burned deep into her national consciousness, Finland had held her own attack in grim anticipation of the proper moment. At long last, he thought with scant joy, it was getting under way.

Russian demands had not ended with the surrender of Karelian and Arctic territories, nor those along the Gulf of Finland, nor with the long term leasing of military and naval bases at Hanko. Instead, more and more was demanded – the return of private property taken from Hanko by Finnish refugees before Soviet occupation; complete Soviet control of the nickel mines at Pechenga; demilitarisation of the Åland Islands; the right to send trains across Finnish territory, and more. And each demand was a further denial of Finnish sovereignty and reinforcement of Russian claims to hegemony over its former province.

And we agreed to each new demand, gave them exactly what they wanted, Erko thought grimly as he listened to the drawn out booming of the assault guns. What choice had we?

Since the summer of 1940 and the defeat of France and England, Finland had been forced into ever closer relations with Germany. The unexpected Russian occupation of Bessarabia – another example of totalitarian expansionism – and demonstrations organised by Finnish communists, followed by Russian charges that the Finnish government had suppressed the Russian-supported Association for Peace and Friendship with the Soviet Union, had made it amply clear that Finland's independence was to be terminated very soon.

Erko had remained on the staff of Field Marshal Mannerheim after the Winter War and, at his request, had swallowed his anti-German prejudices and assisted in negotiations with Reichminister Hermann Goering's personal emissary, Lieutenant Colonel Joseph Veltjens, for German permission to fly supplies from Finnish territory at the head of the Gulf of Bothnia to their bases at Kirkenes in Norway.

But Germany had hardly proved less demanding than Russia. Veltjens was also charged with negotiating, on the most favourable terms possible, an option for the nickel mining concession at Penchenga. In return, Finland would receive German military equipment and supplies in the expectation that she would join Germany in any war against their mutual enemy. Even though the German government professed time after time to have no intention of attacking Russia, it was clear now that Hitler lied. But then, he thought with a cynicism learned since 30 November 1939 – the day Helsinki was bombed by Soviet aircraft – what else was to be expected in this day and age?

And so the Finnish army was poised to sweep across the border at dawn on 10 July 1941 into what had once been, and was to be again, Finnish Karelia. The objective of the Second Jaeger Battalion that first day was a point five kilometres inside the Russian border, between Vyartsilya and Korpisel'kya. They had expected heavy resistance from the Red Army, but in fact encountered virtually none. A few border guards fired and ran and Erko quickly discovered that entire Soviet divisions had been withdrawn from Karelia and sent south to stem the relentless German drive.

Erko's orders had been to attack from the south side of the village of Vyartsilya. Accordingly, the Second Jaeger Brigade formed up in the trees some four hundred metres from the village, and Erko waved two companies out to either flank to create an extended skirmish line. At his signal, brigade rode forward at a walking pace for three hundred metres and dismounted. Every third trooper took his and two others' horses and faded back into the forest, while the remainder slipped forward into positions along and across a gravelled road that entered the village from the west.

With the road cut, Erko began to close in on the village. A single machine gun, mounted in the local post office but badly handled, barred their approach. A trooper crawled in close enough to throw a hand grenade through a side window. The explosion blew every window out and the machine gun stopped abruptly, only to be replaced moments later by rifle fire. With a gesture of resignation, the trooper tossed in another grenade which brought the roof down and set fire to the building.

Local people began to emerge from hiding and Erko set a detail to sorting the native Finns, who had remained behind in 1940, from the Russian settlers moved in after the occupation. He was not surprised when some of the native Finns now claimed to be communists and Russian citizens. Erko had to break up a fight between his soldiers and a local man, a particularly obnoxious loud-mouth. Erko had always thought it remarkable that after the Civil and the Winter Wars there were still Finns who saw in Russia the salvation of their country.

No sooner had he calmed that situation when screams drew him towards a small barn to find an hysterical young woman on her knees in front of her husband, a Russian lumberjack, standing against a wall, hands raised above his head and plainly expecting to be shot at any moment. Even so, the man appeared embarrassed by his wife's behaviour.

Erko was unnerved by the hysterical girl and looked for help. Several women stood to one side watching and he appealed to them to calm her down. But they shook their heads.

'The little bitch is a traitor,' one sneered. 'She took up with him the moment he appeared in the village. Now she's pregnant and they aren't even married.'

'Spare me your Lutheran morality,' Erko snarled, angry at their callousness, and unable to endure more screaming, he yanked the girl to her feet and slapped her hard across the face. She stopped abruptly, hiccuped once and stared at him as if dazed.

'I do not intend to shoot your husband,' he said in a calm voice. 'But if you don't shut up, I will do so immediately.'

The warning sobered her and she collapsed against her husband, sobbing. He rolled his eyes at the soldiers, glared at the women but kept silent. With a sigh, Erko ordered the couple segregated and sent back to field headquarters where a political officer could deal with the situation.

At dawn they continued southeast, until at 1000 hours Erko received orders to move directly south and assist in the investment of the village of Tolvayarvi.

The horses were well-rested and they arrived at Tolvayarvi shortly after noon to find the attack well underway. Elements of the Fifth Division had surrounded the village earlier and were taking heavy artillery fire. Erko's battalion was ordered to move into the line on the north of the town to reinforce and widen a narrow salient thrust into the Russian lines.

The ground was far too marshy for trenching and they were forced to endure Russian artillery fire for twenty minutes before a Finnish battery arrived and began a gun duel. The majority of Erko's troops were youngsters tasting combat for the first time but, even so, Erko was pleased with the way they endured the heavy fire. The Winter War veterans had all been distributed throughout the revamped army to provide a hard core of experience during the rapid expansion of the year before.

Erko hated an artillery barrage more than anything else. The trembling uncertainty, the knowledge that no matter what precautions you took, there was still the statistical fact that if the barrage lasted long enough, you would be killed, never left him. He forced himself to think about Erika to take his mind from his fear. They had been married almost one year now. She had insisted on retaining her job with the Lotta Svard, the women's auxiliary to the Finnish army, and he had not argued, sensing that she needed to feel useful, particularly now. Time enough later on for the children he wanted so badly.

The rate of fire from the Russian battery began to decline. The single Finnish gun must have scored at least one hit he decided, because he could only distinguish the sound of two cannon now. He studied the village through field glasses. The red houses and barns of the village were gay with white trim in the bright afternoon sun – at least the village had not yet fallen into the usual dilapidated state that so characterised Russian villages, he thought.

Although there was no movement about the houses, Erko knew they were filled with Russian snipers. A series of explosions overran his positions in an instant, then shifted far to the rear as the Russian battery sought for the elusive Finnish cannon. Erko swallowed uneasily and glanced to the right where a corpseman, the cross on his torn armband barely visible, was already hurrying towards a churned up area of the line. Soon, Erko thought bitterly, the entire brigade will have the chance to die;

there were two hundred metres of open field to cross while the sharp-eyed Russian snipers took target practice.

He had just given his officers orders to alert the men to be ready, when a runner brought a welcome change of orders. A company of the Fifth Division, probing to the south of the town, had sighted Russian troops marching quickly, almost in panic, into the trees. The town was now deserted except for a single cannon service as a rear guard – and quite effectively, Erko thought with chagrin. All elements were therefore to move forward immediately to occupy the town.

Erko was weary beyond belief by the time his sector was secured, the men fed and sentries posted. His orderly had brought him a tray with a thick stew and fresh coffee and it occurred to him that he hadn't eaten since dawn. Lying now in a strange bed in a strange house waiting for sleep, he had fallen prey to thoughts dredged from the darkest recesses of his mind. He knew they were only symptoms of excessive fatigue but that did not make them any less real.

His worries were self-centred and concerned his own death, or worse, mutilation. Erko feared mutilation more than anything in the world, and at times like this he could become almost irrational at the thought of being rendered helpless for life. Of all the various mutilations, he thought, blindness would be worse than death. He found it impossible to imagine what it would be like to never see a forest in winter, or a sunset, or Erika. He was not half so afraid of death, which to him meant only the end of existence; but to be blind, or paralysed, living, but helpless to participate in life...

He tried to think instead about Erika, dwelling particularly on the week they had arranged in the early spring. Erika had borrowed a friend's holiday cabin some ninety kilometres northwest of Helsinki and they had spent six entire days together without sight or sound of another person. They might have been the last two people on Earth – which would have suited him well enough.

There had been little time for a honeymoon the year before as he had been sent to Leningrad to assist in the reparation negotiations, and afterwards to Berlin. Since then, the demands of their various assignments had kept them apart except for an occasional day or night snatched whenever possible, sometimes weeks apart. The six days of solitude had done them both a world of good and eased some of the strains in their marriage. Lying now in the sweltering bedroom, Erko could almost feel Erika's body beneath his fingers, her breath on his cheek. Damn! He shifted restlessly. Thinking about her was hardly soothing.

Erko got up and went outside to smoke a badly needed cigarette. A sentry passed and he returned his soft greeting. The sky was clear overhead and the warm breeze rustled leaves somewhere. The short mid-summer night was translucent with pale starlight. What had happened to the girl and her Russian lover he wondered? It was obvious she loved the man to distraction, but the pained expression on his face at her hysterical outburst suggested that she was little more to him than a convenience. Now why had he thought of them? Had he subconsciously seen a parallel to his own marriage to Erika?

She had been his assistant at the start of the Winter War, a pretty, competent and intelligent young woman. He had had dozens of assistants before, many of them women, but somehow she had come to mean so much more. He clearly remembered discovering how much when she had almost been killed during a Russian bombing attack on Helsinki. The British military attaché, Charles Atkins, had saved her life then.

Erko remembered rushing to the hospital as soon as he heard, only to meet her coming down the front steps, perfectly all right, and in his relief he had blurted out a proposal of marraige. It may have been a spur-of-the-moment impulse, but it was one he had never regretted, although he often wondered if her response had been just as impulsive.

There was no great passion between them as they had discovered during their subsequent days together and besides, he was getting a bit old for that sort of thing. But there was an easy companionship, much the same as when she was still his assistant. Erko drew a deep breath and carefully stubbed the cigarette out. No sense in standing out here beating his head against a stone wall. Dawn was only two hours away.

In the first six days of what was coming to be called the Continuation War, Finnish forces penetrated sixty-five miles inside the Soviet border, retaking most of what, before March 1939, had been Finnish territory. But the eastern shore of Lake Ladoga was hilly country and heavily forested and there Russian resistance stiffened.

Nevertheless, by 16 July, Erko's company had cleared the last Russian defenders from their sector. Returning to camp, he passed a bedraggled line of Russian prisoners shuffling to the rear. There were not many; nothing like the thousands taken during the Winter War, or that the Germans claimed to be capturing in Russia proper.

They had been continually in action for six days and Erko expected to stand down for rest and re-equipment. Instead, a staff officer was waiting for him with new orders and the following day the Second Jaeger Battalion rode along the lake to take part in the investment of Salmi, the last Russian defensive strongpoint west of the pre-1940 border.

The Finnish Sixth Corps was moving on Salmi and Erko found his Brigade in the vanguard. The Sixth Corps had split into two columns, one marching east via Kyaznyaselka towards Tulm Lake, and the main force moving straight on in a forced march that pushed the Russians hard and did not allow them time to establish defensive positions.

Johan Erko was struck again and again by the contrast as well as the similarities with the Winter War fifteen months before. The weather was the biggest difference. The days were clear, sunny and quite hot, rather than the Arctic cold that had almost destroyed four Russian armies. But, as in the first two months of the Winter War, the Russians seemed incapable of making an effective stand – although Erko knew this to be misleading, as the Karelian Front had been stripped to support fronts further south. This alone said a great deal for the Kremlin's reading of Finnish intentions and their reliance on Marshall Mannerheim's oft-repeated statement that Finland had no intention of proceeding beyond her pre-1940 borders, no matter the provocation.

Salmi was invested by the evening of 18 July. Erko received orders to make an early morning attack on a hill north of the town, which was occupied by a Russian 76.5 millimetre gun positioned to delay the Finns while the last of the Red Army forces were evacuated across the lake.

Shortly after 0300 hours, the sky began to lighten. Erko and a sergeant-major worked through the brush to a point where they could study the hill through the trees. After an hour the sergeant nudged Erko and indicated a spot just below the crest. He focused his glasses and saw an intermittent glint of light, probably from a bayonet. Shifting the glasses right and left, Erko spotted a dozen camouflaged soldiers. He suspected more were dug in on the forward slope.

The sergeant-major was a woodsman from near Savonnlina and he led Erko on a careful reconnaissance that avoided accidental contact. Partly by luck, partly by skill, they discovered that the reverse slopes, whether by accident or design, had been left undefended.

Erko quickly moved two companies from the First Battalion into position on the undefended northeastern slope, leaving the rest of the brigade between the gun's position and the town, before the Russians discovered their mistake. He also sent a runner to field HQ with word that he was opening the attack well ahead of time to take advantage of the undefended line.

At 0530 hours exactly, B Company opened fire on the defended southeastern slope – as the Russians expected them to. At the same time, Erko himself filtered A Company up the undefended rear slope, finding it considerably steeper and higher than it appeared either on the map or from the bottom. The Russian gun returned B Company's fire immediately and by the time A Company reached the crest, it had marked the extent of Finnish lines about Salmi.

The sergeant-major tugged at Erko's sleeve and pointed down the slope. Almost obscured by trees, he caught a glimpse of Russian infantry moving into position – too late. Grimly, he ordered the advance to resume and left a squad of troopers as a rearguard.

The slope eased into birch and fir thickets which impeded their movement towards the gun's position. Erko hoped to God the runner had reached HQ; if they succeeded in taking the hill, they would need strong reinforcements quickly or the Russian troops who had arrived too late would simply follow them up, and kick them off.

The 76.5 millimetre cannon was the mainstay of the Red Army's arsenal of medium artillery pieces. The Finns themselves used the same weapon, most of which had been captured from the Soviets during the Winter War. The position was defended by a company of riflemen and a single machine gun disposed on the slope below to pour heavy and sustained fire from concealed trenches onto an attacker. Fortunately, no thought had been given to defending the rear of the position.

Erko waited impatiently while A Company filtered into position to ring the gun and flank either end of the trenches. When the sergeant-major signalled all was ready, he waited for a lull in the firing, then blew two sharp whistle blasts. A withering volley of fire poured into the trenches, cutting down the majority of defenders.

Consternation reigned. A few Russian soldiers took cover against the trench walls and returned fire, but the balance were caught in the open. It was over in moments and with no loss to Erko's forces. There were four Russian survivors, one badly wounded. Every member of the gun crew had been shot dead.

Without a moment wasted, Erko ordered the gun shifted while a signal was sent down to B Company. The hill was heavily forested and the troops had the devil's own time humping the cannon around and back to a point where Erko had a clear view of Russian vehicles loading men and supplies in the town two kilometres distant. A dirt road ran along the lake front for half a kilometre and ended at a quay where a lake steamer was already loading. A second steamer could be seen making for the quay.

Erko wished desperately that he possessed an experienced gun crew instead of a cavalry company composed of reservists and new enlistees. Eight years before, he had attended a two week artillery course and that was the sum total of artillery experience in the entire brigade. While the sergeant-major made assignments and investigated the cannon, Erko struggled to remember how to calculate range and trajectories while using the unfamiliar Russian tables and comptometer.

A corporal rushed up to report that a convoy of lorries was moving out of the town. Erko turned his glasses in that direction and saw a plume of diesel exhaust hovering about the first lorry as men climbed aboard. He swore in frustration, snatched up the sheet of paper with his calculations and ran to the gun. He brushed the sergeant-major aside and fumbled to set the coordinates, double-checked their settings, then bodily moved a trooper out of the line of recoil.

The gun roared as he jerked the lanyard and Erko's eyes fastened onto the thin trail of smoke marking the round's flight until it smacked into the lake with a tremendous splash, several hundred metres over the target. Red-faced, he halved the setting and saw the shell fall short by a hundred metres.

Even so, the convoy stirred like a disturbed ant colony. Lorries manoeuvred to gain room on the narrow road. He fired again and the third shell landed on the far side of the road fifty metres beyond the lead lorry. Erko lowered the range another half.

The fourth shell exploded so close to the second lorry that the driver was either killed or lost control as it slewed onto the verge and tipped over. Men crawled from the back and ran for cover. His scratch gun crew hadn't waited for his orders but were loading and firing as fast as they could. The shells dropped in profusion about the convoy, unfortunately doing little damage. Only two more lorries were hit and both burned fiercely. Erko became so interested in the results of their amateur gunnery that he forgot about the Russian troops on the slope up which they had come until he heard rifle shots. He ran a few metres up to the crest to see his own rear guard stumbling through the brush and he threw himself behind a log just as a bullet splashed him with splinters.

Russian troops were moving across the crest towards them. Two of his men were hit immediately, and as he checked the left side of the line a third flung up his hands and fell back, a neat round hole welling blood in the middle of his throat. Erko cursed himself for a fool and shouted for a defence line to be formed.

The brigade sergeant-major raced along the line, pushing troopers into cover and ordering them to open fire. The cannonade continued and the roar and muzzle concussion confused Erko. A foot kicked his leg aside and he started, half in fright, half in anger. Two troopers threw themselves down beside him, one cradling the Soviet light machine gun.

The loader grinned at Erko as they set it up and slapped a belt into the breech. The gunner jerked the bolt handle to feed the first round and said something as he pressed the trigger. His words were lost when the machine gun swept a swathe of clipped branches, exploding tree trunks and screaming men. In less than a minute the counterattack was smashed and Erko hurried back to the gun.

A column of black smoke rose in the still morning air over the lakeshore. Through field glasses, Erko saw four lorries burning furiously while a fifth managed to bump around them and race along the lakefront road. Stick figures streamed towards the trees along the village perimeter as the motor convoy dispersed. The gun crew shifted to the docked steamer, but after the third shell it began to move away. The gun muzzle rose and the next shell fell well beyond the ship. The following round exploded on the empty dock. Erko thought the gun crew might be getting the feel of things and refrained from interfering.

The trooper acting as observer shouted a correction and a shell grazed the ship's bow and exploded in the lake; but she ran directly into the next round which tore a huge hole in her side at the waterline. An explosive plume of steam blew the stack off and carried it over the stern to smash against a warehouse. The steamer listed and a moment later settled to half her depth at an angle to the quay, effectively blocking it. The gun crew immediately fired on the second steamer but she, exercising great prudence, was already withdrawing.

Silence swept the hill. Erko, feeling as if he had been fighting for weeks without a break, was astonished to see that it was not yet 0700 hours. The smell of cordite was strong but a freshening breeze began to disperse it. For a few moments only the wind moving lightly in the birches and an upwelling of bird song celebrated the cannon's silence. The spell was shattered when the brigade sergeant-major trudged up to report. With a sigh, Erko heaved himself up and went back to work.

That evening, the Second Jaeger Brigade entered Salmi and secured it.

The Ukraine July 1941

The German camp was quiet in mid-afternoon. Dogorov studied the neat collection of field tents through the last pair of field glasses left in the battery and ignored his empty stomach. The July heat was wet and intense and only a single somnambulant sentry paced the perimeter. He was especially interested in the collection of military vehicles, lorries and the single staff car about which a few mechanics worked. He guessed the rest of the garrison would be sleeping or at work inside the tents. He had been watching the camp since early morning, a small, rear area transport depot located a kilometre from a Ukrainian village.

Since the battery had crossed into the Russian Ukraine the villagers had seemed a bit friendlier. But he knew the peasants were as likely to betray them to German security units as feed them. Nothing the peasants told them could be trusted and Dogorov had learned to conceal the strength, or rather the lack of it, of his force. Instead, one or two men with rural backgrounds were sent into a village posing as farmers, or wounded soldiers returning home, to learn what they could.

The previous evening, one of his men visited the nearby village and learned that most of the garrison had been sent north to sweep for Red Army stragglers. Since they badly needed food, ammunition and clothing, Dogorov decided to attack in mid-afternoon when experience had taught him the Nazis were less alert than at night.

During the past month, his men had become hardened guerrillas. The weak, or those not fully committed, had been killed, or died of disease, or enemy action, or had deserted. One he had recaptured and hanged. The soldier's death struggles in the noose had served to convince the others that he meant business.

Until now, Dogorov had limited their raids to undefended villages for food and clothing, but in the wake of the Nazi advance there was little to be obtained from the peasants. Feeding forty-three men on the run had proven so difficult that Dogorov had been reduced to this desperate gamble.

But his confidence in these artillerymen turned guerrillas had grown. They were no longer an amorphous mass of peasants and factory workers swept into the army net for lack of civilian jobs or skills. They were hardened, disciplined soldiers who had stood up to the worst the Germans could throw at them.

He had sited a German machine gun they had captured two weeks before in a skirmish with a special detachment searching for Soviet stragglers, so as to enfilade the tents, and before dawn he had sent a small party to the other side of the camp. He looked at the wristwatch taken from a dead German officer, a fine Swiss chronometer – two minutes to 1500 hours. Glancing along the line, he caught glimpses of grim faces hidden in the foliage, all watching him. He raised one hand as the seconds ticked down. Beside him, one of the four soldiers, picked for his marksmanship, took careful aim at the sentry.

As the second hand edged towards the Roman figure for twelve, two rifle shots rang out on the far side. Only three seconds early he thought, as the sniper's rifle crashed at his side. The German sentry pivoted, arms flung out and fell. Dogorov led the charge, shouting.

Machine gun fire slashed the tents to tatters as they raced across the forty-metre wide cleared area surrounding the camp. Nazis died as they sat up on cots or burst from their tents and then Dogorov and his men were among them even before the alarm could be given.

Dogorov ran at a German officer who appeared in a tent opening, pistol in hand. In panic, the man shot and missed. Behind Dogorov a rifle fired past his shoulder and the officer collapsed. Without thinking, Dogorov snatched up the man's pistol. Bayonets made quick work of the survivors. One German soldier burst through the back of a tent and raced into the woods, weaving from side to side. A dozen shots missed him as he disappeared into sun-gilded undergrowth.

The firing from the vehicle park grew in volume before several grenades punctuated the fighting and the rifle fire ended abruptly. More explosions followed as the flanking party began demolitions. Dogorov blew his whistle and men ran towards him. A few last shots were fired to finish survivors.

Dogorov viewed the scene with satisfaction. The dead, all in German uniform, lay everywhere. Their own casualties were limited to two, both wounded, one in the leg, the other in the chest. Every man had been assigned a particular item to find – weapons, ammunition, food, clothing, boots, medicine and bandages. After gathering as much as they could carry, Dogorov and Siderov split the men into demolition units. Handgrenades were wired to lorry engines, tents were splashed with petrol and set afire. Siderov trotted up, grinning, with two machine pistols and handed one to Dogorov.

'We've destroyed all the trucks and equipment and set fire to the sheds where the spare parts were stored. I found these,' he indicated the machine pistols, 'in a crate. They still have grease in them.' He passed Dogorov two canvas bandoliers of heavy ammunition. 'My men are bringing as many as they can carry. Hell of a lot better weapon for this kind of work than bolt-rifles.'

Dogorov agreed and sent Siderov to wire together a crate of artillery shells that two soldiers had found while he searched an officer's tent for clothing to replace his own that was falling to pieces. He chortled over socks and boots that fit well enough, and a heavy, grey-green uniform tunic that was tight across the shoulders and chest. He tore off the insignia and started to bundle a pair of trousers when Siderov's whistle blew. With regret, he abandoned the trousers and raced out.

Dogorov suspected that there was an ammunition dump about somewhere, but there wasn't time to look for it. He had allowed exactly fifteen minutes for the assault and demolition of the camp. They had discovered the hard way that the Germans overlapped areas of responsibility for rear area garrisons so that one always covered another. There was just time enough for Siderov to prepare the usual surprises with the Germans' own mines before he blew the three short whistle blasts that meant reassembly.

Siderov hurried back, laughing, and Dogorov grinned. It had gone off like clockwork so far; they would pay shortly, but for now it was good to savour the triumph. They had struck back and hard this first time. He took a last look around, then nodded to the sergeant who would remain behind to set off the demolition charges, and led the group across the open space and into the trees at a trot.

Five minutes later, a sharp explosion, followed by a thunderous series of bangs swept shock waves through the forest. A demolition charge must have found the hidden ammunition dump, Dogorov thought with satisfaction.

The forest was thick with undergrowth, the ground marshy and the air heavy with the sulphurous stench of the swamp and decaying vegetable matter. The heat was worse beneath the trees and the damp soil exuded a fine mist that made breathing difficult. The men shuffled on at a half-run, half-walk, burdened with tins of ammunition and crates of rations.

The horses were being held three kilometres southwest of the Nazi camp and Dogorov was anxious to reach them. Once the burdens were shifted to the horses, they would be able to travel twice as fast. There had been no sign of pursuit as yet, but already Dogorov had heard aircraft.

They reached the horses within an hour, loaded the stolen supplies and marched on. At midnight, Dogorov allowed an hour's rest. The nights were growing appreciably longer in mid-August and the last two hours of travel had been slow as a result. A full moon was due to rise at 0200 hours and he allowed the men to sleep until then. Dogorov did not bother to set guards; there hadn't been a single sign of pursuit as yet and the men badly needed sleep.

Twice during the following morning Dogorov thought he heard the distant baying of dogs and knew that bloodhounds were tracking them. At mid-morning, he heard aircraft again. The dogs seemed closer and Dogorov knew that he could not put it off any longer. He had discussed the situation with Siderov, who agreed. The Germans were far fitter and better rested than his half-starved men.

They halted twenty minutes later beside a spring-fed stream that ran down from one of the few areas of high ground in the forest. The men drank thirstily and refilled their water bottles. Quietly, Dogorov called the sergeant, a regular from the old days of the Tsar's army, to one side and asked him to select three men. The sergeant stared at him a moment as if he might object, but the film of acceptance slid across his eyes and he walked off.

The two wounded and one man sick with fever were selected. They assembled without argument and listened as Dogorov gave them instructions and a map reference at which to rendevous tomorrow at dawn. All four knew that the reference point was false; if they survived long enough to be captured they would be unable to betray the main body, but the Germans would lose an hour or more checking the false lead.

When the battery went on, the sergeant and his three men were stolidly digging concealed rifle pits with fields of fire to the rear. They would wait until the Nazis had passed before they opened fire. Dogorov had given them their target priorities – dogs first, then officers. With luck, they could delay the Nazis for an hour or more. He saw that they were each issued a German machine pistol and a dozen magazines of ammunition. He wished them good luck and led the party out without looking back.

They never heard the dogs again.

Smolensk 5 August 1941

The representative of the Soviet Information Bureau - Sovinfo - who met Torsten Fredriksson at Moscow Airport was among the surliest of individuals he had ever encountered. Also the fattest. The man was even more suspicious of him than the customs officer who examined his passport and belongings with painstaking thoroughness. Every item of clothing was gone over and a needle was used to probe the sides and bottom of his suitcase. When the man produced a screwdriver to take his typewriter apart, Fredriksson snatched it back.

The startled customs man sputtered and the Sovinfo guide roared at Fredriksson to remember that he was a guest of the Soviet Union and subject to its every law. Without a word, Fredriksson repacked his suitcase.

'My good man,' he said pleasantly when the guide ran out of threats. 'Would you be kind enough to arrange for me to board the first aircraft returning to Stockholm? I will remain here until one becomes available.' He lugged the suitcase to the wall, folded his coat for a cushion and sat down on the floor.

The guide sputtered new threats and the customs officer rolled his eyes. A senior official appeared, listened to the conflicting stories while Fredriksson smoked and kept silent, then sent for his superior.

Fredriksson saw immediately that this was a most senior official. He wore a relatively well-tailored suit, a pair of handmade shoes, severe wire-rimmed glasses and there was silence the moment he appeared. He listened to the supervisor, the customs man and the guide, nodded and went away to make a telephone call. When he returned twenty minutes later, he spoke sharply to the guide and sent the others back to work. He apologised to Fredriksson and agreed it was not necessary to take the typewriter apart as every part - if one turned it upside down - was visible from the outside. He then escorted Fredriksson through the terminal to a waiting car and when the guide started to shoulder his way into the back with him, the senior official pushed him rudely towards the front seat.

Fredriksson had wanted to use the more direct SAS flight from Stockholm to Moscow that crossed Finland, but his Moscow hosts had insisted on the once weekly flight via Aeroflot. To avoid unpleasantness since Finland, as well as Germany, was at war with the Soviet Union, the pilot had gone well north into the Bering Sea before turning south to land at Murmansk. They landed again at Vologrod to refuel before limping into Moscow twenty-one hours later. The minimum cabin service was supplied by a doughy female attendant who served lukewarm tea after each take-off and vanished into a curtained section at the rear for the balance of the flight. She spoke only Russian and Fredriksson's command of that language was far too limited to deal with her obvious hostility.

The drive into the city took them along streets busy with military traffic. Armed soldiers and policemen were in such profusion that Fredriksson wondered if there were anyone at the front. The guide answered his questions reluctantly and volunteered nothing.

The guide's official Zis stopped before the greenish façade of a huge, pre-Revolution hotel, across the square from a building he recognised as the Bolshoi Theatre. A small sign in French beneath the Cyrillic marque identified the hotel as the Metropole. Immediately below was a smear of black paint, already beginning to weather, and when he peered hard, Fredriksson saw the dim outlines of the hotel's name as transliterated into German.

At the reception desk, his passport was again examined in detail by the clerk who then tapped on a door behind the reception desk and poked his head inside. A moment later, a fussy individual with dangling pince-nez hurried out, snatched the passport, studied it with even more attention, then shot a series of rapid-fire questions at Fredriksson – in Russian. Fredriksson smiled and pointed after his guide who had wandered towards the kiosk that sold foreign cigarettes and other duty-free goods. The man with the pince-nez charged across the lobby while Fredriksson winked at the desk clerk who quickly busied himself with the card file.

Twenty minutes later, Fredriksson was delivered to the elevator with a muttered farewell from his obese guide. Fredriksson was happy to see the man leave in spite of the fact that they had not arranged a schedule for the following day. He shrugged. At the moment all he wanted was a bath, a meal and sleep.

The floor porter shuffled him down a long, dusty corridor to a tiny room thick with the odour of infrequent and none-too-thorough cleanings and which overlooked an alley. The clatter of crockery from the kitchen and dustbins being emptied came clearly through the closed window. The room was stifling and the steady hum of a wall-mounted radio loudspeaker that had no on-off switch irritated him instantly.

As he watched rusty, lukewarm water trickle from the single tap, he thought that this was not the first time he had encountered shabby and insulting treatment after having forced his attentions on a government – in particular, a very uncomfortable hotel in Addis Ababa provided by the Duce's government in 1936. But for God's sake, the Soviets had *invited* him to come!

The following morning, Fredriksson woke early and went down to breakfast. The waiter brought a pot of real coffee and brown crystalline sugar but the service deteriorated from there. He supposed it was because he thanked the elderly man in Swedish rather than Russian that his breakfast eggs were overdone and the edges burned. The hot toast wasn't and the porridge was inedible. He was trying to attract the waiter's attention when a tall man with a shock of ill-disciplined hair stopped at his table, bowed slightly from the waist and held out a hand.

'My name,' he said in excellent French, 'is Ilya Ehrenburg and I am honoured to meet such a distinguished Swedish journalist as yourself, Monsieur Fredriksson.'

Surprised and pleased, Fredriksson rose to shake hands. 'The honour is mine,' he replied in earnest. 'Ehrenburg is a respected name in journalism. Please, won't you join me for breakfast?'

'A pleasure.' The waiter materialised instantly at his side with a menu which Ehrenburg studied a moment, then spoke rapidly in Russian. Without batting an eyelash, the waiter removed Fredriksson's dishes and hurried towards the kitchen.

Ehrenburg laughed at his expression. 'Would I be wrong in thinking that you have not been treated with all possible courtesy since your arrival?'

'That, Mr Ehrenburg, would be an understatement.'

The Russian held up a hand. 'Please, as we are going to be together for some time, call me Ilya, and may I call you Torsten?'

'Of course, but..?'

'I have been selected as your guide and interpreter. It has been decided that assigning Comrade Boris Dimitrievich Koukoulya as your guide was not in the best interests of the Soviet Union and so he has been given another assignment.'

'Particularly if we are going to the front,' Fredriksson answered with relief. He liked this tall, craggy man already. And he *was* familiar with his work. In spite of the repressive practices of Soviet government and censorship, Ehrenburg was widely travelled and had an international reputation as a journalist.

'I must admit there has been a good deal of outright hostility,' Fredriksson told him. He described the airport incident.

Ehrenburg smiled in sympathy and the waiter hurried back with a wheeled tray from which he distributed dishes quickly. This time the eggs were cooked to perfection, the toast light brown and crisp and there wasn't a lump to be seen in the porridge.

'You must understand,' Ehrenburg said between bites, 'that we here in the Soviet Union are fighting for our very lives. It is common knowledge that even though Sweden professes strict neutrality, so-called "Swedish volunteers" have joined the treacherous Finns. In fact, they have replaced an entire Finnish Division besieging our naval base at Hango. So from this you can perhaps understand why citizens of Sweden are not so popular at the moment.'

Fredriksson nodded. 'But in Sweden our government has no right to tell our citizens they cannot aid the Finns voluntarily, or the Soviet Union, for that matter. What we Swedes do, how we think, is a matter of individual not governmental choice.'

Ehrenburg agreed good-naturedly enough. 'Certainly, I understand. But many of us in Russia are in no mood to be understanding at the moment. A natural reaction to circumstances, you must admit.'

They would be leaving promptly at noon by train for the front, the Russian told him. When Fredriksson tried to determine where they were going, Ehrenburg shrugged.

'I do not know myself.'

Fredriksson baulked. 'How the devil am I supposed to write about conditions in the front lines if I don't know where I am?'

'Ah, you see,' Ehrenburg laughed, 'one front is much like another. You will find our itinerary quite firm. You must get used to the way things are done in Russia.'

Fredriksson considered for a moment. 'Then,' he said slowly, 'perhaps it would be better if I returned to Sweden. I am not accustomed to having my movements dictated. Not even the Germans presumed to do so.'

Ehrenburg called his bluff. 'My dear Fredriksson,' he said, showing a bit of steel beneath the affable exterior. 'Few Western correspondents have been admitted to the Soviet Union since the war began and, until now, none have been given permission to visit the front. I am sorry, but you will find that everything is subject to military security these days. We in Sovinfo have our duties to the nation, and that includes obeying the dictates of military security without protest, no matter how foolish we may think them. The salvation of the nation must come before the interests of the individual. Even in the West, that is so. If you wish, I can arrange return transportation to Sweden for you. In the event you decide to come with me, wear sturdy clothes and boots and travel lightly.'

As far as Fredriksson could tell, the crowded troop train, its windows painted over for security reasons, ran west from Moscow.

All afternoon it trundled on, stopping often and for no apparent reason. When it did, they were twice allowed to descend beside the tracks to stretch their legs and then he saw an empty land slumbering beneath shimmering heat waves that were the only movement within the vast horizons. The sky was absolutely cloudless, the blue washed by glare into burnished copper.

In early evening, the train left them on the platform of a small halt. Ehrenburg lit a cigarette. 'Relax,' he counselled. 'We have a time to wait.' Fredriksson sat down on his suitcase and after a while, lulled by bird song and the too-warm breeze, fell into a restless doze.

Aircraft passing overhead woke him. 'German bombers,' he heard Ehrenburg's voice in the gloom. 'On their way to Moscow. Since mid-

July they bomb every night the weather is clear. You would find it an unpleasant experience, I'm sure.'

'I've already had the pleasure,' Fredriksson mumbled, his voice thick with sleep and thirst. 'I've endured German bombs in Warsaw and London and British bombs in France.'

He found a water tap beside the halt and let it gush until the rust-filled pipes cleared. The water was lukewarm and he stripped off his shirt and washed.

A lorry appeared at ten o'clock, pin-points of hooded headlights barely visible across the steppe. Ehrenburg spoke to the driver when it stopped beside the platform. 'This is our ride, my friend. The driver tells me that we can expect dinner when we arrive.'

'Thank God for that,' Fredriksson muttered. 'I'm starving.'

They drove for hours along an invisible track, the lorry lurching and bouncing like a ship in a choppy sea. The quarter moon rose but its light was barely bright enough to show the collection of battered hovels that was their destination. Fredriksson was so tired when he stumbled down to the dusty road that he had trouble focusing his eyes. There was no wind and the atmosphere was airless, humid and warm.

Ehrenburg found a sentry who led them to a peasant's hut converted to military headquarters, manned by a duty officer who stared at their civilian clothing in suspicion. But when he read their credentials, he gave a shout of joy, hugged Ehrenburg and shouted orders that woke the place instantly. Someone appeared with two plates heaped with hot stew and a pot of tea. While they gorged themselves, the officer and men fired question after question at Ehrenburg who answered as best he could. The rapid-fire Russian was too much for Fredriksson and he was too busy eating to feel offended at being left out. Afterwards, the officer cleared everyone away and led them into the other room where he kicked three men out of the only bed. Fredriksson was asleep before the first flea bit.

He woke abruptly to an air-raid siren and rushed outside, boots in hand, to see laughing soldiers running towards slit trenches in the fields. Fredriksson was shoved into one half-filled with mud and by the time he cleared his eyes, the soldiers were leaning on the parapet watching bombs fall in and about the tiny village.

After the bombers left, all streamed back to the village to examine and comment on the meagre damage. Fredriksson was surprised at the number of soldiers the village housed – an entire brigade, at least. Camouflaged lorries, motorcycles, cannon and even tanks were everywhere, parked under trees along the single muddy street.

'Ah, there you are.' Ehrenburg sauntered up as Fredriksson finished scrapping mud from his clothes with a borrowed trench knife. 'How did you sleep?'

'Well enough, but I don't think much of Russian alarm clocks.'

Ehrenburg chuckled and led him to the mess tent where officers and men were eating together. 'First breakfast and then we must be on our way again.'

Again, he was recognised and in moments was surrounded by a throng of men all trying to speak at once, most thrusting pictures of themselves into his hands.

An officer – a commissar, the journalist explained – prevailed on the men to leave Ehrenburg in peace and took upon himself the task of collecting photographs and names. Ehrenburg promised to have them sent to the addresses written on the backs. 'And, of course, I'll do my best to see that as many of your names as possible are listed in my *Red Star* column,' he ended his impromptu speech. The soldiers gave a cheer and left them alone.

As they ate breakfast in the reddish dawn, Ehrenburg told him, 'It seems that the German bombers come every morning at the same time. They only bomb the village, so the soldiers take cover in the fields. Apparently this has been going on since the village was designated as a rear staging base.' As if to punctuate his statement, the muttered thunder of guns far to the west reached them.

As they strolled back to the hut where they had left their belongings, Fredriksson recalled again that he had only a hazy idea of where they were, as did Ehrenburg – or so he maintained. Fredriksson thought, given the nature of the previous day's stop and start journey, that they had come about two hundred kilometres west and perhaps south from Moscow. The internal geography of Russia was somewhat hazy in his mind but, if he was right, then they were near Smolensk, a key objective in the German drive on Moscow.

He glanced about the village filled with hundreds of soldiers and at the camouflaged tents scattered across the fields holding thousands more. Suddenly the horizons seemed impossibly distant, the few wind-twisted trees struggling for existence menacing, the straggle of alders marking a summer-dry water course frightening. The empty immensity of this harsh, hot land overawed his Western European sense of proportion and he was afraid that if he were killed, no one would ever know, or care.

They drove steadily west past long columns of Russian soldiers slogging towards the same unknown destination.

Most were so young that it seemed every high school in Russia must have been emptied. Their equipment was new and they marched in regular order, confidence evident in their bearing. They were the finest of the Army reserves, Ehrenburg told him, volunteers who had received basic training in school and who had spent the interval since the invasion doing advanced training. 'Now they are going to meet the enemy that has dared to desecrate their motherland.'

Ehrenburg often spoke as if rehearsing copy for his newspaper columns and Fredriksson noted that he tended to do so more often the nearer the front they came.

The column stopped only to refuel and at such times they were allowed to stretch their legs and relieve themselves along the dusty roadside. At one stop in the early afternoon as they shared the tasteless rations they had procured that morning, Fredriksson tried again to elicit their destination.

Ehrenburg shrugged. 'How can I tell you what I do not know myself? I know only that we will see an important battle. If the authorities allow, you will be told where it was when we return to Moscow.'

Fredriksson suspected that only if the Red Army won would he be told.

By evening the guns were appreciably louder and the horizon alive with flashes indistinguishable from summer heat lightning. They spent another night in a peasant's hut and for a long time, Fredriksson lay awake in the dark, squirming as much with apprehension as fleas.

For the first time in weeks, he thought about Jeanette Rodale and what might have become of her. In the year since the fall of France and her abrupt disappearance a month later, he had put in train discreet inquiries, all of which produced nothing and he had returned to Paris in December to check with the French police and contacts in the Germany security forces. And with her friends. Fredriksson was certain that if Jeanette had been arrested, he would have discovered that fact by now.

Jeanette was the sole heir to a manufacturing and retail sales empire that was one of the largest in France and the Germans had a great deal to gain by pampering her. Jeanette had two passionate interests: art – she was an accomplished and talented painter – and her own brand of socialism, or what she in her utter political naïveté thought of as socialism. But her political concerns found little concrete expression beyond long and involved discussions within a narrow circle of friends. She was French to the core and the Socialists were little better off economically for her interest. The Germans certainly had little to fear from her.

Her friends were another matter. Most had bigger mouths than brains and could conceivably have involved her in some ridiculous plot. Fredriksson had located one, a not-too-bright sometime musician who had been unwilling to talk to a foreigner. In frustration, Fredriksson had made a grave mistake; he had threatened him with arrest. Instead of being frightened, the boy beat him up with unexpected skill and disappeared. When he asked an old friend in the Brigade Criminelle of the Police Judiciaire to intervene and pick the boy up for questioning, they had been unable to find him. He had even approached a long-time contact in the Gestapo who had promised to make discreet inquiries. Again, nothing had been uncovered.

Fredriksson finally fell asleep puzzling over possible motives for

Jeanette's disappearance. She knew he had planned to return to her flat in a few days, yet it had been closed and the brief note read almost as if she expected him to receive it only by chance.

In spite of the motor transportation, their pace was little faster than that of a marching man. But then the Russians have never been intrigued by speed, Fredriksson thought. Even their trains rarely moved faster than sixty kilometres per hour. It was possible, Fredriksson found, to converse with the troops marching along the road with Ehrenburg as his translator. Time after time he was told by the eager young men that in Germany the working class was strong and would soon come to its senses and overthrow the Fascist officers, government officials and Ruhr millionaires who had begun this war. The German soldier is advancing only because he will be shot if he does not, one boy, barely seventeen and a proud Party candidate and Komsomol member, told him.

They were steadily drawing nearer to the front. Russian aircraft roared overhead and damaged tanks were hauled to the rear on huge trailers. Occasionally, a lorry painted with red crosses clanged past. The columns of marching troops began to break into smaller units that streamed across the fields as far as one could see in either direction. The roar of artillery was much louder, yet the first spurt of black earth and shuddering explosion came as a shock. They had come within range of the German long range artillery. Military police, mostly women with rifles slung across their backs, shouted the thickening traffic on.

Fredriksson had been a close observer of the battlefield in Abyssinia, Manchuria, Spain, Poland, Norway, Belgium and France for seven years, but he had never seen anything equal to this. In some ways the scene resembled an eighteenth-century painting – one of those monstrously huge canvases designed to cover palace walls. The lines of marching men wreathed in cannon smoke were similar to their earlier brethren, except that there was no longer even a hint of that clockwork precision or the brilliant uniforms and standards that so easily caught an artillery observer's eye. Nor was there the gallant stupidity of sabre-wielding dragoons – the rifled musket had disposed of that insanity ninety years before. Opposing generals now sat miles behind their lines and sped their orders by telephone, telegraph and wireless, rather than from nearby hills with mounted messengers. Only the taste of dust, the smell of sweat and fear and the gnarled hand that inexorably squeezed one's insides into nausea remained the same.

And he was a fool for being here; his colleagues were content to remain at military headquarters where, pampered and well-protected, they were supplied all the information needed for their one-sided stories.

A lorry three ahead exploded with a vicious crack and burning debris rained across the convoy. Yet traffic barely paused, circling the flaming torch that had once carried thirty living men and was now their funeral pyre. As they passed, Fredriksson saw the lorry half on its side. The faint breeze strengthened at that moment and the flames parted. He shuddered at the sight of corpses fried to benches along the sides.

At a crossroads, another lorry burned and a body lay beside it. Not far away, a second body, arm encircled by the red band of a police detachment, was missing its head. As they lurched past, Fredriksson saw the dead figure was a woman with skirts twisted around muddy, scorched thighs.

Without warning, a flight of four Stukas swooped on the convoy. Machine guns slashed the column and Fredriksson reacted by instinct. He dove from the still-moving lorry and scrabbled into the field, remembering again the terror of a similar attack near Dunkirk. The Stukas came again and their machine guns sighed like tearing cloth and left men, animals and vehicles dead, dying, screaming and burning. He risked a glance and saw his lorry burning fiercely – along with his suitcase. Unconsciously, he had grabbed up the case with his portable typewriter and notes.

The Stukas disappeared as suddenly as they had come. Fredriksson glimpsed them racing off to the west. His head ached with concussion and his lungs burned with acrid gasses. A noncommissioned officer with the red triangles of rank on his collar was chivying troops to their feet with hysterical shouts. As he stumbled back towards the road, Fredriksson counted eight bodies.

Ilya Ehrenburg found him and, with a strained grin, inquired as to his health. 'Imagine,' he said, 'and we are still ten kilometres from the front!'

They managed to find a ride in another lorry until an hour later they were stopped at a check point. Ehrenburg argued with a military policewoman and showed her his papers to no avail. He even told her who he was, but she claimed never to have heard of him. A dejected Ehrenburg returned.

'We can go no further. General Zurinko has given new orders.'

The sound of artillery was very loud here and through the trees Fredriksson could see the flash of guns. They were only a hundred metres from the Russian batteries. Ehrenburg sensed his apprehension and noticed the battery for the first time. 'Let's get the hell away from here before those guns annoy someone,' he muttered.

The field seemed like any other; grain beaten down by boots, sod torn up by wheels and treads. Small piles of sandbags were strewn about and it was some minutes before Fredriksson realised that he was looking at the roofs of underground bunkers.

They spent that night in a dugout crammed with soldiers who would be moving up to the front in the morning. A radio played softly somewhere and the banal refrain that he had heard over and over again since his arrival in Moscow, 'The Sacred War', filled the overheated air. Ehrenburg had translated it for him and the words spoke of Russia determined to destroy the invaders and save the motherland.

Fredriksson slept badly, as badly as the young men around him. They were the same, or similar, to the ones seen marching towards the front all day, only now their confidence had been replaced by strain. Restless movement filled the stuffy dugout and more than one cried in fitful sleep. How many of them would be alive tomorrow night, he wondered?

Towards midnight it began to rain and within minutes the dugout was knee-deep in water. Those who had been sleeping on the floor stumbled about the crowded hole cursing and looking for a dry place to sleep. Ehrenburg had appropriated the table the evening before and slept through it all like a baby.

At first light, a sergeant woke them with hoarse shouts and the dugout emptied quickly. Shivering with fatigue, Fredriksson followed. The rain had stopped only to be replaced by fog and it was cold. Long lines jammed the area between the cotton ribbons that marked off the privies which the rain had caused to overflow. The stench was overpowering and more than one nerve-tight stomach gave up the struggle to retain its contents. No other latrine system had been dug and military policewomen stood beyond the tapes to enforce the strict army sanitation rules.

Ehrenburg scared up a small canvas wash-basin and a scrap of soap and Fredriksson stripped and washed while the irrepressible Red Army correspondent found two dry sets of uniform, complete with waterproofs. He also produced two sets of correspondent's collar tabs and safety pins.

'We had better wear these uniforms - and tabs - from now on,' he explained, grinning, 'or we will have rifles shoved into our hands.'

Afterwards, they stood in line for breakfast. 'Dry clothes, a warm blanket and morning tea. Ah! What a life. I need little else to satisfy me,' Ehrenburg chortled.

'I would add toothpowder and dry cigarettes,' Fredriksson sighed.

'Well of course, if you prefer to live soft,' Ehrenburg responded.

After a skimpy breakfast of tea, cold porridge with sausage mash and black bread, they walked to a headquarter's dugout where Ehrenburg engaged a full colonel in vigorous conversation, twice pointing to Fredriksson.

Fredriksson understood just enough to realise that he was negotiating permission for them to proceed to the front lines and, for the first time in his career, he hoped devoutly that it wouldn't be granted. The officer seemed of like mind, but Ehrenburg persisted until the man threw up his hands in disgust and wrote out two passes. Ehrenburg snatched them up before he changed his mind.

*

The fog thinned as the sun rose higher, then disappeared quite abruptly at 0900. The heat grew intense. The countryside steamed and Fredriksson's wool uniform was soaked with sweat within minutes.

The ground, uneven beneath the wet grass, was full of hillocks and gullies that made walking difficult. Ahead, a forest of aspen glistened in strong sunlight, a beckoning oasis whose shadowed interior promised relief from the heat. Fredriksson could not believe the number of men and vehicles that covered the plain around him. Thousands, no hundreds of thousands, moved forward in long lines that curved north and south about the patch of woodland. Lorries and tanks, scout cars and motorcycles scurried and trundled through the ranks. Overhead, aircraft streaked low across the fields towards the west and the sound of gunfire.

Tentatively, a German shell warbled in and exploded. Heads turned and steps faltered but a sergeant's shout whipped them on. Of a sudden, the land dipped towards the trees and, as if his reaching that line were a signal, salvoes of artillery shells fell on them.

Fredriksson burrowed into the grass as the world erupted. Shell after shell exploded and the sizzle of shrapnel and the concussion of high-explosives deafened him. Shells slammed in without the usual warning scream – eighty-eight millimetre shells, he guessed. The Germans were using the eighty-eight, designed originally as an anti-aircraft weapon, and whose shell travelled faster than sound. In France, the British had joked that if you heard it coming, you knew it had missed.

The pounding went on and on and occasionally he heard a scream above the roar and caught glimpses of medical orderlies crouched low against the whirling shrapnel as they scurried from casualty to casualty. There was no panic; no one ran. Some had scooped shallow depressions in the earth with their hands or entrenching tools, others curled into a foetal position, hoping to present the smallest possible target.

Many times before in similar situations, Fredriksson had wondered how and why soldiers endured such danger, such agony, without revolting. The Russian soldier was said to possess an overwhelming love for Mother Russia, a claim he had always dismissed as a lazy historian's fable. Yet, even Stalin – possibly the least romantic man that ever existed – had dropped his appeals to socialist fervour to invoke the spirit of Poltava, of Borodino and Sebastopol in the defence of Mother Russia. Hadn't he taken to addressing the Russian people as brother and sister, rather than as comrade?

Abruptly, the bombardment shifted away from their immediate area. After a moment of stunned silence, officers hurried back and forth along the line, prodding men up. Fredriksson stumbled on aware at first only of huddled bodies left behind, then, on either side, of dun-coloured soldiers rising and flowing towards the woods lying like a traffic barrier before them. Ehrenburg appeared, his face twisted in anger and fear. The Russian dropped a hand on his shoulder and fell into step beside him, neither man capable of uttering a word.

Smoke rose from the trees and he saw ominous flashes of light among the shadows. Another flurry of artillery exploded and as quickly moved on. The Germans were firing box patterns and shifting them about seemingly at random, but in actual fact according to mathematically-pointed grids designed to kill and maim the greatest number of men.

Woods enfolded them and Fredriksson was startled when the odour of plant mould, green leaves and hot sunshine overcame the cloying stench of death and high explosive for a moment. Smoke drifted among the trees like fog and the underbrush had been beaten through with paths.

Shrapnel whirred without warning and bits of leaf and wood rained about them. Fredriksson sensed that he was suffering from shock. He had experienced this same unreality before, as if his tie to the earth had been severed and he was moving about the planet as an invisible observer, immune to harm. It was a common experience, he knew; one of the mind's many tricks for survival.

The trees ended abruptly and the land grew into a rise and artillery fire was murderous in the arena thus formed. The miasma of high-explosive sickened him; the sharper, sulphurous smell of gun powder – the smell of hell – combining with the stench of churned earth, the sweetness of blood, the odour of burned flesh, and faeces and urine.

Lines of men became robots disappearing abruptly beyond the rise. The noise was an incredible mix of whining shells, terrifying explosions, of small arms fire and machine guns, tanks, aircraft – all made thin by the overwhelming size of the battlefield until it had become a single, ululating scream, too often mimicked by a maimed and dying man.

Abruptly, Fredriksson saw that he was crossing the rounded crest onto a shallow slope that swept down into a narrow valley only to rise again to a matching hill a thousand metres on. The ground between had been churned into a nightmare. Trenches were raw brown sores edged with barbed wire entanglements like scabbed flesh. Not a trace of grass remained to be seen in the blasted, muddy, tortured earth. It was like looking at a black and white photograph of the Somme on the fourth day, he thought in awe. Never had he seen such desolation, never even imagined it.

Periodically, toy soldiers rose and ran forward, their brave shouting lost in the noise and distance, before the scythe-like sweeps of machine guns swept them away. Something brushed his jacket and a neat hole appeared in the fabric between his arm and ribs.

Fredriksson sprawled head-first into a trench. Impelled by instinct, he scrambled forward to crouch against the wall as another barrage of artillery shells blasted the trenches. What was he doing here? He hadn't even a steel helmet; none of them had. All the Russian soldiers he had seen so far wore soft garrison caps . . . A shell exploded above the parapet and a piece of jagged wood tore away the chest of the man beside him. The soldier, a grizzled, middle-aged man with the wind-burned face of a farmer, looked down at his ruined chest. His lips moved as if to ask what had happened, but there was no air in his shredded lungs and before Fredriksson could react, the man died.

Whistles blew and a boot crashed against his ribs. Soldiers in brown uniforms threw themselves over the edge, shouting. Bodies cannoned back as the trench emptied and Fredriksson staggered up, edging his head above the parapet to see the latest wave of Russian soldiers shamble across the churned mud towards the German positions.

They fell like grains of wheat spewed out by a harvesting machine. Still the survivors trotted on, rifles held at trail, shouting with grim defiance. Only a few reached the German trench, and they were quickly shot or bayonetted.

Fredriksson slid back, sickened by the slaughter, to find that the trench had filled again. A soldier snarled, thinking him a coward. Another, wearing sergeant's triangles on his collar tabs, grabbed his arm, then mumbled what must have been an apology when he saw the correspondent's insignia. Another soldier had time only to grin before the whistles sent him and the rest out of the trench.

Fredriksson watched as again the line swept forward and just as quickly melted away. He saw the sergeant who had grabbed him fall to his knees. For a moment he thought the man might get up again, but instead he lay down carefully. An artillery shell exploded and obliterated the area an instant later and when the smoke cleared away there was nothing at all to be seen.

Three more times the insane attacks went forward until the distant figures that were Germans stumbled out of their trenches and ran, clumsy with exhaustion, towards the ridge behind them. More Russian soldiers scurried across no-man's land and swept along by the press, excitement and terror, Fredriksson found himself sliding down into the German trench.

It was a charnel house. Not even in Abyssinia had Fredriksson seen so many dead and dying men in one small area. They lay in heaps, bodies slumped across one another as if engaged in a murderous football scrum. Blood everywhere, hardly recognisable as part of the muddy mixture of earth, splintered wood and torn flesh. There were a few still alive and as he watched, a Russian soldier bayonetted a wounded German as the man tried to crab away on one hand and a twisted leg, the other hand held out to ward off the steel. A metre away, an overwhelmed medic bandaged a young boy who screamed with his eyes closed. A little way beyond lay a dead stretcher bearer, his throat torn open by a German bayonet.

The trench was filling with Russian soldiers. Bodies were dragged away to clear space and the abandoned German machine guns manhandled around to cover the ridge. Whistles blew and hoarse shouting sent raiding parties either way along the trench to expand the bridgehead.

Fredriksson knew the Germans would mount a counterattack within minutes and, without a qualm, he climbed out of the trench and started back towards the illusory shelter of the Russian trench and the woods beyond. A hand caught at his sleeve and he turned to see Ehrenburg's strained face.

'We were separated,' he mumbled. Then remembering, he forced a grin. 'An excellent story, hey?' His voice caught and as he turned away to hawk and spit, Fredriksson saw tears coursing through the dirt on his cheeks.

The German counterattack came within the hour. Artillery blasted the trenches with such fury that every German gun in the sector must have been turned onto those coordinates, Fredriksson thought as rolling clouds of flame and smoke systematically obliterated the ground.

The barrage lasted five minutes and immediately a wave of German infantry running behind a dozen tanks appeared. It was over in minutes. The Russian soldiers, who had not had time to consolidate their hold on the trench, let alone fortify it to the rear, were overwhelmed and the trench was back in German hands once more.

'My God.' Fredriksson marvelled at the power of the German guns as he watched the few survivors crawl back in the fading light. Then Russian tanks rumbled past – squat, bulbous shapes with immensely long cannon. The light was bad and further obscured by a thick haze of smoke and dust. Even so, he saw German Mark III and Mark IV tanks appear to engage them. The Russians were badly outnumbered but two Mark IIIs exploded into fireballs with their first shots. A third Mark III darted in and fired at a range of less than a hundred metres and he saw the glowing trail as the shot struck and caromed off the Russian's armour plating.

The Russian tank's turret swung about with astonishing speed and fired one shot. The Mark III disintegrated; the next instant a Mark IV tank scored a direct hit on the Russian's rear deck and it too blew up. A single Russian crewman struggled out and ran for the cover of a burned-out lorry.

Ehrenburg muttered to himself as he made notes in the fading light. Fredriksson shook his shoulder and pointed to the tanks. 'I've never seen that model before. What the devil are they?'

'Our new T-34 tank,' Ehrenburg announced proudly. 'The most advanced in the world. The Hitlerites have nothing like it! It is with these T-34 tanks that we will sweep to Berlin!'

But not that night. The German counterattack developed into a front-wide offensive that sent the Red Army reeling back. By dawn Fredriksson and Ehrenburg had retreated fifteen kilometres in the dark with a panicked reserve division whose commander was determined not to be caught up in another, by now, classic German encirclement.

Fredriksson returned to Moscow five days later. He did not see Ilya Ehrenburg again and no one was able to tell him what had become of his guide. A final interview, a prerequiste to leaving the Soviet Union, was conducted by a young political officer who refused to answer most of Fredriksson's questions, including the location of the battle.

The political officer insisted that the location made no difference. 'You were asked only to view the fighting quality of the Soviet soldier. No other Western correspondent has been allowed to the front and so you should feel privileged. It is now your duty to the world proletariat to write about that spirit which means the ultimate triumph of the Soviet Union over the cowardly Hitlerites, under the courageous leadership of Joseph Stalin, our ...'

Fredriksson picked up his hat and stood to go, his anger overwhelming him. Thousands of men had died in the last few days while this smug bureaucrat, safe behind his desk in his perfectly pressed uniform, manicured fingers sore from shuffling papers, dared presume to tell him what to write.

'You dishonour the men who gave their lives,' he shouted at him, 'with your prattle of fighting spirit and your asinine remarks about how poor a soldier the German is. Go to the front yourself and see what it's all about, you bloody bastard.'

The commissar stared at him in shock.

Fredriksson paused at the door. 'Don't you dare to tell me about the worth of the Russian soldier! I've seen that for myself. And the rawest recruit among them is worth a hundred of you rear echelon bastards any time.'

Four NKVD men were waiting at his hotel. They brought with them a message from the director of the Soviet Information Bureau, his passport and a ticket on an SAS flight to Stockholm that same afternoon. Fredriksson knew he had broken every rule governing the conduct of a neutral correspondent with his outburst but he did not regret one word of it.

But surprisingly enough, the director's message made it clear that his words were not being interpreted as an anti-Soviet, anti-Communist attack. The NKVD men were helpful and polite as he packed and they drove him to the airport and accepted glasses of vodka while he waited to board. Someone, somewhere, he thought, had appreciated his comments to that rear-area hugging bastard.

*

Not until he returned to Stockholm was Fredriksson able to deduce for certain that he and Ehrenburg had accompanied elements of the Soviet Sixteenth Army into battle near Smolensk. The encirclement they had barely escaped had bagged most of the Sixteenth and Twentieth armies – an estimated 310,000 prisoners in all. Radio Berlin claimed that General Guderian's Second Panzer Group alone accounted for 38,000 prisoners, 3,000 armoured vehicles and 3,000 more artillery pieces.

Thoughtfully, Fredriksson ended the three-part account of the Battle of Smolensk in his 'From Across the World' column for 26 September 1941 with the observation that:

> . . . Hitler stands poised on the cutting edge of victory, just as did Napoleon at Borodino 129 years ago. His string of victories is unbroken in the east but autumn weather is bearing down and the rains will start soon. And in mid-October, winter.
>
> Still, Smolensk has fallen, the last great fortress before the capital. Hitler's military genius has not yet failed, nor that of the German army.
>
> Russia and Great Britain reel in uneasy alliance, battered by and separated by two thousand kilometres of victorious German Army, Navy and Air Force. September, October, November, December. Are these the final four months of Western European civilisation as it is now constituted?

Kiev September 1941

Prager left the conference and strode across the dusty field to his tent where he tore off his tunic and shirt and flopped onto the cot. He lay with his hands behind his head, staring at the molten dots of light in the pale canvas. He was so tired and frustrated that he restrained tears with great difficulty. His exhaustion was a physical pain; his head pounded, his eyes were gritty, his stomach burned and bouts of shivers passed through him so that his ribs ached and every internal organ screamed in protest. He desperately needed sleep yet his body would not let go, could not ease up after weeks of strain and effort at the highest pitch.

In six days his panzer battalion had moved three hundred kilometres while involved in continuous fighting. He had slept in snatches, ten minutes here, twenty there as they tore through the desperate resistance put up by the remnants of three Soviet armies strung out along the approaches to the Dnieper River, southwest of the city of Kiev.

The First Panzer Group in concert with the German Sixth Army had encircled and destroyed the Russian Sixth, Twelfth, and part of the Eighteenth Armies at Uman southeast of Kiev. Now, instead of being withdrawn for rest and badly needed maintenance, Prager had just been given orders to turn and drive north to meet the Second Panzer Group pushing down from the north.

What the hell was the matter with them? Why can't those fools in Berlin understand that tanks and men cannot run forever without maintenance and rest? For God's sake, his battalion had started the campaign with equipment and men exhausted from that damnable Balkan jaunt! And there had been neither time, nor equipment, nor replacement parts to repair the damage that six weeks of hard fighting in Yugoslavia and Greece had done. Yet his battalion, as badly off as they were, was in immeasurably better shape than others in the division, operating with captured French, Belgium and Czechoslovak tanks and lorries.

It was no use, Prager thought and sat up groaning. He rinsed his face and head in the canvas basin and stood for a moment, eyes closed, letting the cooling water drip onto his bare chest and shoulders. The interior of the tent was sweltering. There was damned little shade on the steppe and no relief from the heat at night. Tempers were fine drawn and brittle.

A staff colonel had come down from HQ from somewhere in Poland – he hadn't heard where and couldn't have cared anyway – with the new orders and had nearly gone back in a box. Prager understood what von Rundstedt hoped to accomplish with the proposed pincer movement, but there were limits to what men and machines could endure. Kliest, the Group commander, was a panzer general and ought to know better.

My God, Prager thought, if his own First Panzer Group was any indication, the Second Panzer Group must be in even worse shape. They had to drive three hundred kilometres against determined opposition in order to close their share of the ring, while his battalion had only a hundred or so more to do. He gave in then and pulled the vodka bottle from his pack and filled a cup. Only vodka could relax him when he was this exhausted. He snorted, remembering how he had often dismissed his father's Russian front stories of the last war as exaggerations; if anything, his father had understated conditions.

On the night of 16–17 September 1941, Prager stood in the turret of the lead Panzer IV, trying to follow the shielded flashlights of military policemen guiding him towards the river. The night was heavy with humidity and thunder muttered. Flashes of light flickered along the horizon but it was impossible to differentiate between summer heat lightning and artillery. The air smelled of rain and he hoped to God it was so. Anything to break this everlasting heat!

Ahead lay the Sula river, the last Soviet-defended position this side of the Dnieper. As they advanced across the invisible fields, only the darker shapes of trees against the sky betrayed the fact that they were not lost on a vast ocean. The rumble of Panzer IIIs and IVs competing with the guns and thunder was curiously soothing. The tank bucked, throwing him against the hatch coaming, and only then did he realise that they had passed the last military policeman.

Heavy overcast added to the intense darkness and Prager began to navigate with compass and map lit by the turret's shielded red lamp. Five kilometres to the river, he had been told; their task to spread out along the bank, hull down to meet a suspected concentration of Soviet armour and artillery.

Without warning, high velocity shells slashed overhead with a hissing, tearing roar and exploded half a kilometre behind his rearmost tank. The night sky lit up with the concentrated barrage until it seemed as if every gun in the Red army had been registered on their jump-off point. Thank God, he thought, they had got off early.

A moment later the German counter-barrage began and the sky above the river and approaches was crisscrossed with white and red slashes. The safest place to be, Prager thought, was right here, halfway between the two artillery formations as they battled to destroy one another.

They reached their position shortly after midnight and still a bit ahead of schedule. An infantry platoon had proceeded them to mark the area with tapes and they were quickly guided into position. There was little to do then but wait and see if the Russian attack developed. Prager stood his crew down, all but the radio operator, and climbed out of the tank to check that the infantry positions were adequate for his defence. He found the lieutenant in charge of the infantry detachment and by flashlight under a stifling blanket, compared maps. Then with nothing more to do but remain awake, he seated himself far enough back on the turret so that the raised lip of the hatch opening cut against his legs. More than once he had used the discomfort of this position to help him stay awake.

Involuntarily, his hand touched the letters from Sonja tucked into the inside pocket of his black panzer jacket. A packet of six letters, dating from mid-July had finally caught up with him.

Her news was cheerful and for that he was thankful. She wrote of a British bombing raid on Hamburg which had done little damage, according to the radio and newspapers, but had resulted in the destruction of sixteen British bombers. His friend and best man at their wedding, Joachim Brenner, had visited her while on three days' leave before departing for the front and had come to Hamburg to see his mother. He looked very handsome, she wrote, in his new black and silver SS parade uniform with polished high boots and the Sturmbannfuehrer's rank gleaming on his collar. Sonja had enclosed a photograph of the two of them standing by the river beneath the cherry tree, laughing at the camera while Brenner, in parade dress uniform, held the remote cable release in his right hand and encircled Sonja's waist with his left. Brenner had drawn an arrow on the photograph to indicate his major's rank, a reference to an old joke between them.

The photograph of the two laughing people he loved best in the world, with their arms about one another beside the summer banks of the Wandsee River, released a powerful surge of nostalgia. Prager cursed himself for a fool and tried to force Sonja and the letters from his mind, but she hovered on the fringes, distracting him.

He moved restlessly, hitched himself around and stared in the direction of the river. Prager heard a rattle followed by what sounded like a shout. He sat up and listened hard, trying to screen out the roar of the artillery. There, he thought he heard someone call again, from his left, upriver. He had stationed his tank on the end of the line and there should be nothing else in that direction. Making up his mind, he leaned down inside.

The driver peered up at him and Prager showed him his drawn pistol. 'Sit still, Hans, and keep your eyes open. I thought I heard something to the left. I'm going for a quick look.'

Hans nodded but his expression in the red light was disapproving and Prager knew he was right. He should call in the infantry and have them investigate, but he badly needed the distraction. Before the driver could object verbally, he dropped to the ground and, after warning the sentry post, moved off diagonally towards the river.

The earth rose in a natural levée as he approached the river some one hundred metres beyond his tank. Thick bushes lined the crest and from there he could see the river's glint again. He eased down the bank to the shingle verge and knelt, listening.

The far side was invisible. The cloud cover had thickened, obscuring the last stars that had been visible on the western horizon. Artillery flashes and star shells provided a weird, flickering light that moved shadows and objects about as if by witchcraft. Prager knelt in the sand beside the river for several minutes, then convinced that he was hearing things, he started back up the bank. A new sound, a motor, caught his attention.

Prager hesitated, undecided, hating himself for his fear – which was for Sonja as much as himself. The old bugaboo of leaving her friendless and abandoned in an enemy land if he were killed had bothered him terribly of late. With an angry grunt, he climbed back to the bank's crest and padded along the top, making as little noise as possible.

A rocket burst over the river and he saw something edging down the bank half a kilometre further on. In the instant before the flare died, he spotted a tank. The river was low after the summer's heat and the Russians would have little difficulty in crossing here.

Prager raced back to his tank and radioed a concise report to division headquarters, *en clair* so as not to waste time in the coding process, then, without waiting for orders, told Hans to start the engine and drive northwest along the bank at slow speed. He gave quick orders to the rest of the battalion on the command frequency, plans forming in his mind as he spoke.

Prager divided his force in half, silently cursing the loss of two tanks earlier in the day. Six tanks would attack the escaping Russian force while the other five remained in position in case this proved a diversion for a larger breakout.

The night was oppressive with menace. Prager halted his attenuated column to check his bearings. He had marked their firing positions on a line between a rock outcropping and a stand of bushes screening the small inlet. Satisfied they were in the correct position, he spoke softly into the microphone, waited a moment, and fired a red flare.

He heard the driver's whoop and the tank surged forward, bursting through the screening brush. The gunner reached up to slap his leg and he fired point blank at the single Russian tank, an old KV1 which blew up with a concussion that cracked along the river bank and stunned the Russians. Prager could not have asked for a better entry.

Steady streams of machine gun fire and round after round of 75 millimetre shells smashed into the startled Russians. Prager was vaguely aware that several hundred men at least were milling about in the shallows as he shouted orders into the microphone.

They fought bravely but rifles and machine pistols were no match against tanks and they never had a chance. A few managed to escape by swimming the river but most died where they fought. By the time a motorised rifle company arrived, it was all over.

Prager stalked through the debris at the crossing point to where two infantry officers were laughing at documents their troops were gathering up.

'Do you know who these people were?' one asked. 'You've just eliminated the staff of Colonel-General Kirponos, the commander of the Kiev defence as well as the entire Russian Southwest Military Front. One of those,' he hooked a thumb at the jumble of bodies around the smashed boats, 'is probably his.

'We've not only taken Kiev tonight but you've captured or killed the HQ staff before they could run away.'

Dogorov moved along the trench, alerting his men to pull back. The way was knee deep in mud and the night as black as the inside of hell. A cold, stinging rain scourged this remnant of General Bagramyan's scratch force, the survivors of the Fifth and Twenty-Sixth Armies escaped from Zhitomir and the Thirty-Seventh charged with the defence of Kiev.

Dogorov and the twenty-three survivors of his battery had rejoined the

Red Army on a hot, sunny Sunday, two weeks previously. They had walked out of a patch of woods with a white flag tied to a stripped sapling, confident of a hero's welcome, and were promptly fired upon. Three men were killed outright and they retreated ignominiously to the woods. It had taken most of that day to convince the local Red Army commander that they were Russian soldiers who had escaped from behind enemy lines and not deserters or Nazis in disguise. All of which should have warned him of the kind of reception they could expect.

They were disarmed and beaten with rifle butts, then caged behind barbed wire in a muddy swamp in which at least a thousand more Red Army soldiers, also escapees from Nazi-occupied territory, were being held.

For two days they were not fed. Their equipment, including blankets, was taken away, and they slept in the mud. Dogorov was called for interrogation on the third day. He was given a sheaf of paper and a stub of a pencil and told to set out his activities during the past two and a half months in detail. He finished the document at mid-afternoon and was given a glass of lukewarm tea. His bladder was near bursting. The guard muttered an oath at his request but led him out the back and pointed to a patch of muddy ground near a shed.

The actual interrogation was conducted by a middle-aged officer of the Thirty-Seventh Army, wearing the sleeve designation of a commissar. He questioned Dogorov minutely about his weeks behind enemy lines, beginning the day *after* the invasion. Not once did he ask a single question relating to the events of 21 June, or earlier. When Dogorov tried to describe the disposition of the regiment on the first day, the man simply stopped writing. Afterwards, he went on with the interrogation as if Dogorov had not interrupted.

Why had he allowed his command to be taken by surprise? His indignant answer that he certainly had not, was ignored. Had he not come from behind enemy lines? Well then? Did he not realise that he accused, verified his guilt and judged himself all at once?

Dogorov could see that his explanations were falling on deaf ears. He strove to make the man understand that they had not surrendered to the Nazis, but had fought every step of the way. He described their suffering from hunger and wounds, and how only twenty of his entire battery of 148 men had survived those terrible weeks.

The commissar's response was to instruct him not to refer to the German bandits as Nazis. 'They are known as *Hitlerites*. Their political system has nothing whatsoever to do with socialism and it is forbidden to misrepresent them as so-called national socialists.'

The commissar shuffled papers while Dogorov stared in disbelief. A sense of unreality settled about him. He thought of all they had suffered, just so that he could stand in front of this pompous party hack and be instructed like a schoolboy in the proper terminology to apply to the enemy.

The commissar's distrust was plain enough in his contemptuous expression. 'So then, if you were surrounded, if you were out of touch with Soviet forces as you claim, why did you not proceed to Minsk, or even Smolensk? Both cities were certainly closer,' he shouted. 'Explain that, you lying traitor!'

For the first time, Dogorov realised that this was more than a simple mistake. He was on trial for his life! They really did suspect him of being a turncoat! He knew that if he could only explain, things would straighten themselves out, but in his wretched, exhausted state he could not find the words.

The commissar scribbled his signature on a card and pressed a button on the desk. Immediately, the door opened and a guard stepped in. The officer flicked the card across the room to him. 'Take this scum away.'

Surprisingly enough, Dogorov was neither taken to be shot nor to prison; instead, the guard marched him back to the holding compound where the survivors of his battery, all but Lieutenant Siderov who had been taken away at the same time as he, stood at attention against the fence. The guard spoke to another who approached with a scrap of paper and a piece of torn map.

'Here, you,' the man snarled. 'Take this rabble to where it says on there,' he tapped the paper. 'Such devils as you insult real Red Army men.'

Dogorov had never in his entire career been spoken to in such a fashion by an enlisted man. But he knew instinctively that to react would cause his men to suffer. Instead, he dismissed the sergeant before he had a chance to say anything more.

A thin overcast had moved in as they marched through the bombed-out city and into the southeastern suburbs. They were thunderstruck at the devastation, unable to understand how so much damage could be done to so heavily fortified a city. The cloud cover reduced the sun's glare and heat but increased the humidity. An hour later, they had left the last blocks of houses behind and were directed to an assembly point hidden in a thick patch of woods. There they waited until long after dark before being issued three days rations, a full water bottle, a threadbare blanket smelling of rust and mildew, and rusty Model 1892 Mosin-Nagant rifles to which the bayonets had been welded, relics of the Great War.

They marched again and were passed from voice to voice for endless hours until, after midnight, they reached a line of trenches. Their guide led them down into the mud and filth and with a muttered, 'Good luck,' disappeared. It began to rain hard shortly before dawn and as a consequence none of them got much sleep.

At dawn, Dogorov discovered that they had been delivered to a *Strafny*, or punishment, battalion which occupied the most forward portion of a trench system constructed in overlapping circles about the city. It seemed that someone in the vast security apparatus extending back to Moscow had hit on an effective – and useful – way of eliminating undesirable elements.

During the next three days they were under continual shell fire but were denied hot food, dry clothing or blankets. Officially, they existed only as long as it took them to die; no sense wasting resources on scum was the obvious attitude. Probing attacks occurred often, day and night. These were usually preceded by a short artillery barrage that barely ended before the first elements of the Nazi – no, Dogorov corrected himself, Hitlerite – attack reached their trenches.

On the fourth afternoon, a heavy barrage began to roll along the Russian lines. Dogorov waited for the counterbarrage to begin. Instead, the ferocity of the German fire increased and Russian guns fell silent. By dark, the nineteen men who had entered the trenches with him had dwindled to nine. One man, the youngest in the battery, his wasted face pallid in the light of star shells and artillery bursts, gave him a half-hearted smile and tried to joke. Dogorov had tried to send him to the rear with a message but the boy politely refused. Dogorov did not press; he understood that he preferred to die here, with his friends, rather than among those who had deserted them.

A cold anger suffused him at the waste and the arrogance of their treatment. They had been thrown away, disposed of to relieve the State of the burden of their trials, left to the Hitlerites for execution.

The rain, which had slackened and then stopped during the afternoon, began again at sunset. Lightly at first, it quickly turned into a torrential downpour. An officer appeared on the trench lip, silhouetted against the ravening sky by flares. He shouted instructions to pull back in ten minutes above the noise of the barrage, rain and wind, then disappeared. Dogorov did not know who the officer was or where he had come from and was far too exhausted to care. Lightning and thunder were indistinguishable from the flash and roar of cannon as Dogorov stumbled along the trench alerting the five survivors to be ready to pull back. He came to the end where the last man, a soldier whom he did not know, stared at him with wild eyes.

Dogorov edged his head above the level of the trench and stared at the darkness. Rain swept on a cold wind spattered his face and he slid back down – just as an artillery shell exploded at the bend in the trench and a solid wall of furnace air slammed him sideways and the trench wall collapsed.

A heavy, wet mass moulded itself across his body, pinning him down. Something flopped wetly onto his shoulders, pressing his face into the stinking mud.

His lungs raged with deprivation and the icy mud burned his skin; but his legs were free and he struck out grimly as the mud began to fill his nostrils and force its way into his mouth. His foot encountered something hard and he hooked his boot about it, hardly knowing what he was doing, and pulled. The mass holding him down shivered and with a superhuman effort, he pulled again. Mud cascaded away and he was free.

Dogorov remained on hands and knees, spitting mud, gasping for air, then turned aside to vomit. Afterwards, he held his face up and the rain washed mud from him in sheets. For an instant, he was filled with gratitude that he was still alive, then he laughed abruptly. Little difference it made. He felt around for his helmet and encountered the fading warmth of a body – the shell-shocked soldier beside him in the trench. In a daze, he turned the soldier over and his hand encountered a jagged sliver of metal protruding from the neck. His muscles spasmed as if he had been electrocuted and Dogorov found himself a metre away, crouching against the trench wall, shaking with horror.

A voice swore softly above his head. He started to call out, then realised the oath had not been in Russian. Dogorov held his breath. A pair of boots slid down, banging against his bare head and knocking him into the water and mud. A match flared, died and a voice grunted as it moved away.

The trench filled with German soldiers, all shouting at once. A body thumped against him, yelling hoarsely. He heard, felt, sensed another helping the man to stretch out and Dogorov caught the sound of his spasmodic breathing. The man jerked upright, gabbled something halfway between a scream and a sigh, then fell back, one hard elbow jabbing against his thigh.

A rifle fired, the noise a tiny snap against the background thunder and artillery. Indeterminate moments later a whistle blew and the trench emptied.

Cautiously, Dogorov raised his head. Only Russian bodies were left, and the single German soldier, propped against the trench wall. Dogorov touched his throat, sought for a pulse and found none and felt a curious emptiness. Why? he wondered. The more dead Germans the better. But the murderous cynicism did not help.

In the molten light of a flare, he saw that the tunic of the Red Army soldier who had fallen on him was torn where a bayonet had been used to make certain he was dead. Why hadn't they bayonetted him . . ? and then he realised that he was still wearing a German tunic; there were no Russian uniforms to issue to those in *Strafney* battalions.

Dogorov had no idea how much time passed as he leaned against the parapet while the cold rain sluiced away the insanity. After a while, he sensed that he was suffering from shock and exhaustion and that if he remained here much longer he would die of exposure, or a German bayonet.

He saw the dead German's steel helmet. He brushed some of the mud away and put it on. The unfamiliar weight and balance helped to steady him. He hadn't the vaguest idea what to do next and stood indecisively. Dogorov sensed that the German attack had driven into Kiev itself and that the Red Army forces were therefore on the verge of extinction. No orders had come down to them all day. Had the Red Army died where it stood – and he chuckled at the incongruity of the thought, a politician's concept, not a soldier's.

He moved cautiously along the trench as far as a command bunker and stooped to enter, but the stink of scorched flesh stopped him. Having seen the aftermath of German flamethrowers before, Dogorov had no wish to repeat the experience. He backed away hastily while struggling to control his heaving stomach.

Rain pelted him in a maddening flurry and he scrambled to a clump of trees that stood some one hundred metres to the rear. For three days he had watched as every leaf, every shred of bark, every branch was blown away until at sunset today there had remained only twisted sticks poking the sky.

He crawled over Russian and German dead and twice was challenged, by whom he could not tell. Both times, he faded into the darkness and rain. Endless and impenetrable barbed wire barred his way, forcing him to long detours and he lost his sense of direction. He crawled *plastuny* style, remembering the endless 'glass house' sentences to which everyone in his cadet class had been sentenced sooner or later, for punishment and toughening up.

The sky began to lighten and vague shapes emerged. Even so, he literally stumbled against the log wall. Dogorov's heart slammed painfully and he gasped for breath. More rain slanted down as he leaned against the wall, not daring to move. What if it were occupied by Hitlerite troops? Even so, he forced himself to move, to feel his way along the rough wall until his hand encountered the cold slickness of wet glass. Peering in, the place appeared deserted. Across the way, he could make out the vague loom of another building and remembered that they had marched through a village on the way to the front.

The door was partly open. The interior had a desolate air of death and was thick with the stench of cordite, burned wood and the sweetish smell of human decomposition. In the only bedroom he found the source –an old woman lying on a bed, obviously dead for some time. Beside her sat a younger woman with an aged face. She stared down at the old woman in bruised exhaustion and in the dawn light her face was pale and bloodless.

Dogorov spoke to her but she did not acknowledge him. Stepping closer, he saw that a stray bullet or a shell splinter had struck her in the temple, killing her instantly. He shuddered. In both Finland and Russia he had seen men dead in every imaginable contortion, but the sight of this woman killed while tending – or mourning – the old woman shattered him.

A patrol of German soldiers drifted past, smoking shielded cigarettes and laughing softly. This sector must have been secured, he thought. Which meant that he could not remain in the house a moment longer. He forced his mind to work, to think, to ignore the fear that threatened to paralyse him and the weariness that made him want only to find a dry place to lie down and sleep.

Through a back window, he saw a long field and a line of leafless trees in the growing light which might well mark the river's course. There was no chance of crossing in daylight, but he would have a try tonight. In the meantime, he had to have shelter, some food and rest. A small wood shed next to the privy offered the only possible place of concealment.

The house yielded some scraps of kitchen fat from a tin above the stove, a tiny bit of maize and a twist of stale black bread. He mixed the maize and fat, spread it on the piece of bread and ate it as he studied the yard. When a flurry of rain hid the trees, he let himself out and sprinted to the shed.

There wasn't room inside to lie down but it was dry. Working as quietly in the cramped interior as possible, he shifted firewood to form a screen before the door. He sat back, sobbing with weariness and closed his eyes, only to start awake in terror every time a soldier used the privy. In between times, he was plagued by dreams of burning men and vehicles. How much had been reality and how much exaggerated memory, he never knew.

In the middle of the afternoon the door was kicked open and he nearly screamed. German voices laughed and joked as wood was dragged out. The wood he had stacked in front of him disappeared but in the gloom he was not seen. Afterwards, Dogorov wondered what had been done with the women's bodies.

Sometime around midnight, Dogorov emerged, bent and stiff with cold. In contrast to the night before, only a few guns still fired along the northern fringes of the city. Cleaning up the last pockets of resistance, Dogorov thought with bitterness.

A single sentry paced a desultory beat in the road separating the two rows of huts. Would they have posted sentries along the river bank? When he pushed through the last screen of bushes, the river stretched before him, a flat expanse of blackness, its surface stippled with the rain. He listened for a long while, then stripped off the German tunic, helmet and boots and thrust them into the trees and limped into the water.

The shock bit his body like cold iron. The strong current snatched him away from the bank and he let it carry him, realising he was too weak to do more than stay afloat. Dogorov was a good swimmer, a strong swimmer, but not even the spring-fed lakes near Moscow where his mother and he usually spent their summer holidays had prepared him for this.

At water level, the blackness was impenetrable. He had no idea in which direction he was moving or if he was moving at all. Pain isolated him from all other sensations. The first vague thoughts crept into his mind, whispering how easy it would be to let go, to stop struggling. Pain would cease; after all what lay ahead for him if he did survive? Only endless mortal danger and further terror. Russia was lost. Kiev had fallen and Leningrad and Moscow would soon follow. And the Red Army would surrender to the tender mercies of Hitlerites who strangled men and women with nooses in village squares, who murdered *babushkas* and their daughters in their huts, who machine-gunned helpless men, women and children. Who would wish to live in that kind of world?

The river's width was endless. He floated and paddled it seemed for hours, weakening with every stroke until his mind played tricks on him. He was racing his mother to the tiny island that marked the centre of the lake belonging to the ministry. At other times he was trying to swim a Karelian lake with Finnish troops pursuing in motor boats. When his foot brushed mud, he could not believe it. The transition from dream to reality was uncertain and it took all of his remaining strength to drag himself onto the mud bank. He turned over on his back, so cold that he knew he was dying.

A booted foot kicked him from the edge of unconsciousness. Rough arms dragged him up and when he tried to speak, he was struck across the mouth. His last thought was the despairing realisation that he had swum to the wrong side of the river.

East Asia 28 July – 15 November 1941

From the deck of the destroyer *Hakaze*, Hoi An seemed hardly deserving of the term 'port'. A few godowns lined a rickety wharf beyond which thatch and tin roofs clustered in a profusion of narrow, smelly streets filled with chickens, naked children and shiftless people.

Lieutenant Saburo Takeda, *Chutaicho*, commander of A Company, Sixth Special Naval Landing Forces based at Sasebo, Japan, watched as his men clambered down cargo nets draped over *Hakaze*'s side into boats. The Rising Sun ensign at the stern flapped once in the desultory onshore breeze that had come and just as quickly died with the dawn. Already the heat was a malign presence.

The Task Force had sailed from Japan four days before with instructions to land at Lon Chan in southern French Indochina. The *Hakaze*, with two army infantry companies and Takeda's company of Special Naval Landing Forces aboard, had been detached at the last moment and, accompanied by two mine sweepers, sent north to land troops at Hoi An, a coastal town south of the major city of Da Nang. Imperial Japanese forces were occupying French Indochina to use as a base to secure their supplies of oil and minerals in the face of recent American and British actions that had cut off oil supplies and jeopardised their position in Southeast Asia. They had been told they would meet little, if any, opposition from French forces in view of this second request for assistance from the Vichy government. The first had been the previous summer when Japanese tropps had been asked to prevent a Chinese invasion of northern French Indochina after the new French government had arrived at an arrangement with Nazi Germany.

Takeda had only recently reconciled himself to this command. His transfer to the Special Naval Landing Forces had come as a disappointment on his return to Japan. He had been a member of a special negotiating team sent first to Warsaw in July 1939 to explore, in secret, certain arrangements with Poland in the event either nation was attacked by the Soviet Union. But talks had been cut short by the German and Russian invasions of the country. He had then spent the next eight months travelling with a high level investigatory committee in Europe and North and Central America assessing military preparedness and morale.

Prior to his departure, he had requested submarine training but instead, on his return to Japan in July 1940, he had been ordered to Sasebo Naval Base to join the Number Six Special Landing Force as a company commander. After twelve months of intensive training and the constant expectation that they would be sent to China, they had finally received orders to entrain for Yokohama five days ago. Their destination had remained a secret until just before dawn.

A salvo of artillery shells suddenly tore the sky apart above their transport and exploded harmlessly in the bay. The unexpected attack brought shouts of amazement and Takeda bellowed down into the landing boats for silence, then swung himself onto the cargo net just as the transport destroyer's guns began to roar.

Shells from the squadron burst about the docks and Takeda saw what he thought were French troops running along the wooden structure as the boats churned furiously towards the wharf. The destroyer and mine sweepers had anchored close in and as the landing boats closed on the pier five minutes later, a machine gun opened up from the line of godowns. Somehow in the confusion, one boat carrying army troops had drawn ahead. Splinters flew from its gunwales and two men tumbled overboard.

Then the boat was below the French gunner's line of sight and the firing shifted to Takeda's boat.

He fought down a surprising surge of fear as bullets kicked a line of splashes past their stern and shouted at the four men in the bows to open fire. He was amazed that his voice was cool and controlled as he clenched his hands to hide their shaking.

Swift figures darted up the ladder to the wharf. One man spun back and plunged into the water. Another crumbled as he clawed his way over the edge. His comrades pushed past and rushed beyond Takeda's sight. Then his boat was at the ladder and his men were swarming up, urged on by the petty officer's blows. Just as they reached the top, two sharp explosions ended the firing. Hand grenades, Takeda thought and pulled himself over the splintered edge of the creosote-soaked timbers.

Smoke poured from a godown and flames burst through the roof. Several men in French uniform staggered out and were shot down instantly. Two sailors rushed forward with bayonets to make certain they were dead.

Takeda formed his company up on the dock in short order and double-timed them to the end of the wharf. The men were in high spirits but he could feel the strain beneath the grins and whispered jokes. If he allowed them time to think, fear would set in, making them overly cautious. None, including himself, had ever before been in combat.

Although inaugurated in the late 1920s and employed in China, the Special Naval Landing Forces were still an unproven concept. They were sailors trained to function as soldiers, but in an assault capacity, amphibious or otherwise. They were a handpicked élite chosen for physical size and condition, intelligence, a strong patriotic belief in the Emperor and the imperial destiny of the Japanese Empire, and trained after the manner of British and American marines.

Takeda's company entered the tangle of godowns and warehouses at a fast trot. Ahead, Takeda heard sporadic rifle shots. He ran beside the forward platoon, sword clutched against his hip to keep it from banging his legs, pistol drawn.

They broke out of the dock area abruptly. A broad boulevard, bare of all traffic and pedestrians, edged the town and craters still smoked where artillery shells had exploded minutes before.

Takeda ordered the company to ground and he took a position at the corner of a tarpaper and tin-roofed shed to study the street ahead. An unnerving silence lay over the town in the wake of the artillery barrage. His objective was the municipal offices, but to reach them he must cross the boulevard. And the memory of the French machine gun's steady tacking made him cautious.

Takeda saw in a lorry parked against a loading dock the answer to his dilemma. Moments later, using it as a mobile shield, the company charged down the street, dropping riflemen at intervals and a machine gun emplacement midway along to command either end. The street was searched quickly by squads leap-frogging one another, but they turned up only frightened civilians who spoke no Japanese.

The town of Hoi An, an overgrown village, was a confusing maze of haphazard streets, but Takeda had made a sketch map from the few aerial photographs shown to them during the briefing and he managed to find the main square without incident. As the sailors piled out of the lorry and ran to take up positions around the square, Takeda drew his sword, guessing that the sight of cold steel would do more to cow potential opposition than his pistol. A few locals watched the sailors in wonder and he was surprised to see that the Vietnamese did not look at all Chinese, as he had expected.

An elderly European in white shirt and tan trousers limped towards him. Takeda glanced around quickly to make certain his men were in place, then rested his sword point on the ground, cupped both hands over the pommel, rocked back on his heels and waited with what he hoped was proper hauteur for a Japanese officer. The European offered his hand. Takeda stared him down.

'Why have your soldiers fired on representatives of the Imperial Empire of Japan,' he demanded. 'We come in answer to your government's plea for assistance and you allow your soldiers to shoot at us!'

The French official's surprise at being addressed in his own language was pushed aside by Takeda's obvious anger.

'I don't know,' he quavered. 'I have nothing to do with the army. I am simply a clerk in . . .'

More Vietnamese were gathering and Takeda saw an opportunity to demonstrate that the hated European's day in Asia was over. Unfortunately, his orders demanded that all French officials be treated with courtesy and respect as they would continue to govern subject to Japanese decisions.

He compromised by ordering two men to escort the Frenchman into a nearby government building. Then he had a machine gun set up on the second floor from where it commanded the area. A moment later, the Japanese flag was sent up the flag pole, with the French tricolour below. The point was made, he decided.

Takeda marched his company along what had optimistically been called a road leading to the village of Phou Woa, ten miles west of Hoi An. He was accompanied by a frightened young French civil servant whom he judged worthless under the best of circumstances. They had been marching for only two hours but even so the Frenchman was exhausted.

They had not encountered a single peasant since leaving the slum of tin huts on the outskirts of Hoi An. The land was hilly and alternated between stands of trees, the name and species of which the Frenchman was too frightened to remember, and shimmering rice paddies. Occasionally a path led off the main road and Takeda sent scouts to investigate. Each time they returned to report that the path ended in a stand of trees or a rice paddy.

The village was hardly deserving of the term as it was little more than a collection of bamboo huts, arranged in two straggling lines, beside the dusty road. Takeda glimpsed open fields through the trees on either side.

He counted fourteen huts, hardly enough to justify a company of 296 men, he thought. No cooking fires coiled smoke into the morning sky and not a dog or child was to be seen.

He kicked aside a woven mat that functioned as a door and stooped inside a hut, wrinkling his nose at the powerful smell of unwashed humanity and years of stale cooking, which appeared to be done at a firepit in the centre. Sleeping mats lined the walls but there was no other furniture. He touched the firestones. Still warm.

He shouted for the Frenchman as he pushed out into the blinding sunlight. The man hurried up and bowed. Takeda saw that he was so frightened his teeth were chattering.

'Where are all the people?' he demanded. 'Where has everyone gone?'

The Frenchman explained that this was one of four outlying villages surrounding the larger central village, still a kilometre or more along the road. 'In times of trouble...' He flinched, but Takeda motioned impatiently for him to continue. '... all the people gather... in... in the central village.'

Takeda wished he had been given more information about the country. He had been told what to expect from the European elements but nothing about the native population, other than that they would welcome their Japanese liberators.

Exasperated, he called to his senior warrant officer and gave him instructions to deploy the first and third rifle platoons into a skirmish line. He glanced at his wristwatch. If he sent the second platoon to circle the main village, he decided, they would need thirty minutes to get into position. In the meantime, he would have the heavy machine gun platoon start moving forward slowly. The news of three more satellite villages made him uneasy about his exposed position in country he knew little about.

The road led between stands of trees that alternately pressed close on either side, then fell away to reveal stretches of rice paddy with more trees lining their far borders. Difficult country in which to maintain security, Takeda thought. He moved slowly, allowing the men on the wings of the skirmish line time to keep up in the jungle-dense undergrowth.

A stunning concussion smashed at his ear drums. Shells exploded along the road with ear-splitting crashes and dust, and bits of trees, and vegetation mixed with shrapnel, sprayed them. The heavy machine gun platoon disappeared into cover as more shells pounded the area.

Either the gunner's aim was poor or he was inexperienced as most of the shells fell harmlessly. His senior warrant officer, Gohay Ueda, dived into the ditch where Takeda crouched to report the mortar teams ready to fire. It was ankle deep in stagnant, foul-smelling water, but he paid no more attention to it than had Takeda. Takeda shouted the order to open fire and the two 50 millimetre Model 98 mortars began raking the trees on the far side of the paddy and flanking parties scurried out to reinforce the first and third platoons who could be seen running along the boundaries, just inside the trees.

The cannon fire stopped abruptly and a few minutes later Takeda saw the first platoon signalman climb onto the paddy bank. The French gun had decamped, he read the semaphore message. Swearing under his breath, he ordered his own signaller to have the first platoon extend their search area to the north.

When the French interpreter was brought forward, he was shaking and babbling hysterically. Takeda was embarrassed by the man's cowardice. But at least his sailors would see with their own eyes that Europeans were physically and emotionally incapable of resisting the superior morality and might of the Japanese Empire.

They entered the village with weapons ready and deployed for skirmishing. The second platoon appeared out of the trees on the other side at the same time and Takeda took comfort in knowing that two 7.7 machine guns covered the village on converging angles.

What he supposed were the village elders came forward and bowed, all eyeing his muddy, damp uniform. Takeda ignored them and motioned his sailors forward. They raced from hut to hut, driving out anyone they found inside. The Frenchman somehow summoned enough courage to still his shaking as he explained to the village elders that the Japanese had come at the request of the French government to assist in keeping the peace and to protect them from the Chinese bandits.

Takeda thought he detected blank stares at the mention of Chinese bandits but put the reaction down to fear. One of the elders started to speak, but Takeda whipped a hand downward in a clear signal to remain still, then he stalked about the square, peering at these strange, frightened people. The French official demanded to know who had fired on their Japanese protectors, his voice filling with superior indignation as he regained his courage. Takeda suddenly turned and slapped him across the face. The Frenchman stumbled back, staring at him more in astonishment than in pain.

'Listen to me, you cowardly, pale-faced scraping of dog-shit,' Takeda roared in French. 'You no longer rule in this country.' He knew his words would not be understood by the Vietnamese but his actions were clear enough. 'Never again will you abuse Asians because of your ill-conceived sense of superiority or I will hang you by your wrists and use your worthless body for bayonet practice, do you understand?'

The Frenchman, near to fainting, managed to nod. A sailor jerked him upright and Takeda ordered him explain that Japanese sailors would remain to protect the village complex from bandits. Quarters and food would be provided by the villagers in return.

'What are they saying?' Takeda demanded as the elders began to whisper among themselves.

'They say,' the Frenchman whimpered, 'that they have never heard of Chinese bandits. They do not know where these stories come from. They do not understand the reason why soldiers come here from Japan. They do not even know where Japan is.'

Takeda gave him a grim smile. 'Ask who fired at us if not Chinese bandits,' he said. 'Surely not people from the village?'

The elders exchanged wary glances at the translation and the headman eyed him with an expression of ill-concealed disgust. Anger exploded through Takeda. We risk our lives to free these people from European colonialist oppressors, he thought, and they refuse to appreciate what is being done for them. Such an attitude will mean trouble later.

He snarled an order to the senior warrant officer and pointed to the headman. Ueda jumped forward and grabbed the old man before he could react and tripped him to the ground. He snatched a cleaning rod from a rifle and wrapped a cord around the elderly man's legs. At Takeda's nod, two sailors dragged him around the dusty space while the warrant officer kept pace, beating him with the steel cleaning rod. Takeda counted twenty echoing thuds before he ordered the punishment stopped.

The French official crouched and vomited and the women hid their eyes and wailed. Takeda did not like treating an old man in this fashion but many lives were at stake, Japanese, French and Vietnamese. It was better that one old man suffer rather than dozens and possibly even hundreds, die. These people must learn that they would be punished if they refused their wholehearted cooperation.

When he asked again who had been responsible for the shooting, it was clear that the beating of the headman had had a salutary effect on the villagers. He learned that a small group of French soldiers had passed through the village the day before, from the direction of the coast. The villagers had been told only that an enemy had attacked and that the soldiers were going to drive them away. They had cautioned the village about helping the enemy and in the morning the soldiers left the village. Some had been observed moving among the trees across the rice paddies.

Army troops arrived two days later to replace them and Takeda was handed orders from the Naval Commander in charge of the Sasebo Sixth Special Landing Force at Lon Chan to return with his company to Hoi An immediately..

The Sixth Sasebo Special Naval Landing Force sailed for Japan at the end of the week. Takeda heard through the rumour mill that they were to be refitted and landed on the China coast just north of the border to support operations against French army dissidents who had taken refuge there. But two days after their return to Sasebo, the China coast operation was cancelled when the Vichy government prevailed upon French forces to stop hostile acts against Japan.

The thought of returning to a routine of training and more training was more than he could bear, Takeda thought one morning as he reviewed his company. The excitement of action in French Indochina had given him a taste for more.

He stamped into Force Headquarters an hour later and requested to speak to the Commander. The Executive Officer, Lieutenant Ienaga, grinned as he returned the salute.

'Just aching for more action, are you?' Ienaga shuffled through some papers on his incredibly messy desk and came up with a form. 'Orders for your company to prepare to embark. Destination, Manchuko.'

Takeda was flabbergasted. 'Manchuko!'

'Exactly. The army's stretched a bit thin and they've asked us for help. A momentous occasion in itself. The Admiral said, "Send that fire-eater Takeda. I want my best company commander in there. If he screws up, I'll hang him by his balls."'

Ienaga tossed the forms across the desk. 'Expect to be there at least three months. Detailed orders are being cut now. You will embark in ten days. I suggest,' he shuffled through another pile, 'that you take a few days' leave. Commander Yamara said to make certain that you do.' Ienaga leaned across the desk. 'He also asked me to say that you comported yourself with honour in Indochina.'

Lieutenant Saburo Takeda stepped down from the crowded train in the Osaka suburb of Kadoma. In the middle of the afternoon, before the evening rush hour, the station was quiet. The air was warm with the scent of summer and he stood on the platform a moment, remembering the last time he had been home – before leaving for Poland in the fourteenth year of Showa, July 1939.

Takeda decided to walk the mile and a half to his parents' home rather than hire a taxi. The unpaved road led through a market district filled with people taking advantage of the last fine weather of the season. The odour of vegetables, fruit and meat were heavy in the cool air. The road climbed towards the hills and stores and offices gave way to neat houses screened by hedges. Children raced past, laughing. Everything was neat and clean, he had the impression of walking through a vast park.

He was surprised to see that his father was at home so early in the afternoon. The old man was puttering about the hedge he had pampered for thirty years and did not see Takeda open the gate. His youngest brother, Michitaka, stepped out of the house at that moment, expression kindling with surprise. Takeda signalled him to be quiet.

'*Diamasho*,' he said quietly and bowed very low. His father turned quickly, an expression of surprise and pleasure sweeping his face and they embraced.

'What a surprise,' the old man managed. 'Why did you not send us a letter or a telegram?' His mother flurried out and embraced him, while at the same time chastising him for not writing.

'But I did not know myself until this morning that I would have leave,' he tried to explain. 'And I thought to surprise you.'

His sister Ryuko appeared and he embraced her while his brother Michitaka continued to pump his hand as they all talked at once. His father finally commanded attention and he removed his shoes and was ushered into the house.

Ryuko slipped in with the tea and rice cakes. She had changed into an *obi* while the water boiled. His father had a thousand questions and they sat talking for two hours. He described the opening stages of the German attack on Poland as he had witnessed it and then the leisurely drive he and Admiral Suga had taken through Czechoslovakia into Germany afterwards, escorted by a German officer. They had flown from Berlin to neutral Switzerland, then travelled by train to Lisbon, where the Pan American clipper had flown them to New York.

His father was most interested in this part of the story and listened carefully as he described the mixed reception they had received – warm and courteous in New York and cold and almost hostile in San Francisco. 'We were given a tour of the Brooklyn Navy Yard and entertained to dinner by naval officers led by an Admiral of rank equal to Suga.

'You may find it difficult to comprehend, Father, but it took four days to ride across the United States on a train, at speeds of one hundred kilometres per hour and more. Mountains, grasslands, cities, deserts, one after another, so many that I lost track. America is immense but it lacks the martial spirit that characterises the Japanese. The newspapers and radio news programmes were full of stories about demonstrations for peace and members of their Congress demanding that the United States remain neutral at all costs.

'In San Francisco the whole atmosphere was different. We were not allowed to see the naval yards nor travel to a city called San Diego to see the new Pacific Fleet base. I saw signs in shops that said Orientals were not permitted to enter. We were watched closely and the excuse was that we were in danger from the thousands of Chinese that live in the city. We flew to Mexico City and then on to Panama and Guatemala in Central America.' Takeda snorted. 'Those countries are nothing more than economic slaves of the Americans. They are backward and weak and their governments are merely tools of the Americans, especially their big corporations. Hatred for the Americans in those regions is greater than hatred for the British and Dutch in Asia, but the people are even more powerless.'

'Chinks,' his father snorted. 'The damned Chinese are the ones who have given all Orientals a bad name in America with their dirty, grasping ways.'

The elder Takeda had served in the Imperial Army through two wars; the Sino-Japanese war in the 1890s and the Russo-Japanese war in 1904–5. He had been present at the battle of Mukden and had been decorated personally with the Order of the Golden Kite, Third Class, for heroism. His prejudices regarding the Chinese had been set early and he never referred to them in any other way than the disparging Japanese slang term, *chink*.

But Takeda knew his father was only partly right. Prejudice against all Orientals, in all non-white people, was deeply ingrained in Americans. Insulting and restrictive emigration laws remained in effect against all Orientals and the Japanese, American-born or immigrants, were treated as second class citizens in the West Coast states. And it was even worse in the Western Canadian provinces, he had been told.

'We flew by Pan American clipper to Hawaii, Wake Island, Guam, Manilla and, finally, to Tokyo,' he concluded. 'In Hawaii, we went to see the new naval base at Pearl Harbor. But there were only a few destroyers and a sea plane tender in port. Most unimpressive.'

Only when Takeda had satisifed their initial curiosity was he able to obtain family news that had escaped his father's frequent letters. Michitaka had two days before been accepted into the army aviation programme to be trained as a bomber pilot. Takeda teased Ryuko about young men to see her blush and learned that she would begin a business course in the spring.

His father shook his head in disapproval but Takeda noticed his mother's triumphant smile. 'But you see, father,' he laughed gently. 'Times are changing. War with the Americans comes ever nearer. And when it begins, we will need everyone. Women can fill clerical and administrative positions and thus release men for the real business of war which is fighting. When the war is settled, women will be glad enough to resume their normal place in society.'

'Oh you think so, do you?' his sister protested indignantly, but Takeda hushed her with a gesture. Their father would be offended by squabbling.

Later, when he was alone with his mother, he asked her about his father's health. Reluctantly, she admitted that it was poor. He had suffered with a bad chest cold in the spring and the physician feared it might turn to pneumonia. It had not, but he had been left very weak and without ambition. 'He no longer stays all day at the shop,' she admitted. 'He has taken in a young assistant whom I think wishes to buy the business.'

Takeda was astonished! This was indeed bad! His father had spent years building the business which was as dear to him as his family. In 1915 his father had been badly wounded when his regiment was ordered to occupy the former German-controlled district of Shanghai. He had been discharged as unfit from the service with a small pension, which, with the annual annuity from the Golden Kite decoration won in 1905, at least assured Takeda that his parents would not starve or go without shelter if he and his brother should both be killed.

His father had established a small repair business in Osaka, in 1916. Over the years he had specialised in electrical appliances and built a reputation for excellent service and reasonable charges. Takeda had spent many hours after school in the tiny shop waiting on customers and learning the tricks of appliance repair. His father loved the business as something he had created with his hands and skill.

That evening, Takeda went for a walk and discovered that he was glad to escape from the cloying affection of his family. Perhaps I've been away too long, he thought as he strolled through the familiar neighbourhood which evoked his childhood. Perhaps he had lived a regimented life so long that he had forgotten how to respond to intimacy. He was afraid that he would embarrass himself by giving offence to his family.

He passed the lower school he had attended so many years ago. In that peculiar love-hate relationship that existed between the United States and Japan, it had been modelled on the American elementary school as an experiment. He had been allowed to attend because his father was a military veteran and war hero, and he remembered that it had been the occasion of his first lesson in humility, sternly administered by his father when it was discovered that he was lording his good fortune over his playmates. He smiled at the memory, although at the time the experience had been both painful and traumatic.

He paused at the gate. Beyond the building, barely lit for night-school classes in an effort to save fuel, he could see the playing field – playground they had called it after the American style – where he had played baseball and football. Further along the road was the *dojo* where he had studied the martial arts.

It was all so familiar; the memories ached. He even recalled one diminutive teacher, like his father a veteran of the Russo-Japanese War, who could usually be induced to expound at length on the concept of *Yamato damashi*, the spirit of Japan, and its superiority to Western concepts of life and duty, whenever the calligraphy or moral superiority lessons became boring.

The ending bell rang clear in the cool evening air. Takeda lit a cigarette as the students flowed down the walk. A thin breeze brought the smell of rain from the Osaka-wan, the bay. Osaka might well be an overcrowded metropolis, where traditional Japanese values were drowning in the demands of the modern world – as the cynical writers of the day were so fond of proclaiming – but here on the city's fringes, it was easy enough to imagine oneself in the past.

A familiar figure passing through the gate caught his eye. She stopped a moment beneath the gate lamp to speak to a companion. As she turned, Takeda recognised her.

'Pardon me,' he hesitated. 'Are you Mariko Sumata?'

The light was even poorer here away from the dimmed street lamps but he could see her eyes widen as she recognised him. Takeda was then astonished to find that he was tongue-tied.

'I . . . I am Saburo Takeda. I lived next door . . .'

'Saburo!' The way she pronounced his name caused strange feelings along his spine and, suddenly, he had never felt so foolish in his life.

'I did not know you were home on leave. Ryuko did not say a word . . .'

'I . . . did not know myself until this morning . . . I . . . may I walk with you?' he blurted.

Mariko nodded and he fell into step beside her. Perception overwhelmed him; the light scent she wore tantalised him, the sound of her western dress and high-heeled shoes tapping lightly on the pavement and the fact that she came only to his shoulder.

He managed to ask what she was studying in night school, then asked her again after she explained.

Mariko laughed at that and repeated herself. Her voice was light, carefully modulated, and she spoke with a precision he had not heard in years of living among military men who slurred their words and punctuated every sentence with profanities.

She told him about her courses in radio broadcasting and her work as a clerk in an Osaka dental clinic. Still Takeda barely absorbed a word, marvelling instead at how she had changed. She was, he recalled, six years younger. When they were children, she had followed him about, hoping to be allowed to participate in the older children's games. No matter how often he had chased her away or played what he realised now were cruel practical jokes, her hero worship for him had never wavered. He had not seen her in five years, since his graduation from the naval academy. His father and mother had invited neighbourhood guests to a reception and he recalled Mariko had stood to one side, awkward in school uniform, thin with adolescence and spotty skin, not quite a child but certainly not a woman. And he, basking in attention, had hardly spared her a word.

Takeda spent the following day lounging about the house and working in the garden. The change from the strict discipline and tension of military service was a novelty at first, but as the day wore on he began to chaff at the unexpected freedom. In the Navy, every moment was filled with duty. The periods of inactivity that punctuated civilian life seemed to him a terrible waste of time. So much could be done, he thought, if the civilian population could be disciplined and organised as was the military. He threw down the hoe and lit a cigarette.

Takeda suspected what was wrong – Mariko. Ah, now it was out. But why? Why should he care about a neighbour girl younger than himself? He knew little about her other than that she was studying radio broadcasting. A modern woman? Full of western influences? Like his sister? Takeda snorted, picked up the hoe and attacked the row again.

That evening he made excuses to his parents and slipped out for an hour without his sister knowing, thus avoiding her unmerciful teasing. He was dressed in civilian clothing and a policeman eyed him as he hung about the school yard gate. When Mariko did finally appear her smile was warm and she did not seem surprised that he should be there. And again, he was struck dumb; he had not the faintest idea what to say. For hours he had visualised the meeting and the clever things he would say to her; he had even composed a Haiku to recite in an offhand manner at the appropriate moment.

To end the awkward silence, Mariko questioned him as they walked about the war in China and, to his chagrin, the army's role there. The army was the last thing any naval officer wished to discuss with a pretty girl.

'They say at the radio station that the landing of our forces in Indochina has greatly angered the United States. Does that mean we will soon go to war with the Americans?' She glanced at him, and in the glow of a street lamp he saw the anxiety in her expression before she ducked her head to avoid his close scrutiny. 'I have two brothers, you know. I would not want to see them hurt or . . .'

Her comment surprised and angered Takeda. He had been taught since earliest childhood that there was no greater honour than to fulfil one's *ko-on*, obligation to the state, and to die in battle for the Emperor. He began a sharp remark concerning her lack of patriotism but stopped. She was, after all, a woman. How else would she view the possibility of war?

'War is coming,' he said in a portentous voice. 'The United States is determined to strangle Japan and prevent her from taking her rightful place in Asia and the Pacific. The Americans cannot seem to understand that Japan wishes only to follow the same path which they themselves blazed. Southeast Asia and China are vital to Japan's survival; they are not vital to the United States, otherwise she would have gobbled them up by now. I had the opportunity to discuss the problem of China with American naval and army officers and most agreed that America's future lies in Europe, not Asia.

'Unfortunately, there seems to be a powerful faction in the United States who insist, in spite of all logic to the contrary, that Asia is America's to exploit. The freezing of Japanese assets in the United States only serves the purpose of this small clique by bringing war ever nearer.

'We Japanese have a strong desire to build a better life for all Asians, not merely for ourselves. We are assisting our fellow Asians to throw off the yoke of European and American imperialism. Westerners will never understand this as their history is one of exploitation, of constant warfare, in order to establish markets and trade. But Japan has never sought to dominate any nation. We have never established colonies in other lands, and in those areas in which our soldiers are presently, we have publicly announced that their visit is temporary only.'

Mariko slowed her steps and he looked around with surprise to find that they had reached her gate. He had spent the entire time expounding on military and political philosophy...

'I... I must go in now,' she told him shyly. 'I am honoured that you came to wait for me at the school and that you would take the time to explain such matters to me.' She glanced up at him and in the dim light from the streetlamps, he almost thought he detected a hint of amusement. 'Perhaps when you once more return home on leave, I will see you again?'

Takeda felt the feathery brush of her fingertips and the gate closed softly behind her.

'What a fool I am,' he groaned.

The Korean port of Hungnam was shrouded in icy rain as Lieutenant Saburo Takeda led his company of the Sixth Sasebo Special Naval Landing Forces down the gangplank. Dirty grey was the predominant colour. The docks, he noticed with distaste, were exactly what you would expect of Koreans. Rusting machinery, broken crates, scattered garbage, shiftless workers.

A miserable corporal shivering inside a waterproof saluted and introduced himself as Takeda's guide. There was no transport, he was told. They must march to the railway station where a train was waiting to take them north.

The train at least provided shelter from the rain. But little else. No provision had been made to feed them and the cars were ancient and appeared to have been purchased from the Russians in the last century.

There was no provision for heating and the windows were sealed permanently. The benches were hard wooden slats and the lavatory facilities were holes cut in the floor. The cars all smelled of damp, sweat and urine.

The train clicked slowly across grasslands beaten flat by the steady rain. There was nothing to see beyond an occasional village where mongol-featured peasants in quilted jackets watched them pass with sullen, hating expressions. Welcome to Manchuko, Takeda thought. The most important jewel in the Emperor's crown. Whoever had termed it that had never seen Manchuko.

Harbin, the capital, was also damp, cold and completely without interest. Another corporal found him as he was disembarking his men. He brought a change of orders; Takeda was now to proceed directly to his post on the border to replace the army garrison at a village with the unpronounceable name of Xiganzi.

'They are loading ammunition and supplies for you now, sir,' the corporal told him. He led Takeda and his 296-men company across the station to where an ancient steam engine, attached to three equally ancient goods wagons, waited. The corporal saluted apprehensively, as if he expected Takeda to dragoon him, and disappeared. Takeda climbed aboard the train and swore. Not even fresh straw had been laid for them and the cars were ice cold and without heaters or stoves.

That evening the train chuffed out of the station through an incomprehensible maze of switching yards and battered by the persistent rain, ran north.

The village of Xiganzi was a collection of leather yurts, sod huts and a dozen wooden houses, most of which had been taken over by the Japanese. The army lieutenant was so grateful to see Takeda that he threw his arms about him.

'I don't envy you your assignment,' the lieutenant admitted in a burst of honesty. 'I have prepared a detailed report which you will find in the desk. I'm sure you won't believe half of it – but you will in a few weeks.'

The army troops filed aboard the moment Takeda's men and supplies were off. The lieutenant climbed into the engine driver's compartment and as the train began to back down the single rail track in the direction of Harbin, Takeda saw him urging the man to greater speed.

Xiganzi was forty kilometres south of the regimental garrison and military district town of Aihun, on the northeastern slopes of the Lesser Khinghan Mountains. The fast-running Nemoche River, a lesser tributary of the Amur, ran past the village. The river and the railway track which crossed it here was the sole reason for the village's existence. At this altitude, the cold, even without the rain, was biting and he was grateful that they had been issued cold weather gear before leaving Sasebo – extra woollen blankets, insulated mess kit and canteen covers and the old-style sleeveless wool overcoats.

Takeda inspected the barracks and found them neither better nor worse than he had expected. Previous garrisons had sealed up the cracks and windows and built clay fireplaces to burn peat, so at least they were adequately housed. The garrison cookhouse was inhabited by two surly Chinese who made it plain they brooked no interference. The elder, a broad shouldered, middle-aged man with a moustache drooping nearly to his waist, ranted at Takeda in Chinese while waving a slicing knife and he beat a hasty retreat. It was a basic rule which any garrison commander appreciated instinctively – do not offend the cooks.

Takeda's servant volunteered agreement in the manner of all undisciplined Chinese, whether servants or not. He was an elderly Mongolian who claimed to have served successive Japanese commanders since 1932 and, before that, Chinese garrison commanders. It was obvious that he had once received a classical education, and his Japanese was nearly flawless.

'In my youth, I studied for the Manderinate and so learned the value of bending as the reed before a wind. I can assure you Lieutenant Takeda, that Ah Wan is an excellent cook. And as there is little else to look forward to in this desolation . . .' His shrug conveyed his message more eloquently than his words.

Takeda's company was responsible, he soon discovered, for policing an area of more than a thousand square kilometres, stretching from the Amur River which ran northeast deep into the Lesser Khinghan Mountains and south into the grasslands.

Three days later an automobile arrived in the village. Takeda hurried out, adjusting his field cap and shouting orders. But it was only an army chauffeur with a letter from the area commander instructing him to come to Aihun. The forty kilometre drive took most of the day. By that evening, Takeda felt as if he had spent the hours in a cement mixer as he stumbled out of the car in front of the dingy brick building over which the Japanese flag hung in sodden folds. The road – he refused to dignify it by that title – was a camel track that wandered over the rugged hills with little regard for distance or time. The streets of Aihun were little better but at least there was mud to cushion the ruts.

Takeda reported to an elderly army colonel who regarded the naval anchor device on his cap with distaste. 'I specifically requested a unit trained in assault tactics,' he snapped peevishly, 'and they sent me a sailor!' The colonel shook his head and sighed.

'I suppose I will have to make the best of it.' He sat down behind his desk and motioned Takeda into the rickety side chair. 'I ordered you to report, Lieutenant Takeda, so that I may amplify your instructions. You will patrol your assigned border area regularly as laid down in your standing orders. However, in this part of Manchuko, contrary to what the public is told, the enemy is not the various Chinese armies. The real enemy are the Russians and their bandit allies.

'About the first you can do little more than urge them to return to their side of the river. You are to do nothing that may be construed as a threat. The Russians have a habit of testing us from time to time. Harbin does not think they are looking for an excuse to invade, but tensions are high after the fighting last year and their local commanders would be glad of any excuse to shoot. Since Moscow arrived at an accommodation with Hitler, they have been encouraging this state of affairs. Is that clear?'

'Yes sir, it is.'

The colonel regarded him closely for a moment, then cleared his throat abruptly. 'Good! Now, bandits are another matter. Most are communists sent into this area by Mao-tse Tung to stir up the local people. We know they receive supplies and munitions from the Russians, although they deny it. Twice, large detachments of bandits have been observed crossing the river.

'The bandits are to be wiped out to the last man and woman whenever and wherever you find them. It will not be easy. They hide among the local people and threaten reprisals to keep them under control. They butcher anyone they suspect might betray or oppose them. They rule by terror and are very good at it. So if you must make a mistake, do not err on the side of caution.

'When you capture a bandit, wounded or not, execute him publicly with the bayonet and display the body in such a manner that the locals will understand that they are not invincible, but that the Japanese army is.

'I also want you to understand one further thing regarding the Russians.' The colonel fixed Takeda with a grim stare. 'I don't know how you naval types view what is going on in Manchuko, or China, and I do not care. The orders regarding Russian incursions come direct from the Prime Minister himself and are endorsed by the war ministry. I am authorised to punish any officer who deliberately disobeys those orders. Do I make myself clear?'

'Yes sir!'

So it was true, Takeda thought. The army is finally cracking down on dissident young officers who insist on making policy in the field. Perhaps the government has had enough of assassinations and adventurism.

Takeda led the first patrol himself two days later. A grating wind blew steadily through the foothills and the long grass flowed in waves. The ground was rocky and full of gullies and rills, so that marching was difficult. There were no roads and few tracks and from the lowering grey sky came bursts of intermittent rain.

Yet the foothills were far from barren. Twice the first day they saw herders with flocks of sheep on the hillsides. Each time Takeda sent soldiers to bring the shepherd to him, but no matter how slowly he spoke he was unable to make them understand his questions. He resolved that in future an interpreter would accompany each patrol.

They spent the first night in a village of felt and leather tents. These people, he thought as he sat beside the fire eating strongly spiced mutton from a communal bowl, were only a few years removed from steppe-roving Mongols. They were not Chinese, but Mongolians with coarser facial features in which the bony structure was more pronounced. They were stockier and more powerfully built than the slender Chinese. The Manchurians showed little interest in the Japanese sailors, providing food and shelter as a matter or custom rather than duty.

A young man entered the tent, bowed in greeting and sat down beside him. In halting Japanese, the boy explained that he was a student returned to his parents' village for a few days. He studied in Harbin, he explained proudly, at the Japanese school. He apologised for his as yet poor command of the Japanese language but offered to serve as Takeda's translator.

Takeda questioned him about the village, striving to contain his annoyance at the boy's halting speech. His vocabulary was limited and he often fell back on Chinese or Mongolian words which then had to be laboriously explained. But in the end Takeda was able to gather that this was one of several such villages scattered through the foothills. Their livelihood was their sheep and they moved with the flocks between mountain slopes and plains as the seasons advanced and retreated. Until recently, the boy told him, they had been allowed to cross the Amur River to graze their herds. Now the Russians fired on them if they came too near the banks.

'The old people do not understand,' the boy laughed with the scorn of an adolescent, 'about nations and governments.'

Takeda asked about bandit incursions in the area and the boy laughed again.

'No bandits. No bandits no more. Japanese soldiers kill all.' He smiled with satisfaction and offered Takeda a bit of mutton. But Takeda had had enough. The overpowering stench of unwashed bodies, sheep, wood smoke and ancient cooking grease had nauseated him. He got up and pushed out into the icy night air.

After gulping several deep breaths, his headache eased. Bah! he snorted. To have to spend months among people such as these! They were barely human. Pigs! They even lived like pigs! Even the boy who had been given the benefit of a Japanese education had not escaped the pattern.

On the third day, they entered a small but prosperous village located at the bend of another small river, the Zunhayaa, which flowed into the Amur some thirty kilometres north. The entire population turned out to greet them, shouting in Japanese to welcome the astonished sailors into their homes. The village of Kuamoto had been established four years ago by settlers who had volunteered to build a Japanese community in northern Manchuko.

That night they ate traditional Japanese foods and were entertained well into the late hours. Although the villagers came from rural backgrounds and most of his company had been recruited in the cities, they got along splendidly, and when they marched out in the morning the entire village turned out to see them off, pressing packages of food and bottles of locally produced saki on each man.

By the time the patrol ended, it was clear to Takeda that the native inhabitants of Manchuko held little affection for Japanese or Chinese, regarding both alike as conquerors. The Japanese settlers were tolerated but there was no intercourse between the two races. In the south, in China, open warfare prevailed against the Japanese but here in the north it was only the Chinese communist bandits that threatened.

Takeda was summoned to headquarters at Aihun a month later. Any break in the monotonous round of patrol and administrative work was a godsend and he climbed into the car eager to be gone, in spite of misgivings over the summons.

For once the weather was clear. A bright sun streamed across the foothills, folding them in deep shadow, and the wind-blown grass ran like green sea waves. A guard accompanied the driver. He did not speak once or put down his rifle until they reached Aihun long after dark.

The garrison commander greeted him affably and invited him to supper. Takeda was impressed with his comfortable wood and stone house near the centre of the town. A new brick wall was crowned with clipped bushes to protect a beautiful raked garden and provide privacy. Inside, the house was traditionally Japanese; paper screens closed off rooms and bamboo mats and *futons* were placed for eye appeal as much as comfort. Two Chinese girls helped Takeda remove his belt and holster, jacket and shirt in exchange for a luxurious Chinese silk robe and small cups of rice wine.

'A bath perhaps, Lieutenant Takeda?'

The colonel led Takeda to a stone bath house in which a deep wooden tub steamed invitingly. The two Chinese girls served as admirable bath attendants. The steaming water was so relaxing that Takeda found himself nodding off. The colonel laughed and announced supper.

The two girls served fresh catfish from the Amur and Takeda complimented the colonel on their training. He smiled with pleasure. 'This one is Sha-lin, the other is called Me-lin. She is the taller of the two.'

They must be twins, Takeda thought and as they left the room, he found himself wondering which was which.

'I have spent a great deal of time with them,' the colonel nodded, pleased with Takeda's compliment. 'They have become to me as my daughters. I will take them with me when I return to Japan.'

Takeda slept soundly after the rigorous trip. In the morning the girls appeared, one with a tray on which were a basin, soap and towels, the other with tea. One murmured an apology and left after pouring the tea.

Takeda drank the delicate infusion while the girl who remained, unfolded the towels and dipped them into the basin in which a piece of sweet-smelling white soap floated. Rain drummed on the roof, but in the room a brazier had been lit while he slept and it was pleasantly warm.

When he finished the tea, the girl stripped away the futon and indicated that he was to lie back. With the wet towels and soap she washed him thoroughly, then undid the ties of her robe and let it fall. Takeda caught his breath at the perfection of her body. Pale light slanting through the oil-screen window transformed her skin to ivory. Small, perfectly rounded breasts were lightly tipped with rose and her boyish hips seemed to slip into his hands as if by magic.

She teased his neck and chest with her tongue and stroked his hard, muscled body with feathery touches that made him gasp. Fear that he might offend his host by taking one described as a daughter disappeared as she wriggled onto his chest and opened her thighs. Afterwards he lay watching as she cleansed him with the last towel. Then she slipped into her robe and let herself out without a backward glance, leaving Takeda bemused.

At breakfast the colonel asked if he had enjoyed Me-lin. Takeda found himself blushing furiously but the colonel laughed and clapped him on the shoulder. 'You are a young man with a young man's needs. Me-lin is a young woman with a young woman's needs. These Chinese are not as reticent about sex as we Japanese. Better you should find relief in each other than with the locals here or in Xiganzi. These Chinese are as full of the pox as the Europeans.'

Afterwards they walked through the streets to army headquarters followed by armed guards. People bowed as they passed but there was only false respect in their manner. Behind his desk once more, the colonel was all business. 'Please examine these carefully,' he said and placed a packet of photographs in front of Takeda. The first shocked him badly. It showed a headless body of a woman. She had been stripped, her arms and legs spread and tied to stakes. Her belly had been slashed open and her head, eyes staring sightlessly, lolled a few paces away. The rest of the photographs, fifteen in all, were similar and showed men, women and even children to have been tortured and killed in equally brutal ways.

'Where..?' he managed and pushed them away.

'The village of Kuamoto,' the colonel replied.

A moment passed before Takeda's mind cleared enough for him to remember that Kuamoto was the Japanese settlement on the Zunhayaa River which he had visited at the end of his first patrol.

'All in the village were slaughtered, people and animals alike. The atrocity was discovered two days ago when one of our transport aircraft flying from Harbin to Aihun grew curious about the smoke and flew down for a look. I was informed as soon as the pilot landed. I had a doctor and troops fly back with the pilot and sent for you. The photographs arrived very early this morning.

'Your written orders are being prepared now. Communist bandits are responsible. Therefore, you will search for and find them. When you do, you will take them prisoner and bring them to Aihun for trial and execution. If it is not feasible to bring them here, you will execute them immediately, in accordance with standing instructions.

'You may not pursue the bandits onto Russian territory but will take every measure short of that to capture these brutal murderers. Do you understand your orders, Lieutenant Takeda?'

Reality was far worse than the photographs. The soldiers guarding the village had received orders to leave everything exactly as they found it until Takeda arrived. As the Special Landing Force sailors disembarked from their trucks, they were formed into ranks.

The soldiers watched as the sailors marched through the village. Men, women and children had been horribly butchered. Gaping wounds were infested with flies and blood stained the grass black. The soldiers who had been digging graves stopped and watched them, grateful for the chance to rest. Perversely, the sun was hot in the cloudless sky and the stench was horrible. Takeda gave orders that no one was to avert their eyes; no one was to cover their nose. He wanted the sight and smell burned into their consciousness forever.

A Kemptai official waited for him in a tent upwind from the village. He poured a cup of rice wine and thrust it into Takeda's shaking hand. 'I've been in Manchuko for three years,' he said in a wooden voice. 'I seen this sort of thing before, but never so vicious, so . . . so . . .' Words failed him.

Takeda said nothing. He drank the wine quickly and, without asking, the policeman refilled the cup. Takeda remembered the kindness the villagers had shown them the month before . . .

The official was a little man, rotund with cheerful features made ugly by anger. 'Massacres are not unusual among the Chinks,' he said. 'But they have always killed each other up until now. Usually, a few men are beheaded and all the women raped.' He shrugged. 'It is done to keep the villagers in line. They have never dared attack one . . . of our settlements . . . before . . .'

He paused to regain control, then went on in a brisk tone. 'The bandits are officially described as "communist". You should understand that the description is political. They may call themselves communists and may or may not have anything to do with politics. None of them could tell you who Karl Marx was, or Lenin for that matter. They are bandits, nothing more, of the kind that have infested Northern China for thousands of years.'

He pulled a map around so that Takeda could read it and pointed to a small red cross. 'We had information that their camp was twenty kilometres northeast of here in the foothills. Aerial reconnaissance showed the camp to be empty. We have informers scattered through the area and they report the bandits are making for here.' He indicated a spot on the Amur to the northwest, in the opposite direction from the camp. The map symbol for a Russian border outpost showed on the other side of the Amur.

'There are three villages along their route; here, here and here.' He pointed out three settlements along an irregular path ending at the ford. 'All are native villages and they will raid at least one.'

The policeman seemed to know the area well enough. Takeda was aware that the army held the Kemptai in contempt because their intelligence and police activities too often overlapped. In addition, the Kemptai was charged to be alert for deviant thinking among the military. But Takeda was concerned only with finding and punishing the bandits.

'What do you recommend?' Takeda asked. The map showed the terrain growing rugged where a spur of the Lesser Kinghan thrust towards the river.

The policeman traced a route that led to within twenty-five kilometres of the ford. 'The terrain is suitable to this point for travel in trucks. If you leave now, you should arrive before midnight. It then depends on whether or not your troops can march the remaining twenty-five kilometres before dawn.'

He waited for Takeda's comment and when there wasn't any, continued. 'Otherwise, your other choice is to chase them from village to village. As you can see, they could strike at any one. If they know they are being pursued, they will simply make straight for the river. They already have a two day headstart. If they cross the river, you will have to wait weeks and perhaps months for them to return.'

Takeda knew he was right. He also knew that the only thing certain was that the terrain would be far worse than the map indicated. But there was no other choice.

'We will make straight for the ford.'

The Kemptai official smiled for the first time.

The Sasebo Sixth Special Naval Landing Force reached the foothills after a torturous twelve hour drive and began the twenty-five kilometre march without rest or food. One truck had broken down and was left behind, its complement of troops crowded into the remaining three. Twice during the endless night a truck had to be manhandled from the mud, but in spite of their exhaustion the sailors worked with a will. The mutilated bodies of their countrymen served to goad them on, as Takeda had known they would.

The Kemptai official's estimate of a twenty-five kilometre march to the ford was undoubtedly correct, but the horrible terrain and darkness nearly finished them. Starlight, obscured by a high, thin ice layer, barely relieved the primitive darkness and they reached the ford just as the sun broke above the horizon.

Takeda chose his position carefully, less than a kilometre from the border. He searched the area thoroughly with field glasses to make certain they were unobserved, either by bandits or Russians. A high wall of spur ridges barred the foothills and sloped steeply to the river. The ford was an extension of the gully they occupied, a dry stream bed running down to the river and ending in an alluvial sand bar. From the top of the ridge, Takeda located the Russian border post and observed guards going about morning duties.

After a thorough search of the area about the ford to make certain that the bandits had not already crossed, Takeda sent two platoons inland to watch the other two possible approaches. His chief warrant officer, Gohay Ueda, commanded the second platoon, a steady veteran of the Indochina campaign whom he knew he could depend on to think for himself as well as follow orders.

The Kemptai official had marked the location of a large Soviet Army garrison some ten kilometres inland, which was connected to the border post by a road. When Takeda expressed uneasiness that they might intervene, the policeman assured him that it was highly unlikely.

'The Russians tolerate the bandits only for the damage they do us. There is no real love lost between the Chinese Communists and their Russian brothers. In fact, the Soviet Union has made no secret of its support for the Nationalist Government. It will take a great deal more to provoke them than the capture of a few outlaws – as long as you stick to our side of the Amur. They certainly cannot afford trouble with us now.'

Takeda was not wholly convinced, especially after he spotted telephone wires running from the roof of the border control post inland.

The day had begun hot and bright, but within two hours a heavy cloud had siphoned in over the mountains and a chill wind swept down the gully to the river. Takeda did not allow fires for fear of betraying their presence and so the sailors huddled in their greatcoats and silently cursed whatever gods or fates had brought them to this pass.

The bandits were expected to intersect a rutted track several kilometres above the ford – shown on the map as an auxiliary caravan trail – no matter which village they chose to raid. Having come this far without pursuit, Takeda hoped they would have eased their guard in the expectation of sanctuary across the river.

It was well past midday before a runner dropped down beside him. 'They are... coming, sir,' he panted. 'Warrant officer Ueda counted forty-three bandits... all heavily armed.'

The watery grey light and the dull-coloured steppe grass made it difficult to see the bandits at a distance. But shortly Takeda saw the column mount a rise where they were silhouetted against the lighter cliffs. He sent the runner on to warn the two platoons above the ford and waited.

On the slopes not a movement was visible that would have betrayed them, until Takeda signalled. The entire column was well into the gully before he blew two sharp blasts on his whistle and the first volley tore the column apart and emptied a dozen saddles before the bandits knew they were being fired upon.

The bandit leader spurred his horse towards the river, but a second volley sent another dozen or more men and horses down. Takeda had picked the two best marksmen and stationed them beside him with instructions to wound, not kill, the bandit leader if at all possible. Both men concentrated on the lone horseman who seemed to have kept his head while the others panicked. Two shots were fired almost together, the first struck the bandit through the right hip and the second killed the horse. The mass of men and horses wheeled and shouted in confusion as disciplined rifle fire played havoc in their slovenly ranks. Individual sailors knelt or stood to fire at will. A handful of riders managed to bring their terrified horses under control and charged up-slope, swinging swords and rifles. They were shot from their saddles within twenty metres. Others tried to break away by riding between the lines, but the platoon flanks had already curved together to close the trap. Two riders managed to break through and disappeared over the rise to the ford.

The surviving bandits dismounted and began to return the fire, but the sailors held the high ground and their marksmanship was far superior. One man threw down his rifle and raised his hands. Takeda was flabbergasted. What did he hope to gain? But the action swept through the terrified bandits and the survivors followed suit.

Takeda blew the command to cease fire and the sailors ran downslope and used rifle butts, bayonets and boots to herd the survivors together. Twenty-three remained alive, most badly wounded. The bandits were kicked into line and made to strip naked. Their hands were tied together and they were roped neck to neck in a single line. One of the survivors, a thin, intense man with a wispy moustache and pale skin, tried to speak to them in Japanese, but he had been shot through the lung.

Takeda finally understood that he was claiming that they were soldiers, regular members of the Red Army who were hunting the bandits. He demanded that they be treated as prisoners of war.

Takeda snorted. 'A true soldier does not disgrace himself with surrender,' he snarled. 'He fights to the death. And your so-called Red Army exists only as bandits, nothing more. You will be punished for the massacre of Japanese citizens at the village of Kuanmoto.' When the man tried to protest, Takeda slashed him across the face with his pistol. 'March them to the river,' he ordered.

The bandit leader was found still alive, although unable to move his legs. Takeda ordered him dragged behind a horse and his screams echoed down the gully.

At the ford, they had a clear view of the Russian border post, and more importantly for Takeda's purposes, the Russians had a clear view of them. Several trucks had arrived and he could see Russian soldiers running to take up positions along the far bank. The river was perhaps 150 metres wide at this point and shallow enough that he could see sand bars. Through his field glasses he saw several Russian officers, one or two of high rank, peering back.

Takeda had decided before leaving the village that he would exercise his own discretion in the matter of the bandits' execution. It seemed to him that part of the responsibility belonged to the Russians and therefore it was only fair they should share the spectacle. And in any event, it was too far to Aihun. The lesson would have better effect on the Russians than the citizens of the regimental town.

Grim-faced, Takeda had the captives marched onto the sand spit and the last man tied to the first so that they formed a circle. The bodies of the dead bandits were dragged down by horses and stripped. Those too badly wounded to stand were tied to those who were not. The bandit leader was taken to the water's edge and propped into a sitting position. When all was ready, Takeda ordered twenty-three of his sailors forward. They took up positions, each man facing one of the bandits and at his measured orders drew and mounted bayonets.

The bandits understood then and began to scream and beg for mercy. At Takeda's whistle, the sailors lunged; the bandits surged to and fro, jerking one another down, choking and crushing one another as they sought to escape the blades. The sailors went at the chore with a vengeance, stabbing each a dozen times or more in a frenzy of revenge for the helpless women and children of Kuanmoto.

When the last bandit was dead, Takeda ordered their bodies dragged into the river and set adrift, still tied together. The Amur ran fast and smooth for the next two hundred or more kilometres and the sight of the dead bandits, preceded by the luckier ones cut down by bullets, would be an efficacious lesson for all and sundry.

Takeda turned his glasses on the Russians and saw that they were watching stolidly. The Kemptai official had been correct; they had made no attempt to interfere. He walked to the bandit chieftain and stared down at him. Takeda was surprised to see that he was a relatively young man, clad in a dirty sheepskin coat and hat with a crude red star sewn to the up-turned visor.

The man was only half-conscious and Takeda kicked him awake. He unleashed a stream of voluble Chinese, in which Takeda recognised one or two curses. He almost grinned. No one could swear like a chink.

He had toyed with various means of slow execution that might serve as some small revenge for the brutal and inhuman murders which the bandit leader had surely ordered. But the bayonet executions had sobered him. For such cruelty to be efficacious, it must serve a purpose. The execution by bayonet of the twenty-three had served as a warning to the Russians. The torture and death of one more would serve no futher usefulness here.

He stirred the bandit with his foot. Would he survive the long journey to Aihun for execution? Takeda shrugged. If not, the display of his body would do.

Gorlovo September - October 1941

Captain Mikhail Gregorvitch Dogorov was arrested as a spy.

Still wet from the river, he was handcuffed and thrown into the back of an enclosed lorry with several others. But not until after dawn did he see that all wore officers' uniforms from which the collar rank insignia had been ripped. They were not allowed to speak to one another, a dictate reinforced by a bovine-faced NKVD guard who kept fondling his machine pistol.

The lorry stopped late the following night and all were ordered out. Dim blue lights provided just enough illumination to show a railway siding. The prisoners were led to one side to relieve themselves, then back to the railway track. They had not been fed since their journey began and Dogorov had eaten only the scrap of black bread and fat the previous day. A guard responded to their bitter complaints by scooping a pan full of water from a nearby puddle for them to share.

Although it was raining hard, they were made to stand in the open. After an hour, Dogorov was so light-headed from hunger and exhaustion that he collapsed in the mud to lie staring without comprehension at a furious guard who threatened to shoot him unless he stood up. He fell asleep thinking that death would be a blessing.

Something was pressed into his hand and he opened his eyes to the dim glow of a lantern – a hard piece of black bread. Without waking fully, he wolfed it down, drank the water handed to him in a dipper and fell asleep again, wondering why the world clicked and rocked.

When he woke once more, he felt somewhat better. His stomach hurt as badly as before but the vertiginous weakness was gone. As the light grew, Dogorov saw the interior of a goods waggon, its floor covered with musty, dirty straw. Following the example of others in the waggon, he burrowed into it and was surprised to discover how warm it was.

The train stopped twice that day to allow them to relieve themselves and drink. But they were not fed again until evening when thick pieces of black bread tasting of sawdust, and a weak concoction he supposed was tea, were distributed by the guards. The car contained twenty-nine men and Dogorov learned that, without exception, all were accused of collaboration with the enemy. As best he could determine, collaboration was defined as having escaped from behind enemy lines.

The following evening he was astonished to see Lieutenant Alexander Ivanovitch Siderov descend from another waggon. Dogorov managed to attract his attention and they squatted on the wet cinders, half turned away from one another and spoke quietly as they drank the tea ration.

Siderov had also been put into a *strafny* battalion after his interrogation, and like Dogorov had managed to reach the far bank of the Sula, only to be arrested by his own side. Rumour in his goods waggon had it that they were being taken to a prison camp southeast of Moscow. All were, as Dogorov surmised, accused of collaboration with the enemy.

A whistle shrilled and guards went up and down the train shoving the prisoners towards the waggons.

'God go with you,' Siderov said tightly and Dogorov hurried to his waggon, marvelling that after all they had been through together, he had had no idea that Siderov was a religious man.

On the evening of the third day, the train stopped below a small village near Gorlovo, or so the rumours said. It was raining again as the prisoners were marched into the darkness. Near midnight, they stumbled into a barbed wire compound and were formed into lines. An hour later, a roll call was taken and they were fed a thin vegetable soup, issued a paper-thin blanket and told to lie down.

The soup only sharpened his hunger and Dogorov squatted in the mud with a hundred other men, the soaked blanket his only shelter, and sought vainly for an explanation for their barbaric treatment. He was being punished and he did not know why.

Doubts that had troubled him in the Pripet marshes in those first days returned. How could the Party and the national leadership have been so negligent? There had been clear signs of an impending attack for months yet, repeatedly, they had maintained it was not so. English spies were blamed for attempting to provoke the Soviet Union into a war with

Germany but never again, they had been told, would Russian soldiers serve as cannon fodder for British Imperialism as they had in 1914–1917.

And what kind of leadership was there in a government that insisted that Kiev be held when it was clearly impossible? There were no natural obstacles to anchor a defence line and the Hitlerites had proved over and over again that their highly mobile forces could turn any flank. Yet two entire armies, 500,000 men, had been destroyed simply because Moscow was unwilling to admit an error in judgement.

During that endless night as he shivered in the pounding rain, Dogorov reached the nadir of his belief in the party, in the government and in himself.

At dawn they were made to stand for three more hours in freezing rain while a new roll call was organised. Then they were fed more of the same thin gruel in wooden bowls without spoons. Sick, wounded and healthy alike, they were forbidden the barracks during the day.

During the third afternoon following his arrival in the prison camp, Dogorov's name and serial number, but not his rank, was called over the loudspeaker. Shaking with exhaustion, cold, hunger and fear, Dogorov made his way to the gate. He was told to follow a faded red ribbon tacked to stakes which led along a muddy path winding between weathered buildings, often out of sight of guards. As he walked, it occurred to Dogorov that it would be easy enough to escape. He could simply step over the tape and disappear into the forest. But where would he go? His pre-war ration book and internal passport had been taken from him at Kiev. Without them he would not last a week.

He recalled an historical film drama about the Great War which he had seen some years before in Odessa. In it, a Russian soldier had escaped from an Austrian prison camp and made his way to Moscow to enlist in the Red Army. The man had survived winter weather, Austrian troops and gangs of White Guard marauders before the inevitable triumph. At the time, the story had seemed plausible enough; now he realised how great was the gulf between reality and make-believe.

The ribbon led to an unpainted clapboard building. He knocked hesitantly on the flimsy door and walked in. A guard took his name and motioned him down a corridor to an open door where an NKVD officer shouted at him in irritation and motioned him to stand in front of the desk. The NKVD man read slowly from sheets of paper, his progress indicated by a slowly moving finger that pointed to each word. Occasionally, the man rubbed his hands together over a tiny charcoal brazier, the only heat in the room – perhaps in the whole building – whose bowed and warped walls seemed to intensify the damp.

The NKVD agent finished and looked up. Without warning, his face twisted into an expression of contempt and Dogorov flinched as he slammed a fist on the desk.

'You swine!' he bellowed. 'Confess your crimes, now!' He hit the desk again for emphasis. 'Confess, you bastard! The State has more important things to do than play about with the likes of you!'

The months of hardship, the days of agonising humiliation and hunger and cold collided in one intense rush and Dogorov exploded. The NKVD man was so astonished that he jerked back and his chair nearly tipped over as Dogorov bellowed incoherently. He shouted for a guard while Dogorov tore papers from his desk and hurled them about the room, screaming obscenities and imprecations. The guard burst in and drove him against the wall with his bayonet and looked helplessly around at the NKVD officer as Dogorov's anger trembled on the verge of hysteria.

'When everyone else threw down their weapons and ran,' Dogorov screamed, 'I led my men through the Pripet marshes all the way to Kiev and left behind a trail of dead Hitlerites! We fought at Kiev until there were none of us left. We endured torture, hunger and cold. We were deserted by our fellow Red Army soldiers, insulted by officers and now the police accuse us of collaboration with the enemy . . !'

Other guards rushed in and Dogorov was overpowered. Someone stuffed a garrison cap in his mouth, choking off his shouts, and his breath. When he continued to struggle, a doctor was sent for. One of the guards, alarmed at the bluish tinge that was creeping into his face, yanked the cap from his mouth.

'. . . you have the nerve to call me . . . us . . . collaborators . . . you rear area rats, you cowardly . . .' The hat was replaced.

The doctor injected Dogorov and he began to calm down. The guards and clerical staff dispersed, shaking their heads in wonder. Such an outburst was most unusual they told one another; so uncultured.

The shaken NKVD official studied Dogorov who slumped in the chair, head clutched in his hands. The doctor raised an eyebrow as if asking what was to be done and the officer dismissed him impatiently. After a moment, he told the guard to wait outside as well. Dogorov's anger had passed, or at least been subdued by the narcotic.

The NKVD officer's first inclination was to give him an Article 58.l.b. sentence without wasting any more time. A bullet in the back of the neck would teach the *swollich*, bastard. But he hesitated; not one of the thousands of prisoners, officers or enlisted, that he had processed since the end of the Finnish war had dared protest in such a fashion. So, perhaps this man rated a bit of study.

He reread the meagre *papka* on Dogorov that had been compiled by the Thirty-Seventh Army Commissar and forwarded to Moscow a few days before the fall of Kiev. The contents were slender enough, but something caught his eye that he had missed before. The name Dogorov; this man claimed to be the son of the hero Dogorov who had taken the Petrograd Telephone and Telegraph Exchange without firing a shot, and who later had been captured, tortured and hanged by the Whites under the traitor Denekin.

The dead Thirty-Seventh Army Commissar had noted the claim but his scepticism was plain enough. It had been his opinion that the man calling himself Dogorov was in reality a turncoat, a Russian of German extraction, now working for the Hitlerites. He had been sent back to conduct sabotage and espionage in the Red Army – treason under Article 58 and punishable by ten years hard labour under Section 1.a, or death under Section 1.b, of the Criminal Code of 1926.

But could this be the son of the hero, Dogorov? The NKVD man sighed. He vividly recalled the dangerous and heady years of the Revolution and civil war when he had served under the man who might well be this one's father, and he remembered the night they had been ordered to capture the Telephone Exchange. The elder Dogorov had collected volunteers and some rifles and at breakneck speed they had driven from the Smolny through a city blacked out against Zeppelin Raids. Behind the barricades surrounding the entrance were veteran soldiers from the front. But Dogorov had talked them round; when their officer had tried to stop them, they had shot him down like a dog.

He cleared his throat and closed the folder. 'If you are calm now, we will continue. But I warn you, one more outburst and it will go hard with you.'

Dogorov barely nodded and the NKVD officer wondered if the doctor had given him too large an injection. He was far enough behind schedule as it was.

He went through the list of usual questions; name the officers in your command who were or are traitors to the Soviet Union; name also the enlisted men; describe their traitorous activities; answer, why did you not report such activities immediately? Never mind to whom; is it the fault of the Soviet Union that you were encircled behind Hitlerite lines? Such questions only prove your guilt. Why else would you be there but to arrange with your Hitlerite masters to stab your motherland in the back?

Dogorov shook his head at each accusation and mumbled responses to each question. Certainly guilty, the NKVD officer thought. He reached for the stamp to mark the file 58.1.b when, almost as an afterthought, he asked, 'What was your father's nickname?'

Dogorov raised his head for the first time and stared at the NKVD officer. 'I beg your pardon... my father's nickname?' He shook his head. 'I don't know... I barely knew him. I was five years old when he was murdered.'

The NKVD officer grunted and inked the stamp.

'My mother once ... called him Vanya, I think. I don't know why. His name was Gregory ... She said hardly anyone called him Vanya but her. Most knew him as Grigor.'

The NKVD officer's hand hesitated. He had called his old commanding officer Vanya, and he remembered once, on a freezing night northeast of Voronezh in the winter of 1918, Vanya Dogorov had shown him a wrinkled photograph of a beautiful woman holding a small boy, dressed in a sailor suit. They were posed against the lime trees in the Smolny Gardens.

Dogorov took a deep breath and tried to sit up. 'My mother is a high ranking official ... in the Ministry of Foods and Nutrition,' Dogorov muttered. 'She is in Leningrad ... can vouch for me.'

'Nonsense!' the NKVD officer snapped, but with declining conviction. 'Leningrad has been cut off by Hitlerite forces. Only the highest priority telephone calls are allowed through.'

'Then you must send my fingerprints,' Dogorov mumbled like a man awakened from a sound sleep, 'to Moscow ... compare them to my army records.'

The officer pushed a buzzer on his desk. 'They have better things to do in Moscow than to check fingerprints of every spy who claims to have been a Red Army officer,' he snorted. As the guards prodded Dogorov up, the NKVD man bent a stern frown on him. 'And even if they match, that would still not tell us the extent of your collaboration with the Hitlerites, now would it?'

After the door closed, he toyed with the stamp once more. Damn, he thought, it was too dangerous. What if the man turned out to be a turncoat after all? He was taking too great a chance. They would shoot him as well. But, if he was the son of his old commanding officer, the man who had saved his life that time along the railway line from Volgorod to Murmansk ...

Angrily, he yanked the fingerprint card from the folder, scribbled instructions on a form and threw both into the out-box.

Dogorov was returned to the prison compound. The following day he wrote to the prison commandant for permission to be present at the hearing which would decide his guilt or innocence. He received no answer and a few days later learned from other prisoners that there were no further hearings. The NKVD officer who conducted the interview decided your fate, and the decision was invariably guilty. In despair and frustrated anger, Dogorov could only wait and contemplate his fate – ten years at best, an executioner's bullet at worst.

News filtered into the prison compound in trickles. The Germans were said to have mopped up south of the Dnieper and were turning north. Nearly all the rumours agreed that Moscow was the next target and would fall before the winter freeze began in mid-November. Dogorov was surprised to discover how many officers in the prison compound were openly sympathetic to the German cause – if the Hitlerites won, they told him, some of them might yet survive. He was beginning to understand why the security organs were so terribly suspicious of anyone returned from behind enemy lines.

Such thinking bothered him greatly. Why, he wondered, would anyone wish for Russia to be conquered simply to spare themselves? More than once during the long days that followed, he found himself drawn into furtive discussions that went on wherever men huddled under the icy rain or scorching sun. Often, the talk was of the Great Man's mismanagement. Dogorov had never before heard anyone criticise Stalin, not even in fun, as it was a serious crime under Soviet law. It was an article of faith, instilled since childhood by every school, club and organisation that he had belonged to, that government decisions under the leadership of Stalin were always correct. Such decisions represented the will of the working class and the dynamics of the Marxist dialectic simply did not permit the government to make wrong decisions.

When he tried to argue, knowing looks were exchanged. One man, an officer in the artillery like himself, tried to convert him to their way of thinking.

'Comrade, I will make the assumption that you are not a spy,' he began, but someone interjected.

'What difference would it make if he was?' The group laughed.

'How can you say the government makes no mistakes?' the man continued. 'What about the surprise attack in June? You knew it was coming; I knew it was coming; anyone with eyes and ears knew it was coming. Yet my regiment was visited by party workers on the twentieth of June, the very day before, who told us it was all a British plot! I suppose next you will claim that the Red Army never makes mistakes? If so, why were all our marshals and top generals shot between 1937 and 1940?'

Dogorov tried to protest that his words were being twisted, but the artillery officer ignored him.

'Stalin has defined talent in a socialist society surrounded by capitalist enemies as the natural aptitude for survival. I will grant you that Stalin surely has that. His greatest aptitude is killing others before they kill him. Why else do you think we are here?'

The question took Dogorov by surprise. 'Because we have been accused of collaboration . . . because we haven't papers . . .'

The others laughed but the artillery officer frowned them into silence. 'No, comrade,' he said softly. 'It has nothing to do with such ridiculous charges. We are here because we were trapped by the enemy; we were trapped by the enemy because we made the mistake of believing what Stalin told us. As a consequence, we were overrun. The fact that we fought clear only makes us a terrible liability in the eyes of the Great Man. Do you think he wants us walking about representing thousands of examples of his stupidity? Hell no! There are dozens of camps like this one all over the Soviet Union for getting rid of us, because Stalin knows that soon we will begin to ask embarrassing questions. Such as why were we not warned the Germans were about to attack? Or, why were we not allowed to take up defensive positions along the borders? Or, why did our frontier fortifications, built up over so many years at such painful cost, collapse at the first puff?

'Did you know that General Dimitry Pavlov and the staff of the Western Military District were shot because the Germans broke through? Well, my friend, I served for nine months on General Pavlov's staff and I personally passed on two specific requests to Army Command in early June, begging them to let us move into forward defensive positions. I also saw the answers. *No*! – straight from Moscow. Such actions would be provocative, they said. They tell us that we cannot take proper measures to defend our positions, then they shoot us because we are overrun. What kind of logic is that? No, my friend, the Great Man has to be rid of us. He cannot afford to have anyone, least of all trained military officers, know that he is not infallible.'

The news of Pavlov's execution shocked Dogorov even more than the artillery officer's blasphemy. General Dimitry Pavlov was – had been – one of the most respected men in the Red Army.

Thinking about the conversation later, Dogorov resolved to avoid such discussions in the future. There were bound to be any number of spies in the camp – both Hitlerite and NKVD. He had already placed himself in jeopardy with that insane outburst in the interrogator's office, but if there remained even the remotest chance that he could be given a prison term rather than a sentence of death, such conversations would eliminate it forever. To cover himself, he wrote a report and included descriptions of the participants. He gave the report to a camp guard and requested that it be shown to an administrator – meaning an NKVD interrogator. The guard took the report without answering and as he had nothing with which to bribe him, Dogorov never learned whether or not it was delivered.

Three weeks later as he paced the open space between the fence and the point where two huts met, Dogorov heard someone hiss. Turning, he saw Siderov leaning against one hut so that he was out of sight from the main administrative block.

Dogorov had no idea that Siderov was even in the same camp. He had not seen him since the train and when he tried to hug him in greeting, Siderov fended him off.

'I only have a moment, Mikhail Gregorvitch, and you must not be seen with me. Sit down with your back against the building as if you are resting and listen.'

Dogorov felt obscurely pleased that Siderov had addressed him by his name and patronymic rather than by rank. 'I had no idea you were here. It's good . . .'

Siderov interrupted. 'I've been sentenced. They gave me a 58.1.a, ten years for unspecified crimes against the State.' He laughed harshly. 'Can you imagine? They suspect that I am a German agent but the bastards can't prove it and so they are putting me into a prison camp as a precautionary measure!'

Dogorov looked up to see bitterness twisting his face, but then Siderov forced a smile. 'Ah, but it won't be so bad, Mikhail Gregorvitch. Surely it can't be any worse than stumbling around the Pripet with an empty belly? And the work won't be half so hard.'

The import of the sentence hit Dogorov like a blow. If they sentenced his second-in-command to ten years, then surely they would shoot *him*!

Siderov read the realisation in Dogorov's expression and squeezed his shoulder in sympathy. 'Good luck my friend. They gave me five minutes to collect my things. They'll be looking for me already.' He stared at Dogorov a moment then hurried away.

Dogorov started to shake.

A week later, Dogorov was called to the administrative compound for a second time.

Since that last meeting with Siderov, Dogorov had experienced hell. In spite of raging hunger, his knotted stomach rebelled at even the thought of food. He had slept only in spasmodic catnaps and now his body was too exhausted to conceal his fear as he stumbled along the tapes to the interrogation office, prepared to admit anything that would end this uncertainty. A bullet would almost be welcome, he thought. At least there would be an end to it.

Again, the unguarded path taunted him. He had only to step across the tapes and the forest was less than a hundred metres away. But it might as well have been a thousand kilometres.

A bored clerk pointed down the hall after checking his name against a list and went back to his copy of *Red Star*. Whether Dogorov lived or died, whether he even existed, was of no concern to him. And why not? Dogorov thought bitterly; the State has declared that I am a collaborator.

A guard standing outside a door some way past the interrogator's office motioned to him. 'In here, you.'

Dogorov paused and tried to take a deep breath. His mind darted about in panic; is this how it happens – beyond that door is there a man with a pistol waiting for me? He had heard muffled shots at all hours of the day and night often enough in the past weeks. Why didn't I take a good breath of fresh air outside? At least the sun was not shining; that would have made it all the harder to bear. There were no friends left to say goodbye to. At least they could have allowed me to write to my mother...

He closed his eyes a moment, then squared his shoulders and stepped through. At least I will die a man, he told himself, and stepped forward.

He was in a grimy lavatory. Someone told him to strip off his clothes and he did so, shaking so badly that he ripped two buttons, he thought at least they could leave him the dignity of dying clothed. A bar of soap was pushed into his hand and he was shoved through another door, into a shower. The water was lukewarm and he stood staring from the grey soap to the water splashing from the double shower heads, in shock.

'Wash!' a voice shouted and he ran the gritty soap over his skin. It refused to lather but he rubbed it over and over his body and scalp, abrading the dirt away, dazed, not knowing what to think, not daring to hope. The water shut off abruptly and he was handed a thin towel. Outside, an attendant waited with a razor and clippers. His beard was shaved and his long hair cropped almost to the scalp. The attendant daubed his head with a foul-smelling liquid that stung and his abused nose identified it as turpentine. They were treating him for lice!

Afterwards, he was given a fresh uniform with an artillery captain's insignia and outside in the main office he was handed an overcoat and an envelope containing orders to report to general headquarters in Moscow for reassignment. The envelope also contained a travel voucher, *propiska* – identification booklet – and a packet of rouble notes which represented pay backdated to 22 June.

The clerk only shrugged when he tried to ask why. Still in a daze, Dogorov stumbled outside. The air was bracingly cold with a mid-autumn chill and he could smell snow in the offing. He walked along the muddy road to the main gate, trying to understand what had happened. On his left was a section of wired compound, but the yard was not visible, only part of a windowless barracks.

Sudden anger tore through him at the injustices he had suffered, that so many thousands were also enduring this very moment, simply for having done their duty in failing to surrender. Siderov, his own second-in-command, had been sentenced to ten years... But his anger ebbed quickly. As with his longing to step over the tapes and run away, anger at the juggernaut of the Soviet Union was foolish because it was useless. As well be angry with the sky because it rains, he thought.

Dogorov stopped for a moment and stared at the barracks building; the system was correct, he told himself. It was the human element that was at fault. The artillery officer had been wrong; such injustices as this camp were aberrations in the system and in the end always righted themselves.

So what if he had suffered?

What difference if a few individuals did? The guilty would be punished

– and if a man were truly innocent he would ultimately be exonerated. Siderov had that to look forward to.

In the long run, the fate of an individual mattered little. What did matter was that the Soviet Union and the socialist experiment endure and be proven correct.

Dogorov showed his orders at the gate, received the guard's salute and set out for the distant railway station and its cafeteria.

Kharkov Front October – November 1941

Major Freidrich Prager, temporarily commanding the First Panzer Regiment of the First Panzer Group, drove his battered units in a wide sweep northwest of Dnepropetrovsk after crossing the Samara River. The brigade had been temporarily detached to support Seventeenth Army operations along the Donets River between Kharkov and Slavyansk.

The white sun blasted the landscape, shrivelling everything to dust even this late in the season. From sunup to sunset, day followed day in oppressive heat and glare. Uniforms were soaked with perspiration an hour after dawn. Maintenance schedules on all equipment – tanks, lorries, weapons – were so far in arrears that no one paid attention to them any longer. Every spare part, every spare moment snatched from the endless hours of the march, had to be devoted just to keeping equipment functioning.

Tank engines long overdue for complete overhauls even before the battle for Kiev two weeks before, belched constant clouds of black smoke. Piston rings were so badly worn that few cylinders maintained rated compression, and cylinder walls were scored by the insidious dust. Filters had long ago worn out and every village passed was ransacked for silk scarves and blouses to make new ones. Every automobile found was torn apart for spark plugs, filters, used engine oil, petrol, headlamps, batteries and even windscreens.

Prager no longer bothered to request spares. Mountains of parts grew in rear areas but the speed of the advance and the concomitant toll on equipment, coupled with the lack of roads, railways and increasing partisan activity, had slowed resupply efforts to a trickle.

Sixty years before, with a paranoia that was traditional, the Russians had decided to lay their railway tracks to a different gauge from that used in the West, thus making them useless to any invader. Russian track had either to be relaid to European standard gauge or freight transferred from German to Russian goods waggons at the borders.

Then too, the Russians left little behind that was useable despite the precipitous speed of their retreat. Time after time Prager's panzer crews had been pressed into service as firemen to save a burning town or village. The Red Army invariably destroyed everything as they fell back and, innumerable times, they killed Red Army soldiers in the act of firing a town or farm. Scorched earth, prisoners called it; it had worked against Napoleon 127 years ago and Charles XII of Sweden 150 years before that, and it was working against Germany now.

What difference, Prager thought, if their own people starved to death or died of exposure? With the calculating brutality inherent in the Slav, the burden of feeding the civilian population was forced onto the German army. Strict orders had therefore to be issued that the Russian civilian population was *not* to be fed by German forces. Rather, each district was given a quota of food and manufactured goods to supply to Germany first as in reparations, and then any excess could be used to feed themselves. Prager approved of the plan; without such an incentive, civilians, infected by twenty-three years of parasitic Bolshevism, would simply sponge off German forces.

On 8 October, they halted briefly at midday for rest and food. The steppe stretched as flat as a plate in any direction, empty and featureless except for an occasional wind-stunted tree. Actually, the 'flat' aspect was an optical illusion. The steppe was jagged with gullies and washes, depressions and sudden dips that played hell with vehicle suspension systems. Idly, Prager dug down through the carpet of grass and decaying sod to the fine black earth, warm and bone dry after months of summer sun.

He knew nothing of agriculture or soils but guessed that with water and proper cultivation this could be among the richest farm land in the world. Why hadn't the Russians done more to exploit it? They had driven through several collective farms since the renewed offensive began on 21 September, all in the same condition. Buildings burned, the livestock driven off or killed and thrown into wells, yet such damage was negligible compared to that caused by years of neglect. Machinery half buried in the long grass – rusted to uselessness – appeared to have lain like that for years. Those buildings there had not been time to burn were unpainted and dilapidated. And while lines of tangled, unrepaired fence ran for miles, so little of the land was under cultivation that it would have been considered a crime in Western Europe.

The Russians were wasting a land full of promise and riches. The Fuehrer was right when he claimed this land as a German birthright. After all, it had been theirs once, two thousand years before. The German people knew how to use land properly. The Russians could not be allowed to waste such a precious resource any longer. Those who care must fight for his share, Prager told himself, otherwise they would be trampled by those who did not.

The enervating heat combined with exhaustion and he dozed fitfully, troubled by the distant rumble of guns. They were not near enough to rouse him until a sudden crescendo snapped him wide awake. The barrage was right on top of them and he vaulted onto the tank, thinking only that the Russians had mounted a counterattack... a raindrop splashed his wrist.

Astonished, he stared at the drop of water carving a narrow furrow through the dust on his skin. He looked up to see that the sky had gone grey; blackish overhead fading to deep brown near the horizon. Thunder cracked and in the distance lightning speared the earth. A cool breeze swept across the steppe and in an instant the terrible heat was gone.

The tank crews rose in disbelief as the rain began, softly at first, then turning to a deluge. They tore off sweaty shirts and trousers and capered naked, laughing and screaming like excited children. Prager stood with his head back, arms outstretched and let the water run down his face, mouth open, eyes closed in ecstasy.

In the beginning, they welcomed the rains. The choking heat and dust faded into bad memory and the regiment surged forward, morale high once more. On the second day of rain, vehicles began to bog down as the tracks which passed for roads across the steppe were churned to mudsinks. At first, the men laughed and joked as they jockied a lorry or staff car out of the mud. Even the horses tackled the chores with a will. But after the novelty wore off, they began to hate the rain as fiercely as they had the heat and dust.

Everything became damp; uniforms, blankets, upholstery. Boots, packs and weapons rusted in spite of oil. The interiors of tanks and vehicles dripped moisture. Skin diseases appeared; spots and boils replaced chaffing as the chief medical complaint, to be followed closely by fungus growths on feet, in the groin and under armpits. Ration packs grew soggy and the contents inedible in spite of their waxed containers, and cardboard boxes split at the slightest pressure.

Boots and belts and anything made of leather grew mildew. Verdigris formed on brass cartridge cases, each of which had to be cleaned daily to prevent them from sticking in the breech of rifles and machine pistols, and steel cases rusted. But worst of all, the constant rain made the roads impassable.

Within a few days even the tracked tanks bogged down. The regiment lost two irreplaceable Mark IVs, both mired above the treads, one canted at a steep angle to port. An attempt to dig them out proved futile when the rain simply washed the mud back as quickly as they shovelled it out. The tanks were abandoned to the engineers.

The First Panzer *Group* was elevated to the status of an *Army* on 5 October 1941, which occasioned numerous snide comments regarding non-existent promotions. It was observed bitterly that the name change only meant added responsibility without the concomitant addition of troops and equipment. The fact that they were an army in name only would soon be forgotten in Berlin.

On 18 October, a reconnaissance patrol sighted the Donets River at a point north of Slavonsk. In spite of the bad weather and equipment problems, Prager ordered the regiment forward without pause to maintain the pressure. But the Russian forces, though disorganised by their headlong retreat, now began to stiffen. Aerial reconnaissance, when the rain permitted, provided the reason. The Russians had run up against the river and the only crossing, a railroad bridge ten kilometres east of Slavonsk had already been destroyed.

Elements of the Seventeenth Army had forced an entire division of the Soviet Twelfth Army into an ever-narrowing bend of the Donets. The river in this area was approached by low hills that fell steeply to the river proper on their reverse slopes. Soviet artillery was dug into the bend and seemed to have registered every square metre within their range.

Prager went forward that afternoon with two armoured cars, one of them an eight-wheeled SD.Kfz 232 equipped with a powerful wireless-transmitter, provided by the regimental reconnaissance company. They reached the crest without being detected and took cover in a screen of wind-twisted scrub trees. Flowing grass, greyish-green in the weird overcast, swept down a precipitous slope to the river. Prager focused his glasses on the far bank.

Visibility was poor in the light rain but he made out a flotilla of boats plying back and forth. Drawn up and in the river, a few hundred metres offshore, were four gun boats guarding the crossing as the Russians attempted to withdraw tanks and equipment. The batteries of the gunboats were an unwelcome addition to the artillery ranged below.

On the lower slopes, the Russians had dispersed their remaining tanks in two rings north along the river, each well dug in to the muddy ground and widely separated to minimise losses from the artillery fire they knew was coming. Prager sketched a quick map of the area beneath his waterproof, carefully estimating distances and angles.

They moved back below the crest and north almost a kilometre where they found a natural depression to shelter the scout cars. Prager took an MP-40 machine pistol from the car's arms rack, summoned the radio operator and made his way to the crest where they hid in a thicket of wind-twisted alder.

It was unusual, he thought, for a commander to be able to see all aspects of a battlefield in mechanised warfare, but the hills and the two rivers combined to form a natural arena. Below, the bridgehead seethed with frantic activity. A river steamer had appeared, pressed into service as a ferry, and even though the rain made it difficult to see, he was certain they were crossing the tanks and vehicles as first priority; he would have done so if the roles were reversed. Beyond, a line of distant explosions marked the farthest advance of the German Seventeenth Army. The Soviets had chosen the field well. A tributary to the Donets formed a natural defensive line between the opposing forces. It was just possible that his regiment of tanks might be able to break the stalemate. Prager sent the radio operator back to transmit the information and request urgent artillery and air support.

Twenty minutes later he received word that the artillery would be in position at 1400 hours. Six *staffel* of Stuka dive bombers had been diverted from Kharkov to his position and would arrive about the same time as the balance of the regiment. Prager ordered the armoured cars moved closer to the thicket and deployed the crew of the second car in both directions along the crest to guard against being surprised by Russian patrols. He hunched his waterproof about his neck, wiped the rain from the Zeiss field glasses, and settled down to wait.

The rain fell harder and Prager worried it might delay the aircraft, or even abort the strike. The Stuka was not an all-weather plane and the Luftwaffe was notorious for refusing to risk its scarce aircraft to bad weather. He had worded the message so as to entice Luftwaffe command by playing up the chance to destroy an entire division, and one apparently without anti-aircraft guns.

At 1400 hours a battalion of the Seventeenth Army's self-propelled artillery, Hummels, mounting 150 millimetre guns, made contact. Prager fed them the first coordinates while they were still en route and ranging shots screamed overhead to explode along the riverfront. An observer arrived a few minutes later. His communications signaller looped the telephone wire around the handset terminals, screwed the nuts down tightly, tested the circuits and passed the handset to the observer who began rapping out revisions without taking his binoculars from his eyes. Others arrived in scout cars and lorries to join him and the guns were walked quickly onto target.

The slopes below turned into a mass of shuddering, erupting dirt, smoke and flame. Shells set for air bursts scythed through the screening infantry. A tank, far too distant to identify by model, took a direct hit and blew up. The explosion was so great that Prager saw the shock wave expand in the damp, heavy air with astounding speed.

The Stukas arrived at that moment. Prager relayed instructions through his radio car and the aircraft wasted no time. They blasted directly over his position to obtain a base line and swooped into the river valley, concealed by mist and rain. In line astern, each *staffel* slashed between hills and loading area and left the makeshift ferry in flames.

The gun boats were able to find some concealment in the rain, but whatever anti-aircraft fire they sent up was completely ineffective as the Stukas rampaged up and down the river after them until all four boats were on fire or sinking. The Stukas turned their attention to the Russian guns then. In combination with the artillery, their rate of fire slackened quickly as one after another position was destroyed. While the Stukas occupied themselves choosing individual targets, Prager searched the slopes below and spotted a small infantry patrol moving towards them. At the same time, the driver of the radio car panted up to report a flanking patrol moving along the crest from the southeast.

Prager relayed the information to the Stukas and moments later, he saw one flight turn inland. They came in low and the patrols melted away as the noise of their guns floated up to him as a single long *carump*. The Stukas searched for and found the second group of Red soldiers attempting to flank them. Again, the long *carump* and the aircraft disappeared into the rain.

At mid-afternoon, Prager ordered the artillery bombardment lifted and sent the tanks of his First and Second Battalions up. Heavy, close-range fire from the mobile artillery had both frustrated Russian counterbattery fire and then smashed them to virtual silence. Prager cautioned the two battalion commanders to keep a wary eye out for anti-tank gun positions that had escaped the artillery barrage or the attentions of the Luftwaffe. In the numerous do-or-die battles he had fought against the Red Army he had learned one could count only on their complete unpredictability. One moment an entire division might throw down its weapons at the first shot, while their neighbours executed a suicidal charge.

The skies drizzled rain and a cold wind sprang up. There would be frost tonight and wounded left on the battlefield would die of exposure. Two hundred metres inland from the river, Prager saw the ant-like figures of infantry reoccupying forward trenches that had been abandoned during the artillery barrage. North, the lead tanks of the Second Battalion were coming into view, supported by infantry from the Seventeenth Army. His own First Battalion had crested the hill and started down-slope towards the river. Suddenly disgusted with the massacre about to take place, he wanted only to see it over. He snatched up the microphone and bellowed the order to advance at speed.

It was a gamble, but he was tired of seeing his people maimed and killed every time a commissar whipped his primitive charges into a frenzy. The distance to the river was less than a kilometre and Prager ordered the First Battalion to split the Russian force by driving straight through to the river bank while the Second Battalion struck the flank. The infantry coming up would smash the enemy against the anvil of the tanks.

The Second Battalion fanned out to attack Russian positions less than a thousand metres from the Donets. A river boat burning furiously at the stern appeared out of the mist, firing at the tanks. One wheeled to face the boat and returned fire. Its 75 millimetre gun was no match for the heavy calibre guns the boat mounted, but the tank's solid footing provided accuracy and the boat was struck repeatedly before it turned away vomiting flame amidships.

With tanks behind and German infantry attacking from the front, the surviving Russians lost heart and began to surrender. Only one position, near a makeshift ramp ploughed down to the river proper, resisted. An anti-tank gun had been well sited and was protected by machine gun fire from infantry attack. A Mark III blew up and Prager saw a single crew member tumble out. Two more tanks closed in from either side and before the Russian gunner could shift his aim, two shells hammered the position to atoms.

Prager drove down to the river bank where tanks of the Fourth and First Battalions met. He found his second-in-command leaning against his tank, a deep bruise visible along his forehead, laughing with the Second's commander. Rain drove hard about them as if to hide the aftermath of the battle, which included a burning tank – not one of his, thank God. And on the river, two boats burned furiously and a third had sunk, streaming bodies and debris downstream. He had no idea how many Russian soldiers had escaped and he did not care. It was over.

Prager reverted to command of the First Battalion as the Kharkov offensive ground to a halt in mid-November, in gumbo mud that mired an endless line of tanks, lorries, scout cars, waggons and artillery pieces – whether horse-drawn or motorised. His own Panzer Mark IV trundled past, ignored by the infantry marching on either side of the road under triple burdens of weapons and equipment and mud. Twice in the space of a hundred metres, Prager passed Mark IIIs, sunk to the top of their narrower tracks as horses and men thrashed wearily to tow them out. The clay soil of the Ukraine soaked up rain in an instant and at the merest pressure squelched it back as a viscous semi-liquid that sucked hoofs, wheels and men into itself. Men lost boots, horses shoes and vehicles suspension systems, oil pans and fuel tanks, as they were hauled out. Prager himself had spent most of the previous afternoon digging out his own tank when even its wider track proved no match for the mud.

Today they had done well. They had managed a walking pace – a weary man's walking pace – by staying off the road. In spite of the rain, Prager remained in the turret watching ahead for the least sign of boggy ground. It did no good to send someone ahead on foot; ground firm enough to support a man's weight collapsed like porridge crust under a vehicle.

A trickle of rain slid under his waterproof and down his neck. Prager had not been out of his wet clothes for three, no four, days now and in all that time they had moved just fifty kilometres, from one side of the front to the other. Inside the tank it was icy-cold and clammy; the heater had stopped working and there was no time to repair it. And engine heat radiating into the crew compartment was no match for the condensation that dripped from, or stood in puddles on, every surface.

Tank crews tied sleeping bags round their shoulders to keep warm and wore waterproofs over them to minimise the damp, but the added bulk only soaked up more water and wet down filling retained damned little heat.

Prager's battalion was being transferred to support another of the interminable infantry assaults against Russian positions on the outskirts of Kharkov. The infantry, the only force still able to manoeuvre in the rain and mud, had endured the worst of the fighting unsupported and their casualties were all out of proportion to their numbers. Weighed down with full field packs and double issues of ammunition, as well as the rest of the paraphernalia of modern war, an hour's march was a gruelling affair and a full day's akin to running a marathon. God alone knew how many had collapsed and drowned in the mud before exhausted comrades could dig them out.

The going had eased somewhat during the past half hour. They were following a low dyke that divided two immense grain fields belonging to a smouldering collective farm that was now behind them. The infantry had also discovered the dyke and *feldgrau* plodded along under their soaking, sixty kilogramme packs, lost in a fog of pain and exhaustion.

The sound of distant guns slowly penetrated Prager's own fog. Russian guns. How did they always manage to be in position? The primitive Russian was capable of almost superhuman feats of endurance and strength, he had long ago learned, but this filthy mud would test the strength of God Himself.

He recalled the endless lectures he had endured on the differences between Aryan and Slavic man. He hadn't believed much of what was said, particularly the business about Slavs being a species apart, as were Orientals, Negroes and Jews. But the more he saw of Russia and the Russians, the easier it was to believe. Slav society was primitive, just as communes and communism were primitive concepts. And in spite of vaunted claims by the Moscow government, the individual Russian was little better off than his sixteenth-century serf ancestor. The addition of a telephone and a radio loudspeaker to a village did not change that fact any more than it had in darkest Africa.

The Russian was indifferent to hardship. Prager had seen enough Russian prisoners to understand that. Kilometre after kilometre, they tramped stolidly towards the rear, expressionless, enduring. Again and again, the contrast between their bovine behaviour and that of the Western European was striking.

The meanest German village was ten, a hundred, a thousand times more efficient, and cleaner, than the best Russian village. Western man changed his environment to secure his comfort and health. The Slav, like the Chinese or the Indian, merely endured what came and blamed his bad luck on fate. The Slavic race occupied the greatest stretch of fertile farmland in Europe – enough to feed the entire continent – yet they could not feed themselves.

As the significance of what he observed in Russia grew, Prager had begun to question his marriage to Sonja, facing for the first time the full implication of their union. She was of the same genetic stock as the inferior breed which surrounded him. Her parents were from the educated class – if you could apply such a term to communist technicians – but surface veneer could not erase the deeper effects of base genetic materials.

Would their children inherit superior racial characteristics from him, or would they be overborne by those of the inferior Slav? Once, he would have been uncomfortable with such thoughts, but now he found that articulation gave them meaning. As a consequence he had stopped rereading Sonja's letters and even shifted them from his jacket pocket to his portmanteau.

Spares, replacements, petrol, rations and mud were his constant preoccupations now. After all, Sonja was safe and comfortable in Germany, with plenty of food and a roof over her head every night...

Dusk gathered. There had been no orders to laager for the night and strict radio silence had been imposed. The sound of artillery had increased in volume, but judging distance in rainy weather was a tricky problem. Depending upon atmospheric characteristics, they could be five kilometres from the fighting or thirty-five. Prager was in a quandary. He had no idea where the front was and continuing in the dark could mire the entire command in mud.

The rain eased to a fine mist an hour later, but the R/T was maddeningly silent. The terrain sloped as they approached the Donets once more, but his map was ancient and lacked detail. The devil! They would laager here. As best he could determine, they were three kilometres short of where they were supposed to be.

The overcast began to clear along the western horizon and the sky glowed pale silver long after sunset. Twice during the night, he checked the sentries and noticed the increasing cold. The sky cleared completely after midnight and the stars turned into steady points of light. There was no rain at dawn and Prager stood in the turret and rubbed feeling into his face and hands. Did winter come this early in Russia?

He climbed down into the frigid interior of the Mark IV, his joints and muscles aching and stiff with cold. Rheumatism, he thought with bitterness, the tanker's real enemy. The sleepy gunner, huddled in his seat, nodded vaguely and Prager handed him the mess tins. The gunner swore without feeling and dragged himself up to find the cooks. The driver was asleep in his seat, head leaning against the bulkhead, but he woke quickly when Prager touched his shoulder. Without a word, he climbed up into the turret and Prager heard his hob-nailed boots clatter on the hull as he jumped down. The engine hatch cover was yanked open to a great deal of wild swearing at the cold.

The engine backfired several times as it wheezed to life. The driver shook his head. 'If the rings aren't replaced soon, she'll pack it in. She also needs a new carburettor. The transmission is . . .'

Prager stopped listening. The litany had become a morning routine, an outlet for the driver's frustration. Instead, he pulled off his mittens and the thin silk gloves he had found in a village house a week before – they always searched deserted houses now for warm clothing and fresh food the retreating Red Army had missed. He washed his face, thought about shaving, and instead brushed his teeth in the canteen cup of water placed on the manifold to heat. He pulled off his jacket, both sweaters, shirt and trousers and long underwear and searched carefully for lice. He found and dispatched a dozen.

It was his turn to bathe this morning – a sponge bath with the canteen cup of used, warmish water in the tank's cramped interior. The usual jokes were made about blue appendages and, like the driver's complaints, they were therapeutic rather than disrespectful.

Prager dried himself with the single, threadbare towel they all shared and dressed quickly, hating the clammy, sweaty feel of clothing unwashed for a month. Whoever had written the rule that officers and enlisted men must never fraternise had never lived in a tank.

Orders reached them at mid-morning. Prager was directed to detach one tank company to support a drive against a factory defended by a workers' militia in the southwestern suburbs of Kharkov. The defenders had already beaten back several attacks, but intelligence predicted they were nearing the end of their ammunition supply.

Prager snorted with derision. He had little faith in a speculative battlefield intelligence report, unless compiled by men directly under his command whose lives depended on its accuracy. Far too often such information was obtained from turncoats who were as likely to be partisans or sixth columnists.

And it turned out that he was right and intelligence wrong, as usual. The militia force holed up in the ruins of the factory appeared to have no end of anti-tank ammunition for their 37 millimetre gun, which was, in theory, marginally effective against the heavily armoured Mark IVs. Still, Prager had a great deal of respect for the gun. In yesterday's battle, two Mark IIIs and a Mark IV from another battalion had been destroyed, and two more Mark IVs badly damaged. They might only be militia troops, but the Russian gunners seemed to know what they were doing.

Prager studied the factory site through his field glasses. Artillery had shelled the buildings into ruins but, as he had observed over and over again in two long years of war, such ruins tended only to create additional cover for a determined force. Left to his own devices, Prager would simply have by-passed the factory, leaving the infantry to dig them out. But he had been ordered to take the factory and there was nothing for it but to get the job done.

The rubble covered an area some four hundred metres square. In the centre, a multi-storey building had collapsed on itself to form an elevation five metres above the rubble. It was an obvious place for an observation post, as not even a direct hit would knock it out. If the observer was killed, he could be replaced quickly enough and the Russians had no end of such cannon fodder.

No, he thought, the anti-tank gun must be destroyed first. Then the machine guns could be dealt with and the infantry could clean up the rest. Prager spoke to the company commander who had taken the severe beating the day before and he confirmed what Prager had suspected – that the anti-tank gun was moved often during the day, even though it would be extremely difficult to wheel the heavy weapon far in that wasteland of broken concrete and twisted steel reinforcing rods. He also informed Prager that at least two of the long-barrelled 20 millimetre anti-tank guns were about as well.

For two days, single tanks had been sent cautiously forward to draw fire while a direct line was held open to the artillery. But the artillery fire never seemed quite accurate enough to destroy the gun; the tanks had been destroyed instead.

It began to rain again. The temperature had plummeted and the rain froze as fast as it touched the ground, covering everything with ice. There was no way to approach from another direction that Prager could see. The demolished remains of workers' flats surrounded the factory site, vague spectres of masonry and concrete exposing their jack-built construction for all the world to see. Entire blocks smouldered and tainted the air with the acrid odour of scorched wood and cloth. What the artillery had missed, Russian partisans and workers' militia moved in to finish at night.

Prager decided to lead the attack himself and hit on a different tactic. After briefing two Mark IV commanders, they moved forward in line astern, leaving the Mark IIIs behind and out of range. His own tank shuddered as the driver fought with the recalcitrant transmission and its treads slipped on icy patches or broke through the frozen crust into boggy mud below.

As they drew into range, he gripped the microphone securely. The hatch was firmly shut and only the observation slit remained unbuttoned;

that was chance enough. Those 20 millimetre guns could not damage Mark IVs, but their gunners had a disconcerting habit of shooting into open hatches and vents. Prager kept his eyes focused on the broad stretch of rubble about the demolished building and cursed the rain that was driving harder now to obscure the target. The other Mark IVs followed behind him as if scouting, their line deliberately ragged.

The rain drove through the slit into his eyes. It was raining too hard. Prager thumbed the microphone transmit button to order the column to withdraw when his eye caught the merest whisp of smoke at the base of a large, up-ended chunk of concrete. A shell exploded a few metres away but he was already driving the turret around and depressing the gun while shouting the range and coordinates into the microphone.

The 75 millimetre gun recoiled viciously and rubble sprayed in all directions as the smoke canister exploded to pinpoint the area. The other two tanks jammed to a halt and wheeled their guns onto the column of white smoke whipping into the wind. Explosions burst about the site; the tank jarred viciously, slamming Prager against the turret padding and steel splinters splattered against the armour plate. The tank lurched again and the gunner cursed. Prager drove the turret back on target.

A flash of flame collapsed the chunk of concrete. The tank jarred again and the gun position blew up with a muted boom. Red flames and black smoke hissed into the steady rain and Prager ordered two more rounds from each tank fired into the area to make certain.

His tank jarred again from the opposite side – my God, Prager thought, there's a second gun . . . He shouted for a withdrawal into the radio just as a fourth round exploded against the rear deck armour and threw him hard against the turret wall. Groggy with pain and disorientation, he tried to stand but was shoved aside. Icy rain swirled at him as the hatch popped open. He had the vague impression of a body vaulting past him but he was too dazed to comprehend. Heat billowed into the turret. Another figure thrust past, mouth working in grotesque pantomine. More heat and flame seared his boots.

Christ God, he groaned, I'm burning! More smoke swirled up into the turret and he began to cough. He reached for the hatch coaming and pulled himself up. Hands reached into the cupola, grabbed him and pulled.

He heard ammunition popping as propellant charges burst their brass cases. Smoke and flame whipped up from inside the tank as he pulled himself out of the mud and scrambled away. Two explosions bounced the tank on its suspension and it listed heavily to one side. The wind veered the smoke away and he saw a curl of blackened steel with jagged edges lying over the rear deck to reveal the ruined engine. He stared at the wound in awe and at the slash of bright metal where another round had scored a deep furrow along the curve of the turret. They had survived four separate hits! What luck, he marvelled. The last one must have been an angle shot; if it had struck squarely . . . he shuddered. All the crew got out, he discovered, but his personal effects including clothing and Sonja's letters were gone.

Leningrad Front November 1941

The front nearly encircled the city of Leningrad. Trenches and fortifications stretched from Shlisselburg at the mouth of the Neva, south through Ivanovskoye, then north again in a great arc to touch the Gulf of Finland. North of the Gulf, Finnish lines slashed across the Karelian Isthmus from Sestroretsk to a point on Lake Ladoga fifty kilometres south of Keksgolm.

On 13 November, Leningrad had been effectively sealed off from the outside world but for a few tenuous telephone lines not yet cut. Occasionally, the foolhardy crew of a lake vessel ran the gauntlet of storms and patrolling Stukas to reach the besieged city. Far too few made it; but they would continue to try until the lake froze at the end of December.

Major Johan Erko, commanding Finland's Second Jaeger Brigade, now dismounted, frowned to himself as the German General-Major tapped the map with a pointer. The 'new information' the General imparted like an expensive gift had done little to mitigate his resentment at being required to fly across the Gulf of Finland and drive three hours to reach German army headquarters, south of Gatchina.

'Our intelligence people have discovered another telephone line and their intercepts of conversations between Leningrad and Moscow,' the General was saying, 'confirm that the city is now starving to death.

'On 8 November, the day the fortress of Tikkvin was captured by the Thirty-Ninth Motorised Corps, thus cutting the final overland route into the city via the lake, the rations for front line troops were reduced to six hundred grams of bread and one hundred and twenty-five grams of meat. Rear elements received four hundred grams of bread. On 13 November, the ration was again reduced. Factory workers then received three hundred grams of bread daily; all others one hundred and fifty grams. Today, we hear that the ration will be further reduced. Factory workers will receive only two hundred and fifty grams daily, which is two slices of bread – imagine, two slices of bread to live on! – while all others will receive one hundred and twenty-five grams, or one slice. Front line troops will receive five hundred grams, rear elements three hundred grams of bread.

'I might add, gentlemen,' the General chuckled in good humour, 'that we understand that the bread baked in Leningrad, by regulation, must contain twenty-five per cent edible cellulose.' He paused for effect. 'In other words, sawdust! They are reduced to eating sawdust, gentlemen. And sawdust nourishes absolutely nothing but termites.' He laughed at his own joke. 'Our intercepts suggest that between two thousand five hundred and three thousand termites are dying each day in Leningrad.

'So! Of course, the communists have given high priority to the evacuation of all non-essential personnel, but we have made it impossible for them to do so. There is no way out of Leningrad except by surrender.'

Erko raised his hand. The General-Major's frown deepened when he saw the Finnish insignia on Erko's uniform.

'The lake, General-Major? How do you intend to keep the Russians from making use of Lake Ladoga?' His stilted schoolboy German had improved a great deal in the last year but he still had to speak slowly to be understood. It was cold in the briefing room and he shivered. Damned Germans, he thought. Don't they even know how to heat a room?

Erko, like all Finns, was appalled at how little the Germans seemed to know about warfare under Arctic conditions. Here it was, the end of November and no German troops had been issued winter gear. They continued to wear summer uniforms while the temperature dipped below zero. His own soldiers had received their winter issues more than a month before.

The General cleared his throat. 'The lake does not give cause for alarm, Major,' he said portentously. 'How can the Russians cross it? Our aircraft sweep the surface every hour of every day when the weather allows. Otherwise, storms make crossing the lake impossible, or a risky business at best. We certainly are not frightened by the possibility the Russians might resupply a city of three million people during winter storms.' He beamed at the sycophantic laughter he drew.

'Forgive me for pointing out, General-Major, but the lake will freeze by the beginning of January and remain so until April or longer. When that happens, we can expect the enemy to make every effort to resupply the city on roads built across the ice which will curve beyond the range of your largest guns.'

He had deliberately said 'your' rather than 'our'. 'Your Luftwaffe will be unable to fly much of the time because of bad weather, but Russian lorries will continue to run.'

There were a dozen other Finnish officers present and they were nodding in agreement. A staff officer tried to intervene to spare the General the necessity of answering, but was brushed aside. 'Major,' he snorted, 'we of the German army are no strangers to war. Our objective is to reduce the city of Leningrad. The Fuehrer has chosen to do so by blockade. He has no wish to expend the lives of thousands of soldiers, yours or ours. I know well that your high command does not agree, but the Fuehrer prefers to let starvation and disease accomplish the surrender of Leningrad.

'We have made careful studies and determined that the Russians will be unable to cross the ice with sufficient supplies to make the slightest difference to our siege. In fact, by attempting to do so, they will extend their own meagre resources beyond the breaking point. The matter has been decided by the Fuehrer! There is no need for further discussion.'

The General continued with the briefing, but there was a rustling at the back and Erko looked around in time to see a Finnish General stalk out. So, he thought, the Germans were beginning to discover they had bitten off more than they could chew.

Three minor attacks designed to eliminate Russian salients were next explained, two on the Karelian front and one just east of Ivanskoye. Erko's Second Jaeger Brigade was assigned to destroy a factory south of Sestroretsk on the rail line to Leningrad twenty kilometres southeast, which the Russians had managed to keep in partial operation. The job would ordinarily have been accomplished with artillery or by the Luftwaffe but bad weather had grounded the latter and the guns required to do the job were busy elsewhere.

Erko hated these small offensive operations. They were wasteful of lives and produced little of value. As he travelled back to his own headquarters near Sestroretsk, he could not help but think that German and Finnish objectives had diverged widely after less than six months of war. The Germans had put every possible pressure on Helsinki to form an alliance, but the best they had been able to achieve was a diplomatic fiction called a co-belligerency. To the outside world, Finland was conducting her own war and acted as if she were surprised to find herself in unintentional company with the Nazis.

North of Lake Ladoga, Finnish forces had reached their pre-1940 borders and stopped. An uneasy stand-to with the Russians had developed; a few rifle shots and artillery rounds were exchanged daily but, beyond that, the Karelian Front was characterised by little movement and less fighting.

The staff car driving him to the airfield passed a bombed-out block of workers' flats and Erko saw German soldiers marching a line of civilians along the street. The lead man wore a placard around his neck; he caught only a glimpse of the sign and the word, *Partisan*, in Russian and German.

He snorted. To the Germans, anyone who looked at them cross-eyed was a partisan. Strange, he thought, how much the Germans were troubled by partisans while there was little such activity in the Finnish sector. But of course the Germans brought it on themselves. They shot or hanged people for the slightest infraction and a Russian civilian was liable to imprisonment at the least whim of their damned secret police.

The line of partisans, some twenty in all, came abreast of his car. Each had a noose about his neck with the free end – to be tied to the gallows beam – looped over a shoulder. Each man had been badly beaten about the face and all were barefoot in spite of the snow and ice.

My God, he thought angrily, the Germans could be barbaric at times.

Erko's headquarters were located in a hotel that had once been a gambling casino when Leningrad was known as St Petersburg and this suburban area west of the city had attracted the best, and the worst, of Imperial Russian society to nightclubs, whorehouses and country clubs. Some of his bored staff officers rooting in the cellar had found casino gambling equipment and, more intriguing, a small storeroom filled with mirrors, pornographic photos and a large assortment of weird appliances which were clearly sexual in nature. From the amount of dust and dirt that had accumulated, they had decided that the equipment had been in storage since the Revolution twenty-four years before.

After the Revolution, the once graceful façade of the three-storey hotel had been redone in the heavy-handed Soviet manner and the interior converted into a sterile workers' association resort. Walls had been knocked out to form three barrack-like dormitories filled with narrow canvas cots; one for men, one for women and the third for children. The dormitories now served his troops who, like the vacationing pre-war Soviet workers, were grateful for the least comfort.

His orderly had a hot bath waiting and Erko drank a stiff vodka as he soaked the bone-chilling winter cold away. But the bath doubled his weariness and his orderly had to wake him. Erko climbed out and dried himself, thinking of the evening conference to come with still more Germans. But at least it was only a few minutes drive away this time – and included a meal.

An hour later he found enlisted waiters in white jackets circulating among the officers with trays of drinks and canapés, so that it seemed very much like the pre-War cocktail parties he had endured in Berlin. The trays were laden with champagne, schnapps and vodka. Light from crystal chandeliers, looted from God knew where, glittered from military decorations and badges and a bevy of German girls in ball gowns flitted about the dance floor like so many butterflies.

Erko stood to one side watching the array of officers stuff food and drink into their mouths and thought of the German enlisted men freezing about Leningrad in inadequate summer uniforms and boots.

His disgust must have shown on his face because a voice beside him said, 'Something tells me, Herr Major, that you and I agree.'

Erko turned to see an officer in his early thirties, with hair so blond it was almost white. His classic Aryan profile held an expression of disgust as he surveyed the room.

The man wore an SS uniform, not Waffen SS, the combat branch, but of a regiment he could not identify. Erko had encountered SS officers before and knew that most were either party hacks incapable of any other job or else unreasoning fanatics, all dressed up in fancy uniforms that imitated those of the army. Erko was instantly wary; denunciation by an SS officer might not hurt him personally, but it would make cooperation between the two armies that much more difficult.

As if sensing his thoughts, the officer smiled. 'Don't worry, Major, I was an army officer before I joined the SS. I graduated from the Gross-Licherterfeld Cadet School in 1932 and I served in Poland and the Netherlands. My name is Joachim Brenner and my rank is Sturmbannfuehrer, which is the SS equivalent to Major.'

He plucked two drinks from a passing tray. 'Shall we drink to the success of Finland and Germany?' he asked.

Erko could hardly refuse and they touched glasses. 'Tell me Sturmbannfuehrer Brenner,' Erko asked, 'what is the real function of this dinner party? I was under the impression that it was to be a working conference, but it seems rather to be a social event.'

'It is both, Major, ah . . .'

Erko supplied his name and they shook hands. Brenner placed his empty glass on the tray offered by another waiter. 'Will you?' he motioned and Erko shook his head. Brenner took another glass for himself. 'It was decided to make this a social event as well to mitigate any, ah . . . shall we say, discord that might develop between *allies*.' He chuckled at the term.

Erko returned the smile in spite of himself. There was no alliance between Finland and Germany and his government strongly discouraged the use of the word allies when referring to relations between Germany and Finland. But Brenner seemed a likeable enough chap. 'I suggest we choose a table,' Brenner murmured as he noticed a German general looking around for his aide-de-camp. 'If you will permit me to join you, I suggest the back of the room. General Kluger is a windy speaker, so if you fall asleep, it won't be noticed.'

The food was well-prepared and plentiful and Erko wondered what the enlisted men spread across the 150 kilometre front about Leningrad would think if they could see fat, useless staff officers gorging on pork and beefsteak, fresh bread and even French wines and Dutch cheeses, while they choked down half-frozen rations.

As Brenner predicted, General Kluger spoke for an hour about the historical imperative of the occupation of the Eastern Lands and the natural juxtaposition of Germany vis-à-vis Finland, before sitting down to prolonged applause. And Brenner proved right again. The dinner and briefing was little more than an exercise in fence-mending. The operation in which his own brigade was to take part tomorrow was extolled as vitally important to the maintenance of the front and posed as an example of German-Finnish cooperation. Erko was sorely tempted to ask if that were so, why German troops were not participating.

After the briefing, the serious drinking began. Being Finnish, Erko was more than capable of holding his own but the operation scheduled for the following morning made it unwise to try. Brenner seemed to drink enough for both as they talked, yet failed to show the least sign that the copious amounts of vodka, brandy and schnapps were affecting him in the least.

Erko found himself describing the progress of his brigade from the Finnish border to their present assignment on the extreme western end of the Leningrad front.

'And not a moment too soon. We were pretty well exhausted by the time they pulled us off the front lines and sent us back to Lahti to refit. Our casualty rate had been high, nearly thirty-five per cent, and we needed the rest. We had two weeks before they moved us here.'

In turn, Brenner told him that he had arrived in Leningrad after three months in the Ukraine, about which he seemed rather vague. Some kind of rear-area position, Erko thought. Perhaps some easy administrative job he would not care to talk about to a combat veteran. But he had, Brenner said seen action in both Poland and the Netherlands when he was still in the army.

'I find the Russian soldier a strange creature,' Brenner admitted. 'Fanatic one minute and brave to the point of foolishness; the next he runs away at a mere rumour.'

Erko laughed. 'Ah, Major Brenner, don't make the mistake of believing that typical. What you have observed are reserve or militia units, some of whom have received no training of any kind. We Finns have fought the Russians three times now, 1918, 1939–40 and now again, and one thing I will say for Ivan – he is no coward.

'Regular Army units and those reserve units with sufficient training and experience are, as you say, brave to a fault, but the Russians have suffered such immense casualties that they are forced to use anyone who can shoulder a rifle. Many times their officers are completely untrained as well. Some don't have even sidearms. We have even encountered one scratch militia equipped with Colt Berdan rifles made in the 1870s. Last week we took three prisoners who were carrying flintlock muskets taken from a museum. So, it is not unnatural to see panic and cowardice in such units.

'I fought the Russians in the Winter War. In the beginning, they were badly led. We were much more mobile and it is very demoralising to be killed from behind. One heard stories of machine gunners chained to their weapons and whole battalions deserting at once, and such things did happen. But after February 1940, when they were given proper leadership and decent weapons and equipment, they became a fierce enemy.'

Brenner described his experiences during the Battle for Holland and he contrasted the occupation of the country to Russia. 'I remain convinced that we gained the support and sympathy of the Dutch people so quickly by concentrating on pacification and restoration. The Dutch came around just that quickly. As soon as they saw that their economy was approaching pre-war levels once more they ceased being obstructive.

'There is almost no resistance movement there, and what little does exist is criminal in nature and preys exclusively on the Dutch people. We did away with the catalyst for such activities by eliminating dissident elements like criminals and Jews and by taking hostages against good behaviour. But here in Russia, as in Poland, the Slav is a different animal. Because of his well-known disregard for human life, the fate of a hostage has little meaning.

'We have discovered in Russia,' Brenner went on, 'as in Poland, that an active programme to counter partisan activities is the best medicine. And speed and intelligence are two keys. We build extensive intelligence networks using paid informers and act instantly on any information they supply us. Only in this instance is the hostage of any value and to impress the importance of such work on our informer, we take the hostage from his own family. Now that is something that he can understand!

'It is surprising how quickly a reliable network of informers can be built up in this way. It is usually necessary to shoot a few hostages at first to show that we mean business but everything settles down quickly enough.'

Erko was vaguely uncomfortable. There was nothing about the taking of hostages that was disquieting. Certainly, in modern warfare civilians suffered as much as soldiers. Historically, civilians had always participated in wars as partisans or guerrillas and often were effective all out of proportion to their numbers in rear areas. But taking and executing hostages invited retaliation and made break-downs in morale and discipline inevitable.

As if he sensed Erko's discomfort, Brenner turned the conversation to other matters and encouraged Erko to talk about himself. Erko described his wife and his marriage and laughed about how they had so far done little but sacrifice to the exigencies of war. Brenner in turn told him that he was unmarried, a career officer. But he had a friend, an Army officer who was married two months before the war in Russia began, to a Russian girl! Now she is living at his house near Hamburg while he served with a Panzer unit in the south of Russia. His tone was clipped, as if he disapproved of his friend's choice, Erko thought.

'I saw her before I left. A lucky woman. There she was, living in the very lap of luxury, not a care in the world, while her country was at war.'

'Surely,' Erko said in surprise, 'if she married your friend she has become a German citizen and has given up her allegiance to her native country?'

Erko felt a sudden flash of hostility from the German, then Brenner was laughing. 'Perhaps you are correct. Already I have been too long in Russia. She is a very nice girl, rather attractive as well . . . for a Slav.'

Erko had become so interested in this contradictory man that he forgot the time and only the appearance of his driver reminded him. He jumped up and made quick apologies.

Brenner walked with him to the door and they shook hands. Prompted by a surge of loneliness, Erko impulsively invited Brenner to visit his headquarters at his convenience. Brenner smiled widely. 'I'd like that very much. Perhaps, I could accompany you on your operation tomorrow?'

Surprised, Erko agreed and promised to send a driver for him.

On the roundabout drive through the blacked-out suburbs, Erko had a chance to think about the forthcoming operations. Pecking, he called it, after a common occurrence in the barnyard when chickens for no apparent reason would turn on one of their number and peck it to death. They made little stabs here and there with their beaks that drew blood. Eventually, the will to resist disappeared and the victim died.

Leningrad was like the victim chicken. Probes and pecks here and there as the blockade was pulled ever tighter. Soon, the city would lose the will to resist and would collapse. Then Moscow would become the victim – only this time, the chickens would not find it so easy to peck their victims to death.

As the car drove up to the hotel portico, he wondered idly what Brenner's function was. He had forgotten to ask.

Brenner arrived before 0530 hours on a captured Russian army motorcycle, leather great coat splashed with mud and face glowing in the icy air. 'I thought I'd save your driver a trip.'

In his dispatch case, he carried three bottles of Napoleon brandy. 'To celebrate with tonight!' he laughed. Erko shook his head in admiration. 'The partisans shoot motorcyclists like rabbits. It's a wonder you made it here.'

'I drove too quickly for them,' Brenner grinned.

Erko took Brenner with him to inspect the three companies who were to take part. The men were in good spirits at this break in the monotony of siege and, having just eaten a hot breakfast, they greeted Erko by name as he passed along the lines.

The troops began to move up at 0730 hours. Erko and Brenner went with them as they filtered into the trenches facing the bomb-damaged factory. Brenner was impressed with the fact that the Finnish bunkers were floored with carefully-fitted split logs to reduce mud and dampness.

They watched the desultory activities in the Russian trenches through sandbagged observation slits as the eastern sky began to grey with the still distant dawn.

Erko glanced at his watch. 'The assault will begin at 0800,' he commented. A cannon roared behind Russian lines and moments later the ground vibrated as the shell struck well to the rear. Brenner glanced up, his expression apprehensive, but Erko shrugged. 'They fire one shell every fifteen minutes or so. I think the ammunition comes straight from a factory closer in to the city. It seems they are allocated only enough to fire at fifteen minute intervals. Or perhaps that is as fast as they can produce them.'

The three-storey factory had, Erko guessed, been built before the Great War. In daylight, its walls had the creamy colour and texture characteristic of Leningrad brick and long rows of high windows marched across its sides, which would have made the interior light and airy if they had not been boarded up. The sides and roof were pockmarked with artillery shells and gaping holes. Aerial bombing, according to the photographs, had nearly eliminated the roof. But the Finnish air force could not support this relatively minor operation and the Germans claimed that every available soldier and piece of field artillery was required for the main assault east of the city, where they were driving for the mouth of the Neva at Shusselberg, to close the ring about the city.

Erko nudged Brenner and pointed. 'There, beside that pile of rubble. Watch.'

Brenner focused his field glasses and a moment later chuckled. A man poked his head above the snow, looked around warily, then scuttled away. A moment later, another followed.

'Workers,' Erko explained. 'The factory is empty by day but operates at night. We've been shelling it for some time but we only have one light field gun and two anti-tank weapons.'

'Why is the factory so important?'

Erko grunted. 'Two reasons, I suppose. It produces machine pistols for the Soviet Army – but I doubt if it turns out many these days. However, the factory and grounds form a salient into our lines. Headquarters is worried the Russians may use it to concentrate an assault force. If we can take it, then we hold an unbroken line.'

'It looks to me like a job for aircraft or artillery,' Brenner said as he swept his glasses along the building.

Erko did not answer; he liked Brenner but still, he was German and would not be pleased to hear complaints about the lack of German support, even though they were long on demands for this action or that. There was enough friction between the two armies without adding to it. Everyone knew the Germans were famous for allowing their allies to bear the brunt of casualties.

The winter darkness began to melt into twilight. The radio operator handed Erko a routine report – Russian reinforcements were moving up to support the factory. The tension was growing palpable. This was the most dangerous of all military operations – an attack across open ground against an entrenched and well-concealed enemy. And there was nothing to do but wait; all dispositions had been made, orders given, eventualities foreseen and nothing left to chance – one hoped. All movement up to the line had occurred during the night. Surprise and speed were essential now if they were to succeed.

Erko motioned Brenner to remain and started forward. White tapes led to assembly points and on to the front trenches. All troops were in place as he pushed into the assault trench hacked out of the frozen ground during the last two nights. His dismounted troopers had been well-rehearsed in infantry tactics, both practice and actual combat. They waited calmly for the most part, smoking and talking quietly. An officer glanced at his watch and spoke. The men stubbed out their cigarettes and moved off along the trench to their final positions.

'They seem very confident,' he heard Brenner say and turned to see the German behind him. A few soldiers gave him a quizzical stare as they filed past.

'I thought I told you to remain behind . . .' Erko began but a flare arced up and, instantly, machine guns began to rattle. A roar rose from the trench as the soldiers clambered out and raced forward. Erko forgot about Brenner. He waved an arm at the three runners dogging his steps and raced up the ladder.

A flurry of mortar shells screamed down onto the factory and clouds of dust, dirt, shattered ice and snow flew up to join with the level rays of the sun edging over the horizon to form an effective screen. At least, Erko muttered to himself, the assault had begun at the proper moment.

As he ran after the soldiers across the frozen mud of no-man's land, the man ahead stumbled and fell heavily. Erko recognised him as a recent replacement, but there wasn't time to stop; ahead, muzzle flashes were visible in the dawn greyness beyond a low wall topped with sandbags.

As he threw himself down, four soldiers broke cover from a shallow mortar crater, two going left, two right. That confused the enemy machine gunner long enough for a soldier to race across the open space to the wall and heave a satchel charge. The explosion flayed Erko with concussion. A section of the wall disappeared and moments later Finnish soldiers squeezed through and began to spread out in both directions.

Erko followed right behind. He stopped to scribble a hasty message ordering up the reserve company to reinforce the breech and turned to give it to a messenger, only to find Brenner grinning at him. There wasn't time to argue with him. A runner pushed past, snatched the message and dashed back through the wall.

He was surprised at how easily they had breached the wall. The Russian machine gun had been a grave threat for the past week. The gunner was an expert shot, using it like a sniper's rifle and more than once he had picked off a man a thousand metres or more in the rear. Erko had considered it a crucial point in the factory's defences as it controlled the approaches along this sector. But only a twisted barrel and a few links of ammunition remained after the satchel charge had done its work.

A sergeant appeared. 'The railway yard is deserted, Major. I think they've pulled back inside.'

Erko pushed through a gap in a makeshift barricade and clambered over burst sandbags. Winter bare bushes were remarkably thick and Erko eyed them nervously as he approached, thinking of snipers, but the sergeant hurried on.

They clambered up a steep mound of snow-covered cinders and cautiously peered over the crest.

Sunlight broke through the dwindling cloud and its level rays flooded the snowplain that lay between them and the factory. The snow glowed orange which faded quickly as the sun climbed the horizon. The factory was clearly visible and the sergeant seemed to be right; the railway yard was deserted. He ran his glasses carefully along the twisted tracks and rusting switch gear and signals and mounds of cinders. All the coal was gone - probably every last chunk had been salvaged against the bitter cold. Bits of lumber were scattered here and there and damaged rolling stock slumped wearily, much of it fire-scarred.

Erko examined a hastily constructed bunker of rails and sleepers. There wasn't a sign of life and the snow showed few tracks. Erko had expected them to make a strong stand along the wall, then retreat to the marshalling yard. 'Now what . . .' he started.

Brenner had reached past his shoulder and pointed. Erko shifted the glasses to the factory. 'Very clever,' he muttered. 'One, two, no three, machine guns,' he announced, checking the windows.

'That's why we got through the wall so easily. They knew they couldn't hold the perimeter so they let us break through to the bunkers. Then when we engage them, they will hit us hard from the flank with the machine guns. One more day of machine pistol production, at least.' He shook his head in admiration.

He thought for a moment, head bent against the searing wind. Brenner and the sergeant exchanged glances. Their single field piece had stopped firing and he heard the distant shrill of whistles as his troops moved towards the marshalling yard. Slowly, silence settled until it became unnerving.

The Russians had bottled themselves up, gambling that their ruse would go undetected. An amateur, Erko thought, is running their show. Probably the factory manager. These damned Russians are so imbued with respect for authority that they never stop to consider if the boss has the proper qualifications; it's enough that he *is* a party member. No professional military commander would trap his entire force in that way.

He scribbled three notes with terse instructions and sent them off with a messenger, then turned back to the factory to make certain of his analysis. The cold wind whipped dry snow along the ground, making vision difficult for a moment, and he thought of what it must be like in there – civilian workers half-trained as soldiers, equipped with inadequate weapons, virtually no food and no fuel for fire, knowing that they were going to die – if not today, then tomorrow. Yet they had held the factory for two weeks.

Erko was jerked from his reverie as the sergeant touched his shoulder. 'Nearly time, sir.'

He glanced at his wristwatch. 'Go,' he said softly. As one, the line of Finns swept forward, running hard through the powdery snow. Erko started forward as the first shots popped from the factory yard. The sacrificial rear guard.

Halfway across the marshalling yard, whistles blew and the troops changed direction suddenly and, ignoring the sparse rifle fire from the bunkers, raced for the factory wall. The machine guns had all been sited on the second and third floor; the Finns gained the wall and began to tear at the barricades blocking the ground floor windows. The machine guns were all but useless as they could not be depressed enough to fire straight down.

Erko saw Lieutenant Erranien smash a hole through a plywood cover with his rifle butt and the man behind tossed in a handgrenade. Both ducked away as the explosion blew the cover to splinters. Troops poured in through the gap, shouting. Other windows were being dealt with in a similar manner.

Erko ducked inside among a tangle of men, and squirmed away to allow others in. He hated this kind of fighting most of all. Close quarters fighting was the most vicious there was as each side understood that quarter could neither be asked nor given.

Rows of machinery, some of it destroyed by bombing or the desultory artillery fire that had been visited on the factory, stretched into the gloom and the floors were slippery with snow. The ceilings were holed and it was possible to see the sky in a hundred places. Scrap paper, refuse of every description and empty cartridge cases littered the floor, mute testimony to the weeks of fighting and destruction. Erko found an office in which the glass had been shot out and decided it would serve as a command post.

He and Brenner kicked broken glass and junk into a corner and shoved desks and filing cabinets against the front wall as a barrier against stray bullets. Erko spread out his sketch map of the factory's interior, assembled from prisoner interrogations. He marked it off into grids and assigned each squad a sector to be cleaned out.

The structure reverberated with rifle fire and the explosions of stick grenades. Shouts and screams could be heard, however faint, and Erko grew silent as the casualty list mounted. Brenner sat to one side, huddled into his leather coat, face and lips pinched in the sub-zero cold and watched, saying little. He sensed Erko's anger and was subdued by it.

After midday, the factory began to darken as the light failed and heavy snow clouds moved in from the Gulf of Finland. Reports of sporadic reinforcements slackened as did the volume of fire. Erko had managed to clear the entire ground floor and push several companies of troops to the very edge of the marshalling yard from where they could see, in the distance, the church spires that marked the northwestern suburbs of Leningrad.

Brenner was keeping Erko's grid chart up to date. In spite of the fact that he spoke no Finnish, he twice went out onto the floor to investigate a particularly stubborn strongpoint. Erko was grateful for Brenner's help but puzzled at the same time over why he would expose himself to such unnecessary danger.

It must go beyond mere curiosity, he thought as he watched Brenner mark off another portion of the grid where a soldier was pointing a grimy finger. Brenner grinned at the man and clapped him on the arm. It was too bad that all German officers couldn't be as personable and helpful.

Erko doubted that Brenner had permission to take part in a Finnish operation, and in actual fact Erko had no permission to allow him to do so. Both might well receive severe reprimands. On impulse, he asked.

Brenner laughed. 'Such rules are made by those who remain safely in the rear. A real soldier pays no attention to them.'

It was on the tip of his tongue for Erko to point out that Brenner was not a soldier, but a political policeman. He caught himself in time.

They secured the factory by evening. Twenty-three prisoners were taken, only those too badly wounded to fight any longer. Soviet attempts to reinforce the militia garrison were forestalled by the reserve company that Erko pushed out to the forward edge of the marshalling yard. Here, the road was funnelled through a narrow gully to the plant which from the Leningrad side occupied the summit of a hill. The reserve company, armed with the two anti-tank guns and two mortars, easily held off the feeble attempts that were all the Russians seemed able to make. Again, it seemed to Erko that the Soviet were willing to exchange territory with the Finns while they threw their main forces against the Germans on the other side of the city.

Erko called up the demolition company assigned to the assault and by midnight explosive charges had been planted throughout the structure. Erko ordered the reserve company to fall back temporarily to the line of the wall. Only as they assembled did he become aware of the full extent of his casualties. He had lost seventy-nine killed and sixty-three wounded out of a reduced brigade-sized force of 1,400 men – nearly ten per cent dead and the battalion's effective strength reduced by another twenty per cent. Was putting an end to ten or fifteen new machine pistols a day worth all those lives?

Brenner nudged him and he looked up to see the engineer lieutenant raise an arm. Whistles shrilled and a moment later the demolition charges began to go off, shattering the building's reinforced concrete shell. As blackness closed in again, huge clouds of dust and masonry particles rose above the site. The darkness hid the full extent of the destruction but the hated silhouette of the factory had disappeared.

The weary troops marched back to their barracks six kilometres away as fresh troops filed up through the wall to take up defensive positions on the edge of the marshalling yard. Erko waited beside his staff car with Brenner. The tall German shifted position and stamped his feet. The air was absolutely still and the silence broken only by the occasional thud of a distant bomb or artillery shell.

'Why?'

Brenner was a vague shadow in misty darkness.

'Why what?'

'Why did you risk your life up here with us today?'

The figure moved slightly and Erko guessed Brenner had shrugged.

Brenner said, 'You are a good officer, Johan Erko. Like me. Both of us are too good for the duty we have been given.' His face was bleak for a moment and Erko wondered exactly what kind of duty he was referring too.

'I suppose I wanted to feel like a soldier once again.'

Brenner straightened quickly and banged a fist on the staff car's fender.

'I need a drink, my friend. Let's go back and open those brandy bottles!'

(Personal note for Hans Svenson, Editor. I am sending this column in the legation diplomatic pouch to avoid the censors. You will see why when you read it – Torsten.)

> From Across the World Torsten Fredriksson, Moscow, via Stockholm, 15 October 1941 – For immediate release: The battle for Moscow began in earnest with an assault on the city's fortified positions, 30 September 1941. German panzer and reconnaissance units are reported to have reached the city's outlying suburbs. Every train leaving Moscow is jammed with humanity. Roads are clogged with people in cars, in lorries or on foot, all streaming east.
>
> The first snow fell in the Moscow region on 9 October and was

followed by heavy rain mixed with sleet and more snow. Many say that summer faded into winter overnight.

The Moscow grapevine, that unofficial but usually reliable and uncensored news source, reports that General Guderian's panzers are moving up the Smolensk-Moscow highway at eighty kilometres per day! Kaluga, less than 120 kilometres west, fell on 14 October and it was subsequently rumoured that the Sixteenth, Nineteenth and Twentieth Armies before that city were destroyed.

In the absence of official news, horror tales creep out of Leningrad and the conquered territories to the west. Perhaps it is the Moscow government's way of bracing the people's will to resist. Whenever the weather permits, the Luftwaffe blasts the city day and night, in spite of heavy losses from the most massive concentration of anti-aircraft weapons ever assembled.

Today, clouds of white smoke hang over Moscow as Government ministries burn files. As I walked the city streets, I saw trams and underground trains deserted by their crews. People rushed on foot to the stations carrying whatever they could pack, abandoning whatever grew too heavy to carry. I saw opportunists selling cardboard boxes on the street corners for thirty roubles apiece. State bakeries and food shops are closed and long lines of desperate people stream into the private market stalls on Chermushki Street. Black-market operators sell food openly from carts and I saw uniformed militia men buying from them. Panic is reaching epidemic proportions and the government is said to be leaving the city.

It has been believed for so long, here and around the world, that if Moscow falls the Soviet Union is finished, that the people actually believe it. Nothing could be further from the truth, but then truth in Russia is a commodity that is rarely susceptible to Western understanding. Truth means whatever the government chooses it to mean, or what the people as a whole, by some mysterious and wholly Russian process of osmosis, choose to believe.

Suffice it to say that if Moscow does fall, the Union of Soviet Socialist Republics will be finished, whether or not the Red Army is defeated. The people will have lost all faith in the Communist Party and its ability to govern. And even here, without the consent of the people, the government cannot exist.

Moscow October 15 – November 30 1941

Captain Mikhail Gregorvitch Dogorov was not certain what to expect when he stepped from the train in the familiar green painted Kursk Station. Snorting trains, screeching whistles, chimes from the tannoy system, shouting porters, harried men and women and a sea of uniforms swirled around him in a confusing mass.

Those not trying to board a train squatted wherever there was space enough for a suitcase or cardboard box. He fought his way up the platform, cursed roundly as he did so and when he reached the booking hall, faced another struggle to get through the doors. He burst out into the frosty air of the station square thankful that he had no luggage to hamper him.

People were queuing up in vast lines that snaked out into the streets and Dogorov was amazed at the sight. Even on a first fine summer Sunday he had never seen anything like this. He grabbed the arm of a railway worker hurrying past to ask what was happening, but the man yanked his arm away with a curse and trotted on.

Dogorov left the station and walked north on Sadovaya to Karl Marx Street where he thought it might be possible to board a tram. It had rained during the early morning and the pavement glistened in the crisp October sunshine. In contrast to the railway station, the streets were quiet. Militiamen watched the desultory traffic from the corners as usual, but Dogorov saw that each was armed with the new PPD machine pistol. The plates – the radio loudspeakers mounted high on the telephone poles at each intersection – played selections of martial music.

At the intersection of Sadovaya and Karl Marx, he saw a guard post surrounded by sandbags from which protruded the barrel of a machine gun. My God! He hadn't seen machine guns in Moscow since he was a boy. The tram stops all had long queues and he turned down Karl Marx. A block along, he was stopped and his papers examined. Beside the militiaman stood a stolid individual in a dark military greatcoat whom he guessed was an NKVD agent. His uneasiness grew.

Dogorov's orders were to report to the Moscow Military District for reassignment. His orders also stated that he was to be quartered in the officers' barracks near Butyrsky Zast. When he arrived, he found it worse than expected. The long hall was filled with men, shouting, laughing, joking and arguing at the top of their lungs. He had had enough of such overcrowding in the prison camp and as soon as he registered and was issued his Moscow ration book, he sought out the barracks' commander and explained that he lived in the city, at his mother's apartment, and unless the commander objected, would stay there, thus easing the overcrowded situation in the barracks.

The commander was a lumpy individual in an ill-fitting uniform, an infantry officer long past his prime and relegated to this thankless task for unknown sins. Dogorov suspected that the war had rescued him from an early retirement on inadequate pay and, as Dogorov hoped, the commandant was more concerned with the demands made upon his barracks than the whereabouts of officers assigned there. Dogorov could almost see the progression of thoughts working their laborious way through rationalisation after rationalisation.

Slow he may have been, but the commandant was no fool. After a short sparring session, Dogorov confided that his mother was a high ranking official in the Food and Nutrition Ministry and the commandant smiled. It was all arranged without words, and he wrote a pass for Dogorov quickly and blotted it with a flourish.

Dogorov left immediately, feeling a slight pang of conscience at having taken part in a subtle form of bribery. The commandant understood that nothing could be done for him now, but later . . . ah, that was a different matter. Storing up favours in the Soviet Union for one's old age was akin to the Western process of building a retirement fund. The Soviet Union took care of its aged, but there were few luxuries involved. Fortunately, he had not had to admit that his mother was trapped in Leningrad.

The walk across the city along the Moscow River in the cool autumn afternoon soothed him. Trees showed the last russets and gold of autumn. Shortly, the rains would start in earnest and the colours would wash away with the leaves and Moscow would take on its characteristic winter-grey colour.

His mother's flat was in a three-storey apartment building constructed shortly before the start of the Great War, between Kaluzhskaya Strand and Lenin Park. She had been granted the spacious three room apartment in the building in memory of his father. After the Civil War, Lenin personally confirmed the apartment in his mother's name, making it to this day, one of the few privately owned flats remaining in the city. Even during the lean years of the 1920s, due to her own position in the Party and the government, Madame Olga Semonova Dogorov's ownership and occupancy had never been questioned and Mikhail Dogorov had always accepted it as her due.

He found the building strangely quiet on this late-autumn afternoon. Even the elderly couple who served as caretakers were gone. The apartment was undisturbed; he had half-expected that it would have been reassigned since his mother's transfer to Leningrad. Apparently, his troubles had not affected her position in the slightest.

He opened the windows to air the musty smell left by summer heat and the damp of autumn. The tiny refrigerator grumbled to life when he plugged it in. After months in the forests and swamps of the Pripet and the weeks in prison camp, this simple tin box topped by an ugly coil suddenly marked the vast gulf between Mikhail Dogorov and the majority of the people of the Soviet Union.

The ownership of an electric refrigerator was a sign of luxury and Party favour. All of his childhood friends had grown up in flats considerably smaller than this. They shared lavatories, baths and kitchens with other families in the building. But then their fathers had not been high Party members murdered by counter-revolutionaries, nor were their mothers officials in the All Soviet Food and Nutrition Ministry. Outstanding service to the Party earned outstanding rewards, he had always been taught.

The flat consisted of a kitchen with a two-burner stove and the wonderful refrigerator, a parlour-living room and his mother's bedroom where the mattress had been rolled at the foot of the bed, the bureau and dressing table cleared and drawers opened to prevent mildew. The closet contained some of her clothing, bits and pieces not needed in Leningrad. And all the furniture remained – a certain sign that her transfer was to have been temporary. In the dresser, he found a very old jewel case that belonged to his mother. The case was beautifully carved from the finest Circassian burl walnut and inlaid with a delicate filigree design in gold. His mother had once told him that it had been made by the famous jeweller, Fabergé, and presented to her by the Grand Duke Michael in 1913 after a performance. Her eyes had sparkled as she recalled those pre-Revolutionary days when she had been a rising young actress.

Inside, nestled among a few pieces of jewellery, was a velvet pouch. He slipped out the fine Swiss gold hunter watch and slowly wound the stem. A metallic ticking began when he held it to his ear and he opened the cover. He would have to discover and set the correct time he thought. His own steel army issue watch had disappeared on entering Gorlovo prison camp. He turned the watch over and read the dedication engraved in fine old Russian script.

'To my dearest Prince Orvolovski from your Maria.' His father had been presented with the watch by Prince Orvolovski himself just before he was executed by a firing squad his father had commanded. Dogorov's mother had never known the entire story as her husband was murdered a few weeks later by White Guard bandits. He slipped the watch into his pocket.

In the parlour he dropped into a chair after shedding his tunic and sat staring at the fading park. What was going to become of his mother now, he wondered? There had been little in the papers he devoured on the train beyond descriptions of astounding Soviet victories – most of which he doubted. Only one city in the occupied territories had been mentioned; indeed, it would have been impossible to tell from the newspaper accounts what areas of the country were occupied by the Hitlerites.

Leningrad was that exception, but the papers had noted only that a

Workers Shock Army had been organised to meet the Hitlerite threat. On the train he had heard rumours of mass evacuations of the civil population. If that were the case, his mother would probably be evacuated when the city government left.

The chill of the autumn evening began to penetrate the flat. He stretched aching muscles. It was useless to speculate. He would gain a better understanding of the nation's situation tomorrow when he went for reassignment. Dogorov closed the windows and sat watching the darkness creep over the city and thought about dinner.

He was jolted awake some time later by the sound of guns. Across the park streams of tracers raced into the sky. He felt, as well as heard, the dull crump of bombs and knew he should go to a shelter. Instead, he sat watching the tracers until the bombs ceased and he fell asleep once more.

The sun was warm the following morning, easing the autumn chill. The sky was such a rare and cloudless blue this late in the season that it seemed all Moscow had turned out to defy the grey panic of yesterday. There were traces of the bombing; here and there a burned-out building or street barricades set up to divert traffic while labourers cleared away debris. But certainly nothing like the destruction he had seen in Kiev.

Headquarters for the Moscow Military District was jammed with uniformed men waiting in patient lines. Dogorov discovered that the longest line was reserved for officers like himself who had been trapped behind enemy lines and escaped. Two whom he spoke to told of queuing for days and a feeling of uneasiness swept over him.

In mid-afternoon, he reached a scarred desk where his paybook and *propiska* were examined by a harried clerk who stamped them and passed him on to another clerk who repeated the process and also checked his name against a huge list. Twice more the ritual was repeated before he was directed to another, shorter line, which meandered along a stuffy hall. The weather remained fine and the afternoon sun warmed the building until it was stifling.

Another hour dragged past before he was admitted to a spacious room in which the windows had been thrown wide. A heavy oak table covered with green baize held a dozen cardboard boxes containing files. At one end, three bored officers and a civilian sat.

Dogorov came to attention and saluted. The officer in the middle opened a folder and Dogorov saw that it was the *anketa*, the detailed biography he had written at Kiev. The man wore the collar tabs of a Lieutenant General of Infantry and was heavyset, verging on corpulence. Even so, his uniform seemed too large. The collar hung loose below his throat and Dogorov noticed an unhealthy pallor to his skin which hung in folds, as if he had suddenly begun to lose weight at an alarming rate. His voice, when he asked Dogorov's name and rank, was raspy and he had to clear his throat several times before he could finish the sentence.

'You were trapped behind enemy lines, twice, it says here?' The officer looked up at him and Dogorov saw that his eyes were deep set and the conviction came to him that the man was dying. The shock caused him to stutter and the other officers exchanged looks.

'Yes . . . yes, sir. I . . . I . . . my artillery battery was on manoeuvres . . .' he took a deep breath. 'My command was Battery A, Third Artillery Regiment, Fourth Army. We were encamped thirty kilometres from our garrison at Brest-Litovsk when we were attacked by Hitlerite aircraft shortly after dawn on the twenty-second of June. We were unable to return to the fort as the city was invested immediately. Instead, we marched through the Pripet to Kiev. We fought . . .'

The General cut him off. 'Yes, yes, Dogorov. It is all detailed in your folder. We are, however, more concerned with why you did not make more strenuous efforts to rejoin your regiment at Brest-Litovsk. Who in fact, authorised your withdrawal to Kiev?'

Dogorov felt sweat run down his sides and the feeling of suffocation returned. 'No one, sir. There was no one to authorise or disapprove. We were completely cut off from our garrison and from our own rear area. To have tried to fight our way through would have meant capture and death and the waste of field guns and manpower.'

The officer eyed him angrily. 'You seem to have a habit of making independent decisions, Captain.' He flipped through several pages in the folder. 'In the Polish campaign, you thought well enough of yourself to authorise your battery to open fire on a Polish artillery position. In Finland, it is reported that you made an unapproved political speech to your battery. And now it seems, you hold yourself to be enough of a military strategist to decide, on your own, to march nearly three hundred kilometres to Kiev. Who authorised you to make such decisions?' he shouted. 'You abandoned your field pieces in any event and of your entire battery, only twenty men turned up at Kiev? Better you had employed them in destroying Germans at Brest-Litovsk than running to save your worthless skins!'

Dogorov was thoroughly frightened now. His entire record was damning. Even the speech in Finland had been reported. And the same charge was being pressed again that he thought had been dismissed in the prison camp. Added to that, he was also being charged with deviationism – independent thinking! He was done for.

The civilian cleared his throat and the General subsided as if the outburst had used his last store of energy. 'It would seem, Captain,' his voice was thin and pitched high, 'especially in view of your record, that your efforts to escape were neither strenuous nor entailed much risk. Perhaps you were aided by the Hitlerites?'

The open accusation of treason was so overwhelming that Dogorov could only gape at the tribunal. 'My . . . actions have been investigated,' he managed, 'and I was cleared of wrongdoing.'

'That is neither here nor there,' the civilian sneered. 'We have heard many such stories as yours. It is amazing how many officers like you managed to return from behind the Hitlerite lines with such ease. We want to know why you found it necessary to run away rather than perform your duty?'

An officer wearing the old style military tunic without rank badges, merely piping in black to indicate that he was a cavalry officer, took up the questioning in a voice that lacked the hectoring tone of the others.

'Can you explain in detail how you came to be overrun in the first place, Captain?'

In a sudden flash of insight, Dogorov recalled Siderov's warning against relying on lack of official action as a defence. Maybe there *was* a vast cover-up in progress as the artillery officer in the camp had so cynically maintained.

He chose his words with care as he described how his battery had taken part in summer war games and so was out of touch with headquarters on the morning of 22 June. He told how they had been fired upon on the outskirts of the city and had destroyed a tank with point-blank cannon fire. Even though it was Siderov who had retained the presence of mind to load and train the gun, he had no qualms about taking the credit in his predicament.

Now that he understood what was expected, he began to regain a measure of confidence. Siderov was gone, disappeared into the prison camps, perhaps even dead by now. It would do no harm to blame him. So, he told the tribunal that it had been Lieutenant Siderov, his second-in-command, who had counselled surrender, but he who had insisted on withdrawing in the direction of Kiev. Subtly and with studied understatement, he described how Siderov had opposed his efforts to engage Hitlerite units patrolling for detachments of Red Army soldiers in the Pripet. And finally, he admitted frankly that he was at a loss to explain why Siderov had been separated from the survivors of the battery who had reached Kiev with him.

When he finished, he could detect no softening in their expressions, but somehow the tension appeared to have lessened. The General studied the folder once more and glanced around the table as if to ask if there were any more questions. The remaining officer, a short, pock-faced Georgian shook his head and went on staring out of the window through the smoke from his cigarette. The civilian ignored him and the cavalry officer scribbled copious notes.

Dogorov was dismissed curtly and told to await further orders. Only when he reached the street and the chill wind of early evening struck at him, did the reaction set in. He stumbled to a low stone wall and sank down, shaking badly. Nausea overwhelmed him and he felt the world slip away in a blackish-red spiral. He struggled against the urge to vomit until it, too, began to recede. He was certain that Siderov's warning had saved his life.

After three days in which he alternated between despair and anger, Dogorov received notification through the post that he had been cleared by the Moscow Military District Examining Committee. Again, a new paybook, *propiska* and ration book were issued. That very morning Dogorov began the rounds of every office that he imagined could help him obtain an assignment. He waited long hours in empty corridors, prowled rainy streets after officers and officials whom he or his mother knew, and even attempted to contact Foreign Minister Molotov.

Applications were accepted and he was told to wait. Personal contacts promised letters to the proper authorities that may or may not have been sent. And the weeks passed with no result. He discovered in his increasingly desperate rounds that there were many like him and that the memory of Stalin's purges were still fresh enough that no one wished to be associated with an officer whose record was clouded. Who knew when the next round of arrests would come.

In the evenings, Dogorov sat in the empty flat watching the anti-aircraft fire light the Moscow skies and ate his meagre supper. As he was not on active duty, his ration had been pegged at the level of Moscow's civilian adults not engaged in defence labour - 800 grams of bread per day. Every morning he divided the day's ration in two, half for the morning, half for the evening, supplemented whenever possible with eggs or cheese - never meat - bought on the flourishing black market. Afterwards, ration-free vodka helped him to sleep.

And Dogorov brooded. Never had anything so affected him. Depression rode him like a hag. All his life had been spent in the service of his nation and party. Now, because he had done his duty as an officer and a communist he had been tainted a traitor. In the prison camp, he had felt that a 'tenner' would at least allow him to contribute to the defence of the nation. Now, he was simply a parasite, the most despised of the entire criminal class.

He also missed his mother. If only she were in Moscow, rather than trapped in Leningrad, she would have known what to do, whom to see. She could have gone straight to V.I. Molotov and persuaded him to help. And in the evenings she would have made the flat feel like home.

He remembered the good times they had shared, the New Year's mornings when they exchanged gifts, and later had sat down with friends to dinners of Zakuski, soups, perhaps a Polish duck or a chicken, with sweets afterward. He also recalled the parade in Red Square to which his mother had once received a permit and, years later, another in which he had taken part with his class from the Frunze Military Academy.

He recalled icy winter evenings when he had done his school work on the old oak table beside the fireplace – before he had gone away to the military academy. And warm summer days when the windows had stood wide to catch the slightest breeze from the river beyond the park, and their holidays in the countryside at the ministry dacha. All those days seemed never to have happened; all the love and affection that had passed between them to have never been.

Just when he began to drink heavily, Dogorov was never quite certain. Drinking was at epidemic proportions in the Red Army and he had done his share of carousing over the years. Vodka, brandy and wine were served at mess and freely available in the new officers' canteens which had been allowed to open once more. But he was always careful of how much he drank, simply because it led to complications. During the purges, he had noticed that certain field grade officers who disappeared were also the most inefficient because of heavy drinking. Had some regimental commanders used charges of political unreliability to get rid of them?

Since his return to Moscow, he had fallen into the habit of drinking in the evenings to forget the day's rejection and to fall asleep. He had long given up the search for a command position; was in fact willing now to settle for any assignment that once more made him feel a part of the national effort.

On the morning of 15 October as he walked down the Lubyanka Hill on Ulitsa Dzerzhinskgo, from the Kitai gorod section towards Dzerzhinsky Square, Dogorov saw a silent crowd watching clouds of smoke rise from inside the walled courtyard of NKVD headquarters. The secret police are burning their records, someone whispered. Dogorov looked around and was troubled by the grim satisfaction he saw on many faces. Secret police were necessary for the safety of the State, he knew. They protected society against anarchists, revisionists and revanchists, to say nothing of the disgruntled and criminal elements of the population who were always so quick to take advantage of the law-abiding citizen's constitutional guarantees.

The city raved with rumours; the Red Army was retreating to the Urals in panic. Everything to the west would be given up to the Germans and their allies while the Red Army regrouped and tried to hold the Siberian provinces. Japan was said to have attacked in the east and was rushing troops along the Trans-Siberian Railway to link up with the Hitlerites. There had been such a rush to leave the city that, for the first time in memory, there were more rooms, flats and houses than there were people needing them.

But the worst, and most disheartening rumour of all he heard that afternoon, was that Stalin himself had left the Kremlin and retreated to Kubyishev with the rest of the government and the foreign embassies.

Dogorov sat in his chair facing the park. Rain mixed with sleet lashed the pavement. The severe weather precluded a Luftwaffe bombing raid and so the city was unnaturally quiet. He poured more vodka and raised his glass in toast to Lenin's park and the silent city beyond. Twice before he had faced a crisis of faith; first had been his decision to cross the Pripet, requiring that he acknowledge the fact that the government and the party to which he had given unquestioning obedience and loyalty had been wrong. The second had occurred in the prison camp when he was forced to the realisation that government and party were conspiring to conceal a dreadful mistake by imprisoning loyal soldiers whose only crime had been to persist in their duty.

Each time, he had justified the Kremlin's action by blaming Hitler for misleading Stalin, then treacherously attacking without a declaration of war. He also understood that a certain amount of repression was necessary to conceal the full extent of their losses, as it would both hearten the enemy and demoralise the Russian people if they became known.

But Stalin's abandonment of Moscow was beyond support. Moscow was the centre of Russia, the very soul of the nation. Without her, there was no Russia, no Union of Soviet Socialist Republics. The other states in the Union were mere appendages, for their own benefit. Tomorrow, he thought drunkenly, he would volunteer to dig tank traps. Anything...

Certain rumours had achieved such widespread credibility that Stalin was forced to the radio the following day to announce that he had *not* left Moscow and that steps were being taken to halt the flow of refugees, restore public services and put an end to black-market speculation in food. Dogorov, making his way down Arbat Street through the bomb damage, listened to the radio broadcast with tremendous relief. The rumours had been wrong, thank God. Stalin had remained behind at great personal risk to lead the nation! Sleet lashed the streets as he hurried towards General Headquarters, inspired to make another appeal, all his depression and misgivings and even his hangover, forgotten.

As he passed a bakery he saw people hurriedly forming a queue to wait for the bakers to report for duty. A bell clanged as a trolley ran through an intersection. A radio plate erupted with the opening strains of the Internationale and the steady ticking of a metronome, signalling an important message. A moment later, the well-modulated voice of Yuri Levitan came on the air. All bakeries and food shops had been ordered to reopen, he announced. All public services and transportation were to be put into operation immediately. Anyone who interfered or failed to do his or her duty would be treated as a Hitlerite sympathiser and a spy.

Dogorov stood with head bowed against the sleet, straining to hear, but the voice was replaced by the Red Army Orchestra and he went on. Stalin had not announced specifically that the State Defence Council had decided to defend the city, but he was adept at reading between the lines, as were most Muscovites, and knew that unless a major disaster occurred, Moscow would be held.

On his way home that evening he passed the Dzerzhinsky Military Academy, near the red brick mass of the Rossiya Hotel, where he had taken his advanced artillery course in 1935. Its blacked-out windows lent a certain grimness to its façade that was undeserved. But then perhaps it was, he thought. Of all his professors at that time, not one had survived the purges. He marvelled at the fact that so many traitorous deviationists could have infected the faculty.

Towards the end of October, the combination of mud and fanatical determination had begun to slow the Hitlerite offensive. Bad weather interfered with their bombing campaign as much as the rapidly increasing anti-aircraft gun defences and as a result a few shamefaced refugees returned. There was still no official news regarding the defence of the city but rumour had it that Marshal Zhukov had been recalled from Leningrad to take charge and he had established an inner defence line encircling three-quarters of the city. From Novo-Zavidovsk in the northeast, it ran through Klin, the Istra Reservoir, Zharvoronky, Krasnaya Pakhra, Serpukhov to Aleksiv in the south and was anchored at Tula.

In the various military units he visited, Dogorov heard rumours of the vast reserves that Zhukov was said to be assembling east of Moscow, from forces Stalin had hoarded since the war began. There existed an unusual undercurrent of resentment and Dogorov even overheard two ranking generals complaining to one another that if these reserves had been committed earlier, the Hitlerites could have been stopped at Smolensk or Kiev. Or Leningrad, he thought.

But even as he sensed the vast offensive stirring, he could not obtain an assignment. As the days passed, disappointment gave way to angry frustration as it became clearer and clearer that it was useless to sit for hours in anterooms enduring the discourtesy of enlisted clerks and low-ranking staff officers. In the evenings, he brooded and drank and longed even for the hardships and action of the Pripet. Just to be doing something, that was all he asked!

Dogorov suspected that he was deteriorating but it no longer seemed to matter. What good was a shaved face and pressed uniform when the Army had no use for him? When the government had turned him into a parasite?

And as the rumours about conditions in Leningrad grew worse, fear for his mother's safety was added to his frustration. It was said that starvation was killing people by the thousands, yet the winter had barely begun. The Hitlerites and their Finnish allies had cut off the city from the outside and only an occasional plane-load of supplies turned up inside the ring.

Everywhere he turned, the flat reminded him of his mother. One night, as he sat half-drunk, it came to him that he was mourning her as if she were already dead. Wild fantasies chased through his mind then, memories of her dressing, bathing, swimming or sunning in the summer. It was impossible for two people to live in such close proximity as they had without incurring intimate moments. And even though he was away at school most of the time after his twelfth birthday, a combination of repressed adolescence, long absences and her striking beauty, had only increased his attachment to her.

On 25 October, Dogorov obtained an interview with the political commissar of the Tenth Reserve Army. He stood at attention, eyes fastened on the grey-green wall above the commissar's bald head as the man read through his file. Finally, the commissar laid the folder on the desk, put his finger tips together and stared at him without warmth.

'You claim to have fought your way out of the Brest pocket to join the Thirty-Seventh Army at Kiev?' he asked, as if the idea amused him.

'Yes sir.'

'And you then escaped from the Hitlerite encirclement of that city and swam to safety? Two extremely lucky escapes, one would conclude.'

'Yes sir.'

The commissar smiled, his tight expression and tone telling Dogorov plainly enough that he was a liar. 'A question of political unreliability was registered against you by the Commissar of the Thirty-Seventh Army.'

'But . . . but I was cleared,' Dogorov protested. 'Twice. And the second time by the investigating committee of the Moscow Military District. Their endorsement is recorded . . .'

The commissar frowned at the file, then shook his head. 'You were cleared by an army investigating committee, it is true. But they, citing the Thirty-Seventh Army commissar's report, made no recommendation regarding re-employment. The NKVD investigator at the Gorlovo prison camp did not clear but only passed you on to Moscow. A final disposition of your case remains to be made at Dzerhinsky Square.' His expression was bleak. 'There are no commands available for such as you. You will be notified if your services are needed. But everyone is required to aid in the struggle for the inevitable defeat of the Hitlerite aggressors regardless of their political classification. I recommend that you apply to a labour battalion for service at the front.'

Dogorov stiffened at the insult and saluted. 'Thank you, sir.'

*

Returning that evening, Dogorov bought a bottle of black-market vodka which he opened as he left the stall. So, a final disposition of his case remained to be made by the NKVD vultures, he thought. The Army's investigation meant nothing at all. He snorted as he trudged along the crowded street. And he had cursed those who had shown relief at the columns of white smoke rising from burning records. Ah, if only his record had been among them!

The wail of air-raid sirens caused a warden to materialise and hound him into the Moscow Metro for shelter. The escalators had been shut off and he stumbled down the steep slippery steps, pressed on every side by crowds that were in turn frightened, impatient, bored. Other wardens shone flashlights and shouted peremptory directions before he was deposited on a platform already occupied by hundreds of people.

A gust of wind swirled dust into his face as a train whooshed into a tunnel. He found a place to sit beneath a giant propaganda poster showing a Red Army soldier driving a dripping bayonet through a Hitlerite soldier with a satanic face. He gave the poster a mock salute and ignored a prune-faced woman's disapproving stare. She slapped her whiny child in retaliation. The ornate lamps flickered and went out briefly, to screams and shouts, brightened then dimmed, but remained lit. The smokey semi-darkness was filled with incessant noise; howling children, explosions rumbling through the tunnels and the air was laden with dust and the stench of fear, oil, smoke, urine, vomit and packed humanity.

Dogorov drank steadily until the all-clear sounded some time after midnight. He ignored a warden's warning to watch for delayed-action bombs and staggered up into the icy night air to find the city on fire. Sirens screamed and the treacherously clear sky glowed red.

The wreckage of a German bomber lay across an intersection, its nose buried in the ground floor of an office building. The tail section had twisted on impact so that the twin horizontal stabilisers were upside down. Rescue workers pawed at the debris, seeking survivors trapped in the building.

Weird shadows flickered and a burst of noise, like an artillery barrage, overwhelmed him. Suddenly, he was running along a lane lined with burning Russian tanks and lorries and screaming, dying men. The heavy stench of burned meat tore at his nostrils and a figure moved to stop him but Dogorov shouted and ran harder.

When he came to his senses, he was huddled in a doorway, shivering with the cold, still clutching the vodka bottle. The street was deserted. Far off, above the buildings, he saw the flicker of searchlights. With fingers so frozen he could barely bend them, he worked the cork from the bottle. The last swallow of liquid ran down his throat, warming him and for a few moments his shivering eased. He leaned against the iron-cold brick and closed his eyes while the terrible pounding headache that had begun in the stuffy, fume-ridden subway suffused his body.

The shivering returned and he forced himself up and began to search drunkenly for a street sign or a familiar landmark. Once someone chased him until he ran onto a main street. He thought he heard Siderov calling a warning, but then the footsteps disappeared and he knew it was his imagination.

Dogorov never knew how he found his flat, nor how long it took. He remembered flinging the empty bottle against a building to hear it smash, but nothing else. He stood before the dark shape of soot-encrusted brick, trying to understand where he was and what he was to do next. The blackout was intense and only dying fires and meagre starlight provided any light. Remembering finally, he fumbled with the door, fighting to concentrate. Somewhere in the recesses of his mind, he knew that if he did not get out of the cold soon, he would freeze to death.

The door opened suddenly and he staggered to the stairs that led up to the first floor. Ice had caked on his boots and he slipped and fell, smashing his forehead against a rubber-edged stair riser. Dogorov tried to get up but lacked the will to do so. He pushed once, then abandoned himself to the blackness, thinking that it no longer made a difference.

The light was blinding. The pain in his head was excruciating and he knew he had been badly wounded. For long seconds, he fought a terrible battle to move an arm. If he was paralysed, he did not want to know, wanted only to die immediately.

But the pain in his head was already beginning to lessen and the light leaking through his tightly-closed eyelids cooled and faded. He found that he was lying on his own bed, fully dressed, although his boots and overcoat had been removed. In fact his overcoat lay on top of the quilt drawn over him.

He last remembered running down the lane of burning tanks, hearing the screams, smelling broiling flesh . . . but it could not have been . . . weeks had . . . He lay huddled on the bed, enduring, drifting in and out of sleep. When he was fully conscious again, a trace of sunshine edged the blackout curtains.

Something had awakened him. Knocking, repeated insistently. He sat up. The room crashed about him and he nearly toppled to the floor. As he struggled to regain his balance and contain the nausea, he had a terrible vision of uniformed NKVD men beating at the door.

Dogorov fell back on the bed with a groan. Everything whirled about him and the nausea was a living thing trying to force its way out. A young woman was standing beside his bed, looking at him with an expression that was half disgusted, half amused. Dogorov vaguely remembered having seen her in past days. She had seemed familiar but he had been either too drunk or too immersed in self-pity to care.

'I hope you are feeling better.' Her voice was low and throaty, almost husky.

She went to the windows and threw the curtains aside. Light streamed in and he gasped in pain. He heard her laugh.

'Serves you right, comrade,' she mocked.

When he was able to open his eyes again, she was standing with her back to the window, enjoying the sun's meagre warmth as it haloed her figure.

'Who are . . . ?' he began, but pain occupied his full attention.

'The one who found you lying on the steps where you knocked yourself silly last night. If I hadn't heard you and looked out, you might have frozen to death. A celebration is fine but not if it kills you,' she finished with asperity.

He lay with his head huddled in his arms, knowing that he should thank her, but too sick, and worse, too embarrassed to do so. He heard her leave the room and he turned over carefully, waiting for the door to close so that he could be alone with his misery. Instead, she rustled about the tiny kitchen. The scratch of a match was followed by the kettle's clink as she put water on to boil. A moment later, she passed in front of the doorway, shaking out his overcoat. While the water boiled for tea, he heard her scraping and washing the dirty dishes which he had left piled in the sink for weeks. Once she swore.

She was a bit older than he had first thought, closer to his age – late twenties perhaps, early thirties – he saw when she came in with tea and clean cups. She put them on the bedside table and motioned for him to sit forward while she plumped the pillows. She had a fresh, light scent about her that was readily apparent in his hypersensitive state.

'This flat is a pigsty,' she said in a conversational tone. 'I thought they taught army officers to take care of themselves?'

Dogorov grunted. He was in no shape for the lecture he deserved. But she surprised him by opening her coat and pulling from her bodice a tiny lady's watch tied to a black ribbon. He saw that she wore a white uniform of some kind.

'I'm late now. And the trams are unreliable these days.' She paused at the door. 'You must take care of yourself. Stay in today. You will feel better tonight.' She went out before he could think of anything to say.

Dogorov slept most of the day – out of despair rather than because of the hangover. He was depressed and frightened that the commissar was right, that only the labour battalions were now available to him.

But as his head cleared he found his determination returning. The Soviet State had spent thousands of roubles training him as an artillery officer and he took that responsibility seriously. He had not panicked and surrendered his command as so many others had. When he finally had to abandon the guns, he had taken care the Hitlerites would never profit from them. And he had fought his way out of the encirclement with the survivors of his battery, all the way to Kiev, inflicting damage on the enemy at every opportunity. Was it the fault of the State that rear-area bureaucrats served it badly?

By evening, he had bathed, shaved and cleaned the flat. He fried his bread ration in some fat and drank several cups of hot tea. He was brushing his uniform when the doorbell jangled.

The woman from this morning peered past him into the room. 'You've cleaned it up! How nice.'

Dogorov wasn't certain how to respond. Conflicting emotions struggled – resentment that she should have seen him drunk and helpless, but then a surprisingly warm feeling that she had cared enough to look in again.

Once more he had the impression that he had seen her before. She had a pert nose that turned up slightly at the end, and wide cheek bones. There was also a bit of a slant to her eyes that betrayed Tatar origins. Her cheeks were red with cold and he noticed that she was shivering.

Greatly daring, he drew her inside to warm herself. The flat was almost as cold as the outdoors as he hadn't yet lit the fire, but it was out of the draughty hall at least. He motioned her to a chair and hurried to fetch tea.

'Turnabout is fair play,' he said smiling shyly and she laughed – a breathless sound that pleased him absurdly.

'Well, I must say that you look a bit different tonight, Captain Mikhail Gregorvitch Dogorov.'

'How do you know my name?' he asked as he struck a match to light the fire.

'I know you very well, Miko.' She surprised him with the nickname his mother had given him as a child. 'You don't remember me do you? But then I was only nine when you went away to school.'

And suddenly Dogorov... did. 'Of course, Vera Andropova Shatnikova! You are the little girl that lived upstairs.'

'Not so little now,' she laughed. And indeed, he thought, she wasn't. Even in a heavy overcoat, he had the impression of an ample figure, which contrasted with his memory of her as skinny and knock-kneed.

For a few moments they talked about their childhood days when the world had seemed so much simpler, but then an awkward pause occurred as both realised they had little more in common than the brief and very lost time of childhood.

Dogorov asked after her parents, wracking his brain to remember who they were and what they looked like.

'Ah, both are safe in Samara, thank God. Father was transferred there at the beginning of this year to oversee a new munitions factory. It was hard on mother as she has been quite sick, a semi-invalid in fact. But at least there is no fighting there and sufficient food for everyone. Not like here. And your mother, Olga Semonova? Do you hear from her? I came to see her just before she left for Leningrad.' Vera bit her lip. 'I do hope she is all right.'

Vera must have detected his surprise. 'Oh, we became quite good friends, Miko. Or I suppose I should call you Captain Mikhail Gregorvitch Dogorov, and salute,' she said with mock gruffness that was a parody of the American cinema child-star, Shirley Temple, who had been such a hit last year.

He laughed in spite of himself and her smile was warm and full of good humour. My God, he thought, how long has it been since I've talked to a woman who was not a damned official?

The room had begun to warm and Vera told him that she had studied to be a doctor when she had been transferred to nursing. 'I was very disappointed at first,' she said shrugging. 'It's all right for now. The State needs nurses badly. But when the war is over, I shall resume my studies. I nurse at the Military Hospital Number Three. I'm a surgical nurse,' she said proudly. 'But what about you? I thought you were going to become Russia's greatest astronomer?'

She began to draw him out, overcoming his reluctance to talk about himself and what had happened to him. He had just reached his escape from Kiev when the old Windsor clock above the cold fireplace chimed the hour.

Vera jumped. 'Oh, I should have been home hours ago. I must still wash my uniform for tomorrow, take a bath and do my hair.' Reluctantly, Dogorov followed her to the door where she turned and pressed a small, warm hand against his arm. 'We can see each other again, if you like,' she smiled shyly. 'I still live in our old flat. The authorities have not reassigned it yet. Perhaps they have forgotten.' Her grin was impish.

Dogorov resumed his rounds early the following morning. His uniform was brushed and pressed and his boots shone as brightly as his scraped chin. He felt a new air of confidence which he attributed solely to Vera. Why, he had no idea.

At the military headquarters of the Twenty-Third Motorised Artillery Regiment, he heard the rumours about the parade for the first time. Initially, he thought them only more of the fanciful stories always circulating in the Moscow rumour mill. But by mid-afternoon he began to wonder. Those who normally scoffed at such tales were instead passing this one along.

The rumour held that the traditional Red Army Parade would take place as usual tomorrow, 7 November, in celebration of the twenty-fourth anniversary of the overthrow of the hated Tsarist dynasty by Lenin and Stalin. But how could it take place with the Germans conducting mass bombing raids on the city day and night, whenever the weather allowed? The number killed would be insupportable. Yet, Dogorov had to admit that if the parade did take place, it would constitute a major propaganda coup and show the world that Russia was more than capable of defending herself.

Vera confirmed the rumours that evening. She banged on his door and demanded as soon as he opened it, 'Have you heard? My section has been selected to march in the parade. I'm so excited that I won't sleep a wink tonight. Can you imagine what the Germans will think when they find out we held our parade under their long, frozen noses?'

She laughed and her fine grey eyes sparkled. 'Miko, will you escort me tomorrow?'

Dogorov protested that he had no ticket. 'I can't just go. There will be security men everywhere. You must have a ticket, and proper credentials.'

Vera stamped her booted foot. 'Of course, I know that. And I think it's silly. The parade should be for the people and not just for those fat old men on Lenin's tomb.'

Dogorov stared at her in astonishment. 'But the authorities can't allow everyone to go just because they want to see the parade,' he protested. 'It would be impossible to maintain security.'

'I suppose,' she sighed. 'But at least you could go with me as far as the hospital?'

'All right,' he surrendered. 'I'll escort you to the hospital.'

'In uniform?'

'Of course! How else?' Vera gave him a quick kiss on the lips.

'Oh, I have so much to do. Let's get an early start, at eight o'clock.'

The door shut behind her and for a long time that evening, he could taste her lips.

The morning of 7 November was grey with snow and drifting mist. There would be no bombers today if the weather lasted, Dogorov thought. Vera left him at the gate to Military Hospital Number Three on Petrovsky Boulevard and joined the other nurses of her section lining up in the courtyard. Shortly, they were marched away.

Dogorov was at a loss for something to do. It would take him only three hours to walk the eleven kilometres to the end of the parade route, but it would take Vera nearly five and it was too far for him to go home. He wandered along streets paralleling the march route for a while but the sharp glances of militiamen made him uneasy. He certainly did not need to be detained on suspicion of spying.

What little he had glimpsed of the parade at intersections caused him to conclude that it was a pale shadow of former years. But the fact that the government dared hold it at all said much for the confidence in the ultimate outcome of the war. The Lenin Library was open and he went inside.

Dogorov stamped his booted feet and swung his arms vigorously to keep warm. He had been waiting for nearly an hour. The sky had grown clearer in the early afternoon and there were large rents in the clouds through which blue sky shone with pale winter sunlight. But the temperature had plummeted and a wind had sprung up. He had not been so cold since the night they had dragged him from the river.

He waited in a small park several blocks from the dispersal point. Some weary civilian marchers, finished with their part of the parade, dragged past towards the various tram stops. Twice he heard the rumble of heavy engines and saw tanks and mobile artillery pieces draw up in nearby streets to wait further orders.

To Dogorov's practised eye it was obvious that the weapons were a mix of new and battle-worn pieces extracted from various depots. A number of the tanks were so new they were unpainted and still showed the scorch marks of welders' torches. He would have liked to have taken a closer look, especially at the self-propelled artillery pieces, but militiamen and armed soldiers were everywhere.

The sun burst through at the horizon and flooded the western sky with orange-red light. Shadows deepened and he ventured closer. Several units of soldiers had caught his attention. All wore white snowsuits and carried skis. They stood about under the watchful eyes of officers, laughing and smoking. Twice he caught snatches of unfamiliar dialects but it was only when one of the soldiers wandered towards the trees to relieve himself that Prager saw his oriental features.

So, it was true, he thought as he watched the ski troops march off. Units of the Far East Army were being transferred to the Moscow front. Stalin was playing a dangerous game. He walked back to the park's centre. The sun had now disappeared and the twilight glow was fading. The cold deepened with each minute. The last of the military bands arrived and fell silent. Tone deaf, Dogorov could not appreaciate their skill but he did enjoy the thumping rhythms of the drums. Then Vera was trudging up the path towards him and he grinned and hurried forward.

She looked exhausted and half dead with cold, yet she could still summon enthusiasm enough to smile and, through chattering teeth, describe the parade as he hustled her out of the park and along to the tram stop. The tram was jammed with other weary participants wanting only to get home and warm themselves. Dogorov managed to crowd aboard one and drag her after him. He wrapped one arm about the stanchion beside the elderly motorman and the other around Vera's waist and held her like that as the tram jerked and thundered its away along the river. When the route turned back into the city, it began to empty and they were able to push inside. There was no longer an excuse to hold Vera and, reluctantly, he released her. She gave him a weary smile.

They left the tram and walked the two blocks to the hospital. Vera still faced ten hours of duty and Dogorov could see that she was near exhaustion. He tried to talk her into letting him deliver a message that she was too sick to work. 'I'll make you some hot soup, Vera. You really shouldn't work tonight.'

'I am all right, really. I've been this tired many times before. And the others won't feel any better than I do. If I'm not there, it will only mean more work for them.'

Dogorov perceived a good bit of steel in Vera. She had a mind of her own, knew it, and used it. At the gates where they had started out six hours before, she thanked him gravely for escorting her, then grabbed his coat collar to pull his head down and kissed him.

The parade was well-publicised in the newspapers and on the radio and it woke the city from its fear. People were no longer so abstracted and churlish. Dogorov even heard laughter in the streets again and the outlandish rumours that had cursed them subsided.

The fronts surrounding Moscow on three sides were stabilising. In the west, the Hitlerite line was pushed back fifty or more kilometres from the city limits so that only late at night was it possible to hear the guns in that direction. The air raids continued; whenever the weather was clear, day or night, the Luftwaffe came like carrion crows. The roar of massed anti-aircraft guns became a cacophony of sound – the sharp barking of the smaller twenty and forty millimetre quick-firing pieces, the hard clapping of the medium calibres and the rolling roar of the heavy calibres seeking high-flying bombers, inundated the city.

Forced to altitudes above five thousand metres by the greatest concentration of anti-aircraft guns ever assembled, the bombadiers' accuracy was poor. Bombs fell indiscriminately on military and civilian targets alike. Hospitals were hit as often as railway roundhouses, schools and workers' flats as well as military barracks.

But the freeze deepened and, as it did, the fighting began to grind to a halt. In the north, however, around Leningrad, there was little change as regards the fighting. Dogorov's worries about his mother grew daily. In spite of the lack of reports on the plates or in the papers – *Red Star*, *Izvestia*, or *Pravda* – he, like most Russians, had become adept at discerning the truth from rumours. And what he deduced worried him greatly. There was no heat or light in the city as the power generating plants had been destroyed or captured by the Germans. Those Leningraders not fighting in the front lines received a ration of 250 grams of bread, fifty per cent of which was, by emergency decree, sawdust. The amount was insufficient to keep a child alive, let alone an adult.

His own 800 gram ration was small enough, but at least he was able to supplement it on the black market. His only consolation came from the fact that his mother was a high-ranking official and so would obtain supplementary rations.

The day following the parade, Dogorov had made his usual rounds and spent two hours that afternoon in a smelly, overcrowded, bomb shelter while an ancient harridan lectured him on the army's failure to protect the good citizens of Moscow.

Vera was still riding the emotional surge of the parade when he returned that night. Her door opened immediately and she called down the stairs to him to come up for a cup of tea. Dogorov was appalled at how cold the room was. The flat had been part of a larger maisonette long ago divided into smaller units. The Shatnikova allotment consisted of two rooms, one six by four metres, the other two by three, against the building's north wall. A large bay window occupied one corner making it impossible to warm the place, in spite of heavy curtains and a blanket hung to block the draught. The carpeting was as old as the building and thoroughly threadbare. The once creamy wallpaper was stained to a dirty beige and the tiny fireplace sent most of its heat up the chimney. Vera wore her nurse's cape against the cold.

'I've only just lit the fire,' she apologised. 'I thought we might have dinner together?'

Dogorov went over and kicked the fire apart, then poked at the sticks of wood until the flames died. 'On one condition,' he said in a severe tone as he collected the wood.

'What condition..?'

'That we go down to my flat where it is warmer.'

Dogorov had not intended to seduce Vera and in fact did not. She seduced him. She produced a bottle of vodka and two thick pork chops and laughed at his surprise.

'I got them "under the counter". From an old family friend who raises a pig or two every year. In return, I see that she is admitted to the hospital whenever her rheumatism is bad. A useful friend to have, wouldn't you say? She told me once that her father had been a game keeper and her mother a parlour maid to a rich family before the Revolution. She told the Cheka where the family had hidden their jewellery and, in return, the government allowed her to remain in the gate house as caretaker when the estate was confiscated.'

The flat warmed quickly and Vera busied herself with the stove, filling the room with the delicious aroma of frying pork chops. When she shed her nurse's cloak, Dogorov was entranced by her figure as she flitted about the stove and table. When the dinner was ready, she poured two glasses of vodka, called Dogorov to sit, and served him a crackling chop and two spoons of mashed potatoes. A slice of brown bread, hardly tasting of sawdust filler, completed the meal.

Afterwards, Vera cleared and washed the dishes, then came to sit beside him before the tiny fire. Dogorov lit two cigarettes and passed one to her. The night was heavily overcast, precluding bombing raids. No sound penetrated the heavily curtained and sealed window. The room was warm and it was almost possible to forget the war.

When the Windsor clock chimed eight, Vera cocked her head to one side to listen, then said in a serious voice, 'I would like to go to bed with you.'

She was a revelation. She was patient, good-natured, laughed easily and wasn't the least embarrassed at his untutored gropings and his haste, and it was soon clear to Dogorov that she was far more experienced than he. The following morning, half fearing rejection, he suggested that she move into the flat with him. Only the two of them remained in the building now and her room was impossible to heat on her meagre fuel allowance. If they shared their fuel and food rations, they might live comfortably. To his surprise, she agreed instantly and he helped her move her things that morning.

Vera sponged and brushed his uniform every evening while he polished his shoes with a tiny lump of shoe polish melted and combined with lard. She even cut his hair short once more and he shaved every morning, using the bit of hot water left over from tea, until his chin shone as brightly as his boots. His walk lost its shuffling gait and he stood straighter and once more spoke with authority so that he was not so easily dismissed by clerks.

In the third week of November, Dogorov was summoned to the headquarters of the Fourth Reserve Army. He took the tram to the end of the line and walked for several kilometres before hitching a ride in a military lorry. He was received by a panel of field grade officers who seemed friendly enough. They had reviewed his record and had only a few questions, most of which pertained to his service in the war with Finland. It soon became apparent to Dogorov that he was being tested for his depth of field experience.

He answered each question fully, seeking concrete examples from operations in which he had participated. As the proceedings drew to a close, he sensed that the officers, all with long field experience to judge by the type of questions asked, were favourably disposed towards him.

That evening, he was in a buoyant mood. On the way back to the flat he bought a kilo of black-market sausages and a box of chocolates that later proved so stale as to be inedible.

He was so certain that he would be offered a position that Vera burst into tears at their impending separation. But by the end of the week, when he still had not heard one way or the other, he crossed the city again, this time walking the last fifteen kilometres, only to discover that the barracks were empty and the fields that had contained motor vehicles and artillery pieces were now barren under a flat blanket of new snow.

Vera came off duty at midnight and found the flat ice cold and Dogorov, wrapped in his greatcoat, passed out in a chair with an empty vodka bottle on the floor beside him. Vera guessed what had happened, but this time there was considerably more disgust mixed with her concern. When she could not wake him, she covered him with her cloak and went to bed.

The next morning she built the fire and, when the room had warmed, removed her nightgown and gave herself a sponge bath. She was conscious that Dogorov was watching but she ignored him. When she had finished, she covered herself with a robe and lit the gas and put water on to boil for tea and porridge. She set the table for two and when the food and tea was ready set it out.

After a few moments, Dogorov hobbled to the table and sank down in his chair, holding his head in his hands. He sipped the tea but ignored the porridge. Vera's quiet determination to act as if nothing out of the ordinary had occurred shamed Dogorov and he began to eat.

After she had cleared the dishes away, Vera turned back the blankets, removed her flannel robe and lay down. Dogorov rubbed his unshaven cheek but when she grinned at him, laughed and tore off his clothes, hangover forgotten. Afterwards, they lay drowsily in each other's arms and talked.

'I made a mistake in remaining in Moscow,' he said. 'I should have requested permission to travel to the Caucasus. Away from Moscow and the security organs, I could have obtained a command. I'm sure of it.

'Perhaps I should still do so,' he mused, 'before they think to issue a warrant for my arrest.'

Vera lay across his chest, comforting him with her body. There was little she could say to deny it. The state security apparatus was all-encompassing. No one escaped and she was afraid for him. Sooner or later the security organs would remember – or be reminded by a block warden, or one of the many other official and unofficial informers – that an officer was living in a private flat in Moscow, with no means of support beyond his ration, and doing no work useful to the State. Someone would check his file and decide that the State was better off if he were sent to a labour battalion or to prison. Vera shivered at the thought. She had heard tales of the camps from doctors who occasionally treated prisoners.

Time was running out. Men in NKVD uniforms, with machine pistols slung across their backs, would appear one day soon and that would be the end of him.

*

One morning in late November, Dogorov was washing up the supper dishes. Vera had left a few minutes before for her work shift. The knock on the door startled him and he put down the dish as adrenalin pumped painfully through his body. So! They have come, he thought. Automatically, his glance went to the army duffle bag containing his spare uniform and boots, bedroll and housewife, candles and matches, three changes of underwear and stockings, two packets of newspaper cut into squares for toilet paper and several small jars of fat, jam and bread. The duffle bag would serve equally as well at the front or in a prison camp. Dogorov took a deep breath and tried to calm himself. It required a supreme act of will to open the door.

A miserable shivering army corporal stood there. The boy's face and ungloved hands were beetroot-red with cold.

'Captain Mikhail Gregorvitch Dogorov?' he stuttered.

At Dogorov's nod, he thrust a grey envelope into his hand, saluted and left. Dogorov heard his boots clack on the marble stairs but not until the outer door slammed did he recover his wits. Then he closed the door to the flat and in a spasm of fear, tore the end from the envelope and shook out the cheap grey paper which fluttered past his hand to the floor. Groaning, he picked it up. He was, he read in astonishment, ordered to report to the Forty-Second Artillery Battalion, General Headquarters Reserve, to command Battery C, on November 29 1941 – tomorrow!

Dogorov sank down beside the cooling fireplace, unable to believe his luck.

That evening, Dogorov took Vera to dinner at Mikhail's to celebrate. He had tried to obtain reservations at the Praha, but it had been struck by Hitlerite bombs during the past week. Even so, it cost a bribe of fifty roubles to obtain a table, leaving him just enough in his depleted wallet to pay for dinner.

The evening was bittersweet. Both knew there was little chance they would see each other again before the war ended. As part of the GHQ reserve, his regiment could be sent anywhere, at any time. The rumours that Vera's hospital would soon be evacuated to the Urals were all but verified. And because of the approaching separation, neither quite wanted to admit what the other had come to mean. They had made, Dogorov thought, an unspoken agreement not to speak of a future relationship.

The restaurant accepted their ration coupons and a further bribe to produce what for war-time Russia was a veritable feast. Tinned caviar from Aralsk, fillet of sturgeon from the Black Sea, *piroshki*, beefsteaks and for desert, cream pastries spoiled by a suspicious taste of lubricating oil.

Dinner was a success in spite of its strained atmosphere. Dogorov was even able to point out to Vera several high ranking military officers, among them Marshall Vorshilov, a few tables away.

Afterwards, they walked home through the bitter evening. The sky was icy clear and in the western suburbs the pale fingers of searchlights strove for German bombers. The rumble of exploding bombs filled the frozen air and the sky was bright with flashes.

Once more in the flat, they were suddenly shy of one another. Awkwardly, Dogorov built the fire and poured glasses of vodka, finishing the bottle. They toasted one another silently, and then Vera was in his arms. He held her for a long time without speaking until the flat had warmed. Then, still without a word, they undressed and got into bed. The cold sheets made her giggle and that broke their reserve.

In the morning when he woke, Vera was gone. A note rested on the mantel, against the clock. It said only, 'Goodbye, my darling.'

Mobility is the keynote of war

Napoleon

Slavets November–December 1941

Slavets grew out of the gloom and snow flurries into a double line of log huts and a few clapboard houses, grouped on either side of a frozen mud track. A burnt-out Russian tank, a KV1A, was mired halfway to the turret on the edge of the village. In all, Prager counted twenty-four dwellings and eight barn- or shed-like buildings. The present population, according to army census, totalled 122 – old men, women and children. All the men between fifteen and fifty-five had been taken away by Soviet recruiting parties during the autumn.

Prager discovered that a panzer rifle company had also been quartered in the village, to provide security for his tank battalion and to police the surrounding countryside, which included an extensive tract of forest two thousand metres north and east of the village. The balance of the First Panzer Regiment had been distributed to other villages within a twenty kilometre radius of headquarters, established at a slightly larger town called Berestivo.

The riflemen had not been idle, he discovered. The village hall had been converted to a headquarters with offices set aside for his staff. Telephone lines had been strung to the neighbouring villages and a central switchboard connected them to both regimental and divisional headquarters at Kharkov. Regular patrols had already been instituted and the countryside was reported quiet.

His battalion's normal complement had been reduced to 372 from its June high of 785, but replacements were expected any day. Prager made a tour of inspection immediately with the young lieutenant commanding the riflemen, Klaus Mahr, a gangly, sandy-haired boy so young it seemed painful, until one looked into his eyes. Prager subsequently discovered that Mahr, who had first seen action in Poland, had fought in France and Greece, and had been in the Russian campaign since the beginning.

The riflemen had taken over two of the four clapboard houses and two log huts as barracks. Prager evicted the Russian civilians from the remaining two houses and pointed to four log huts nearby. 'I'll have those last four as well.'

Mahr waved and a sergeant and six men began banging on doors and chasing the inhabitants into the road. Personal effects were thrown after them. When one woman insisted on trying to re-enter her home, a soldier knocked her down. Mahr shouted in anger and the sergeant cuffed the soldier and booted him on to the next house. The woman scuttled inside to emerge a moment later hugging a framed photograph. Surrounded by her children, she hurried away along the road.

'At least the communists taught them how to share,' Mahr grinned. 'I increase any villager's basic ration if they take in a dispossessed family.' He glanced anxiously at Prager for his approval. 'It keeps them from going over to the partisans.'

'Excellent thinking. You've a head on your shoulders, it seems.' Prager was astounded at the pomposity of his words and was glad that it was dark. He could feel his face glowing with embarrassment.

Mahr led Prager to the sheds. 'I thought these would be perfect for your maintenance people.' He shoved open a door and shone his torch inside.

The sheds appeared well constructed, with asphalt floors. Several windows, their glass panes now broken, would provide good light during the day. He noticed oil stains on the floor.

'Before the war,' Mahr told him, 'the Ivans kept a highway maintenance gang here.'

Prager snorted and Mahr laughed. 'From the look of what passes for roads, God knows what they did with themselves. Anyway, when the fighting started nearby, they went off with the roadgraders, lorries and the tools, but neglected to burn the sheds.'

Prager used his torch to examine the place closely. 'All three are just alike,' Mahr offered.

There was room to move two tanks inside at a time, he saw. The floors were littered with trash, as was to be expected, but a working party could have it clean in an hour. Damn! What a stroke of luck! No need of canvas shelters where fingers froze within minutes.

'This place will do fine, Mahr, once it is cleaned up.' Outside, a few pinpoints of light shone from the windows of the converted barracks where the blackout needed improvement. He saw a sentry heading for the door and so kept quiet.

'All the comforts of home, sir.'

'Except women, hey Prager clapped him on the shoulder as they walked back to the headquarters building.

'Well, sir, if you have no objection to Russian women, there are plenty of them about.'

The following morning, Prager was swallowed up in the half-forgotten drill of a fixed base. The panzer riflemen were responsible for security and patrols but, as senior officer, Mahr had to clear operational orders with Prager. By the end of the week, the tank crews had settled in comfortably and the garrison was running smoothly.

It had snowed for one entire afternoon and the village resembled a picture postcard scene, Prager thought to himself one evening as he strolled to the maintenance sheds. The cold was not as bad as he had expected. There was plenty of fuel and supply lorries shuttled in regularly. His greatest problem, he foresaw, would probably be boredom.

And so it remained until the following week when Mahr brought a Russian civilian to see him. The man was elderly with the reddish, weather-seamed skin of a farmer, accentuated by a bristling white moustache.

'This old man came to me with a report of partisans in the forest,' Mahr explained.

Prager glanced at the old man, who touched his forehead. 'God's truth, excellency,' he said in laboured and heavy German.

'How do you speak German Prager demanded, hiding his surprise.

'I was a prisoner in the last war, excellency. I worked on a farm near Magdeburg. They were very kind to me. In Russia now, we have only godless communists,' he made the sign of the Cross and started to spit until he remembered where he was.

'Pigs who call themselves partisans have moved into the forest. We cannot cut wood without paying them a tax and they steal our food at night, the devil take them, spawn of Satan!'

Prager made certain that the old man gave them the correct location of the partisan camp as closely as he could. He had served in an artillery regiment during the last war and so was familiar with maps. Afterwards, Prager had the old man placed under guard and he and Mahr planned a quick operation to bag the partisans before they established too secure a base.

That night, the company of riflemen and two make-shift squads drawn from his tank crews and mechanics entered the forest at widely separated points. They were in position shortly before dawn, just as a bitterly cold rain began to fall. At 0800 hours exactly, Prager and Mahr both fired flares from opposite sides of the enemy camp and the troops rushed the area with fixed bayonets. The fighting was over quickly. The partisan band had included twenty-three men and four women. Eight men and one woman survived the attack and Mahr marched them into the village soon after dawn. All civilians were turned out to witness the executions ordered by Division as both warning and retribution. The villagers cheered the firing party and dragged the bodies away afterwards for burial in a common, unmarked grave. Prager watched the burials, certain that the menace of partisan activities was at an end. The enthusiasm the villagers had shown for the executions had convinced him of that.

As autumn degenerated into winter, there was no further trouble in the area. The villagers were organised into working parties to cut firewood. Normally, wood was cut all through late summer and into the autumn, during and after the harvest, but fighting had made that impossible this year. Adequate firewood meant the difference between life and death and the village women and old men did not need urging to cut and stack the wood against the buildings, both for added insulation and storage.

November passed quickly enough. Prager found it a pleasure to see the exhaustion and the bruised look about eyes, the hollow cheeks and slumped shoulders of his men disappear with proper rest and food. Replacements were slow in arriving but fresh food was plentiful for a few weeks after the freeze. Prager had eaten bland rations for so long that he had almost forgotten the taste of real food.

A new Mark IV Panzer clanked into Slavets one morning, its sides still chalked with messages from the workers at the Rheinmetall-Borsig at Wimag. It was the first new tank the battalion had received since Kiev. Prager had made maintenance work first priority, followed by training sessions morning and afternoon for the tank crews. He also organised lectures within the battalion to discuss Russian combat methods - and particularly anti-tank techniques - during the evenings, well aware that idleness among enlisted men led swiftly to a breakdown in efficiency and discipline, especially when garrisoned in a village filled with women whose own men had been gone for months. In conjunction with Mahr's troops, he also began an extensive series of defensive positions around the village.

A batch of letters arrived from Sonja on the last day of November, the latest postmarked 14 October 1941. He began with that one to make certain that everything was all right. Satisfied, he arranged the letters in chronological order, skimmed each for bad news and finding none, settled down to read them slowly.

The absolute normality of her letters at first served as a balm. She wrote of the fine summer weather, of rainstorms on the river and how they reminded her of the first time they had made love. She proudly described how she had painted the house herself, sewed three dresses and even planted a garden which supplied her with fresh lettuce, tomatoes, carrots and peas.

She wrote disarmingly of her attempts to send him fresh vegetables, and the postal clerk's refusal to accept them because they would go rotten. She did not feel bad however as she had been assured by the clerk that front-line soldiers received the best food that Germany produced. Prager snorted, remembering weeks of dried rations, tinned salt beef and canned sausages.

Prager had been afraid that Sonja's natural feelings against war in her homeland would be apparent in her letters. But it might as well have been fought on the moon for all the notice she took of it. Only at the end of each letter did she acknowledge the war when she begged him to be careful and not expose himself to unnecessary danger - exactly what any good German wife would have written.

The letters were devoid of complaints and only by reading between the lines – the garden and the clothes-making activities for instance – did he sense that shortages were beginning to appear in Germany. Sonja did mention an increase in British bombing raids on Hamburg in one letter but dismissed them as ineffectual. His house on the Wandsee River was too far from the city and its industrial targets to be of concern but, even so, Prager folded the last letter feeling vaguely dissatisfied and not certain why. Perhaps her letters had been too normal. Not once had she asked for news of his concerns or activities, or even of any battles in which he might have participated.

But the letters did cause his misgivings of past weeks concerning the wisdom of marrying her to disappear. He had been a fool to doubt, he told himself. That night, he lay for a long time on the narrow field cot, racked with longing for her. The letters had re-ignited his physical needs once more and he remembered Mahr's off-hand comment concerning the easy availability of Russian women.

The rumours began in early December. Army Group Centre was said to have gone over to the defensive about Moscow and the advance halted from Karelia in the far north to the Crimea. Temperatures fell well below zero and it was worth a man's life to stand guard-duty alone at night.

In spite of repeated requisitions, they had not yet been issued winter uniforms and the troops were beginning to look like tramps. Hand towels were worn as scarves, spare blankets and even tablecloths supplemented summer-weight greatcoats. Gloves were improvised from any cloth or leather that could be found. Some of the Russian women were doing a lucrative business knitting mittens. The village sheep were shorn out of season, and Prager had to issue strict orders against using firewood to keep the men warm in their sheds.

And despite the medical orderly's best efforts, three cases of frostbite developed in the first week of sub-zero temperatures, one severe enough to send the man to the rear for amputation of both feet, ears and several fingers.

The resupply effort, which had looked so promising, fell off as the weather worsened. New engines, transmissions, tracks and other vital equipment arrived slowly and there was little to be done for the vehicles until they did. In spite of the lectures and construction work on the defensive positions, the men were still idle too much of the time. But there were only so many who could be sent on patrol or assigned to guard or fatigue duty, and Prager and Mahr quickly ran out of makeshift tasks which had included weatherproofing the barracks and cutting firewood.

Trouble began about the same time as the rumours of reverses in the north. Certain of the men began bullying the native Russians. There was little enough either Prager or Mahr could do about it except to issue strict orders to the NCOs and restrict contact as much as possible. Unfortunately, some of the replacement NCOs in both units were no longer the high calibre of the pre-war men and not a few had originally been conscripts.

If the enlisted men were not kept busy, Prager certainly was, as he juggled training, maintenance, guard duty, equipment and manpower schedules, rosters and requisitions, as well as the projections of equipment required for future operations. At the same time, he found himself growing depressed. He had requested a month's leave hoping to return to Germany for the holidays and pointing out that he had been in continuous action since 22 June. It was denied without comment at Army Group level.

The denial served to fuel a growing worry and he began to feel that his misgivings in June were now being borne out; despite their rapid advances and the unimaginable number of prisoners taken – equal to the initial estimate of the total fighting strength of the Red Army – the war would not end this winter. With every day that passed, Prager grew more certain that they faced another summer of campaigning in Russia. A second request for leave was also denied and drew a mild reprimand from the regimental commander who reminded him that he was not the only newly-married husband in the army.

Prager was working one Sunday morning two weeks before Christmas when Oberfeldwebel Hans Bethwig knocked on his door to report that one of the First Battalion's replacements had just been arrested.

'For God's sake,' Prager exploded. 'Haven't I enough to do without this kind of nonsense. Arrested for what, Sergeant Major?

Bethwig stared past him at the wall. 'Murder, sir.'

Bethwig had no other information as they hurried across the frozen square. 'I saw Schutze Arvo Weldman being marched to the Panzer Rifle barracks. Lieutenant Mahr sent me for you.'

Mahr's face was grim as he waited in the anteroom. An iron stove glowed a dull red in the corner, overheating the room as usual. Prager shed his greatcoat and gloves immediately and followed Mahr into the inner office, after telling Bethwig to remain outside.

He remembered that Private Arvo Weldman was a mechanic from Ebingen. He had a sullen face and a heavy Swabian accent and had arrived the previous week in one of the few drafts of replacements they had so far received.

Weldman was sitting in a chair and did not rise when the two officers entered until one of the guards cuffed him. Everything about him was heavy and sullen, Prager thought; features, shoulders and ham-like hands deeply engrained with dirt and grease. His face was disfigured by three deep scratches along one cheek and a yellowish-black bruise that darkened his forehead. His hands were manacled and the two riflemen on either side both had facial bruises. One looked as if his nose might be broken.

Prager glanced at Mahr. 'The charge?'

'Rape and murder of a village woman – hell, a girl. I doubt if she was fourteen years old.'

'How do you know this?' Prager demanded.

'I'm sorry, Herr Major,' Mahr's voice turned formal. 'My men broke into the hut as he was choking her to death. I saw the body. The girl had been badly beaten – brutally in fact. She was naked and it was obvious that she had been raped. Buggered too.'

Mahr looked at Weldman and his eyes were bleak. 'It is one thing to kill women and children during a battle, Herr Major,' he rasped. 'But quite another to do so deliberately and with great cruelty.'

'Do not lecture me, Lieutenant,' Prager snapped. 'I know my duty.' He reached out and yanked Weldman's chin up. 'You are accused of rape and murder. You will be tried by court martial. Do you have anything to say for yourself?'

Weldman's eyes flickered for a moment with what might have been fear but he shook his head. Prager turned abruptly and strode from the room.

Prager convened the court martial the following evening with permission from Divisional headquarters. A medical officer drove down in the morning and examined the body. Prager took him across to the rancid-smelling hut where the body was still sprawled on the bed. The medical orderly had done a preliminary examination and discussed his findings with the doctor. Neither the young rifleman or the doctor seemed at all disconcerted by the girl's naked and savagely beaten body and Prager reflected that they had probably seen far worse in the past six months.

Evidence of torture was clear enough. The corners of her mouth were cut and bruised where she had been gagged. Her wrists and feet had been abraded by the cords Weldman had used to tie her and which the orderly had left in place. Cigarette burns marred her not-too-clean skin and there were numerous knife cuts on her breasts, abdomen and buttocks. Her body was a mass of bruises and Prager recalled that Weldman's knuckles were cut and bleeding. A length of wire had been twisted tightly about her neck until it had almost disappeared into the skin.

'Nice fellow,' the doctor said. 'He must have tortured her half the night. I'd guess that she was choked unconscious several times before he finally killed her.' He indicated a noose hanging from a ceiling beam and the orderly nodded agreement.

Prager left them to it.

*

Lieutenant Mahr, three other officers appointed by brigade headquarters and Prager constituted the board of a summary court martial. A captain had come from the Second Brigade east of Slavets. Prager had met him once or twice before and knew him to be a competent, if not decisive, combat officer. The major who arrived from brigade HQ at Berestivo was a thoughtful individual with thick glasses and a near-sighted way of staring at anyone who spoke. He had been named as president of the court martial board but seemed happy enough to defer to anyone who wished to speak.

The third officer was another captain, also from Divisional headquarters and a lawyer. 'I'm just here to help interpret the law,' he chuckled. 'And see this bastard shot, assuming of course he did what he is accused of.' This last was said with a grim smile. He too had seen the body.

The evening before, Prager had requested that Sergeant-Major Bethwig serve as Weldman's advocate. Bethwig was an old-timer and a veteran of the 1914–1918 war. He was competent, intelligent and respected throughout the brigade.

An hour before the court convened, Mahr reported that not one villager had been seen since Weldman's arrest and that he had therefore ordered an assembly. A head count revealed that four village men were missing.

'Gone over to the partisans, as old as they were,' he predicted grimly after he had arrested the families and sent them by lorry up to Division for interrogation.

As they filed in to take their places, Prager saw that the narrow room was packed with men from both the rifle and panzer companies. Since Weldman had not been well-liked, Prager concluded that they had come out of boredom and curiosity rather than concern.

Yet, since the killing, Prager had detected an undercurrent that he did not like. In the first weeks after their arrival, the soldiers had shown sympathy for the Russian villagers, particularly those evicted from their homes. Many had voluntarily cut wood for the winter and repaired huts, especially for families whose men were away in the army or had been captured or killed. But that attitude had changed lately to active antipathy as rumours of partisan activities in other sectors reached them. And now this.

Sergeant-Major Bethwig surprised him. After the doctor presented his findings and the two riflemen testified to having seen the accused in the act of choking the victim to death, Bethwig rose and acknowledged the accuracy of the reports.

'I do not wish to challenge the facts as stated. Instead, I wish to introduce in defence of the accused the right of any German soldier to interrogate a Russian citizen in any way he sees fit.'

Prager gaped in astonishment as Bethwig continued, not at all abashed by the stir he was creating. To support his contention, he cited as evidence the Fuehrer's recent 'Commissar Decree', which declared all members of the Communist Party, all subversives, partisans and others considered dangerous to German intentions, subject to immediate arrest and execution by any member of the German armed forces.

'Private Weldman will swear that he suspected the woman of being a link between the partisans and the villagers and that he was only carrying out our Fuehrer's orders by interrogating her concerning partisan activities in the area. Due to his zeal and inexperience, she died during the interrogation.'

A gale of laughter swept the room and Weldman turned and shook hands like a prizefighter. The major banged the table with his fist. 'I'll clear this room,' he roared, 'if discipline is not maintained.' He stared at Bethwig, unable to keep the disgust from his voice.

'Sergeant-Major, you ask us to believe that this man, a recent replacement with no battle experience, no experience of Russia at all or of local conditions, was able to identify a fourteen year old prostitute as a partisan? If so, your defence lacks credibility, Sergeant-Major Bethwig.'

Bethwig stood his ground. 'Nevertheless, sir, that is our defence. Private Weldman was acting in a manner consistent with our Fuehrer's decree.'

The major had no choice but to accept and Bethwig continued. He led Weldman through a carefully rehearsed testimony, in which he admitted that although he had tortured the suspect – how easily the dead child becomes the suspect, Prager thought – he had only done so because she had acted in a suspicious manner. When the prosecuting officer pointed out that Weldman was not known to speak Russian or the girl German, Weldman maintained with a straight face that they had communicated through the use of signs and the few words each knew of the other's language.

When the prosecutor questioned him about torturing the girl, Weldman gave an obviously memorised speech which drew nods of agreement from the spectators. The words were obviously written by Bethwig, but Weldman discoursed on torture as an interrogation technique. 'It is well known that torture is not condoned by law in the Third Reich, but then neither is it specifically forbidden. And it is in fact used by the security forces of the government and Nazi Party, of which I am proud to be a member of long standing, in matters pertaining to State Security. Therefore, the Fuehrer's own decree plus the precedent of State employment condone my interrogation of a partisan agent and enemy of the Reich.'

The court retired to Prager's office where he stared at each officer in turn, attempting to sense the direction of their thoughts. Without waiting for the president to open the discourse, he slammed a fist down on the desk, making them all jump.

'Damn it, I won't have it. Bethwig has made this animal out to be an agent of the government and therefore authorised by the Fuehrer, no less!' He pawed through a pile of papers and tossed a mimeographed sheet onto the desk. 'There it is. Read it for yourselves. The decree does not apply to individual soldiers. In fact, it empowers only legally constituted security forces to deal summarily with subversives, not every fool in uniform with a gun. My God, if that were the case, any soldier could torture and kill any Russian he even suspected of being a partisan. We'd have a blood bath on our hands that would make Attila the Hun's activities seem a kindergarten exercise.'

The others sat mute.

'Well, say something one of you!'

Mahr cleared his throat. He was the junior officer present, but it was plain enough that the other three weren't going to commit themselves first.

'To date, we have had no trouble with the local population. But if this man isn't punished, we will.' His words were blunt enough. 'I suspect that the four village men have gone to the partisans because of this killing.'

The captain nodded reluctant agreement. 'We've had the same experience in the Second Brigade area. As long as the locals aren't treated badly, they'll not help the partisans.'

'On the other hand,' the Major said, as he polished his glasses, 'the girl was a whore. What are the chances that she was an agent for the partisans?' The Divisional HQ captain held up a hand to contain Prager's explosion.

'Look here, I'm an outsider and perhaps I see the affair in a clearer light. You have assumed that she was not a partisan only because you are concerned with punishing the man who murdered her. Well and good. But I'm looking beyond that. I think the problem is threefold – firstly, there's the issue of a contemptible murder. Secondly, the security of our armed forces and ultimately, the Reich, is intimately involved with the need to determine whether or not she was a partisan, no matter how spurious the claim. The third and final problem has to do with discipline. If you solve the first two and ignore that, you will have served justice but lost the confidence of your men. You saw how they reacted.'

Prager nodded grudgingly. 'Thank you, captain. I understand that, but as you say, the primary responsibility of this board is dealing with Weldman. He is a murderer and a sexual pervert. As such, he is a time bomb. Greater considerations of Reich security can be dealt with elsewhere. As to discipline of my battalion, I can assure you that I will see to that.' The lawyer shrugged and Prager restrained a nasty comment.

'I'll sum up, then,' the major said. 'This Weldman tortured and murdered the girl, prostitute or not. Two eye witnesses testified they saw him strangling her with wire. The doctor has testified that particles of Weldman's skin and hair were found beneath her fingernails, that the scratches on his face were caused by her nails and that samples of semen taken from the girl and from Weldman have proved to be identical. And we have testimony from others in his squad that Weldman often talked of raping Russian women and performing various sexual acts that can only be described as aberrant. I think it significant that in none of the testimonies given by others of his squad, was it once mentioned that Weldman suspected this girl or any other villager of being a partisan.'

The lawyer nodded. 'A succinct summary, Major. I suppose there is nothing left for us to do but vote.'

The captain from the Second Brigade said slowly, 'I agree with the Major. One must think of the wider implications of this affair. If this Weldman is executed, it may well have an effect on the morale of our forces throughout the area. After all, they have fought very hard for six months under the worst possible . . .'

Prager interrupted to snarl, 'Weldman hasn't seen any fighting. He arrived here from Germany a week ago. Enough of this nonsense, gentlemen,' he swept the table with his glance. 'The evidence is plain. Weldman raped, tortured and murdered that child. I vote "guilty as charged".'

Weldman stood at Bethwig's urging when the officers filed into the overheated room. Prager could see beads of sweat on his forehead and hoped to God they were caused by fear.

The major wasted no time in formalities. 'Private Arvo Weldman, we find you guilty of the rape, torture and murder of one A. V. Sharapova, a fourteen year old female minor residing in this village. You are therefore sentenced to death by firing squad. The execution will take place this evening at 1800 hours, subject to confirmation of this verdict and sentence by the divisional commandant.'

Weldman stared at them in shock and Prager suddenly realised that a death sentence was the last thing he, Sergeant-Major Bethwig or the audience, expected. A guard grabbed for him and missed as Weldman collapsed. They dragged him off sobbing for mercy. Disgusted, Prager went to his office to telephone a report to Division.

Lieutenant Mahr entered as he was speaking and Prager waved him to a chair. Mahr fished beneath his jacket and brought out a bottle of vodka which he divided evenly into two canteen cups.

Prager replaced the handset, picked up his cup and raised it in toast. 'I used to hate this stuff,' he muttered. He drank quickly, then again, and put the cup down, thinking of his father-in-law. I wonder, he thought, if anyone has shot that bastard yet?

'They've confirmed the verdict and are dispatching a motorcyclist with written orders. Weldman is to be shot as scheduled this evening. The garrison is to be assembled as witnesses.'

Prager stared into the cup and in a formal voice said, 'Lieutenant Mahr, you will select and command a firing party of ten men, five from your rifle company, five from my panzer battalion.' Over the cup's rim, he saw Mahr take a long drink. 'Have you ever deliberately shot a man?' he asked.

'A Russian officer,' Mahr said after a while. 'In August, north of Kiev. He was standing in a bunker doorway with a pistol, nothing more. There were eleven men with me. He hadn't a chance and knew it. We didn't have time to waste and when he wouldn't surrender, I shot him myself. Inside were wounded nurses. He was protecting them.' Mahr shuddered at the memory. 'My God, he was a brave man.'

Prager knew that there would be no problem with Mahr. 'Division will draw up a proclamation in German and Russian and it will be posted throughout the area by tomorrow.'

Lieutenant Kurt Mahr waited in the snow with the firing squad. The ten men chosen to compose the firing party were plainly unhappy with their role. A restless movement in their line was aborted at his snarled command.

Mahr had selected the firing party early in the afternoon. Prager had visited the barracks where they had been isolated and laid special emphasis on the fact that the condemned man had been tried according to military procedure, found guilty of his crime and sentenced to death, which sentence had been confirmed at Division headquarters.

'One rifle will contain a blank cartridge inserted at random,' he said. 'So you will do the condemned man no favour if you miss deliberately. And,' he warned, 'I will punish any man I suspect of doing so.'

The village street was lined with men from the panzer battalion and rifle company, drawn up in four rigid lines, two to a side. No villagers were in sight but a twitch of a curtain or a door or shutter being eased aside made it plain they were watching.

A frigid wind whipped ice crystals the length of the road. Two electric arc lights had been brought out from the maintenance sheds and their harsh glare cut a tunnel through the darkness to the chair placed against a log barrier. A generator's whine ululated with the wind.

A door opened behind Prager and, without ceremony, the prisoner was brought out, his hands tied behind his back. That Weldman was terrified was evident in his shambling gait as he was dragged by the arms along the road between the lines of shivering men. Prager had stationed himself so that he could watch the lines as the prisoner passed.

Weldman was a coward; he was in such a state of abject terror that the instant he saw the chair, he all but collapsed. One of the guards muttered something and jerked him upright again. Prager saw a number of men avert their eyes.

As they neared the chair, Weldman began to struggle. Mahr stepped in to help but Weldman was a big man and he managed to throw off one guard. Mahr had stationed two more nearby for just such an occurrence and they moved in quickly. Between the five of them, Weldman was shoved down onto the chair and quickly bound. Mahr bent down and hissed something into his ear. Weldman stopped struggling and looked from Mahr to Prager, then, with a terrible sigh of resignation, he closed his eyes and slumped against the ropes.

Prager had never participated in an execution before. The legal office at Division headquarters had thoughtfully included the proper manual with a copy of the death warrant and he was astonished at the numerous details involved in executing a man. When thousands were being killed every day, it seemed obscene to submit the death of one more to such bureaucratic detail.

Weldman began to sob, his face twisting and untwisting in a rictus of terror and the guards stepped away from him in distaste. Mahr nodded to the chaplain, but as he came forward Weldman threw himself from side to side in the chair shouting, 'No, no, please no!' over and over again. The chaplain glanced helplessly at Mahr who motioned him back.

Mahr took a deep breath and drew a sheet of paper from his pocket. He read out the charges and the sentence steadily enough as Weldman continued to alternately sob and scream. When he finished, Mahr turned, gripped Weldman's shoulder and shook him. The condemned man stared around, eyes wild in the arc-light glare. Mahr asked if he wished to say anything. Weldman's mouth worked but produced only incoherent groans. Prager wanted to turn away from the disgusting spectacle but forced himself to stand at rigid attention.

Mahr drew a handkerchief from his pocket. A guard stepped in to steady Weldman and as the bandage touched his face, he started back so violently the chair nearly overturned. But once the bandage was secure, Weldman did not move again.

Ordinarily, Prager would have entrusted the next step to Sergeant-Major Bethwig, but after his performance in the court that morning, he was no longer certain of him. Instead, Mahr nodded to Sergeant Fuchs, a war-time enlistee but a steady man nevertheless, who wheeled and passed in front of the firing party. He took each rifle, opened the action and turning his back, inserted a cartridge into the breech, closed and locked the bolt, put the safety on and handed the weapon back. One rifle held a blank cartridge when he finished.

Fuchs called the firing party to attention and, at Prager's nod, Mahr gave the first command and the firing party raised their rifles. At the second, ten rifles were aimed at the figure twenty metres away and Prager watched closely, as did Mahr and Fuchs from opposite sides to make certain that none wavered.

Without hesitation, Mahr gave the command to fire. The roar of ten rifles sounded terribly thin and unimpressive in the black night. Weldman jerked spasmodically and the chair collapsed. His body heaved against the ropes as Mahr stepped forward, drawing his pistol. Prager was astonished at the man's resilience. Nine 7.92 millimetre bullets had smashed his body, yet even as Mahr cocked his Walther pistol and in one smooth motion, stooped and fired a bullet into his forehead, Weldman was still alive.

Routine took over.

The firing party marched away to receive their ration of cognac and the burial party, detailed to dispose of the body in a grave blasted out earlier, came forward. Prager watched the rest of the men trudge off to their quarters under the close scrutiny of noncommissioned officers and noted that some of their sullenness had disappeared. That Weldman was a coward and had died badly was less forgivable it seemed than that he had tortured and murdered a fourteen year old girl.

Prager shook his head at the mentality of the common soldier. But their reaction proved he had been right about the necessity for executing Weldman. The least breakdown in discipline under such circumstances had to be punished swiftly, and in the harshest manner allowed by law. If one man were allowed to go unpunished, or worse, was punished insufficiently, discipline would be jeopardised and worse crimes would result.

German forces were spread too thin to control a population actively against them. Allow such atrocities as the murder of the girl, no matter that she was a whore, to go unpunished and the natives might begin to support the partisans. Once that began, it would snowball as the army was forced to take reprisal action.

So far, the severity of partisan exactions and the outright banditry of their undisciplined elements had forced the locals to the German army for protection. As long as the army continued to deal fairly, even to the extent of paying for blankets requisitioned by the troops, there would be no major trouble. There were even plans being laid for the army to assist with the spring planting, and local industries throughout the region were being put back into operation. A nearby collective farm was in the process of conversion to a farm cooperative, modelled along German lines.

It had been just the opposite in Poland – as Prager had seen at first hand – where the SS was responsible for maintaining civil order. Their approach was so heavy-handed, even savage, that two years later, the country was a hotbed of partisan activity and sabotage.

Fortunately, in Russia the army had been allowed to retain control of the rear areas. Like the autumn operation against the partisans, Weldman's quick trial and execution would go a long way towards offsetting the Soviet propaganda Prager knew was aimed at the villagers in German-liberated territory.

The Pacific War December 1941 - February 1942

Lieutenant Saburo Takeda dried his face with a hand towel and tossed it to his orderly. He was conscious of the vague figures of his company in full combat gear standing at parade rest. The humid night pressed on them with smothering intensity and the hiss of the sea alongside was full of menace. Their objective, Bird Island - Wake Island as the Americans called it - was invisible in the darkness.

During the evening briefing, they had been shown a montage of aerial photographs of the wrecked Pan American Hotel, burning fuel tanks and poorly camouflaged gun emplacements, which had refreshed Takeda's memories of the island. Others, taken by Japanese military and diplomatic personnel flying the Pan American Clippers that used the island to refuel, showed it to be only lightly defended. And since the American Pacific fleet had been smashed at Pearl Harbor three days before, no serious opposition to their landing was anticipated. Especially since naval aviators based on Truk had reported downing the island's last pursuit aircraft the day before.

Takeda sensed eagerness emanating from the men of his company assembled in the blue glow of battle lanterns. They had been recalled from Manchuko only three weeks before and they were in top form, eager to join in their first real land action against the Americans. All across the Pacific, from Hawaii to the Philippines to Malaya, naval, air and land forces were establishing the supremacy of the Japanese Empire. Yet Takeda was conscious of his own resentment at being relegated a part in so minor an operation as the occupation of Bird Island. An hour or so of shelling and they would wade ashore with less danger than he had encountered in Indochina a year ago. He was almost certain he had been chosen to participate in this invasion because he had what the Navy would surely consider pre-war knowledge of local conditions - he had been on the island for a few hours nineteen months ago while the Pan American Clipper on which he had been flying was refuelled and serviced.

The conquest of the Philippines and its powerful American garrison was underway. Guam had fallen and after the occupation of Bird Island,

Takeda suspected Midway Island would be taken as a preliminary to the invasion of the Hawaiian Islands themselves. Then, the Empire of Japan, solidly astride the shipping lines to Asia, would call the tune. No longer would the Americans exercise their repressive influence over Japan, or indeed all of eastern Asia. With the raw materials of the Pacific Basin solidly under her control, Japan was destined to become the most powerful nation in the world, thus wiping away forever ninety years of insults and Western imperialist interference.

The ship's siren whooped twice. All about them, the sea came alight as the ships of the task force – the cruiser *Yubari*, the destroyers *Mutsuki, Kisaragi, Yayai, Mochizuki, Oite* and *Hayate* – opened fire while turning to port to steam down the southern flank of the islands at about 6,000 yards.

Bird Island was really a coral atoll composed of three islands – Wake, Wilkes and Peale – arranged in the form of a V, the open end of which pointed northwest, while Wilkes and Peale formed the legs. Aerial reconnaissance had revealed only three gun batteries, one apiece at the ends of the V and the third at the juncture of the legs, on Wake itself.

While awaiting the assembly of the task force at Ruotta Anchorage at Kwajalein, Takeda had studied Operation Order Number 1, dated 5 November 1941, detailing forces and tactics to be used in securing Bird Island. The task force was to consist of two cruisers, six destroyers, and four transports, two of which were converted destroyers and the other two, *Maru,* or commercial shipping vessels.

Thirty-six bombers of the 24th Air Flotilla had struck the island on a round-the-clock basis since the start of hostilities on 8 December. Now, after this final bombardment, the landing force would embark in small boats for the final assault. Takeda was irked that his company was scheduled to land in the second wave, but the other company commander was senior to him and had wangled the honour.

The muzzle flashes of the task force, sailing in line astern, had moved towards the horizon. Takeda was entranced by the spectacle of night-time naval gunfire. So far the Americans had not returned the compliment. Were they so badly demoralised they feared to give away their positions, thus inviting a devastating avalanche of steel and explosive? But then it was well known that Americans could not withstand sustained artillery fire.

In the glow of the battle lantern, his watch read 0600. The lead ship, *Yubari*, had reversed once again and seemed closer in this time. She was silhouetted for a moment against a blazing fire – probably oil storage tanks. *Yubari* fired a broadside but even so, Takeda saw the light flare on her afterdeck and grunted with surprise when she turned and headed out to sea at high speed. The flare grew brighter until her upper works were outlined in flame.

Takeda saw a quick succession of flashes at the apex of Wake, marked on American and British charts as Peacock Point. He turned to remark to his second-in-command just as a violent explosion tore apart a ship less than five hundred yards away. He was stunned; the converted destroyer carrying the first wave of the landing force had blown up!

Their own ship keeled violently to starboard. Noncoms shouted for silence in the ranks drawn up on the foredeck. The eastern sky was greying with the approach of dawn and ships close in grew in definition. There was nothing to be seen of their sister ship but swirling debris rapidly being left behind. The destroyers formed again into line astern to charge the shore batteries. Takeda swore, frantic at the stupidity of a commander who could order such a manoeuvre. Naval gunnery was the great love of his life and its most basic tenet forbade ship-borne guns to charge land-mounted guns.

A salvo struck around the lead destroyer. A moment later, three shells smashed her bridge and bow and she blew up with such force that even across the miles of water, the concussion stunned. Shells slammed into the second destroyer and she veered away while the surviving ships spewed smoke to screen her.

Signal lamps flickered and the invasion fleet turned ponderously back out to sea. Takeda watched, helpless in an agony of shame. How could such a disaster have happened? It was insupportable . . . a disgrace of the first magnitude!

A faint cheer drifted across the sea and he turned to see the *Yubari*, barely discernible in the blood-red dawn, leading the destroyers in once more to attack – a gallant but foolish action. The heaving seas hid them for long minutes but when the column was visible again, Takeda saw smoke pouring in thick volumes from another vessel and the squadron was coming out again at high speed. The splashs of near misses spouted in his binoculars.

His watch showed 0720; in little more than two hours, the entire invasion force had been thrown back by a handful of men and a few old cannon. Takeda could not grasp the extent of the disgrace. Although he had no part in the action, he felt the responsibility as keenly as any naval officer directly involved.

And it was not over yet. Without warning, machine gun fire raked the decks of their ship. Sirens whooped and anti-aircraft fire slammed skyward but the American aircraft which had taken them totally by surprise was gone.

The American fleet had been destroyed at Pearl Harbor as had all aircraft on Bird Island, so there should be none nearer than Midway to support the Americans! And no American aircraft that he knew of had that range. One after another, four aircraft attacked the ancient light cruisers escorting the troop transports, tiny irritating mosquitoes unperturbed by the fierce anti-aircraft barrage until their bombs were exhausted and they disappeared into the dawn red sky.

At Ruotta anchorage a few days later, Takeda learned that a total of 340 men, sailors and soldiers had been killed, including many of the company of Special Naval Landing Force aboard the converted destroyer-transport who were to have formed the initial invasion force. Two other destroyers had been sunk and a transport beached and lost. Both old cruisers had also been badly damaged.

How suddenly our confidence has been shaken, Takeda thought. We who have attacked and destroyed the American battleship fleet at Pearl Harbor, eliminated their air fleet in the Philippines, attacked and occupied the island of Guam, invaded Malaya and all without serious hindrance, only to be thrown back by a handful of ill-armed American marines on a spit of island in the middle of the Pacific. As he contemplated the disgrace, he knew they had brought it upon themselves. How often had they been taught that only proper preparation and quick and consistent execution wins battles. They had failed to heed this most basic of all lessons and the taste was bitter.

Takeda squinted against the powerful early morning sun on 21 December 1941 as he watched his company at morning callisthenics. He was alert for slackers, but every man was streaming with sweat and in spite of the heat, going at it with a will. He could feel the rumble of ship's engines through the deck and the rolling lift of the open sea.

The reorganised and greatly strengthened task force streamed from the Ruotta lagoon at dawn for Bird Island. The lines of ships seemed endless; the disgrace of their repulse would not be repeated. Alone of all the task forces striking first blows against the Americans, they had failed; but, and his thoughts were grim, they would soon redeem their disgrace.

Reconnaissance had reported no reinforcements reaching Bird Island, but there were rumours of an American carrier task force steaming from Hawaii. It was plain that Rear Admiral Kaijoika and his staff were worried. In the briefing only an hour ago, they had discussed the possibility of further air attacks by American aircraft flown from carriers. The 24th Air Flotilla had been ordered to find the American carriers as quickly as possible.

The main force consisted of: two aircraft carriers, *Hiryu* and *Soryu*; three heavy cruisers, *Kingugasa, Aoba, Koko*; *Furutaka, Tone,* and *Chikuma,* due to arrive from the Pearl Harbor strike force; three light cruisers, the repaired *Yubari, Tatsuta,* and *Tenryu* and eight destroyers, *Mutsuki, Yayai, Oite, Mochizui, Asanagi, Yunagi, Urakaze,* and *Tanikaze.* Three troop carriers, a converted destroyer, a Maru transport and one seaplane tender completed the invasion force.

The day was sunny and warm but the ocean breeze modified the heat above decks. Below, where the invasion force was confined on the converted destroyer except during exercise period, it was oven-hot. Loin cloths were allowed and the men lay quietly in their bunks or gambled in a desultory fashion. The task force commander – with the American carriers in mind – was keeping all ship's crews at general quarters, thus requiring the troops to stay below and out of the way.

The task force rendezvoused off Bird Island before midnight on 23 December. Orders were passed quietly for the Special Naval Landing Force to embark. Takeda marshalled his men and led them on deck, stumbling and cursing. The task force commander had ordered a complete blackout. There would be no signal lamps and no preliminary bombardment to warn the Americans of their return.

The 24th Air Flotilla had flown heavy bombing missions since the task force had withdrawn on 11 December and aerial reconnaissance showed that most of the permanent structures and all gun emplacements had been destroyed. Takeda was sceptical; the airmen had made those exact same reports prior to the first invasion attempt.

He had taken great pains in the address to his company the evening before. Ordinarily, he would have denigrated the enemy's skill and bravery, but not this time. The Americans had repulsed them easily and had fought as fiercely as any Japanese. The shore batteries had braved the fire of charging cruisers and destroyers and given an excellent account of themselves.

Takeda had commanded too long to even think of insulting his subordinates with less than the truth. They had fought in Indochina and Manchuria and were seasoned veterans and would not flinch when he told them to expect a hard fight.

'Bird Island is a key element in the Pacific defence of the Empire,' he had told them in sober assessment, 'just as it is to the Americans in the defence of their interests. We, however, will succeed in capturing the island because our skill and dedication is superior. But you may expect them to contest the islands to the death.'

Takeda had purposely avoided the stock propaganda phrases dealing with the lack of moral fibre among the Americans, or the influence of Hollywood as a tool of Moscow-directed Communism, or their racially-inherited lack of courage. Nor had he mentioned the fact that because the Americans were a mongrel race, one composed moreover of the dregs of a decadent Europe, they lacked spiritual commitment. Not only were such truths self-evident, but his men had heard them too many times before. Instead, he had concentrated on making certain that they understood what was required of each and every man.

The seas were running heavily as they embarked in the small landing boats. The pre-dawn darkness added to the difficulty of forming up and the tinny sound of the motors seemed no match for the ferocity of the seas. The run into shore was endless and even the most seasoned sailors were sick. Takeda fought with his stomach to avoid disgracing himself and strained his eyes into the darkness for the first flicker of white marking the reef line where the ocean combers broke. In this wild night, Takeda was certain the American defenders would not detect them until they were actually on the beaches – if they got that far, he thought as he grabbed the gunwales in the vicious seas.

'There,' a voice whispered, relief evident, and Takeda saw a faint white blink in the darkness. As the boat rumbled closer, the line grew towards the horizon. At the same time, he heard the hollow pounding of waves on the fringing coral.

The lead boat penetrated the reef without incident. Takeda's boat followed and shortly the seas eased as they ran into the sheltered waters south of the three islands. Takeda formed his company quickly and started up the beach. The blackness was as dense as velvet; he heard voices, words indistinguishable in the wind. A shout and a flare erupted.

Takeda dove for what cover there was as the flare burst low and rifle shots kicked up sand. A machine gun chattered on their flank and Takeda shouted the order to open fire. A withering, disciplined blast poured into the darkness directed towards the flashes.

Takeda tried to analyse the composition of the force blocking the way inland. The enemy's rifle fire had been relatively weak; it was the machine gun on their right that was the real danger. Was the American garrison attempting to draw him into a trap? Takeda hesitated a moment, weighing the alternatives as the eastern sky showed the first flush of dawn. He had to do something quickly while full darkness lasted.

The least likely supposition was a trap. The Americans would have no idea where they would land and they certainly did not have sufficient forces to garrison the entire coast. Therefore, it seemed most logical that they were facing, at best, a handful of riflemen and one machine gun.

Takeda's training had emphasised quick decision making and he did not hesitate now. He shouted orders for a bayonet charge and was the first one to race up the sloping beach as fast as the soft sand permitted. A second flare burst, but higher this time, and he saw a single trench with four pale faces, eyes shadowed to ghoulish holes, staring at him. A rifle cracked and he felt a faint concussion as the bullet whipped past his head.

He fired his automatic pistol at the trench, more to make them keep their heads down, than in the expectation of hitting anyone. The four defenders rose to meet them, firing their rifles as fast as they could work the bolt handles. The Special Naval Landing Force ran over them with hardly a pause and a few moments later a grenade exploded on his right and the machine gun ceased firing.

Light grew quickly. Takeda glanced at his watch – 0550. The carrier plane strike was scheduled for 0600. A second machine gun hammered them from the left and his company scattered into the sparse cover offered by the sand and scrub. The Americans were putting up a defence consistent with their actions two weeks before.

They were met at every turn with small arms and light machine gun fire, but within an hour of the landing, his company had occupied the ruins of the Pan American Hotel and flushed out three snipers. Wave after wave of carrier aircraft, serving as mobile artillery, had blasted strong-points in response to commands relayed via the fleet. The Americans had sited their weapons for best effect but they lacked the mobile artillery needed to stop the invasion force.

At 0630, a bugle call floated insistently in the early morning air and the firing died away. A few minutes later, Takeda was astonished to see an American officer moving from position to position with a white flag. As he did so, the defenders rose from trenches and ruins, hands raised in surrender.

Takeda barely retained sufficient presence of mind to order his men to meet them. As they were lined up and searched, he could not rid himself of the feeling that somehow he was being contaminated by their cowardice.

One American, a sergeant, stepped up and saluted. Takeda nearly slapped him for his insolence but the man did not deserve even that much attention; instead he stared past him, uncomfortable in his presence. The man's uniform was filthy and spattered with oil and he wore an empty holster. His boots were dusty but of good quality as was the rest of his uniform. He did not appear to be hungry and was clean shaven and his ammunition belt was half full.

The man spoke, in English, and when Takeda ignored him, persisted until he snapped an order to a soldier who used his rifle butt to drive the American back into line. Takeda could see the same disgust in the expressions around him. Even though they had been told repeatedly that the Americans, Dutch and British would surrender rather than die, it was difficult to believe. Who could understand a military tradition that did not consider surrender a disgrace, no matter the circumstances? He could feel only disgust and hatred for such a betrayal of military tradition and honour.

Two more Americans, one wearing the gold leaves of a major, came towards him with a white flag attached to a mop handle, followed by a Japanese army officer. The Japanese officer saluted. 'The Americans have surrendered, sir.' He managed to keep his voice neutral. The American officer was of higher rank but Takeda did not salute him.

'Do you speak English?' the American asked.

Takeda, who until that morning had not heard English spoken for nearly two years, was swamped suddenly with the memory of the racial slurs and veiled insults he had suffered on the American West Coast in 1939 and 1940. Even now the attitude of this officer made it plain that he found it distasteful to surrender to a Japanese.

'Yes, I speak English,' Takeda replied evenly. 'But you must speak to me only in Japanese.'

The major blinked and his face reddened with anger. He started to say something but Takeda turned to the Japanese army officer who explained that the American wished to go about the island to make certain that all the American troops received and understood the order to surrender.

The sun's glare hurt Takeda's eyes as he squinted up at the taller American. Was he planning some kind of treachery? Always, he had been taught that American marines were fanatical fighters who were sent into battle drunk or drugged. But the man's eyes were clear, his speech unslurred and there was no smell of alcohol.

Takeda nodded curtly and ordered the man escorted by armed Japanese soldiers. 'If you are fired upon,' he said to the army officer, first in Japanese and then in English, 'kill him with a bayonet.'

The invasion force was fully ashore by 1000 hours. Aerial reconnaissance had reported no sign of American ships within the several hundred mile search area. As he thought about the American officer and his escort Takeda was inexplicably reminded of a night in Warsaw, only a day or so before the war in Europe began, when he had dined with a group of Western military attachés. The memory of the evening still rankled and he felt again a hollow surge of humiliation as he recalled how the American civilian and the British officer had so arrogantly dismissed Japan's claims in the Pacific and Asia. Automatically, they had assumed these areas preordained to remain under British or American control for all time.

They had not quite laughed when he had enumerated Japan's own claims using exactly the same logic by which they justified their 'rights', but their opinion of him had been made plain enough in their expressions of paternal tolerance. Well, Mr American, he thought, let's see what you think now? If the lessons of the Russo-Japanese War were lost on you, perhaps these will not be! We Japanese will teach you yet how to act, and die, properly.

The return to Japan was in stark contrast to the outward voyage. In late November the mood of the fleet had been one of apprehension overlaid with a sense of bravado. Then it had been difficult to comprehend that they were really going to attack the powerful and arrogant American and British Empires. But events of the past month had dispelled the sense of inferiority cleverly ingrained into the Japanese people by the Europeans for nearly a hundred years.

In three weeks, the Empire's area of direct control had expanded ten-fold, its area of influence a hundred-fold. And the United States had been proven a cowardly paper tiger powerless to stop them. Japan was no longer a third rate country, held in economic and spiritual subjugation by the white colonial and industrial powers. Never again would she be dictated to from the capitals of Europe and America.

Takeda saw the time when the Empire would control half the globe. His father, a lifelong ultra-nationalist, had always maintained that Japan's power should extend from the American West Coast to the far western borders of Asia. Someone had to fill that power vacuum and better that it was his own nation whose motives he understood and trusted. Takeda and his father differed only in their view of who the immediate enemy was; his father held it was the godless communism of the Soviet Union, just as it had been the Tsar's Russia before 1917. But both agreed that one had only to look at the restlessness of colonial people throughout Asia and Africa to know that the white man's day was nearly over. From the Philippines to India, from Timor to Manchuria, the coloured races waited only for a leader – the Emperor of Japan!

The Americans were being herded up from below for exercise. Takeda watched dispassionately as they were formed into a ring and made to shuffle around the rim of the main hold. They were a miserable lot, he thought and why not? They had forfeited their honour and now were less than pathetic in their filthy bits and pieces of uniform. Dirty and unshaven, the American marines looked like the bums he had seen along San Francisco's Skid Row.

Takeda believed in the Code of Bushido – the way of the warrior – as did the majority of the officer corps. He had first been taught its spare code of discipline in primary school. His memories of adolescence were a mixture of stern discipline and beatings administered by non-commissioned and commissioned officers alike, first in military school, then in the navy, for the slightest infraction – exactly the way he disciplined those under his command.

All traces of soft thinking had been beaten from him and he had nothing but contempt for the desires and materialism of civilian life. He was a warrior of the Emperor and his life task was to assist in building the Japanese Empire into a powerful tool for human change and discipline. The lectures on Bushido that he had heard perhaps a thousand times directed his thinking.

But his teachers had been careful to make him understand that not everything Western was abhorrent. Science and technology were Western inventions far superior to many traditional Japanese practices based on decadent Chinese systems. A *katanga* could not defeat an armoured tank, but a thirty-seven millimetre cannon could. And what

Western man developed, the Japanese, by applying the superior cultural and social values of their society, could improve.

Similarly, the traditional spirit of the Samurai, as embodied in the Code of Bushido, had been cultivated in all branches and ranks of the armed forces and, in combination with Western military techniques, had produced a superior soldier to whom surrender was the ultimate disgrace and for whom to die well in the service of the Emperor was the greatest joy. Since the election of General Tojo Hideki as Prime Minister, the entire nation now participated in the glorious struggle and ninety million souls formed a central arsenal of the spirit as well as the body.

Takeda was well aware that the military, and particularly the Navy, high command, were divided over the course the war should take. A powerful faction led by Admiral Yamamoto felt that Japan must win quickly as she lacked the resources and manpower to defeat the United States in a prolonged war. It was their position that all resources must be bent to this task alone and everything else made subordinate. Takeda agreed.

There was a fine line between fanaticism and common sense, he knew, and the United States was three hundred times the size of the Japanese homeland and had three times its population. Even the Code of Bushido could not make up for that difference.

America must be defeated quickly. Yet watching the prisoners shuffling about the deck, Takeda thought that they were a puzzling people. They had fought valiantly, and thrown back the first invasion force – perhaps due to Japanese overconfidence, as some maintained. But there was no denying that the Americans had fought well. Yet less than two weeks later, they had surrendered after two hours of fighting. It was puzzling; which America were they to fight?

The harbour and docks at Sasebo were jammed with warships of every class and description. Troop transports loaded around the clock and destroyers, minesweepers and light cruisers bustled in and out of the bay. An aircraft carrier slid silently past them in the channel, massive, sinister. Overhead, aircraft patrolled ceaselessly to guard against submarine attack. Now that Great Britain and the Dutch government in the East Indies had also declared war, the enemy fleet had grown in numbers, if not necessarily in quality, *vis-à-vis* the Japanese Imperial Navy.

Takeda's company was moved once again into barracks and he was called to the regimental commandant's office, congratulated for his part in the invasion and given five days leave. In peacetime he would have been glad enough of the leave. Now, he was loath to take it even though this might be the last opportunity to see his family again for years. According to the rumour mill, they would soon be going into action again and destinations ranged as widely as the Philippines, Alaska and Australia.

Hard fighting lay ahead to clear the remnants of Western imperialism from Asia.

It had snowed the previous night and traffic between the base and the station was badly snarled. Takeda made it only because the train itself was delayed. The porter, an elderly man with the 1905 war ribbon on his lapel, bowed him into the crowded compartment where a young woman hopped up quickly to offer him a seat.

As the train hurried north through the snowy landscape, Takeda was conscious of the deference paid his uniform and rank. He was also conscious of the girl standing before him. It had been a long time since he had talked to a woman and he tried without success to strike up a conversation. She had a pleasant, round face and lustrous hair which was unfortunately worn long in Western style; even so, she was attractive enough in knee-length dress and wool coat, although he would have preferred the traditional *obi*. Whenever she turned, the coat revealed the sheen of silk stockings and the temptation to run his fingers along calves nicely rounded by high-heeled shoes, was overwhelming. But she was so overcome by the attention he paid her that she could only giggle whenever he spoke and he soon gave it up as a bad job. Obviously, her parents had not taught her traditional respect.

In spite of the heavy snow, the train was only ten minutes late into Osaka. It was growing dark when he walked out of the station crowded with commuters and the sharp wind mingled the smell of the icy city and the sea, a decided contrast to the summer perfume of his last visit. The atmosphere seemed hushed as he walked through the soft snow to Kadoma. Lights glowed in windows and he pictured contented families celebrating the latest victories of their armed forces.

On the train, he had sensed the jubilation and pride among the civilians. The newspapers were full of – somewhat exaggerated – stories of Japanese successes throughout the Pacific and Eastern Asia. Takeda had been amused to see that the correspondent for the *Ashai Gurafu* had turned canvas tent camps on Wake Island into fortresses and described Americans captured there and on Guam, as weakened by the effects of the tropical sun on their pale skins.

His homecoming was marred by a disagreement with his father whose first question when tea had been served was why hadn't the Navy pressed on to invade Hawaii? His mother sighed as she withdrew.

Takeda attempted to explain that never had there been the intention to invade the islands, only to destroy the American fleet. 'We simply do not have the manpower to garrison an island chain as large as Hawaii with all our other commitments. To do so would strain our supply lines to breaking point. And neither is it necessary at the moment.' His father's expression remained sceptical.

'There are other ways to force an American withdrawal from the Pacific,' Takeda went on. 'Bird Island is only one brick in the wall of island fortresses we are building across the Pacific which, when completed, will prevent a future American advance. You will see, father. The Americans will turn their attention to the war in Europe.'

His father ignored his arguments and continued to condemn the faint hearts in the Navy who drew back from continuing the offensive. He contrasted the Admirals with the Army Generals who spoke constantly of advance, advance, advance. 'It was a mistake to attack the Americans first,' he maintained angrily. 'But once we had done so, the attack should have been pressed to the ultimate.

'You will learn, my son, what we discovered in China and Manchuria thirty and forty years ago; one wins wars only by advancing. The Hawaiian Islands must be captured and the West Coast of the United States attacked. The Americans must be kept off balance until what little will they have to fight disappears. It is more important to attack and attack the United States than it is to conquer British and Dutch possessions. Bah, they are preoccupied in Europe. What danger can they be to us?'

Takeda tried gently to argue with his father. 'The British and Dutch control rubber, manganese, oil and other materials vital to our war effort and to our industrial productivity in peacetime. We have inflicted grave damage on the United States by sinking her fleet and it will be two to three years before she can rebuild. By then the Empire will be so powerful that no one will dare attack us.'

His father refused to accept the logic. 'Russia is the true enemy,' he snapped. 'She has already made an alliance with the Americans and the British for help in Europe. And then when they have finished with Germany, they will fall upon us. Instead of assisting the Germans to destroy Russia, we waste our efforts in the south, in Malaya and the Dutch East Indies, as if either were a threat to the Empire. Time enough for them when we have dealt with our real enemies.'

Takeda tried again. 'You must understand, father, that much has changed since 1905. Our war with the Americans is a naval war, one in which the supply lines binding island to island are more important than the islands themselves. In this new kind of war a single aircraft carrier is worth far more than a dozen divisions of soldiers. Our strategy must be to eliminate America from the Pacific, at the same time absorbing those areas which have raw materials vital to our success until our position is impregnable and our fleet and army are powerfully entrenched.'

But his father was plainly unwilling to accept his arguments, so Takeda hid his feelings and changed the subject. He was troubled; not by the fact that they disgreed – they had always done that on military matters – but that his father was becoming a querulous old man unwilling to listen to another point of view.

To escape the cloying attentions of his mother and sister the following afternoon, he went for a walk. At the end of the block, he passed the lower school glowing with light in the overcast winter afternoon. Through the window he could see the bent heads of children hard at work and on the playground, snow-suited gnomes raced about under the instruction of teachers, shouting anti-American slogans.

He took a tram into Osaka and walked along the busy streets, noticing that the food markets did not seem quite so full of customers or food. In front of a bakery, a long line of women watched him pass; several bowed silently to his uniform. Traffic was light and it was growing colder. He stepped into a food stall and ordered a cup of tea and a rice ball.

The proprietor grinned uneasily. 'There is no rice, honoured sir. Only tea.' Takeda assented and the man served him and asked eager questions about the war. But Takeda was tired of talking about the war and his answers were short and noncommittal. The proprietor left to wait on other customers and he finished his tea quickly and left.

As he walked, he was aware of how uncomfortable he was in the company of civilians. He was sure that some of those women had blamed him because they had to queue to buy food. And wasn't the manner even of those who bowed, reserved? Foolish women he thought; they resented having to queue while their sons gave up their lives without complaint. And the food stall proprietor had talked as if the war were designed solely for his own amusement.

He found himself in a small park. A line of pines screened the city's noise and he dusted the snow from a bench and sat down. Perhaps he should go to Tokyo and join the other officers in his regiment who had also been given leave. At least there they could drink and argue, engage in political discussions and get drunk without civilian interference. But for some reason, the prospect did not appeal to him this time.

Always before, he had been an eager participant. Such affairs had almost become a ritual. On returning from combat, or from a particularly gruelling training exercise, they would rent a suite in a good hotel. A survey party would have bought as much saki and Scottish whisky as they could afford so as to avoid the hotel's invariably inflated prices. They always began at a *geishaya* with a fine meal that lasted as long as anyone was capable of eating and talking. The following day, all would troop along to the *Ginza* in search of a bath house where the female attendants might occasionally double as prostitutes.

He had declined the invitation this time to go home instead – to argue childishly with his father. Then to discover that his younger brother Michitaka had been unable to obtain leave from his bomber training school near Hiroshima, his sister Ryuko was busy with her own affairs and his mother's usual attentions suddenly annoying.

*

It was Ryuko who, that evening, directed Takeda towards the solution to his ennui.

'Mariko has asked about you often. Do you remember Mariko?' she asked with a coy smile.

Takeda was surprised at how quickly her face sprang to mind. 'Of course.' He tried to keep his voice noncommittal. 'She lived next door to us before I went away to school. Didn't I talk to her when I was home a year ago?'

His sister giggled. Why did all young girls giggle so much these days, he wondered with annoyance; then was instantly ashamed of himself. And why should she not? She was young and quite pretty and she knew nothing yet. Better to enjoy her childhood. It would end soon enough.

'Mariko is very interested in your career, big brother. She is always asking if we have heard from you? But of course, I do not see her much now that she is living in Tokyo.'

'Tokyo!' he exclaimed. 'Why Tokyo? Kadoma is her home.'

His sister laughed. 'How old fashioned my big brother has become. Don't you remember that she was studying for a position in radio? Well she has one now, as an announcer for Radio Tokyo.'

Takeda lay awake that night, thinking about Mariko and how she had changed from the thin, shy girl who lived next door. He also recalled that she had been quite strong-minded and how she had laughed when a year ago he had asked how soon she planned to marry and begin a family. So many of the young – and he automatically exempted himself from that category now that he had passed his thirty-first birthday – no longer felt bound by the old traditions.

Takeda boarded the train to Tokyo the following day, to join his friends, he told his parents – and himself. But Ryuko smiled knowingly and when she kissed him goodbye that morning, she actually winked at him. His sister, he thought, was far too mature for her years. But of a sudden, Takeda realised that his baby sister was nearly twenty-three and as much a woman as Mariko. He shook his head over the lost years as he stared through the window at the rushing landscape.

Takeda had never really cared for Tokyo. It was too big, too impersonal and somehow too un-Japanese. Yet he enjoyed his infrequent visits, providing they remained short. He took one of the many taxis lined up outside the Tokyo Central station. The cloying odour of coal gas hovered under the portico and the driver seemed as glad as he to reach the street where the winds had free play.

He had reserved a room at the Dai Ichi Hotel by wire. At the sight of his naval uniform, the desk clerk was polite, but distant, and Takeda guessed that his fellow officers had already made a nuisance of themselves. He was shown to his hotel room by a bellboy barely old enough to reach the door latch.

When he joined the others after a short nap, he found them absorbed in two-day-old hangovers; his reception was accordingly muted. Someone passed him a saki bottle and he was urged to catch up. A desultory card game was in progress. Three officers were asleep, two on the floor and one on the couch, and the rest were talking idly about the latest changes in the government, but without enthusiasm, as the new ministers were mainly army officers. The rooms stank of alcohol, sweat and an undertrace of vomit and urine. As the afternoon wore on and the winter sunlight dimmed, Takeda's disgust grew.

But saki always seemed to lubricate his brain and by mid-afternoon, he had arrived at the cause of his boredom. On arriving home, he had expected to be treated as a hero but instead, his father had criticised, his mother had treated him like a child while listening to his tales with fond benevolence, and Ryuko had shown little interest in his accomplishments and very little respect for his rank. Ryuko had become too much the modern woman and Takeda did not pretend to like her rejection of traditional Japanese values. Neighbours listened politely, but at the first opportunity interrupted to complain about the hardships of civilian life in wartime and about the growing shortages of rice and vegetables. It seemed to Takeda that it had not yet really penetrated the civilian mind that Japan was at war with a ruthless enemy.

That evening, he was persuaded to accompany the others to dinner at a *Kagurasaka* restaurant, but within an hour it showed signs of turning into another drunken brawl. The patience of the restaurant owner was being sorely tried, as was that of the geishas serving them, and Takeda knew that soon the police would be called. He had no wish to undergo another fight with the police who resented military officers and so, with head spinning from too much wine, he left.

The temperature had dropped below freezing and snow flurries drifted across busy streets. The frigid air helped to sober him and he walked with the crowds along the narrow thoroughfares, garish with neon. Street vendors danced through the crowds shaking paper fish, simple toys, bunches of wilted flowers and nauseating assortments of fried and steamed foods. Many of the vendors were Korean and Takeda took care to avoid them.

There had been talk of blackout precautions, but only talk. The newspapers gleefully reported the American blackout of their east and west coasts and, of course, the British blackouts had been the subject of innumerable political cartoons for years. But how could American aircraft reach the Home Islands? Where would they come from?

As he moved along streets crowded with soldiers and sailors on leave, Takeda was surprised at how far the censors had retreated in past years. Outside every night club, photographs of nude women were showcased in all manner of poses, even though their private parts were obscured by pieces of black paper.

Prostitution had always been a thriving business in Japan, but never openly, yet before he had gone two blocks, he was propositioned four times and a dozen pimps, many of them boys of ten or eleven, vied for his attention with unlimited promises. Takeda was suddenly disgusted with the changes five years of war had brought to Japan. He brushed away a laughing girl who tried to take his arm, and went back to his hotel.

Late the following afternoon, Takeda stood outside the entrance to the Radio Tokyo building. Hundreds of people streamed from the doors making it impossible to check every face. He had intended to apply to the receptionist until the possibility that Mariko might not remember him – or might not want to see him – had caused him to hesitate and then it was too late as the mass exodus began.

'Are you looking for me, Captain Saburo Takeda?' a soft voice asked and he jumped. There was a bad moment when at first he did not recognise the pretty young woman smiling at him. Mariko seemed smaller, yet more mature. Her cheeks were fuller, her eyes larger and her complexion paler than he remembered until he saw that she was wearing foundation and eye makeup.

Her hair was shrouded beneath a fur hat and her Western-style coat came almost to her ankles, beneath which were fur-rimmed, high-heeled ankle boots. Standing against the backdrop of bustling crowds, a faint trace of breath whispering from parted lips, her lustrous eyes shining in the fading light, he thought her the most beautiful woman he had ever seen.

The avalanche of impressions caused him to stammer like a school boy as he tried to acknowledge her greeting and explain that he just happened to be passing.

Mariko nodded demurely. 'Ryuko wrote to me that you were coming to Tokyo. I hoped that you might want to see me again.'

Takeda was still confused at how suddenly everything was happening, and how at variance with his expectations. He remembered Mariko as a pretty but distant girl, but this Mariko was a beautiful woman happy to see him. Had his silly sister been right after all? And when had she written? He had only left Kadoma the day before yesterday.

They walked through the gathering dusk, drifting snow hushing the city's stridency. For a moment, Takeda felt abnormally free. A sense of well-being swept through him and it was all he could do to keep from cheering his good fortune. He became aware that people were turning to watch him pass. Mariko smiled up at him and the way her face was framed by the soft fur, he thought he had never seen a woman as beautiful. Does she feel as I do? he wondered, and in the next instant was puzzled. Just how did he feel?

They walked for a long while, Takeda conscious of the appraising and admiring stares of passers-by, content merely to be with Mariko until he noticed that she was shivering.

'Perhaps,' he said in a lordly and daring manner, 'we should find a restaurant and have dinner.' It was not really a question so much as an order. Mariko nodded.

'I would like that very much.' She looked up at him as they passed beneath a street lamp and he saw that her eyes were wide with anticipation.

But as soon as the words were out, he cursed himself silently. Damned fool! You don't know where to take a nice woman in Tokyo! The places he had visited with his fellow officers were obviously out of bounds for a woman as sensitive and sheltered as Mariko. In the strangely liberal conditions of wartime was it even possible to find somewhere suitable?

Mariko must have guessed at his thoughts as she smiled. 'May I suggest the Doh Hana. It is a fine restaurant with an excellent menu.'

Gratefully, Takeda accepted the suggestion and she told him it was only three blocks away. 'It will be quicker to walk than to look for a taxi cab.'

As they entered the restaurant, the attendant saluted respectfully and the maître d' bustled up as their coats were whisked away. Takeda turned, prepared to receive his bow but to his surprise, the man bowed first to Mariko and greeted her effusively by name.

Expressing his pleasure that she had again chosen to honour their restaurant in a torrent of compliments, he led Mariko directly to an excellent table, held her seat with a flourish and snapped his fingers for waiters. Takeda was left to follow along behind and seat himself.

Waiters surrounded Mariko, offering matches when she removed a cigarette – a cigarette in public! – from her bag, tidying up the table and polishing the already gleaming plates. The head waiter ventured a question, contriving to bow, smile and flirt with her all at the same time. Then, as an afterthought, he turned to Takeda. 'And your escort?' The question was addressed more to her than to him but Takeda ordered a scotch and water in a brusque voice and the waiters settled napkins, rearranged dishes and bustled off reluctantly.

Mariko laughed at his expression which was a combination of astonishment and annoyance. 'I read the news for Radio Tokyo and my picture is often in newspapers and magazines. And we are not that far from the radio station. I often come here.'

Takeda's annoyance began to ease and he shook his head ruefully over his arrogant assumption. A waiter interrupted again before he could answer, but when he had gone, Takeda inclined his head in parody of a

Chinese mandarin and asked her forgiveness for his unpardonable boldness and stupidity.

'I had no idea that you had become a famous personality.'

Mariko frowned. 'Please, I am not. I am a voice on the radio and my picture is in magazines. The fact that I have little privacy in public is a most unpleasant part of my job.'

Takeda was suddenly conscious that he did not know what to say. He had expected to find an acquaintance from childhood alone in the big city, confused and afraid and grateful for a friendly face from home.

Instead, Mariko was very much in command, recognised, bowed and spoken to with respect while he was ignored – it was not the naval officer accompanied by a pretty woman whom people in the streets had turned to watch. He remembered the Zen teachers of his youth, and their canes. They would have found more than sufficient reason for punishment in his arrogance this evening.

Takeda found himself fighting a sudden desire to rush from the restaurant. All his life, he had been taught that naval officers were among the élite of Japan. He had fought in Indochina, in Manchuria and the Pacific and acquitted himself with honour for the Emperor and Japan. Yet he had been lectured by his father and coddled by his mother. Then when he thought to impress a pretty young woman – one, moreover, who had hero-worshipped him as a child – she turned out to be the hero and he a mere decoration. And what was worse he discovered, was that understanding what had happened did not relieve his embarrassment, nor his resentment, and for a moment, as irrational as it was, he hated Mariko. She had become a famous radio personality while he had scorned knowledge of such nonsense, or of anything that did not bear on his military career.

He hardly dared meet Mariko's eyes and, as if she sensed his thinking, she touched his arm. 'I should have warned you. But it is so difficult for me to accept that everyone knows who I am. I should have remembered that you were away fighting and would not know.'

Takeda glanced up. Was she taking the blame for his foolish arrogance?

Mariko blushed. 'I wished only to impress you,' she admitted in a whisper. Takeda suddenly remembered the number of times he and his friends had sent Mariko running home in tears, and was ashamed. She met his eyes squarely, something he had not the courage to do, and with that strange conjunction of thought he had already noted, continued, 'When I was a child, I followed you about and made a nuisance of myself. You thought I was a foolish child. When we met last summer, I saw that your feelings had not changed. You were were so handsome in your uniform. You had fought a battle and I . . .' She faltered. 'I wanted you to like me, and not to think of me as you did when we were children. I wanted so badly for you to write to me. And when you did not, I wished to do so – but that would not have been seemly.' She stopped in confusion as the waiter came to the table, pad and pencil poised. When he began to offer suggestions, Takeda nodded impatiently and told him to bring what he thought best.

The moment was lost and they sat in awkward silence. Takeda knew he should say something but he did not know what. The waiter returned with rice cakes and they bent their attention to their plates.

Afterwards, he walked with her to the dormitory for unmarried female employees of Radio Tokyo. She stood beside him, shifting from foot to foot in the cold, fur collar drawn tightly about her face. He thought again that she was the most beautiful woman he had ever seen. He wanted badly to see her again. By virtue of having served in so many Western countries, Takeda was a bit more sophisticated about women than most men of his time and position in Japan. Sexual experience was easily gained, but only among prostitutes or women of low class. A casual acquaintance with a young woman of marriageable age was uncommon and sex unthinkable, an insult to both families. Most marriages were still arranged by the parents and there were still brides and grooms who did not see one another until the wedding ceremony.

Takeda wanted desperately to tell Mariko how beautiful and desirable she was, but he was afraid that he might frighten or even mislead her into believing his interest was in marriage.

She turned to go and, impulsively, he held her arm and blurted out, 'Mariko, I wish to see you again!'

Her smiled dazzled him. 'Tomorrow evening,' she said softly, 'at seven, after my last broadcast.' She hurried away before he could recover from the shock of what he had done and the heavy doors closed behind her like the gates of a mediaeval castle.

Takeda paced outside the Radio Tokyo building the following evening. His temper was short, having endured a great deal of chaffing from his fellow officers when he had refused to spend the last night of leave together. All day, he had anxiously reviewed every word he and Mariko had spoken the previous evening, fearful that he might have misinterpreted a response or worse, committed himself in a way he had not intended. In doing so, he had alternated between anguish over his own lack of sophistication and an intense elation that she had wanted to see him again.

The crowd of home-bound employees streaming from the building thinned until by seven p.m. it had stopped and Mariko still had not appeared. Through the revolving glass doors, Takeda could see an elderly night watchman pottering about the lobby.

By seven-thirty, apprehension had turned to anger and he banged on the locked lobby doors. The night watchman hurried forward, waving his hands. 'Closed!' he shouted. 'Tickets on sale tomorrow. Come back then.'

Takeda unbuttoned his overcoat and the sight of his officer's insignia brought an instant change of attitude. Inside, he demanded that the watchman telephone the studio. His anger grew as he waited; what did she think she was doing? First she had led him on with lies about how she had admired him as a child and how she wished to impress him, make him think well of her, then had insulted him, had made him wait in the snow! Was this how she achieved revenge for the petty insults of childhood? Did she think that because she was a radio star that she could . . .

The watchman replaced the receiver on the hook. 'I did not know it was you, honoured sir,' he said nervously and scuttered around the desk to hand Takeda a note. The folded paper, in what could only have been Mariko's handwriting, said that she had been unexpectedly detained for an important broadcast and would he please come up to the studio. It was timed for six-thirty that evening and he glared at the watchman.

The man apologised profusely. 'Unfortunately, the day watchman had gone off duty without informing me of the note. Would the respected naval officer please accept my apologies? I will bring the matter to the attention of the management tomorrow without fail.'

Takeda ignored the apology; the old fool had probably just forgotten the message. He brushed past him into the open lift. The watchman hastened to push the proper button and close the door, calling instructions by which to find the studio after him. The lift ground upward and as it did, Takeda's anger cooled. By the time he reached the specified floor, he was feeling foolish at his suspicions and that made him angry all over again.

He found his way through the confusing maze of corridors to an open office door. A young woman smiled and invited him in. She indicated a chair and as he sat down he saw Mariko through a large plate glass window sitting at a table on which stood a microphone. She was reading from a sheet of paper and seated opposite was an elderly man in a general's uniform, whom he recognised from newspaper photographs as one of the Prime Minister's military advisors. The secretary turned the volume up on the wall speaker behind her desk and Mariko's voice filled the room.

Takeda felt pride wash away the last of his anger; Mariko sounded professional and cool, not at all abashed at speaking to such a powerful general. But then the import of her words penetrated. Mariko was reporting that the invasion of the Dutch East Indies had begun.

'Actual details are not available as yet,' she said, 'but it is reliably reported from sources within the Imperial War Department that today, 11 January 1942, our troops have landed in Borneo and overcome all resistance. The Dutch colonialist oppressors are falling back in panic in the face of the heroic Japanese army and the native population is rushing to welcome our victorious troops as liberators. Allied warships dare not attack the powerful Japanese armada cruising in East Indian waters. To provide further information, General Eota has graciously consented to speak to us all tonight.'

The general acknowledged the introduction and read a short statement in which he described, in extremely general terms, the invasion of the Dutch East Indies, using many more words than Mariko had to say the very same thing. 'We have done so out of compassion for our Asian brethren,' the general concluded. 'The arrogant Dutch have occupied the lands and waters of the East Indies far too long. Today, the Empire of Japan ends this insulting domination. The Japanese people grant the people of the East Indies new status as members and partners in the Sphere of Greater Co-Prosperity. We shall not rest from our labours until all Asia is likewise freed from the domination of the white man.'

Mariko then asked the general a series of questions, reading each from sheets of papers which the general handed to her. He read each answer when she passed it back, expression grave and voice properly military and reassuring. Once she looked up and saw Takeda through the window, and smiled, as if in relief.

When the programme ended, General Eota accompanied her into the waiting room. The great man frowned at Takeda's naval uniform and it deepened into a scowl when Mariko greeted him warmly and introduced him as an old and dear friend.

Instead of returning Takeda's greeting and bow, the general demanded, 'Are you aware that all armed forces leaves have been cancelled?'

Takeda swore under his breath. 'No excellency, I was not. Thank you for informing me.' He suddenly felt like a first-year naval cadet again.

It was obvious that Mariko was distressed by the news and of a sudden, Takeda wondered if it were true. Surely she would have known, since an order to all military personnel to return to bases, camps and airfields would have been broadcast over the radio. Then he saw the proprietary way the general stood close to her and a surge of dismay went through him.

The general snapped. 'I suggest then, Lieutenant, that you return to your base immediately.'

There was nothing that Takeda could do but submit. He saluted and started to say goodbye to Mariko, but she took his arm and with a distracted apology to the general, drew him into the hall.

'I am so sorry I did not know.'

Takeda was having a great deal of difficulty restraining his anger. Whether true or not, he had been given a direct order by a superior officer and he had no choice but to obey. But he was certain the general had lied to get rid of him...

Mariko walked with him to the lift. When it came, it was empty and impulsively, she stood on tiptoe and kissed his cheek, then stepped back, both hands before her face to conceal her embarrassment.

A mix of emotions assaulted Takeda and left him speechless. As the lift doors slipped shut, he heard her whisper, 'Please write to me. Please?'

Behind the broad, inviting beaches of northwestern Timor, the land degenerated into swamp. The heat and humidity, after four days of soft sunshine and gentle tradewinds, was overwhelming. Takeda sniffed the mix of decaying vegetation, stagnant water and heat with disgust.

This was his fifth combat amphibious landing and never had he seen such extensive preparation. After a thunderous artillery bombardment, they had embarked in the pre-dawn and moved ashore cautiously, expecting to contest every square centimetre of beach. Instead, they had met with no opposition at all.

On 20 February 1942, Takeda established his company five hundred metres inland, at the point where the land turned to swamp, and sent out consecutive patrols which found only native Timoreans who offered no resistance. With the help of an interpreter, a Javanese nationalist, curiously named Jakob Suranyo, educated in Rotterdam as well as at various Dutch prisons, Takeda questioned the dozen or so people that were brought in. None knew anything about the size or location of Dutch forces, nor seemed to care. Even when the interpreter beat two women in front of their husbands, the stories did not change.

The general had not lied after all; the recall message from Sasebo was waiting at the hotel. Takeda had managed to catch the last train south that night and arrived in time the following day to march his company aboard a troop transport. They had sailed within hours. The squadron anchored in Cam Ranh Bay three days later and the ship, with his company aboard, sailed due east the day after arrival, ending once and for all the rumours that they were going as reinforcements to the army in Malaya, and started a new series concerning the Philippines. The ship transporting them joined a task force organising in the Bay of Davao. His only glimpse of the Philippines was a series of low, heavily-wooded islands that ran on seemingly forever and the dark mass of Mindanao, faintly menacing in the overcast. The illusion was further heightened by a stench of rotting vegetation, like foetid breath.

They landed against light Dutch opposition at Manado in the Celebes and again two weeks later at Kendai. They were slated for a landing at Makassar which would secure the Celebes on 7 February, when they were detached and rushed across the Banda Sea to land north of Dili on Timor, the largest of the Lesser Sunda Islands.

Special Naval Landing Forces were organised along army lines; each company contained four platoons and on the march, one was always forward scouting, one was divided into two squads to provide flank security and the other two marched, sandwiched between. Takeda's orders were to occupy a village twenty-five kilometres west of Dili. An army battalion would be moved up to replace them as soon as it could be landed and they would march south towards Kupong to link with a Special Naval Landing Force parachute battalion moving north from there.

So far, there had been no sign of enemy troop movements. Aerial reconnaissance had identified an army camp near the village but low-level investigation had shown it, like the airfield at Dili, to be empty and it was thought the Dutch troops had been withdrawn to guard the oilfields inland. The only thing they knew for certain, Takeda reflected, was that the Dutch had strong forces somewhere on Timor.

As the morning grew older, the heat increased, lulling them with the rhythm of the march. It was nearly a month now since he had last seen Mariko, but not a day passed that she had not occupied his mind, sometimes to the exclusion of more important matters. Two days ago, he had even been reprimanded during a staff meeting for inattention.

For days he had struggled to push her from his mind, refusing to write to her even when her first letter reached him on the ship. Yet just before disembarking, he had written – a brief and formal note that said little more than that he was well.

The letter had embarrassed him. With the exception of his mother or sister, he had never before written to a woman, and those letters were actually addressed to his father. How would Mariko receive the note? Would she be angered by the piece of cheap notepaper only partly filled with formal phrases? But perhaps that was best he told himself. Perhaps she would not bother to reply and thus it would end. Yet at other times, he castigated himself for his stupidity and resolved to write a more gracious letter as soon as the moment offered.

They had been climbing since mid-morning and at noon, the thick undergrowth which had impeded their progress began to fall away to reveal a level plain dotted with trees. Takeda halted the company along the rutted track they had been following. It continued across the plain, which he judged to be at least six kilometres in diameter. The air was steamy with humidity and the sun, unhampered now by the trees, struck at them ferociously.

Takeda squatted down to study his map while the warrant officer established guard rounds and sent out scouting parties. The sketchy map he had been given did not show the plain nor, he suspected, a great many more terrain features and he considered circling its edge to keep to the cover of the rain forest. But when he estimated the distance, he saw an additional six hours march would be required.

His orders allowed no leeway. There were times when it was better to delay, he knew, in order to be certain of reaching one's objective at all, but delays had probably caused the loss of more military operations than any other single factor in history. Takeda chewed his moustache for some moments. With no Dutch aircraft to worry about, he need fear only direct assault. And the plain was open enough that he could not be ambushed. He made his decision; they would go straight across.

Takeda felt as an ant must feel when crossing a sand pit. The intense sun beat down, hotter even than he had experienced in Indochina. Only a few stunted trees dotted the plain. The waist-high grass that impeded their progress was full of insects that fell off onto their uniforms and crawled into the smallest opening and itched and irritated like mad. They marched for an hour before the forest on the far side began to appear nearer. Twice, thunderstorms swept across the sky, but brought only a few moments' relief; afterwards, the sun par-boiled them in their wet uniforms. The ground was uneven beneath the concealing grass and twice they struck marshy patches where the ground was so yielding that two sailors lost shoes in the stinking mud.

They were less than a kilometre from the trees when the aircraft screamed down on them and lashed the columns with machine gun fire. Takeda had ordered the company to march with double intervals between each man, but as the march dragged on, the men unconsciously tended to bunch together until the exasperated noncoms, hoarse from shouting and fists raw from blows, had stopped trying to keep them separated.

The aircraft cut swathes through the men before pulling up in steep climbs for a second pass. Takeda spotted the gold triangle insignia of the Dutch forces and cursed. So, the landing field was deserted was it?

The stubby aircraft dropped towards them again and Takeda recognised them as American-made Brewsters, obsolete and slow, no match for the Zero, but with self-sealing fuel tanks and armour-plate, effective for straffing ground forces. It was known that the Dutch had purchased a few for their European air force in 1940 but they had never been reported before in the East Indies.

The machine gun platoon managed to get one of their guns into action. Takeda shouted at them not to fire but his voice was lost in the engine's roar. The second aircraft jinked right before he could reach them. Bombs exploded and sprayed the machine gun position with shrapnel. Takeda thought they were going to make a third pass but instead, both aircraft disappeared over the trees north towards the landing beaches. He shouted for his communications man to radio a warning to the landing fleet and ran.

The machine gun crew lay dead, one man with a leg blown away, another without a head. Three of the four bombs had missed but one had killed another six men. The machine gunning had accounted for another ten and fifteen more wounded. Eighteen dead and fifteen badly wounded; heavy casualties even before it had properly begun.

Five of the wounded were too badly hurt to continue. Takeda detailed a corporal with four sailors and one medic to get them into the trees. The more lightly wounded he started for the coast, immediately instructing them to see that help was sent with stretcher bearers for the badly wounded.

Furious at the disgrace of losing so many men, the company pushed hard in spite of the heat. It was already mid-afternoon and there remained ten kilometres of forest to penetrate before reaching the village. But as if it were determined to make up for the sparse vegetation on the plain, the undergrowth increased in density. The track wound through green solitude between banks of tall, thin trees whose canopy allowed the ground foliage to flourish. Takeda hated being forced to remain on the track but he had no other choice.

Scouts ranged behind as well as ahead of the column, moving now in single file. After the aircraft attack, Takeda feared an ambush. Intelligence had been wrong on every count so far; he had lost thirty-three dead and wounded, more than eleven per cent of his force, in a matter of minutes to aircraft that supposedly did not exist.

At sunset, two scouts came in to report sighting the village. Takeda moved the column along the track to the point where the undergrowth began to thin, then spread them out into two skirmish lines that enveloped the village on three sides. The men formed up with a will, eager to revenge their dead and he went forward with the scouts in the dying light to study the village through field glasses.

It was composed of eight long bamboo and thatch structures housing several families. He saw two substantial wooden houses which were European in design. The few people visible were Moslems, he inferred from the turbans the men wore. The women wrapped themselves in strips of cloth to form sarongs that left shoulders bare. Children wore no clothing.

There were no Europeans in evidence and, in fact, the door to one of the European houses stood open. Did that mean the soldiers had gone as well?

The track they had been following all day ran through the village and six houses had been built on either side of it. Cleared land to a depth of one hundred metres surrounded the village for agricultural use. Three women were still at work with short-handled hoes in one of the western fields.

As the last of the daylight faded, Takeda sought hard for any evidence that the villagers were aware of being watched, or were concealing Dutch soldiers. If they were, he thought grimly, his heavy machine guns would take care of them. Takeda could not afford to lose a single sailor more. To this end, he had prepared the heavy machine guns to rake the village without warning if he found the slightest hint of ambush.

As night fell, Takeda became aware of the restless anger among his troops and he understood and shared it. During the two years in which he had commanded Company A of the Sasebo Sixth Special Naval Landing Forces, it had become a tightly-knit team. They hadn't suffered a single casualty in Indochina or Manchuria, had seen only four wounded at Bird Island and nothing more than minor injuries at Manado and Kendai. The loss of eighteen killed had been a shock that had to be avenged if they were to regain their self-respect.

The tropical night was stifling. The very earth breathed a humid miasma of foetid air, rotting vegetation and the cloying scent of mould as the day's heat was given up reluctantly. At Takeda's signal, the troops began moving towards the village, guided by the light of cooking fires. His orders were to halt on a line thirty metres short of the huts and hold, but he had only reached a point seventy metres short of the nearest hut when he heard a shout and cries of alarm.

Takeda fired off a flare to flood the village with harsh, white light and the skirmish line swept forward, shouting. A shot was fired, by whom it was impossible to tell, and a hail of rifle fire swept the village as screaming sailors rushed forward with bayonets fixed. Takeda ran towards the European-style houses, shouting '*Banzai*!' A grenade roared and flame lanced up the side of a thatched house, illuminating troops chasing villagers with bayonets. A sailor grabbed a young woman running from a long hut. He threw her down as a sarong-clad man ran at him screaming in anger. Taken by surprise, the sailor sidestepped and drove his bayonet into the man, yanked it out and stabbed again. The young woman scrabbled away, screaming, but another sailor caught her by the ankle and tore her garment away.

Takeda was distracted then as another group of sailors fired into a cluster of people, then charged with bayonets. Takeda held back for several minutes to allow his men to work off their anger, then began to blow his whistle to restore order.

The toll had not been as great as he feared, he decided an hour later as he paced the village. Only fifteen civilians had been killed and a dozen others hurt, two seriously. Two of the long huts had burned to the ground but his sailors exhibited only minor injuries. He surveyed the village in the light of the dying flames and was satisfied.

There would have to be punishments of course, for undisciplined behaviour. He snorted. The army might tolerate that sort of thing with their lower standards of conduct, but the Special Naval Landing Forces were an élite group which could not countenance indiscipline, no matter how much he understood and sympathised.

His senior warrant officer, Gohay Ueda, reported the village secure.

They could begin interrogations in the morning, he decided. He did not expect to learn much since the European houses appeared to have been empty for a week or more and there was no indication that Dutch troops or native levies had been quartered here.

All in all, he thought, he was satisfied with the evening's work.

Takeda studied the eighty or so villagers assembled in the main square as the morning sun began to climb over the forest to the east. Already its fierce heat had started sweat beneath his uniform tunic. Takeda rested his hand on his sword hilt. The villagers were a sullen lot, he thought and would bear a close watch. Some wore grimy bandages, but others did not appear to have treated their wounds at all. He doubted if there was a woman over ten years old who had escaped rape the evening before; most had now been pushed behind their men, and children clung to the sarong-like wraps the adults wore.

He nodded to Ueda who shouted an order. Two guards thrust through the crowd, dragging the village headman after them. The elderly man was badly frightened and he all but collapsed when thrust to his knees before Takeda. Speaking slowly so that Jakob Suranyo, the interpreter could keep pace, he announced that the Dutch no longer ruled Timor.

'You are now subjects of his Imperial Majesty, the Emperor of Japan, who is warring with the colonial powers of Europe to free you and your children from centuries of oppression,' he told them. 'Such a task may require harsh measures from time to time unless the strictest obedience is given to all Japanese forces.

'If you obey, you will be treated well as are all law-abiding subjects of his Imperial Majesty. Accordingly, you are expected to forswear all allegiance to your former Dutch masters.

'Japan is triumphantly driving the Dutch, Americans and British from Asia. Under Japanese guidance and administration, Timor and the East Indies will become an equal partner in the Sphere of Greater Co-Prosperity.

'This far-seeing cooperative economic venture will replace colonialism throughout Asia. Already, the former French colonies of Indochina have joined willingly and the peoples of Malaya and Burma are flocking to the banner of the Rising Sun, repudiating their former English masters and inviting the assistance of Imperial Japan.

'We are happy to assist our Asian brothers and in return ask only that you help those who are risking their lives for you. You must reveal the hiding places of all Dutch soldiers. You must tell us where weapons are hidden, and all food supplies. Possession of radios is forbidden for now and it is also forbidden to shelter European civilians for any reason. All must be turned over to Japanese military forces so that their safety can be guaranteed and so that they may be put to useful tasks.

'You must also, when called upon, assist Japanese forces in any way demanded. You must provide food and living quarters for all Japanese soldiers. You must provide transportation and entertainment.'

Takeda stared down at the village headman and nodded to the two guards who helped him to his feet.

'Where are the Dutch soldiers?' the translator asked sternly. The old man hesitated, then babbled in his own language. Takeda glanced at the interpreter.

'He says there are no Dutch soldiers in the village, and there never have been. Only one Dutch policeman visits the village every two weeks. And a public health nurse who comes once a month. Of course, he lies.'

Takeda ignored the Javanese and bowed to the headman who reacted with astonishment at this courtesy.

'Tell him,' Takeda said to the interpreter, 'that we must remain in his village. He is to provide quarters and food. I will also want two strong young men to act as guides and they will be paid for their work.'

Suranyo started to argue with Takeda about the necessity of paying the guides, but Takeda stared at him until he ducked his head in obedience and translated.

The headman quickly agreed. He offered Takeda a place in his own home which he declined, striving to keep the distaste he felt at the offer from his expression. An officer of the Imperial Japanese Navy did not live in a grass hut like an ignorant savage. He would remain in this larger of the two European houses and the senior warrant officer and petty officers would use the other.

Were the villagers unconcerned over the deaths and injuries suffered the evening before, or were they concealing their resentment? Search as he might, Takeda could find no trace of anger on any of the placid faces staring up at him in the hot sunlight. It had been that way in Indochina and Manchuria. Cattle, he thought. They were all cattle; no wonder the Europeans had found it so simple to rule.

A runner arrived at noon. The army battalion that was to replace them had been delayed for two days and Takeda was ordered to remain in the village. Aerial reconnaissance had spotted small bodies of enemy soldiers in the vicinity of the coast. One band was only twenty kilometres north of Takeda's position in the village. It had not been possible to establish their direction of march but it seemed reasonable to assume that they were moving towards him, perhaps to combine forces with other small groups to attack Japanese positions.

Takeda marked the location of the sightings on his map and plotted probable routes. If they were in fact moving towards the coast, the village, sited on the edge of the last of the rugged terraces mounting towards the interior, would lie within their line of march. He sat for a while, considering various possibilities and, when he was certain he had not overlooked any, began to draft orders.

By evening, Takeda had reorganised the hastily-constructed defence lines of the night before. He established two rings, the outer separated from the inner by a hundred metres of open ground. The two light machine guns were posted on the inner line to provide converging lines of fire and the mortars had been sighted to drop bombs from twenty to two hundred metres in advance of the inner line. Tonight, the trenches would be dug by the villagers.

He had done all he could, he thought as he mopped sweat from beneath his cap. From a distance, the cleared area appeared as grazing land for the few scrawny cows the village owned. The Dutch would not suspect the existence of Japanese defences until they were fired on.

But Takeda had no intention of allowing the enemy to strike first; he had also assigned eight squads to patrol sectors up to twelve kilometres east of the village. Their function was both to obtain information about the area and to locate Dutch or local levy combat forces.

In the event contact was made, he had given strict orders to offer harassing fire only and fall back on the village, while dispatching runners to warn him, thus drawing the enemy onto the village where he could destroy them from fixed positions.

Impatiently, he ordered the exhausted soldiers and villagers back to work. The sooner the defences were finished, the sooner they could all sleep.

Lieutenant Saburo Takeda strode through the village followed by his senior warrant officer and two armed sailors on the second morning of the occupation. He had bathed and put on a clean uniform, properly ironed by his orderly. The sun had risen a few degrees above the horizon, but the silence was unbroken save for the sound of their footsteps.

In the trenches dug during the long night, sentries stiffened to attention as he passed. Beside each, two more sailors slept in contorted positions. Takeda gave no more thought to their discomfort than he would have to his own.

Normally, the village would be bustling with activity by now, but the trenches had taken until nearly dawn to prepare. Soon, he would order the civilians woken. The village must appear normal if the Dutch aircraft which had attacked them two days before returned.

For a moment, he considered the possibility of inducing a Dutch air attack. The resulting civilian casualties would be heavy and might well change the villagers' attitude to their former colonial masters. What did the Timoreans really think of the Dutch colonialists? he wondered. According to his Javanese translator, they hated the Dutch, but was that really true? The Timoreans were not the same racial stock as the Javanese and he suspected that there was little love lost between the two.

Jakob Suranyo, the Javanese interpreter, was a professional revolutionary, possibly even a secret communist, and he could be expected to say only what he thought Takeda wanted to hear; in this case that the villagers were anti-Dutch and pro-Japanese. But Takeda remembered the way in which the headman had spoken of the Dutch police and public health nurse. There had been no trace of anger or hatred in his voice.

That evening, the village headman spoke in low tones with the other village elders while the interpreter sat nearby, listening. Across the way, a gang of young men had finished tearing down the remains of the roof on one of the burnt houses. Beams had already been cut and laid ready for use. Takeda sat on the verandah of the largest European house, smoking a cigarette and enjoying the light breeze as the short tropical twilight dwindled. Torches were lit as the dusk deepened and to a rhythmic chanting, roof beams were lifted into place with a surprisingly sophisticated block and tackle of native design. A native woman glided softly towards the porch with a large bowl of curried chicken and rice.

Her graceful movements reminded him of Mariko and he visualised her clad in a bright native sarong which fastened just above the breasts to leave bare her lovely shoulders. Impatiently, he brushed thoughts of Mariko away, and the Javanese woman as well. War was no time to think of women, he scolded himself.

As he ate the greasy, ill-prepared food, festering with unfamiliar spices, he thought about the meagre information the patrols had gathered during the day. None had made contact with the Dutch, although one patrol had found tracks made by marching men wearing boots or shoes. For once though, intelligence seemed to be right; the tracks indicated they were heading towards the coast. Certainly if they intended to attack the village, they would have done so by now.

Takeda had tried to place himself in the mind of the Dutch field commander who must guess that he could only be the advance guard of a major force. Would he attempt to capture the village or would he bypass this potential enemy strongpoint and strike at the beachhead? Imperial Japanese forces had been ashore for three days and were now at the most vulnerable stage – they had moved inland beyond the cover of naval guns and were not yet properly supported by their own field artillery. So, if the enemy commander could force the Japanese to withdraw, the propaganda value alone would be incalculable. While he could not hope to hold all Timor, he might make it so expensive for Japanese forces that reinforcements would be required from other operational areas such as Borneo, Java or even the Philippines. Because of the Americans' unexpectedly strong resistance on the Bataan Peninsula, Japanese forces in the East Indies were stretched perilously thin.

Takeda finished the curry and wiped his moustache thoughtfully. If he were the Dutch commander, he would certainly bypass the village – as all the signs suggested they had – and attack the coast. The village could be reduced by aerial bombing when necessary.

The senior warrant officer appeared with the interpreter in tow and Takeda acknowledged his salute.

'He,' said the warrant officer, hooking a thumb at the Javanese, 'says two young men are probably missing from the village.'

Suranyo's attitude suggested that he was doing Takeda a great favour by reporting the fact.

'Are you certain?' he asked softly.

Suddenly, the Javanese was more frightened than he had ever been in his life. He had expected Takeda to bluster and shout and he stuttered as he tried to explain that he had made a head count the evening before but had not counted again until this evening.

'You did not make a count this morning?' Takeda asked, his voice oily with suppressed anger.

'No . . . no, sir.' Then Suranyo tried to brazen his way out. 'You worked us all so hard that I was too exhausted . . .'

'You fool!' Takeda exploded. 'Then they have been gone as long as twenty-four hours! By now, the Dutch will know of our defences and the forces at my disposal!'

He slammed the table in frustration. No wonder there had been so few signs of the Dutch. They had simply bypassed the village, knowing that it was strictly a defensive position, and moved on to the coast. He stared at the Javanese whose expression still held a hint of defiance.

Takeda forced himself to think calmly for a few minutes, then ordered the headman brought. The interpreter confronted him with the evidence of the headcount. The old man glanced at Takeda, face expressionless, and shrugged. He spoke briefly. 'He says,' the interpreter's voice was sarcastic, 'that they have gone to the coast to fish and will return in a few days.'

Takeda knew instinctively that the man was lying. 'Ask him if they have not gone to warn Dutch soldiers instead?'

The headman's eyes flickered, but he shook his head stolidly. Takeda knew that his fragile-seeming appearance was a blind. In any society, only the most stubborn and headstrong rose to leadership. This old fool would probably die before he told the truth. But a lesson had to be given, Takeda knew, otherwise the Empire would lose all control.

He ordered the villagers to be herded into the square and more torches brought. While he waited, Takeda fumed at the stupidity of these people who were driving him to such measures. He had come to free them from Dutch oppression, yet at the first opportunity they betrayed their liberators. These people were Moslem, and so it was unlikely that they were communists; the Dutch colonialists, who feared communism as much as nationalism, would have seen to that.

Takeda motioned to Suranyo to step up beside him on the verandah and snapped, 'Translate word for word what I say. Do not add or take away anything. Word for word, do you understand?' The Javanese nodded.

'Two of your young men have gone to fight for the Dutch soldiers,' Takeda addressed the villagers. 'They have betrayed *us,* your liberators. The entire village has remained silent and so you all participated in this betrayal.'

He motioned to Ueda and two sailors dragged the headman forward and forced him to his knees in front of the verandah. The senior warrant officer drew his sword and tested the edge with a thumb. The villagers pressed back and he heard angry murmurs. Takeda waited to let the tension build into fear.

'Your headman knew that the two had gone to the Dutch! Yet he did not come to tell me. He has betrayed the Japanese Empire, of which you are now an integral part. The penalty for such treason is death!'

The headman looked up, his eyes mirroring his surprise as the Javanese translated. Takeda nodded and in one swift stroke, Ueda severed the man's head before he could protest. The head fell with a solid thud. The warrant officer grasped it by the hair and held it while the body convulsed at his feet. He turned, displaying the head to the sobbing women and shrieking children.

'The next time,' Takeda warned, 'I will execute ten of you in like manner.' He jabbed the translator who was staring in horror at the body. 'Tell them,' he shouted furiously. The translator did so and when the villagers started to disperse, Takeda shouted an order and the soldiers stopped them.

'Tell them also,' Takeda growled at Suranyo, 'that it was your carelessness in not discovering sooner that the men were missing that caused their headman to die.'

The little Javanese stared at him in disbelief but Takeda shouted, 'Tell them!'

Suranyo stuttered several times and when Takeda heard the villagers begin to mutter, he knew that they understood and nodded to Ueda. The warrant officer pounced on the Javanese and tripped him to the ground. A sailor handed him a rifle sling as four others spread-eagled Jakob Suranyo and tore his sarong away. The warrant officer stroked the leather sling across his palm and in one smooth motion, whipped it high above his head and snapped it down across the man's naked buttocks. Suranyo screamed, a high-pitched womanish sound, and again each time the sling fell until the eighteenth stroke when he fainted. A sailor twice had to dump buckets of water on him before the forty strokes could be finished.

*

'Our efforts will be concentrated along the track leading to the coast,' Takeda told the three warrant officers. 'You, Warrant Officer Yamana, will march independently to the coast and report the situation to headquarters by no later than 1500 hours.

'The Dutch know that the two villagers will be missed sooner or later, that we will guess what is happening and will pursue them. They will therefore attempt to ambush us. So that they may also watch for reinforcements moving to the village from the coast, they will place the ambush on the inland side of the plain. Warrant Officer Aoka will lead a ten-man patrol five hundred metres in advance of the main body. The Dutch will surely allow Aoka to pass in order to fire on the Second Rifle Platoon which Warrant Officer Ueda will lead to simulate the main party.

'I, however, will follow with the Third and Fourth Platoons five hundred metres further behind. As soon as the Dutch open fire, Ueda will take up defensive positions. Aoka will double back and I will strike from the rear. By surrounding the ambush party, we should be able to make short work of them. The Heavy Machine Gun Platoon will remain behind to guard the village.'

Takeda cautioned them to exercise precise control of their men. 'Remember, I want prisoners for interrogation.'

The fierce heat sapped their strength quickly. This close to the equator, there was no variation in temperatures to mark seasons or bring relief and only the monsoon in the summer months made the difference apparent. The humidity was so high beneath the forest canopy that it seemed they were wading through a fine mist, and the vegetation was so dense that it was impossible to see more than a few metres to either side of the narrow trail. The air was filled with raucous bird cries and mysterious rustlings kept them in a perpetual state of suspense. His hatred of the jungle was beginning to reach paranoic proportions, Takeda realised.

They broke out onto the plain at mid-morning and found Aoka's patrol and Ueda's Second Platoon waiting for them. A sickening feeling that he had been outsmarted had been growing in Takeda during the last half-hour. He had been so certain the objective of the Dutch troops was a harassing raid along the coast. Instead, could it have been the village?

For the first time in his military career, Takeda hesitated. There was too little information on which to base a correct decision, he raged to himself. How could he be expected to know which was the right choice? The two warrant officers squatted a little way off, talking quietly and eyeing him surreptitiously, as if they knew of his inner struggle, and that angered him the more. He had left only the heavy machine gun platoon of fifty men to defend the village and, as he refolded the map, he saw that his hands were shaking and realised that beneath his anger, he was badly frightened.

The tired sailors double-timed back along the trail. Takeda made no attempt to hide his mistake – it was far too obvious. As they ran, he recalled the arrogance with which he had described his plan and overrode his warrant officers' objections in such a manner that no one had dared ask further questions. Wave after wave of sickening shame washed through him and he knew that if the village were lost, he would have no recourse but to commit suicide to redeem his failure. There was no place for fools in the service of the Emperor.

A small stream slipped across the trail half an hour from the plain and clearly the men expected to be allowed to rest here, but Takeda shook his head grimly when Ueda ventured to request permission.

The first ranks splashed across, bunching up as they slowed to climb the shallow bank. Just as they gained the top, machine gun fire raked the column and hand grenades splashed around them.

Later, Takeda determined that they weren't massacred only because an anxious machine gunner opened fire a moment too soon and the hand grenades exploded in the water which absorbed most of the shrapnel. In spite of the Dutch having achieved total surprise, there was little confusion as his sailors responded to years of training. Instinctively, they fanned out along the stream bed, staying as low as possible. Takeda saw a petty officer sprinting downstream, a rifle squad at his back, racing to outflank the machine gun. The petty officer crumpled but the men ran on and disappeared into the trees.

Takeda dropped behind a tangle of dead brush and a fallen tree. Three men threw themselves down beside him. A tripod slapped into the sand and water, splashing him, the gunner dropped the Type II light machine gun onto the tripod and secured it and the feeder snapped open the cover, draped the linked cartridges across the open breech and slammed the cover shut.

Takeda scrambled away to give them room. The machine gun opened up and leaves and pieces of branches exploded wherever the sleet of slugs tore into the trees. Rifle fire poured at them from either side of the trail and from his new angle, Takeda quickly noted how limited it was in spread. The Dutch had not extended their lines sufficiently, preferring to concentrate their fire. Either they did not have enough men to do so, or their commander was terribly inexperienced.

Against regular army troops the ambush might well have succeeded; against trained, disciplined and combat experienced Special Landing Force sailors, it was doomed to failure. Within minutes, firing broke out on the right – the rifle squad had outflanked the machine gun and it fell silent after the muffled explosion of two hand grenades. A warrant officer, Ueda, Takeda thought, led an immediate charge; three men fell but the rest disappeared into the jungle.

It was over in minutes and Takeda had lost eight more men killed and six wounded. He counted twelve Dutch bodies and six native Timoreans, and four Dutch and three Timoreans had surrendered. All were well armed and the stubble on the European faces indicated they had been in the field for several days. With them, serving as a guide, was one of the young men from the village.

Takeda studied him and the young man's defiant stare wavered and changed to fear. Well might you be afraid, he thought. But for you, eight of my men would still be alive.

'Rope them together,' he ordered. 'Aoka, take six men and bring the prisoners to the village after us. Don't leave any behind. Kill the wounded who cannot walk. It is important that you reach the village as soon as possible. Do you understand?'

Takeda reformed the column and they hurried on. As he ran, he wondered why the Dutch soldiers had surrendered? What was the matter with these Europeans? Do they expect us to feed and house them? A soldier's duty is to fight and die, not surrender.

Takeda pushed ahead with the main body. The fact that an ambush had been laid on their return route told him that the village had been taken. The small numbers of enemy involved though suggested that the Dutch commander had underestimated the Japanese forces as seriously as he had underestimated European ability. There were two questions uppermost in Takeda's mind now; how large was the force holding the village and had any of the ambush party got away to warn them? As a matter of course, he had sent scouts racing ahead but had little hope that they might overtake any survivors.

They approached the village an hour later and without allowing the exhausted sailors to rest, Takeda ordered them into a skirmish line which he then filtered into the forest, well back from the village. They moved to the edge of the cleared land and waited.

Two scouts found him and reported no sign of Dutch soldiers. Nor any sign of the heavy machine gun platoon. Otherwise, they had learned nothing that might cause alterations to his plan.

Takeda was conscious that he had less than 210 men left now, all spread in a thin crescent about the village. He worked his way forward to a point where a low dip in the damp ground was screened by a fallen palm trunk. Lying full-length in the dip, he was able to peer beneath the trunk and, well-concealed, study the village at length.

The long huts baked in the afternoon sun. Occasionally, a villager appeared and a few chickens scratched about beneath a hut. Ants discovered him and midges and a plague of other insects. The sun slipped through gaps in the canopy to burn his back and neck and his arms grew cramped with the strain of supporting his weight. But Takeda remained in place, motionless, punishing himself.

In late afternoon, he was finally rewarded. A dog appeared and wandered towards a hut. It stopped a short distance from the ladder and Takeda turned his glasses on it in time to see its ears flatten in alarm. The dog barked and almost immediately something flew out of the hut and struck it hard in the flank. The animal ran off, yipping.

Ueda and the prisoners reached them just as dusk was falling. The Europeans were exhausted and slumped to the ground immediately. The wounded were missing; Takeda did not ask what had happened to them. The village boy who had betrayed them lay on the ground, a bit apart. His arms had been tightly bound and were badly swollen and he shivered continuously from fear.

The last trace of twilight fled and the darkness became palpable. Takeda paced the line again, delivering the word to his warrant officers that they would attack at 2000 hours exactly. As the minutes ran down, tension drew a tighter grip on him; several times he came close to retching and only the fact that others were watching enabled him to maintain control.

Takeda refused to think of the outcome. If they won, he had redeemed himself. If they lost, he would commit *seppuku*. His nerves drew finer, stretching nearly to the breaking point. He shuddered continuously and in spite of the heat, was cold. Takeda could not understand it; he had never before experienced such apprehension – he refused to admit that it might be fear. The Dutch soldiers in the village would be waiting for them, he knew. They would know their ambush failed. But he had no other choice. He must recapture the village at all costs.

At 2000 hours, he saw figures rise carefully from concealment and begin to filter across the cultivated ground. They appeared as no more than shadows moving swiftly against the dark mass of the jungle. A flare burst and he heard shouts from the village. At the same instant, the large eighty-one millimetre mortars coughed and explosions blossomed among the village huts.

Two heavy machine guns chattered – Takeda identified them as his own Type 99s taken from the heavy machine gun platoon he had left to guard the village. A long, curving line of Japanese sailors ran forward shouting and Takeda ran with them, fear and nerves forgotten. The mortars pounded the village, concentrating on the machine gun positions. A line of Dutch riflemen appeared among the huts. They got off only one volley before they were overrun. Mortar fire had again ignited several huts and in the reddish glare, he saw his sailors sweep into the village from three sides.

He rolled a hand grenade beneath the first hut he came to and ducked away as it exploded, shredding the thatched walls. He glimpsed a figure in the doorway of the next, saw the muzzle flash and felt the sharp whoosh of air as the bullet sliced past. Instinctively, he dashed towards him to take advantage of the time needed to cock the rifle bolt, and tripped. As he sprawled headlong, two more shots followed one after another past his head and shoulders.

Shaking with fear, he rolled quickly into the shadows and fired twice at the door with his pistol, but the figure had disappeared. Dutch soldiers materialised from everywhere at once. People ran screaming, children dragging behind. The fighting degenerated into a savage mêlée of hand-to-hand combat with bayonet, rifle butt and knife. Takeda saw Warrant Officer Aoka attacked by two Dutch soldiers, beaten to his knees and shot through the head. A moment later, both were dead, hacked down from behind.

A man leading his wife and two children ran from a burning hut straight into a machine gun burst that killed them all. A woman was bayonetted when she sprang up suddenly to run, another was struck with a rifle butt as she held up both arms to ward off the blow.

Then, as suddenly as it began, the fighting was over. The enemy disappeared and Takeda's sailors moved warily from hut to hut, thrusting bayonets through the walls and tearing the covering away. They ordered anyone out they found inside and shots cracked nastily if the villagers did not move quickly enough. Takeda had issued strict instructions against rape; there was no time to be wasted in case the Dutch counterattacked.

The heat from the burning huts beat against their faces, driving them all back. Flames soared tens of metres high and lashed the dried thatch roofs with unholy fury. Every structure in the village was on fire, including the two European houses. Takeda shouted for them to be saved and the sailors used their bayonets ruthlessly to herd the surviving villagers to work beating out the flames with rugs, clothing and even their hands.

They saved the largest house which Takeda had made his headquarters. All but one of the other structures in the village were a total loss. Embers smouldered and the night's blackness closed around them. Torches were lit and the villagers, under the watchful eyes of his exhausted but elated sailors, began dragging the bodies of dead Dutch soldiers to a pit being dug on the edge of the village.

One wounded soldier was found unconscious and added to the prisoners taken after the ambush. Takeda counted twenty-three dead Dutchmen and suspected another ten or so had managed to get away. Nearly thirty-five villagers had been killed or badly wounded but Takeda felt no remorse. They had brought it on themselves, he thought.

At dawn he inspected the damage thoroughly, then turned his attention to the villagers being gathered before his door. A nose-twisting odour emanated from the burnt thatch and particularly from the hut used to store grain. The Dutch prisoners had been started for the coast at first light under heavy guard for interrogation, further depleting his strength. But their information might prove vital.

The radio operator, grinning from ear to ear, brought him a message. The Dutch had today surrendered the East Indies and instructed all Dutch forces to cease resistance at once. A second told him that they would be relieved by the army the following day. Takeda crumpled the two notes, amused at the workings of fate.

He watched from the verandah as his sailors prodded the villagers into line. The house had been cleaned, the walls and floor scrubbed and the fire damage repaired. A lingering odour of burned wood and cloth filled the place, but then he would not have to use it much longer.

The men and women who had dug the grave were being led towards him at bayonet point. The air was thick with fear and Takeda meant to keep it that way. He had tried to appeal to their sense of nationalism, had tried to instil respect for the Imperial Japanese forces who had bought their freedom at terrible cost to their own lives. Now he would instil fear to ensure their cooperation.

The Dutch arms had been gathered and stacked on the porch under guard. Takeda sauntered over to inspect the usual assortment of bolt action rifles, revolvers, bayonets and knives, while allowing the tension to build. Two rifles caught his attention. Both had slender barrels and short wooden stocks. The midsection of each was large, round and contained a sheet-metal door. The stampings on the receiver were in English – Johnson Automatic Model of 1941, Made in Providence, R.I., U.S. – which surprised him. Had the Dutch purchased American weapons? The rifle seemed heavy and the fat midsection, at the point of balance, made it awkward to carry.

He pushed the door in and saw several cartridges nestled inside. When he cocked it to chamber a round, the bolt did not lock open. Instead, it ran forward, flipping one cartridge out and inserting another in the breech. The rifle was semi-automatic, he thought in surprise – no wonder the Dutch soldier had been able to fire three rapid shots at him!

Takeda turned then to the distasteful task that awaited. The sailors had herded the thoroughly cowed people all together now with shouts and threats that Takeda made no effort to moderate.

The boy captured after the ambush was dragged forward and thrown sprawling in the dust. Jakob Suranyo's voice quavered as he translated the charges against him and only a stern look from Takeda drove him to finish.

Takeda then spoke slowly so that the interpreter could translate. 'Because of this fool,' he indicated the boy, 'good Japanese sailors have died. And people from this village were killed. He has betrayed his Asian heritage,' he shouted, 'to assist the white Dutch oppressor. He sought advancement in the eyes of your former colonial masters at the expense of sixty lives of my men and your neighbours.'

When he paused to catch his breath, the villagers murmured and stared angrily at the boy and Takeda concealed a smile. How easy it was to shift their hatred.

A woman began to wail and tried to push forward but was roughly shoved back. Other women screamed and struck at her and she collapsed in tears. The boy's mother, he suspected.

He faced the villagers. 'Do not,' he said sternly, 'make the mistake of thinking that this boy is alone responsible. All who knew that he and his companion had gone, and did not report it, are guilty as well.' No one dared meet his eyes.

'Under emergency occupation law, I have the power to sentence every person in this village to death for complicity in treason.' The villagers began to surge back with shouts and moans and his sailors waded in with rifle butts and bayonets.

'Instead, every tenth grown man and woman will be shot.' He nodded to Warrant Officer Ueda who began counting. As he did so, sailors ran forward and jerked the people out of line and herded them towards the large grave. The boy was the last, dragged along to join the eleven unfortunates who were huddled together, staring fearfully at the rifles of the grim-faced sailors. Ueda set his expression and turned to him and Takeda saw that he hated what must be done as much as he.

'Who will do hard things? He who must?' Takeda snorted. Hadn't he quoted that in answer to the American more than two years ago in Warsaw? How true it was. The word of this execution would spread throughout the island and many fewer people would die when they understood how useless it was to fight against Imperial Japan and avoid freedom.

He nodded and the shooting began.

Tula Front December 1941 – January 1942

Dogorov left the train in the village of Derovenko, forty kilometres northeast of Moscow. A military policewoman in a grey great coat with the letter P inside a black and red diamond on her sleeve and a brand new PPsh machine pistol slung across her back, directed him to the camp.

A fierce wind drifted snow as he trudged with his duffle bag slung across his back along the barely-visible road which ran across flat, empty fields. Only an occasional stand of trees showed in the frozen mist and the pale ball of the sun was haloed in the pearl sky. After an hour's walk, the camp appeared. Its perimeter was festooned with wire and hard-eyed guards barred his way at the gate. His bag was searched and his papers were examined with care. He was passed through, but the procedure was repeated at the administration centre by a *Starshina*, a sergeant-major, before he was led across a compound to a long barracks constructed of logs.

Inside, he was shown to a curtained door by a corporal who knocked on the frame, pushed aside the green baize and announced Dogorov by name and rank.

An elderly man wearing a colonel's uniform looked up, his annoyance at being interrupted changing to a welcoming smile. He dismissed the corporal and shook Dogorov's hand eagerly.

'It's good you've come,' he said and shouted for the orderly to bring tea. 'Here, make yourself at home. Take off your coat. You must be frozen.'

There was barely room in the cubicle for a desk and two chairs. Dirty, creased manilla folders were stacked everywhere and maps overlapped one another on every bit of wallspace. An antique silver samovar with a cracked spigot stood precariously on one edge of the desk, which was littered with sheets of graph paper containing lists and the familiar calculations of angles of fire and trajectories.

The colonel saw the direction of his glance and smiled. 'My name is Ernst Nicholavitch Lysacker,' he introduced himself. 'They called me out of retirement, temporarily, you understand, in December 1939.' He shook his head with humour. 'We've been terribly short-handed since the regiment was raised this past September.'

A female orderly pushed aside the curtain and without a word handed in mugs of hot tea. When the curtain fell back into place, Lysacker winked and drew out a bottle of plum brandy. He tipped a small measure into both cups, then settled himself to read through Dogorov's folder, muttering whenever he saw something that pleased him.

'You were graduated from Frunz, I see, in 1934. Good, good! And the Dzerzhinsky Military Academy for Advanced Artillery Studies. Excellent. Also, you were in Karelia. I was further north, at Petsamo. Oh, the Finns gave us a time, I admit.'

When he came to the section of Dogorov's file detailing his escape from the German encirclement at Brest and Kiev, his good humour faltered. He closed the cover and studied Dogorov for a moment.

'I will be frank with you, Captain Dogorov. I am worried about your experiences in the Ukraine. You have been cleared, of course, by the Army but not by the security organs. There may be further difficulties.'

Dogorov listened nervously, wondering what excuse Lysacker would use to dismiss him. 'I don't understand, Colonel? As you say, I've been cleared. I did not surrender my command at Brest and I fought my way out of Kiev. What more could be asked?'

Lysacker said nothing for a moment. 'Please do not misunderstand me. I do not doubt that you are a patriotic and loyal officer. But our regimental Commissar, Colonel Lev Raiken, is a bear for propriety. He is also, if I may say so, a bit of a fanatic. Your predecessor is serving a ten-year sentence because Colonel Raiken found evidence of sabotage and obstructionism. Oh,' he waved a hand dismissively, 'the evidence was sound, if minuscule. No doubt about that. I tell you this only because I am concerned with the smooth functioning of our artillery regiment.' He hesitated for a moment, then smiled. 'I'll take a chance. You've no idea how badly we need a trained artillery officer.'

Dogorov was relieved, if dismayed. The commissars had gained so much power since the start of the war! At the same time, he felt a growing anger. Would he never be allowed to perform his duties? Must he always have to defend himself against unwarranted accusations? But he knew the answer to that as well as anyone.

Following his interview with the colonel, an orderly led Dogorov across the compound to a barracks reserved for officers, a frame building sided with clapboard and swirling with draughts. The floors were split yellow pine, sloppily fitted and half covered with sacking rugs.

Each officer shared a cubicle, a smallish room three by four metres and containing two narrow cots, a single chair, a shared bureau and washbasin. Wire hooks served as a closet. The window was solid with frost. What luxury, he thought. At Brest he had been quartered in a barracks with two hundred other officers.

A young man with a shock of dark, curly hair and a large nose looked up when Dogorov pushed aside the curtain. Dogorov dropped his duffle bag and nodded to the other officer as he stood and extended a hand.

'You must be the replacement officer for Battery C. My name is André Smirnovitch Sinhovsky, Captain. I command Battery A.'

Dogorov hesitated, then shook hands. Sinhovsky immediately cleared papers and books from the other cot which he had been using for a desk. 'We didn't expect you so soon,' he grinned. 'I hope you managed a ride from the station? It's a long, cold walk today.'

'It was . . .' Dogorov loosened his greatcoat but did not remove it. The entire building was icy cold in spite of the glowing stove he had seen in the hall. He unpacked his duffle bag, shook out and hung up his spare uniform.

'We are short on orderlies at the moment,' Sinhovsky said. 'There are eight of us sharing old Subarov. Poor soul, he's rushed off his feet, but he's a good-natured grandad and does his best.'

'I'm sure,' Dogorov replied, and if Sinhovsky caught the superior inflection, he ignored it and launched into a brief account of himself.

'I knew that war was coming, so I thought if I joined up as an officer, I might stand a better chance of surviving. I hoped to attend flying school since I belonged to a flying club in Moscow, but with its usual perverseness, the army sent me to artillery school.

'But then perhaps it was all for the best,' he sighed. 'I had a dear friend who became a pilot. The Hitlerites shot him down on the first day of the war. It was a crime to send them up in those ancient I-35s against so fine an aircraft as the Messerschmitt 109. I have another friend who is a navy pilot. He flew in the first bombing raid on Berlin, in August,' Sinhovsky said proudly. 'But he too was killed, only last month.'

Dogorov tried to shut his ears to Sinhovsky's monologue. There were too many things he needed to think about without having to listen to a talkative Jew.

The curtain whipped aside. A thin man with a hawk-like face and eyes stared in at him. His collar patches lacked gold lace and he wore the five pointed red star of the political commissar on his sleeve. For a long moment, he studied Dogorov.

'I am Colonel Lev Raiken,' he said in a hoarse voice. 'I understand you have just joined our regiment.' Raiken was obviously not enamoured of the niceties of politeness. 'I have just read your file. You were behind the Hitlerite lines?'

Dogorov nodded. 'Yes sir. We were on manoeuvres when the Hitlerites . . .'

'No doubt,' Raiken murmured, dismissing the story with a wave. 'You also escaped encirclement at Kiev?'

This last was not so much a question as an accusation and Dogorov struggled with a surge of anger before nodding meekly. 'That is correct Comrade Colonel.'

'Hmmm. How very lucky for you. Do your duty, Captain Dogorov, for Russia and the party, and we will get along.' Raiken stared at him then disappeared as abruptly as he arrived.

Dogorov sank onto the cot, trying to maintain a composed expression while burning inwardly at the man's insulting behaviour. Raiken's ill-concealed hostility was frightening. He thought when he received this posting that the threat of prison camp was behind him.

'*Swollich*, bastard,' Sinhovsky muttered under his breath. He did not meet Dogorov's eye immediately but instead jumped up and glanced through the curtain. 'Let me tell you something about Colonel Lev Raiken,' he whispered. Surprised, Dogorov stared at him.

Sinhovsky spoke quietly so that Dogorov could barely hear. 'In October, we were north of Volokoamsk. One day we received orders to lay down a box barrage on a certain map reference, beginning at 0700 hours.

We opened fire on schedule and Colonel Lysacker arrived at my battery, with Lev Raiken in tow, just as the counter-battery fire began. It was plain to me that our brave commissar did not like to be so near the front. We took several rounds very close and in fact one killed a gunner in your Battery B. My friend, Sergi Belenko was standing beside me. He drew my attention to our fearless commissar and I saw that his pants were wet at the crotch. Later, he wrote an anonymous poem and pinned it to the mess bulletin board, but someone must have ratted on him.

'Raiken got even last month by accusing Sergi of conspiring with the enemy. The charges were false but Raiken got two enlisted men – both Komsomol spies – to swear to them. Colonel Lysacker did not know the whole story and so took Raiken's charges and so-called proof at face value. Sergi was lucky he got a tenner instead of being shot. So you watch your step.'

Dogorov drew a deep breath. So that was the kind of man he was dealing with. A fanatic and a weakling who could not bear ridicule – or even the thought of ridicule.

A week after his arrival, Dogorov received a post card from Vera – one of the government-furnished kind with printed messages to tick off and barely enough space for a line or two of handwriting. It said only that she could be reached through a post office box address in Moscow. In other words, her hospital had finally been transferred beyond the Urals. Dogorov had expected the news yet it still left him with the feeling of once again being cut off from everyone he knew. His mother had disappeared into the hell of Leningrad, his friends in the Third Artillery Regiment were dead, scattered, or in prison, and the only person he knew in Moscow from his childhood was now gone, perhaps forever. The Soviet Union was an immense country and even without the war, the chances that they would ever meet again were remote.

The artillery regiment, composed of two veteran batteries and the rest newly organised from draftees, were completing refit and retraining when Dogorov joined them. A month of rest combined with extensive training had shaken them into a well-disciplined, if largely inexperienced regiment. There had been ample time to winterise equipment and develop tactics to deal with mud, ice and subzero cold. The officers, however, were mostly new replacements – many of the experienced ones who had survived had been sent to form the nuclei of new artillery regiments – and therefore, Colonel Lysacker welcomed Dogorov's expertise and put him to work immediately. Commissar Colonel Raiken did not interfere directly, although he was always ready with a snide or disparaging remark concerning Dogorov's abilities or his loyalty to the Soviet State.

Because of Raiken's interest, the other officers tended to avoid

Dogorov and he did not blame them. Only Sinhovsky – one of the few experienced officers Lysacker had been able to retain – did not mind what the commissar thought; Dogorov's gratitude was tempered by the fact that Sinhovsky was a Jew.

Dogorov did make friends with the three mess girls, and one in particular, a homely, mousey little thing who wore huge spectacles. She was very thin beneath the shapeless padded uniform coat but, occasionally, he caught the subtle scent of soap as she passed.

At first, he felt sorry for her and teased her gently. She responded with shy smiles that transformed her face and soon he found it easy enough to make her laugh. The other officers ignored her in favour of her more outgoing sisters who were always ready to trade insults and coarse jokes. She was known simply as Valenka and one evening Dogorov discovered that she came from a tiny village in the Urals, north of Sverdlosk. She was also exceedingly shy and Dogorov, in an excess of boredom, set himself to draw her out.

Her full name was Valentina Orlova Shemenkova. Her father was a woodcutter and they lived on a collective. She knew only that her great-grandparents had been sent to the Urals for revolutionary activities during the reign of Tsar Alexander II and was intensely proud of the fact. To Dogorov's surprise, she was better educated than he. Her mathematics were only average, as she did not possess any particular talent in that direction, but she was well-versed in history and literature, two subjects of which he knew very little. One evening, she admitted that she wanted to be a writer. After much persuasion, she showed him one of her short stories.

Dogorov agreed to read it as a lark, expecting only a childish essay. In fact, it was about her woodcutter father and his comical dealings with an ignorant official of the lumber collective. Dogorov was certainly not a literary expert, but he could see that the characters were drawn with a discerning eye for human foibles and the language was crisp, sparse and imaginative. He read the story in a single sitting and praised it inordinately, to Valenka's pleased embarrassment.

Dogorov discovered an almost paternal urge to protect Valenka from the coarseness of the military camp and the officers' mess, which to his surprise was reciprocated. Valenka made a pretence of arranging the silver at his table one evening while she whispered that she had overheard Colonels Raiken and Lysacker arguing about him that afternoon.

'Comrade Raiken wants to arrest you while he conducts a new investigation of your background. But Colonel Lysacker refused to agree as there was no new evidence,' she said.

Realising that she must have listened outside Lysacker's cubicle, he protested in alarm. 'Valenka, you could be shot as a spy if they found out! I'm grateful for what you did, but I forbid you to take such a risk again.'

Valenka poured coffee into his cup. Dogorov, without thinking, took her free hand just as Raiken entered the room. Dogorov saw him from the corner of his eye and managed to contain his start of guilt. Valenka's body was turned in such a way that Dogorov was certain that Raiken had not seen that he was holding the girl's hand.

Rules against fraternisation between officers and enlisted personnel were as strong in the Red Army as in any other although, at the front, the practice among officers of taking a front wife – an enlisted female servant or orderly, or even a female officer – as mistress, was winked at. But this was not the front and excessive concern on his part could make trouble for her, could even result in her transfer.

Dogorov released her hand quickly and picked up the cup. After one sip, he put it down. 'Next time you bring me coffee,' he snapped, 'see that it's hot.' He did not dare look up but turned back to his newspaper. He heard her gasp and dart away and he knew she thought she had offended him with her gabble.

He felt Raiken's eyes on him and only by a great exercise of will, did he prevent himself from looking in his direction.

On the second of December, a German motorised unit in a sudden thrust penetrated the city limits of Moscow. A small but fierce battle was waged in a churchyard before the Hitlerites were driven back. Someone noted that the towers of the Kremlin were just visible from the church steps when the heavy cloud cover cleared momentarily. *Red Star,* the army newspaper, carried a photograph of a burning scout car and the bodies of three dead German soldiers. They formed the gruesome high water mark of the German offensive against Moscow.

Rumours from the occupied areas spoke of starvation, of forced labour and cruelty beyond imagining. All infractions of Hitlerlite rules it seemed were punishable by death. Reprisals for partisan actions often involved the massacre of entire villages. One rumour that sped through Moscow concerned a village in the Ukraine. The entire population of 156 souls – men, women and children – were said to have been driven into the church which was then set on fire. Anyone trying to escape was shot. It was said that screams could be heard for hours.

Leningrad had become a place of horror. Tales of mass starvation were given credence by a government-drive to raise food and warm clothing for the citizens of the besieged city – this in Moscow, itself on starvation rations. Dogorov had had no news of his mother since the chance telephone call in August, nor had anyone at the Food Nutrition Ministry in Moscow been willing to give him any information. His only comfort was that, as an official, she would not starve.

The few bits of good news came only from the south where Soviet forces had counterattacked and driven the Nazis out of Rostov. Everywhere else along the five thousand kilometre front, the Germans were pushing ahead or holding their gains of the summer and autumn. Only in the far north did the Karelian front seem stable – and that because the Finns were content with having regained territory lost two years before.

On 6 December Dogorov woke earlier than usual and, while Sinhovsky snored on, he dressed and trotted across to the mess hall, swearing at the bone-biting cold. As early as it was, Valenka was already setting out cups and saucers and from the kitchen he heard the clatter of dishes and pans and smelled bacon frying. This was a good opportunity, he thought, to explain why he had cut her off so sharply a few days before.

Valenka brought him a cup of coffee and said in a hesitant voice, 'Good morning, comrade . . .'

A blast of sound over the loudspeakers cut her off. '*Vnimaniye! Vnimaniye!*' An excited voice ordered all officers to assemble in the mess hall in ten minutes and the radio went silent again. Valenka set the coffee pot down and darted away without a word. She was back moments later with a tray piled high with slices of bacon, fried bread, a large bowl of porridge covered with yellowish cream and even a fried egg.

'Eat it quickly,' she whispered breathlessly, 'before the others arrive.'

Dogorov squeezed her hand and began to eat. Quick thinking on her part! If for some reason they should be ordered to move out immediately, the others might have to do with a cold breakfast!

He had just finished the egg and bacon when Colonel Lysacker appeared, followed by a moment later Raiken, who scanned the room with a grim expression. The other officers of the regiment poured in quickly, taking seats and shouting for tea or coffee. The three mess girls scurried about, breathless with exertion.

As soon as they were all assembled, Lysacker pulled a chair to the centre of the room, climbed up and announced that the long-awaited Red Army offensive had begun.

'This morning at 0500 hours, our soldiers swept forward on all fronts against the Hitlerite positions! Our first reports speak of surprising gains.'

Loud and prolonged cheers swept the room and voices demanded to know how soon the regiment would move up to the front. Lysacker cooled them abruptly with the announcement that there were no orders as yet.

'The Forty-Second Regiment will remain in reserve for the time being,' he said in a voice devoid of all emotion. He stepped down from the chair and Commissar Raiken, his face unusually flushed, began a long, confused speech about duty, honour and the inevitability of a Soviet triumph under the leadership of the party. In keeping with the new line, he did not mention Comrade Stalin once but emphasised the collective nature of the party leadership.

During those first weeks of December, Dogorov fretted and paced as did the other officers and men of the regiment. Tempers grew short and sullen as they saw their chance to strike a death blow at the Hitlerites slipping away. The Siberian units – they had seen their advance guard on 7 November – moved past their camp in long lines of lorries and horse-drawn carts crammed with white-clad soldiers, skis roped to roofs.

Now, as then, Dogorov watched them pass with an uneasy feeling. The Japanese had proved a tenacious and fierce enemy in early 1939 and now, after three years, they would be immeasurably stronger. With the major portion of the Soviet power occupied in the west, there was little to prevent the Japanese from stabbing Russia in the back in support of their Hitlerite allies. As the flow of Far Eastern divisions continued, Dogorov guessed at Stalin's desperation. More than anything else, those endless lines of trucks and sledges told him how close Russia was to the final disaster.

On the third day of the offensive, the usual programme of martial music on Radio Moscow was interrupted. A voice announced a message of importance would shortly be broadcast. The familiar metronome began to tick and moments later a new voice read out a government statement that Japanese naval and air forces had destroyed the American Pacific naval fleet at its base in the Hawaiian Islands, a place called Pearl Harbor. The music resumed and everyone glanced surreptitiously around to see how they were supposed to take the news. What did it mean, Dogorov wondered? Certainly, the Americans were now free to help the British, but in the Pacific, thousands of miles away. And American hatred of the Soviet system was too well known to expect them to give any help.

So, when the announcement came on 11 December that Germany had also declared war on the United States, Dogorov took that as a sign that the Americans were being pushed into the European war against their will. The fact that the Americans 'had extended a fraternal hand of alliance to Soviet Russia', did little to modify his opinion. What did surprise him was just how great had been Stalin's gamble. He must have denuded the Far East of *Siberyaks* – troops stationed in the Siberian provinces. Had he known of the impending Japanese attack on the United States? In any event, it was clear enough that there would be no Japanese attack against the Soviet Union. She would be far too busy with the Americans.

The new winter offensive infused hope, Dogorov sensed. Beginning on

11 December, there came a great outpouring of propaganda broadcasts in which the progress of Soviet troops was announced from day to day, something so unprecedented that everyone wondered if the government had not lost its collective mind.

The main counterattack had been delivered against the centre of the Hitlerite line about Moscow and the gains had been impressive. Already Soviet forces had reached Stalinogorsk and the Germans were reported to be falling back in disarray. The officers' mess buzzed with speculation; the majority favouring the theory that the Germans had been weakened both by the speed of their advance and by the sudden onset of sub-zero cold and blizzards. Their own Russian counterattack was spear-headed by the Siberian divisions to whom the Moscow winter must have seemed spring weather.

By the middle of the month, Red Army forces had reached Klin and Kalinin. All along the line, the pressure on the enemy was severe and unrelenting. The radio announced that in the north, around Leningrad, the Hitlerite forces had been pushed back beyond Tikhvin and the Germans were said to be retreating. But as no announcement concerning the relief of the city was made, Dogorov's fears for his mother were hardly eased.

Training intensified. Two- and three-day field problems were the norm. Titbits of news were snatched eagerly from the radio or *Red Star* and every time they returned to camp the questions flew fast and thick.

On 24 December, Dogorov's battery stumbled into camp at the end of their third three-day field problem in two weeks. As soon as their equipment was cleaned and stored away, Dogorov dismissed the battery and went to the baths. The attendant gave a grunt of sympathy as he helped him peel away his filthy winter uniform and Dogorov collapsed gratefully onto the bench and motioned for the fire to be stoked. Since there was no one else in the bath house, no one argued with him over whether or not it was too hot.

An hour later, bathed, shaved and dressed in a clean uniform, he squinted at the snow-laden sky as he trudged wearily across to the mess for coffee and food. It was past the usual dinner hour but he had hopes that Valenka would be on duty and could get him a bite to eat.

The mess was almost empty as most of the regiment was still out on various field problems and Sinhovsky's cot did not appear to have been slept in the previous night. With surprise, he noted a decorated Christmas tree in the corner. Whatever in the world had induced Commissar Raiken to approve that decadent religious symbol?

Valenka came in with coffee and a tremulous smile and he winked at her. She relaxed visibly then and he suddenly realised that he still had not explained why he had dismissed her so abruptly that night – was it really as long ago as three weeks? His anxiety over the offensive had driven all else from his mind, plus the fact that he had barely seen her since, because of manoeuvres.

As he ate the warmed-up stew she found for him, the mess began to fill with those regimental officers still in camp. A discussion immediately started about the offensive and soon moved to the war in general. When the discussion reached the role of the United States, opinion seemed to be evenly divided between those who felt the Americans would exert little or no effect on the course of the war and those who held that she would tip the balance between the contending forces.

Dogorov was tempted to voice his own opinion in line with the former view. It was plain enough that war would be fought and decided here on Russian soil, not in the Pacific Ocean, or even in Western Europe. They could expect no more help from the Americans, he thought, than they had received from the British. After all, what were the British doing after two years of war – chasing about the North African desert with a few divisions while Russia bled whole armies from the heart. Why should capitalists pay more than lip service to any such alliance? Just as he was moved to say something, he saw Raiken enter the room and take a seat near the door where he would not be noticed but could hear everything being said.

Better to keep one's mouth shut, Dogorov told himself. The party had not established the line to take regarding American participation. Dogorov saw Raiken's eyes moving from speaker to speaker, categorising each for later consideration.

On New Year's Eve day, Dogorov received a letter from Vera from which the postmark and return address had been cut away by the censor. Dogorov read it through, puzzled at her tenuous tone until he realised that she must have written it before leaving Moscow. Even so, he recognised that she too had guessed that their chances of ever seeing one another again were almost non-existent. In three pages there was no endearment more intimate than *Dorogo*, dearest, nor did she once refer to the hours they had spent making love.

In all honesty, Dogorov had to admit that he had not committed himself either. Thinking back, it seemed as if both had unconsciously agreed that living together was nothing more than an interlude in which they had supplied one another with sex and mutual comfort. He shrugged and tossed the letter into the stove as he passed.

In the hour before dinner, the mess was deserted. Like himself, most other officers were finishing reports or out on field problems. Valenka was not on duty, which was just as well with him. He was in no mood to talk to anyone. A mess attendant brought a bottle of vodka and a glass. He felt a strong urge to get drunk tonight and New Year's Eve provided a perfect excuse. He was surprised that his thoughts kept returning to Vera

Everything was a myth, he told himself. The superiority of Stalin's leadership, the dedication of party, government and military officials and even what he thought of as his love for Vera. Damn her! If he got drunk enough, maybe he wouldn't think about her.

The mess began to fill as others wandered in. Most nodded a greeting but no one sat at his table. Dogorov, by now in a fine state of maudlin self-pity, did not mind; they were all afraid of Commissar Raiken, which was perfectly understandable.

Valenka appeared from the kitchen, pulling a long white apron over her uniform. She smiled at him and began to set tables for dinner. Dogorov knew she was watching him but ignored her. He had finished more than half the vodka and the dingy, white-washed room had begun to recede and he was happy. After all, hadn't he proved useful to the State once again? For the moment it did not matter what Commissar Raiken thought of him. Once Valenka passed his table but his forbidding expression turned her away.

A plate was set before him and he pushed the food about with his fork. As the evening drew on, the radio began to play music and several officers danced with one another. Dogorov was not aware of it, but Raiken wandered past several times, sharp eyes measuring. Once he stopped beside the table and spoke. Dogorov, not knowing and not caring who it was, muttered a reply and turned away. Valenka, watching from the kitchen, saw Raiken's face flush with anger.

Just before midnight Dogorov suddenly felt nauseated. He pushed himself up and stumbled to the door. No one paid him any attention, even Raiken who had cajoled one of the other mess attendants onto his lap and was shouting out a chorus of *Stenka Razin* with the rest.

The cold air braced him for a moment but he stumbled going down the icy steps. Somehow, Valenka was kneeling beside him, holding his shoulders as he vomited. Afterwards, he cleaned his mouth with snow and she helped him to stand. Half supporting, Valenka led him across the parade to the barracks and guided him down the stuffy hall to his own cubicle. The building was utterly silent and, for a change, almost warm. He dropped onto the cot, one hand over his eyes, mouth open and Valenka thought for a moment that he had fallen asleep. As she turned to go, Dogorov muttered and she bent over to hear better.

He patted the side of the cot and without hesitation she sat down. 'Valenka . . . I did not mean to speak so harshly . . . night you warned me . . . Raiken. He was watching us . . . I meant to tell you before . . .'

His voice trailed away as Valenka felt her heart bound; the incident had puzzled and depressed her. A dozen times she had castigated herself for her stubborn feelings for this man who seemed so mixed-up and full of self-pity. There were others who could offer her far more, and were ready to, including both regimental commanders. The war was a godsend to a poor girl like herself and she should be taking advantage of it.

Without thinking of the consequences, she smoothed the long, untrimmed hair from his forehead and kissed him lightly. Dogorov touched her cheek and returned the kiss. For a moment, she was conscious of the sour taste of vomit on his lips, but then a burst of emotion deep inside her threw every other consideration into limbo. With only the briefest hesitation, she pressed against him.

His lips opened and she felt the tentative touch of his tongue. Without experience in sexual matters, she was so surprised that her lips opened involuntarily. His tongue swept into her mouth and she shuddered. Dogorov fumbled the buttons of her tunic open and touched her breast. Valenka did not know how it happened, but her jacket and blouse disappeared and he was pulling off her boots and trousers.

Moving gently, Dogorov kissed her breasts and stomach. She had long speculated about sex and men with girl friends at home, but as all were as inexperienced as she, it seemed they had got much of it wrong. And search as they had in the local library, there were no books to guide them. She had listened to her army comrades describing the men they had engaged in sex with but the coarseness and anatomical details had repelled her. Never had anyone said a word about the feelings that raged through her body now, at once frightening and reassuring, painful and so pleasurable that she could not control her response.

A trace of moonlight filtered through the frosted window and he saw her dark eyes watching him. He kissed her again gently and pushed deeper. She cried out but he smothered her sobs with his mouth.

Dogorov could not believe his own audacity. If he hadn't been drunk... he had never before taken such liberties with a woman. Afterwards, he thought how wrong he had been about her. When her clothes were stripped away, he saw that she was far from thin. Beneath the bulky winter clothing was concealed a perfectly proportioned figure. Her breasts were full and rounded, almost pear-shaped with pink, well-defined nipples – Vera's had been dark and bloated. Her hips were slim but soft and swelled gently from waist to thigh. And the freshly scrubbed smell of her was as much an aphrodisiac as the sight of her body. How she managed to stay so clean he could not guess.

The following day, New Year's Day, Valenka was off duty until the evening. They walked in the still forest, arms about one another, and talked. They decided to keep their affair secret until they reached the front, but even so Dogorov felt a stab of anxiety. Sooner or later Raiken would again attempt to arrest him. If he succeeded, Valenka might be implicated as well.

He glanced at her from the corner of his eye, trying to conceal his concern. Valenka's cheeks were alive with the frost and her lips bruised and full after their night of lovemaking. Her eyes were shadowed and sleepy and he felt a stirring within him that was more than the need for sex. He puzzled it out and concluded with surprise that it was similar to the protectiveness he felt for his mother.

Vera was self-sufficient enough, he thought, to make her own way in any situation. But Valenka, while willing, was not as strong. He doubted she possessed the strength to survive under front conditions and the thought of her in a prison camp made him sick to his stomach.

They found a woodcutter's hut above a small stream that twisted and turned a frozen path through the forest. Inside, it was dry and firewood was stacked beside the stove. Giggling like children, they built a fire and, as the hut warmed, Dogorov spread his greatcoat on the floor for a mattress.

'*Snovym godom,* Happy New Year,' she whispered.

Dogorov laughed. '*Snovym schastyem.* Are you superstitious?' he asked. 'My mother used to say that you would spend the rest of the year with whomever you were with on New Year's Eve.'

Valenka smiled. 'Good!'

They spent the afternoon in contented lovemaking. After weeks of artillery practice, the utter stillness of the forest was soothing. Pearlescent winter light diffused among the leafless trees to create a ghostly twilight and darkness had crept among the trees before they realised the day had ended.

The regiment spent two more weeks in reserve before orders came for them to move into the line east of Tula. Dogorov had anticipated this day for months. The sense of impending moment, the knowledge that he was at long last going into battle as part of a regular army command infused him with satisfaction and well-being and gave him a renewed lease on self-respect. Even Raiken seemed to have lost interest in him, ignoring him since New Year's Eve, perhaps accepting his innocence at last. Dogorov had even come to blame the delay in reassignment on Army bureaucracy. After all, they had to keep track of ten million men and women!

The regiment's lorries formed a single long column on the frozen roads and they had been driving for fourteen hours when it began to snow just at 1800, reducing their speed to a snail's pace. The world, already circumscribed by darkness, closed in as swirling meteorites of snow pelted the windscreen. Dogorov had just drifted off to sleep when he was jolted against the dashboard as the lorry stopped abruptly. The regiment had only converted in mid-November from horses to vehicles and most of the drivers, former teamsters, had not yet mastered the simultaneous use of brake and clutch.

Swearing under his breath, Dogorov used his shoulder to bang the door open and jumped down without a word to the half-frozen driver. Battery C had been placed second from the end of the column. He was tired of jolting along in the lorry and was glad of any excuse to stretch. And besides, there was the possibility of seeing Valenka who was in a supply lorry somewhere ahead.

Abruptly, he came on a lorry nose down in a drainage ditch. The road ahead was empty as far as he could tell in the swirling darkness.

Flashlights gleamed as soldiers attached a cable to the following lorry and a man slithered down the bank to wrap it around the axle of the disabled truck. An angry security sergeant stood by, swearing at everything and everyone. Both lorries engaged reverse gear and a dozen soldiers strained for footing at sides and tailgate. Several more ran up with pine branches and thrust them under spinning wheels.

The wheels of the lorry still on the road caught and it began to hump backwards, drawing its disabled partner up like a pre-historic monster from the ditch. Its rear wheels gained the edge of the bank, caught and the lorry backed out under its own power.

The security sergeant ran to the cab, yanked the door open and shouted for the driver to get down. An officer also wearing security insignia materialised. He nodded to Dogorov and listened as the sergeant made his report.

'This *swollich*,' he hooked a thumb at the driver, 'fell asleep and ran off the road, Comrade Lieutenant.'

The driver's face was pale and he was shaking so badly he had to lean against the lorry. Blood had run down the side of his face from a deep gash before congealing in the intense cold.

The officer turned to Dogorov. 'We must get the column under way again, Captain,' he snapped and nodded at the trembling driver.

Dogorov nodded curtly. 'Take care of it now.'

The lieutenant shouted and the sergeant swung his machine pistol butt up into the driver's midsection and kicked him hard as he doubled over, gasping with pain. He continued to kick the terrified boy to the side of the road. Dogorov shouted for a new driver and when he ran up, ordered him to turn the headlights on full. Trees leapt from the darkness and they were all momentarily blinded. The sergeant checked the magazine of his machine pistol and motioned for the hapless driver to stand in front of the ditch so that the light was full on him. The soldier stumbled into place, one hand up to shield his eyes from the glare, the other out as if he could forestall the bullet. The sergeant fired once and the boy slumped as if suddenly very tired and the headlights went out. Dogorov shouted for the column to get moving.

As each lorry drove past, the sergeant stood with his flashlight shining down on the dead man – a warning to other drivers not to jeopardise the offensive. Falling asleep at the wheel was sabotage and sabotage was punishable by immediate execution. When the life of the nation was at stake, there could be no allowance for individual weakness. As his own lorry came abreast, Dogorov jumped aboard and noticed with grim humour that his own driver was doubly alert.

The regiment reached their assigned position at midnight. A fierce wind had sprung up to sweep the fresh snow into an abrading ground blizzard against which Dogorov struggled with head bent to position each gun, then supervised the fusing of shells and the laying of telephone lines. He also reminded each gun commander to watch for signs of frostbite among his gun crew. There was no excuse for frostbite; covering all exposed skin, wrapping the extremities with loose cloths and wearing felt *valenki* overboots, to keep feet dry, were simple and effective precautions.

Frostbite was a serious offence. If negligence was the cause, the offender was transferred immediately to a *strafny*, a punishment battalion, where he could expect the minimum of medical treatment since he hadn't much longer to live in any event. *Strafny* redeemed themselves by leading assault waves against fixed positions, manning machine guns in the face of overwhelming enemy assaults or by attacking tanks with dynamite or gasoline bombs strapped to their bodies. *Strafny* also cleared enemy mine fields by the simple expedient of marching shoulder-to-shoulder across mined areas. New regulations also decreed that an officer who allowed excessive frostbite cases in his command was to be court martialled and shot.

Colonel Lysacker called all officers to his tent for a pre-dawn briefing. He unrolled a large-scale map of the area and pinned it to his field desk. 'This, gentlemen, is our operational area. We are instructed to bombard enemy positions beginning at exactly 0700 hours. We will fire a fixed pattern on the following points.' He reeled off a list of coordinates and assigned batteries to each. 'We will not fire registration shots in order to preserve surprise, so we can expect heavy counterbattery fire immediately. It is only fair to tell you that our predecessors, the 103rd Regiment, were not so much withdrawn as wiped out in a similar action two days ago.'

Lysacker produced a bottle of vodka and poured a measure of the spirit into a dozen glasses that stood ready on his desk. He motioned the officers to help themselves and Colonel Raiken gave the toast to the Red Army. Lysacker nodded and continued.

'The infantry attack will begin at 0730 hours.' He pointed to a series of lines on the map that dipped into a heavily forested area less than half a kilometre from the Russian front line. 'The Hitlerites are dug in throughout the forest. We will shift coordinates at exactly 0725 hours to open narrow lanes through the mine fields.'

Dogorov saw that their fire would fall just ahead of the first line of trenches and any mistiming would have disastrous results for the infantry. He shivered slightly, very glad that he was in the artillery.

'The second infantry wave will follow as soon as the trenches are secured. If the first wave fails, the second wave will secure the trenches and the third wave will move up in support. And so on until they succeed. The Hitlerites are known to be particularly strong here and equipped with winterised gear.' Indeed, the map showed that the Forty-Second Regiment had been placed at the exposed tip of a narrow salient thrusting well into the German front lines. The Germans would be expecting just such a blow as they were preparing to deal, Dogorov thought, and it was entirely possible that, in addition to counterbattery fire, they could expect a tank assault.

'It should be obvious that this is a pivotal point in the offensive. If we succeed, we will have turned the Hitlerite flank and with luck, we might even unhinge their position in this sector. Are there any questions?

From time to time during Lysacker's monologue, Dogorov was uncomfortably aware that Raiken was watching all of them through slitted eyes, but when the commissar raised a cigarette to his lips Dogorov saw that his hand was shaking. Twice, Raiken's glance had rested on him for uncomfortably long periods. He felt a surge of fear; why after two weeks was Raiken paying attention to him again? Had he discovered his affair with Valenka? Raiken was obviously frightened this near to the front and a frightened man was doubly dangerous. He remembered Sinhovsky's remarks about the officer he had replaced, the one the commissar had sent to prison for a tenner...

Daylight was limited to about seven hours at this time of year – 0800 to 1500 hours. Working in temperatures that had dropped to forty degrees of frost, Dogorov had driven his men to establish the battery position so that by 0600 hours he was ready to run his observation posts as close into the Hitlerite lines as possible. Unfortunately, the ground was level and heavily forested and afforded the observers little advantage. He expected no opportunity for independent fire, but it was best to be prepared.

He drew a deep breath and experienced the mixture of elation and fear he had come to know so well in Finland. The elation stemmed from the fact that his entire professional training from age twelve on had been directed towards just such moments as these and that he was once again a part of the vast Russian military machine whose task was to protect the land against all enemies. The fear was as much due to the prospect of personal failure as it was to the possibility of being killed or maimed.

The four batteries of the Forty-Second Regiment were aligned in an arrowhead formation, pointed directly at the German lines, and Battery C formed the point. Their regiment was aligned with neighbouring regiments in much the same manner so that the entire division could project a concerted mass of flame and steel at the enemy. Providing that every battery registered and fired accurately and that counterbattery fire did not open wide gaps too soon, it would be impossible for flesh and steel to survive their barrage for more than a few minutes. The Hitlerites must either run or die – in theory.

One by one his observation posts and each gun commander checked in until, by 0650, Battery C was ready to open fire. The minutes ground past, the tension increasing.

The barrage began far to Dogorov's right, but a minute early, as an overeager battery commander – or one who had failed to correctly set his watch – opened fire. As the second hand of his father's old hunter swept towards 0700, a mounting crescendo of noise and light moved towards them. Dogorov shouted the order to open fire into the telephone connected to the guns of his own battery just as the second hand touched twelve.

As one, the three 105 millimetre guns jerked against their trails and belched flame and steel projectiles. The gunners bent to the task of reloading and firing again. A sense of elation overwhelmed Dogorov and he stood grinning like a fool, ears covered with mittened hands as the guns raged and transmitted their pain through the ground in anguished vibrations. He had taken part in massive bombardments in Finland, notably, the siege of Viipuri, but those had merely been of brigade strength. Here, before Tula, entire divisions of artillery, guns ranging in calibre from the workhorse 76.2 millimetre to the new 122 millimetre Model 1941s, pumped shells into the German lines as fast as the gunners could load and fire.

He huddled behind the sandbagged revetment, telephone headset clamped to his ears, and tried to sort out the tangle of tinny voices. Observers had little to report as their view was still obscured by darkness, by the trees, by roiling smoke along the forest's edge, flares of light, sprays of shrapnel and flaming debris boiling from the conflagration.

The first counterbattery fire came finally at 0715 – we caught them asleep, Dogorov thought grimly. The ranging shots were long and he nearly failed to hear the racketing sound the shells made as they slashed above the trees to explode hundreds of metres to the rear. The winter sky was losing its hard edge and softening with dawn. German aircraft would be aloft soon, he thought – if they weren't already searching for the muzzle flashes of Russian cannon. Dogorov hoped that the Red Air Force was waiting for them.

A tree cracked viciously and its top disappeared as splinters of steel and wood showered the battery. Concussion hammered him, threatening to split his head and he scrambled in the snow, clawing for the earth's shelter. Something icy and abrasive poured down his collar and he twisted in panic, swiping it away, and saw that the sandbags, shredded by shrapnel, had showered him with half-frozen sand.

Another barrage ripped the area and he forgot the sand as choking fumes cascaded over the position. Gas! he thought in panic. Were the Germans using gas? There had been rumours for weeks... He had fumbled his gas mask out of the case before he recognised the sharp, acrid odour of high explosive.

That moment of panic sobered him, reminded him of his responsibilities and sent him running from gun to gun to reassure the crews with his presence. Heat and an acrid stench overwhelmed him and he fell. Tears gushed from his burning eyes and nausea ripped his stomach. His mind was suddenly wrapped in a sticky blanket. Legs and arms refused to work and his skin was covered with something wet and clinging. He tried to brush it away from his face and rapped his own nose hard. The sharp pain brought him to his senses and he wiped his streaming eyes.

Smashed metal, torn trees and earth, a leg ripped from a body and looking rather ludicrous lying by itself in a puddle of reddish slush. The 105 millimetre cannon he had been running towards, together with its crew, had become a smoking black hole half filled with water.

A curious numbness took him; the stench was overpowering and he realised he was sitting in a puddle of mud and snow with a coat sleeve shredded to tatters. Fearfully, he pulled the cloth aside but the skin beneath was untouched.

A sudden spasm of vomiting shook him and afterwards he slumped forward, supporting himself on one arm, gasping for breath and very near to passing out. Only then was he aware that the horrible raging sound of gunfire was gone, even though he could still feel the frozen earth vibrating.

Dogorov pushed himself up with great difficulty. The sky brightened and darkened in strange rhythm as he staggered forward. Tree branches slashed his face and he sat down abruptly, realising that he had been going the wrong way. Something warm tickled his cheek and he brushed at it absently, then got to his feet and started again.

A subsonic roar began and grew in volume. Things about him ran in and out of focus and he had the impression that he was walking several metres above the dipping, swaying ground. A face materialised, mouth working soundlessly. It was joined by another and Dogorov thought hard before he recognised Commissar Raiken. Dogorov's attention narrowed to his fleshy lips before, presently, they too faded from sight.

A great, bushy beard obscured the face looming above him like a swollen moon. He was reminded of a picture he had seen as a child and which belonged to the family of a playmate. They had been religionists and the picture, hung over the stove, showed a stern, elderly man in a long white gown and flowing beard who, his friend told him, was God. But then Dogorov was puzzled by the fact that the upper portion of the figure's face was hidden by a white hood pulled low on his forehead. Does God wear a snowhood, he wondered? A surprisingly gentle hand pressed him back.

'Can you hear me?'

The voice echoed and re-echoed from a great distance. He nodded but whoever it was, God or man, motioned for him to lie still.

A small flashlight shone into Dogorov's eyes and the figure turned his head from side to side to examine his ears. Dogorov felt the pressure of a bandage. When he reached to touch it, his hand was pushed away.

'A small shrapnel wound. A graze. Do not be concerned.' The pain began then, the ultimate assurance that he was indeed alive.

Valenka's face appeared, her expression anxious. He tried to reassure her by nodding, but it hurt too much. When she saw him looking at her, her face blazed with that sudden smile that always startled him by the way it transformed her features.

He found that his ears were clearing of the painful pressure. The doctor asked one or two more questions and packed up his paraphernalia.

'Rest here for an hour, then resume your duties. You were quite lucky. There doesn't appear to be serious damage. But if your headache should become worse or you begin bleeding, lie down immediately and send someone for me.'

When the doctor had gone, Valenka knelt beside the cot and kissed him on the eyes and lips and when Dogorov tried to sit up, she pressed him back. 'You've suffered enough, Mishka.' She used her own pet name for him. 'The doctor ordered you to rest and you must. I've seen concussions before. Too much exertion can cause a brain-storm.'

She moved to a tiny alcohol stove, sifted tea leaves into a tin cup and poured it full of boiling water. Dogorov drank the tea greedily and lay back against the rolled blanket Valenka slipped behind his shoulders. She hovered about, touching him, gazing at him, unable to believe that he was still alive. Dogorov told her that at first he thought the doctor was God and that he had died, making a joke of it and although her emotions threatened to overwhelm her, she forced herself to laugh. Valenka wanted nothing so much as to burst into tears in his arms, then make love to him and at the same time she was so angry that she wanted to beat him, to strike him and scream that he was a fool for risking his life.

Dogorov rested for fifteen minutes and despite Valenka's protests, got up. He clung to the wall, waiting for the narrow bunker to stop swimming and the earth to stabilise. Valenka stood against the table that held the stove, one hand pressed to her mouth as if to force herself to remain silent while he took a few steps up and down the narrow space. His vision was clearing rapidly and the roar in his ears had become a high-pitched whistle that was annoying, but was fading into the upper registers.

He struggled into his greatcoat and bent to kiss Valenka's unresisting lips. Outside, the frozen air and the clear, growing light braced him a bit. He saw by his watch that he had been absent from his battery for forty minutes and he set off at a shambling walk. He passed the site of the destroyed gun five minutes later and the dismembered leg shook him as he scurried on. He was breathing heavily and his heart was pounding by the time he burst through the screen of trees to the next gun in the battery. He was clammy with sweat and needed desperately to rest. The gun was silent. Struggling to focus his eyes, he saw the gun commander holding a bloodsoaked bandage to his head as he argued with someone – Raiken! An unmistakable expression of relief swept the soldier's face as he spotted his battery commander. Raiken turned quickly and Dogorov saw that his eyes were starting and his face twisted into a rictus of fear. He began gabbling as soon as he saw Dogorov, pointing in the direction of the German lines.

Dogorov could hardly understand what the man was saying. He leaned against the cannon's trail and wiped sweat from his face and listened to the commissar's hysterical shouting. A German shell exploded nearby, the physical shock of the concussion stunning in its intensity. The air was thick with fumes and as the crash and roar of guns and exploding shells penetrated his deafness, another shell fell forty metres to their right and a third, beyond that. The Germans were searching back and forth along a line, he knew. Soon they would raise or lower the elevation and repeat the pattern.

Raiken's shouted words gradually began to make sense. He was ordering the battery to pull back. 'The Nazis are counterattacking with tanks!' he screamed. He was so rattled that he had forgotten to refer to the Germans as Hitlerites. 'Our assault has been smashed...'

Dogorov tried to make Raiken understand that was only to be expected. 'As our bombardment,' he shouted above the din, 'destroys their front line positions, their counterbattery fire will increase. We must continue to maintain our fire, otherwise the Hitlerites will...'

But Raiken wasn't listening. He had turned back to the gun crew, screaming; then suddenly conscious that he was nearly incoherent, he swallowed hard and with visible effort, drew himself together. He turned back to Dogorov.

'Captain.' His voice was high-pitched and strained. 'I am giving you a direct order. You *will* pull this battery back, now. I am withdrawing the entire regiment before we are destroyed!' Another flurry of near-German misses punctuated his words and Raiken screamed.

Dogorov stared at him and the gun crew turned away. For an instant he was tempted to obey. If he withdrew the battery, the line would crumble. His excuse would be that he was only obeying orders and Raiken would be blamed and they might shoot the commissar for cowardice. In any event, he would no longer be a threat to Dogorov. But a withdrawal at this moment could very well jeopardise the entire offensive. 'Our orders, Comrade Colonel,' he said twisting the title with contempt, 'require that we remain in the line and continue to fire until relieved or killed.'

'No.' Raiken shook his head violently. 'No, no, no! I am ordering you...'

'Give me that order in writing,' Dogorov shouted, 'countersigned by Colonel Lysacker and I will do so, but not until!'

For a moment, he thought Raiken would dissolve into hysteria but from somewhere the man dredged up a final measure of self-control. He drew a deep, shuddering breath and, for the first time, seemed aware that others were listening. Dogorov pulled him out of earshot.

'Get hold of yourself,' he snapped. 'You are a soldier now and not the general secretary of this or that. Soldiers are paid to die, not to run.' He pushed him towards the trees and the rear and turned back to the battery, dismissing Raiken for the moment. With any luck, he thought, the coward would not survive the battle.

German counterbattery fire was literally shooting them to pieces. Listening to the guns, Dogorov judged that less than half remained in action. Then, one of those unexpected lulls that occur when all guns are reloading at the same time brought the ominous rattling of treads and powerful petrol engines. The German panzers were moving! Where was their damned aircraft? He flogged his battered body and mind to work.

All telephone lines were out – cut by the fierce counterbarrage – both those forward to the observers who were probably dead by now, as well as to the rear and regimental headquarters. Dogorov had no idea if the main thrust of the Hitlerite counterattack would take place against their sector or not, but they were for it in any event. They were less than a kilometre from the trenches and the panzer tanks would zip through what remained of the infantry without pause.

Shells ripped the trees again and the air was filled with splinters, rock, frozen earth, shrapnel and the acid smell of high explosive. A gun blew up in A Battery, two hundred metres away. A black smoke column roiled into the early morning grey sky. The men about him were coughing, some doubled over and vomiting, and in many eyes he saw the same raw fear that had infected Raiken and he knew they were thinking only of the commissar's orders and how they suddenly made excellent personal sense.

The first of the panicked infantry poured from the forest, faces twisted with fear, running blindly. Later he learned that five assault waves had been cut down to a man as they slogged across the snow-covered stubble field towards the woods; five suicidal attacks that merited only a single paragraph in the after-action report, the merest sentence in the battle summary and nothing in the history books. Something over twelve thousand men on both sides died in less than two hours that January morning – twelve thousand more among millions killed and maimed.

In spite of Raiken's order to do so, Dogorov did not run with the infantry; although that morning officers of far greater seniority and experience than he did. Instead, he raced from gun to gun in his battery, pistol in hand, shouting at the gunners, knocking terrified men from the control seats and depressing gun muzzles to point blank range as Siderov had done that first day of the war. He fired the first shot at a Mark III Panzer which materialised in the trees. The shell holed the turret. His second blew it to pieces.

They used their 105 millimetre cannon as anti-tank guns that morning and the four batteries that formed the assault front, with only seven guns still operational, destroyed twelve German tanks and smashed the counterattack.

Only isolated memories remained in his mind afterwards; a gunner twirling the tracking wheel to spin the cannon muzzle onto the target. A gun roaring and in the same instant, a tank erupting in flame as it literally blew inside out. Brilliant sunshine and bone-numbing cold in the clear morning air. Gunners cheering, voices thin in the bright sunshine and sub-zero air. Mutilated bodies everywhere; Red infantry, Hitlerite tankmen, his own artillerists. Yet he kept them at the guns, pounding shell after shell into the trees to explode at random distances, filling the forest with man-killing splinters of steel and wood to decimate Hitlerite infantry following the tanks.

The fierce counterbattery fire was forgotten as they loaded and fired, loaded and fired. A runner was sent back to battalion headquarters to report and bring up more ammunition, the counterbarrage shifted away from them to the rear and finally the counterassault failed and only smashed tanks, flaming wreckage and bodies remained.

He looked at his watch; 1140 hours. My God! he thought, we've been fighting for more than four hours yet it seemed only minutes had passed. He slumped against a splintered tree to regain his breath. He knew that he must reorganise the gun crews, redistribute men to replace killed and wounded for the next attack which would certainly come soon.

There would be heavy preparatory fire first. Could he obtain orders to move the battery back . . . ? Perhaps Raiken had been right after all; perhaps they should have fallen back as he had ordered. But Dogorov knew that would have been the worst course of action to follow. Withdrawal under heavy fire would have necessitated the abandonment of guns and ammunition and would probably have turned into a rout and the death toll would have been far greater in the end. Better to force the men to remain at their positions, at gunpoint if necessary.

Dogorov pushed himself up, staggering with dizziness so that he had to lean against the tree. Double images bothered him and he tasted blood in his mouth. He forced himself to walk along the line, complimenting the men in a restrained manner, speaking to individuals by name, joking and noting exceptional instances of heroism, all the right things an officer was expected to do.

As dusk crept in, Dogorov realised that the Hitlerite counterattack had been broken by his battery's point-blank fire. The attacks that followed were weak and designed only to keep them off balance while the battered defenders withdrew.

But were the Hitlerites pulling back all along the line or just in this sector, he wondered? They had held strong defensive positions all through the December offensive. Why withdraw now?

Apparently, divisional command was of the same opinion as, shortly after dark, another series of infantry assault forces moved up through the regiment into the forest. Grim, silent men ghosted through the darkness directed by soft commands from their officers. They stared at the brooding guns and the haggard artillerymen huddled in sleeping bags and passed by without a word. The dark procession put Dogorov in mind of the fairy tales his mother used to tell him of ghost legions marching to fight the barbaric enemies of the Russian people.

At midnight, he received orders to move his own battery forward one kilometre at dawn. The Hitlerites *were* falling back then! Two lorries, engines snorting in the iron-hard cold, shuffled into the clearing, one towing a replacement 105 millimetre cannon and the other a field kitchen. Hot food, what luxury! Dogorov thought. The cooks lit stoves and were soon ladling out hot stew and *kasha* and gallons of boiling tea.

At 0600 hours, his orderly roused him from the uneasy sleep into which he had fallen. Dogorov unbuttoned his sleeping bag and raised himself on one arm, so groggy that he could not remember where he was. He felt as if he hadn't slept for a month. He rubbed a handful of snow on his face to wake up and got out of the bag, groaning with the pain of cold-induced aches and the return of the rheumatism he had first experienced in Finland. In the distance, he could hear the sharp mutter of German guns. They must be firing to keep our Red Army men awake, he thought.

The night sky was crystal clear. Stars glittered and the air was like frozen metal. He stamped his boots and beat his gloved hands together, wishing that he could have a bath. The communications sergeant snapped on a flashlight and shielded the beam with a bare hand. The man was a peasant from the Archangel region and no matter how cold it got, he never seemed to notice. The light beam illuminated new instructions ordering the battery to move immediately instead of waiting for dawn.

With great difficulty, he restrained a curse. The Germans must be retreating faster than first supposed. Now, if they could only drive the Hitlerites clear back to the border as quickly as their Soviet forces had been thrown eastward! Perhaps the Red Army could repeat the feat of that earlier Russian army in 1815, and drive the invaders into headlong retreat? After all, who could compare Hitler to Napoleon?

But caution was necessary. The Hitlerites could be intending to suck the Red Army deep into the salient before pinching it off to trap three Soviet divisions, a standard German manoeuvre. A dozen times since June they had pulled it off, at Brest, at Zhitomir, at Kiev, at Smolensk and on and on. His regiment's own position, facing to the southeast, lay squarely in the path of any flanking attack – such as the one he had beaten off only this morning. Dogorov studied his map as the battery prepared to move, then convinced his analysis could be right, sent a request for additional support to Colonel Lysacker, pointing out the possibility of a strong flank attack.

Twice, the battery was held up in the dark as engineering parties worked feverishly to clear a road through the thick forest. Shielded headlights cast deep shadows on either side and he sensed rather than saw the smashed tanks and dead bodies, the debris of the previous day's assault.

An engineering senior lieutenant told him that the Hitlerite forward positions gave every indication of having been abandoned on a moment's notice. 'We found papers and maps and even officers' luggage. They made some attempts to destroy their bunkers but,' he shrugged and grinned, 'they built them too well. They even left paraffin stoves behind.' He told Dogorov to warn his men that some of the bodies were probably booby-trapped.

It wasn't often, Dogorov thought as he shone his flashlight about, that one got a look at the damage one's weapons had caused. Whole trees had been sheared off and those still standing were studded with bits of shrapnel. Everywhere twisted steel and human remains were tangled together. His flashlight passed across one dead Hitlerite and he turned away quickly. The man's face and half of the chest had been torn away. The body was so badly mutilated that it was impossible to tell if it had been young, old, blond, dark, male or female.

The order to open fire came again at 0700 hours and the forest vibrated to the howl of an entire artillery division. For the second day, the sky was a cloudless blue bowl. No one heard the high, distant drone of bombers nor the sharp reports of anti-aircraft guns, but the bombs fell wide of their positions and tortured trees flickered in their hellish glow.

There was no time to worry about enemy aircraft. Unless they smashed the German lines open for the infantry to drive forward, they could again expect heavy counterbattery fire as the Hitlerites reestablished their gun positions.

'Tea, Captain Dogorov?'

Startled, Dogorov tried but could not prevent the smile that spread across his face. 'Valenka!'

Two nearby gunners exchanged grins and suddenly found reasons to be elsewhere. Valenka poured hot tea from the huge thermos flask she carried on a strap over her shoulder.

'Valenka, you are not allowed in the front lines . . .'

'I know, Mishka,' she whispered, 'but it is important. Really.'

Dogorov held her gloved hand a moment, then stooped quickly to kiss her. Valenka darted a nervous glance about the clearing and Dogorov laughed as she tried to pull away.

'Listen to me! Listen! Colonel Raiken is coming to arrest you.'

Dogorov grunted in surprise and released her. 'How did you find that out?'

'I overheard him accuse you of cowardice, of trying to run to the rear during the counterbattery fire. The doctor verified that you were in the regimental bunker but was not allowed to say more. Colonel Lysacker had no other choice than to agree.' She glanced towards the trees. 'He was only waiting for the NKVD escort when I slipped away. He could be here at any minute.'

Dogorov's mind whirled in confusion. He had almost forgotten yesterday's incident but, of course, Raiken never would. To conceal his cowardice, the commissar had to arrest him. Even though there were witnesses, who would dare testify on his behalf? Whoever did so would find himself in a prison camp in short order.

'Valenka, you must get away from here.'

She shook her head and backed away but Dogorov grabbed her arm. 'Listen to me,' he hissed angrily. 'Raiken certainly knows about us. He will arrest you if he even suspects you came to warn me.'

'I don't care about that. I want only . . .'

'Damn it, Valenka, I'll need all my wits just to save myself. If you are arrested as well, he will threaten me with your imprisonment, so for my sake, you must go.'

Valenka hesitated in an agony of grief and indecision, then brushed his cheek with cold lips. Dogorov stared after her as she ran into the trees, twisted with sudden loss. He sank onto the camp stool and dragged the position map to him, tea forgotten.

He was suddenly overwhelmed with the same feeling of helplessness he had experienced in the prison camp when called for interrogation. There, it had been emphasised by the single strand of wire that mocked him with the fact that the security organs needed only a symbol to control his fate.

Here the forest mocked him, as poor a barrier as that single strand of wire. A kilometre or so away lay the German lines waiting to welcome an officer-deserter who would provide details of the Red Army artillery dispositions. But desertion to the Hitlerite cause would be far worse than a term in a prison camp. He could never betray his country and party, no matter the provocation.

Colonel Raiken was accompanied by two burly men in full winter uniform, minus snowcovers. Dogorov looked up with what he hoped was an expression of innocence.

'Captain Mikhail Gregorvitch Dogorov, I arrest you in the name of the Soviet State for cowardice and for desertion of your post under fire. Take him,' Raiken snapped. The NKVD agents sprang forward to grab his arms and yank him to his feet. The crew of Battery C stared for a moment then turned away to busy themselves with something else, anything else.

Here and there, Dogorov spotted a contemptuous glance directed at him and realised that even though every member of the battery knew the charges to be false, that in fact it was Raiken who had acted the coward, some were still prepared to believe the commissar because he represented the government! A man has only to be arrested these days to be judged guilty, Dogorov thought – 'Why else arrest him if he weren't guilty?' people would ask. 'Surely the organs have better things to do than arrest innocent people? Where there's smoke there's fire, I always say.'

Dogorov attempted to retain his dignity by shaking off the NKVD men but they clung tenaciously and rather than engage in a wrestling match, he gave in.

'It will do no good to try and run away again, Dogorov,' Raiken barked. 'There is nowhere for you to go, except perhaps to your fascist friends.' No one in the battery was watching now and Dogorov thought that he might as well have ceased to exist.

'You bastard,' Dogorov ground between clenched teeth. 'You're nothing but a self-serving bureaucrat who thinks the Soviet State exists for your benefit only, you filthy swine, you coward...'

Raiken's face went white then red with anger. 'If he says another word, boys, gag the bastard.' Raiken turned away and one of the NKVD men punched Dogorov hard in the kidney to start him moving.

As he lurched forward, Dogorov shouted, 'I'm surprised you found guts enough to come up to the front lines again!' He was rewarded with anonymous laughter from the trees.

The commissar turned and ran at Dogorov who tried to duck but the NKVD men held him stolidly as Raiken hit him several times in the face and kicked at his crotch. Dogorov twisted aside just enough to catch the blow on his thigh but the kick knocked him to one knee. He spat blood from his split lip onto Raiken's boots.

The laughter was louder now and Raiken, suddenly aware that he was being seen beating a helpless man, whirled and without a word hurried towards the rear. The two NKVD men pulled Dogorov up and followed.

When they reached the narrow track the engineers had cut during the night, Dogorov saw that Raiken had a motor car waiting, an old, high-topped saloon. A line of infantrymen moving up to the front eyed them uneasily and Dogorov noticed the young lieutenant's hostile glance. Well, it no longer made any difference, he thought. Raiken did not intend to take him back for trial anyway.

It had never before occurred to him but the security organs were not constrained by Soviet constitutional guarantees and rules of evidence. A bullet in the head and who would care? Not the two NKVD men hurrying him along. Afterwards, if there was any question, Raiken had only to claim that he tried to escape. Who would question a political commissar?

He was shoved into the back of the motorcar and one of the NKVD men climbed in after him. Raiken took the front passenger seat. The motor started with difficulty because of the intense cold and Raiken cursed the driver. His anxiety was becoming so apparent that even the guards were now contemptuous.

The Russian bombardment went on, deafening in intensity as they drove along the muddy, slush-filled track past the burnt-out German tanks and body-collecting details with their graves and the registration clerks laboriously filling out printed cards in pencil for each Red Army body. A pile of Hitlerite bodies, frozen into contorted attitudes, had been stacked beside the road and Russian bodies were piled in the same fashion opposite, so that they formed a gruesome pair of gateposts. Dogorov did not want to think that within the hour he would be one of them.

Raiken urged the driver to greater speed and turned to say something to the other guard in the back. His teeth, yellowed and rotted by years of neglect, were revealed whenever his lips curled – vicious explosions slashed across the road and concussion slammed Dogorov's head against the window. The car swerved into the snow-banked verge, they ploughed a spray of snow and dropped with a sickening thud.

Another explosion burst on top of them and Dogorov was showered with glass. The area boiled with exploding snow and mud, splinters of steel and smoke. Dogorov lay still in the sudden silence that followed, cataloguing the various parts of his anatomy and wondering at the splashes of blood on his greatcoat. He pulled himself upright. The man beside him was hunched against the far door, unconscious or dead, he did not know or care which.

When he tried to open his door he found it was jammed against the ground. The driver was slumped across the wheel and only the back of Raiken's head was visible. The odour of petrol penetrated his nostrils –

petrol! The motor was still running. The shock of the discovery cleared his head immediately. The off-side door beyond the NKVD man was partly open. He crawled across the body and battered the door with his shoulder until it opened enough for him to slip out.

Dogorov dragged himself away; as he reached the slope down which the car had dropped, he heard a scream for help. Gasping for breath, he half-rolled so that he could see the car. Raiken's face was partly visible through the passenger window.

Dogorov clenched his teeth against the pain in his thigh where Raiken had kicked him and staggered back to the car. He could now see that the driver's face had been replaced by a mask of blood where the flesh had been torn away by shrapnel. Raiken saw him, scrabbled at the window and screamed again for help. Dogorov peered in to see that the steering wheel and gear lever had been twisted to one side, entangling the commissar's legs. He reached for the door and heard something sizzle in the engine compartment.

Beneath the engine, raw petrol was pouring in a stream from a broken fuel line. Suddenly, flame whooshed straight up from the engine compartment. Raiken screamed and redoubled his efforts to batter the door open.

Dogorov took a step back, then another; the world began to narrow into a long, dark tunnel focused on the motor car. The flame issuing from the bonnet danced towards Raiken and his screams turned thin and full of terror. Dogorov knew he had only to break the window, bend the gear lever aside and pull him out.

Flames appeared beneath the car following the fuel line back to the tank ... If Raiken died, there would be no charges against him. How many others had Raiken sent to the prison on trumped-up charges so that he could hide his cowardice? He was a disgrace to the party, and to the Army. There was no room for individualists when Russia was fighting for her life, no room for individualists in the party, ever ... he scurried away as the fuel tank blew up with a muted boom.

Flames rushed into the passenger compartment and for an instant he saw Raiken twisting in agony, then he tripped and sprawled in the snow. The sky had darkened, leaving only a pinpoint of light. Heat from the burning motor car swept over him and in the moments before he lost consciousness, he felt warm and comfortable.

On 26 March 1942, as Dogorov was recovering from burns and multiple shrapnel wounds in a Moscow hospital, he was decorated with the Order of Surov. It was then he learned that Colonel Lysacker, promoted to Major-General, had recommended the award for his action in stopping a German counterattack during the Tula Front offensive with point-blank cannon fire, without regard for his own life. But the medal did little to assuage his depression. Valenka had disappeared somewhere in the maelstrom of the Tula Front.

From Across the World Torsten Fredriksson, somewhere on the German Front About Moscow, 8 January 1942 – For immediate release: The German High Command in Berlin, no less than the German Army commanders on the spot about Moscow, have been surprised at the scope and ferocity of the Soviet Winter Offensive. Like everyone else, they had been certain that once winter clamped down, both sides would use the respite to rest and rebuild. But the Soviets are showing no intention of doing so.

After the German drive on Moscow ground to a halt in December, there were numerous probing attacks and small unit actions of the kind every army employs to gather intelligence and keep the enemy off balance. But in early January, Soviet attacks have increased both in number and ferocity and there are reports here of Soviet prisoners taken from divisions thought to have been stationed in the Far East.

Estimates of the total number of Soviet Army divisions made before the Germans embarked on Operation *Barbarossa* were based on the supposition that up to ten per cent of the total Russian population could be called up without doing irretrievable damage to the Soviet economy. From this, it was calculated that Russia had seventeen million men available for military service.

The German High Command to date has reported Red Army casualties for the six months of the war since June 1941 – which one can only accept at face value – to be seven million dead, wounded and captured, which means that more than 150 divisions have been destroyed. To this must be added half a million casualties suffered in Finland in 1939–40. Reliable German sources therefore estimate that the USSR still retains six million in its army, one and a half million in the air force, half a million in the navy and half a million more in reserve. But, as European Russia comprises less than half the Soviet Union, large numbers are needed to garrison Siberia, to guard against a Japanese invasion across the Manchurian border and to serve in supply and logistics capacities. Another million, perhaps?

If accurate, these estimates account for seventeen million Soviet men.

Therefore, it seems inconceivable that the Soviets can produce sizeable strategic reserves, yet where are these new divisions coming from? If the Russians are releasing their Far Eastern Divisions to fight in Europe, they have to be replacing them somehow – unless the Kremlin has decided that American entry into the war will tie down the immense Kwantung army that now occupies Manchuko.

If these estimates are wrong, then Russia is doomed. But if right, the Russian bear is far from defeated.

The Eastern Front January - April 1942

Winter clamped down hard in January. The temperature dropped until it averaged thirty degrees of frost, day and night, and still winter uniforms and equipment did not arrive. Anything wearable was requisitioned from the locals whenever the opportunity presented, particularly *valenki*, thick felt overboots that were amazingly warm and waterproof and which were shared out among the sentries and patrols.

Major Friedrich Prager's troops scorned primitive Russian huts and living conditions and Prager noted in his diary that 'we Germans are perhaps too fastidious. The peasants are full of an amazing variety of vermin as are their clothing and living quarters. A single night spent in a peasant hut is sufficient to provoke an infestation that will last until the spring thaw. But they do stay warm.'

The greatest danger came not from the enemy but from their own supply system. German issue footwear - a combination of leather jackboots and wool socks - were deadly. The boots froze, the constant chaffing wore holes in the wool socks and skin contact with frozen leather produced frostbite within minutes.

Army Group South issued instructions for coping with the cold instead of proper winter clothing. Prager stared in disbelief at instructions to tear strips from blankets, shirts, trousers and even tents to make foot wrappings in the Russian manner to replace scarce wool socks. Unfortunately, there was little from which to make such wrappings as every blanket and bit of clothing the men possessed was worn day and night in an effort to keep warm. And such items as tents, duffle bags and tarpaulins had long been thrown away in the past summer's headlong advance.

Prager sent requisition after requisition begging for cold weather uniforms, but the answer never varied. 'Winter clothing is issued on a priority basis to active combat troops only.' As Prager's battalion was ostensibly in reserve, they did not rate winter clothing.

Every day brought new problems. To survive the harsh winters and cramped living conditions, the Russian peasant sank into what seemed to Prager a deep apathy one step above hibernation. The presence of the garrison disrupted this survival mechanism and the incidence of violent arguments and fights rose. At the same time, the work efficiency of the peasant, never high to begin with, dropped to near zero.

On 1 January, Lieutenant Mahr left with his rifle company for the Moscow front. Prager was sorry to see him go, not only because his seriously understrength battalion must look to its own security now, but because he had grown to like the younger man. With him, Prager had felt that he could be himself whereas he had to keep that distance with his battalion officers that a good commander needs in order to maintain discipline and respect.

After Kharkov, he had arrived at Slavets with twelve operational tanks, four Mark IVs and eight Mark IIIs. Two scout cars and a dozen lorries had been requisitioned in late December with four of the tanks for the north, including the brand new replacement. Five tanks were inoperative for lack of spare parts, leaving only three. Yet he knew he was credited in the Order of Battle listing with a full battalion.

Officially, Prager's unit was resting and refitting. But there was little more rest to be had here than at the front. When not patrolling, they strove to keep their remaining vehicles working, foraged for food and firewood and tried to winterise the barns and buildings that served as barracks.

Direct enemy attacks on the battalion began in mid-January. At first they were limited to sniping incidents involving sentries. Then a motorcycle dispatch rider was ambushed on his way to divisional headquarters. His naked body was found in the snow full of bullet holes and bayonet wounds. His uniform, dispatch case and equipment, including motorcycle, were nowhere to be found.

Prager reported the attack to regimental headquarters and requested immediate reinforcements as his seriously understrength and under-equipped panzer battalion was in no position to deal with partisan attacks. His request was forwarded to Division who replied simply that he must be responsible for battalion's security as there were no reinforcements available. Prager threw the message across the room.

The battalion's morale declined as the incidents increased. Twice, pitched battles were fought and three prisoners were taken, all civilians who called themselves partisans. They inadvertently revealed that Moscow no longer based their appeal to the Russian people on the tenets of communism but rather on the defence of the Motherland. Old battles from Kulikovo to Poltava, from Borodino to Odessa were invoked to spread patriotic fervour and the prisoners spoke of freeing Russia from the hated Teutons. Moscow had revived the thousand-year blood feud between Germany and Russia. But then, Prager thought, hadn't German troops marched into Russia to purge the world of Godless communism with its anti-Christian goals and unnatural economic and political policies?

At the end of January, long-delayed letters arrived from Sonja. The same convoy, forging through a two-day blizzard, also brought a meagre issue of winter clothing which Prager quickly reserved for use by sentries only.

That evening, Prager locked himself in his office and sorted the five letters by date and then, as usual, opened and skimmed the last to make certain that everything was all right. A wave of homesickness swept him at the sight of Sonja's handwriting and he had to put the letter down while he blew his nose and composed himself.

The first letter was dated in early September, the last at the end of November. All were numbered and he saw that he had letters fifteen, nineteen, twenty-six, thirty-five and forty-three, to slot into the batch he'd received last November. The rest, presumably, were somewhere in the chaotic mail system that had only begun to sort itself out after their rapid advances of the past summer and autumn.

Sonja wrote of nothing in particular, merely described her daily life, knowing instinctively that this was what he most wanted to read. She again mentioned the increasingly frequent bombing of Hamburg and noted that she often watched from the garden and assured him that there was no danger as the house was far from the city proper and the docks which were the main targets.

She had volunteered for war work and been assigned nursing duty at a military hospital. The work was distressing, she wrote, but satisfied her need to assist her adopted country in any way possible. That did worry him as it brought her directly into the city and put her in danger from the bombers. He ached to know more but knew that she could not tell him in a letter. He was surprised in fact, that the censors had not excised comments about the British bombing campaign.

The first time through, Prager did not see it and only when he reread the letter a third time did he spot the tiny red check mark beneath the word *adopted*. A censor had taken note – and a chill swept him. Of course the Army knew that Sonja was a foreigner and a Russian, even if she was now a German citizen by marriage with patent signed by Minister of the Interior Wilhelm Frick and the wife of an officer serving on the Eastern Front. An officer moreover, who had connections in high military circles. But postal censors were employed by the Gestapo.

Perhaps the censor's pencil had inadvertently rested there; perhaps it meant nothing at all.

In the first week of February a heavy partisan attack almost overran the German garrison at Shemstovo, a village fifteen kilometres north of Slavets. Prager reluctantly placed his battalion on full alert – a full alert which he knew he could not sustain for long. Night-time temperatures of thirty to forty degrees of frost made it impossible to expose sentries for more than fifteen minutes at a time.

Everyone – fitter, driver, clerk and cook – served in rotation, but with frostbite cases, sickness and accidents, his battalion was down to less than 250 effectives, not enough for the round of patrols and sentry goes, as well as regular duties.

Two days after the attack on Shemstovo, Prager reduced the full alert, but warned his officer and NCOs to make certain that the sentries stayed awake and alert at all times and that the men were encouraged to be sensitive to any change in the villagers' attitude.

This last proved counter-productive within twenty-four hours when two enlisted men were brought before him for bullying villagers. In one case the elderly villager who had reported the partisan camp in the forest in November, took exception to the way he was ordered to produce his identity papers and had protested. He was severely beaten and sustained a broken arm and bruises. Prager knew that the young soldiers responsible had reacted from fear and exhaustion and that punishing them would lower morale further and might even provoke retaliatory incidents. Yet something had to be done to pacify the villagers.

After several discussions with regimental headquarters, Prager transferred them both to a logistical unit in Kiev and issued an extra ration of food to the injured man's family.

The winter was becoming worse than anything Prager could have imagined. By contrast, the Russians – peasant or soldier – seemed to find nothing extraordinary about the cold. A major supply convoy was ambushed between divisional headquarters and Slavets and when Prager examined the site, he found evidence that the Russians had lain waiting in the snow and sub-zero cold for hours. Rumours began to circulate within the battalion that the Russians, being sub-human, were able to endure far colder temperatures than Germans.

The cold added greatly to the problem of keeping the worn-out tanks in operation. Once a tank was moved from the heated maintenance shed, the engine had to be kept running or lubricated joints froze solid within an hour as the cold turned lubricating oil to sludge and stiffened grease. No winterised lubricants were available, but Prager discovered by talking to an elderly villager who had once been a taxi driver in Stalingrad, or Tsaritsyn as he called it by its old name, that sunflower seed oil kept lubricating oil liquid at very low temperatures.

Prager ordered that every hut and barn in and about the village be searched for sunflower oil and seed and a total of thirty-five litres of oil and half a ton of sunflower seeds were confiscated in the sweep. A press built by the maintenance crew extracted three more litres of oil from the seeds.

He had the sunflower seed oil mixed half and half with lubricating oil and tested in a tank engine. It worked well enough as long as the engine was run for one hour in twelve at temperatures above thirty degrees of frost, or three hours in eight below that. But the bearing grease problem defied his best efforts. The only solution was a blow torch applied to hub and axle.

In the second week of February, Soviet mortars pounded Slavets. Three hours before dawn, the first shells whistled in to explode on the village outskirts, waking Prager with a start – they were fifty kilometres from the front! Where had they come from? By the time he reached the command bunker, the shelling had stopped.

A polished sun rose at 0830 hours to flood the snowscape with rose. As the day drew on, Prager made the rounds of sentry posts, concentrating on those facing the forest north of the village. There was no sign of movement and no resumption of shelling so he called for aerial reconnaissance. But by the time the aircraft arrived, the light was going and the pilot had to return to base.

As dusk thickened, Prager stood on the edge of a trench, studying the impenetrable fir forest, a thick black line in the field of his binoculars. The rubber eye cups were iron hard in the intense cold and he had wound a strip of cloth across his brow to prevent them from freezing to his skin. Blue shadows stretched a dozen times normal length and the setting sun contained no perceptible heat. The wind cut like a razor and, even in his huge sheepskin greatcoat, the sentry beside him shivered.

Two huts had been struck by mortar shells, killing the four people inside – a young mother and her two daughters and her old father-in-law. Both burned ruins showed black against the tinted snow, like rotten teeth. On the edge of the village, a working party strengthened the breastworks, laying blocks of snow like bricks. A line of shivering women, children and old men passed buckets of water from hand to hand to pour over the snow wall to create a crenellated and vaguely mediaeval fortress wall that was nearly bullet proof.

Prager stopped beneath a bare apple tree to shelter from the wind while he lit a cigarette. The harsh Russian *mahorka* tobacco rasped at his throat. He tried to imagine Slavets without snow and found himself longing for spring.

It could be worse, he thought, staring at the nearly buried KV1 hulk. I could be further north at Leningrad; or worse, outside Moscow. At least here we have log huts.

The following morning was Sunday and during church services, a sergeant-major hurried in to report that a sentry had observed men moving in the open near the forest. Prager left immediately.

The air was bitingly cold and he wore only his uniform tunic, but there wasn't time to go for his greatcoat. The sentry handed him the field glasses and Prager warmed the eye pieces against his chest. A sullen sun rested above the eastern horizon, its light dingy. He studied the snow field but saw nothing.

'You are certain of what you saw?'

The sentry answered through chattering teeth, 'Yes sir. Two men, bent low, running towards the forest. They were too far away for a shot, sir.'

Prager nodded. The man was a veteran and knew the value of an accurate report in such circumstances. 'Good work.' He saw the relief man peering out of the bunker. 'Go and get warm.'

Slavets lay approximately four kilometres northeast of a tributary to the Dnieper, unnamed on his map. Somewhere in the confines of the forest which followed the north bank of the river, were the bandits – they called themselves partisans but Prager suspected they were either Red Army soldiers trapped by the lightning German advance, or deserters whom a few civilian malcontents, mostly communist party members from the surrounding villages, had joined. Prager thought they must be receiving supplies from the Red Army as occasionally aircraft engines had been heard in that direction on clear nights.

The map symbol for the village of Shemstovo caught his eye fifteen kilometres northeast – on the eastern border of the pine forest where the garrison had almost been overrun by similar bandit attacks, as had the garrison at Ulanov a few kilometres further on.

Prager tried to dismiss the thought forming in his mind. Foolishness. The Russians were proponents of the traditional European method of linear warfare and had never been inclined to other methods. Hadn't the Finns shown just how inflexible they were? It was inconceivable that the Russians would waste resources on isolated bandit gangs behind the German front in the hope they might do enough damage before they were destroyed to make them worthwhile.

A rough hand woke him; Prager huddled deeper into his sleeping bag, reluctant to emerge from its warmth.

'Wake up, Major,' a voice hissed. 'We are under attack.'

A half moon silvered the snow and rimmed the trees and village huts with ice when he stepped outside. Around him, troops were tumbling out of their quarters and running to the trenches. Prager reached the main fortifications on the northern side of the village with the first soldiers. Rifle bolts clattered and apprehension drove him to pass an unnecessary command to hold fire.

The forest was ink black in the meagre light and the sky bright with stars in spite of the moonlight. The Milky Way streamed overhead and Orion strode towards the western horizon. The snow-covered fields were featureless in the flat moonlight and so it was difficult to spot the Russian figures streaming from the forest on skis.

For a moment he was held in thrall by the sight of hundreds of men gliding towards him, the ghostly first wave less than five hundred metres distant. They came in disciplined lines, four distinct waves, each two hundred metres behind the other. Someone shouted and he looked to his left in time to see streaks of fire rising from the forest. He dove into the trench just as the wave of mortar fire descended on them.

Crouching low, mouth against the ear of his senior sergeant-major, Prager shouted orders to open fire on the advancing troops with mortars. The sergeant scuttled away and the harsh coughing of their own mortars began. Keeping low, Prager moved along the trench ordering the riflemen not to waste ammunition. The Russians had chosen the wrong night, he thought. The moon was far too bright.

At the end of the trench he turned back to the village, stopping twice to scan the snow field. The first wave of Russian attackers had disintegrated under rifle and mortar fire, but the second wave was advancing steadily enough. He swore. The bandits were pressing as if they were Red Army regulars. Where had they accumulated so many men? In the four waves that he could see, he guessed there were at least six hundred, almost a full battalion!

Prager ran to the maintenance sheds where, in spite of the fuel shortage, he had kept one tank on standby with its engine running one hour in eight. The tank's crew was waiting with hatches open and he vaulted onto the rear deck.

'Up to the main line,' he shouted, 'but stay in the trees. They have mortars!'

The tank commander waved in understanding. As they lurched free of the ice, Prager almost lost his balance and clutched a turret handhold just in time. The Mark III pivoted and ground forward to the beaten path that marked the main road and lumbered towards the end of the village. The commander pointed to a small orchard and Prager nodded vigorously and jumped off.

The Mark III eased into position, splintering the slender trees and the engine noise died to a rumble. Prager heard the turret motor whine as the gun swivelled, lifted and after a pause for the gunner to aim, fired with a vicious crack.

He had the impression of a reddish streak ending in an explosion just beyond the first line of advancing Russians. The gun muzzle dropped a degree and fired again. This time, the shell ploughed the snow and exploded among the plodding bandits. The next shot was also on target and the gun began to fire rapidly, traversing in short jumps. The tank commander stripped the frozen canvas cover from the machine gun, banged it loose on its ring, cocked it with a jerk and began to shoot.

The field turned into an inferno and a sleet of steel melted the remainder of the first wave and then the second. Still the third came on and, in a brief lull when the gun was being reloaded, Prager heard hurrahing coming across the open fields.

But the concentration of fire was too great even for their fanaticism and the third wave faltered at three hundred metres, then turned back. The fourth wave also broke apart and ran. As they reached the trees, Prager saw two men emerge in the strong moonlight and wave them back. Both must be officers, he thought, attempting to rally their men. When the first panicked Russian ran past, one officer drew his pistol and shot him in the back. The other officer followed suit and in moments they had stemmed the panic. Prager watched, appalled.

The Russian troops began to reform. The throbbing mass separated into two disciplined lines once more and Prager realised that he was watching trained, regular soldiers and not a raggle-taggle bunch of partisan bandits! His own troops had stopped firing and were laughing and shouting to one another in self-congratulations, but Prager had a sudden premonition that it wasn't going to be all that easy.

He ran towards his headquarters, intending to order as many tanks up to the line as possible. As he passed the barn near the tree where he had stopped a few days before for a cigarette, he heard the rapid, paper-tearing sound of Soviet machine pistols, which in the frozen air had a brittle, snapping quality. Two German soldiers ran towards him, shouting. Behind poured a dozen white-clad figures.

One of the soldiers ducked behind a log hut, snatched a stick grenade, twisted the cap and heaved it into the path of the oncoming Russians. As they dove for cover, the second German soldier continued on and Prager shouted at him to find and bring reinforcements.

The Ivans were less than fifty metres away when they saw him and shots drove Prager into the shelter beneath a large tree. He cleared snow from his face in time to see a Russian kneeling in the open, taking careful aim. Prager yanked his Walther pistol from its holster, ripped his mitten off, aimed and squeezed the trigger.

Nothing happened. The intense cold had gummed the lubricating grease inside the bolt. A shot whizzed past his head and he scrambled to the far side of the tree. Panic raced through him and he barely restrained the deadly urge to run. What could he do..? His only weapon was useless. The iron discipline beaten into him at the military academy took over and his mind began to function once more. There was a way, he saw, visualising the mechanical design of the P-38; he jerked the slide back and ejected the magazine, pushed the takedown lever open and fumbled the slide forward and off. The lug release pin was frozen into place and he jabbed at it with his thumb before it moved reluctantly and the barrel came free. He broke his mechanical pencil shoving at the firing pin to force it into the forward position. Two more shots slashed the tree as he reassembled the pistol with frozen fingers.

Prager shoved the magazine back into the gun and locked the slide open, then carefully edged around the tree's base until he could see the Russian, who now had started towards him in a crouch. He aimed the pistol and with his left thumb, pushed the slide release down. The slide snapped forward and the protruding firing pin fired the chambered bullet. The shot went wild but the startled Russian vaulted for cover.

Prager pressed the firing pin with the pencil and it moved easily; the heat from the fired cartridge had freed it. He edged back around the tree in time to see another Russian raise his head above a snow bank, then duck. He aimed at the spot and waited.

The head appeared again. All he could see was the top of a fur cap. He depressed the front sight until he was sighting several centimetres below the crest of the snowbank and squeezed the trigger. The pistol recoiled, the barrel flipped up obscuring his view but his fingers were too cold to have squeezed the trigger properly and he doubted his accuracy, even though the head did not reappear.

Prager rolled back to the near side of the tree. Six more cartridges in the pistol and eight in the spare clip. And the Russians had automatic rifles – he would have given anything for a grenade, or warm hands.

As if the sentry had read his mind, a stick grenade spun towards the hut and exploded with a vicious crack. The corner collapsed and figures in white ran away. He emptied the pistol fruitlessly as a dozen German soldiers appeared, firing at the Russians who had taken to their skis.

The corporal blew his whistle and troops ran towards the huts, kicked doors open and turned everyone out. Children screamed and women wept and old men cursed them as they were forced to line up in the snow and were thoroughly searched. His troops laughed or complained about searching the women, depending on age and attractiveness, until Prager, livid with rage, shouted for them to behave.

When they found no evidence that the Russian infiltrators had hidden in the village, Prager concluded that the half dozen or so who had attacked from the rear must have lain in the snow all night, far enough out not to be seen by the sentries. Their white coveralls would have made them nearly invisible until they attacked, killing two of the four men serving sentry duty. Prager had come on the scene just in time to break the impetus of their attack. He gave orders that a sharper night watch was to be kept on the flanks and that each dawn the snow fields were to be swept with machine gun fire.

The midday light dulled and the sky lowered with claustrophobic intensity. Snowflakes swirled intermittently, threatening a storm. Prager sensed something ominous building and, on the way to his headquarters, he stopped at the armoury and drew an MP 40 machine pistol and a pouch holding four thirty-two round clips of 9 millimetre ammunition, promising himself never to go anywhere again without it. Being killed in a tank battle was one thing, but each time he realised how close he had come to death by a rifle bullet, he started to shake. It was illogical, he realised, but he could not rid himself of the self-induced terror.

He paused on steps clogged with frozen snow and looked towards the forest. Dark specks that must be bodies cluttered the fields and he counted forty-seven through his field glasses. Then conscious that he was in plain view of any sniper with a good telescopic sight, he pushed inside and drew the blackout curtains. He pulled both sweaters he possessed on over the three shirts, again regretting the loss of the heavy underwear that burned with his tank at Kharkov, replaced his tunic and struggled into the summer-weight officer's greatcoat again. He wrapped the skirts of his coat around his legs and bound them in place with twine to form a kind of legging. He was now wearing every bit of clothing he owned and he was still freezing.

When Prager returned to the trench facing the forest, he found the boyishly-young lieutenant commanding the tankless A Company lying behind the thick ice wall studying the area through binoculars.

'They will come back,' the lieutenant grunted, 'as soon as the commissars finish whipping them into shape. Did you see how they shot anyone who turned back? What a hell of a way to fight a war; if the enemy doesn't kill you, your officers will. What was all the shooting about a while ago, sir?'

Prager described the Russian attempt to infiltrate the lower end of the village. 'I can't understand what they are trying to do? They act as if they want to occupy Slavets? But what good will that do them? They can't possibly have enough ammunition and supplies to hold it this far behind the front.'

'Nothing the bastards do surprises me any more. God damn, I'm cold.' The lieutenant rolled over and beat his hands together.

'I'd like a look at some of those bodies,' Prager mused. 'They attacked like soldiers, not irregular bandits.'

'Here they come!' several voices shouted.

Prager did not need field glasses to see Russians skiing from the forest in two waves, each man several metres from his neighbour. 'Damn!' the lieutenant breathed as they drew closer. 'Look at that. That second line isn't even armed!'

It was true, Prager saw, yet the unarmed Russian soldiers skied on with just as much determination. 'My father fought on the Eastern Front in the last war,' he muttered. 'He saw the same things then. When the Russians don't have enough weapons, they tell the foot soldiers to take rifles from those who are killed or wounded.'

The lieutenant snorted in derision. 'Uncivilised bastards; the world won't miss them!'

When the range closed to eight hundred metres, the machine guns began to fire in short, murderous bursts and no one reached the two hundred metre mark. The second line, two hundred metres further behind, had also broken but only to pick up weapons.

Prager laid a gloved hand on the ice wall, rested the machine pistol on his hand, turned the selector switch to single shot and began to fire. This isn't a battle, he thought, watching his targets stumble or fall, it's simple slaughter.

The second line disappeared and to his astonishment, a third materialised in the gathering dusk. And behind came a fourth. He was frightened now and he knew what had caused that haunted look in his father's eyes whenever he spoke of facing a Russian human wave attack. It was beyond savage, he thought as he changed magazines; it was simply inhuman. How could anyone go so calmly, so willingly, to certain death?

Shouts for more ammunition began and gasping bearers raced back and forth with the heavy ammunition containers. How did the Russians motivate their men so? Why do the Ivans allow it? Why don't they revolt and kill their officers as they did in 1917? Was the Soviet high command mad? Hadn't they learned anything?

Snow swirled around the ghostly lines and the machine guns fell silent as targets disappeared, the gunners far too cognisant of their limited ammunition supply to waste any in blind firing. Prager hurried to the maintenance shed to see what was holding up the last two tanks still operational. Fitters and crews worked feverishly and fires burned beneath them to warm engines and gear boxes. A mechanic divided a bucket of hot sunflower seed oil between the Mark III and Mark IV and starter motors whined faster as the oil penetrated.

The warrant-officer in charge reported they would be ready in five minutes. Prager described the assault forces moving towards them in the heavy snow and the man turned away shouting urgently at his crews even before Prager finished speaking.

An engine ran up raggedly, its driver nursing it to keep it from stalling. In this cold, a stall meant that fuel lines would have to be warmed individually to start the petrol flow again. The Mark III commander signalled he was ready and Prager clambered up to the turret as it began to roll towards the doors, shouting orders to go to the south side of the village in case of another attack from that direction. He jumped down as it rumbled into the night.

The Mark IV was started five minutes later. Its engine ran poorly but would, he judged, get it into position behind the breastworks facing the forest to support the Mark III.

At 1900 hours, the snow stopped. The wind strengthened as a high pressure area cleared the sky and the stars shone hard and unblinking. At first, the newly fallen snow was swept along the surface in silent swirls, but as the wind strengthened, it snatched it up again into a curious ground blizzard that abraded exposed skin raw in minutes. When Prager noticed his own face begin to burn, he ducked out of the wind and massaged his nose, ears and forehead to restore circulation, gritting his teeth at the pain.

Warnings were passed against neglecting frostbite precautions and Prager made the rounds himself to see that the weary men were following procedure. They had run out of frostbite cream a week ago and had to make do with lard, collected from the village.

The third assault came at midnight, under cover of the ground blizzard. The enemy crept within two hundred metres before they rose ghost-like to the piping of officers' whistles and surged forward, some on skis, the rest struggling through the waist-deep snow on foot. Prager's machine guns again scythed their ranks to pieces. The white overalls that had concealed them against the snow now exposed the enemy against the black-grey sky. Even so, the Soviets came on, rank on rank, their thin hurrahing audible in the lulls of gunfire.

Prager had never experienced anything like these massive infantry assaults and estimated that upwards of seventy Soviet soldiers had been killed since dawn. Had they an inexhaustible supply of men? Radio reports told of similiar attacks on other garrisons and he began to wonder if the Red Army had not broken clear through the front and this was part of a general assault?

He sent orders to the two tanks to shell the edge of the forest where the enemy lines were being formed up and five minutes later, shell explosions burst against the dark trees, brief flashes that robbed him of night vision.

There were no further assaults that night. Prager stood the garrison down from full alert at 0200 and left the trench himself shortly before 0400 and returned to his office. The fire in the stove had gone out and it was as cold inside as out. He built a fire, starting the damp wood with handfuls of useless orders sent down from division. A few months ago, he would never have dared do such a thing, he thought as he shoved another handful of paper into the flames. Forms were sacred to an army – until the fighting began. The water in the tea kettle had frozen and he put it on the stove and sank down on the bench.

They had been lucky. Only luck had saved them from being overrun in the first assault, and a determined defence from prepared positions had saved them in the second. The room was beginning to warm and he could hear ice cracking in the kettle. Thank God the Russians had only mortars. Artillery might finish them. Yet for all their fanaticism, the Russian assaults had been ill-prepared. How in the name of God had they expected their men to succeed in crossing two thousand metres of open ground against prepared defences?

Even his troops were angered at the way the Russians had thrown their men away. How strange, he thought. Even as his soldiers did their best to kill an enemy, they hated the wholesale slaughter forced on them.

Prager was contemptuous of the so-called 'brotherhood of soldiers' said to exist between fighting men of all nations. No war had ever ended because the common soldiers of both sides had refused to fight. There had been occasions in 1917 and '18 on the Eastern Front when demoralised Russian troops had thrown down their weapons, but elated German and Austrian soldiers had taken advantage and when the Treaty of Brest-Litovsk ended the fighting, Germany had gained more Russian territory in the final few weeks than she had in the previous four years of fighting.

And in the hell of Verdun in 1915, a half a million French and German soldiers died in six months, yet the fighting had continued – a matter of honour, it was said.

The attack on German garrisons were general all through the area south of Kharkov. A combination of Soviet regular army units and partisans had taken advantage of the bad weather, poor communications and widely-dispersed nature of the German occupation forces to open a limited series of counterattacks – limited from the standpoint of Army Group HQ, but certainly not from that of the individual garrison commanders.

There were no further attacks all that day and Prager used the respite to improve his defences. A second line of trenches were hacked out and an ice wall built along the southern side of the village. The peasants assisted grudgingly and only after the threat of reprisals. Prager resolved to keep a closer watch on them and wished to God he could simply eject them from the village.

The next attack took place at dawn the following day. Again, seemingly endless waves of suicidal Russians swept towards them from the forest. His tired troops were no longer astonished at the foolish bravery confronting them, nor did they rail now at the stupidity of the Russian commanders. Prager saw instead a dull anger beginning to grow as reluctant admiration succumbed to hatred for the sheep-like fools running to certain death.

On the fourth day of assaults, the Russians somehow supplemented their two small mortars with a field piece. Prager was standing on the north barricade at dawn, shivering in the wind as the forest emerged from the gloom. The first registration shot rattled across the sky and exploded beyond the village. Soldiers and peasants alike erupted from the huts and ran for the shelter trenches. The gun was quickly brought on target and a hut disappeared in a blaze of kindling.

Each assault was now preceded by artillery fire of fifteen minutes duration. As day succeeded day, it settled into a routine that rarely varied. Artillery fire began at dawn and the first assault wave appeared at the edge of the forest. The gun and mortars stopped when Russian troops had approached to within a hundred metres of the village defence line. The sequence was repeated at noon and at dusk, usually without the infantry attack. Each time, Prager cursed impotently; the village was being shot to pieces and he could do nothing. The seventy-six millimetre gun of the Mark IV and even the fifty millimetre gun of the Mark III had sufficient range to reach the forest, but he could not spare the ammunition.

Prager's garrison was being forced into a smaller and smaller area. His patrols were now fired upon almost from the moment they left the village. The snow was far too deep to use tanks in support, even if he had the spares to make them operational and the petrol to run them.

Because of the weather and Soviet attacks, supply convoys became sporadic. Within two weeks, his ammunition supplies were running dangerously low and fresh food of any kind had disappeared and they were reduced to canned rations barely sufficient to sustain them in the intense cold. But clothing remained his greatest problem. With the exception of the dozen sheepskin greatcoats received in December, no other winter clothing arrived and the soldiers continued to wear inadequate summer weight clothing. Added to the cold was the health factor; it was no longer possible to bathe adequately and lice became a grave problem.

Prager bombarded regimental headquarters with requests for winter clothing, ammunition and food. Over and over, he emphasised the danger that they could be overrun unless sufficient ammunition was received – especially anti-personnel shells for the tanks. He was finally promised a supply convoy at the first break in the weather.

That convoy was reported by radio en route six days later. All the previous night, flares and the arcing trails of artillery shells had lit the sky above the village, presaging something more than the usual battalion-strength attack at dawn. Prager was certain that whatever it was would not happen before then but could not afford to take the chance and so the garrison stood-to on full alert in the bitter cold.

The temperature rose a bit during the night to thirty-two degrees of frost and the clear sky blazed with stars. German soldiers huddled in trenches and bunkers hacked out of the frozen earth, at the cost of more labour than any had ever thought possible. The single Soviet howitzer and the two mortars had so pounded the village that not a single structure remained.

The civilian inhabitants had dug a bunker of their own in which they huddled like frozen moles and waited for one side or the other to prevail. There was little food for them and no firewood to be spared. What little remained, plus that from the shattered huts, was carefully hoarded and burned to keep the sentries from freezing to death during the terrible nights. At dawn, all fires were extinguished as even a trace of smoke brought cannon and mortar fire.

During the six days they had waited for the convoy, two blizzards followed hard on one another, interrupted only by a few hours of crystal-hard weather that lasted just long enough to raise hopes that the lorries were on the way. Prager had long since ordered rations reduced to one thousand grams per man, far less even than allowed an office worker in Germany. The civilians, totally without resources, were allowed eight hundred grams for nursing mothers and six hundred for all others including children. Those were starvation levels for all concerned in this kind of weather.

Army nutrition tables told Prager that people living in such conditions needed a minimum of 1,198 grams daily, and as a consequence frostbite cases rose among the exhausted civilians and soldiers alike at an alarming rate. He lacked the manpower to enforce frost-protection measures among the civilians but ordered any soldier reporting frostbite court-martialled for dereliction of duty. He also ordered the men to pair off when outside so that they could watch one another. Even so, two sentries had been discovered yesterday morning, frozen to death.

As he watched the flares bursting over the village, Prager thought he understood the logic behind the Russian mass assaults. They knew that his entrenched forces were impregnable only as long as they had ample supplies of ammunition. So they were doing everything possible to stimulate wastage. Prager appreciated that the Soviets were more than willing to trade their most numerous commodity, human life, in exchange for enemy bullets and so he limited all rifle and machine gun fire to repelling direct assaults and the dawn machine gun sweeps to clear the approaches of Russian snipers and sappers. The few rounds of tank ammunition remaining were held in strict reserve, as was petrol. Not for the first time did Prager wish for an issue of horses – for transport or food.

Dawn of the day the convoy was to arrive. There was no assault. Even the shelling stopped. The morning drew on, clear and hard and the windswept sky was steel blue and the pale sun provided no warmth. Snow swept across the open fields to assault the barricades and trenches with even greater ferocity than the Russians. Anxious hours passed and eyes went frequently to the southwest where the long-buried road curled towards the district town of Berestivo and regimental headquarters.

Just before dusk, a column of smoke was spotted in the southwest and Prager received confirmation by radio. The convoy had been attacked and three lorries and one tank had been destroyed. The remainder had retired. The weather forecast was for a severe blizzard. Another attempt would be made as soon as it ended. For the first time, Prager was badly frightened.

The blizzard struck in mid-afternoon. Twice in the following days the Russians mounted assaults, but half-heartedly, as if the weather were too much even for them. When the storm ended three days later, the landscape as far as the eye could see was as smooth and unmarked in the watery sunshine as a calm sea.

Huddled lumps of frozen flesh that had dotted the fields by the hundreds had disappeared beneath the fresh blanket of snow. 'We'll smell them in the spring,' a sentry predicted with disgust.

As the cloud cover cleared off, the temperature again dropped below zero. The only thermometer in the village had disappeared during the bombardment weeks before and Prager had no way to measure it accurately, but at mid-morning, the warrant officer in charge of maintenance reported that none of the tank engines could be started. Even the sunflower-diluted lubricating oils had frozen.

In the far distance, Prager watched Russian soldiers construct snow fortifications. They had begun to do so the day the blizzard struck. He saw now that one wall had been built a thousand metres distant from the village's eastern flank. If only he had sufficient ammunition for the tank guns, he thought, they would never have dared try. He was tempted to order five rounds per gun but restrained the urge – that was what the Russian commander wanted him to do.

Prager now had no great hope that a relief convoy could fight through to them. His was not the only isolated garrison demanding assistance and resupply. The Russians moved freely about the countryside and regimental radio reports suggested they were able to mass at any point between Slavets and Berestivo in a matter of hours. The nightly buzz of aircraft over the distant forest was maddening, indicating as it did that the Russians were being supplied by air while the Luftwaffe hadn't been seen in several weeks.

The bombardment began at midday. The initial round of cannon and mortar fire drove them into the bunkers and lasted twenty minutes. There was silence for nearly an hour, then the firing resumed and this time seemed likely to continue indefinitely at the rate of twelve rounds every hour, twenty-four hours a day. The strictly maintained five-minute interval between rounds acted on the beleaguered garrison like a Chinese water torture.

Prager no longer maintained any illusions as to what they had in mind. Having tried to overrun the garrison by sheer numbers and failed, they now intended to starve and bomb them into submission. For the first time, Prager understood how thin were German forces in Russia. Fifty kilometres behind their own lines, still they had been surrounded and cut off by Red Army forces operating with seeming impunity. His garrison had been reduced to a few thousand square metres of territory someone had dubbed *Die Kauldron* – the cauldron.

Prager had determined after careful observation that the Russians had only one field artillery piece, probably a mountain howitzer small enough to be airlifted, as well as the two mortars. Against them he could make use of the cannon the tanks carried and their machine guns, but he had only a dozen rounds per gun and four hundred rounds per machine gun remaining. Even petrol to run the tanks was exhausted and between frostbite, battle casualties and sickness brought on by exposure and slow starvation, he now had less than one hundred and twenty effectives capable of fighting. Providing he reduced rations to eight hundred grams for the soldiers and two hundred for the civilians, they could last four more days. Radio communication with Berestivo had grown sporadic as Aurora Borealis lit the night sky in a dazzling display that no one in the garrison appreciated.

Prager finished the appreciation report, read it through slowly, correcting a word here and there and encoded it himself. He had never felt so helpless in his life. Unless they received petrol, spare parts, ammunition and food in a matter of days, they would be overrun. He had just come from checking the rifle ammunition supplies – less than two hundred rounds per man and they had been firing it at the rate of fifty to sixty rounds per day. And there was the problem of the wounded. Their only remaining medical supplies were aspirins and antacid tablets. In this cold, unless a wound were treated immediately, the tissues often froze and when thawed became gangrenous. He needed to get the nearly two dozen worst wounded soldiers out on the first convoy to reach them and the sixty odd remaining sick and wounded after them as quickly as possible. He snorted. Might as well wish for aircraft to fly them out.

He stared at the ice-bound wall of the bunker, struck by the idea; why not? Because of the snow-bound roads, twenty hours of clear weather were needed for a convoy to reach them, even without a fight. But an aircraft required less than one hour to cover the same distance. The Russians were parachuting supplies to their forces; why in hell couldn't the Luftwaffe do the same for them?

The radio operator was dozing with his headset pushed off one ear. Prager woke him, noting that although he was barely twenty, his skinny face was etched with an old man's fatigue lines. A dark beard had grown in skimpy patches and his tattered greatcoat with its frayed collar and the woman's bandana – babushka the Russians called them – wrapped around his ears and tied beneath his chin made him look more like a tramp than a soldier. One spectacle lens was cracked and he had to tilt his head to compensate.

The boy tapped out the call letters. The earphones lay on the splintered writing surface and Prager could hear the bursts of static whenever he pushed the switch to receive.

Because of atmospheric disturbance, it took an hour to make contact and longer to transmit the report and verify it. For all their labours, their only response was a curt 'message received'. Prager stalked out to the line and stamped up and down behind the ice wall, now and again studying the Russians as they worked on a second, closer, wall at six hundred metres.

He had issued orders only that morning that the four best shots in the battalion be selected. In one hour rotations, whenever there was sufficient light to see, they were given the one sniper rifle the battalion possessed and sent onto the wall to snipe at the Russian workers. One of the sergeants commanding an attenuated company was serving as spotter to the current sniper when Prager reached their position.

The sergeant dismissed the man with the rifle and he and Prager stood together in the fast fading dusk and watched the Russians through field glasses. 'We've accounted for three of them today,' the sergeant growled. 'The bastards. Now they're frightened and even their commissars can't drive them any harder.

'I've been keeping an eye on one of the bastards. He's short and fat, at least he is in that coat of his. I recognise him by that damned great revolver he wears on a lanyard. I saw him shoot a soldier two days ago. Just pointed the gun at the man and fired.' The sergeant shrugged. 'Maybe the soldier talked back, I don't know. Those around them just stared at the commissar until he left. But he still comes out to see how they're doing every morning. I've told the boys that whoever shoots him gets an extra ration and a recommendation for the Iron Cross.'

Amused, Prager chuckled. 'Any luck?'

'Not yet. He's a cagey bastard. Keeps his head low whenever he's in range. He must suspect something because he was wearing a snow smock today. Looked just like anyone else. This afternoon I noticed a cluster of Russians just inside the trees. I watched them for a few minutes. Two thousand metres is a waste of rifle ammunition but it was interesting to see how they divided into groups. I'd be willing to bet that the smaller group were the officers.' The sergeant laughed. 'I thought the Bolshies weren't class conscious. So, I'm going to test my theory in the morning. If I see a fat man in a white smock standing in the small group, with any luck Ivan will have something to celebrate tomorrow night.'

Shortly after midnight, the radio operator woke Prager to read him a message confirming that the Luftwaffe would attempt to parachute supplies shortly after dawn. Reluctantly, Prager left the relative warmth of his sleeping bag to check on the weather. The skies had remained clear, although the high pressure ridge was reported to be moving eastward quickly. Behind, the meteorologists were forecasting another blizzard.

The aircraft came at dawn, escorted by two Stuka dive bombers. Prager, standing in the cover of an ice wall, watched them drone towards the village at high altitude, dawn sun glinting on wings and fuselage. Before him, strips of snow had been marked in black with ash gathered from every firepit, stove and burned structure in the village.

In addition, he had sent three patrols out before dawn to the west to clear out the snipers who infiltrated during the night. There had been a single burst of firing as the sky lightened, but nothing since. The patrols were instructed to remain hidden and serve as a covering force for the recovery parties already crouching in the trenches.

The three aircraft circled the area and the two Stukas peeled off and dove towards the forest. Across the distance, Prager heard the whistle of their sirens. Moments later smoke erupted above the trees and the dull rumble of exploding bombs reached them. The Stukas made a second run then turned sharply over the trees and burst above the Russian ice fortifications to rake them with machine gun fire that threw splinters of ice glinting in the brightening sun.

The larger aircraft, a Ju 52, made a quick run at low altitude across the field which Prager had chosen for the dropping zone. The bomber climbed again and a minute later it dipped low across the fields to the north, too near the forest.

'No!' he shouted in anguish as white parachutes blossomed and crates shot out of the aircraft's side and rocked once before bouncing in a flurry of snow. The Ju 52 climbed fast, turned and came rocketing overhead, waggling its wings in salute as Russian soldiers raced from the forest to gather up the crates the Luftwaffe had dropped into their laps.

Prager assembled noncommissioned officers and the lieutenant commanding B Company – the only officer left to him – in his command bunker shortly after dusk. 'Gentlemen, the Luftwaffe has agreed to make another attempt. They tell us that the sun's glare and the ground fire is such that the pilot cannot see the landing zone well enough to drop his load. Tomorrow, they will attempt to land the aircraft in order to be certain. Therefore, we must build a landing strip a thousand metres long, tonight!'

When the whistles of surprise had died, he continued. 'This may be our last chance. The weather forecast is for a severe three-day blizzard beginning tomorrow night. If we do not receive the ammunition, not to mention the food, we won't survive another serious assault.' As if to emphasise his words, a Russian shell burst close by, showering them with dirt and ice from the bunker roof.

'The aircraft will be equipped with skis,' he continued, ignoring apprehensive glances directed upward, 'however, the last blizzard has made it necessary to compact the surface. We must also mark either end of the landing strip with smoke flares. Therefore, everyone in the garrison who can be spared from guard duty, and every civilian who can walk, will assemble on the west side of the village in twenty minutes, near the remains of the old church. Any civilian who refuses or shirks is to be shot at once as an example to the others.'

The night was bitterly cold. Prager guessed the temperature was below minus forty degrees of frost, and a thin wind had started to blow. The soldiers stamped and muttered in the snow while the civilians huddled under armed guard. Since the siege began, Prager had done everything possible to encourage the civilians to desert to the Red soldiers. There was little they could tell the Red Army men and the fewer mouths he had to feed, the better off they all were. But suspecting the kind of life waiting for them in the woods, the civilians had preferred freezing in the remains of their homes to freezing in the forest.

At 1800 hours exactly, soldiers and civilians were marshalled into three groups of ten across by five deep. At Prager's signal, each group was started forward at one minute intervals so that they formed a staggered front eighteen metres wide.

The first three lines in each group were soldiers, the remainder civilians. More than four metres of snow had fallen so far this winter, most of which had compacted well enough. But the blizzard of the previous few days, combined with a harsh wind had left a surface of powdery snow more than a metre deep in places. As a consequence, the first ranks sank in nearly to their waists.

Prager had ordered no lights and complete silence so they would not alert the Soviets any sooner than necessary, but a muffled chorus of curses drifted back to where he followed the right hand group, compass in hand, counting paces. On the far side of the line, a sergeant with a compass also counted paces and, periodically, the count was passed to the man monitoring the centre group for comparison. Using this method, they were able to keep the line moving on a fairly straight course for the required distance.

The cold was unbearable. It bit through greatcoats and leather boots as if they did not exist. Prager had long ago ordered the men to pry off the metal reinforcing strips at heel and toe in an effort to reduce the incidence of frostbite and every scrap of paper, every piece of extra cloth in the battalion had been torn into strips for insulation and stuffed into boots and coats.

Prager had stuffed his own boots with forms designed to measure agricultural output in the district. They had arrived in the final convoy to reach Slavets, packed in six large wooden boxes with an accompanying note explaining that the forms were being distributed early to allow district commanders to familiarise themselves with the required procedures. Useless forms could be supplied but not winter clothing or spare parts or sufficient food and ammunition, he had raged at the quartermaster in Berestivo by radio.

As they tramped on, Prager anxiously studied the night sky. The wind had moved around from the northeast and was now blowing across the landing strip they were trampling out the snow – the worst possible direction. It was too late to reorient the strip, even if he could be certain that the wind would hold steady from that direction. If it blew too hard, a landing would be impossible.

Snow spurted a pace ahead. He heard a soft grunt and a man staggered in the second line and sat down. A bullet cracked past and someone shouted 'Down!' Angrily, Prager countermanded the order.

'Keep going,' he roared. 'We can't stop.' A sharp-eyed sniper must have spotted their movement against the stars. Prager heard an exchange of rifle fire to the north and then nothing more. The wind gusted, sending a mass of powdery snow into their faces and he stumbled over the body of the soldier who had been shot. There was just enough starlight to see a dark hole in his coat collar. The bullet had passed through his neck, probably slicing the carotid artery. A good death, he thought with envy. As cold and exhausted as the boy would have been, he would certainly have felt nothing. He probably just sat down in the snow, thinking he was tired and went to sleep, unaware that he was dying.

Ahead, a woman whimpered and he heard whispers. The civilians were freezing but there was nothing he could do. It had come to this, he thought; whether you lived or not was unimportant, it was how easily you died that counted. They were all dead anyway, so what did a few hours matter as long as death was painless and quick.

They tramped on. Eight-hundred-and-seventy nine, he chanted half-aloud. Eight-hundred-and-ninety, no eighty. The cold made it difficult to concentrate. He had lost all feeling in his feet, and his hands and teeth ached with the cold. The stars were being obscured by a high thin haze and it was growing difficult to see the compass needle.

He had an irresistible urge to lie down and sleep; Prager could never remember having been so tired. A few minutes rest would refresh him, would help them all. His thoughts were mired in a sticky syrup and he began to float away.

'Major,' a hand shook his arm. 'Major, I count fifteen hundred paces.' The sergeant-major shook his arm again and Prager felt himself being drawn back from a long, dark and warm tunnel. Fifteen hundred paces was the sum they had agreed would approximate a thousand metres because of the difficulty in walking in deep snow.

Prager mumbled an order to halt and heard the word pass up the line. With great reluctance he rubbed snow on his face but he was so cold that he could feel only the gritty sensation of ice crystals.

The thousand metre march had brought them all nearly to the end of their resources. Children, too tired even to whimper, slumped in the snow while their mothers swayed with exhaustion; even the better-fed soldiers were silent, their heavy breathing the only sound beyond the ululating wind.

Prager allowed them to rest a few moments while he forced himself to pace back along the track. The snow had been churned but not compacted as he'd hoped. He closed his eyes a moment in utter weariness and dejection; one more time, on the way back and that would have to do. None could survive a second march. He made his way back to the people huddled against the rising wind and used the butt of his machine pistol and his boots without pity to get them up and moving. No one argued, no one resisted and he drove them like dumb animals.

The wind was an agony; it slashed their faces with frozen snow, abrading every exposed surface. The blizzard was rising; the aircraft would not be able to find them, much less land. But there was nothing else to do, nowhere else to go. Prager fought the wind, the cold and his own exhaustion and drove them like cattle.

He never learned how many died that night; how many simply collapsed in the snow undetected. The children came through best, then the soldiers. The old people died without a sound. All were weakened by lack of food, by the cold and exhaustion caused by the incessant artillery bombardment that allowed only snatches of sleep.

His stomach burned the harder he fought to save them. Twice, sudden pains doubled him over. After a while, his mind focused only on the next step to be taken, the next shout to be given, the next push with a buttstock to be administered, the next woman's arm to grasp and lift to keep her from falling, the next child to be shoved forward, the next gust of wind to be endured. He was carrying a young girl, ten, eleven, twelve? He had no idea how or where she had come from. She was so slight, her face emaciated with cold and hunger, yet she was an unbearable burden he dare not lay down. His mind played tricks; first she was Sonja, then Sonja's mother dressed in black like a crow and then the young girl murdered in November.

Only the lives of the hundred and fifty more people he had driven out here caused him to go on; he knew but for them, he would have given up long ago and laid down to die. And the hardest task of all remained. He refused to think about it, instead shut his mind away, shouted and roared and struggled against the snow and wind.

Prager had given orders that the last of the tea was to be brewed and the remaining rations heated by the sentries left to guard the village. Someone took his arm and a voice was speaking to him in German. Slowly, he became aware that he was struggling with a soldier for possession of the girl. Other soldiers, ghostly shapes in the dimming starlight herded people inside the ice walls.

By God, he thought, they had made it, and he stopped fighting. The soldier laid the girl down and Prager realised she was dead. His knees buckled as the soldier shouted for help and he was dragged inside and a hot mug pressed into his hands. The cup burned his skin through the wool mittens but he clasped it tightly, revelling in the pain, then gulped the scalding liquid. Ever so slowly, the ice mass in his chest began to thaw.

He was helped to sit against the ice wall, out of the wind and the cup was refilled. The little girl's body was taken away by an old man who stumbled blindly towards the steps and Prager ground his teeth together and heaved himself up. It had to be done, now.

He went along the trench, looking at the huddled people, German soldiers and Russian civilians alike, fugitives from hell, all mixed together, helping one another, warming one another as best they could.

I can't do it, he thought. I can't do it. But he knew there was no other choice. *All* would die otherwise; this way at least some had a chance. The lieutenant got up as he approached and leaned wearily against the wall. He knows, Prager thought. It was too dark to see his expression and for that Prager was grateful.

Six hundred metres away were the Russian forward lines, their own people. 'Get them up,' Prager shouted hoarsely. 'All civilians up!'

The soldiers stared at him, stupid with fatigue. 'Get the civilians lined up outside the wall,' he roared. Would they do it; would his own men obey such an order? How many will die crossing that six hundred metres? Prager no longer cared. They were all dead and no one knew it yet.

Slowly, the German troops began to stand. They urged the Russians up. Cries of dismay and groans; Prager shouted louder to drown them out; cursing, ordering, blaspheming.

He drove them until he was nearly mad with rage. Every single civilian in the village was forced outside the walls. Three makeshift stretchers were brought with old people so swaddled in rags it was impossible to know if they were alive or dead.

Prager climbed onto the ice wall and pointed to the northeast, to the invisible Russian ice fortifications. 'Go! Go!' he shouted and shook his machine pistol at them. They understood then amid a chorus of agonised screams and curses. He aimed the weapon into their centre and shouted again. Other soldiers did the same. Order them to shoot, he thought wildly. Shoot them down, now. How much kinder a death was a bullet . . . Slowly, the people moved, an amorphous mass stumbling, shuffling, crying, moaning and helping one another into the wind-whipped snow and darkness.

Prager waited ten minutes, then fired three flares in succession to light the fields and warn the Red soldiers that civilians were approaching. A moment later, he heard the distant rattle of machine gun fire. It did not last long. You rotten bastards, he thought.

*

Dawn came reluctantly. The wind blew steadily from the northeast, too strong for an aircraft to land. The sky was full of scudding dark clouds and it was bitterly cold. The black wind cut through ragged uniforms, froze feet in heavy leather boots caked solid with ice, and burned exposed skin. Prager stood on the ice wall and studied the expanse of ground to the northeast, heedless of snipers. Snow gusted along the surface but it was still possible to see the huddle of bodies only a few dozen metres from the Russian ice well. At least the bastards had waited until they could not miss.

Prager had never known such hatred as he felt now for the enemy across the fields. Had he known all along that the Russians would not accept the villagers? They were communists weren't they? Did the individual count for nothing? The villagers had been useful only as long as they bled German supplies and manpower. When he sent them away their usefulness ended and they became instead a liability. And so they were shot down by their own people.

The forest retreated beyond the haze of ground snow. He swept the glasses around to the northwest and saw the patrol sent out at dawn to check on the landing strip, still struggling towards the far end. A wind gust nearly toppled him. He climbed down like an old man, every bone and muscle protesting the cold and the fear that was exhausting him.

It was horribly cold in the dugout and he thought of Dante's innermost circle of hell – not fire, but ice. That old Italian certainly had that right. There was no proper roof to the dugout, merely a few planks laid across a cellar and covered with snow and debris. Prager had forgotten what it was to be warm.

By nightfall the garrison would either be dead or made prisoner, he thought. He removed the clip from his pistol and counted the rounds – eight, plus one in the chamber. He removed one bullet, inserted it in the empty clip and put that into the spare magazine pocket of his holster, and reloaded the P-38.

In three years of war he had never had occasion to think of death as a matter of choice. Death in battle was the result of random chance and there was little one could do to prevent it, other than to refrain from exposing oneself to intentional risks. Now, death had become the preferred alternative. Prager had no illusions as to his fate if captured. The best he could expect would be a painful interrogation and a bullet. The worst, a Russian prison camp.

They had all heard of the horrors of Russian POW camps, where prisoners were given little or no food and, in many, no shelter of any kind and worked twelve to eighteen hours a day in mines or forests. The Soviet government had never signed the Geneva Accords regarding prisoners of war and so the objective of Russian POW camps was to eliminate prisoners as swiftly as possible.

A shout from the radio operator startled him. The man wrote furiously and thrust the slip of paper at Prager. He stared at the decoded message. The pilot of a Ju 52 was approaching their map reference point. Would they fire flares as soon as they heard his engines? Prager gave the orders and went to check that the ten wounded men selected to be air-lifted out were ready.

Prager climbed onto the ice wall and pulled the scarf away from his ears. For a moment he heard nothing above the keening wind and searched the sky to the west with field glasses. The sky was full of cloud, darkish and threatening from horizon to horizon and the first flakes of snow whipped past; if the pilot left it much longer... he heard the distant throb of aircraft engines.

A Russian artillery shell exploded on the south side of the village, the rolling carump erasing the noise of the aircraft. Prager saw it a moment later, a dark speck well to the north, over the forest. 'Christ, not again!' he roared and clawed the flare pistol from his pocket and fired two in quick succession, then grabbed the nearest soldier and shouted, 'Get to the command bunker. Tell the radio operator to signal the pilot to turn south – south! Do you understand?'

The soldier raced off and Prager saw an instant's puff of smoke near the aircraft – the Russians were firing at it. The aircraft changed direction then – fortunately to the south. Prager fired another flare and sent two men ploughing towards the landing strip to alert those stationed there to light the smoke markers.

Either the pilot saw his last flare or he received the radio message as the aircraft lost altitude and circled towards the village. The patrols, in spite of being half-frozen, were alert. The oil drums blazed up before the messengers could have reached them, to mark either end of the landing strip with thick columns of black smoke. The pilot turned to make his approach from the east and Prager began to breathe again.

The Russians turned their attention to the landing zone. A flurry of shells fell across the landing strip where the markers continued to pour out smoke. Prager laughed; let them waste their ammunition on snow, he thought.

The Junkers disappeared into the wind and snow haze and even the sound of its engines faded. Prager was suddenly apprehensive. Shot down? The Russians might have guessed after yesterday's fiasco that a landing attempt would be made. If they sent a gun... Unable to wait longer, Prager thrashed through the snow towards the landing strip. The wind blew harder, whipping the icy crystals against his back and right side and sudden gusts momentarily reduced visibility to zero. There was no reason for him to run, he thought, but it was better to be doing something...

The aircraft reappeared very low, bounced, dipped, bounced and disappeared for one long heartbreaking moment. He expected flames and black smoke but the aircraft reappeared, its side presented. Down by God!

Prager reached the aircraft as the pilot was being carried out of the fuselage. The left wing was shattered and the fuselage lay at an odd angle because the left ski mount had collapsed. The pilot's face was bloody and his head lolled from side to side as they eased him down. One of the soldiers took off his glove and felt for a pulse.

The soldier glanced up after a moment, fingers still against the man's throat. 'Dead, sir. Must have broken his neck in the landing.'

Prager stared at the body in its leather and fleece-lined flying suit and was ashamed that his first thought was of how warm he must have been and the second, that his wounded were now stuck here to die. 'Clumsy bastard,' he muttered under his breath. 'Start unloading,' he rasped, 'before the Russians attack.'

A stream of men, some pulling sledges, others with boxes or ropes, streamed from the village, all eager to help carry supplies. A line formed and unloading began. The aircraft had crashed six hundred metres from the village and the frozen men struggled back and forth with heavy burdens of ammunition, food and God only knew what else. Prager climbed inside, pushed past those unloading the cargo and into the tiny cockpit.

He had never been inside a Ju 52 before and was astonished at how small and cramped it was. There were dials everywhere and two of what he thought of as steering wheels, curiously bisected. He ignored the bewildering array of dials and instruments and searched for papers but found only an issue aerial map of the Donets' area southwest of Kharkov, with Slavets circled in red pencil and some cryptic numbers in the margin. The pilot had flown alone; the absence of crew making it possible to carry more cargo.

The Russians opened a hasty assault with mortar and cannon fire but they had waited too long. Prager had divided the ammunition between the four defence lines as soon as the fire was identified. Even at the expense of losing the food, he was not going to jeopardise the ammunition.

Someone whooped and shouted his name. Prager ran along the ice wall to where a group of men were gathered about zinc-lined cases of anti-personnel seventy-five and fifty millimetre cannon shells.

'There are thirty more, just like this one, Herr Major!' one of them shouted. And they laughed and cheered as Russian shells screamed in, happy as small children on Christmas morning.

Prager helped carry two crates to the Mark IV dug in hull-down at the corner of the only masonry structure in the village, the now-demolished church. The shells were loaded into the magazines while Prager and the tank's commander discussed lines of fire as the first assault line of Red Army men clambered over their ice wall and began to slog across the snow.

Prager climbed onto the turret. Snow had begun to trickle down again but not so hard as to obscure visibility up to several hundred metres. Not that it would have mattered. The Mark IV had long ago registered lines of fire. Beneath his feet, the tank bucked and vibrated as the turret gearing was engaged and disengaged to free it of ice. The sergeant-commander climbed into the open hatch and clamped a set of headphones over the scarf protecting his ears and spoke quickly. The turret jerked again and the gun rose and steadied. Prager knelt and grasped the coaming and the gun vomited smoke and concussion.

A shell burst with a reddish glow ahead of the advancing line and figures went down like grass before a scythe blade. The turret moved a bit to the right in response to a telephoned report and fired again. The sound lashed Prager like a whip. Two more rounds were fired and the Russian line faltered.

Before Prager could congratulate himself, he heard firing from the southwest. He jumped down from the tank and dashed through the shattered village. As he pushed through a stand of splintered pines and saw for the second time the white shapes of Russian troops clambering over the ice wall. A German soldier, blood streaming from a bayonet slash to the face staggered past, shouting, 'They've broken through, they've broken through!'

Russian soldiers ran towards the command bunker. Prager shook his machine pistol off his shoulder and fired a long burst. Four white figures materialised on the Russians' flank, firing rifles. A grenade followed and exploded with a sharp crack that was instantly lost to the wind.

The same wind brought him a long drawn-out 'hoorah!' and more white shapes appeared before the barricade. Prager hesitated; there was no cover between him and the barricade and he saw his four soldiers, all lying in the snow, methodically shooting Russians as they climbed over the ice wall.

Where had these Russians come from? There hadn't been time since the aircraft appeared to have sent them around to attack from a position 180 degrees opposed to the forest, so this had to be part of a major assault. Had the resupply aircraft caused the Russians to push up the start? Of course, and the main assault had unexpectedly been driven back by the anti-personnel rounds, but these soldiers would not know that. This was a diversionary attack then, intended to confuse them and draw men from the main fortifications – but it had come too late.

Prager turned and ran back towards the command bunker, leaving the four soldiers to hold back the Russians. He sent five men under a corporal to support them, with instructions to return as soon as the enemy were eliminated or driven back.

The snow had stopped, although the wind continued to flurry it off the snowpack. He could see the crashed Ju 52 quite clearly and men still working about it, even though a Russian line was advancing towards them. There was still a good bit of cargo to be brought in, mostly food, and hundreds of litres of petrol in the wingtanks to be salvaged that would drive the tanks and heat bunkers.

Prager ordered the single lorry that had been left to them and a working party to be escorted by the Mark III tank which he pulled from its position. Russian artillery began again, plastering the village in an effort to make them keep their heads down. The Mark III moved out ahead of the lorry, using its treads to tramp a path, but the lorry bogged down within a hundred metres and that seemed to put new heart into the Russian gunners. Shells began to land seconds apart, closing in on the lorry.

The tank commander ploughed towards the aircraft, snow spraying in all directions. He brought the machine around between it and the village and jumped down. Prager saw another crew member, the gunner possibly, climb into the turret and the tank opened fire in a long range duel with the Soviet howitzer and the mortars. Meanwhile, the tank commander, ignoring bursting shells, levered open a compartment on the rear deck and dragged out the tow chain. Prager laughed in excitement; by God, why hadn't he thought of that. The chain was strong enough to pull another tank out of a bog . . . Shells burst so close that snow and dirt obscured what was happening. The commander directed his tank in front of the Junkers with hand signals, attached the tow chain to an engine support and began to back away, moving the powerful tank in reverse towards the village while it continued to fire. Prager made a mental note to recommend the sergeant for the Iron Cross.

The Russians drove another assault at them. The wind gusted fitfully, first blowing a full gale and obscuring everything with flying snow, then dying away to a bare breeze. When visibility permitted, the tank guns fired, methodically demolishing each attack. Prager wiped his field glasses and watched the lines disintegrate as before. The tank had managed to drag the wrecked aircraft to within fifty metres before the engine mount tore loose. While the men about the aircraft worked furiously to pump fuel into the barrels stacked on the truck, the Mark III's machine guns clattered and its gun kept up a steady barrage, searching for the Soviet mortar and artillery positions.

'Ivan looks determined . . .' someone shouted into his ear. He had started to turn when he was hurled aside and buried beneath a white mass. His head roared with agony and he could not understand what had happened. Then, through the roaring, he heard someone screaming, but so far away. The screaming went on and on; a boot stamped his chest, something struck his face and the sky blazed. Hands clutched and he was tugged from the snow. Explosion after explosion went on and he felt rather than heard them. Then he was being carried down a ladder. Darkness. He shouted with terror. Another shuddering explosion and something cold fell on him. More shouting but he did not understand the words. A face swam into view and its lips were moving and he wondered if he concentrated hard enough if he might know what was being said. The face went away; an oil lamp burned for a moment, then was blown out and he discovered he was terrified of the dark.

Prager struggled to sit up, then to stand and could not believe how dizzy he was. He rocketed from side to side like a drunk with no control of his body. His confusion was so great that he did not even know which way to turn; everything was dark and his head was exploding with the roaring noise that confused him, refused to let him think coherently. He was disoriented, dizzy and unable to comprehend what was happening.

Light blazed and he looked up and saw the sky. A figure was silhouetted against the light and he stared at him. Three explosions smashed against his eardrums and the figure teetered. He was shoved violently to one side and the body hurtled through the opening and splintered the duck boards. It wore a white snow smock with a red star sewn to the hood.

'. . . out of here,' someone screamed.

Someone else, Prager saw it was the radio operator, went up the ladder and levered himself over the edge, waved for the next man and disappeared.

Prager's mind began to function. I must have been dazed by the blast of an artillery shell . . . how long ago? Have I been unconscious? How long? Have the Reds broken through?

Prager pushed the body aside and began to climb. Three rungs exhausted him but a boost from behind urged him on. An arm grasped his and hauled and he struggled up the last rungs and half-rolled, was half-shoved, to one side.

He smeared his face with snow hoping the shock would clear his mind. His head ached so badly it was difficult to think. He tugged off his cap and rubbed snow on the back of his head. The pain lessened and the roaring in his ears slackened.

Daylight was fading, he saw. It had been midday when the attack had started. Had he been unconscious for four hours? Prager pushed himself up on hands and knees and looked around. At first nothing made sense. Everything seemed in motion, crazy dancing movements that made him sick to his stomach. He shut his eyes but found that even worse as afterimages cascaded in miniature cataclysms. He tried to stand, to hold on to something for support. The earth dipped and swayed.

The two men from the bunker crouched with him behind the debris. One handed him a machine pistol and Prager nodded, thankful that someone retained some presence of mind. He tried to check the breech to see if a round was chambered but his hands had trouble obeying. Only slowly was his mind beginning to clear.

Later, they saw several Russian soldiers moving about, two carrying wooden cases of ammunition suspended coolie fashion across their shoulders – nine in all, to three of them. Prager wondered vaguely where the radio operator had got to. There was a great deal of shooting off to the right, but he had no idea what it meant. Long blue shadows reaching across the snow disappeared abruptly as the sun slipped below the horizon. Explosions grew out of nowhere – a flash, a column of flame, smoke and concussion that buffeted face and eardrums. The sky overhead turned a clear, deep purple.

He felt as if he had been beaten with clubs and it took every ounce of willpower to again check the breech and magazine in the MP-40 – half full. Sixteen rounds. With an effort, he pointed at the cluster of Russians, then at himself and moved his hand to indicate that the two others should circle in either direction.

The youngest glanced at the other, a middle-aged, stolid countryman from Bavaria who served as headquarters' orderly. Prager saw the boy's eyes narrow with fear, or was it determination? A few metres away, a jutting beam had gathered an eddy of splintered timbers and he motioned the lad to its cover. He started as if to say something, then duck-walked away. The Bavarian was already moving in the opposite direction. Prager saw him ease down behind a battered brick wall.

He slid the machine pistol over the debris, canted it left and down to offset the inevitable muzzle rise, checked to see that it was cocked, lined the sights up on the lead figure and squeezed the trigger. The stream of 9 millimetre slugs hosed the ammunition carriers. He released the trigger, resighted and fired again. Two more went down and a third twisted away, screaming.

Another man ducked and the others ran in every direction, two of them straight into the boy's fire and were killed instantly. A hand grenade flew over the pile of timber and exploded. Something spattered him but there wasn't time to look; more Russians charged from cover firing long bursts that blasted snow, ice and splinters about his head.

There was no time to be frightened. Prager ran, tripped over the boy's body and fell. The bunker entrance was beside his hand and, without thinking, he scrambled for the ladder. His boot missed a rung and he fell hard onto his left shoulder. He dragged himself into the shadows conscious that his left arm was useless. Swearing incoherently and close to gibbering with fear, he dragged the heavy Schmeisser machine pistol onto his knees and pointed it up. He had an impression of a single figure as he pulled the trigger. The weapon pounded his chest, splinters and ice were blasted about the entrance. Grenade! his mind screamed but instead a body fell through the opening. In panic, he fired again and the magazine emptied.

Adrenalin ran out at that moment. His pistol was gone, the machine pistol empty, his life run out. He hadn't even the strength to find cover against the inevitable grenade. Prager resigned himself to dying.

'Major Prager?'

Prager heard his name but the words were meaningless.

'Major Prager!'

He opened his eyes. 'Major!'

The Bavarian's broad red face peered down at him. 'Quick, Major, before others come.'

Prager did not understand, and never would, why he was so angry.

It began to snow again at midnight. Prager hunched behind the ice wall and sipped his fourth cup of hot tea. What luxury, he thought. A hot drink and silence.

The Russians had failed in their all-out assault and Russian bodies lined the perimeter to prove that fact. The guns had ceased firing with darkness and the last Russian troops retreated, he supposed, to lick their wounds for the next try.

Prager's head ached badly as did his left arm, which had been sprained and not broken in the fall as he had first thought. The medical orderly had been killed at the start of the attack so one of the soldiers had made a clumsy job of wrapping his shoulder tightly with pieces torn from a dead Russian's uniform. He kept his arm tucked into his filthy greatcoat which made him feel like a ridiculous Napoleon, but it did ease the pain.

It was difficult to believe that so much had happened in just two days – the landing strip tramped out in the middle of the night; the murder of the Russian villagers; the crash of the Junkers ... Without the machine gun ammunition and anti-personnel rounds for the tanks, they would have been overrun. He could smell the wreck of the Ju 52 smouldering yet – the petrol salvage team had fired it when it appeared the Russians might reach it. Neither the lorry nor the Mark III, or their crews, had survived. A head count an hour ago showed the battalion reduced to 102 effectives and eighty wounded.

The Russians had succeeded in pushing them back again. He got to his knees and rested his chin on his right arm and stared across the wall into the darkness. Starlight glimmered on the churned snow and the humps of bodies. At random intervals a flare exploded and machine guns raked the area to kill infiltrators, using the bodies for cover. Another such assault and they would hold only the village itself.

How long, he wondered? A few days, a week? Would it take that much time to shoot up all their new ammunition. Did the Russians suspect the radio, his only contact with the outside world, had been destroyed and its radio operator, who might have been able to repair it, had bled to death from a splinter wound? If they didn't, he thought, they would soon enough.

Pale light on the eastern horizon resolved into a sliver of moonlight which to Prager's night-sensitive eyes seemed as bright as day. The scattered bodies were easily seen now. How many had died today? Hundreds here perhaps? Thousands all along the front? As the moonlight grew, meagre as it was, the artillery opened up again. The shells made a sound like an express train entering a tunnel before they fell onto the village.

Statistics were their great enemy. The chance of being hit by any single artillery shell was remote – one in fifteen thousand, it had been calculated. But at a dozen shells per hour, twenty-four hours a day, the odds added up inexorably until they summed certain death.

They had occupied Slavets in November with a battalion reduced to 372 men after the autumn campaign. Now only 102 of them remained able to fight. Prager worked the arithmetic in his head; twelve rounds per hour times twenty-four divided into fifteen thousand. Fifty-two days. Some time within the next fifty-two days, every man in the garrison would be killed. He laughed. Fifty-two days. Each of the survivors had already exceeded the allowed statistical limit of luck.

He pressed his mouth hard against his arm, face numb to the iron cold of the ice and struggled to stifle a scream, not of fear but of frustration. He cursed himself for his weakness and cursed the Russian land and the fools that inhabited it. He cursed the frost and the greater fools who believed it could be conquered.

The siege endured even though the Russians never again mounted another all-out assault. It seemed to Prager that they were as exhausted as he and his garrison. A week after the Junkers crashed bringing supplies, the weather cleared for two days and the Luftwaffe returned to bomb and strafe the forest. The sight of their tormentors enduring a taste of misery heartened the encircled garrison.

Twice during those two days, the Luftwaffe flew in more supplies. Ju 52s roared low over the open fields to the west, engines throttled back to stalling speed and billowed parachutes of food, ammunition and a new radio transmitter/receiver directly onto the ruined village. Then they feasted on salt pork, dried biscuit soaked in boiled coffee – ersatz, but welcome anyway – and fresh pastries made up for them especially by Luftwaffe cooks. Two kindly meant, but deadly, cases of schnapps had been dropped as well and Prager put them under strict guard in his own bunker and doled the bottles out at mealtimes only. He would have destroyed every bottle if he hadn't thought it would occasion a mutiny. Alcohol, subzero temperature, malnutrition and exhaustion were a killing combination.

Still they did not receive real winter gear. Instead, small packets of civilian winter clothing – used ski jackets and pants, overcoats, scarves and knitted gloves by the dozens were parachuted to them. Prager used the new radio transmitter to register a strong complaint and the reply caused grim laughter in the bunker. They were told that all winter clothing was being allocated to the Moscow front where winter conditions and fighting were severe.

It had done no good to point out that the temperature had not risen to zero centigrade since New Year's Day, that the wind averaged twenty kilometres per hour and because of the constant frost and enemy action, one tank only remained operational and none of the lorries. And finally, even with air-dropped supplies, their diets remained below 1,200 grams per day, seven hundred less than the minimum listed in the army tables for Class I rations in combat and winter conditions.

Blizzards followed one another all during March. The enemy, gradually regaining a measure of strength, fell into a new routine. Each dawn was greeted with a twenty minute bombardment, followed at noon by another. The day was closed with a final ten minute salute. Then, throughout the night, they continued to fire one round every fifteen minutes to deprive the garrison of sleep. Snipers moved in as close as possible each night and they possessed incredible endurance. They might lie without detectable movement in the snow for up to twenty-four hours before firing a shot. No matter how careful the garrison was, the snipers managed to pick off an average of one man every other day.

Strain was also a killer. Sunken eyes, hollow cheeks, faces seamed with windburn and frostbite, shaking hands and chattering teeth were not due to the cold alone. Privations could be endured, including the danger of relieving oneself in winds that made frostbite a certainty within thirty seconds, but strain took a steady toll.

The happy-go-lucky tanker who had played Father Christmas to the village children, climbed onto the ice wall one day and spread his arms. A sniper obliged with a bullet through the head. Another soldier went over the wall before anyone could stop him. He was allowed to march most of the way to the forest, firing his machine pistol in intermittent bursts and screaming at the top of his lungs, before they shot him down.

A strange lassitude struck Prager at the end of March. Nothing seemed worth the effort any longer. His head ached and his stomach burned constantly with indigestion. Prager spent more and more time in the dugout behind the blanket he had rigged to afford a measure of privacy.

There he simply sat, eyes closed, collar drawn close to his face, until he came to with a start to realise that an hour or more had passed.

The conviction that none of them would survive had burned deeply into his mind and it only seemed common sense to wait quietly for the end, wasting as little energy as possible.

Prager no longer remembered another existence, nor could he recall what it was like to be warm and not hungry. The shape and texture of his previous life was forgotten. He no longer thought about Sonja; she had receded into the past with the rest and he understood now how millions had endured the trenches between 1914 and 1918. Below a certain level of misery, pain, cold and hunger, existence becomes automatic, requiring little conscious effort until the organism exhausts itself and dies.

Perhaps, he thought, it would have been less endurable if there had been enough to eat. But their diet had again fallen below 1,000 grams per day, bringing the numb, dream-like quality of starvation's middle and latter stages.

The Soviet winter offensive had faded away. The enemy still crouched in the forest, still fired artillery shells at them and when the weather conditions were right, provoked them with weak assaults.

Prager had painfully assembled a picture of the extent of the Soviet counteroffensive south of Kharkov. As he had surmised early in January, German forces had been spread far too thinly about the countryside and the ferocious weather had destroyed their elaborate logistical and support plans. The Soviets had found it a simple matter to infiltrate troops through gaps between German garrisons, and partisans had flocked to them. When a sufficient concentration of force was achieved, they struck. If a garrison could not be overrun by main force, it was surrounded and, with the weather as an ally, isolated from reinforcement and resupply and worn down by attrition.

Relatively small Soviet forces were thus able to tie down the entire German front outside the main battle areas and keep it in turmoil at a time when they should have been resting, refitting and preparing for the spring and summer campaigns. We at least have one advantage over Napoleon, Prager thought. The aeroplane held isolated garrisons together and, when the weather allowed, which was rarely, resupplied them. The Soviets also used aircraft to supply their units and thus situational stalemates were achieved subject to clear weather which was measured in hours rather than days.

By mid-March, in spite of strict radio security, Prager thought he had detected the limits of the Soviet counteroffensive south of Kharkov. It encompassed territory within a line below Balakleya and east of the Donets, that ran due west more than a hundred kilometres, then abruptly south past Lozovaya and doubled back nearly to Slavyansk. Major General Mackensen, commanding the First Panzer Army, had begun a relief effort in mid-January but had been hampered continually by bad weather.

The weather began to moderate at long last and the severe blizzards faded and were replaced by frequent snowfalls, lasting several days, but lacking the gale-force winds that produced such bitter frost. Then, in the second week of April, a sudden thaw developed. The garrison greeted the pale warmth of the meagre sun with cheers, certain that winter was at last ending. But this change was only the beginning of an entirely new set of miseries. A ground mist seeped upward in mid-afternoon and snipers moved under its cover to take a fresh toll. Then, as the temperature rose above freezing for the first time in five months, bunkers flooded with melting snow and within two days they were driven out.

At mid-afternoon of the thaw's third day, Prager discovered the reason for the lull in enemy artillery fire – they had been hoarding ammunition for the thaw, knowing the rising water would drive them out. The heaviest artillery bombardment they had yet endured descended and forced them back into the flooded mudsinks.

It proved worse even than the autumn rainy season. At least then it had been possible to take shelter from the rain and one only had clammy clothing and boots to endure. Now the bunkers flooded knee to waist deep and movement raised both waves and curses and it was impossible to dry anything. Uniforms were soaked as was bedding. Boots, which had endured the worst that winter had to offer, rotted and fell apart in a matter of days and the grim joke had it they had held together this long only because they had been frozen solid.

April brought torrents of water that ran everywhere seeking routes to the thousands of rivers, creeks and streamlets suddenly revealed. The stench of rotting flesh hung over the village like a miasma and bodies reappeared as the snow melted, putrid and gangrenous. Roads also reappeared, but as quagmires and further precluded relief. Supplies were air-dropped, including dry clothing and boots, but so many packets fell into flooded areas that they were often wetter than the clothing the men wore.

The thaw ended abruptly in the last week of April. An iron freeze descended even as the weather remained clear. The roads froze iron-hard overnight and, before dawn, Prager had issued a general alert.

The seventy-two survivors of the garrison who had gathered around the command bunker, dispersed into position as the horizon lightened in the east. The cold was bitter and as the light grew Prager saw ice on boots and trousers. His own feet were numb. It had been three weeks since he had taken his boots off and he did not remember when he had last changed his footwrappings and ragged wool socks.

Prager guessed the attack would come from the eastern edge of the forest minutes after dawn when the sun would be shining directly into their eyes. There had been no artillery preparation nor had the weary sentries reported unusual movement during the night but, after nearly five months, Prager knew his adversary well enough to guess that they would realise that this was their last opportunity to destroy the German garrison. Spring was advancing swiftly and when the roads began to dry, the First Panzer and Seventeenth Armies would renew relief efforts.

The artillery barrage began without warning. The first shells screamed down on the perimeter in swift succession, but the sodden earth absorbed the worst of the explosions and shrapnel and the bunkers held. Prager had moved his single remaining tank at midnight and shells aimed at its previous position exploded harmlessly. He shielded his eyes against the sun and saw the familiar, lemming-like figures running towards them across the frozen ground. The machine gunners and snipers ignored the artillery barrage to take up carefully prepared positions from which they began to pick off targets in the first wave.

In the four months they had been under seige, Prager had recorded thirty-two frontal assaults. This made the thirty-third, he thought as the first assault wave reached the five hundred metre marker and the artillery barrage diminished. Still, the men waited. At three hundred metres, the cannon played a final crescendo and he smiled. These Russians were so damned unimaginative. They never varied their routine.

When the badly attenuated assault reached one hundred metres, Prager blew his battered whistle and the men rose out of bunkers and slit trenches and trotted silently into position behind the battered breastworks they had maintained at such cost during the winter.

The second wave emerged from the glare and Prager thought their spacing greater than usual. The sun glare was painful and Prager's eyes watered, making it that much more difficult to see. But he had the impression that the second wave was not as large, nor pressing the attack as furiously. Then it wavered and fell apart.

The end was decidedly anticlimactic. Russian soldiers merely disappeared, leaving bundled rags that were dead comrades in the frozen fields. Like men released from a trance, the garrison stood and gawked. One or two climbed onto the breastworks, then jumped down on the other side. Someone laughed and it proved infectious and they began to cheer themselves hoarse. They had survived! They walked about the shattered remains of the village openly, all danger gone, the enemy defeated and fled.

At midday, Prager sat on a portion of wall that had been reinforced with a baulk of charred timber. He unbuttoned his greatcoat as the sun grew warmer and a tiny splash nearby drew his attention. Ice melting. His mind, numbed by months of terror and hardship, was only now beginning to grasp the abrupt turnabout.

The Soviet force holding the forest had slipped away during the night, leaving only a small party behind for one last attack – out of habit grown unbreakable, or despair? He did not know nor care. Whatever the reason, the Reds were gone and they had survived. Seventy-two of them anyway.

Seventy-two survivors, he thought. He had arrived in Slavets with a total of 372 men. So they had endured a casualty rate of eighty per cent in four months. And since the start of the campaign ten months before, they had suffered casualties of ninety-two per cent. For all intents and purposes, his command, the First Battalion, First Regiment of the First Panzer Army, Army Group South had ceased to exist.

Arctic Convoy June 1942

Lieutenant Commander Rand Dobson, HM Royal Australian Navy, leaned on the bridge railing in a rare moment of privacy and contemplated the cliffs of Iceland sinking into the endless summer sunlight. The wind was soft with spring and the sky deep blue overhead turning to gold on the western horizon as convoy PQ 17 entered the Denmark Strait. They were thirty-five ships – twenty-two American, eight British, two Russian, two Panamanian and one Dutch, shepherded by six escort destroyers, four trawlers, three minesweepers, two submarines and two auxiliary anti-aircraft vessels.

He watched a US Navy *Catalina* flying boat circling over the convoy and, all of a sudden, felt the first stirrings of excitement in a long while as the convoy commander's signal boomed out and tiny black bunting balls zipped up the distant mast and burst into pennants. The signal rating appeared instantly with the translation.

'Signal to convoy, sir. Take up night stations.'

'Night Stations' in name only as they would be sailing in sunlight twenty-four hours a day. But as the sun rolled down to the western horizon, visibility would be reduced sufficiently to justify the usual night precautions.

Dobson nodded, aware that he should have anticipated the signal. I'm rusty, he thought. 'Sound night action stations.'

The bugle blared from the tannoy, followed by a nasal Cockney twang that penetrated every square inch of the ship. Below, on the main deck, sailors burst from hatchways and raced to their respective stations. The signal rating turned the log so that Dobson could sign the entry, then returned to the wheelhouse.

Dobson was first officer aboard the minesweeper HMS *Hara*, his first sea duty since being exiled to Halifax in the spring of 1941. Naval officers with convoy experience were in short supply and the fact that he had been assigned as First Officer, rather than being given a command of his own, was proof that the Admiralty had not yet forgiven him.

For a long time, Dobson had blamed his exile on Admiral Dunbar-Naismith, who had commanded Western Approaches at Plymouth while Dobson was First Officer aboard the minesweeper, HMS *Adelaide*, in the winter of 1940–1941. He had written a report critical of Commander Peters, captain of the minesweeper, only to discover in a polite but searing interview with Dunbar-Naismith that even the basis for his report had been wrong. He realised now that he had allowed personal feelings to colour his appraisal of Peters' actions, but still, he resented the harsh treatment he had received.

In moments of honest assessment, he knew that it was justified, if for the wrong reason. He was being punished for misinterpreting his captain's action, not for panicking at a vital moment and so allowing a U-boat to escape, a fact that he was certain no one else knew about. Even so, there had been many times since when the memory of this inadequacy rose to gall him and he despaired that even if he could obtain a command, that he could exercise it properly.

Dobson had arrived in Liverpool from London barely in time to walk from Lime Street Station to the Adelphi Hotel for the convoy conference, which he had been directed to attend in place of the *Hara*'s captain who was still on leave – his first in fifteen months. He showed his papers to the military policeman inside and was directed to the mezzanine tearoom where a hundred ship's officers in every merchant and naval uniform extant in the North Atlantic Alliance waited for the conference to start. He checked with the clerk for other officers from *Hara* and was surprised to find he was the only one present.

The briefing opened with a review of past convoys on the Kola Run, then a dissertation on weather conditions to be expected in the Barents Sea, and finally a captain from naval intelligence described the disposition of German naval and air forces in Norway. Dobson's responsibilities in past months had been centred on the approaches to Halifax and Sydney, but he had managed to keep abreast of the convoy situation as a whole and so was able to see at once that nothing had changed recently.

The intelligence officer reported no sign that the battleship *Tirpitz* was planning to venture out of the relative safety of her Trondheim base, as she had after convoys PQ 12 and QP 8. *Tirpitz* was a critical factor in the planning of any Arctic convoy, supported as she was by a small but powerful escort group, comprised of the heavy cruiser *Hipper*, two pocket battleships, *Admiral Sheer* and *Lutzow*, and assorted destroyers and light cruisers. But recently it was believed that Hitler himself had forbidden her to operate after convoys since the aircraft carrier, HMS *Victorious*, had been sent to the Home Fleet at Scapa Flow.

Hitler was keeping his naval force in reserve against the possibility of a continental invasion via Norway. A mitigating factor in her presence on the flank of the convoy route was the fact that the German Navy had not shown much aggressive spirit as far as her capital ships were concerned, since Jutland in 1915.

The tone of the conference had been optimistic enough, even though losses had been growing steadily since February. Before that the first twelve convoys had gone through virtually unscathed. But as Allied-supplied equipment began to appear on the Russian Front, the Nazis had begun to take them seriously. Intensive efforts had been made to intercept PQ 12 and the homeward bound QP 8, but in the bad weather and fog of the Arctic winter they had been missed. Convoy PQ 13, on the other hand, lost five out of nineteen ships. The majority of PQ 14 had been turned back by ice, but the cruiser *Edinburgh* was torpedoed and three merchant ships sunk from PQ 15. PQ 16 had lost seven of its thirty-five merchant ships.

What was worse, PQ 15 sailed in April and PQ 16 in May 1942, while the days were lengthening above the Arctic Circle, enabling the Luftwaffe and the Kriegsmarine to press their attacks under optimum visibility. PQ 17 which would sail in twenty-four hour daylight would do so under extremely heavy escort. A support group commanded by Rear-Admiral Louis H.K. Hamilton would contain four heavy cruisers – two of which were American – and three destroyers. And somewhere east of Bear Island, a powerful covering force led by the battleship HMS *Duke of York* with the aircraft carrier *Victorious* would pace them beyond the horizon, daring the Nazis to come out.

After three years of war, Dobson placed little faith in the accuracy of intelligence estimates. The memory of the part, albeit a minor one, that he had played in the Norwegian fiasco in April 1940, when they had all depended so heavily on their intelligence reports that the Nazis beat them into Oslo by one day, still rankled. And it was a view he found shared by the ship's captain, Commander Leon Tarkington, Royal Volunteer Naval Reserve, who returned aboard two days later. Dobson liked Tarkington from the start, finding him to be a brash and irreverent, middle-aged officer, commissioned from the merchant marine ranks at the beginning of the war.

Tarkington had little use for the spit and polish of peacetime naval drill that so many regulars had held over into war. He was interested only in getting the job done as efficiently as possible. And he had the merchant officer's abiding interest in his crew's comfort and well-being which made him popular with the enlisted men, except for those few old-timers and hide-bound professionals who resented change of any kind.

Dobson had been prepared to suffer Tarkington's contempt in silence. His exile to Halifax at a time when every officer with convoy experience was needed for sea duty said without equivocation that he was being punished. In fact, Dobson saw his assignment aboard *Hara* as merely a continuation of that punishment, as it made a command of his own even more remote – for which he felt a curious relief. His exile had done more than teach him humility; it had caused him to brood on what he now saw as a terrible lack of judgement and a disastrous moment of panic on his part.

But if Tarkington was cognisant of his record, he did not show it in his cordial welcome. Dobson was waved to a seat while Tarkington poured two double brandies. A chill summer rain had swept in from St George's Channel and the brandy was welcome.

'Glad to have you aboard, Mr Dobson. Your experience is most welcome.' Tarkington listened closely while Dobson described the convoy conference and they checked the charts and signal routines together. Tarkington even asked his opinion on one or two points and noted his report on the ship's condition with a pleased nod. 'I'd say well done, Mr Dobson. You seem to have things well in hand.'

The voyage from Liverpool to Reykjavik had allowed the ship's company to shake down after their month's leave. Dobson found himself falling swiftly back into the pleasant routine – and boredom – of convoy escort duty. *Hara* was one of the last escorts to arrive and the convoy sailed twenty-four hours later. In the light of PQ 15's and 16's experiences, Dobson fully expected they would have to fight their way to Murmansk from the moment they left Iceland. But instead, the first six days passed uneventfully under cloudless skies and balmy temperatures.

Estimating a convoy's chances on the Murmansk run was subject to a lot of complicated factors. In summer, the great Ice Barrier, the leading edge of the Arctic ice sheet, retreated far enough to enable shipping to pass north of Bear Island, three hundred miles north-northwest of Norway's North Cape. The added distance helped offset the twenty-four hours of daylight by reducing the time the convoy spent within range of Luftwaffe long range bombers by three days. On the negative side, the combination of retreating ice and total daylight doubled the U-boat danger because it kept them at sea four days longer.

The entry of the United States into the war six months before was beginning to make a difference. The US Navy flew landbased *Catalina* patrols from Iceland and Greenland and they had proven increasingly effective against U-boats, whose masters were leery of operating under the threat of surprise attack against which they had little or no defence. The *Catalinas* ranged from Greenland and Iceland along the convoy track as far as one hundred miles north of Spitzbergen, thus keeping the U-boats off-balance at least half the distance.

During the first week of the convoy's journey, the suspicion grew in Dobson that Tarkington was testing him with what he suspected were contrived situations. He was careful not to let his anger show as it was only natural that, when an officer had been under a cloud, he had to prove himself again. Accordingly, Dobson found himself assuming an aloof manner and for some reason this attitude seemed to draw a certain respect from the ratings. Pleased with the effect, he continued to cultivate it.

The attitude of the sailors puzzled him. In the more than two years he had languished among the Canadians, the British sailor seemed to have developed into another breed. Too many conscripts, he thought. They seemed far less willing to accept discipline or give respect. The outward forms were there, usually, but he could sense the contempt beneath. It was as if officers were considered to be oppressors. As an Australian, he seemed to be exempted from the worst of it – perhaps because the British seemed to consider all Aussies as essentially working class – but the attitude boded no good for the future of the Navy, he thought. He made a mental note to discuss it with Tarkington, curious to know if it was his imagination or not.

On July 1, they passed Jan Mayen Island to the northwest. So far there had been no sign of enemy activity and no indication from naval intelligence monitoring of German military and naval wavelengths that PQ 17 was in more than routine danger. Late that afternoon, their constant companion, one of the *Catalina* from Iceland, dipped low over the convoy. The *Hara* was on the starboard flank when Dobson saw the aircraft waggle its wings and turn west towards Greenland and home. They had passed the limits of land-based aircraft. An hour later, they were joined by what became a permanent fixture, a German Focke Wulf Condor, a long range reconnaissance aircraft based in Norway. His optimism had been premature and a sudden feeling of isolation overcame him; what in the hell was he doing here, he wondered. Halifax may have been boring, but it was safe.

At midnight, 3/4 July, Dobson was on watch when a sudden blast of horns and whistles echoed round the convoy startling him and every other escort. American flags unfurled at mastheads and ships' guns fired volleys of salutes to announce American Independence Day.

The celebration, Dobson chuckled, was hardly calculated to endear them to their British allies, especially as a dozen convoy rules had been broken at once. But then, the Americans and British were uneasy allies in many respects. Even so, British, Panamanian, Dutch and even the two

Russian flags were dipped in salute and Dobson wondered with cynicism if they would all be required to salute 7 November with such fervour? Certainly there were many in HMS *Hara* who would do so.

The sun, which had rolled along the horizon at midnight, now began to climb through a dense fog that lay above the surface of the sea like a dirty ceiling. After the blast of celebratory gunfire, the convoy had subsided into placid silence and so the explosion at 0500, which rumbled across the sea, soft, muffled, almost aplogetic, came as a distinct shock. Dobson spotted a mushrooming cloud of black smoke on the far side of the convoy. What the hell, he wondered and dashed to the wheelhouse door. The signalman had the Talk-Between-Ships earphones pressed against his head. He saw Dobson and shook his head.

Dobson debated only a moment; the ship was already at night action stations and the crew needed the few more minutes of sleep before the watch changed. As did Tarkington. Nothing would be gained by going to action stations until the threat was defined.

Five minutes later, the signalman touched his sleeve. 'Ship is *Christopher Newton*, sir. Single torpedo bomber found her in the fog. Convoy commander ordered her crew to abandon and the wreck to be sunk.'

He had been right then, he thought with relief. Dobson had the lookouts warned to keep a sharp eye but no one spotted the lone dive bomber in the fog. First blood, he thought. Happy Independence Day, Yanks.

When his watch ended, Dobson snatched a hurried breakfast and went immediately to his cabin to sleep. Four hours on watch in twelve left little time for both regular shipboard duties and sleep, especially when the ship stood to night stations and he was required to be at his post in the aft fire control compartment.

The blare of a bugle over the tannoy woke him and even as his body instinctively lurched awake, he was aware of the anomaly of bright sunlight pouring through the uncovered port to suffuse the dirty grey bulkhead with gold. His watch showed 1500 hours and, confused, he staggered into the passageway shoving his shirt into his trousers. On deck, a warm afternoon sun glimmered.

He reached the aft fire control compartment and plugged his earphones into the main circuit to report himself present. A moment later, Tarkington's voice came on the line. 'U-boat sighted ahead of the convoy,' he announced in crisp tones. '*Hara* ordered to investigate.'

The deck heeled as he spoke and the background vibration of the ship's engines increased. Dobson leaned forward as the stern went down and he scanned his instruments; all indicated that the ships guns and the new K-guns capable of throwing two depth charges to either side of the destroyer's wake were loaded and ready, as were the torpedo tubes.

A stream of reports flowed into his earphones and Dobson closed his eyes the better to visualise the ship's weaponry. A plotter touched his arm and Dobson glanced at the slip of paper for their exact position and time. He slipped it into his pocket and concentrated on the information flowing through the headphones.

A British seaman's sighting of what he had taken for a periscope had coincided with an asdic signal on the extreme starboard edge of the convoy. It seemed unlikely that a U-boat would show itself in broad daylight, but the escort commander could not afford to take the chance and so the chase continued for forty minutes before *Hara* was recalled.

Dobson hated the idea of being confined in a steel box in the depths of the hull. He much preferred the bridge, where the real decisions concerning how the ship was to be fought were made, not down here in this bloody coffin relaying orders and information and calculating gunnery plots for targets one never saw.

They secured from action stations thirty minutes later and rejoined the convoy. Dobson went up on deck and paused at the rail to light a cigarette and observe the crew while they snatched a few moments relaxation. *Hara* had been at sea for over two years and her crew was well-seasoned. His predecessor had done an excellent job, he thought, before being posted out to the Med to command a Hunt-class destroyer escort. But as professional as they were, there was still that sense of sullen resentment below the surface. If he hadn't noted it in other seamen in Liverpool, he would have wondered if it wasn't peculiar to the *Hara*.

Changing attitudes, and the thought of his predecessor now commanding his own ship, did not improve his disposition and Dobson crushed the cigarette and dropped it into the scuttle in annoyance. That's what came of being a bloody Australian and getting on the bad side of a pommy admiral.

There were four more submarine sightings that day, although none in *Hara*'s sector, and no one had to be told what it meant. The mid-afternoon sighting had probably not been a false alarm after all and the additional sightings suggested they were being stalked by a wolf-pack. And tomorrow they would come within extreme range of Nazi *Condors* from bases at Narvik, Bardufoss, Tromsö, Banak, Kirkenes in Norway and Petsamo in Finland. The bastards would hunt them until they anchored at Polyarny or Murmansk under the protection of Russian anti-aircraft guns.

Then the convoy received the welcome news that heavy fog over coastal northern Norway was expected to ground the Luftwaffe. Although the long range bombers were only one part of the total threat, they were the worst, and there was a perceptible lessening of tension throughout *Hara*. The day passed slowly. The sky was summer calm and only an occasional fleck of foam showed on the wave crests.

Dobson inspected the engine room, then the galleys where the cooks were busily preparing bully beef sandwiches and gallons of tea to be kept hot in insulated flasks against the action that was certain to come. Shortly before he was due to go on watch, Dobson was summoned to Tarkington's cabin adjoining the bridge. Tarkington waved him to a chair and indicated the teapot. Dobson poured himself a cup and Tarkington added a measure of gin.

'To your new command,' he smiled and raised his mug. Dobson started to acknowledge the toast. 'I beg your pardon, sir?'

Tarkington handed him a yellow flimsy. 'Just in from the Admiralty. Captain Sargant, commanding rescue ship *Sanda*, suffered a severe heart attack this morning. His executive officer was badly injured in an accident the day after we sailed and was flown back to Reykjavik. So you've been appointed to her command.'

Dobson struggled for something to say, torn between gratitude for a command at long last and disappointment that it was not in a fighting ship.

Tarkington guessed his confusion. 'A rescue ship is a fine command, Rand,' he said using his Christian name for the first time. 'The Admiralty must think highly of you.'

Dobson nodded, still not trusting himself to comment. He had looked through the list of regular serving officers in the convoy's naval escort the day before they sailed from Liverpool. He was next senior below command level and the Admiralty had simply used that as their selection criteria. He was certain Tarkington was aware of that but was grateful for his kindness in placing the best possible interpretation on it.

'We'll lay alongside *Sanda* in twenty minutes for the transfer. Better pack.' Tarkington hesitated, as if to say more. Dobson, his face beginning to burn, stood up quickly, shook hands and stumbled out into the corridor.

Hara came alongside *Sanda* and the breeches buoy was rigged quickly. Few off-duty seamen watched. He hadn't been aboard *Hara* long enough to build real respect among the crew and the air of aloofness he had cultivated had prompted discipline but earned him no special friends. He was just another officer who served aboard a few days and moved on. If he had been killed, at least the ship's company would have been turned to for his burial.

He was swung over the gently heaving sea and dropped to *Sanda*'s wooden deck without incident. A petty officer saluted and unlaced the canvas breeches. The engineer, the only other officer aboard besides the two doctors, hurried through a hatch wiping his right hand on his overalls and gave Dobson an oily handshake.

'Sorry about the reception,' he apologised. 'We are very short-handed.

I'm Lieutenant Archibald Carson.' He led Dobson into the deck house and up to the bridge. A single rating stood at the wheel and he gave Dobson a tentative smile. The speaking tube blew and the engineer answered it at once then turned with a grimace.

'If you will excuse me, Captain Dobson, we've a bit of a problem with the generator. The main shaft bearings are bad and we've no way to replace it without shutting down for several hours. I'll have to go and see what I can do.'

Pleased and flustered to hear his name preceded by the title 'captain' after so long, Dobson almost missed what the man said. 'Do the best you can, Mr Carson.' He managed the standard naval answer.

After the engineer hurried away, he decided against turning the crew out to read himself into the ship. The change of watches in two more hours would be soon enough and would not disturb the sleep of the men below. Dobson hesitated, then kicked his duffle bag into a corner. Unpacking could also wait. He sat down at the chart table and began to skim the log.

The daily notes made in a spidery hand were routine enough and the only real problem seemed to be the generator. It was on the tip of his tongue to order the engineer to shut it down and fix it once and for all when it occurred to him that the medical staff might need a continuous supply of electricity. Suddenly he felt himself at a loss; there was so much to learn, so much to do, so many pitfalls to watch for.

He forced himself to relax and stop dwelling on his inadequacies. He had commanded a ship before, the *Adelaide*, after Peters had suffered his stroke. And with the exception of the single incident when he froze under the sudden and conflicting demands for his attention and thus lost a U-boat, he had done a creditable job. Mastering the command of a rescue ship should be child's play in comparison.

Normally, there were three officers aboard *Sanda* capable of standing watches. Now, there were two; himself and the engineer. The first task then was to arrange a new watch list to include a petty officer.

It occurred to him that he did not even know the establishment of a hospital ship. What was her crew? How many petty officers? How many medical staff? He knew only that two physicians were aboard. Rescue ships, the real heroes of the system, were for the most part coastal or channel passenger steamers with low freeboard to make it easier to haul exhausted and wounded or burned men from the sea.

Rescue ships freed the fighting escorts to fight and made it unnecessary for the escort's captain to make the heartbreaking decision to abandon sailors in the water while in pursuit of a U-boat. It had been just such an incident in HMS *Adelaide* that had prompted Dobson to file the report that had damaged his career. It was pure irony that shortly afterwards he had been forced to make the same decision himself.

*

Enemy aircraft, HE 115 torpedo seaplanes, appeared at 2100 hours. So much for the heavy fog over coastal Norway, Dobson thought. The sea had taken on a soft golden tone as the sun touched the horizon and long shadows streamed eastward. The bombers were audible for some moments before they were visible and Dobson, standing on the exposed bridge muffled against the chill wind, watched them come, four tiny specks flashing red silver in the sun. A storm of anti-aircraft fire greeted them but the German pilots bored in without hesitation.

The anti-aircraft fire was so intense that three aircraft dropped their torpedoes at long range and veered away. Even so, two were hit and cartwheeled across the sea, shedding bits of wing and tail and flame. The third, damaged, fought for altitude.

The lead aircraft, perhaps the squadron commander, flew on in spite of the flak barrage, attempting to force his way inside the convoy's anti-aircraft screen, where the gunners would be hampered by fear of hitting their own ships. He almost made it.

Still a thousand yards out, the Heinkel staggered as flak shredded its starboard wing. With consummate skill, the pilot landed two miles ahead of the convoy. *Sanda* was in the front rank and Dobson had a perfect view of what happened next. The burning aircraft remained upright on its floats as two yellow life rafts bobbed away. Flames blossomed around the wing roots and a moment later, the aircraft exploded.

A destroyer shot past *Sanda*, siren whooping, but another HE 115 appeared, landed nearby and taxied to the rafts. The downed crew clambered aboard and the rescue aircraft turned into the wind, its propellers whipping long streamers of spray behind. A life raft tumbled away in the blast as the Heinkel gathered speed. It wasn't until then that the surprised convoy gunners recovered. Anti-aircraft fire poured after the rescue plane but it lifted and flew serenely out of range.

Only then did Dobson realise that he had been holding his breath, almost hoping the gallant rescue would succeed.

During the early morning hours, fog shrouded the convoy. Everyone breathed easier, even though the risk of collision was now greatly increased. But fear of collision was a small penalty to pay for protection against aircraft, surface ships and U-boats.

Dobson began a thorough tour in the engine room where the twin diesels throbbed away. The engineering officer had been the ship's engineer in civilian life and knew her intimately. *Sanda* had been a channel steamer before the war, plying between Felixstowe and Dieppe. As she was built in the 1920s exclusively for the Channel route, *Sanda* had only two proper staterooms and they now formed the surgical operating rooms. The enclosed mezzanine ran two-thirds of the length of the ship and had been designated as sick bay. Passenger chairs had all been removed and row after row of bunks, two high, had been bolted to the decking. They were empty now save for the unconscious former captain.

The medical staff consisted of two physicians, one a regular naval officer, Lieutenant Walter James, a veteran of the Arctic convoy run, the other a well-known London surgeon with a commanding presence, Lieutenant David Fletcher, and six medical orderlies. Dobson was pleased to see that the regular naval surgeon did not seem overawed by his noted colleague.

Neither doctor concealed their doubts about the elderly man's chances of recovery. 'Too much stress on a man his age and condition,' the naval surgeon said. 'I'm afraid there's little hope.'

As he made his way back to the bridge, it seemed to Dobson that far too many commanding officers were being killed off by tension, elderly or not. The pressures were far too great. But then the navy list had been full of retired officers in 1939. Britain, and indeed the Commonwealth, were paying the price for the successive Liberal and Labour governments who had emasculated the armed services. Few young career officers had survived reduction after reduction and pay cut after pay cut throughout the Commonwealth. He remembered with bitterness the long years he had suffered in the much-reduced Australian navy, praying for sea duty. And when it came at last, a single mistake had him in a desk job instead of a sea command. In three years of war, he had spent less than ten months at sea. And when command came, it had to be in a rescue ship.

Dobson did not doubt the need of rescue ships nor belittle the dangers they suffered. He had had first hand experience with their lack. But he belonged on a destroyer. He had a natural empathy with German U-boat commanders as he had proved in the North Atlantic two years before.

After dinner, Dobson moved his few belongings from the corner of the bridge into the captain's cabin, abaft the bridge. He kicked off his boots and lay down without undressing, intending only to rest. The balmy summer weather and lack of wind made it seem far too much like a peacetime cruise and he was determined that his crew would remain alert.

The distant sound of anti-aircraft fire and the whoop of sirens woke him an hour later and he swayed onto the bridge, groggy with fatigue. The summer sun had settled onto the horizon and the cloudless sky was blue with gold overlay. Through binoculars, he found the innocent puffs of smoke that marked bursting anti-aircraft shells and guessed from their volume that the siege of convoy PQ 17 had begun in earnest.

He counted twenty torpedo-bombers approaching from every direction. The nearest, an HE 115, held directly on for a medium-sized freighter in spite of the nearly solid wall of anti-aircraft fire. The ship began a turn but too late. Dobson saw the torpedo released and in the flat light it bounded once and, at point-blank range, smashed into the freighter *Navarino* amidships.

She blew up. Simultaneously, the Heinkel was struck and slammed into the sea directly ahead of the escort leader, *Keppel*, who, too close to turn aside, smashed the aircraft under. The rest of the torpedo squadron kinked right and left as tracer shells poured into their formation and their runs became so erratic that only two other ships were hit, the Russian tanker, *Azerbaidjan* and another American ship, the *William Hooper*, before the squadron disappeared east in ragged order.

Azerbaidjan was closest and Dobson gave the helmsman orders for *Sanda* to run down on her. As they approached, the captain appeared on the bridge. The ship was holed but still steaming at convoy speed and they were waved off.

The *William Hooper* was farther back and Dobson saw that their sister ship, HMS *Zamalek*, was already up to her and so he ordered *Sanda* back on course, turned the watch over to the petty officer and went back to the chartroom.

But there was no sleep for him now that it had begun. He had almost forgotten how bad the tension could be as it attacked with a vengeance, tightening abdominal muscles and constricting his throat. He felt his heart thump faster and muscles all through his body tense. It would be this way, he knew, until they anchored safely under Soviet anti-aircraft guns.

And, sooner or later, the U-boats would make their appearance. They were only waiting for the covering force of cruisers lurking just over the horizon to depart. Then, while the six destroyers of the close escort were engaged by aircraft, they could strike.

At 1020, the signal rating woke him. 'The Commodore is ordering the convoy to scatter, sir.'

Dobson stared at the man, thinking he had heard wrong. 'What . . ?' he croaked.

'The Commodore has signalled for the convoy to scatter, sir,' he repeated. His face reflected Dobson's confusion as he thrust the message form at him.

Dobson read it, slid his feet into sea boots and stumped onto the bridge. The sun was directly behind them and low on the horizon as he used his binoculars. Everything appeared normal enough until he saw an escort destroyer running northwestward at what had to be twenty-five knots.

Dobson could hardly believe it, but all about him the assemblage began to open like a vast flower as individual ships turned onto new, predetermined courses so designed that, in a matter of minutes, the convoy as such had ceased to exist.

He found the Commodore's flagship, *River Afton*, with the glasses and there it was, the 'scatter' signal flying at the masthead, emphasised by her foghorn and whistle. Even as he stared, the signal was hauled down and the *River Afton* began to turn away.

Surface ships?

Had *Tirpitz* broken out at last with her escort – the pocket battleship *Lutzow* and the heavy cruisers *Scheer* and *Hipper* and their attending destroyers? If so, they must be damned close!

Only once before that he could remember had a convoy been ordered to scatter. In November 1940, thirty-seven ships of an Atlantic convoy being escorted by a single armed merchant cruiser, *Jervis Bay*, had been attacked by the *Scheer*. The escort captain had ordered the convoy to scatter while he gallantly, and hopelessly, had attacked *Scheer*.

Jervis Bay was sunk but she delayed the *Scheer* long enough for all but six of the convoy to get away. Her captain, Edward Fogarty Fegen, was awarded a posthumous Victoria Cross.

Dobson hurried to the captain's cabin and feverishly dialled the combination to the safe. In the rush of assuming command and familiarising himself with *Sanda*'s specific convoy orders and the procedures for rescue craft, he had ignored the predetermined scatter course in order to concentrate on higher priority matters.

He found the Admiralty envelope and tore it open as he went into the chartroom and laid out the course it contained on the navigation chart. They were ordered to steer well south of Bear Island in a flattened curve that would take them into the Barents Sea and south to Archangel by the shortest possible sailing route.

Christ! he thought. It was bloody suicide in summer. The Luftwaffe would have a field day. At no time would *Sanda* be more than two hours flying time from any base in Norway! How many other ships had been given similar foolish orders? He stepped to the bridge window, ignoring the apprehension on the petty officer's face who had seen the course plot.

The other ships were now little more than smudges on the horizon. He searched the sky but only the lone Focke Wulf Condor that had been with them since 1 July was to be seen, circling aimlessly. Dobson thought that its crew must be as astounded at what had happened as any ship in the convoy.

Sanda was extremely vulnerable, few vessels were more so in the Royal Navy. She carried no naval guns and a quick check of the arms locker revealed two World War I vintage Colt .455 automatic pistols, one for the captain and one for the first officer, and two Model 1927 Thompson submachine guns. And one Lee-Enfield rifle for exploding mines.

The Luftwaffe would appear in force shortly as the Condor would have broadcast the departure courses for every ship in the convoy. He studied the navigation chart carefully, measuring distances and estimating where the greatest concentration of U-boats could be expected. He also marked in the shortest courses between the airbases on the Norwegian coast and the two German destroyer bases at Trondheim and Kirkenes. There was a third at Petsamo in Finland which would be a menace later.

Dobson had no illusions that the cruiser squadron could hold off a battle fleet comprising *Tirpitz* and *Lutzow*, particularly if air attacks were properly coordinated. That was a job for the heavy cover, the battleships and the carrier, *Victorious*, from the Home Fleet. In the meantime, he was caught between two impenetrable barriers – the ice barrier at the latitude of Hope Island and the coast of Norway itself. The Luftwaffe could strike at them anywhere, anytime until they entered the Kola Inlet.

Dobson studied the chart of the Scandinavian coast. Clear weather with intermittent fog had been forecast only a few hours before. It was a terrible enough risk to continue escorted, insanity to do so without.

Damn it! Why had the Admiralty ordered the convoy to scatter? Never had there been a convoy better protected than PQ 17. But he knew the reason; the same threat that kept the Nazi battleship *Tirpitz* hidden in her deep fjord – aircraft. The Admiralty would not risk Home Fleet battleships and the *Victorious* to German long range bombers, anymore than Hitler would risk the *Tirpitz* to those from *Victorious*. And so, somewhere to the west, the two naval squadrons played cat and mouse while he and the rest of the convoy continued towards the Kola Inlet, alone.

If he hugged the Ice Barrier as far as thirty-five degrees east longitude, Dobson thought, he might reach Moller Bay at Novaya Zemlya. The Ice Barrier would furnish some concealment until they could hide in one of the island's many fjords. The problem lay in his orders. Even as *Sanda* ran for her life, she was expected to serve as a rescue ship.

But it was certain suicide to take an unarmed ship through such a heavy concentration of enemy air-, surface- and sub-surface craft.

What good would it do to pick up a few survivors if *Sanda* herself was sunk? Yet if he arrived at Novaya Zemlya alone, a court-martial board would consider that he had played the coward and rushed to safety. No amount of explanation would ever persuade them, safe and comfortable in London or Liverpool, that he had made a correct decision.

To hell with them, he thought. He was not going to waste his ship and the lives of his crew. Only a fool would do so. Dobson gave the helmsman a course that would take them well north to the Ice Barrier. From its meagre cover he could do far more good by making quick sorties south to aid ships under attack. He made a note to double-check *Sanda*'s wireless watches and procedures.

The Ice Barrier is the very fringe of the vast ice sheet that covers the entire Arctic Ocean. In winter, Arctic temperatures weld the ice into a single vast block, but in summer its border melts into millions of separate islands of all shapes and sizes. As *Sanda* plodded north towards the Ice Barrier, she encountered two other ships from the convoy, an American and a

Panamanian freighter, both of whose captains quickly agreed to follow *Sanda*. The Panamanian vessel carried miscellaneous naval stores and the American was a refrigerator ship.

At midnight, the tiny convoy felt its cautious way deep into the ice pack fringe. The strange arctic light made it difficult to see detail at any distance and in his new role as convoy commander, Dobson ordered all available hands on the three ship convoy onto aircraft lookout-duty and suspended anti-submarine watches for the time being. No sensible U-boat commander would risk his vessel inside the ice pack and without asdic, Dobson would have no way of detecting him even if he did.

At midnight, Lieutenant Fletcher came onto the bridge to report that Captain Sargant had just died. 'There was little that we could do for him after such a massive attack. I'm surprised that he lasted as long as he did.'

Fletcher gave Dobson a keen glance. 'I know that you regular Navy laddies are sensitive about your powers of endurance,' he said in a low voice so the helmsman would not hear, 'but you look a mess. Of course, I've also learned that it's no use trying to get you fellows to rest. But Captain Sargant was a perfect example of what happens when you don't. I prescribe a minimum of six hours sleep.'

Dobson shook his head. 'Too damned short-handed.'

The doctor nodded glumly. 'I thought that would be your answer.'

Dobson went to the ship's loudspeaker to announce the Captain's death to the crew.

At mid-morning, Dobson was dozing at the chart table when a lookout woke him to report a ship under attack to the southeast. Dobson stumbled onto the bridge wing and searched across the horizon with gummy eyes until he spotted the thin column of smoke.

Although the distance was more than forty nautical miles, the ship was clearly visible – upside down with smoke pouring into the sea. The eerie mirage effect was quite common on Arctic summer days at sea when the sun's heat created huge refractive cells of air like giant telescope lenses. He could see quite clearly as a torpedo float plane made a final pass under the burning ship, presumably to machine gun the decks and bridge before departing in search of other prey.

Dobson signalled the freighters to reduce speed and proceed on course, then without waiting for acknowledgements, turned to run down on the burning ship. He was certain that U-boats would waste no time on the stricken freighter now. Why should they, he thought bitterly, when they had thirty unarmed ships scattered across the Norwegian Sea waiting to be sunk. He remembered the convoy meeting in Liverpool at which it was predicted that PQ 17 would suffer less than ten per cent casualties.

If ten per cent survive it would be a miracle.

The tanker was down by the bow, lying further and further over on her starboard side as water poured into her and drove thick, greasy smoke through every possible opening in her decks. Two lifeboats drifted nearby and Dobson ordered the rescue party on deck.

They took the survivors aboard, most covered with oil and some badly burned. Four men remained aboard the ship, struggling to launch a Carley float. Dobson stepped into the wheelhouse and ordered *Sanda* to close on the tanker. The helmsman complied uneasily and Dobson suppressed an urge to countermand the order, to turn *Sanda* away.

The helmsman edged her in gingerly until her fenders scraped the blackened steel plates. The tanker loomed ominously. On *Sanda*'s deck the rescued seamen, all with staring eyes in oil-smeared faces, waited to see if their ship would now become their executioner. A wave caught and slammed *Sanda* against the larger vessel. A whirl of horrible diesel fumes and smoke blanketed them and Dobson shouted into the loud hailer at the four sailors who were oblivious to *Sanda*'s presence.

They don't see us! Dobson thought. And they can't hear me over the noise of the fire. More choking smoke rolled about them and flames roared from the holds like massed welders' torches. 'Softly, softly,' he muttered to the helmsman. *Sanda* rocked away and a moment later, the tanker lurched over again. The men on the deck redoubled their efforts to free the Carley float which Dobson now saw was tangled in the wreckage of a winch.

The heat was intense enough to blister the paint on *Sanda*'s upperworks. Dobson spotted the flare gun in its holster beside the voice tube. He shoved a round into the breech of the heavy brass pistol and fired it past the wrecked winch. One startled sailor looked around and saw *Sanda*. Using the loud hailer, Dobson shouted for lifelines to be thrown across. There was no time for a breeches buoy. The tanker lurched again and the deck fell over a bit more. She was going fast.

The four men slipped and slid down the torn deck, helped by the ropes, but the first to reach the rail panicked and dove overboard immediately. Although it was summer, on the edge of the Ice Barrier the water was barely above freezing. Sailors lined *Sanda*'s side and shouted encouragement even as they knew it was hopeless. A life belt splashed a few feet from him and he veered towards it but his movements were growing feeble. His life jacket impeded his movement and they saw him struggle to get it off, then as if knowing it was hopeless, he reached a tenative hand for the line still beyond his reach. A wave swamped him; his head appeared once again, mouth open and gasping for air. Another wave and he went under. This time when he rose, he was face down and unmoving.

The remaining three sailors tied the lifelines about their waists and were pulled on deck. As the last man came aboard, Dobson ordered *Sanda* away at all speed.

She hadn't gone a hundred yards when a shuddering explosion tore the bottom from the tanker. The sea boiled and debris showered them – a chunk of steel plate smashed their stern and sheered a boom from its mount. As the tanker's upperworks settled, portholes and windows blew out and a second explosion tore her stack off. She rolled and went down in less than a minute.

Sanda found the two freighters before midnight and Dobson saw that two more ships had joined them, one an anti-aircraft trawler. He was also pleased to discover that she was captained by a lieutenant senior grade named Dawkins, and so he remained in command of the tiny convoy.

The *Dance* class trawler, HMS *Sheerness*, armed with one four inch and four 20 millimetre anti-aircraft guns in high angle mounts, had already taken up position abeam of the merchant ships where her guns had the best command of the sky. Dobson reported the rescue of all but one of the tanker's crew to the other captains, knowing that it would both hearten the merchant crews and cement his authority.

The rescued men were quickly taken below for treatment and Dobson completed the log entry, stepped out onto the bridge and lit a cigarette in the shelter of the canvas windscreen. The sun danced on the western horizon and dazzling shafts of light were refracted from the ice to highlight the black leads they followed eastward. Broken ice, like scree, edged the leads and at times clogged them straight across so that it rattled and drummed against *Sanda*'s hull. Fascinated for a moment, he watched a slab of ice, clear as green glass, tilt up and slide away to rock and splash in their wake. He finished the cigarette and flicked it away, satsified that he had made the correct decisions; his mini-convoy was now able to give the Nazis a fight, thanks to *Sheerness*.

On the third day following the order to scatter, Dobson watched the heaving, grey seas through bloodshot eyes. Cakes of ice drifted past and occasionally the bow shouldered pieces aside. The helmsman's head lolled on his shoulders as he struggled to stay awake. For three days now, the crew had been at constant action stations with little chance for more than an odd moment's sleep.

The weather had turned unseasonably warm, even for July, and the sun burned down through the endless day, converting the ship's interior to an oven and torturing the twenty-three men in sick bay. They had broken into open water again where the danger of U-boat attack increased to a certainty, making it impossible to open vents and scuppers for fresh air. Their only cover now was an occasional patch of fog that usually burned away as fast as it formed. Dobson watched the morning's high clouds and tried to guess how much longer they would last.

The heat added to the desire to sleep above decks whenever duty stations permitted. That way, if torpedoed, you at least were not trapped below. But the men who functioned deeper in the ship, the engine gang and the galley crew, had no such urge. Especially the engine gang; donkeymen, greasers, wipers, stokers. If they were not scalded to death when the boilers burst or crushed as a torpedo or bomb penetrated, the odds were they would drown as the ship went down.

And even if they reached the deck and leapt into the sea, the chance of survival was slim – as the unfortunate sailor had demonstrated a few days before. Many sailors shed life belts if there was no immediate hope of rescue so that their bodies would not provide food for birds.

Once in December 1940, Dobson had spotted one such eyeless torso, from which gobbets of flesh had been torn away, bobbing in calm seas west of the Faroes and had taken it aboard for a proper burial. All extremities had been nibbled off and the skin had turned leathery under the assault of sun and salt water.

The man had not drowned but had died of concussion, probably killed by a depth charge. Escort vessels were under strict orders to charge the vicinity of a sinking ship and if there was any sign of a U-boat, to disregard survivors in the water. More than once, Dobson had seen the effects of such depth charging when bodies rolled to the surface like dead fish, with their bellies and skulls split open by the underwater blast.

He shook his head to rid himself of such morbid thoughts. They were merely the by-products of exhaustion, he told himself, not growing insanity. His eyes were red-rimmed and lids ground over eyeballs as if both were coated with sand. His tongue was furry with fatigue, nicotine, coffee and constipation brought on by a diet of cold bully-beef sandwiches and lukewarm tea. Paradoxically, the sea was beautifully calm, turquoise green and pregnant with ice floes, a day, in short, to delight the worst sailor.

Somewhere south was Norway and drawing closer, Luftwaffe hunters in the guise of long range Condors. Dobson hated the Condors even more than submarines. One could strike back at the U-boats, could evade their torpedoes, could destroy one caught on the surface by ramming or gunfire.

But not the Condor which sought you out, then circled well beyond range of anti-aircraft guns to call in the killers. Even CAM ships, armed freighters carrying catapult-launched Hurricane fighters, were no deterrent. By the time a Hurricane was launched and climbed to altitude, the Condor, if alert, had disappeared over the horizon or into cloud to play an intricate game of hide and seek until the interceptor's fuel was exhausted and it ditched in the sea with all the attendant dangers to the pilot.

At midmorning, the lookout shouted down from the masthead. Dobson stepped onto the bridge wing, turned his glasses on the given bearing and saw a mirage repeating the incident of two days before.

A column of smoke rose from a ship as aircraft darted about it like wasps. A flare blossomed about the freighter and a vast cloud of white smoke appeared. When it cleared away, there was nothing to be seen. A mirage had again shown them the loss of another ship beyond the horizon.

Dobson's own mini-convoy had now reached the most dangerous point in the run to Murmansk and Archangel – directly north of Bear Island and within easy range of Nazi air bases at Tromsö, Banak, Petsamo and Kirkenes. As the sinking beyond the horizon confirmed, even short range fighters could reach them now.

Dobson was torn with indecision. His standing orders required that he attempt to rescue survivors no matter the cost. Yet if he did so, he risked being spotted by air reconnaissance who had only to backtrack his course to discover the tiny convoy. For only the second time in his life – both times within three days of one another – Dobson determined to ignore a standing order which had been issued in London, a thousand miles and a month and more away from the scene of combat. He would continue on course through the ice pack with his charges. He might not ever get another ship again but at least this one stood a chance of surviving.

Twice more during the long day, freak mirages allowed *Sanda*'s crew to watch ships as much as a hundred miles south being destroyed. Each time, the ship's company grew quieter, more morose. Men avoided one another's eyes and tension grew. They all knew that he had made the right decision, that Dobson had first to consider the lives distributed among the five ships, and the stores, weapons and supplies vital to the Russian army which they carried. But that did not make it any easier to watch ships burn and sink and know their crews were burning, drowning or freezing to death.

The Condor appeared in late evening. The sun, strained through cloud, glinted from its metal skin as it circled against the feathery sky at twenty-thousand feet. Dobson watched with dread as it orbited slowly eastward with them.

Sanda had exchanged positions with *Sheerness* who now led in line astern through the narrow leads in the ice pack. Dobson had dropped back to instruct each master personally that they were not to open fire except on his express orders. At the Condor's present altitude and distance, it would only have been a waste of precious ammunition. He also ordered each ship to maintain a thousand yard separation; great enough to make it difficult for the bombers and torpedo planes to strike them all at once, close enough for each ship to lend the fire of its single anti-aircraft gun to that of *Sheerness*.

The Condor stayed with them, at times moving further north, at others, dropping so far south that Dobson was certain she was going to meet oncoming bombers, but she always drifted north again. He calculated that the bombers needed only two hours to reach them, but by mid-morning, nearly nine hours after their discovery, they still had not arrived. Too busy elsewhere, he thought bitterly. The Condor would keep them fresh enough.

Dobson remained on the bridge. The Arctic air held a spring tang and the sun, inching back up the morning sky, turned the water from gold to orange to green to blue, but he remained oblivious to the beauty. Reality was inextricably bound up in the circling Condor as the day wore down to twilight. Again, the golden evening mocked him, reminded him of similar evenings when he had walked the cliff tops and watched the sun sink into the Australian hills above his home while darkness gathered from the sea.

Fear had drawn over the ship like a smothering blanket. His own throat was so dry that it was painful to swallow and try as he might, he could not force himself to concentrate. Disjointed thoughts that made no sense filtered through his mind. His movements were jerky and he was afraid to speak lest his voice quaver. He sensed someone standing at the wheelhouse entrance and turned to see one of the petty officers, McCargill.

'Begging your pardon, sir,' McCargill said, 'but AB Swithmore 'as gone round the bend like, sir.'

Dobson's blank stare caused McCargill to hasten to explain. ''e's climbed into one of the lifeboats, sir. 'e won't say nothing. Just sits there.'

Dobson felt as if his body had recently died, leaving his brain to function alone. 'I'll have a look,' he grunted. 'Take my place here.'

But as he left the stuffy wheelhouse, Dobson realised that he was grateful for the interruption. Swithmore's problem at least offered something concrete with which to grapple. On the main deck, he walked past silent huddles of men, some wrapped in blankets, sleeping. A few of the less badly wounded had joined them. Those still awake watched him pass without expression and some shielded the tiny sparks of cigarettes behind their hands as if afraid that he would reprimand them. Perhaps the sole benefit of the long Arctic twilight was that it allowed the men the comfort of a smoke.

He found Swithmore crouched on the thwarts of number two lifeboat, clutching a small leather bag, his life belt strapped tightly over his pea jacket and sea boots placed neatly beside him. *Sanda* was a small vessel and her crew totalled thirty-seven. To help pass the time Dobson had read every crewman's personnel file. He recalled that Swithmore was barely eighteen when he had joined the Service in 1939 and in the past twelve months alone, had served in four convoys. His last cruise had been in a destroyer with a North Atlantic Convoy that had lost eighteen out of forty-two merchant vessels. He had landed at Liverpool after ten days of continuous fighting only to be transferred into *Sanda* who had sailed the following day for Iceland. During the past year, Swithmore had never had more than four days leave at a time. If anyone had the right to a nervous breakdown, he thought, surely young Swithmore did.

Dobson climbed into the lifeboat and placed a hand on the boy's shoulder. It evoked no response. Swithmore continued to stare straight ahead, blinking very slowly, oblivious to Dobson's presence and indeed to anything else.

'You sit here a while and relax,' Dobson said softly. 'As long as you like.'

Dobson faced the sailors who had gathered. 'Leave him be,' he said in the same tone of voice. 'He won't jump overboard, not while sitting in a lifeboat.'

Swithmore's breakdown produced an unexpected depression in Dobson. For the first time, the enormous danger of their position overwhelmed him. He had experienced fear many times before during the interminable rescues of British troops from French ports in May and June 1940, during mine sweeping operations in St George's Channel that same winter and on the North Atlantic convoys.

But there was a difference; then he was the hunter with the hunter's advantage and well-armed; now he was unarmed and hunted and fear was no longer momentary but continued at the same level, day after day.

In addition to the fear of death or maiming, he was haunted by the fear that he might panic and lose control as he had come close to doing the night HMS *Catalon* chased and sank an E-Boat, and when *Adelaide* came unexpectedly under his command. What if it happened again?

Someone was shaking him awake. He found himself on the deck staring up at the rating who had the helm. I must have passed out, he thought. The man peered at him and Dobson saw that he was badly frightened.

'I . . . I'm . . . all right,' he pushed him away and got up. Sudden nausea gripped him and he leaned against the cold glass. My God, he thought. I'm right on the edge.

The Luftwaffe came at midnight.

The cloud had thickened, dimming the evening light, but not enough to hide the convoy. Patches of fog crept among the waves. They came in from the west, as expected, flying low in the glare. HMS *Sheerness* saw them first at four thousand yards. She opened fire with her twenty millimetre anti-aircraft guns and within seconds, the freighters followed her example.

The attack developed in standard pattern, as he had known it would from his reading of similar attacks. There were eight bombers in all and they divided, two to a ship, and ignored *Sanda* for the moment. There was no waste motion as the torpedo bombers followed one another in line astern towards their targets.

The meagre anti-aircraft fire seemed far too little to deter them and indeed the bombers did not seem inconvenienced in the slightest until one exploded. His wingmate faltered and released his torpedo prematurely. The target had been *Sheerness* but she evaded the torpedo nicely without slackening fire.

But the following flight was more successful. The lead pilot held true to the last possible moment, releasing his torpedo at two hundred yards. The aircraft passed so low over the freighter's superstructure that Dobson thought it would strike. The Panamanian had already begun to turn, water boiling beneath her counter, but at that distance, she did not have a chance.

The torpedo tore into her amidships; for a long moment there was absolute silence, then a sheet of flame blew her in two. The bow kicked forward and sank too swiftly for anyone to escape. The stern bobbed away, lifting and dipping the torn midsection. A lifeboat was swung out. Dobson saw a crewman with an axe cut it loose and the boat fell with a crash that he heard clearly over the half-mile that separated them. Five men leapt into the water and swam for the bobbing, half-swamped boat. Three clambered in and turned to help the fourth. The stern section shuddered, swung slightly to the left and rolled. The movement brought the lifeboat directly beneath the single propeller, still spinning lazily. The stern slid down and with all the inexorability of a falling tree, the monstrous bronze blades slashed the lifeboat to splinters. The stern section belched a final gout of air and wreckage and mangled bodies boiled up.

The other two merchant ships evaded the torpedoes and the bombing squadron climbed for altitude.

The fog gathered substance as the bombers came again, following their squadron leader as before, but this time breaking apart further out, having gained a measure of respect for *Sheerness*'s anti-aircraft fire. They concentrated on the trawler this time and came at her from three directions at once. *Sheerness* did not stand a chance.

The leader dropped his torpedo at four hundred yards. As he turned away, a wing crumpled and the aircraft cartwheeled and exploded. Daunted, the others released their torpedoes further out, but *Sheerness* could not outmanoeuvre them all and she blew up with astounding ferocity and disappeared.

Dobson stared at the spot where she had been a moment before as water boiled and pieces of wreckage rained down. He wanted to scream in frustration and then to retreat inward like the boy crouched in the lifeboat. *Sheerness* had been their single hope of survival, her anti-aircraft guns the only effective weapons between them and destruction.

Dobson, with one convulsive mental effort, shook off the despair that was trying to overwhelm him. He would not, under any circumstances, allow himself a repeat of the incident with the U-boat.

'We'll search for survivors,' he snapped to the helmsman. At the same time, he shouted for the signal rating to transmit an order to the surviving freighters to close on him. Conventional practice kept the ships dispersed to make it harder for attacking aircraft. Without *Sheerness*, only by concentrating the meagre fire of the two remaining forty millimetre anti-aircraft guns did they stand the slightest chance.

The Ju 88s did not re-form for another attack but flew off south. Low on fuel, he thought. But there would be plenty more to take their places. Nevertheless, he was relieved. Even the briefest respite to a condemned man is eagerly grasped, he thought.

They found a single survivor from *Sheerness* a member of the black watch, a young stoker whose hair and clothing had been burned away. He died an hour later, 'of shock, exposure and burns,' the naval surgeon, James, told him. 'I can't understand how he had managed to get out before *Sheerness* went under, or even survive the shock of cold salt water on his flayed body.'

Thin cloud moved in an hour later, forcing the watching Condor lower and lower until it was within range. The gun crews aboard the merchant vessels blasted away but could only drive her off. As he stood on the bridge wing in the sudden cold, Dobson knew the Condor would return. Fog eddied about the surface, thin, insubstantial. Would it thicken? Was there fog over the Norwegian coast? The radio receiver crackled softly but was voiceless, as if the Admiralty had shut down, as if Britain had disappeared.

He went inside to the chart table where he kept a running notation of their snail-like progress along the great arc beyond Norway. The Nazis knew where they were. No matter if their airfields were socked in, they knew the convoy's speed and direction. The bombers should have returned by now, unless someone had decided not to waste aircraft fuel on them, but to vector a U-boat onto their course instead, or destroyers. It would be like shooting fish in a barrel. The three ships had absolutely nothing with which to defend themselves against a U-boat; not guns, nor armour nor speed.

A few more hours, a day at the most, was all the time they had. The Condor need only check on them periodically to detect minor changes in course. He studied the Ice Barrier once more and an idea began to form. Slowly at first, and then with increasing speed, he worked out his mental calculations in detail on the chart. It just might work, he thought when he finished. And if not, anything was better than waiting to be slaughtered.

He wrote out a careful message and called for the signal rating to transmit it by Aldiss lamp. The rating read it through and stared at Dobson as if he were mad, and then grinned in delight as the light dawned. 'Aye, aye, sir!'

After an exchange of astonished signals, the three ships steamed due west as far inside the ice pack fringe as possible, the broken ice drumming against the hull in discordant percussion. Dangerous business, he knew, but so then was dodging bombs and torpedoes.

At exactly 0900 of the fifth day since the convoy break-up, Dobson ordered the merchantmen to shut down all boilers. He did not want even the slightest wisp of smoke to betray them, he told each captain as he steamed past the two ships in turn. Lieutenant Carson, his engineering officer, went gleefully down to change the troublesome generator and Dobson signalled instructions for white paint to be issued from the Panamanian's cargo and for each ship to be painted white, stem to stern, waterline to waterline.

He had worried that simply reversing course for a few hours would not allow them to escape as the German aviators might be up to that trick. But if at the same time, the three ships were to disappear into the pack, white against white, they might just stand a chance.

By late evening they were finished. Another hour was spent getting up steam and as the Arctic light deepened and fog swirled lightly across the wave tops once more, *Sanda* led off, picking her way fastidiously through leads filled with dark water only a few degrees warmer than the solid ice around them. Dobson studied the following ships, pleased at his own cleverness as they ghosted through the summer twilight.

A Condor was spotted at 0300 hours. The German pilot was lower than normal Dobson noted, obviously searching for them. He had the signalman use semaphore flags in the shelter of the deckhouse to signal all stop. For an hour, the German circled over the area, dropping as low as five thousand feet at one point. The temptation to shoot at him was overwhelming but they remained motionless, Coleridge's 'painted ship upon a painted ocean...' Dobson hoped.

Even the glass in ports and windows had been painted white or else shielded with white canvas so that not even sun glare could betray them. When the Condor finally disappeared over the horizon to the west, the release of tension was palpable. Dobson heard cheering from his own crew and faint across the water, from the other two ships and smiled. Most un-navy like, he thought, but good to hear.

Ten minutes later, the American freighter signalled to ask why they did not get under way? Dobson's answer was three words, 'Wait and see.'

His patience was rewarded. The Condor suddenly reappeared twenty minutes later like a massive bird of prey, skimming close over the ice and watching for the least sign of movement in the pack ice.

*

At dawn, Dobson gave the order to proceed east but by mid-morning the ice had thickened, forcing them even closer to open water. During the rest of the day and all that night, they moved fitfully. Dobson was reasonably certain that he had confused the searching Condors; they were now almost one hundred nautical miles behind and twenty north of where they should have been, but that was hardly enough to ensure safety. A chance sighting by a Condor if they were forced into open water once more would place them in immediate jeopardy.

Dobson had no idea of what might have happened to *Tirpitz* and her escorts. There was no radio traffic at all, except on the frequencies used by the German navy and air force. Had the Home Fleet sailed in time to trap her? Had she escaped again? What of the cruiser squadron and the destroyer shield that had accompanied PQ 17? The most logical supposition was that *Tirpitz* had disposed of both in view of the silence the Admiralty was maintaining.

They reached a point one hundred nautical miles east of Hope Island. Novaya Zemlya was five hundred miles east and the entrance to the White Sea an equal distance south. Archangel lay at the end of a long inlet on the White Sea, well within range of Norwegian and Finnish-based German bombers. Every U-boat north of Norway and east of Iceland would be congregating off Cape Kanin to finish off survivors. Without anti-aircraft and anti-submarine escort, any attempt to reach Archangel was sheer suicide.

On all three ships, nerves were stretched to the limit by exhaustion, lack of sleep and the poor nourishment afforded by cold tea and preserved beef sandwiches, and by the wearing fear that every hour might be the last. Men shambled about their duties like zombies. Tasks that should take no more than ten minutes often consumed an hour. Lookouts fell into trances that were not sleep, not wakefulness.

But when they broke out of the ice into open sea at 2000 hours, the weather became cooperative for the first time since leaving Iceland. Streamers of mist curled along wave tops and as the night wore on the cloud increased and rain squalls, cold and chilling, shielded them from aircraft and U-boats.

For twenty-three hours they steamed across the empty, storm-ridden Barents Sea at twelve knots, until at 1600 hours 12 July 1942, Dobson shepherded his charges into the shelter of Moller Bay on the western coast of Novaya Zemlya. There they found two more ships from Convoy PQ 17, both exhibiting extensive damage. One ship's bow was crumpled and torn half away, whether from collision or bomb blast Dobson could not tell. He sent the medical staff off to see to any wounded.

Beyond the range of German bombers now, U-boats were the chief danger and he ordered all four ships to anchor as close in to shore as possible. One of the new freighters was armed with an anti-aircraft gun while the other had two World War I vintage Lewis guns for protection against strafing aircraft. Dobson gave specific orders for all four ships to train their guns on the inlet and post a twenty-four-hour gunnery watch.

With his charges secured, Dobson inspected *Sanda*. He saw men drugged with exhaustion sleeping everywhere there was a bit of space, others staring blankly at him as he passed. The young sailor, Swithmore, no longer occupied the lifeboat and Dobson was too exhausted to find out what had happened to him at the moment. His own fatigue had now gone beyond simple exhaustion and he was conscious of moving gently in and out of a surreal world in which men spoke and their voices echoed. He had no appetite and could not remember the last time he had eaten. He shivered constantly and stumbled unless he concentrated on taking one step at a time.

Dobson finished his inspection as the motor launch returned with a dozen badly-wounded merchant sailors from the damaged freighter.

'They are all impressed with our "Great White Fleet",' Surgeon James grinned as he saluted. He went on to report that three men had been killed outright in the two dive bombing attacks the ship had endured and he had brought the severely wounded back to *Sanda* for surgery. As he talked, Dobson leaned against a stanchion, striving to remain alert.

The doctor broke off in mid-sentence and before Dobson could protest, he put a hand on his chest, pushed and caught him when he swayed back and started to fall.

'Captain Dobson,' the surgeon snapped, 'it is my duty to warn you that you are close to a physical breakdown from exhaustion. I suggest you get your head down in your cabin for at least eight hours.'

Dobson laughed at him. 'Eight hours! Sorry Doctor, but this ship, indeed this convoy, is my responsibility. It's out of the question.'

James snorted. 'This is no time to debate the issue with you, Captain. If you collapse, which you will shortly, you will be of no use to anyone.

'A ship's doctor is empowered to certify any crew member unfit for duty, including her captain, if in his opinion a valid medical reason exists. I have already certified one captain this voyage and I do not wish to do so again.'

Dobson struggled to understand what the man was saying. Was he threatening to certify him unfit for duty? Mutiny! He'd have him under arrest first . . . Then he was conscious that he was staring at the spot where the doctor *had* been. Good Christ in heaven, he thought, he had fallen asleep on his feet. A seaman appeared at his elbow and murmured, 'The doctor asked me to help you to your cabin, sir.'

Dobson had only enough presence of mind left to order a mattress laid for him in the chartroom. As he climbed to the bridge, he knew that James and Fletcher were both right; for God's sake, he had Captain Peters of *Adelaide* as an example of what happened when one pushed oneself past all sensible limits.

After five days straight on the bridge, with no more than a few hours of sleep snatched here and there, Dobson found that now that he was willing to sleep, he could not.

His mind whirled with a thousand concerns, from the boy who had huddled in the lifeboat to the fuel reserves of the merchant freighters. And to add to his troubles, Lieutenant Carson had reported that the spare generator they had replaced a lifetime ago, now had a broken armature which would have to be rewound.

Dobson finally slept some time after midnight only to wake abruptly three hours later. He lay without moving, letting his senses gather his surroundings. A reddish light trickled into the chart house and through the open door he saw a petty officer standing watch. What had awakened him? Nothing seemed out of the ordinary and the petty officer's posture betrayed nothing more than boredom and duty.

Sanda was riding uneasily; the sea was getting up in the bay. Soundings needed to be made, he thought. Their only chart had been drawn in 1858 and the depths indicated were sketchy away from the harbour mouth. If we have a full-fledged Arctic gale . . . Dobson wanted to get up, to make certain that everything was in order, but his body refused to cooperate. He closed his eyes again for a moment while he gathered strength. He had already slept longer than he should have and he felt worse than when he had lain down. Damn doctors! The thin shivering that had possessed his chest and shoulders for two days was also worse and his mouth was dry and angry with the taste of acid and sleep. His clothing stank. How long had it been since he had even washed his face? And he was hungry as well as thirsty but the thought of another bully-beef sandwich and coffee was more than his stomach could stand.

When he opened his eyes again, the light was brighter. The chronometer on the bulkhead read 0521. Dobson got to his feet like an old man with arthritis. A different petty officer nodded and the ship's uneven motion made him stumble.

Beyond the water-spattered glass, a grey waste of Arctic water and barren hills was stabbed by torrents of rain. The seas were running to six-foot swells and he stepped out into a cutting wind that reminded him of midwinter. The bay was a maze of conflicting wave patterns which the heavy-laden merchant ships rode far more easily than *Sanda* and he thought about the wounded below.

After visiting the sick bay and assuring himself that the wounded were as comfortable as conditions allowed, Dobson went to his cabin for the first time in five days. The air was musty from disuse and moisture had condensed on the steel bulkheads. He ignored the air and icy dampness and stripped. Cold water ran from the taps but he filled the basin anyway and with a cloth and soap washed himself all over and shaved. He dressed quickly in clean, if damp, clothing and boots and was back on the bridge within ten minutes.

The steward brought him a steaming mug of coffee and a platter heaped with fried eggs and bacon. He had forgotten that now that they were anchored, the kitchen fires could be lit once more. The wonderful odour caused his stomach to cramp suddenly and he took a tentative bite of eggs. For a moment, he could not swallow and tears started. With an angry gesture he brushed them away and forced himself to chew and swallow. Gradually, as he pushed food into his stomach, the tension eased and he was able to finish the meal.

As he was finishing, a whistle blasted a warning and he shouted for battle stations to be signalled and sprinted onto the bridge wing in time to see the bow of a grey and blue camouflaged destroyer nose into the bay. For a terrible moment he thought they had been trapped by German destroyers, and then a red flag broke at the masthead. A second Soviet destroyer followed.

The overcast gave way at that moment and summer sunlight sparkled on the white caps. The Soviet destroyers both blew their sirens and the freighters answered with steam whistles until the bay echoed and re-echoed. A pack of startled seals shot into the water and sea birds fluttered in confusion.

Three days later, four merchant survivors of PQ 17, with the rescue ship HMS *Sanda* trailing behind, sailed up the Dvina River and anchored at the quays edging the Archangel waterfront. The escorting destroyers had dropped away once their charges were into the river and now the meagre cover flight of three P-40 Tomahawk aircraft in Russian colours flashed away without acknowledgement.

The huts and warehouses along the docks ran for miles under the leaden skies. A cold wind blew along the waterfront as Dobson studied the battered surroundings and innumerable guards with slung machine pistols stamped and shivered. Only seven other foreign cargo ships were visible, most showing the scars of marauding aircraft or U-boats. He closed his eyes for a moment, as if that would help contain his anger – at the Admiralty for ordering the convoy to scatter and at the Soviets for refusing to send escorts to meet them. God only knew how they had been persuaded to send destroyers as far as Novaya Zemlya.

It was worse even than he had expected. Of the thirty-four merchant ships that left Iceland with convoy PQ 17, only eleven had reached Archangel. Sixty-eight per cent of the convoy had been destroyed, far and away the most disastrous loss on the murderous run to Russia.

Constant summer daylight was the enemy as much as the Luftwaffe or the Kreigsmarine U-boats and destroyers. The Luftwaffe could strike twenty-four hours a day and he suspected that when the toll was counted, it would show that the worst damage had been done by aircraft. And still, they faced the long run home along the same track. Dobson turned away from the battered ships as they were nudged into position by tugs. As mooring lines snaked down, Russian guards in padded uniforms took up positions.

Twenty-three ships lost, he thought, sick with the knowledge. Below him, the first of the too-few wounded sailors *Sanda* had saved were being brought on deck for transfer to a Russian hospital. He had, at least, used his head and brought his charges through. He had disobeyed strict orders and for that he would accept his punishment. But he had finally redeemed himself in his own eyes for allowing that U-boat to escape in 1941.

The final blow came later that day when Dobson learned that *Tirpitz*, the cause of the disaster, after an abortive sortie, had returned to her berth in Altenfjord without ever having fired a shot.

Stalingrad July - December 1942

Major Friedrich Prager pulled at his sticky shirt as he trudged across the field to the waiting Fiesler-Storch. He had never experienced such heat before. The steppe was burnt black under the sullen sun which beat down day after day to suck every drop of moisture from man and land alike. He climbed into the aircraft, wincing at the touch of hot metal, and settled into the cramped seat behind the pilot. When the mechanic shut the cockpit flap, the temperature jumped again. The engine barked into operation, the pilot waved the chocks away and the aircraft gathered itself and leapt into the overheated air.

The message had arrived late the previous evening ordering him to divisional headquarters at Kharkov. His clerk found an observation aircraft going in that direction, so at least he didn't have to endure the ten-hour lorry ride in the heat.

The Fiesler-Storch began to bump and bang. Twice, the bottom fell out and his stomach came close to revolting. He protested weakly but the pilot only shrugged. 'It's the air, Major. Nothing I can do about it. If you feel sick, there's a paper bag in the side-pocket. The ground crew would appreciate your using it.'

A staff car waited to drive him to headquarters as he staggered out of the aircraft. The pilot made certain that Prager was clear, then wheeled back onto the grass strip and took off on the next leg of his trip. Prager drew several deep breaths and leaned his head back against the seat as the car drove off.

He had expected it to be a little cooler along the river but, if anything, it was hotter, and certainly more humid. There was a good deal of military traffic on the roads but relatively few civilians to be seen. The condition of the city surprised him. Almost nothing had been done to clean up the battle damage from the year before and if the city centre was in somewhat better repair, it was only because it had escaped the brunt of the fighting. The civilians they passed were in rags, faces pinched with hunger. Once when the car stopped for a convoy of army lorries, a group of silent children gathered a little way off to watch. A few soldiers threw sweets and cigarettes to the children who gathered them in with the avidity of sharks.

'Replacements,' the driver snorted. 'They'll learn.'

Prager nodded agreement. These same children assisted partisans and those cigarettes and sweets might well show up on partisan dead in the next few days.

At headquarters, there seemed no shortage of anything. The sentries wore new uniforms and carried the new GEW 41 semi-automatic rifles with ten-round clips, while the infantry company assigned to his Panzer brigade had only the five shot, bolt-action 98K rifles to use against Russian troops armed largely with PPD and PPsh machine pistols. He kept his expression neutral at the sight of the sleek, well-fed and-tailored officers and was self-conscious in his worn, dirty uniform with the frayed cuffs and collars and badly sewn rent in the knee.

Divisional headquarters was located in a former radio broadcasting station. Russian civilians, nearly all women, mingled freely with German staff and as he was directed along the corridors, he saw attractive secretaries outside most offices and wondered how in the name of God they maintained any security at all?

He was directed to the proper office and as he entered, felt the frosty nip of refrigeration. At the front, every cartridge, every spare part was at a premium, yet there always seemed to be shipping space available for essentials like air conditioning, he thought with disgust.

He saluted the caption behind the desk who stared him up and down. 'You might have at least shaved, Major,' the captain snorted. 'General Falkyn insists that certain standards be maintained by his officers.'

Prager took a deep breath. 'My apologies to the General,' he said through clenched teeth, 'but our ration of soap hasn't arrived yet this summer.' He pushed the swinging gate so hard it slammed against the captain's desk, and stomped through into the conference room.

The large room was filled with officers of every rank and

description. At one end a movie projector rested on a wheeled cart and a uniformed female projectionist stood patiently beside it. A long table had been spread with a selection of breakfast foods – croissants, Danish rolls, fruits that he hadn't seen since the start of the war and two large containers of coffee – real coffee, his nose told him! He dropped his cap on the buffet and ignoring everything else, snatched a cup from the sideboard.

At the first sip, he barely restrained an exclamation of surprise. It *was* real coffee!

'The Americans buy it from Brazil,' a voice at his shoulder said, 'and send it by convoy to Persia. The Russians bring it by rail into the Caucasus and we take it from them there. A roundabout route of supply, but effective nevertheless.'

Prager turned to see a tall, dark-complexioned man in the uniform of an Italian infantry officer who looked vaguely familiar. But then what he had taken at first glance for dark skin was really wind and sun burn, exactly like his own. The man wore the *Winterschlacht im Osten* medal and the *Corpo Spedizione Italiano* and the *Campagna d'Africa* ribbons. But it was a scar of frostbite on his forehead more than any decoration that marked him as a combat veteran of the 1941-42 winter.

'I believe, Major Prager,' the officer said in slightly accented German, 'that we have met before, in Warsaw, before the war.'

Prager peered at him. The face was certainly familiar enough and then his usually excellent memory came to his aid. 'Ah yes, Marchetti, Alfredo Marchetti, is it not? You were the Italian military attaché and a lieutenant at the time. I see you have twice earned promotion. My congratulations.'

Marchetti chuckled. 'How very good of you to remember, Major. I myself had to ask who you were. My memory is terrible,' he shrugged. 'What can one do?'

Prager gestured to the coffee urn. 'May I pour you a cup, Major? I suspect that for you, as for me, real coffee has become a luxury.'

'By all means.' Marchetti did not have the heart to tell him that his troops were still being issued their regular coffee ration. He took the cup and inhaled the fragrance before tasting it. 'A bit weak, but then we Italians prefer our coffee thick.'

'If I recall correctly, we last met at a cocktail party at the American Embassy in late August of 1939,' Prager said, turning to survey the room.

'Correct. In fact, we were arranging a dinner party for that evening when you were called away.'

'Ah, I remember now. Let me see, there were quite a few of us at the time. The British attaché, a Swedish journalist, an old friend of mine, a

Japanese naval officer, a former American flying officer, yourself and a Russian officer.'

'That's right,' Marchetti laughed. 'I had forgotten the American but I do remember the others, particularly the Russian. As it turned out, he had just been recalled to Moscow. I wonder what has become of him since?'

Prager took out his cigarettes and offered one to Marchetti who declined it politely. 'The trouble with serving as a military attaché is the terrible possibility of meeting old friends on opposite sides of a battlefield one day. I did in fact run across the American after the war began. He somehow managed to remain in Warsaw following the surrender and fell foul of our occupation authorities who had decided that he was a British spy. I helped to extricate him from the country.'

Marchetti nodded. 'I do recall him now that you mention it. Rather brash, I thought. He and the Japanese officer argued about who should rule the Pacific. Perhaps you remember Charles Atkins, the British attaché?'

Prager nodded and Marchetti continued. 'While I was in Rome on leave this past spring, I was visited by your Swedish journalist friend. We had dinner and talked about the war and the people we had known and he mentioned that Charles Atkins had been killed on Crete in May, 1941.'

Prager went very quiet. After a moment, he took a long breath. 'I liked Charles Atkins. I always found it difficult to think of him as an enemy. Now, I suppose it doesn't matter.'

Someone shouted for attention as a group of staff officers entered. Feet clicked and they were ordered to find seats. Prager hastily refilled his coffee cup and Marchetti followed suit before joining Prager at the back of the room.

The senior of the two generals in the group wore the crimson piping of the Obercommando der Wehrmacht, the other, field grey but with SS runes on his collar, which Prager thought of as a mockery. Both men bowed when introduced by a colonel who retired stiffly to the covered map display. Marchetti studied the others in the room; most were senior officers, colonels and above, but there were sufficient numbers of field grade officers of all ranks that he did not feel out of place.

'Gentlemen,' the general began, 'how very good to see you all in such excellent health. I have flown from Berlin to acquaint you with the objectives of our autumn campaign which will shortly be unleashed. You will then return to your units and brief the officers who could not attend. The constraining factor will, of course, be the rains expected about the first of September. But by then you will have captured the objectives which I shall now describe to you. The Fuehrer, I am instructed to say, states categorically that this and the coming winter campaign will end the war.' The general waited for the expected applause, but it was anything but hearty. Prager and Marchetti exchanged sceptical glances.

The colonel uncovered a large map that showed the central and southern portions of the Soviet Union.

'These, gentlemen, are the autumn campaign objectives. Beginning with the right flank, the Crimea will be cleared of all enemy troops. Army Group A has already mounted a concerted drive towards the Caucasus and some of you will join it. Its objective is the capture of the Caspian Sea oilfields.

'Autumn objectives,' Prager whispered to Marchetti, 'because Timoshenko's attack on Kharkov in May upset Berlin's timetable.' Marchetti snorted in answer.'

'Shifting north,' the pointer tapped, 'the Sixth Army will clear the area between the Donets and Volga Rivers all the way to the city of Stalingrad, thus guarding the flank of Army Group A as it thrusts deeper into the Caucasus.

'The Fuehrer's conception is quite plain is it not? And brilliant as well. At a double stroke, we secure our oil supplies, destroy the major Russian communication and transportation centre below Moscow and obtain the vast farmlands of this region. After this campaign is completed in the autumn, we will have several options open to us. The most logical would be a quick thrust through Persia to remove the British and link up with General Rommel's Afrika Korps, which will by then have completed its drive through the Middle East.

'Turkey, outflanked on three sides, will then have no choice but to join the Axis. And when she does, British positions remaining in the Middle East and Africa will no longer constitute a threat and the loss of India must follow. Without India, Britain will not only lose her will to fight, but the means by which she obtains the raw materials to do so.'

Prager was familiar with the general outline of the India plan, having worked on various portions of it in Berlin in 1937. Then it had sounded too fantastic to be taken seriously, a schoolboy's daydream. But no longer. Germany had conquered all of Western Europe, most of North Africa and half of Russia since then. Political miscalculation had kept them from Moscow the previous winter, but the autumn and winter campaigns promised to settle that affair.

The SS general spoke next and he described the unexpected strength of the Russian opposition encountered during the previous winter, 'But,' and he thumped the table, 'thanks to the Fuehrer's great leadership, we maintained our positions through the winter and in spite of overwhelming odds and a coward or two, we held.'

All coughing stopped and no one scraped a chair in restless movement, no papers rustled and the atmosphere went tense with anger and outrage. The staff general shifted nervously but the SS general ignored it.

You bastard, Prager thought. What the hell do you know about it, you lousy toy soldier? The general was referring to the case of General von Sponek who had commanded the Forty-Sixth Infantry Division at Kerch in the Crimea. In December, von Sponek had found himself in a deep salient, surrounded on three sides by heavy Russian forces. His ammunition was almost gone and his troops had received no winter clothing, despite the fact that the temperature at times dropped to forty below zero. They were in clear danger of being cut off and had taken severe casualties and to save the remnants of the Forty-Sixth, von Sponek had ordered a retreat.

The fact that General von Sponek had led the parachute landing at Rotterdam and wore the Iron Cross with Crossed Swords had not saved him. Hitler personally ordered the SS to arrest him. He was tried and condemned to death and only a last minute reprieve saved him from the firing squad. His sentence was reduced instead to life imprisonment.

The Nazi Party and the Fuehrer had given the army notice by this action that no excuse would be accepted for failure and no retreat allowed for any reason, unless personally approved by Hitler himself. If duty required every man to die where he stood, then by God, they would die.

The briefing droned on for another hour and Prager fretted at the inactivity. His battalion was in the midst of re-equipping with new Mark IV tanks, but instead of a blessing, they were a nightmare. Never had he seen such poor workmanship and half of the vehicles had been so cannibalised during the long journey east from the Ruhr that their engines could not even be started. Even the treads had been stripped from three tanks.

Marchetti stole frequent glances at his wristwatch. The struggle to understand the General's rapid German was tiring. Why the devil was he here? His infantry battalion was operating under Italian command a hundred kilometres north of Kharkov. What brilliant piece of asininity were the Germans planning this time? All through the spring and early summer they had pounded Russian lines, earning respectable advances, but nothing like that needed if they were to end the war this winter.

Marchetti forced himself to pay closer attention as the general described the latest product of the Fuehrer's fruitful mind, and swore under his breath. These damned Germans were completely unable to understand that their vaunted Adolph Hitler might well be a political genius on the order of the Duce, but like the Duce, as a military planner, he was a disaster.

Unfortunately, Hitler's luck in the beginning had convinced far too many who should have known better that he was indeed a military genius. Anyone who undertook an unbiased review of those so-called successes could hardly fail to see them for what they were – a combination of Allied stupidity and the most incredible luck. The Rhineland, Austria and Czechoslovakia were simply the result of British and French cowardice. Even in Poland, Hitler, not yet confident of his supposed genius, had allowed his generals to fight without much interference. Accordingly, the army had achieved a superior concentration of force against a weak Polish army who, in any case, had no natural geological barriers on which to make a stand.

The superior mobility of the small mechanised portion of the German army had enabled them to knife through the Poles like a hot blade through butter. But if the Poles had possessed even half the mobility of the Germans they might well have engulfed the tenuous Nazi armoured screen and rolled them all the way back to Berlin.

The French high command, still mired in the glory of the 1914-1918 war, had refused to concentrate their own, much superior, armour even when it became clear that the Germans had simply bypassed the Maginot Line. Flushed with success in Poland, Hitler had inserted himself into the operational aspects of the campaign in the west and his influence was evident immediately; according to rumour, it was he who had issued the order to halt on the Aa canal line outside Dunkirk and thus allow the British Expeditionary Force – the bulk of the entire British Army – to sail away.

Hitler's political sensitivity, like the Duce's, may have told him that twenty years of pacificist and scandal-ridden governments in France had so weakened and demoralised the nation and the army that they were incapable of defending themselves, but that was as far as Hitler's actual contribution had gone, Marchetti thought.

He recalled the frequent talks with his father at the old villa in the hills above Civitavecchia during his spring leave. Never had he seen the old man so pessimistic.

'The entire government has gone mad,' he had complained. 'The Duce has fallen under the spell of that madman in Berlin. All he can talk about is the wonderful work Hitler is doing to rid the world of communists. Thank God, the Duce hasn't followed so far along that he has begun to murder Italian Jews.

'We are over-committed in North Africa, in the Balkans and now in Russia. I have argued with him, as have others, that Italy cannot sustain such an extensive war. We need raw materials from Africa and oil from the Middle East simply to sustain our internal economy and those are now denied us. But the Duce is impervious to logical arguments; it is as if he expects angels from heaven to fly down with gifts of oil and chromium. No, I exaggerate – he expects the Germans to supply us! Hah!

'It no longer makes any difference that I supported him from the earliest days. That I stood by him when those madmen of his murdered Giacomo Matteotti because he was a socialist. He is surrounded now by Nazi flunkies and even Ciano has been cut from the inner circle. In fact, Ciano has incurred particularly dangerous enemies among the Nazis, idiot that he is. And all the while, that fool Rommel romps about the desert without a thought to consolidating his lines of supply before advancing again. After all, he has only to demand from his Fuehrer that Italy send more and more!'

His father had turned his chair to face the diorama of lead soldiers the two of them had spent so many happy hours constructing when he was a boy. My God, how long ago in time that was, and how short in years.

But his experience in North Africa and Russia had confirmed his father's opinion. The first time the Germans had come up against a determined enemy with time to organise – the British – they had been stopped in their tracks in September 1940. Then, Hitler's true timidity and lack of long-term planning had exposed him as an amateur to anyone who cared to see. Rebuffed at the English Channel, he had lost interest in Britain and turned east.

Marchetti suspected that Hitler feared the reaction of the German people if he suffered an overwhelming rebuff, or even if he were forced to pursue a campaign of attrition such as an invasion of England might become. Instead, he had pinned his hopes on another quick victory. Perhaps he thought England would ask for an accommodation if they saw Russia, their last potential European ally, defeated. Was it for that reason that Hitler had exposed Germany and Italy to the horrors of a two-front war? If so, it merely suggested to Marchetti the capacity of the German leader and army for self-deception.

A plume of black smoke rose on the horizon. A tank clattered past, raising clouds of choking summer dust, but the men were too tired to curse. Off to their left, two flights of Stukas roared east over the heavy wheat fields. They had marched every day for two weeks and every day it was the same – sixty kilometres between 0300 and 1300 hours when the heat became too intense to continue. Marchetti's second pair of hand-made boots, purchased in Rome in the spring, were wearing out rapidly. He had supposed that two pairs would be sufficient for the year. The issue boots his troops wore were in even worse condition and many had taken sturdy Russian boots from dead soldiers or even prisoners.

Marchetti had always pictured Russia as a land of extreme cold, long winters and ravenous wolves. The winters were bad enough and so were the wolves, but he had never imagined how bad the summer heat was. The steppe was worse than the Libyan desert. At least there it had been dry, but in Russia it was so humid, the air so laden with moisture that it was difficult to breathe. Sweat rotted equipment and uniforms, rusted weapons and caused dozens of different skin diseases from boils to fungus infections of the feet and groin.

The sun blazed from a cloudless sky for weeks on end without a drop of rain to cool the parched earth. Water courses snaking across the steppe were bone-dry and trees were such a rarity that men fought over their shade. Worst of all, a perpetual thirst assailed them as there were never enough water carriers to supply even the basic ration.

Marchetti had instituted desert rules on the second day of the march. The men were allowed one mouthful of water per man per hour to prevent murderous dehydration. Each man's canteen was inspected at the beginning and end of the day's march and those whose canteens were dry were required to perform the onerous details of establishing camp before they were allowed to drink again or rest. As the march drew on, the men hardened and grew experienced at rationing themselves, yet there always remained a surplus of culprits at evening inspection.

Three weeks after their march began, they came in sight of a tributary of the Donets that still held water and that evening the men had sufficient to drink for the first time. Marchetti stood on the bank watching as his naked charges capered in the water. A faint breeze stirred against his own naked skin and Marchetti shivered, delighted with the coolness, yet reminded that in Russia nothing was ever as it seemed. It was already August and soon the rains would begin. And then the cold would deepen day by day until the rain became snow and winter would be on them again.

His brigade had seen little fighting during most of the past winter. They had been stationed behind the front lines in a rural area north of the Rumanian sector, above the city of Odessa. They had got along quite well with the local people, perhaps because so many of his own men were peasants like the locals, and instinctively understood their concerns.

What little fighting they had seen amounted to no more than an occasional skirmish between patrols and partisans who were relatively inactive in their sector compared to those garrisoned by the Rumanians and Germans. Their greatest enemy had been the eternal cold and the constant blizzards which had isolated them for weeks at a time. If not for their good relations with the local Russians, they would have suffered a great deal more from starvation or the cold than they had, like their Rumanian and German neighbours had, in fact.

The spring rains which cleared the roads turned them to impassable mud, halting all action. It was then that he had managed to secure a month's leave while his company was withdrawn for rest and refitting. On his return, he had found them fat and lazy and set about to remedy that.

The conference at which he had met Freidrich Prager again after three years had marked the turning point and brought their 'holiday' to an abrupt end. Orders to move up to the front came almost immediately. They had marched out two days later north and east through areas long under German occupation.

As they plodded along day after day, they were struck by the gaunt appearance and sullen attitude of the few Russian civilians they encountered. Entire towns had been destroyed in the previous summer's fighting and few showed any evidence of rebuilding. And it was even worse when they crossed the Donets. At times, Marchetti felt as if he were passing through a futuristic landscape of great devastation such as H.G. Wells had envisioned. Only jack-booted, steel-helmeted robots with machine pistols across their chests seemed to inhabit the burned landscape and only the front areas showed evidence of life – a grotesque paradox.

Marchetti watched the sunlight fade over the Chir River. The grass on which he sat was bone dry and brown but the dirt beneath was rich and black. On the other side, the steppe rolled east until it lapped against the great Don itself. To the north and south were the twin objectives of Berlin's frantic planners, Voronezh and Stalingrad, the anchors of a vast defensive line designed to shield their new Caucasian holdings.

He tried to picture Stalingrad as a modern industrial city, but images of his native Milan interfered. The two would differ greatly, he knew, even though Milan was the most industrialised of all Italy's cities. Stalingrad would be cluttered with heavy socialist architecture and heroic figures cast in ferro-concrete, while Milan was a museum of the most delicate marble and granite sculptures. The Soviets glorified humanity in the amorphous collective while his own people did so in terms of the individual.

What lay beyond Voronezh and Stalingrad, he wondered? More steppe as far as the Pacific? The map did not show it, of course, since it was one of the efficient German sector maps, but it did not matter. They had been told at Kharkov that while the Soviets would defend both cities tenaciously, they lacked the depth of reserves to do so successfully.

The staff general from Berlin had dwelt lovingly on the details. Army Group B would drive on Voronezh and then south down the Donets Corridor to Stalingrad, while Army A, to which Prager's battalion had been attached, crossed the Don between Rostov and Tsimlyanskaya, a dozen or so kilometres south of the confluence of the Don and the Aksai Rivers. They were to drive southeast to Stavropol and the Caucasus, then turn east to parallel the mountains all the way to the Caspian Sea.

The war had lasted too long, Marchetti thought. At home, everything was falling apart. Young men unable to avoid the draft, or who still believed in the Duce's visions, had been taken away by the army; others had disappeared into the cities or the countryside. Factory production had fallen because there were insufficient workers and quality had become a joke. There were no private vehicles in operation any longer, unless of course, you had connections to the very highest echelons of government – and his father no longer possessed such connections.

And the strong, broad-shouldered father of his childhood had become a shrunken, sick old man who must ride to the doctor's clinic on the handlebars of his gardener's bicycle. There was so little fuel that all but four rooms in the house had been closed and master and servants lived together. His father had foreseen the food shortages and ordered the back lawn of the villa ploughed and vegetables planted. He had also secretly bought chickens, three pigs and a cow to supply meat, eggs and milk. Even so, the servants had to take turns spending long hours in food queues for such essentials as olive oil, sugar, salt, spices and flour. New clothing was non-existent and even tooth powders and brushes had disappeared from the shop shelves.

His father was a very sick man. Cancer of the pancreas, the doctor had confided in the solemn tones reserved for impending death. Less than a year, he told him and Marchetti hoped passionately that he would be allowed to go home once more before the old man died.

His father's approaching death gave Marchetti that much more to brood about. He sensed how horrible it was for his father to find himself failing a bit more each day. All his life, he had been a powerful man, active in the management of the estate and factory. Now he was confined to a single room in an empty, freezing house, isolated from the friends and contacts of a lifetime, facing an irrevocable sentence of death alone. But he was never one to rail against fate; he accepted the cancer just as he had everything else in life that he could not change, including the lingering death of his wife and the slow subversion of the fascist dream by Mussolini and that cohort of uniformed fools with which he had surrounded himself.

In the days before the war, when Mussolini still counted his father among his staunchest supporters, Marchetti had often met the great man at government and party functions with his father. Then, the Duce, a dignified if pompous figure, had appeared to him the greatest revolutionary leader since Garibaldi. Hitler and Franco both claimed to have been inspired by his example. But in the past two years, all had fallen apart and Mussolini stood revealed to the critical eye as an empty-headed braggart, his promises smothered by the corruption of his own party. Heaven help us, Marchetti thought. Italy and Germany were led by a former private and a corporal respectively who, courtesy of their own press reviews, had been declared military geniuses.

Marchetti himself had once believed in the party's promises of a new and powerful industrialised society built on respect for the nation, government and the individual. He had ignored the fact that Mussolini's 'better-life-tomorrow' promises sounded very much like those of the Church which he had abandoned after his final year with the Jesuits. He could smile now at the failure of both institutions to turn him into a carbon-copy believer. The Jesuits had used beatings and cold-water enemas, the party bribes, sinecures, peer pressure and, if all else failed, threatened the bullet just as the Jesuits threatened an eternity of hell. Some things must be accepted on faith, both thundered at him in their efforts to produce one more unthinking fanatic.

We have all changed since 1939, he thought. Some for the better, most for the worse. He thought about Prager. How had the German changed since those days in Warsaw? Military attachés were diplomats and actors and as such the real person was rarely glimpsed, only the external image.

But Prager seemed hard, rock hard, as if the humanity had been burned out of him. The stories he told of the previous year's fighting, and especially the winter battles, had left Marchetti with a sick feeling. His experience had been nothing compared to what the German had endured.

He had seen his share of fighting and killing in North Africa and in Russia. He had seen Red Army men marching rank after rank against entrenched machine guns, but then his own countrymen had done so in North Africa and so had the British, French, Italian, Austrian and Turkish troops during the first war. Was there some kind of hypnotic mechanism that suppressed the instinct to live when, as a part of a large group, the individual was forced into extreme danger? He recalled vividly his desperate ten-day march across the Libyan desert ahead of advancing British forces; ten days with no shelter against the winter and so little water and food that death would have been a blessing. The British treated prisoners well; everyone knew that. So what had denied him the relief of surrender, forced him to drive the survivors of his demi-company on and on?

He and Prager had compared their experiences in the officers' club that night in Kharkov where they had caused a stir by swaggering in, sunburned almost black, uniforms worn with the unmistakable evidence of hard action. There were severe glances and subdued comments *sotto voce*, but they ignored everyone and finished three bottles of vodka. Prager fell asleep in his chair and he had stretched out beneath the table. In the morning, SS security police tried to arrest them and were left behind with cracked heads.

To be sure, conditions had improved drastically this past summer. Winter clothing was already being stockpiled, new and more powerful weapons were being issued and there were rumours of a tank bigger and better armed than the Panzer Mark IVs. Special rear area security units of SS guards and German police had been established to deal with partisans and Russian railway tracks were being reduced to European gauges at fantastic rates to ease the supply problem. The Luftwaffe had established mastery of the sky and the U-boats had all but destroyed the American and British merchant fleets in the North Atlantic and Arctic Oceans.

So why was Prager so sceptical? He had nodded towards the SS men filling the club until they outnumbered regular Army officers more than two to one. 'Too many bastards about,' he had muttered and refused to say anything more. Marchetti understood. His father, with his contacts in the *Servizio Informazione Segreto* had already decided that the Axis had lost the war, in part due to the venality of its leaders who insisted on personal gain and power before the needs of their nations.

They camped beside the Chir for two weeks as August turned into September. To the south, the distant sounds of siege guns waxed and waned. Aircraft raced back and forth across an incredibly blue sky filled with lazy cumulus clouds towering fifteen thousand metres and more. There was plenty to eat and drink for a change and new German uniforms and equipment were issued to them. Even films were shown at night against a white sheet rigged on the side of a lorry. No orders came and there was nothing to do. Other units of troops, mostly German, arrived and disappeared but they, in their isolation on the extreme southern end of the Italian Eighth Army line, were left undisturbed.

Marchetti conducted exercises and practised assaults on a line of tents representing buildings. They had originally been scheduled as part of the final assault force on the city of Stalingrad but now were to be relegated to garrison duty; a task that did not displease him since he had long since lost any illusions about the romance of battle. After three years of war, his ambition had narrowed its focus to returning himself and as many of his men as possible to Italy, alive.

Their idyllic existence ended with the month. Orders arrived for them to proceed to a map reference point twelve kilometres northeast along the Don. They marched the following morning and were greeted that afternoon by the commander of Marchetti's brigade, a rather ineffectual colonel, and a hard-faced German who accepted Marchetti's salute with a motion so sketchy as to be insulting. The German was introduced as Major Karl Zindermann. Once inside the HQ tent, the colonel offered coffee and asked after his father and the state of his men but the major broke in impatiently.

'Listen to me carefully, Major Marchetti. You are being assigned to a sensitive point on the line in this area. Your colonel tells me you are the best he has. You will take your battalion here.' He pointed to a small jog in the river's course below the city of Kletskaya, immediately on the Rumanian left.

The major's opinion of the Rumanians, and by inference, all non-German troops, was plain enough. Marchetti had encountered this attitude before and glanced at the colonel, expecting him to reprimand Zindermann. But he only stared at the map with a fixed expression.

The major went on at some length describing the disposition of troops, lines of supply and, in minute detail, Marchetti's duties which amounted to little more than guard duty. Marchetti was insulted by Zindermann's attitude but following the colonel's lead, kept silent.

The briefing did produce something positive; for the first time since the conference, Marchetti gained a detailed picture of the Voronezh-Stalingrad offensive and his resentment was submerged in the flow of information. Voronezh had been taken quickly enough to anchor the northern end of the line, but Marchetti sensed that the Stalingrad portion of Operation Citadel had fallen behind schedule.

By the end of the third week even the long march seemed preferable to the unutterable boredom of the trenches. Marchetti's battalion overlooked the Don from shallow bluffs a few metres above the placid river. The apparently empty land on the other side was burned brown under the summer sun. It was dotted with heat-wilted trees and ran into the burnished distance.

There was no shade on their side of the river within a kilometre. They spent the first week cutting the tough sod and digging trenches, the second week in widening and deepening the trenches and bunkers and then, because there was nothing else to do, shoring them with wood cut from distant trees and carried to the river. Marchetti insisted that trenches be led back behind the bluffs so that at no time would anyone be exposed to sniper fire. The decision paid off; at the start of the third week, Russian snipers took up positions across the river.

It was then that he began to appreciate the German weapons they had been issued. The heavier 7.92 millimetre GEW 98 and the GEW 41 semi-automatic rifle, as well as the nine millimetre Parabellum P-38 pistol he now wore in place of his nine millimetre Corto Beretta, gained the respect of the Russian snipers in short order.

It began to rain during their fourth week on the line. The previous day had been a marvel of early autumn with a mild sun and a cool breeze off the river. All Sunday afternoon, the battalion had filtered men down to the river in groups of fifty to bathe and swim in a sheltered inlet protected from sniper fire by a Spandau machine gun.

The rain began before dawn on Monday and, by mid-morning, had turned into a downpour. It slackened that evening and on Tuesday the sun was hotter than ever. Rain water disappeared into the parched ground and humidity hazed the steppe.

The supply lorries failed to show that day and Marchetti was not surprised. He accompanied the battalion supply clerk to the food depot and gloomily observed the small reserve they had managed to stockpile.

'These damned Germans,' the clerk complained. 'Because we are Italian, they don't give a damn. I've demanded extra rations to build a reserve until I'm blue, but nothing happens. The drivers just laugh and pretend they don't understand. They understand well enough when they want coffee, the bastards.'

Marchetti often sat at the entrance to the command bunker and listened to the mutter of heavy guns in the direction of Stalingrad. It was obvious to all by now that the assault had fallen far behind schedule, but the Germans had clamped a complete blackout on news and even the German lorry drivers did not seem to know what was going on. They had plenty of information about the drive into the Caucasus – Mount Elbruz had been sighted and German armour was almost within reach of the Caspian Sea – but nothing concerning Stalingrad.

Occasionally a German army newspaper found its way to them but Marchetti believed little of whatever it contained. News from Stalingrad was of individual or small unit actions and there were no overall progress reports. Twice, he had visited other Italian battalions on their left but it was the same there. Even the Rumanians had no news.

Even so, Marchetti pieced together meagre bits of rumour, discarded the absurd, wondered about the veracity of the remainder and still did not like the emerging picture. The Russians seemed to be holding onto the city by their fingernails. Fighting was street to street, even building to building and casualties were extremely high on both sides. Marchetti toyed with calculations based on Red Army losses versus probable and even exaggerated estimates of the size of the Red Army before the war and the possible reserves that could be generated from a population of two hundred million. It was clear enough that the Russians were at the end of their string. Stalingrad, if it continued, must suck in the remainder of the Red Army not already committed to battlefields that ranged more than three thousand kilometres in length from the Caucasus Mountains to the Arctic Circle. His confidence began to grow in spite of the delay in taking the city. The Russians obviously knew that this was their last chance and were expending their utmost effort.

The rains returned that Thursday. They fell all day in thin, lacklustre showers that at first were refreshing after the renewed heat. Thursday was also notable because, after nearly five weeks in the line, Marchetti received orders to withdraw two companies from the battalion to a map reference point fifteen kilometres to the rear for rest. Somewhat astonished at this wholly unexpected generosity, he complied without question, left his battalion chief of staff in command and went with them for a break in the routine.

Tanks rattled along the road spattering mud everywhere, followed by lorries crammed with troops. It seemed strange to be marching counter to the stream of men tramping the road verges into muddy morasses. They passed a dozen supply depots which had been camouflaged from air attack with netting and Marchetti noted their locations angrily.

At noon they halted and the men immediately rigged shelter halves against the rain and built small fires of bits of twigs and paper over which they brewed coffee. Marchetti had picked a shallow ravine for protection from the surprisingly cold rain and wind and a few minutes later, another group of soldiers appeared wearing the standard rubberised waterproofs of the German army. They were covered with mud and their faces were drawn with exhaustion. Marchetti sipped his coffee and watched them settle down on the other side of the ravine. They looked as if they had been marching for weeks, he thought and serve them right. It was their damned war. But then he noticed the officer raise a hand to beckon someone. The waterproof fell away to reveal a flag insignia sewn above the SS runes on his cuff. The flag had the red field with the blue and white cross of Norway.

The Norwegians dug out rations and he saw that they had only cold water to wash them down. He beckoned to his sergeant. 'Norwegians,' he said. 'They look like they've had a bad time.'

The sergeant muttered, 'SS bastards.'

'Cold and hungry Norwegians,' Marchetti emphasised. 'Since we'll be in camp tonight, I think I can spare them some coffee.'

'Coffee!' The sergeant stared at him. 'You want to waste coffee on SS?'

Like all units who had endured combat and hardship over a long period of time, Marchetti's battalion had shaken down into a close team in which orders were given sparingly. Every man knew his job and did it because they were professionals and because failing to do so might cause someone else to suffer. The slackers had long since disappeared – killed, wounded, missing, reformed. Marchetti did not need to order his men to share their coffee and hot rations with the Norwegians and would not have in any event, because the food and coffee were theirs to use as they saw fit. He simply spooned the last of his own supply into the pot. The sergeant muttered a curse under his breath, stared at Marchetti and then across at the Norwegians, shook his head and added some from his own supply. He glanced ruefully at the battered pot and shambled along the line to explain to the others.

A few minutes later, he returned and picked up the pot. Marchetti called after him, 'Your reward will come in heaven, Sergeant Negroni.'

'Not too damned soon, I hope,' he growled and walked across to the Norwegians. Many of the others followed with their own pots. Marchetti sipped the steaming liquid in his own cup – he had refilled it before Negroni had finished his explanations. It was all right to be generous, he knew, but there is no need to be a damned fool.

Cries of pleasure greeted the Italians when the Norwegians realised they had brought real coffee. The two groups mingled and soon were sharing soggy ration packs and cigarettes. After a few minutes, an officer came across to where Marchetti sat. The Norwegian saluted and Marchetti shifted aside under the shelter and motioned for the man to sit.

They quickly discovered their only common language was German, which neither spoke well and so their conversation was interlarded with Norwegian and Italian words and a great deal of gesturing. The Norwegian's name was Hans Jurgensen and he was a lieutenant commanding Company C of the Viking Regiment, Sixth SS Division. They had been detached from the rest of the division, which was further south in the Caucasus, for reasons unknown, and sent up to the line at Stalingrad. They had been on the march for nearly a week since leaving the railhead and were due to enter the line on the northern end of Stalingrad proper following three days rest.

Marchetti told him frankly that he thought it curious that Norwegians were fighting for the Germans and Jurgensen snorted and with no hint of defensiveness told him, 'We aren't fighting for the Germans, we are fighting communism. When the British and the Americans formed an alliance with the Russians, we decided that someone had to draw the line. Only the damned Germans were fighting, so what other choice was there?'

Marchetti's expression must have shown his scepticism because Jurgensen shrugged. 'I know you must find it difficult to believe that we could be fighting on the same side as those who have occupied our country. But you must remember two things; first, the British were only one day away from the same invasion and two, if the Allies win, the Russians will gobble up all of Europe. I do not want the Russians in my country nor in Sweden or Finland or Denmark. Germans are bad enough but at least we share racial characteristics and heritage.'

Marchetti understood as he was as concerned as Jurgensen over the menace of Russia if the Allies should win the war. The Americans especially were likely to give the Russians a free hand in Europe. What difference would it make to them, five thousand kilometres away?

Marchetti offered the Norwegian another cup. 'My God,' Jurgensen muttered, 'I haven't tasted real coffee since before the war.'

Jurgensen told him that he had been a Norwegian army officer before the German occupation. 'I fought at Lillehammer and retreated north with the Norwegian Fifth Infantry Division and the British 148th Brigade to Andalsnes. Then the British abandoned us like they did the French, two months later.

'So, I surrendered because there wasn't anything else for it. I went into the Veidal Concentration Camp near Bodo when they found out I was an officer and a university lecturer. I was released in May 1941 and in July was offered the chance to join a special Scandinavian SS unit to be used only against Russia.'

Jurgensen grunted. 'Anyone with half a brain could see that after France, Russia was next. I thought to myself, maybe this is the chance to stamp out communism once and for all. And besides, the university was closed and I was tired of doing nothing.

'Very few of us were members of the *Nationjal Samling*, the Norwegian Nazi Party, at the time. Mostly, we are those who know the Soviets really mean it when they say that communism will soon rule the entire world. Look what happened to the Baltic States, to Bessarabia, and Finland. Believe me, that was only the beginning. If the Russians should win, all Europe is in deadly danger.'

Jurgensen laughed at his own rhetoric. 'It has been so long,' he apologised, 'since I've had someone to talk to.'

'Not at all,' Marchetti told him. 'Please continue.'

'Well, we were sent to Sennheim in Alsace to train. We lived in French army barracks that weren't half bad. In February 1941, we were shipped to Vienna for more training and finally to Heuburg, in Germany. We knew something was about to happen then.

'The invasion of Yugoslavia began and they sent quite a few of us along to gain combat experience. I tell you, I was really impressed! After I saw what happened to Yugoslavia and Greece, I knew that German armour would go through the Russians like a dose of salts. But damn it, there never seems to be an end to the bastards. You kill a thousand Russians and find a thousand more right behind them. You occupy a thousand square kilometres of land, and see another thousand which must be captured.

Everywhere you turn there are partisans sniping at you from trees, setting mines in the road, poisoning wells and burning villages and farms to destroy anything that could be used as shelter.'

Suddenly conscious that he was sounding desperate, Jurgensen stopped talking. He essayed a nervous laugh to assure Marchetti that he was in control of himself, then sat staring at the fire, his cooling mug of coffee forgotten.

The Norwegians marched out thirty minutes later. The constant threat of death made such contacts bittersweet. Marchetti had discovered long ago the intense need war creates to reach out to fellow human beings to assure oneself that one is still alive and still human.

Relationships such as these were abnormal in the sense that they were promoted by war where friendships were declared on a moment's acquaintance and, within hours, deepened into a life or death commitment. But intense and emotional as they were, such friendships were transitory. When a comrade was killed, the grief was overwhelming but usually short-lived because there was simply too much death. When military service was over, few such relationships, strong as they seemed, survived. Most soldiers shook hands, promised to keep in touch, and never saw one another again.

The autumn rains began in earnest and the countryside along the Don turned into a quagmire. Hour after hour Marchetti sat in his bunker, which was half-filled with water in spite of all their efforts at a drainage system, and wondered why Stalingrad refused to fall. Had something gone wrong? According to the plan, the city should have been occupied before the rains. Rumour had it that Stalingrad had become a meat-grinder. Personally, he had seen little of the Russians all summer except for prisoners or snipers.

His battalion formed the northernmost extension of the lines about Stalingrad and the southernmost end of the Italian Eighth Army line on the Don. They were flanked on the southeast by the Rumanian Third Army. Attacking the city from the southwest was the Fourth Panzer Army while the German Sixth struggled in from the northwest. As best he could determine, opposing them were the very much weaker Soviet Sixty-Second and Sixty-Fourth Armies. Axis lines touched the Volga at points above and below the city – at Ryonk in the south and Yerzovka in the north. Rumour had it that all of Stalingrad, but for a kilometre-wide strip extending from the *Krasny Oktober* factory to the Tsaritsa River in the south, was in Axis hands. Perhaps so, he thought, but why then did Russian artillery grow louder by the day?

At the end of October, Marchetti was ordered to report to brigade headquarters, who sent him along to division HQ at Starobelsk where he was informed that a request had been submitted by a Norwegian SS unit operating in Stalingrad that he be sent to them as an official observer. Marchetti stared at the divisional intelligence officer, wondering if someone were not playing a bad joke on him.

'Why you?' the obviously puzzled colonel asked.

Marchetti read the order and found he was instructed to report to a certain Lieutenant Hans Jurgensen in the front lines west of the *Krasny Oktober* factory, where the fighting was said to be the bitterest.

It took Marchetti three days to make the two hundred kilometre trip from Starobelsk to Stalingrad. He had to pass through an astonishing number of military checkpoints and at each his papers were carefully examined and verified before he was allowed to continue.

When he asked why at one post, he was told that partisans were using the uniforms and papers of dead German soldiers to make their way safely about in the rear areas. Later, when he mentioned this to Jurgensen, the Norwegian laughed.

'Partisans, hell! They are there to prevent desertions. German officers of my acquaintance tell me that desertion has become a major problem. And why not when orders for even a minor assault can amount to a death sentence? I've even heard rumours that a few officers have been shot by their own men. Shades of 1917!'

The Norwegians were uniformly dirty and exhausted. The three days rest they had been promised had turned out to be a figment of someone's imagination and they had been marched into the line as soon as they arrived. Marchetti had guessed at the desperate nature of the fighting but for once it seemed that even the rumour mill had been guilty of understatement. As they ate a meagre dinner of canned rations and drank the Georgian wine Marchetti had bought in Starobelsk, he studied the young Norwegian officer.

His face was deeply lined and dirt embedded in the skin suggested he hadn't bathed or washed regularly in weeks. His eyes were furtive, darting here and there and twice, when artillery shells whistled overhead, he froze; only his blank eyes followed the audible track of the shell. Marchetti also noticed a faint tremor in his hands. The Norwegian's eyelids blinked convulsively at times and a tic, of which he seemed unaware, twisted his lips and thrust his chin forward. He chain-smoked black Russian cigarettes and drank the wine quickly, almost with contempt, then produced a litre of vodka.

'The only good thing about this place,' Jurgensen muttered. 'They give you all the vodka you can drink. It comes up with the ammunition. Couldn't survive without either.'

That evening, Marchetti attended a regimental briefing with the Norwegian. The others were German and he noticed how the two of them were subtly isolated. Without exception, all but he were hollow-eyed and gaunt, filthy with vermin and in the narrow space, stank. The briefing was conducted by a colonel in little better shape than they. Marchetti watched their apathetic responses and was strongly reminded of North Africa during the British breakthrough in the spring of 1941, when the Italian army had worn that same furtive, haunted look of men who don't know for certain that they have lost but suspect so.

The briefing officer described the operation scheduled for first light. The regiment would assault a factory labelled as Point Thirty-Four on the map. Photographs showed a field of rubble surrounding a gaunt, pocked concrete building in what must have been an area of similar buildings now destroyed.

The colonel nodded to Jurgensen. 'While we are busy about this task, our Norwegian comrades will have the honour of capturing this Soviet artillery observation post.' He pinned another large photograph to the wall which showed a single tower of reinforced concrete that appeared to have withstood the best efforts of German artillery and aerial bombardment to date.

'The Russians use this tower as an artillery observation post and we must have it for the same reason,' the colonel rumbled on. 'The attack on Point Thirty-four will draw Russian fire and reinforcements allowing the Norwegian SS troops to attack and capture it. Remember,' the colonel admonished, 'that building is less than half a kilometre from the Volga. Everything we do in this area can be seen and artillery fire directed at us from the east bank.'

The plan was described in detail; after heavy mortaring and point-blank cannon fire from five tanks, the regiment would assault the factory – Point Thirty-Four – while the Norwegians attacked the Soviet observation post. 'A machine gun here commands the approach to the tower and will have to be removed. You must do this quickly before the observers in the tower realise what is happening.

'Two red flares will be fired as the signal to begin,' the colonel said. 'I have procured a flame-thrower squad which will join you at first light. When the action has been successfully completed, Obersturmfuehrer Jurgensen, you will fire two red flares and the artillery observation team will join you. Everything must go like clockwork,' the colonel said mechanically, as if he did not believe it himself. 'We have artillery support for only twenty minutes at 0930 hours.'

Marchetti was appalled, and as they walked back to the bunker he sensed that Jurgensen was as well. The attack described by the briefing officer was tantamount to suicide. When he ventured as much, Jurgensen laughed.

'Just another day on the line at Stalingrad. Notice that we uh... foreigners get the dirty job? You don't see any fine German boys charging snipers' nests over two hundred metres of open ground do you? It's just our bad luck they used up the last of their Ukrainian volunteers last week.'

Jurgensen was silent until they came in sight of the bunker. 'At least after tomorrow you will have an idea what to expect.' He clutched Marchetti's arm and in the moonlight the Norwegian's face had a haunted cast. 'I think you were surprised when my invitation arrived? Well, I had an ulterior motive. I need you to tell your people that these Germans are crazy. The Russians are getting ready to go over to the offensive – hell, we can see them moving troops up to the riverbank every afternoon. After dark, they come over in boats. Anyone can see their flares as they swarm across. We've heard Luftwaffe pilots telling of whole armies moving towards Stalingrad, but these jackasses act as if the Russians are going to throw down their guns and run away. Well, I can tell you that won't happen. These aren't the same Russian soldiers we fought last year. They don't need commissars shooting slaggards to hurry them to the line any longer.

'You must tell your superiors what you see here. We should have pulled back weeks ago and let the damned city starve until the Caucasus was wrapped up and reinforcements were available. But the madman Hitler has decided that Stalingrad is more important than the Caspian oilfields, or even Moscow! So, we are all going to die, you included unless all the non-German contingents act.' He spat in the mud. 'All the Germans swore an oath and they will die before they go back on it, the stupid bastards.'

Jurgensen paused to catch his breath and looked around to make certain there was no chance of being overheard. A cold wind gusted their greatcoats and Marchetti shivered, as much at Jurgensen's prediction as at the cold. What had happened to the man, he wondered? He sounded half deranged.

'I asked for you to come because I found out your father is an important man in Rome. Something has got to be done or we will lose the war and all Europe will be taken over by the Russian communists. I cannot protest as we are SS troops and subject to SS discipline. I do not report directly to my Norwegian superiors but through the German divisional HQ, and who knows what lies those bastards add to my reports. But you can because the Italian Eighth Army is independent. Tell them just what you see here and urge them to do something before it is too late.'

Marchetti lay awake for a long time, listening to the roar of artillery. It was a good deal louder here, the result of concentration as well as proximity. Shells exploded throughout the sector in random pattern and it was impossible to guess where the next would hit. The only relief came when the enemy artillery shifted to a different sector. You knew then that someone else was being shelled, Marchetti thought, but you did not care so long as it was not you.

Marchetti remembered the shelling in Libya, in the autumn of 1940, at the camp he commanded south of Sofafi when they had come under attack by a large British patrol armed with mortars and Bren guns. He recalled now most strongly that peculiar feeling of helplessness that came from being under shell fire.

In the beginning you told yourself that nothing was going to happen to you. After all, the universe was you; without you there was no world, no war, nothing, and fate or God or good luck or whatever would protect you. Someone else would be killed or maimed but not you. Then the first near miss happened and the feeling of being unique vanished as the cordite fumes choked you and your heart pounded so that you feared a heart attack as much as a shell burst. Your stomach knotted with fear and maybe you urinated or defecated involuntarily. Marchetti's memories of the trenches that particular night were made up of fear and the cloying smell of explosive, screams and excrement.

Another string of shells exploded nearby, marching towards the bunker faster than thought. Marchetti lay rigid, waiting, as he knew everyone else in the bunker was doing. Yet there wasn't a sound, as if everyone but him were sound asleep – and he knew it wasn't true. The explosions ended, shifted elsewhere he thought, but there was no relief.

It was a funny thing, fear. After the first time, it never seemed quite so bad again even though it was. Perhaps the brain could only absorb so much and one either went insane or learned to live with it. He, as so many others, kept the terror at bay simply by containing it, holding it, hiding it within himself while outwardly endeavouring to appear normal. Perhaps after a while one even tricked oneself – to a very small extent.

They were roused at 0600. After a hurried breakfast of cold beef and bread and a single cup of lukewarm ersatz coffee, they moved in pitch darkness to the assembly point. Jurgensen had tried to make Marchetti remain in the bunker but he refused.

A bitter wind blew from the direction of the river, whipping ice-hard snow crystals into their faces. In spite of the darkness, their objective was almost visible as they moved towards it. The constant explosions of artillery rounds bathed the structure in flickering, reddish light.

They passed a tank hunkered down behind a pile of rubble. Marchetti smelled hot metal, lubricating oil and cordite and the familiar rumble of its engines suddenly seemed abnormal in the hell that flickered about them.

They slipped on ice and cursed and resettled weapons. Marchetti had taken an extra bandolier of ammunition and four grenades which he had shoved into his pockets where they dragged like lead weights. He was cold to the bone and deadly weary, as if he hadn't slept in weeks. His feet were half frozen and his greatcoat was inadequate to keep out the searching wind.

Just short of the last trench, a dark-faced man in uniform and greatcoat, smelling raw and dirty, passed out bottles of vodka. Ahead, the blasted ruins of the tower loomed as the eastern sky lightened with dawn.

Marchetti was appalled. He had never before seen such a wasteland of tangled steel and shattered masonry. A German officer, a colonel, hurried up and he and Jurgensen conferred. When the German pointed, Jurgensen swore violently, then turned away. Marchetti raised an eyebrow.

'No flame-thrower. Maybe the SS slept late this morning, or maybe they were frightened off.' Jurgensen spoke in bitter German so that the colonel could hear, but the man only shrugged and hurried on. 'The bastard's ordered us to attack anyway. The machine gun is a hundred and fifty metres or so ahead. The son of a bitch.' Jurgensen stared after the German's retreating back. 'I'd like to shoot him myself. The Russians have hung onto it for nearly two weeks.'

No wonder he hates the Germans so much, Marchetti thought as he studied the jumble of broken concrete, timbers and reinforcing steel rods that formed the machine gun strongpoint. Two cracked sections of concrete had fallen to form a roofed shelter of sorts. He could just make out a thin gap along the top of the rubble beneath the concrete slab of roof. Just enough room for the barrel of the machine gun.

With growing apprehension, Marchetti studied the rubble piled on either side in such a way that it formed a runway or gully leading directly to the slit. Above and beyond, extensive ruins offered ample concealment for snipers. And beyond that, the three-storey tower two hundred metres further away provided an ideal shooting platform. Marchetti breathed a curse in Italian.

The Norwegian may not have understood the words but he did the intent. 'Exactly,' he muttered. He was silent a moment, staring, then shook his head. 'Christ in heaven, if only we had that damned flame-thrower!'

The Norwegian SS troops stood or squatted in the rubble which offered concealment from the tower. Marchetti looked from Jurgensen to the soldiers and back again, knowing exactly how Jurgensen felt at that moment. The Nazis treated them all as second-class troops, as auxiliaries to be used only for garrison duty – or cannon fodder.

The Norwegians were armed with their own weapons and equipment, bolt-action Krag rifles and 11.25 millimetre pistols modelled after the American Colt .45 semiautomatic pistol. Their uniforms were issue SS, but the quality was poor. All had mixed bits and pieces of Russian uniforms, boots and equipment and a few even carried the Russian PPsh submachine pistol with its huge seventy-one round drum magazine.

Jurgensen looked at him and took a deep breath, then turned and shouted a command in Norwegian. A squad of men shuffled to their feet and, not daring to look at one another, came forward and crouched to hear his instructions. They moved with that sense of economy that all combat soldiers develop as a result of too little sleep, poor and insufficient food and an enemy's constant attempt to kill them.

One by one they moved forward around the screening mound of rubble, keeping well to the shadows. The dawn light was growing fast and the sky to the east glowed with shades of red and orange. The light suffused the rubble, lending a sickly, almost futuristic cast to the scene.

Marchetti glanced at Jurgensen but he was watching the progress of the squad over the rubble. The leader held up a hand and the others stopped when they reached the end of a rubble-berm. Beyond there were several metres of open ground before the gully started that led in tortuous fashion towards the bunker. Without warning, the leader dashed across the open space and dived into the gully. The machine gun fired quickly but he scrambled down the slope, wriggled around and burrowed low.

The machine gun blasted the end of the berm this time, forcing the Norwegians to duck against shrapnel and ricochets and Jurgensen shouted for covering fire. They had one mortar which was almost useless against the entrenched machine gun but two bombs thudded off nevertheless to explode on and around it. The machine gun did not pause in its probe of the berm.

'This is insane,' Jurgensen snarled half to himself. 'We need a heavy gun, a thirty-seven millimetre at least, but the bastards claim they haven't one to spare.'

The sun edged over the eastern horizon and the fading red sky was cloudless. Marchetti saw the lone man in the gully look up and knew he was thinking that in a few more minutes the sun would expose anyone trying to reach him to the sniper in the tower. It would also be in the machine gunner's eyes, not that it would matter much as all he had to do was fire periodically to keep him pinned down.

Jurgensen shouted another squad up and gave them quick orders. They too exchanged glances, then moved out as ordered. They separated, as had the previous squad, but instead of moving towards the gully, skirted the berm and began to crawl forward through the rubble, using every bit of cover possible to approach the strongpoint from above and behind. Marchetti understood that Jurgensen was attempting to get them to the strongpoint before the sun climbed higher, but the distance proved too great and the rubble too thick.

A second man from the first squad raced from the berm's cover and dived into the gully. The Russian machine gunner was again a shade slow and Marchetti saw the soldier squirm down the slope and twist around to lie panting in the shadows. The leader of the second squad, approaching from above and behind, tugged a hand grenade from his pocket. He was still twenty metres from the strongpoint but a maze of twisted steel and barbed wire blocked his way. He twisted the igniter, held it at full arm's length and threw.

The grenade landed short, bounced once before the stick struck the ground and, like a rugby or an American football, darted to one side and exploded, throwing up a harmless spray of rubble and shrapnel. The man who had thrown the grenade jumped up and raced forward firing his Russian machine pistol from the hip as rubble spattered down. Marchetti saw chips spray from the bunker just as the soldier stumbled and fell headlong in that nerveless sprawl that meant he was already dead.

Jurgensen shouted to the others to hold their positions and swore volubly in Norwegian. 'Now they are all pinned down and they have no way to get back until dark.'

When Jurgensen moved away to talk to one of his men, Marchetti found a small hole through the rubble that offered some concealment while still permitting a constricted view of the bunker and the rubble on either side. He tipped his helmet forward to bring the curve into play. A bullet striking the helmet's rounded portion might skip away if the angle was right, rather than penetrate.

The hole allowed a good, if limited, view to the left of the strongpoint and the tower, or what remained of it. And he could see a Norwegian rifleman curled behind a broken piece of masonry while beyond him, another moved towards better cover. He found the two men pinned in the gully; neither had moved from their awkward positions. The machine gun fired a short burst at that moment and he saw rubble dance above their heads. Apparently the machine gun could not be depressed further, thank God.

Marchetti used the pair of small but powerful folding field glasses his father had given him when he came home from Libya and focused them on a soldier lying in full sunlight. The sun had moved well above the eastern horizon and washed away the deep, concealing shadows.

The body was motionless, half turned towards them on its left side. He saw a tiny patch of blood under the collar bone. Marchetti tapped Jurgensen. 'Sniper,' he said quietly and pointed. From the other side, Jurgensen swore.

Marchetti turned the glasses on the man behind the body just as a bit of dust spurted past his leg. He must have realised at that instant that he was under fire as he twisted to one side, but a second bullet struck his helmet and sent it skittering away and he flopped once and lay still.

Jurgensen looked at the soldier, his expression reflecting his helplessness. The killing ground was living up to its name, Marchetti thought. The heavy machine gun fired again and the men in the gully pressed harder against the bottom. It seemed to Marchetti that the bullets had struck a bit lower this time. Were the Russians propping the gun up to decrease the muzzle angle?

Three men dead in less than five minutes; potentially seventeen more by the end of the day. Marchetti backed away from the rubble mound and moved so that he could focus the glasses on the tower. He shaded the lenses carefully with his hand so that they would not flash in the growing sunlight. The tower, through the glasses, was a tangle of masonry and steel reinforcing rods, perfect cover for a sniper. It was at least two hundred metres away, child's play for a good shot with an accurate rifle, a telescopic sight and good cover. Marchetti studied the building, guessing from the angle of the shot that killed the last man, that the sniper was on the third and top floor.

He searched the pocked surface for five minutes before he caught the barest trace of movement. There, he thought with grim elation, above a broken window ledge where a shell or bomb had exploded inside the building and blown out the frame and a part of the wall. The remaining rubble offered excellent concealment within a space of two or three metres on both sides of the angle.

A cosy spot, Marchetti thought. A place to lie down and rest, perhaps a small stove for heat and to cook some soup – all the comforts of home. He pointed out the sniper's nest to Jurgensen.

'If you can eliminate him, your rifle squad can flank the strongpoint and drop hand grenades from above to distract them inside long enough for the two in the gully to get at least one grenade through the slit.'

Jurgensen nodded. 'But how do I get *him*. We can't attack the tower because the machine gun covers that damned open area. If we wait for tonight, the sniper will have picked them off . . . damn it, it was stupid to send so many men out there . . .'

Marchetti knew it was not, that he would have done exactly the same. 'Artillery?'

'I've asked again but the answer is still no. They haven't any to spare. I think a big push is shaping up in the neighbourhood of the railway station and ferry terminal and everything will be moved down there when they finish with the factory.'

'Do you have a sniper's rifle?'

Jurgensen shook his head. 'I've asked a dozen times for one but it never comes. Nothing ever comes from the Germans, damn them, but orders to go out and get my men killed.'

Marchetti grunted and handed Jurgensen his MP40 and took the Krag rifle the Norwegian carried. He opened the magazine box mounted on the side, rolled the five rounds into his hand, then opened the bolt and caught the cartridge in the breech as it was ejected.

He examined each for concentricity and tossed one doubtful cartridge to Jurgensen who juggled the machine pistol to catch it. Marchetti slipped the remaining four rounds into a pocket, reversed the rifle and peered through the barrel, turning it slightly this way and that, searching for imperfections in the bore or minor bends in the barrel. He then tested the trigger pull for creep and crispness of let-off. Satisfied, he rolled the cartridges back into the breech and worked the bolt.

Jurgensen watched with scepticism as he climbed the rubble and manoeuvred two chunks of masonry to form a head-high barrier which he then bridged with a piece of timber. Marchetti eased the rifle through the opening and braced his chin on his hand to study the tower.

The window was at a slight angle and so he thought the chances good that the sniper would be crouched to the right where he could watch the trapped Norwegians. One shot; there wouldn't be a second chance.

Marchetti searched away from the tower and located a makeshift target, a piece of wood poking above the jumble of broken concrete at what he estimated was two hundred metres. The rifle, he noted, was the Model 1894/12 made at Konigsberg in 1924. It was equipped with the old-fashioned tangent sight that had a shallow V notch which he set carefully for two hundred metres. The V gave as clear an image as could be expected, but much poorer than the sight picture he was used to on Italian and German rifles. He rested the forestock on his gloved hand and the gloved hand on the edge of the rubble mound, sighted carefully and squeezed the trigger.

He felt it grate at mid-pull but the let-off was crisp enough. The rifle jumped and when he looked, the wood was missing a chunk on its right side, confirming the Krags reputation for excellent accuracy with the 6.5 x 55 millimetre service cartridge.

Jurgensen knelt beside him and focused his glasses on the tower. Marchetti told him where to watch. 'The moment you see the slightest movement, tell me because I won't be able to see more than the window itself in the notch. I am going to aim at the bottom right-hand side.'

Jurgensen grunted agreement and hunched forward onto his elbows. 'Nothing,' he muttered after a moment. Thirty seconds or more went by. 'Nothing.'

The struggle to keep the front sight in focus became a chore. The rear sight persisted in developing a double image, one superimposed slightly above the other, which Marchetti found increasingly difficult to bring together. With a gasp, Marchetti finally drew back to rest his eye. As he did so, Jurgensen muttered, 'Now.'

Marchetti swore, rubbed his eyes and re-aimed.

Now his trigger finger began to ache and in spite of the cold, sweat formed beneath his uniform and on his forehead. The sun was moving higher causing the sights to glisten and again he had to stop. Again, Jurgensen muttered, 'Now.'

Muttering under his breath, Marchetti lit a match and carefully blackened the front and rear sights with soot. Jurgensen watched without a word. Marchetti knew he was trying not to increase the pressure, but his forbearance had the opposite effect.

He resettled the rifle on his gloved hand, drew the stock tight against his shoulder and laid his cheek hard against the comb. His trigger finger took up the slack. The sights settled on the window and he concentrated on the front sight, ignoring every impulse to glance over it. The sun was stronger now but the blackened sights improved visibility. The window was still a blur past the front sight but it had lost some of its tenuousness.

'Nothing,' Jurgensen resumed the soft chant. The sights began to swim again and the motion of the front blade relative to the window described the familiar figure eight.

'Nothing.'

Marchetti ignored everything; the cold stone cramping his left hand, the growing ache in his right shoulder, the icy feel of the walnut stock against his cheek, the pain where the rubble dug into his ribs.

'Nothing.'

He tried to picture the Russian sniper crouching against the window frame, motionless except for the minute movement of field glasses as he scanned the rubble below for another victim. His long Mosin-Nagant rifle with its telescopic sight would be propped securely into a rest to assure accuracy. He hadn't any need to worry about a betraying flash of sunlight because the sun was directly behind him.

'Nothing.'

Who was he? Some mad killer let loose from a Soviet prison? Doubtful. Snipers had to be excellent marksmen. And marksmanship was skill acquired only by practice – thousands of rounds fired per year. Criminals rarely had that kind of patience and he supposed that, like those from other nations, Soviet snipers were generally normal, stable individuals with a high degree of skill, probably professional hunters...

'Now.'

Marchetti was so lost in pain and concentration that he almost did not hear Jurgensen's command. His conscious mind woke with a start and he saw the front blade steady on the black blur of the window, saw the top come level with the rear notch and the light equalise on either side and, almost without conscious volition, his finger squeezed the trigger.

The recoil broke his concentration and he ducked down, dragging a protesting Jurgensen with him. 'If I missed,' he shouted, 'he'll return the shot and you'll be dead.'

They scurried along the rubble, keeping very low until Marchetti spotted a place where they could watch with relative safety. Both used their glasses. The window took on solid definition as Marchetti focused. There was no sign of movement behind the window frame. Jurgensen lowered his glasses first and they exchanged glances. Marchetti led the way back to the firing point and crouched down, Jurgensen beside him. They heard the machine gun fire another short burst.

Jurgensen took a deep breath and scrambled up the rubble. He took his helmet off and balanced it on the muzzle of Marchetti's machine pistol, then eased it up for an instant. Nothing. He crawled a few paces to the left and repeated the manoeuvre, making it look like a careless soldier moving behind the rubble. If the sniper was still alive, the next time should draw him, Marchetti thought.

It did not and Jurgensen sighed in relief. 'I think you got him. How did you learn to shoot like that?'

'I attended a private academy when I was a boy. We were all taught to shoot. I took a Bronze medal at the 1936 Olympics.' He exchanged the Krag for his machine pistol.

Jurgensen eased onto the rubble and called to the men in Norwegian that the sniper was dead. 'Get a move on,' he shouted, 'before they replace him.'

Marchetti saw the lead man hesitate, then with a convulsive effort, fling himself forward. He scrabbled across the open space to the next bit of cover, waved and the rest of the squad followed, converging on the strongpoint from behind. There were no shots from the tower and all made it safely to cover.

Two Norwegians scrambled under the overhang and pitched grenades into the slit. The explosions blew dust, debris and shrapnel from every opening and the two soldiers crouched in the gully raced forward, one on either side. Another stick grenade was flipped through the slit and again a solid whomp blew out dust and smoke. A figure in a dirt-brown uniform tried to claw out through the slit and was shot through the head. Three SS men disappeared inside the makeshift bunker. Two more shots echoed before they reappeared, waving to indicate that all was secure.

The stench of burned flesh issuing from the strongpoint was stomach-turning. Nevertheless, they shoved in past the mangled remains of four bodies and Jurgensen gave a sharp order in Norwegian. Several men reluctantly began to haul the dead bodies outside.

They discovered that the slab of concrete did not offer the shelter from the rear that it had from the front. The tower was clearly visible over the hectares of rubble and Jurgensen wasted no time. He called to his sergeant to form up two squads while a third remained to hold the strongpoint against a Russian counterattack.

'This time,' Jurgensen told Marchetti bluntly, 'you are staying behind. I want to make certain you write that report.'

Marchetti watched them go towards the tower, taking advantage of every bit of cover until they disappeared. Then he examined the damaged Russian machine gun which he recognised from numerous captured examples as a 12.7 millimetre DShK Model 1938 Heavy Machine Gun. This one had a dent in the barrel – probably from hand grenade shrapnel. He poked around in the rubbish until he found the heavy canvas bag containing the spare barrel and the tools needed to service the gun – copper hammer, punches, oil bottles and wiping rags.

Since there was nothing to do now but wait, he decided to put the gun back in service. With its wheeled mounting and the stacks of metal ammunition cans he had seen against the back wall, perhaps Jurgensen could make use of it since the damned Germans wouldn't give him any support.

He had learnt long ago that all weapon designs follow certain mechanical principles and logic. The first rule was always to unload the piece first. The DShK had a rounded magazine cover held in place by a latch at the top rear. He flipped it up and pulled at the rounds wound round the feed sprocket. They refused to move. There was a small switch sticking up from just behind the feed sprocket and when he pushed it, the sprocket wound backwards and the four cartridges in the magazine slid out.

It took ten minutes to work out the exact procedure for field stripping the machine gun. A dog-eared manual was crammed into the bag but only the pictures were of use. He finally figured out that he had to brace the gun and use all his strength to pull the gas tube forward and turn it clockwise. The barrel came out the same way and he was sweating before he got the new one seated properly and the gun reassembled. He laid the cartridges into the sprocket, worked the rotating cam and snapped the cover closed. Then, with the help of one of the soldiers left behind, he got the gun turned around to cover the approach to the river and the tower.

Through field glasses, he found that the Norwegians had moved to within fifty metres of the tower. He studied the shattered building carefully, but the strong sunlight had deepened the shadows to opaque black and it was impossible to see if anything or anyone was moving about its base or in the two windows visible.

A soldier reared up suddenly to throw a grenade and it puffed smoke and dust deep in the rubble. A cold wind stirred more dust and made its way across the wasteland into the strongpoint to search out every bit of exposed skin. Marchetti shivered and buttoned his coat collar against his throat. The contrast of bright, cloudless sky and the icy devastation was ludicrous.

Something winked at the second floor window of the tower. Marchetti trained his glasses on the window and saw spits of flame visible against the dark background. The Russians had put a machine gun up there, he thought. Had it been there all along, or only since he had killed the sniper? He sought among the rubble for the Norwegians but saw no one. Pinned down, he thought. Well maybe he could arrange a second surprise for the comrades.

He settled himself on the gun's tractor seat and grasped the spade grips. He had never fired a machine gun of such heavy calibre and had no idea of the ballistics or how hard it would be to hold the gun onto the target. He had used the eight millimetre Breda Model 37 Heavy Machine Gun in training and at Sofafi South, but it was half the calibre and weight of this monster. He took a deep breath, lined the sights up and wondered if the Russian gunner had loaded tracer rounds. He stared at the cartridges, some of which were black-tipped, but he did not know the Soviet colour codes.

He pushed the trigger; it resisted and he pushed harder before remembering the safety. Cursing under his breath, he pushed it off and glared at the grinning Norwegian serving as feeder. This time the gun fired and the sights jumped. He let up quickly and had the impression of whitish smoke trails pounding the vicinity of the window. Accurate!

He fired again, a longer burst, and saw pieces of masonry fly off the wall. He corrected, fired again and thought he saw a tracer round penetrate the window before his view was obscured by dust and dancing pieces of concrete. Marchetti ducked and curled himself as tightly below the gun as possible. He heard someone scream and then the concrete shell was filled with the snap and scream of machine gun bullets ricocheting around the interior.

Marchetti fought his panic; of course the Russians would return his fire. They would be more than aware that the strongpoint had been taken . . . this was a sighting burst . . . he counted to three, then shoved himself back into the saddle. It was the work of a moment to realign the sights. This time, he fired a long, heavy burst, working the muzzle in very short circles so that the window disappeared in a cloud of cement dust and flying pieces of concrete. He kept it up until the belt was exhausted, ignoring the damage the sustained firing was doing to the weapon.

When the belt end whipped into the breech, he threw himself down and under the gun again, cringing against the returning fire. But nothing happened. After a moment, he opened his eyes. Still nothing. Had he succeeded in knocking out the machine gun? He counted slowly to thirty, then unfolded himself. His feeder was doing the same and they eyed one another across the gun's trail. The soldier's expression said very clearly, 'you are the officer'.

Marchetti crouched beneath the opening and took off his helmet, then straightened until he could see through the opening. A quick glance told him nothing. He took a deep breath and eased up for a longer look. A figure was running away from the tower's base and a moment later an explosion flashed and rolled towards them. There was no answering fire from the machine gun on the second floor but dimly, after the explosion's boom passed, he heard the distant snap of rifle fire.

Marchetti slumped down, ignoring the soldier's quizzical glance. The man did not speak German, so there was no use trying to explain. Let him find out for himself.

The tower was secured by mid-afternoon and the rumble of heavy guns sounded from the south where a new assault was warming up. Marchetti watched the four men stumbling over the rubble as they made their way back with two makeshift stretchers. It was plain enough from the way they took their time that the stretchers held dead bodies.

One Norwegian had been killed in the strongpoint when the Soviet machine gun had returned Marchetti's first burst but, other than a few scratches from shrapnel and debris, there had been no other casualties. Four men dead assaulting the strongpoint, killed by the sniper and two assaulting the tower – relatively light casualties for this kind of savage fighting, Marchetti thought. Thank God his own company was on the river line further north, where they had only to contend with artillery barrages.

But then he saw that Jurgensen was one of the dead. Shot through the head, a stretcher bearer explained in halting German, during the last assault of the tower. A few Russian soldiers remained alive when they burst in and one had shot him from the shadows at the top of a stairwell.

Marchetti nodded and turned away quickly so that the Norwegian soldiers who were gathering around would not see his tears. He stumbled up the gully and slithered down the far side of the rubble slope from where they had started earlier in the morning. He stopped, lit a cigarette, then brushed at his eyes and looked away across the bright, sunlit expanse of broken concrete and shattered trees as the anger began.

He had experienced such hatred only once before, at Sofafi South when Captain Maroni had ordered him to move the camp back to its original indefensible site, and again when he had seen Maroni sprawled at ease in the officers' mess after he had marched his shattered company for two days to the next camp north and endured a three-day lorry ride back to the coast. He had nearly killed Maroni then, and would have if he hadn't been prevented by other officers.

Jurgensen's life had been wasted in the same way those of his soldiers killed at Sofafi South had been. Stalingrad is just a political game played by two savage dictators who care nothing for the good men they are throwing away, he thought with hatred.

Marchetti dropped his cigarette and glanced with surprise at the snow flurries. Jurgensen would get his report, he promised. If he had to deliver it to the Duce's office personally.

*

Marchetti returned to his unit two days later. Compared to what the Norwegians were enduring, his isolated position on the Don seemed a holiday resort. He could look out through the bunker's observation slit and see nothing but river and brownish flat land marching clear to the horizon. And other than sporadic artillery bombardments, the line had been quiet for some time. The Rumanians to the south seemed to be absorbing what little punishment the Russians were capable of administering beyond the Stalingrad front.

He studied intelligence reports that had come in during his absence but there was no indication as yet that the Russians meant to reinforce their Don line. At Eighth Army headquarters, the army command and its German advisors seemed confident that the enemy had reduced its forces in other sectors to the bare minimum in order to feed the voracious maw of the city battlefield. For a few days there was talk of mounting an offensive across the river to flank Soviet lines northwest of Stalingrad, but nothing came of it. What, he wondered, had ever possessed the German High Command to agree to abandon the drive on Sartov that would have resulted in the isolation of Moscow from the production centres of the Urals and Siberia? Hitler, Marchetti was convinced, had little real conception that modern war meant occupying production capacity, not land.

Marchetti was less sanguine. Even a casual glance at the map showed the Soviets to be in an excellent position to launch an attack against the flank of the German Sixth Army. The Axis line ran west-northwest from Stalingrad proper on the east, across the open steppe between the Volga and the Don, to Kachalinskya. The river then jogged north for a short distance before turning northwest again almost as far as Rossosh, a distance of nearly four hundred kilometres. In effect, the Sixth Army had carved out a vast salient, with its farthest advance east not quite anchored on the Volga. If the Soviets possessed sufficient forces, they could attack south against the flank of the entire Sixth Army, he thought.

But when he mentioned the possibility, he was laughed at. One staff major had clapped him on the shoulder. 'Where the hell are they going to get the troops for such an attack? Why we've already destroyed the equivalent of their entire pre-war army? How many more can they possibly have in reserve? One, two, a few divisions of artillery and perhaps infantry? If you were Stalin, where would you send what few reserves you could scrape up? Moscow, Leningrad, the Caucasus? Stalingrad? The war is almost over. A few weeks ago some German mountain troops even had time to climb Mount Elbruz, the highest in all Europe, and raise the German flag. What a blow to Russian morale that must have been, hey? Come and have a glass of wine before you go and tell me how you...'

Imperceptibly, winter slipped south across the river. Midday flurries became wind-whipped ice crystals and each succeeding dawn saw the ice along the banks of the Don creeping closer to the centre of the broad river. Then one day, the sun did not melt the night's new snow and by the end of that week Marchetti measured fourteen centimetres outside the bunker. The following day, the temperature rose abruptly and in the afternoon it rained. When the temperature fell below zero again that night, everything was coated with a thick layer of ice, including a sentry who had frozen to death – their first winter casualty.

Marchetti stared at the quartermaster sergeant in disbelief. 'This has to be a mistake...'

'I'm sorry Captain, but I double-checked all the way to Army headquarters. It's true. We are required to give back all German-issue equipment. They seem to be losing it at Stalingrad faster than they can ship it in,' he finished bitterly. The German lieutenant standing beside him snorted angrily but kept silent.

Marchetti's own anger was threatening to boil over. He could not believe that the Germans were capable of anything so petty. The order included not only German uniforms and weapons, but cold-weather gear such as tents, stoves and other equipment which they had installed in their bunkers months ago. But standing behind his supply sergeant and the shivering German lieutenant from the quartermaster corps was a heavy-set German military police officer, a captain whose wine-red face almost glowed in the dim light of the bunker. He swung his hands together to keep warm in their heavy leather and fur gloves and Marchetti thought of the knitted wool gloves that were all his men would now have to wear.

'The collection must begin today,' the German lieutenant said. 'The lorries will arrive this afternoon.'

Marchetti stared at the signatures on the document. It had been issued a week ago by Army Group B headquarters and was signed by ranking Italian officers as well as by General Hoth, so it would do no good to complain. He silently cursed his spineless superiors who knuckled under so easily to the Germans.

'Replacement equipment will be issued item for item, I take it?'

His supply sergeant raised his eyebrows and the German quartermaster officer looked uneasy. 'Uh, no Captain. The replacement equipment will not arrive until tomorrow...'

Marchetti stared at him in astonishment. 'What the hell do you mean, tomorrow? Do you expect my people to turn over their weapons, shelter, cold-weather clothing and gear and get nothing in return? What if the replacements do not come tomorrow? What if they do not come for a week, or more?'

'I . . . I don't know, Captain. I was just ordered to come and get all German equipment. Someone else is . . .'

'Come, Captain Marchetti,' the German military police officer said in execrable Italian and motioned impatiently towards his staff car where three more military policeman sat inside. Marchetti noted that the engine was running, and probably the heater as well. Behind the staff car were two lorries.

'I am ordered to take this equipment to Depot Number Three by 1600 hours, today.'

'And just what do you suggest that my men do? Without cold-weather clothing, they will freeze to death. How do you expect them to defend themselves in case of a Russian attack if they have no weapons?'

The military policeman shrugged. 'That is not my problem. I have my orders. You will begin the collection now.'

Marchetti stepped around the table that served as a desk and tapped the German policeman on the chest with stiffened fingers, forcing him to step back as he spoke.

'If you want the equipment my people have, then you make damned certain they have something adequate to replace it with. Understand?'

The German smirked and turned to signal his men in the car but stopped with his hand in mid-air.

'Don't do it, Captain,' Marchetti hissed, 'or I'll shoot your fat guts out.' The German stared incredulously at the Walther pistol jammed into his stomach and dropped his hand.

'Now you listen to me, you fat fool. I don't care what your orders are. Until my men are re-equipped, you take nothing.' From the corner of his eye, he saw one of his sergeants step up beside him, hand on holster flap. More soldiers came into the bunker from where they had been listening, all with weapons ready.

The German opened his mouth but Marchetti shook his head. 'Don't say it, you bastard. Just leave while you are still alive. And if you come back without replacement equipment, I'm going to send you on a little scouting expedition . . . across the river.' He jabbed with the pistol muzzle and the military policeman backed away. The German lieutenant shook his head but kept his mouth shut.

His troops crowded around to watch the Germans drive away and to hear what had precipitated the standoff and Marchetti wondered how he was going to tell them.

Two German lorries rumbled over the rutted track the following morning, escorted by a sizeable German military police detail. Marchetti had posted sentries and he met the lorries and their half-track-borne escort with a full company drawn up in combat order.

An Italian staff officer stepped down and waded through the newly-fallen snow to Marchetti. He barely acknowledged the salute before launching into a tirade to which Marchetti listened with resignation. But when the colonel finished without ordering him to Army headquarters, he smiled. If Eighth Army command had meant to discipline him, he would have been ordered out immediately. So this was only a show to impress their German comrades and he smirked at the heavy-set German police officer he had chased off the day before.

'Colonel,' Marchetti replied in careful Italian so that the German could understand, 'I think we both know how foolish this situation is. As battalion commander I can do no less than see that if my men must give up their clothing and equipment, they receive usable replacements immediately. Otherwise they will die, either from exposure or Russian bullets.'

The staff officer, an elderly colonel, peered at him from under frosted eyebrows and drew him aside. 'Major Marchetti, you are damned lucky that your father is who he is and that the Eighth Army is in great need of experienced field commanders. Otherwise, you would now be under close arrest and your career at an end. As it is, your record has sustained a very heavy black mark.'

Marchetti grinned. 'Perhaps you are correct, Colonel, but there is a more important problem than my career. My soldiers do not understand why General Garibaldi permits the Germans to take their clothing and equipment and leave them defenceless and naked. I find it impossible to explain satisfactorily, Colonel.'

The colonel reddened with anger at his insolence but Marchetti was past caring. Jurgensen's death had taught him that much. 'These damned Germans think we Italians are not worth shit. Perhaps Eighth Army headquarters feels the same way, heh Colonel? Well I'll tell you, sir, when our soldiers are properly equipped and led, they are among the finest in the world and I've seen far too many die to prove it. The Germans treat all their allies in much the same way they do their enemies,' he said bitterly. 'First they beg for help and promise the moon, then they kick us and insult us after we agree. I recently saw a Norwegian officer and seven of his men die uselessly because the Germans could not be bothered to move a single cannon, or even a tank, to support them.

'Well, Colonel, I am responsible for my men. Watching those Norwegians taught me a thing or two. If that fat bastard behind you wants this equipment, he'd better have replacements ready. If he doesn't . . .' Marchetti waved a hand at his men drawn up with weapons ready. The German military police troops who had remained in the half-tracks stirred uneasily at his gesture.

The colonel huffed and tried to draw himself up to Marchetti's level.

'Major, you are dangerously close to mutiny,' he warned. Marchetti smiled.

'Perhaps you wish to arrest me, Colonel? Think what a court martial that would be?'

The staff officer's self-assurance collapsed. 'Major, you must realise,' he whined, 'that we are totally dependent on our allies, the Germans, for supplies. There is nothing else to be done. The Germans have ordered the exchange. General Garibaldi receives no support from Rome, only message after message demanding this victory or that and orders that bear no relation to reality. So, do not think that a public outcry on your behalf would save you from the firing squad. Rome is three thousand kilometres away and impervious to logic.'

The exchange took two hours in the bitter cold. At Marchetti's insistence, his men came one at a time to exchange gear and weapons. The battalion armourer inspected each Mannlicher Carcano rifle and rejected forty-three as unfit for service. The German officer's face was purple with anger at the end of the two hours, but the Italian staff officer remained aloof, ashamed of the proceedings. Marchetti nodded to the forty-three men standing to one side, still in possession of MP-40 machine pistols.

'When you bring serviceable rifles, Captain,' he smiled, 'you may exchange them for those weapons.'

The colonel was finally moved to anger by the German's insistence that they give them up now and backed Marchetti's decision. He swore at the German captain and ordered him to the lorries. The Nazi screamed at his driver and the lorries jockeyed around in a circle, swaying and bumping over ruts until they were headed back down the track. The German captain clung to the running board of the lead truck, shouting curses and threats until a severe jolt knocked him into the snow. Marchetti prayed for a Russian sniper but the captain caught up with the lorry, pursued by laughter, and disappeared into the cab.

It was obvious that the quality of Italian military equipment – once purchased in great quantities by dozens of nations – had degenerated. Boots were made of thin, poor quality leather and their interiors lined with cardboard. Most of the Mannlicher Carcano rifles were dated 1941 or 1942 and were full of cosmoline which the men eyed with distaste. Maintaining a semblance of cleanliness under these conditions was difficult enough; having to clean grease from the weapons would make the task impossible.

The workmanship was poor, Marchetti noticed; bluing thin or nonexistent on receivers. Machine tool marks were evident and the stock wood was of poor quality, hurriedly and imperfectly dried. Recalling the quality of pre-war Italian weapons, Marchetti shook his head at the contrast and made a mental note to hold rifle practice that afternoon. The poor quality of wood, metal and workmanship would make them terribly inaccurate, he suspected.

They had exchanged good German winter clothing for standard issue Italian uniforms rather than the winter clothing he had hoped for. The colonel had promised that sufficient winter clothing for the entire battalion would arrive within the week, but Marchetti knew better than to rely on anyone's word for a quartermaster's performance.

A series of snow storms lashed the Don region in early November and Marchetti was reminded of the descriptions of the river and the surrounding farm and pasture land in Mikhail Sholokov's, *And Quiet Flows the Don* which he had read some years before. He was convinced now that they would have to bear a repeat of the previous winter, but this time in holes rather than in log huts. By the end of the week, temperatures were falling to twenty and thirty degrees of frost at night.

Marchetti sensed that the Russians were gathering for an offensive. He had no firm evidence, merely an uneasy feeling brought on by night activity across the river. Sometimes it was possible to hear the roar of powerful engines, muted by distance, and once he thought he smelled diesel fuel.

Eighteen months of campaigning in Russia had taught him that nothing was ever as it seemed. The Russians were adept at concealing both intention and movement and his sentries and patrols reported little sign of Russian troops across the river. Occasionally, a wisp of vehicle exhaust could be seen against a clear sky if the wind was dead calm. Otherwise, the white landscape rolled into the blue distance as empty and unwelcoming as the surface of the moon.

But it only needed a moment's carelessness to understand that they were there. A helmet raised too far above a trench wall or a figure not quick enough while scurrying from bunker to bunker drew the pop of a distant rifle and often enough a dead body sprawled in the mud. Finally, Marchetti had had enough.

He obtained two kilos of coffee from the battalion quartermaster and arranged a trade with a greedy German supply officer who dabbled in the black market. The coffee – one of the few luxuries still in good supply to the Italian troops – bought a brand new Mauser rifle with a ZF-41 sniper scope. Marchetti personally mounted and sighted the rifle and zeroed the sights at four hundred metres, his estimate of the distance across the Don to the Russian trenches.

Over the next two nights, Marchetti had a rifle pit scooped from the frozen soil and protected with a double thickness of sandbags over which bucket after bucket of water was poured until it was harder and more resistant than armour plate. A small opening was bored through the ice and sand wall to form a narrow slit four centimetres high by twenty long. The slit opened on the inward side to a metre square which allowed plenty of room for shoulders and rifle. From across the river the narrow slit would be invisible, even to the most powerful field glasses.

Marchetti climbed into the protected space at noon and studied the landscape on the far bank through his binoculars. It was similar enough to that on their side; thin gravelled beach leading to a bank ranging from two to five metres in height. There were no trees along the river itself but several stands were visible inland. Since their side of the river was slightly higher, long humps in the snow were visible to him that he was certain were Red Army trenches. Twice, his guess was confirmed when he saw a careless head moving about.

But he was after bigger game. At mid-afternoon, just before dusk, his patience was rewarded by movement. As the light changed and melded he saw a shadow where it should not have been.

Change of shifts, he thought. Like a factory, the bastards. He worked the Mauser's action to free the congealing oil, then pressed five cartridges into the magazine and inserted a sixth in the chamber, closed the bolt and set the safety. The short, straight stock nestled into his shoulder and he wrapped his left arm through the sling and stretched full-length on the blanket lining the floor of what he thought of as the execution chamber.

The forestock rested neatly on the padded wooden stand he had carved the night before and he had only to shift his right arm to change the angle of fire. Marchetti focused carefully. The power scope provided a bright circle of light in which the long hump was clearly visible. A helmet appeared quickly and was gone and he had the impression of a face beneath the metal rim. Since they had lost their German weapons, he had forbidden probing shots at the Russians – no need for them to know that they had been poorly re-equipped – and as a consequence, the Russians had grown careless.

Dusk was falling swiftly and even through the scope, the scene faded away. With a sigh, he sat up, opened the bolt and ejected all six cartridges. Tomorrow.

Immediately following his staff meeting in the morning, he returned to the execution chamber. A sense of excitement had infected the headquarters company. His participation in the 1936 Olympic Summer Games was known throughout the battalion and the rumours said that thousands of lire had been wagered in a complicated pool.

By 0900 hours, it was light enough to begin his vigil once more. Again, the sky was incredibly blue, even if the sun offered little heat. He studied the shadows and waited. At noon, he spotted the briefest flicker of shadow and examined the snow in that area until he found the darkish shadow that could very well be the Russian sniper's aperture. Or was it just a blemish in the snow? If he was wrong the sniper would be warned and he would have to begin the game all over again.

Marchetti summoned a sergeant and gave him careful orders. The sergeant repeated them, then slipped down the trench to a point some ten metres away. Marchetti saw him signal, then dash across to the next bunker. The sergeant had timed it nicely; not as fast as to cause the sniper to hold fire, not slowly enough to chance being hit. As the brief puff of smoke testified. He had been right – and he squeezed the trigger. The Mauser shoved hard against his shoulder and cheek and the sharp crack in the confined space deafened him.

Marchetti waited, field glasses glued to the spot. There was no movement, no sign that the bullet had struck the snow on either side. He shouted to the soldier stationed outside as a relay. Down the trench, the sergeant poked a helmet up on a stick to draw fire and nothing happened.

Marchetti rolled over, grinning, and slid out of the execution chamber. Scratch one murdering sniper, he thought.

19 November dawned crystal hard with temperatures below thirty degrees of frost and Marchetti woke to the sound of massed artillery.

He dressed quickly, cursing the icy bunker. He had placed his boots on the shelf above the stove but it was so cold that they were barely warm. Outside, a dawn breeze stirred the new snow and stars were scattered across the paling sky, except where the entire northern horizon was lit by flickering cannon.

His second in command, Lieutenant Ambruzzi, a young seminarian snatched up in the draft and serving as his chief of staff, stumbled up beside him. 'What is it?' his voice was anxious.

'The Russian counteroffensive, Lieutenant. The counteroffensive our German friends said would never come.' The first artillery shells whined over the Don to search the rear. Marchetti took a deep breath. 'Now it begins,' he muttered.

For a week, the Russian counteroffensive swelled in strength. Intelligence reported strong Soviet forces from the east thrusting deep into the salient created by German, Rumanian and Hungarian forces. In addition to the official reports, there were dozens of rumours that Russian forces had also attacked from the south. If true, Marchetti thought, staring at a map of the Stalingrad front, they obviously intended to pinch off the Sixth Army as he had foreseen weeks before.

But along their portion of the Don front, other than periodic and heavy artillery barrages, there was little action for the moment. Probing Russian patrols met Italian patrols, exchanged a few shots, a few casualties and retreated.

Marchetti became aware of signs that suggested the Rumanian lines on his right were giving way under the terrible pounding. It was clear that the Rumanians, totally unequipped to deal with such a massive assault, tried to fall back in an orderly manner to secondary defensive positions, but the Russians followed so closely with combined air, armour and artillery assaults that they never had a chance to man the new lines before the Soviet tanks overran them again. In vain, Marchetti reported to Eighth Army Headquarters that he was completely unsupported on his right flank.

On 24 November, Marchetti gave Lieutenant Ambruzzi strict instructions to hold at all costs should the Soviets attack. He then set out with a driver in an automobile, an ancient Model A Ford requisitioned from a nearby collective farm some weeks before, for Starobelsk, hoping to gain an appreciation of the situation along the Don, convince someone that he was precariously exposed and at the very least, obtain artillery support.

There had been no new snow for two days and little wind. The sun dazzled in a cloudless sky and the alternate freeze-thaw cycle had packed the old snow hard as ice. The Model A hiccupped and coughed along a track made by the convoy lorries following the traffic signs the methodical Germans had erected – Halt, Slow, Forbidden – as if they were travelling an autobahn.

Traffic grew heavier as they approached headquarters, although most of it was streaming west. Many of the vehicles bore Rumanian markings and Marchetti saw German military police waving them past contemptuously. Traffic soon grew so heavy that snarls were inevitable and they slowed to a running, then a walking pace and finally to a halt. Every few minutes they were able to jerk forward until, finally, they passed a disabled lorry being pushed off the road by a light tank being used as a snowplough. Traffic speeded up then until the sun gradually disappeared and it began to snow heavily.

Hour after hour, they ground on, passing ghost figures in field grey moving towards the front and others trudging towards the rear. Once the car stuck in the new snow and the soldiers who helped them out understood neither German nor the few Rumanian phrases Marchetti had learned.

Finally, an officer who spoke a bit of German told him they were Flemish, part of an SS detachment who had been marching for two weeks. The officer knew only that they were ordered to Stalingrad, to find the front lines, make contact with units on either side, and dig in. He seemed to think the city was little more than a village near the river. Appalled, Marchetti disabused him of that notion, explaining that the city was more than eight kilometres wide and sixteen long. He gave him directions to the airfield at Pitomnik where the Sixth Army had established its headquarters and wished him luck.

Italian Eighth Army Headquarters was a madhouse. Field telephones buzzed incessantly, people raced in and out and heavily-armed troops stamped about outside in the deepening cold. There was no food except for the staff and special passes were needed to enter the mess halls. No facilities for any but immediate staff had been provided and the lavatories were open spaces in the snow, protected from the wind by banked snow walls. Angry military policemen had been stationed at intervals around headquarters and were turning back anyone without legitimate reason for being there. Twice Marchetti convinced harassed, exhausted and half-frozen officers that he was there on legitimate military business but a noncommissioned officer, an old line regular Marchetti realised by his bearing and manner, refused to allow him to go further.

'You must wait your turn, Major, like all the rest. General Garibaldi is in conference with his staff. I myself can tell you everything you need to know. Yes, they realise that your battalion is exposed on its right flank but there is nothing that can be done about it. There are no troops and no artillery to spare, most of all no artillery. The Soviets have broken through in a dozen places both north and south of Stalingrad and it is said that less than eight kilometres now separate the two Russian armies. An offensive against our own positions along the Don is expected at any moment. When it comes, the staff will decide if we stand or how far we must retreat.'

Marchetti stared at him, aghast. 'The German Sixth Army is nearly encircled?'

'Yes, Major,' the sergeant replied wearily, as if for the fiftieth time. 'The damned Rumanians ran like hell, from all reports. There has been some talk of pulling back, but nothing has yet been decided.'

The news stunned Marchetti. He tried to make sense of what he had heard but the babble of voices, the shouting, the buzzing of phones, the roar of engines and artillery, as well as the shock, confused him. How in the name of God could the Russians have broken through to that extent? Of course the Rumanians had broken – anyone would under such a pounding as they had been taking – but surely the Germans hadn't entrusted them to hold vital parts of the line alone and without reinforcements?

'Major!' the sergeant said sharply.

Marchetti was aware suddenly that he was still staring at the sergeant. 'It would be best if you returned to your command and prepared to pull back. I've seen this sort of thing before, in North Africa.'

Dear God, so have I, Marchetti thought.

'You won't get better advice but if you insist on waiting, I can arrange for a staff officer to tell you the same thing – tomorrow, or perhaps the following day.'

The sergeant turned away to answer the importunate questions of another officer, and, sickened, Marchetti fought his way out of the stuffy building. The memory of the long retreat across Libya ahead of British tanks was still fresh in his mind, even after two years. But in North Africa there had been a difference; if the worst came to the worst, one could always surrender to the civilised British. He shuddered to think how the Russians would treat prisoners captured along the Don or before Stalingrad.

He found his driver arguing with a German military policeman and demanded to know the problem. The policeman saluted his rank, if reluctantly.

'He is trying to confiscate our staff car,' the excited driver babbled, pointing to the battered Model A. Staff car indeed, Marchetti glared at him but the driver took no notice. 'I tried to make him understand that it is yours, *Maggiorie* but he does not understand Italian and I speak...'

Marchetti silenced him. 'What is the problem, *Unteroffizer*?' he asked in German.

'This automobile is confiscated by order of General von Paulus,' the man snarled, but he refused to look Marchetti in the eye.

'Show me your authorisation,' Marchetti snapped, 'and stand to attention when you speak to an officer.'

Marchetti knew that German military police were given virtually unlimited authority in a combat zone, even to the extent of conducting on-the-spot executions under certain circumstances. It was a brutal system but one that worked to keep the German field army the most disciplined in the world. Even here, within sight of Italian Eighth Army Headquarters, they held sway as in theory, anyway, General Garibaldi was under the command of Army Group Don.

The soldier snorted at his demand and started to unsling his rifle. Marchetti caught his arm and stepped in close. 'Think twice, soldier,' he growled. 'I am an officer in the Italian army. If you do not show me your authorisation immediately, I will arrest *you* for attempted theft of military supplies in a combat zone. In the Italian army, as in the German, the penalty is death.'

The policeman's pose crumbled at the threat. His face drew on a haunted look and he tried to twist his arm away. 'You can go...' he had started to whine when Marchetti punched him in the face. The soldier slipped and went down beside the bumper. Marchetti hit him again when he tried to get up, took his rifle away and gave it to his driver who was watching him as if he thought he had gone mad.

They marched the soldier back across the trampled snow to the headquarters. The sergeant looked up in surprise when Marchetti, followed by his driver, pushed the German in. His face hardened as he listened and he lifted the telephone handset and spoke quickly. A moment later, two Italian military policemen appeared and hauled the German away.

As they drove away from Eighth Army Headquarters, Marchetti thought to himself that if the desertions are beginning, it must be worse than anyone thinks.

The Russians did not aim a sudden blow against Marchetti's position, rather they increased the pressure day by day. At first, the thin ice on the Don kept Russian patrols infrequent, but as the cold deepened at the end of November and the beginning of December and the ice thickened, both numbers and size of the Russian probes increased.

Marchetti had met several of the Rumanian officers and found that, while all were good fascists, they were also hostile to the Germans. Additionally, their equipment was abominable. Many of their weapons dated from the First World War. Marchetti had himself seen several of their artillery pieces which were captured Russian guns still bearing the Tsar's Tula Arsenal proof marks.

In addition, many of the Rumanian officers were ill-trained and cared little for those under their command. Most of the enlisted men were conscripts full of resentment and fit only for labour service. Even so, they had held up far better under the awesome Soviet pounding than he would have thought possible.

Marchetti knew their turn would come sooner or later. Even before the headquarters sergeant had offered his gratuitous advice, Marchetti, as uncomfortable with his exposed position along the Don as he had been in the Sofafi South camp two years before, had, without orders, already prepared secondary defences two kilometres west along a series of shallow ridges overlooking the denuded grazing lands sloping down to the river.

The tattered Rumanian lines finally gave way completely and his patrols brought in reports of Soviet tanks and other tracked vehicles followed by infantry, pouring across the river in waves. Marchetti, accompanying one patrol stared open-mouthed at the spectacle. Vehicles, horses and men formed a continuous stream and Soviet aircraft flashed low overhead. Canteens had even been set up to provide hot food and drink. My God, he thought, no wonder the Rumanians had collapsed. And this was only a small part of the Soviet effort on the extreme left of the Soviet assault line. He could not conceive of what it must be like closer to Stalingrad where the main breakthrough had occurred.

He also learned with sickening assurance why his own positions had got off comparatively lightly. The Soviets need only send a small percentage of the army pouring through the gap to encircle and destroy him whenever they happened to think about it.

The Russian pincer movement was completed two days later and the Sixth Army at Stalingrad found itself encircled. In Stalingrad proper, the Red Army garrison, reinforced by a massive night effort to shift men, equipment and supplies across the frozen Volga, moved over to the offensive.

On the far northern end of the Stalingrad line, where Marchetti's battalion remained dug in, supplies of food and ammunition were more erratic than usual. Radio contact with both Sixth Army and Italian Eighth Army headquarters was lost for three days and of the two runners he sent out to make contact with units on his left, only one returned to report that he was unable to get through. Strong Russian forces had finally encircled them almost as an afterthought.

The rumours began: the Sixth Army had either surrendered or had broken out and abandoned their Italian and Hungarian allies; Germany was signing a separate peace with Russia; Italy had left the war; the Americans had invaded North Africa. Marchetti paid no attention to any of them; he had learned in Libya that it was impossible to separate fact from fiction under such conditions.

Marchetti had seen the signs before in Libya. High confidence giving way to uncertainty, then to hopelessness as the army fell to pieces. What angered him now, as then, was the knowledge that the process could be stopped if Army headquarters provided a frank appraisal of the situation and then followed up with logical and systematic orders. Instead, they remained silent, perhaps fearing that morale would be destroyed by bad news, never understanding that the absence of information only creates misinformation.

The weather degenerated as quickly as the encircled Eighth Army. Freezing mists appeared that erased details beyond a few metres and covered every surface with ice. Marchetti gave strict orders that all weapons were to be stripped of every trace of oil and grease and he passed out the small supply of cold-weather lubricant he had located earlier in the autumn and hoarded until now.

The growing shortage of food was his greatest problem. They had managed to open a narrow corridor through the encircling Soviet lines north, parallel to the Don, but supply convoys found them at ever decreasing intervals and he was forced to institute a rationing system.

Several of the men had been carpenters in better times and he had put them to work building sledges from the meagre stands of birch fringing the river in their sector. The sledges served for transporting ammunition and hot food, on the few occasions when it was available, and the wounded and dead. Replacement clothing and boots became nonexistent and they were reduced to stripping Russian corpses as well as their own dead.

Marchetti was surprised to see how lightly the Russian soldier travelled. Rations were often no more than a small bag of millet or parched corn, a paper twist of sugar and another of salt, a handful of tea leaves or a bit of coffee and hard, dried biscuits. They wore heavily-padded canvas coats and trousers and felt boots over issue leather boots which appeared clumsy but were surprisingly warm and waterproof, especially when well-greased and packed with straw or dried grass.

During the long second week in December it seemed that the Russians were toying with them, although Marchetti guessed they were really occupied with more important matters. Attacks were limited to less than regimental strength and might or might not be announced by an artillery bombardment. The shelling began before, concurrently, or even during, an attack and as often as not subjected their own troops to fire. Marchetti puzzled over this apparent callousness for some time before he realised that the Russians were in fact laying down artillery fire in such a way as to create narrow lanes which the Red Army men travelled with relative safety.

At other times, there might be no bombardment at all and then the Russians materialised from the mist clad in white snow smocks, wave after wave slogging or skiing forward across the ice until sustained Italian fire wiped out the majority and drove the rest back. He shuddered to think of the bodies the Don would carry to the Black Sea in the spring.

Between attacks, Marchetti was forced to employ up to half of his dwindling troops at any one time to patrol or to forage for ammunition and food. As hungry as they were, no one ever argued the fact that ammunition had the higher priority.

Then, on 15 December, they were driven out of their defensive positions by a sustained barrage and infantry assault supported for the first time by tanks. The attack developed so quickly that the forward positions were overrun almost before Marchetti realised what was happening. There was time only for an *en clair* message to Eighth Army Headquarters before he ordered the battalion to fall back on their secondary positions.

They were saved when in the afternoon a freezing mist descended across the Don area. Artillery fire became sporadic, then stopped. Tanks bogged down in the waist-deep snow and his own men infiltrated the Russian lines and knocked out a dozen more with petrol bombs and hand grenades before the tanks withdrew.

By nightfall, they had reached the rear defence lines. Marchetti guessed that someone across the Don had decided to liquidate this minor nuisance on the flank of the Red war machine. Marchetti began to think about a retreat as far back as the Donets, wishing now for the summer heat he had cursed during the advance.

Inexplicably, the Russian attack was not resumed the next day, nor the next. General Garibaldi himself appeared at midmorning on the third day in a ski-equipped Saiman 202 reconnaissance aircraft. This visit of the Eighth Army commander marked the extreme concern with which developments along the Don and at Stalingrad were at last being viewed in Starobelsk and Rome, Marchetti surmised.

He had not seen General Garibaldi, an acquaintance of his father's, since his own return from Stalingrad when the General had listened impatiently to his report and the conclusions he had reached. He had passed Marchetti's written report to an aide without so much as a glance and Marchetti guessed it had gone into a wastebasket before he had left headquarters.

General Garibaldi examined his positions quickly, chastised him for failing to retake his original fortifications, congratulated him on his foresight in having prepared a fall-back line, and pinned the *Medaglia al Valore Militare*, the Distinguished Service Medal, on his greatcoat. Then he dropped the bombshell.

Hitler had directed the formation of Army Group Don under General von Manstein. At the same time, he had forbidden the Sixth Army to break out of the Stalingrad cauldron. Instead, Manstein was ordered to break to reinforce von Paulus in a desperate attack codenamed *Wintergewitter*, Winter Storm.

'We are to support Army Group Don to the full extent of our resources. Your orders, Major Marchetti,' Garibaldi said as he tapped the map, 'are to hold at all costs. All costs, do you understand?'

Marchetti waited for the specific order forbidding him to retreat, but Garibaldi gave him a sharp look then stamped out of the bunker and hurried towards the aircraft. So that's the way it is, Marchetti thought to himself.

As the aircraft faded into the overcast, he realised that he had been given no chance to complain about the supply problem or the lack of orders. But then, when a general does not wish to discuss such subjects, they usually remained undiscussed. The medal of valour was meant to be the token replacement for the food, ammunition and clothing they were denied and, perhaps, an apology for having failed to take his report seriously. Marchetti unpinned the medal and threw it away.

Christmas Eve brought a blizzard, a salute from the Russians in the form of a fierce artillery barrage and a long delayed telegram from headquarters, informing him that his father had died on 27 November 1942.

Marchetti crouched in the shuddering bunker and stared at the creased, oil-stained scrap of paper, thinking that the old man had died nearly a month ago, alone in a freezing old house under a pile of blankets, not knowing if his son was alive or dead. Marchetti could only think of how such a lonely death was a terrible waste at the end of his father's life. To have lived so long, to have had such influence on the shaping of modern Italy, to have known such wealth and power, and then to end in failure, shunned by the very man he had helped raise to power, rejected by the party which he had helped build, hungry, cold and wracked with the terrible pain of cancer.

After a while, Marchetti got up, feeling the cold in every joint. He dropped the message into the stove and watched the flame dance, turn blue when it found the sulphur in the cheap paper and curl into black ash. Like his father's life, he thought. Like all life in the end. Marchetti wondered why he could not cry, could not feel sadness for his father? Perhaps it was because he was going to die soon as well.

The bombardment began at 1800 hours and was concentrated along the two kilometre stretch of line occupied by Marchetti's battalion. When he was convinced that this was the final Soviet assault, he wrote a report detailing the steps he was putting into effect and shouted for a runner. A heavily-bearded man stirred and pushed himself away from the wall where he had been sleeping. He crouched beside Marchetti as he finished the note in the light of the single candle, the last of their supply.

The soldier's name was Anthony Spillito and he could not read. Marchetti patiently dictated the gist of the report until he had memorised it in case something happened to the paper.

'You are to say to the adjutant to General Garibaldi or to the General himself and no one else, that we can no longer hold our positions. That I expect the Russians to mount a very strong attack at dawn. You will tell him that I am pulling back two kilometres to this line of woods here, six kilometres behind our present positions.' He pointed the feature out on the sketch map he had made below the report. 'Make certain that they are aware of these map coordinates. Tell him also that I expect the Russians will follow quickly and that unless we are reinforced, they will overrun us by tomorrow night. Now repeat.'

The soldier did so, stuffed the message into the pocket of his filthy blouse, buttoned his greatcoat and saluted. A shell landed fifty metres or so away, Marchetti judged, and the concussion, transmitted through the frozen earth, jarred his teeth painfully. Spillito paused at the ladder.

'Happy Christmas, Major,' he grinned.

The Russian barrage increased in ferocity as midnight neared. Happy Christmas to you too, he thought. And to you, Ivan. The candle stub was nearly gone and its feeble light barely reached the table edge. The main part of the battalion had already started the retreat and the headquarters staff crouched in the entrance, waiting for him.

He took a last look to make certain that nothing usable had been left and that all papers, documents and files that could not be carried were piled in the centre of the floor. Satisfied, he unscrewed the cap from the last tin of paraffin oil and sloshed it over the table, papers, wooden floor and walls, reserving this last, bitter task for himself. This was the fourth time since November 1940 that he had retreated, had abandoned everything to the enemy. Each time was harder. Without a backward glance, he went up the ladder into a night so cold and windy that it snatched the air from his lungs and left him gasping for breath.

Just that afternoon, one of the fall-back bunkers had taken a direct hit, killing all twenty-two men inside. There now remained fewer than 160 men in the battalion which had been 750-strong in June.

The barrage had moved left of their actual position – incredible that in two weeks of constant patrolling and probing the Russians had never managed to pinpoint them – and he gave the orders for the headquarters staff to move off. He took his last hand grenade from the gas-mask pouch, twisted the igniter, tossed it down into the bunker and stumbled after the others. The grenade went off with a hollow boom and for a brief instant, the snow glared blood-red before the roof collapsed. Scorched earth in reverse, comrades.

Marchetti estimated the temperature at more than sixty degrees of frost. Winter would finish them at Stalingrad, he had little doubt. Manstein's attempt to relieve the Sixth Army and drive the Russians over the Volga had failed ignominiously, even before it had begun, because Alexander II's immortal General Winter had taken a hand once again. Subzero cold, bad weather, fierce Russian counterattacks and lack of supplies had stopped the armoured thrust far short of its goal. In fact, the relieving force had been all but cut-off themselves and survived only after a desperately-fought retreat.

At headquarters, someone had told him that Goering had bragged to Hitler that the Luftwaffe would supply all the needs of the Sixth Army and the Army of the Don by air. But not once had Marchetti seen anything but Russian *Stormoviks,* which harassed them during the day with machine gun and cannon fire from tree-top level.

As he plodded along in the darkness, head down against the fierce wind, he thought about the revenge he would now be denied. The entire *Corpo di Spedizione Italiano* had been betrayed from the beginning. They had no business bearing so large of a share of the fighting in Russia when Libya, Tunisia and Albania remained to be defended. But the Duce was concerned primarily with his political image viv-à-vis Adolph Hitler and so they had gone to Russia where promises had not been kept, replacements never arrived and supplies and pay were constantly in arrears.

Every action in which he had participated had been poorly planned, poorly carried out and then ignored, whatever the outcome. And for a year and a half they had buried comrades one after another – for what?

The Germans had made a hash of their southern thrust. Not only was Stalingrad now lost to them but their entire flank was exposed to the largest collection of armies ever assembled. Once the Russians finished at Stalingrad, Marchetti knew they would be unleashed south and west.

He pulled tighter the tattered strip of blanket which he wore as a muffler and thought again about Goering's boast to supply the forces at Stalingrad from the air. The man was a fool, an ass. One had only to glance at a ten-year weather history of the Volga bend region to know that conditions were suitable for flying only ten per cent of the time from December to early May.

Even that restriction could have been dealt with if the Luftwaffe had possessed long range bombers capable of flying from Germany, but everyone knew that Hitler, in his prescient wisdom, had cancelled long range bomber development even before the war to concentrate on the production of medium load, medium range bombers. The only thing in plentiful supply at the Stalingrad cauldron was vodka because, as Jurgensen had once said, 'It makes the dying easier.'

The cold numbed them to the bone and he knew that if anyone stopped moving they would freeze to death in minutes. The sky flickered with red and white flares and the glare of exploding artillery shells pursuing them. Marchetti had positioned himself at the rear of the ragged column, with the wounded, so that he could encourage stragglers. He found himself carrying one end of a stretcher; never until then had he realised what an intolerable burden a man could be. The stretcher had a life of its own, twisting and turning as the bearers clambered through the snow, tripped over obstacles or lurched through the ice crust. The weight pulled down from the shoulders and in no time, an intolerable ache ran through his arms to frozen hands, and down his back to his pelvis.

While he carried the stretcher, he was aware of nothing else but pain. The wounded man's spasmodic cries when a bearer stumbled soon became endurable and Marchetti found an unreasoning hatred for him growing as the night dragged. He struggled on, counting the steps, rifle banging against his hip where it kept slipping from his shoulder. When they stopped, he reslung it across his shoulder and perversely it dug into his back.

He suggested they use four men to carry the stretcher but the front bearer, an experienced medical orderly, shook his head. 'Only be worse,' he panted. 'Four people floundering... in the snow... getting in each other's way... better two.'

They changed often, every thousand paces, but even so, the task was horribly debilitating. His fingers ached with cold when locked around the stretcher poles and there was no way to warm them. When the time came to change bearers the first time, Marchetti almost cried out as the sudden release of weight and the cold cramped shoulder and back muscles. He struggled to work his fingers and the pain of returning circulation was excruciating. Then for a few minutes the relief of not having to carry the stretcher sustained him.

The snow grew deeper the farther from the river they went, forcing them to lift legs high at each step. He ordered all able-bodied men to march directly ahead of the stretcher teams to trample the snow, but it did little good. It was fresh, and in the sub-zero cold, far too powdery to compact.

Some time after midnight, artillery shells careened across their track in a ferocious barrage. Flares fizzed and sputtered in the black night and glared painfully from the snow. They threw themselves flat and Marchetti heard someone scream. He squirmed into a tight ball, rocking himself into the snow as if it would shelter him from shrapnel. As explosions set the frozen ground to vibrating like a monstrous bell, he closed his eyes and fought with his fear.

The certainty that he had miscalculated grew. He had not expected the Russians to attack until dawn. Then his troops should have had at least two hours in which to withdraw while the Russians occupied the abandoned Italian defences and waited for orders to push on. That was the way it had always gone before because the Russian officers were notorious for their lack of initiative. But someone in authority must have guessed that the Italians were in no position to stand up to such an overwhelming attack and ordered a close pursuit. More of the bad luck that had dogged him since their arrival in Russia.

Explosions raged and ears bled from concussion. Gases from exploding charges seeped along the ground, choking them, driving them up for fresh air so that whirling shrapnel could slice them to pieces. Then the barrage passed on as suddenly as it had come. Marchetti found himself on his feet, shouting, kicking, pulling and punching those around him until they too were up, responding to subconscious commands instilled by long training. His head ached so badly that he wanted to vomit and he was so cold and exhausted from sleeplessness that it required conscious effort now to lift one foot after another. He took one end of the stretcher again because it was his turn and they plodded on.

Marchetti was freezing to death; his body shivered in a desperate attempt to warm itself, but it was so cold and he was so weak that shivering only wasted precious energy. The shelling had stopped but the flares seemed nearer. Had Russian troops taken up the pursuit again? They hadn't weapons left heavier than the single Schwartzlose eight millimetre machine gun and he was certain that some of the men had thrown away their Carcano rifles. And in the swirling darkness, he had no idea how many of the headquarters company were still with him.

What was he to do? Surrender was out of the question. Might as well die on the steppe as in an open barbed-wire cage. Even if one survived the cage, the march north to the Arctic mines would finish them off. The Russians had made it plain enough that they did not want prisoners. Better to die as a soldier of Italy.

He was reduced now to moving one foot after another only with the most total concentration. It was his turn again on the stretcher and the burden tore at his shoulder and back muscles. It was so cold that his brain seemed to have congealed; he tried time after time to count a thousand paces so that he could call a fair halt but the number always eluded him and he had to start over and over again until the bearer in front protested he could not go another step.

They began to pass bodies in the snow. The first time, after checking that he was dead, they ransacked the soldier's pack for ammunition and food. Marchetti did not know who the man was and lacked the strength to find and take his paybook. They repeated the procedure for the second body but after that, no one bothered to do more than check for signs of life. Marchetti had no idea what they would do if they found someone alive. The thought was vaguely troubling but after a few moments, it too slipped away.

They had been marching for hours in the howling wind and even the artillery bombardment and the flares were nothing more than sky glow. The wind swirled the distant thunder of guns at them occasionally but otherwise there was only the terrible keening it made on its thousand mile passage from Siberia. He was lost. They should have found the forest hours ago.

Once he stopped to rest and went from man to man making certain that each scrubbed his face with snow to ward off frostbite and that whatever served as a wind mask was fastened snuggly. But only a handful remained and when they started again, two refused to get up and there was nothing he could do but leave them behind.

Marchetti was not certain just when he came to the realisation that he was dying; perhaps when the sky lightened to reveal an endless waste of howling white. He had no idea where they were and the few men who were still with him had given up asking. The glass in his compass had broken during the bombardment and he did not even know which way they were marching. It was thirty kilometres to Starobelsk from where they were on the Don. How many of those had they covered? In the right direction?

Curiously, his shoulders and back no longer ached. He thought that rather strange until he realised that the stretcher was empty. His hoarse shout failed to stop the man in front and the stretcher poles were jerked from his hands. Marchetti shouted again but the others plodded past, some with eyes closed, the rest with expressions blanked by their snow masks.

We must go back, he thought in anguish. We must find him... He turned irresolutely. The steppe was murderously white and without feature. The wind swirled snow at him and stung his eyes and exposed skin. He took a step. Where? Where should he look? How would he find him? And if he did, what would he do? The man was probably dead, even before he fell off the stretcher. What did one more matter; they were all dying anyway, wandering in circles. The best they could hope for was to fall asleep quickly – the worst, to be taken by the Russians. The last man went past and Marchetti followed.

He stumbled through the snow, the wind numbing his back where it thrust against him, trying to knock him down. Marchetti thought that was funny; even the elements had conspired with the Russians to kill him.

He thought of his father dying alone a month ago. Who would have thought that he would have followed so soon. His father's death had seemed terrible only . . . when, last night? My God was it only last night, a few hours ago . . . ?

The light had not brightened beyond first dawn, but then he no longer had any conception of time. He had been marching throughout eternity. Dante was right, he thought, when he described the Ninth Circle, the inmost compartment of hell, as a place of ice and snow. Perhaps his father's death had not been so terrible after all . . . He became aware that he was alone, that the others had disappeared. When . . . had he turned the wrong way . . . ? The realisation crushed him.

He hadn't the strength now to rub snow on his face but then there was no need to worry about frostbite any longer. He laughed at himself and was instantly afraid. He did not want to die. Was this how the great anti-communist crusade ended? Was the entire Christian army of the West to freeze to death in Russia?

All tracks had disappeared into the pervasive white light and he no longer knew where sky ended and land began. His eyes had absorbed the very whiteness into themselves. He had read about it somewhere, sometime – in the Canadian Arctic, it was called a 'Whiteout'. He tried to remember more of what he had read but the thought leaked away.

How far? How much farther to what? I'm going nowhere. Maybe I'll walk in a circle back to the river, but he knew he wouldn't. They had come too far during the night. He was right-handed and so he would veer to the right, unconsciously veer to the right as his steps described a great circle, around and around and around . . .

Where had the others gone? Were they dead yet? He was an officer; it was only right that he should die last. And why not. Wasn't he responsible for them? They must die first so that he could fulfil his obligations.

Curious, he thought. I'm not afraid now. In fact, when I lie down, I will feel relieved. But why am I not afraid? I have not been a religious man for years, since university . . . I renounced God then. Shouldn't I be afraid of his retribution for my treason?

But he was truly not afraid, only tired. Infinitely more tired even than in Libya. Soon, I will stop and lie down. I wouldn't have done that in

Libya. Then I can go to sleep. The sun is warming me I think because I don't feel the cold any longer.

For some reason he thought of the daughter of the Chilean diplomat with whom he had swum nude one soft summer evening in Spain. Afterward, they had made love on the beach, sheltered behind a screen of rocks from the mild breeze, revelling in each other's body, in each other's eagerness, the warmth of the night and their youth. He had never seen her again but he thought of her now. For some reason he felt a touch of that warmth, that feeling of wholeness and confidence he had felt then.

Why in these circumstances, he did not know. Perhaps he might make it after all. He did feel better; the thought of her had renewed his will to live. How far had he come . . . ? If he made an effort, if he took one step to the left for every ten steps forward, that ought to straighten him out . . . Soon the sun would be high enough to tell him which direction . . . it was only thirty kilometres to . . . half a day's march . . .

He tripped and sprawled in the snow. Cursing, he struggled to get up but the snow refused to support his weight. His arms pushed through and he floundered until he managed to roll onto his back.

Marchetti heard a sound, almost a groan. He struggled up and in doing so, his hand encountered the body over which he had tripped. He hesitated, hating what he knew he was going to discover. 'Go,' he told himself. 'Leave him. There is nothing you can do . . .' He moved closer and saw a young soldier, huddled into himself, half-glazed eyes staring at him. Redemption! Redemption, by God! For leaving the wounded man behind . . . Marchetti laughed. 'You'll get a medal for this!' he shouted and collapsed laughing beside the soldier.

After a few minutes, the hysterical laughter edged away. He rubbed his eyes and stared at the dark figure beside him. 'Get up,' he muttered. 'Get up!'

Eyes stared back at him, barely understanding, then the head moved in a negative shake, slowly as if the spinal column were in need of lubrication. 'Can't . . .' the figure breathed.

Marchetti swore and hit him in the face. 'Get up, you bastard!' he whispered. 'Get up!'

The eyes brightened for a moment, then closed and the boy tightened his arms about his chest. 'No . . . let me alone . . .'

Sudden anger poured through him and Marchetti sprang up and began to kick him, over and over again until the boy uncurled himself and scrabbled forward, mewling. Marchetti cursed, cursed the boy and himself. He knew he should leave him; the boy would be dead in minutes. It was his own bad luck that he had stumbled over him. There was no way that he could leave him – redemption awaited.

Giggling at the enormity of the divine joke, he grasped him under the arms and with a violent heave, wrenched the limp burden up. He slapped the boy hard across the face, again and again, over and over until the boy roared with anger and pain and tried to push him away.

'Stay awake, you rotten bastard, you filthy son of a filthy whore. Move your damned legs,' he screamed and berated him with the filthiest curses he could muster. They stumbled forward together, hanging onto one another. 'Again,' Marchetti screamed. 'Move, you lazy, ignorant piece of shit.'

They fell into a rhythm that by its very jerkiness served to keep them awake. As they tottered forward, falling often, pushing themselves up, screaming and cursing at one another, striking in maddened fury each time they fell, he admonished himself against taking God's name in vain even as he thought that his curses lacked bite without it. The boy sobbed and Marchetti taunted him, laughed at him, called him a crybaby, promised to send him home to mama.

But it was no good. The wind and snow blasted at them from all points of the compass. The strength they gained from fury and frustration dissipated quickly and they fell more often. Long ago his feet and hands had gone numb. Now his legs had disappeared and ice was creeping up his chest and he could no longer think coherently.

He was lying in the snow. Where had the boy gone? Had he left him behind? Tears stung his eyes. The ungrateful bastard. He had saved his life, and been abandoned. Marchetti struggled up and started forward once more. One step to the left, he told himself and began the count again... one, two, three...

The snow was warm. He was warm. How had that happened? He was aware that the blizzard still raged but he could no longer hear or feel it. The wind had gone, disappeared, and the snow did not sting anymore.

He was comfortable for the first time in days – months, by God. He ceased to wonder what had happened and enjoyed the luxury of being warm and comfortable once more. He had always liked these moments before sleep when warmth stole in and you began the long, soft slide to oblivion. As a child, and even as a man, he had often tried to prolong the moment by concentrating on an imagined incident of which, of course, he was the hero.

Marchetti closed his eyes and saw the sun-warmed body of the diplomat's daughter whose name he had long forgotten, and drifted slowly, inexorably into sleep, and death.

'All the business of war, and indeed all the business
of life is to endeavour to find out what you don't know by what you do; that's what I called "guessing what was on the other side of the hill".'

Duke of Wellington 1769-1852

Milne Bay September 1942 – December 1942

The glaring expanse of steel-blue water, the source of the killing humidity, hurt Lieutenant-Commander Saburo Takeda's eyes as his troops marched down the hill through the town of Rabaul to the small boats that awaited them at the docks. Hot, miserable and hungry, Takeda was filled with misgivings about this mission even before it had properly begun.

His Sixth Special Landing Force company had undergone a bewildering series of alerts and preparations in the months since they had been withdrawn from Timor and he had received his promotion. First, they had been scheduled to participate in the May invasion of Midway Island, but that had been cancelled the week before the fleet sailed into the greatest naval disaster that had ever befallen the Japanese Navy.

The navy had suffered a severe blow to its prestige, as well as its strength, with the loss of its best aviators and four aircraft carriers. Even so, the Army, with what could only be described as blind incompetence as well as patent disregard for the navy, insisted that strategic goals established long before the war be carried out, and so the island campaigns were ordered to continue.

Next, his detachment had been ordered to embark as part of the landing force for Operation FS; the capture of Nauru, Ocean Island, Samoa and the Fijis to complete the Central Pacific end of the Island Defence Ring. But with the defeat at Midway, FS was cancelled. The navy no longer had the resources to mount twin campaigns and the South East Area facing Australia and New Zealand and protecting the Philippines was considered of paramount importance.

Then, they were slated to take part in the capture of Guadalcanal, which would secure the flank of the invasion force moving to capture Port Moresby, but at the last minute they were once more diverted, this time to participate in Operation RI, the subsidiary invasion of the Papuan peninsula at Buna and Gona.

The plan for the South East Area segment of the defence chain seemed incredibly delicate to Takeda, as the establishment of one fortress depended upon the capture of another. Buna and Gona were trading centres at the eastern end of the primitive island of New Guinea in the Australian-occupied half of the island, known as Papua, and their only value lay in the fact that they secured one end of the trail over the nineteen hundred metre high Owen Stanley Mountains to Port Moresby, which was to serve as a naval and air base from which to attack northern Australia.

But again, for a fifth time, orders were received at the last minute eliminating them from participation in the invasion force. Thoroughly frustrated and depressed, Takeda had spent a miserable summer at Sasebo training his already overtrained unit, while his classmates spread throughout the Empire earning commendations and promotions in active combat.

Then, early in August, Takeda was summoned to Tokyo. The train ride was long and subject to frequent stops because of troop trains moving towards the coastal ports. He noticed, as they rumbled past road crossings and through cities and towns, that civilian motor traffic had become almost non-existent. The British destruction of the Borneo and Malayan oilfields had been a wanton act of destruction that must be punished, he thought.

A civilian businessman, leaving the train at Osaka, bowed and with a smile handed him a copy of the *Mainich Shimbun*. Takeda glanced through it idly, his first look at a civilian paper since returning to Japan. The war news was good. The paper told of great victories from Burma to the Aleutians to Savo Island and extolled the bravery and sacrifice of servicemen in glowing terms.

The Foreign Ministry had begun talks with the representatives of the freed nations, Burma, Vietnam and Malaya, regarding early independence. Even the Philippines had been included, although there was still fighting in some of the outlying islands. But the government obviously meant to keep its promises. Independence was to be granted at the earliest possible moment.

Tokyo's main station was jammed and he had to fight his way through the crowds. There were no taxis to be had and buses were as congested as the station and filled with the nauseating odour of coal gas emanating from the cart-mounted charcoal furnaces towed behind each vehicle.

Inside the Naval Administration building, he was directed to an office on the third floor where a smooth-faced naval aide ushered him into the office of Admiral Miyamo. Takeda bowed and was motioned to a chair.

The naval aide opened a map on the admiral's desk and left. The admiral regarded Takeda for a long moment. 'I am familiar with your record,' he said finally. 'It is unpleasant to be subjected to the series of stops and starts which you have experienced recently, but I have an operation that requires your skills and abilities.'

The admiral peered at him over the top of his glasses as if to see what effect this meagre flattery would have. Apparently satisfied when Takeda maintained his expressionless attention, the admiral continued. 'You are familiar with our overall plan for the Pacific? Our first priority was, and remains, the establishment of an impenetrable defence line extending from Burma to Australia to Hawaii and north to the Aleutian islands in an unbroken arc. Only when this line is fully implemented and guarded by the navy will Japan be secure.'

Takeda nodded dutifully. Why is he wasting his time telling me what every schoolchild knows? he wondered.

'Due to the short-sightedness of certain Army colleagues,' the admiral continued, 'we have endured setbacks that are potentially dangerous to the nation. You are aware of Admiral Yamamoto's belief that Japan cannot win this war against the United States if it should last beyond one year?'

Takeda nodded. While the admiral's beliefs were by no means shared by everyone in the navy, he was of the same mind. He had seen just how huge was the United States. Their manufacturing capability was certainly no secret and simple logic must tell one that, unless an impenetrable defence line was established which the Americans could only break at too great a cost to themselves, they must eventually win. Takeda believed strongly in the national destiny of Japan and the superiority of Japanese fighting spirit, but he was also practical enough to see that there were limits.

'We are approaching the end of that year and still victory eludes us. In the meantime, the United States grows stronger,' the admiral grunted. 'We were defeated at Midway; there is no other term for it. A good naval officer must face and base his decisions on facts, not emotion.

'Our defeat at Midway has complicated the picture and heartened the Americans. They recognise Midway as a decisive battle because of our carrier losses. They may be right as we are, at the moment, not in a position to interdict American supplies through the South Central Pacific to Australia, where we face a growing menace from the forces of General MacArthur.

'But, if we can bring the enemy naval and air bases in northern Australia under constant bombardment and threaten them with an invasion, we can tie down great numbers of Australian and American forces at little cost to ourselves and thus disrupt their plans to attack north through the Solomons to the Admiralties, the Moluccas and ultimately, the Philippines.

'The capture of Port Moresby is therefore vital to the completion of our defence perimeter. Because of bad weather and distance, our aircraft cannot reach Port Moresby from bases in the western part of New Guinea to support a naval landing, and so operations were mounted to capture Buna and Gona.

'It is most unfortunate but the weather has become our major problem on New Guinea. We have no means of forecasting weather in the Milne Bay area so that our aircraft may operate effectively. The skies can be absolutely cloudless over the western end of the island but a minor typhoon could be blowing by the time our aircraft reach the Buna-Gona area. We have stationed a submarine in Milne Bay but it is unable to surface long and often enough to be effective.

'So, it is vital that we secure an advanced meteorological station in the area of Milne Bay. If we can ensure the accuracy of our weather predictions, we can operate our aircraft so efficiently that the Allies will be thrown back from their beachheads.'

He tapped a pencil alternately on Port Moresby and Milne Bay. 'The Allies must fly from Australia under the same conditions, but they have established a network of coastwatchers, Europeans who have remained behind in the islands and are protected by native elements. These coastwatchers provide excellent coded meteorological information to Australia on a daily basis.'

The admiral studied Takeda a moment, as if measuring him for the task ahead, then spread another map on the desk, this one showing the tip of the Papuan peninsula and Milne Bay. The entire end of the island was shaped like a fork with two tines, between which small islands were scattered. A great number were shown at the eastern end of the bay and one was circled in red crayon.

'This is your destination, Tandona Island, in the extreme western end of the Louisiades. You will leave Rabaul by destroyer and, if necessary, proceed to Rabi Island where you will embark in small boats for Tandona to establish a meteorological and communications base. The islands are far enough removed from the main island of New Guinea that you should be unobserved if you run in at night. Your command will include a meteorological specialist and as soon as you have established yourselves you will transmit weather information to Rabaul on a daily basis. A radio operator specialist will accompany you so that headquarters at Rabaul can begin to receive useful information as soon as possible. You will be under the tactical command of the Southeastern Fleet and be considered part of the Combined Special Naval Landing Force for the time being. But your orders will come from this office only.

'As soon as operations at Port Moresby are completed, a destroyer will be sent to Tandona with army personnel to replace you. Subject to your report, further bases will be established.'

The Admiral then introduced him to his planning staff who briefed Takeda in detail and supplied him with orders requiring him to sail from Sasebo in three days. 'You will find, Commander, that your commanding officer has been informed, your company alerted and preparations begun for your departure.'

Takeda left naval headquarters confused and upset. Confused because he did not understand what was happening in Tokyo. The army and the navy were feuding to such an extent that an admiral felt free to make cynical comments to a junior officer and furthermore the campaign in the Solomons, as it was outlined in the briefing that followed their conversation, was little more than a patch applied to previous patches. It was clear to him that the enemy was continually being underestimated. We may have smashed their battleship fleet at Pearl Harbor he told himself as he walked, but it was aircraft carriers that counted today. And the Americans fought us to a draw at the Coral Sea and at Midway they turned back our invasion fleet with their carriers and sank ours.

Admiral Yamamoto is right. This war will be won by raw materials which the Americans have and we do not. The Americans also have three times our numbers and a hundred times our factories and shipyards. They can afford to spend years chipping away at our defensive perimeter while they rebuild their fleet, and fight the war in Europe as well.

Takeda was further depressed because once again he was being sent away from the main part of the war. Milne Bay! he thought with contempt. What chance would he have there to contribute? But Takeda was a naval officer and knew it was not his place to question his superiors. Such behaviour could be left to the ill-disciplined army.

If they were to embark for Rabaul in three days, there was no time to travel to Osaka to see his parents. What rotten luck. His father's last letter was in so shaky a hand that he could barely read it. His sister had written several days later to say that their brother, flying in Burma, had not been heard from for two months.

Takeda hesitated on a street corner. As it was only mid-afternoon and the train did not leave until 1800 hours, there would be time to see Mariko. But would she wish to see him? Her letters had been so very correct, almost formal, as if she were writing from duty rather than affection.

Loath to endure another bus ride, he walked to the radio station. Takeda told himself as he did so that it was foolish to pursue a woman as famous as Mariko. His ego still twinged whenever he recalled his embarrassment at discovering that it was Mariko who had been the centre of attention and not himself the night they had gone to the restaurant.

The receptionist's expression was dubious when he asked to see Mariko Sumata. 'I am sorry, Commander, ah Takeda,' she glanced at the card he had filled out, 'but Mariko is so busy. Perhaps I might direct you to our public relations . . .'

Takeda managed to keep his temper under control at the insult. Who did she think he was? 'Please inform Mariko that Lieutenant-Commander Saburo Takeda is in the lobby and wishes to see her.' He snapped the order as if he were on his own parade ground.

The startled receptionist ducked her head and picked up the telephone and a few moments later Takeda was escorted to Mariko's dressing room by a young boy, a page they called him, who politely offered a seat.

'Miss Sumata is in the studio at the moment, sir. She asks that you wait for her here. May I offer you a cigarette?' The boy produced a pack of French Ovals and added hastily when he saw Takeda's frown, 'Oh, no sir, these are for visitors. I am not allowed to smoke.'

Fully half an hour passed in the uncomfortably feminine room that smelled of perfume and powder and silk garments before the door opened and Mariko swept in, followed by two women and a man. The man, thin and consumptive-looking, carried a clipboard and wore a watch about his neck on a cord. He was arguing with Mariko but she ignored him and hurried to Takeda. As he stood, she hugged him and kissed his cheek as they did in Hollywood movies.

Takeda was embarrassed at this open display of affection but the others ignored the incident. He tried to step back but Mariko turned, still clutching his arm and made rapid introductions. The two women were production assistants and the man was her director.

The women smiled but the man barely acknowledged the introduction and continued to argue until Mariko snapped her fingers.

'I will not listen to another word. I have made my decision. You will find three additional minutes. Now I would like to be alone with Commander Takeda.'

The man shrugged and threw out his hands. 'All right, Mariko, I'll see what I can do.' He hurried out, having forgotten Takeda's presence, but the women left with smiles directed at Takeda.

When the door closed, Mariko stood on tiptoe to kiss him again, further embarrassing Takeda and smudging her lipstick. She laughed gently at his expression and drew him down beside her on the couch. Mariko wore a silk kimono and from the disturbing softness of her body through the fabric, he wondered if she had anything on beneath.

'It has been so long,' she smiled. 'Please tell me what you have been doing in the past months, and why,' she smiled again, 'you have all but stopped writing to me?' Her perfume flustered Takeda. Her hip pressed against his on the small couch and there was nowhere for him to go. He could not help but notice how flawless was her ivory skin and when she touched his hand delicately with her fingertips, it was all he could do to repress a sigh.

'Are you upset with me?'

The question completed Takeda's destruction, but a knock at the door saved him.

Mariko snapped, 'I do not wish to be disturbed . . .' but the door opened anyway and the director stuck his head in. 'Sorry Mariko,' he apologised. 'We are wanted upstairs, *right now*.'

Mariko muttered an expletive under her breath that shocked Takeda. 'Tell them I will be there in five minutes,' she said firmly. When the man started to argue, she snarled, '*Five minutes!*'

The door closed and she turned back to him. 'If I had known then what I know now about this job, I would never have left Kadoma. I am sorry, but I must go. We are preparing a special programme for Sunday evening and have scheduled several high-ranking military officers and government officials. How long will you be in Tokyo? Can we have dinner this evening, no,' she bit at her lip, 'tomorrow evening? Please, tomorrow evening?'

Takeda managed his first coherent sentence. 'I have to return tonight. The train leaves at 1800 hours . . . six o'clock.'

Mariko's expression was stricken. 'Damn! I thought you might be staying for several days . . . oh, this is terrible! I won't even be able to go with you to the train . . .'

Takeda stood up quickly. 'It's my fault. I shouldn't have barged in and disrupted your schedule.' He reached for the door but Mariko caught his hand.

'When will you be in Tokyo, again?'

'I don't really know, perhaps soon,' he waved vaguely.

She rose as he started to turn away, stood on tiptoe to kiss him soundly.

Takeda had never been kissed in that way before. Not even by the adopted daughters of his commander in Manchuria. In fact, he had not known it was possible to be kissed that way.

Mariko stepped back with a faintly triumphant smile. 'You will write to me regularly,' she ordered. 'Or I will be very cross with you.'

The door opened again and the director stuck his head in. 'Mariko!' He pointed to his watch.

As he took the lift to the ground floor, Takeda knew he had been correct. Mariko lived in another world. And her language was shocking! She was becoming too much a modern woman. But as famous as she was, he thought in confusion, she seemed to care for him. Hadn't the kiss proved that? No properly brought up Japanese girl – and Mariko had been brought up in the traditional manner – would ever kiss a man like that unless she cared very deeply for him. He saw her brief letters now as moments snatched from frantic days. The fact that she had found time to write at all, especially when he had nearly stopped doing so, was further proof.

In the lobby, the receptionist bowed but made a show of glancing at her wristwatch as Takeda walked past. But he didn't acknowledge the gesture, only turned so that she could see the lipstick smear.

They had arrived two weeks earlier to find Rabaul soaked in the heat and humidity of summer's end, worse even than the East Indies. There were no trucks to haul their baggage, according to the young ensign who hurried up, panting as if from a long run. His white uniform was soaked with sweat and filthy, but Takeda restrained an automatic reprimand when he saw the etched lines of exhaustion about the boy's face. Rabaul, Australia's main naval base in the Coral Sea, had been captured in January and had become the Empire's strongest naval and military base in the South East Area.

Rabaul was typical of the European planter towns he had seen in the East Indies – long cement-block or metal buildings, white-washed to reflect the sun and narrow streets lined with western-style houses so totally unsuited to the climate. The majority of buildings were in ruins and what remained were pocked with bullet and shrapnel holes. New Japanese construction was going on everywhere and the town had a bustle and energy it would never have experienced under its white masters. The harbour was full of war ships and cargo vessels and served as an alternate naval facility with Truk, 1,300 kilometres north.

Takeda had been told that they would remain at Rabaul for only two days, but no one had informed the harbour or garrison authorities that he was arriving or what his needs would be and he was forced to scrounge his own shelter and food. He fumed angrily at the foul-up and waited three fruitless days just to hear a senior officer tell him they were sorry but they had no orders, and no one to spare in any event to help him. Takeda took matters into his own hands.

The next day he marched his company from village to village along the New Britain coast and confiscated three large fishing canoes. But word of his coming spread by the next morning and all the fishing boats mysteriously disappeared. Not even severe beatings produced them. So Takeda hit on a new strategy. He sent his senior warrant officer, Gohay Ueda, in command of two of the canoes already captured to lie off the coast before dawn while he marched his company into the village. The ruse worked well enough and four more boats were captured in as many days. Pressure on the harbour authorities finally produced a pair of motor launches – converted whale boats.

The seven canoes and two launches needed extensive maintenance, which required five more days, but eventually he had got them all safely aboard the destroyer that would run them to within three hours of Tandona Island. His only piece of luck had been the destroyer captain who had agreed to a slight detour and thus saved them several more wasted days on Rabi Island.

The officer of the deck saluted smartly and told off a messenger to lead the company below. 'The Captain wishes me to say, Lieutenant-Commander Takeda, that you are most welcome to enjoy the hospitality of the wardroom. He regrets that he cannot be here to greet you but duties about the ship require his presence elsewhere and he hopes that you will understand.'

Takeda was shown to a cabin below decks. An officer was asleep, naked and covered with perspiration, on the bunk below an open scuttle. The barest trace of breeze eddied in but it only seemed to add to the stifling quality of the cabin. Takeda had been awake all the previous night and probably would be again tonight and he looked with longing at the top bunk. But that pleasure was still some hours away. He left his duffle bag and went out to see to his company.

At 2000 hours, Takeda was awakened by a mess steward. The bottom bunk was empty and darkness had fallen beyond the empty scuttle. Groggy with heat, he managed a sponge bath in the tiny basin and grimaced with distaste as he put his wrinkled, dirty and sweat-soaked khaki uniform back on and went out. On deck, the heat was instantly wiped away by a cooling sea breeze. Warrant Officer Gohay Ueda was waiting for him and he gave instructions to have the men prepare to embark at midnight, then went below to the empty officers' mess. Nevertheless, a steward placed a large plate well-filled with rice and fish and a pot of hot tea on the table and left him to it. Takeda ate hungrily. On Rabaul, to conserve their rations, they had lived for two weeks on fish they caught themselves and on canned and dried rations drawn only after a lengthy battle with the commissary department.

Just as he was finishing, the general quarters bugle call sounded over the loudspeakers and he felt the vibration of the destroyer's engines increase. The ship was suddenly filled with the rush of running feet and the sound of blowers speeding up. His name came over the loudspeaker and he was ordered to the bridge.

Takeda stepped through the screen door to find the captain engaged in conversation with the executive and navigating officers. A striker called the captain's attention to his presence and he beckoned to Takeda.

'We have sighted,' the captain began without preamble, 'what may be an enemy ship. We are here,' he pointed to the chart and Takeda saw that the navigator's plot led to a point some twenty kilometres northeast of Milne Bay.

'We have had reports,' the captain continued, 'of an American task force moving into the area and this may be it. My orders are to avoid all contact and to report. Therefore, I must change course,' he indicated with the pencil a new route that would take him north in a long curve towards Guadalcanal and Savo Island.

'Because of the danger of encountering the enemy, I would advise you to abandon your mission tonight. We will be returning to Rabaul in four days time. You could attempt it then.'

Takeda stared at the map. Tandona was forty-eight kilometres away from their present position. At three kilometres per hour, the best the motor launches could manage pulling the unpowered fishing boats, it would take them sixteen hours. Dawn would find them only half-way there. But, if they remained aboard the destroyer, there was no telling how things might change in four days.

He studied the Milne Bay chart. If they made directly for the coast they could reach it before daybreak. They could then lie up for the day and complete the trip tomorrow night. They would lose nothing and would gain three days. And the better acquainted he was with the Milne Bay area, the better he could perform his task.

'I prefer to embark my men now, Captain,' he said and explained what he had in mind.

The tiny flotilla towed by the two whaleboats chugged through the black night. There was no moon but the stars blazed, providing almost enough light for Takeda to make out the features of the man before him.

Two hours after leaving the destroyer, the lookout had sighted a dark bulk against the horizon. Takeda ordered the engines stopped but the crew of the second whaleboat did not hear the order and puttered on. Not daring to be separated, Takeda cursed and ordered speed resumed, hoping the ship would pass without hearing them.

With a cloudless sky and the boat's compass, Takeda had no trouble navigating. He altered course two hours before dawn and landed them on the northern tine of Milne Bay. They dragged the canoes across the sandy beach and concealed them in trees and dispersed and camouflaged the motor launches with wrack and canvas.

A sea breeze mitigated the tropical heat somewhat as it grew steadily during the morning. Takeda posted sentries and lookouts and the men ate and slept until mid-afternoon. After the months of frustrating delays and false starts and the killing work and heat of Rabaul, a day of idleness was most welcome. It had, Takeda thought, a holiday flavour.

At noon, the breeze died and the heat grew until it was difficult to breathe. Takeda tried not to think of the inviting sea. He did not dare allow bathing until after dark and then there would be no time as they would need every minute of darkness. Twice, he had been awakened by the steady drone of high flying aircraft. Patrols? Had the mysterious ship seen them after all? If a reconnaissance plane spotted them, fighters and bombers would be drawn to the area and it would be only a matter of time until they came under enemy attack.

As the short dusk faded to night, they ate a hurried meal of dried fish and rice and launched the boats. Takeda checked the helmsman's compass reading and heading against his own and the two strings of boats puttered into the bay.

The night dragged on and the men grew restless in the cramped boats. They averaged thirty men to a boat and no matter how one turned, there was not sufficient leg room and the impossibility of resting one's back grew into excruciating torture before many hours had passed. Those unfortunate enough to be assigned the canoes were in even worse condition. The canoes were extremely narrow and reeked of fish.

Takeda had hoped to land on Tandona Island well before dawn, but the second motor launch's engine broke down and the flotilla was delayed while the crew tried and failed to fix it. Takeda swore and watched the sky begin to grey in the east. They had at best an hour before it would be light. He gave orders for the disabled boat and its string to be towed by his boat, assisted by oarsmen. As they got under way again, Takeda fumed at their lack of speed.

The sun was well up by the time they sighted Tandona. They had passed innumerable small islands but their smooth, broad beaches had offered no hiding places for the boats and the vegetation was too sparse to provide sufficient cover.

Every man in the company watched the skies nervously and when they finally beached the boats and canoes in the gentle surf, no one had to be urged to get them unloaded and concealed as quickly as possible.

Half the supplies had been hidden and all of the ammunition, but only half the food and medical supplies, when they were startled by the roar of aircraft engines. A high-winged flying boat with Australian markings, using the island itself to screen its approach, burst over them. Its machine gun fire spattered about them but did no damage and the aircraft disappeared in the morning haze. Takeda stared after it, sick with disappointment and frustration.

Furiously, he drove the men to move the equipment and supplies inland as far as possible from the landing site. They had, he thought, two, perhaps three hours before bombers reached them from the nearest enemy bases on New Guinea. He shouted and cursed and struck with the flat of his sword at laggards until, less than ten minutes later, four aircraft – P 40s – rocketed in from the sea at twenty metres altitude. Their machine guns yammered and smashed boats and sailors indiscriminately. Bombs skipped down to explode in the trees and Takeda threw himself flat beneath a fallen log as shrapnel and machine gun bullets slashed the jungle vegetation.

It was over in moments and the aircraft disappeared as abruptly as they had come. Twenty had been killed outright and three more so badly wounded they died before sunset. Two fishing boats were burning and a third had been shot to pieces. The working motor launch was untouched – their only piece of luck – but most of their medical supplies and half the food had been destroyed.

A stunned web of unreality wrapped about his brain as Takeda stared at the horror of bodies thrown about by the force of the bomb blasts and machine gun fire and the twin columns of black smoke rising skyward like beacons. He finally managed to rouse himself and give orders for the fire to be smothered with sand. But five minutes later, a second flight of P 40s blasted in to pound the beach.

Takeda had no choice but to abandon the boats remaining on the beach and the supplies they contained. His shouted orders could barely be heard above the roar of aircraft and machine guns and bombs but discipline prevailed and the men charged into the cover of the trees. Platoon and petty officers sorted them out, loaded them with supplies and got them moving inland.

Tandona Island was twelve kilometres in diameter, large enough to hide on, but hardly big enough for nearly three hundred men to find sufficient food on which to subsist for long. They had brought with them a sixty-day supply of rations, had lost a little more than half, leaving them with only enough for thirty days. Takeda had planned to eke out their rations from local resources – fishing, hunting and fruits of various kinds which he was certain would flourish on the jungle islands. Special Naval Landing Forces were trained in the technique of living off the land and while it had never yet been necessary for them to do so, he was certain the company could.

Away from the beach, the land sloped upward quickly across three high terraces to five hundred metres above sea level. Takeda had been stunned by how quickly the fighter aircraft had responded. The nearest Australian air facilities were at Port Moresby, but surely that was beyond flying range for such fighters? Why had they been operating in the area and better yet, where had they come from? Was there a new enemy airfield in the area? No, he thought, most likely they had been en route to Buna when they were diverted by the PBY reconnaissance plane's report. But could he expect ground troops soon? If so, then his first need was to establish a defensible position and the island's interior, all high ground, simplified that matter – somewhat.

At mid-afternoon, Takeda allowed the exhausted men to rest below a clearing and with Warrant Officer Ueda, he climbed on to the clearing. A thin streamer of black smoke still trickled from the smouldering boats and supplies. A speck that was an aircraft circled lazily and as they watched, flew off to the southwest. The sea was deserted in every direction but for the scattered islands in the Louisiades Group.

As tired as they were, he and Ueda forced themselves to explore the immediate area. The jungle thickened on the southeast-facing slope where huge trees rose straight for twenty metres and more to provide a humid, semi-twilight beneath. Takeda decided to establish the main camp here. Ueda did not offer comments as befitted a good subordinate, but it was plain that he approved of Takeda's selection.

They rested a few moments before starting down again. Takeda's shirt was wringing with sweat and he was extremely thirsty. Fresh water was going to be their major problem, he thought. They had not seen any water at all during the climb and he wondered if the islands' only supplies came from rainwater. If so, they would have to fashion cisterns of some kind.

The shadows beneath the trees were deepening into premature twilight before the company had completed the camp. Climbing above the clearing, Takeda studied the bay. The sun was setting in a burst of orange and gold that set long tropical streamers of cloud glowing with neon colour, but the beauty was lost on him at the moment.

The New Guinea coast was visible as a thin smudge in the splendour of the dying sun. Somewhere over there Japanese units, including the Fifth Special Naval Landing Force from Kure, were participating in a mission that should have been his. By now, they would have moved inland from Buna and Gona, he thought, along the Kodoka Trail and over the Owen Stanley Mountains towards the prize of Port Moresby. Meanwhile, he was stranded on an insignificant island in Milne Bay without enough food, no water and twenty-three dead and wounded.

They ate a spare meal of rice and fish cakes, cold, as Takeda did not dare risk fires. Afterwards, he sent two platoons back to the beach to establish lookout posts in the morning. The rest of the exhausted men were ordered to suspend their rubberised ground cloths on sticks to catch any rain that might fall. Only then were they allowed to sleep.

Takeda lay awake, mind idling as he waited for sleep to banish his anger. All summer he had watched Special Naval Landing Force company after company depart Sasebo to garrison islands in the Pacific, to establish bases in New Guinea and conduct landings on the Chinese Coast, while he sat idle.

He had hung tenaciously onto every word describing the fighting in the Philippines and watched with glee as the Americans retreated down the Bataan peninsula into the island garrison of Corrigedor. But again, an unexpectedly spirited defence had required that the Empire commit far more resources and men than had been anticipated. Only after their commander, MacArthur, had run away had his army surrendered. Takeda had often puzzled over this curious predilection of Westerners for surrendering. Did they not believe in what they were fighting for? A man who fought for what he believed in should prepare himself to die for his beliefs.

As drowsiness at last crept over him, his mind turned to home and the missed opportunity with Mariko. What a fool he had been. A few minutes to send a telegram and she perhaps might have been able to arrange time for him. It was clear that she wanted to but she had a wartime job to do as well. While it was certainly not as important as his, still it needed to be done.

What did he want from Mariko? Should he write to his parents and ask that they speak to hers about marriage? Was he ready for that step, or should he wait until after the war?

*

At morning inspection, the men looked remarkably fit and healthy after the ordeal of the past two weeks. It had not rained during the night and so Takeda continued strict water rationing.

After the flag raising ceremony and bow to the Emperor, Takeda swiftly gave orders for shelter, water, firewood, scouting and food gathering parties to be made up. As he watched them leave, a petty officer followed by the radio operator approached.

The man's face was stricken and he hardly dared look at Takeda as he bowed. 'The radio was damaged in yesterday's bombing,' the petty officer reported fearfully.

Takeda stared, unable to believe what he was hearing. He himself had supervised its packing. Anger gathered in the deepest recesses of his being and surged outward. His hand went to the hilt of his sword, his face contorted and he nearly lost all control. The radio operator stood with head bowed, unable to face him, certainly expecting at the least a blow from his fist.

Their only reason for being in Milne Bay at all was the radio. Without it, they were useless as was any information they might gather. Takeda fought to control himself. Giving way to rage, however cathartic, would surely convince the men that they were in a hopeless position.

His voice was choked with anger as he asked if the radio could be repaired. The petty officer and radio operator exchanged frightened glances. 'I don't know, sir,' the operator said. 'Several valves were smashed and so were two spares.'

Takeda had wanted to bring a second of the Type 94 3A radio transmitter and receiver but no more were available. Instead, he had ordered that spare valves be carefully packed and brought along. 'It looks hopeless, sir,' the petty officer ventured.

Takeda remembered the many times he had watched his father repair radios in his tiny Osaka shop. His father liked to say that there was always a way to repair anything, whether or not the proper parts were available. It only required ingenuity and that made the difference between a good repairman and an average repairman.

'You will find a way to repair the radio or build another,' he told the terrified radio operator. 'You will not fail.'

Takeda dismissed them and turned his mind away from this latest disaster. It did no good to brood. If they were to perform their mission, he must be strong and allow no lapses of discipline or morale. He must see that all duties were performed correctly. He suppressed his own growing despair and went resolutely to work.

Takeda had established as the first priority, anti-aircraft detection rules and practices. No one was to show himself in the open, all clearings were to be avoided and no one was to shoot at an aircraft for any reason without his direct permission.

At mid-morning, Takeda hiked down to the beach where he ordered the burned boats left in plain view and had those considered repairable hauled inland and concealed. Salvagable equipment was removed but all else was left as it was in the hope that the Allies would decide they had abandoned the island during the night.

He ordered an observation bunker established on the rounded peak that formed the highest point on the island. The petty officer in charge of that detail even found and transplanted three small trees that screened the bunker perfectly without obscuring the lookout's view.

A reconnaissance aircraft flew over the island in late afternoon, too high for its nationality to be discovered, but Takeda proceeded on the assumption that it was either American or Australian. The flight of bombers that blasted low over the island thirty minutes later, scattering anti-personnel bombs, left no doubt as to their origin. No one was hurt in the raid but it was plain that his simple camouflage had fooled no one.

The two exploration parties sent out that morning returned exhausted and thirsty to report that they had been unable to discover fresh water anywhere on the island. But the island was covered with lush vegetation, Takeda argued with himself. Surely that meant frequent rain falls which dictated catch basins and streams. Takeda ordered all canteens collected and placed under armed guard. When the water remaining was measured, it amounted to seventy-five quarts, roughly half a pint per man for one day only.

The lack of additional water supplies since boarding the destroyer three days before was beginning to tell. Takeda could not recall ever having been so thirsty. His tongue was beginning to swell and he was experiencing odd bouts of mild dizziness. Urination had become painful and his body throbbed with dull, unfocused pain. The evening sky in the west mocked them with colourful clouds as the sun set in blazing display, but above them, the sky was diamond clear.

September was the end of the dry season in these latitudes, Takeda knew, but dry season was a relative term. The monsoon would start in mid-October but it hardly seemed likely that it would rain before then. If it doesn't, he thought grimly, we are dead men.

It did not rain again that night and in the morning Takeda directed that each rifle squad search for water. He held back two squads whom he had collect all ground covers and canteen cups and led them down the slope to the terrace they had crossed on the way up from the beach.

High trees provided light shade over a small meadow. Takeda was loath to chance working in an area so open, but he had no choice. He ordered shallow pits, a metre in diameter and twenty centimetres deep, excavated and the dirt distributed carefully in the surrounding grass.

In the centre of each hole a canteen cup was placed, the rubberised ground cover was stretched over the hole and its edges weighted with rocks. Then a small stone was tossed into the centre, causing the cover to sag above the canteen cup. Finally, cut grass was scattered over the ground cloths as camouflage.

The dark, rubberised cloth absorbed the sun's heat and raised the temperature in the hole beneath to distil water from the soil. The moisture condensed on the underside of the cover and dripped down into the canteen cup. It was a slow, awkward method, Takeda thought, but might stretch their remaining supplies another day.

By the evening of the fourth day, their sixth without fresh water, Takeda knew it was hopeless to remain on Tandona any longer. If there were freshwater supplies on the island, they hadn't been able to locate them and sooner or later, Allied troops would land to search them out. There were other, larger islands at this end of Milne Bay and certainly one of them would have fresh water.

Warrant Officer Ueda had managed to salvage or repair four fishing canoes and enough petrol and spare parts from the damaged motor launch for at least eight hours at low speed. Takeda decided to make the trip in two sections on successive nights, as there was not room enough in the boats to take them all at one time.

He selected Warnoa Island, one and a half hours west. The water was divided and the bulk left to the group staying behind. Half the heavy equipment and the radio and spares were loaded and they set out just before midnight. The passage was smooth enough and as if the gods had decided to relent, the sky clouded over and it rained hard for a few moments before midnight.

The men went crazy as the fresh water poured down and they caught it in their mouths, helmets and canteen cups. Even so, it was impossible to save more than a few litres before the rain moved away. But it was enough to put new heart into them.

Two hours before dawn, the five boats were swept silently onto the beach by the gentle surf. The rain had restored vigour and discipline and they moved quickly into the trees to establish a defence perimeter. Takeda sent the motor launch and canoes back to Tandona after a quick reconnaissance. He did not expect to find the island inhabited and when the patrols returned to report no sign of human habitation, he allowed the men to sleep.

They found a stream within an hour of the flaming sunrise and Takeda ordered all canteens filled but allowed no one to drink until the water purification tablets placed in each had taken effect. In spite of all his care, four men had developed dysentery and were already proving a burden.

There were already too many wounded – damaged goods – and he had punished the offenders harshly.

Their main camp was established on a bluff overlooking the beach, with a clear view west and south into the Coral Sea as well as east to the New Guinea coast. A freshwater stream ran nearby, dropping sheer for several metres into a small pool that emptied itself quickly. As the stream ran down through the rocks, it formed larger pools which were handy for bathing yet were concealed from the air by trees. Everything they did now, everywhere they went, was determined by the amount of concealment available.

Takeda's greatest worry since the radio had been smashed was that they would be given up for lost. It was hardly likely that the navy, hard pressed as it was for ships, would waste one in a search of Milne Bay just for them. Tokyo would merely assume they had fallen foul of the enemy task force the destroyer's captain would have reported.

So, Takeda decided to send two of the canoes, each with a party of ten men, to Rabi Island to report. When they left two nights later, both boat commanders carried identical reports and lists of supplies required, which included rations, a new radio and spares, medical supplies and heavy infantry weapons.

The boats left at one hour intervals after dark and on slightly different courses with instructions to lie up well before dawn each day. At least, he thought, this pre-monsoon season will give them quiet seas and no storms. He caught a last glimpse of the second canoe as it cleared a small headland.

Warnoa Island was much larger, nearly eighty square kilometres in extent and had plenty of free-running streams. It appeared, however, singularly free of edible wildlife. Takeda spent the first day scouting for an observation point that was shielded from the air but allowed a wide view of the New Guinea coast and the waters in between. If they were lucky, their night move from Tandona had gone unobserved and not until the Allies actually mounted an invasion and explored Tandona would they look for them elsewhere.

A scouting party found a flat shelf, several hundred metres wide, jutting from the southwest slope of the low volcano that crowned the island. It supported a thick stand of trees whose top branches were interlaced to the extent that the sky was barely visible. In the relatively cool shadows beneath, there was little ground cover and the soil was thick and loamy. Takeda ordered three observation posts established at equidistant points along the shelf's rim from which observers could keep the New Guinea coast under continuous daylight observation. On the opposite side of the volcano, near the peak, he established the meteorological station. Both sites had nearby streams providing plenty of fresh water. His only real problem now, he thought, was the lack of a radio.

Enemy aircraft came at midday and laid a string of bombs directly across the camp. Takeda had gone to the beach to take sun sightings with a sextant and heard the aircraft in time to find cover.

Six B-17s with Australian markings struck the camp and even at a distance of three kilometres, the earth jarred to the explosions of bombs and the plume of smoke and dust rising from the slope made the volcano seem alive again. The aircraft, still in formation, wheeled out to sea then swept inland again, changing formation to line astern. They came in low, one at a time to machine gun the slope at the exact location of the camp. When the bombers disappeared to the southwest, Takeda raced back.

Everything was a shambles. Tents had been ripped to shreds by machine gun fire and shrapnel. Although food and ammunition had been widely distributed, much of it had been destroyed. Thirteen men had been killed and he now had twenty-three wounded on his hands, most so badly damaged they were of no use to anyone.

Takeda forced himself to pace through the camp, fighting the shock that threatened to overwhelm him. He was so stunned by this unexpected blow that all he could think about was how would he ever be able to cremate those who had died honourably and box their ashes for the return to Japan.

For a long while, his mind refused to grapple with the prime question – how had the Australian pilots known which island they were on and how in all the mighty square kilometres of savannah and jungle had they known which exact spot to bomb?

Had they been spotted while crossing to Warnoa? But even so, that would tell the enemy only which island they were on. Had one or both of the canoes sent to Rabi Island been captured? He could not believe that any Special Naval Landing Force sailor would allow himself to be taken alive, or if so, would betray his comrades.

A spy – a coastwatcher on the island? How else could their location have been pinpointed so accurately – and so fast? Takeda forced himself to examine this new supposition dispassionately. The same reasons that made the Louisiades an excellent weather observation post for Japanese forces would make it equally valuable to the Allies, and Warnoa was located so that all ship and much aviation traffic in and out of Milne Bay could be kept under continuous daytime observation. So it made sense that the Allies would keep a close watch on the area to the extent of placing a coastwatcher on Warnoa itself.

Takeda shouted for Ueda and gave terse orders for an armed reconnaissance party. That night they built the cremation fires deep in the forest. If the glow was seen, Takeda thought, it made little difference.

They moved the camp at dawn to a less sheltered, less comfortable location near the base of the volcano, overlooking a narrow gorge leading down to the beach. This time, Takeda established a double line of pickets, the first one thousand metres from the camp, the second two hundred. Now, no one could approach close enough to give away their position to less than a square kilometre in area – far too large for effective bombing.

Takeda's tent and most of his possessions had been destroyed in the bombing. He retained his sword and pistol belt, but everything else was gone except for the uniform he wore, his sextant and field glasses. The pictures of his family and one Mariko had sent to him at Sasebo, the thousand stitch prayer flag from his mother and sister and his copy of Tao were all lost.

The reconnaissance party returned at dusk and Ueda reported little success. 'We spotted the remains of a very old camp,' he shrugged. 'It was impossible to tell how old. Perhaps natives from New Guinea come here in their canoes.'

Takeda was now faced with two alternatives. He could move to another island or he could eliminate the enemy coastwatcher; either was only partly satisfactory at best. There might be another coastwatcher on whichever island they chose to move to, particularly if it was as large and self-sufficient as Warnoa. If they could find and kill the coastwatcher on the other hand, the island had plenty of water and, with any luck, sufficient food to feed them. He could expect the Allies to invade but Warnoa offered excellent defensive possibilities and he thought they might hold out until after their relief arrived.

That night, Takeda plotted his campaign carefully. Rather than one large patrol, he organised two series of five eight-man patrols and stripped them to bare essentials, rifles, bayonets, a blanket apiece and sufficient rations for three days. Each patrol was led by a petty officer or senior private who were instructed to track down the coastwatcher, capture or kill him and return with his radio and whatever spare parts they could find, and his food supply.

The patrols moved out before dawn and he watched them melt into the darkness with some foreboding. They represented thirty per cent of his remaining force and they would be largely out of touch for up to three days. In the meantime he busied himself with the requirements of camp and defence. Slit trenches were dug and vital equipment, their meagre food and ammunition supplies were hidden in camouflaged pits under cover of darkness and bunkers were started so that when the bombers returned at mid-morning, they were ready for them.

Again, they roared in from the sea, hardly troubling to hide their approach. But Takeda's tactics paid off; bombs fell in twin strings on the old campsite. The coastwatcher, if there was a coastwatcher, had not seen their move.

*

At dusk, a sentry trotted into camp to report a canoe had been sighted among the smaller islands to the north and appeared to be making for Warnoa Island. Takeda led the squad to the beach himself. Darkness was complete when they arrived and the guide confused his directions so that they startled the sentry post. A dozen shots were fired at them before they were able to identify themselves.

Takeda was furious and beat the guide. If the canoe contained an enemy scouting party, they could hardly have failed to be warned. Nevertheless, he spread the men along the beach after cautioning them to maintain a sharp lookout. Shortly before midnight, a full moon rose and Takeda was somewhat soothed by the silvered beach and burnished black water. A soft trade wind rustled the palms and dried the perspiration from his blouse.

A sailor hurried up to report in low, urgent tones to a petty officer who came in turn to Takeda. 'They have landed two kilometres along the beach. This man says they are wearing helmets and have rifles.'

That, thought Takeda, eliminates the possibility of natives.

The soft sand impeded their progress and all were breathing hard when they reached a point of land beyond which the canoe had landed. A freshwater stream ran down the volcano's slope to the sea and crossed the beach at this point. Three sailors were keeping watch on the canoe which had been drawn up on the beach.

Takeda personally took their report. 'We saw them move inland through the brush and tracked them for several hundred metres. There are six of them and we could not tell who they were. They did not speak and the moon was not high enough to see their features or skin colour. They went as far as this stream, then disappeared into the brush.'

Takeda felt a surge of elation. For the first time in months, he would be in direct contact with the enemy. I must be cautious now, he thought and forced himself to wait until his heart rate and breathing slowed. Then he divided the patrol into two squads , one to remain near the trees while the other crossed the stream with him to flank the canoe. He was certain the enemy would return before dawn, either to leave the island or to hide the canoe.

His squad took up positions fifty metres equidistant from the canoe and stream. Another hour passed before he heard a foot slip on a rock and a splash followed by silence. Easing the foliage aside, he saw six men moving along the stream bed. They paused where the vegetation gave way to beach, then started towards the canoe.

Takeda placed his whistle in his mouth and took a breath. A voice spoke softly in Japanese as they bent to the canoe.

Japanese! Takeda spat out the whistle and shouted, 'Sixth Sasebo!' The newcomers dived for cover and he shouted the name again and cursed himself for not having thought of assigning a password.

'Are you Lieutenant-Commander Saburo Takeda?' a voice shouted from the beach.

'Yes!' He repeated their unit name. One man stood up warily and Takeda stepped out of the shadow of the bush. The sailor laughed then and kicked the man nearest him. 'Get up and salute your commanding officer. It is us, Commander Takeda. We have returned from Rabi Island!'

They had a sobering tale to tell. 'We made good time at first with the tide pushing us. We could see the second boat following for two hours before we began to draw ahead. After midnight, an enemy vessel approached. We heard its engines and I am certain that it was an American PT boat, although we did not see them pass in the darkness.

'After a while, we saw a flare perhaps two kilometres behind us and then we heard machine gun fire. I am certain they destroyed Petty Officer Inega's canoe. After that, we put ashore on a small island north of Milne Bay to hide for the day. That night, we rigged the sail and when the trade winds strengthened, we made it nearly to Rabi Island.

'As we approached, we could see the flare of exploding artillery shells and even hear shooting, so we dropped the sail and began to row again. I directed the boat to approach what I thought was our main stronghold, but instead we almost ran into the enemy. In fact, we were among them before we discovered our mistake.

'We got out of there in one hell of a hurry and an hour later we saw a destroyer steaming slowly along the north side of the island. We thought she might be American and so were about to put out to sea again until we heard a bugle call. We knew the Americans do not use bugles and so assumed she must be Japanese.

'She anchored in a small bay but we did not dare hail or approach her for fear of being shot at, so we put out a sea anchor and waited for dawn. When the sun rose, we saw that it was indeed a Japanese destroyer. She appeared to have suffered heavy damage and was listing to port and down by the bow. Her forward turret had been smashed, her hull had a great gash across the bow and her bridge had been shot away.

'We started to paddle closer but two enemy aircraft came and bombed and straffed the ship. When she did not fire back, we knew she had been abandoned and so we paddled ashore and reported to the army commander who was surprised to see us but not happy.

'He wished us to join his forces but I respectfully pointed out that we were under orders to report our position, obtain supplies and return and he allowed us to do so when I insisted.'

Takeda wisely did not ask the nature of the petty officer's insistence.

'I reported our position to headquarters at Rabaul by wireless and asked that food, a radio and air support be given to us. They promised these would be sent and directed the local commander to supply us with a wireless and some rations. We then returned without incident. As we approached, we heard shooting and as I thought you might be the enemy, we landed here to try and find out what was happening. But the island proved too large to explore at night and we were going to wait offshore until dawn.'

The radio boosted morale to an astonishing degree. The very much relieved radio operator fiddled happily with the set, adjusting the dials, tweaking tubes and polishing the exterior and only once - under his breath - complaining about the Model 87's age.

That evening, they transmitted their first weather report. Takeda knew that enemy wireless monitoring posts would be searching for them and he timed the operator's transmission with grim impatience.

Strangely enough, there was no response. An hour passed, then two. The wireless operator suggested that atmospherics might have garbled the transmission and grudgingly, Takeda gave him permission to send their identification code.

The operator tapped out the letters three times but the speaker remained maddeningly silent.

Then, just as Takeda was about to give up for the night, a burst of code chattered from the speaker. The radio operator wrote furiously with a pencil stub and when code blocks ended, he flipped the transmit switch and tapped a single acknowledgement letter.

'Translate it,' Takeda ordered.

The operator took a small book from his blouse pocket and laboriously transcribed the message onto a single sheet of paper. It was with great difficulty that Takeda restrained himself from urging the man to hurry. He wanted to pace but to do so would suggest that he was nervous and that would never do.

When the translation was complete, what he read chilled him. The transmission had not originated from Rabi Island but from Rabaul. His original orders and their relief by Army troops had been cancelled for now. He was instructed to operate the meteorological station as long as possible - nothing about being withdrawn. Attempts would be made to supply them by air. They were to mark a landing zone and transmit its coordinates with the code AD the night before. An aircraft would make the attempt at dawn.

The message, Takeda thought, was worse for what it did not reveal than for what it did. Rabi was not mentioned once so the battle must be going badly. Secondly, they were going to attempt to supply them by air, rather than by sea. That suggested that the Americans still held the airfield on Guadalcanal. If Allied war ships were still contesting the Solomon passages there would be no destroyers to spare to relieve, or even resupply them. Thirdly, the message had provided no information on the enemy or their intentions. Was that an oversight, or did Rabaul not know?

But the intent of the message was clear enough; they must look after themselves for the time being.

The radio provided a tenuous link to Japan. In the evenings, Takeda allowed the radio operator to tune in to Tokyo and those not on duty gathered to listen to popular tunes and familiar voices from home. The effect on morale was all out of proportion to the tinny voices resounding across the forest clearing of a South Pacific island.

Takeda would never forget the thrill he felt when Mariko's voice purred through the ether. He had never heard her broadcast before and understood instantly how she had become an overnight sensation in Japan. Her voice, even over the rough loudspeaker, was low and musical and suggested a blend of classical and modern Japanese woman so perfectly that her appeal traversed the spectrum. She could be as respectful as a geisha or as searching as a newspaper journalist, but without offending.

At the end of her twice-weekly show, she read letters from mothers to sons scattered across the Empire. During this segment, she never hesitated to ask generals and government officials searching questions about the safety and well-being of soldiers and sailors. They may have found her questions uncomfortable on occasion, but so great was her popularity that none dared silence her. Mariko was the advocate of millions of mothers and soldiers and no outpost of the Empire was too remote for her voice to reach.

Takeda never told anyone of his relationship with Mariko as he did not wish to share that intimacy. Listening to her voice as she read letters, he always thought about the letter he had sent with the boats to Rabi Island. In it, he had asked his parents to approach Mariko's family about marriage.

Perhaps it was the loneliness of this command, but he thought of Mariko constantly. He could dwell for long minutes at a time on the feel of her hair against his cheek, or the touch of her hand or the softness of her body beneath the silk kimono as she had kissed him that last time. She embodied everything desirable in a woman. He imagined the shape of her body and drove himself to distraction with longing. And he cursed the peculiar mix of accepted sexual principles and traditional Japanese practices that held it perfectly proper for a man to visit a comfort girl but not to make advances to an unmarried woman.

Even if the match was acceptable to Mariko's parents, they could not marry until the war was over. He did not even expect to return to Japan until the fighting was ended and that would not occur until New Guinea was taken and its flanks secured by the Solomons and New Guinea, and then Australia and New Zealand invaded and occupied. Only then would the Americans and the British, hard pressed in the Middle East and Europe, consent to a negotiated peace on Japan's terms.

Perhaps they might then find a small house in Kadoma, near their parents. A house and children would occupy her time and energy while he was away in the Navy. Perhaps an answer from his parents would come in a supply drop, or even from Mariko herself during a broadcast. If anyone noticed the way he hung on her every word emanating from the static-filled loudspeaker, it was never mentioned.

Rain, the first indication of the approaching monsoon, pounded the island hard during the next two days and runoff turned the gorge into a cataract. The rain fell so hard that it was impossible to work. Slit trenches filled as fast as the men dug and they could not cross the swollen, raging streams. Idleness and discomfort when the temperatures plunged caused bickering and twice Takeda ordered Warrant Officer Ueda to administer physical punishments.

He was relieved when the skies cleared and the hot sun burst forth even though the island steamed in misery. At least, they could get on with their preparations for defending the island against the attack that was certain to come. At mid-morning, he heard the B-17s again. They came in low from the sea as before, but this time they circled the volcano and attacked the weather station without accomplishing any great damage. So, Takeda thought, the coastwatcher had been active during the rain, in spite of his intensive patrols. The number of men in the field left him dangerously shorthanded but the elimination or capture of the coastwatcher was first priority.

They settled into routine. The bombers came at mid-morning and sometimes their aim was good and at others bombs fell well outside the target areas – the old campsite, the weather station and the sentry posts along the southwest shore. But so far, the mysterious spy had not discovered their new camp.

The radio operator, anxious to make up for his earlier failure to protect the radio, spent every moment monitoring various frequencies. At the end of the week, he came to Takeda, grinning with excitement. He had picked up a brief burst of code at 13.65 megacycles. The signal was strong enough, he told Takeda, that it could very well be coming from the island. At his own suggestion, he built a signal generator from spare parts cannibalised from the smashed radio and tuned in to the frequency he suspected the coastwatcher was using and transmitted white noise to cover or obscure those broadcasts. From then on they noted the increasing inaccuracy of the bombers until, a week later, they stopped coming.

Takeda was never certain whether the coastwatcher had left the island or the Allied commanders had lost contact with him because of interference from the signal generator. Perhaps they had decided they had wasted enough bombs and fuel. The patrols found few enough signs of the watcher… once a sandal print of the type Europeans wore in the tropics and twice ashes from a small fire. The only man-made structure they found however was a simple lean-to on the eastern slope of the volcano, so weather-ravaged that Takeda suspected it had been constructed by a camping party long before the war.

Takeda called off the search and put the men to more productive use. Work went forward swiftly on the defences he had planned and they began to transmit weather data twice daily. There was no sense in concealing the fact of their existence any longer, he decided. The weather information was vital to the entire New Guinea position.

Their food supplies worried him the most. They had been reduced to a two-week supply after the bombing and more and more men were being diverted to hunt or gather what few edible plants could be found. Fishing, the most lucrative source of food, could only be done at night because of the constant danger from marauding aircraft. A small amount of medical supplies also remained and when the quinine was finished, malaria would strike them harder than the enemy.

The island did support a small herd of wild goats they discovered. The animals appeared well-fed but their flesh had a gamey taste that many of the men found inedible. But as the last stores of rice dwindled, and palm heart and fish, baked or grilled, grew too monotonous to bear, he knew they would eat it.

The invasion began on 20 October 1942. A fishing party spotted the Australian force just before dawn.

'One destroyer which unloaded a battalion, sir. I counted at least six hundred men. And landing craft brought three field pieces ashore.'

In the three weeks they had spent on the island, Takeda had compiled a detailed terrain map. Chief Petty Officer Tanaka, who had been in charge of the fishing party, indicated that the enemy was coming ashore on the western side of the island where the savannah rose gradually from the beach onto the volcano's slopes. Takeda approved of the choice; it was one he would have picked himself. The grass grew chest high and there was little natural cover for defenders to use other than a few gullies and stream beds.

His own camp could only be approached up the gorge unless one was willing to climb the volcano's opposite slope, cross over and descend from above. In which case, they had only to take cover in the gorge which was nearly a kilometre long and in several places was forty metres deep. A stream also meandered along the bottom and made walking difficult.

Because an attempt to approach the camp via the gorge would be tantamount to suicide, dominated as it was by two mortars and one of their two machine guns, he felt secure enough against serious attack from that direction.

Takeda took a deep breath and was surprised to find how eager he was to test the enemy. This was what he had been trained for, what he enjoyed the most – outwitting one's enemy, as he had in Manchuko, on Bird Island and again on Timor. He examined his assumptions a final time and found no flaws in his reasoning. In fact, the enemy had already confirmed his plan by landing on the open savannah. He could expect the field guns to support their advance, then be used to shell his camp when they came within range – providing they could manhandle them up the gorge. The only unknown quantity was air support from New Guinea – how much and how effective? Confident that he could hold out if he received sufficient food, medical supplies and ammunition, he transmitted a warning to Rabaul and once more requested supplies and reinforcements.

A shallow ravine cut across the savannah. Ordinarily, it would not prove a hindrance to non-mechanised infantry, but Takeda had decided to make it his first defence line against an Australian move inland. He had sited his last mortar and the second machine gun to dominate it at its shallowest point and had dug man-traps furnished with pungi sticks – sharpened stakes – on either side. He did not expect to stop the Australians here, only to slow them up.

His company had suffered casualties of almost one third and so were reduced to 197 effectives. The sixty-five seriously wounded or sick were truly damaged goods for whom he could do little but move them higher on the slopes away from the gorge.

The rest of the force he reorganised, combining the five platoons into three and redistributing the remaining mortars, two machine guns and ammunition and the last of the food and medical supplies. The first platoon, under Senior Warrant Officer Ueda, would hold the gorge. He would lead the second himself and Chief Petty Officer Tanaka would command the third platoon and be responsible for striking the advancing enemy on the flank.

Accordingly, he ordered Tanaka to assemble his force and move to the first designated strike point in the grasslands where he judged the Australians would gather to drive against his line on the ravine.

Takeda scouted the enemy shore positions himself. The numbers and disposition of their troops were the key to his tactics and he could not trust the task to anyone else. The Australians had established a defensive perimeter a hundred metres into the savannah. On the beach, enemy troops scurried to unload supplies and ammunition from two landing craft while a third was en route from a destroyer a thousand metres offshore, one of the *Scott* class belonging to the Royal Australian Navy. They mounted, as he recalled, two four-point-seven inch, one three-inch, and two two-pounder pompoms as well as twenty millimetre Oerlikons.

The large guns had a range of seventeen thousand metres, which meant that they could furnish supporting fire anywhere on the island except in the remote interior $_{2}$ and that included the gorge! So, there had been another reason why the Australians had selected the savannah for their landing. Particular attention would have to be paid to neutralising artillery observers.

At midday, the Australians began to move inland in force. They were organised, according to scouting reports, into two parties $_{2}$ the larger heading inland to the volcano as he had anticipated, the other moving along the beach towards the gorge. They were both, he thought with satisfaction, in for a surprise.

The main party had only a single field gun while the smaller party had two. Clearly, he thought, they were depending on the destroyer's guns to shield their beachhead. Better than he had hoped. In effect then, the entire north shore was relatively safe given the inherent inaccuracy of naval guns over long distances without direct fire control.

Takeda reached Petty Officer Tanaka's position at 1300 hours. The overcast had cleared off and the sun baked them in the high grass. His nostrils filled with pollen and dust, and skin irritation added to his apprehension so that he found himself snapping angrily at the least interruption. It was strange, he thought, how later one never remembers the discomfort of campaigning, the heat, thirst, hunger, irritated skin, the stench of unwashed uniforms and bodies and flies, everything that made one's life so miserable. One only remembered the fatigue and the fear, and sometimes the excitement.

Takeda checked the machine gun's field of fire and the placement of the mortar, and fretted at the Australians' slowness. They had, he thought, the look of men experienced in combat. Their equipment was worn and their uniforms dirty and he suspected they had been withdrawn from the fighting on New Guinea especially to recapture this island. From where, he wondered? Buna was closest but they could also have come from Port Moresby.

By 1500 hours, the Australians still had not appeared. Takeda sent out a scout who returned an hour later to report that they had halted only a few thousand metres past their beachhead and dug in. He had counted three Bren guns, five mortars and two field pieces. Takeda sent a messenger to Warrant Officer Ueda on the cliffs above the gorge and rethought his tactics.

When night finally swept in from the Pacific, it did so with the swiftness that never failed to surprise him. He had spent the endless afternoon scouting the Australian positions and working out his plan. The training of the Special Naval Landing Forces emphasised stealth and night movement and he intended to make use of both. The ring of grinning faces visible in the moonlight told him the men were as anxious as he to come to grips with the enemy.

For a moment, Takeda felt the sense of expectancy he had first experienced in Manchuko during the long minutes in which the communist bandits had ridden down the valley to the river, and again in those final moments before the night attack on the Timorean village. At such times, he told himself, there was no other profession in the world like that of a soldier.

Only one word was needed, softly spoken, 'Go.'

They had stripped to shirts and trousers, bayonet, rifle and grenades. The twenty men chosen from his squad spread out and eased forward through the grass. Listening hard, Takeda could hear nothing above the trade winds. The grass waved in the moonlight, as much from the trades as their passage and they circled to approach from downwind.

It took forty minutes to cross the half kilometre of open ground to the first Australian trenches, from which they could hear the muted conversation of the enemy. Takeda smelled the ripe, Western smell of whites on the night breeze, the rank odour of tobacco and the peculiar stench of people who ate too much meat.

He signalled for a halt and waited, listening, trying to gauge the enemy's mood. Were they relaxed? Tense? Expectant? Were they aware of an enemy moving towards them? Five minutes went by, ten. He knew he could depend on his sailors to stay motionless until dawn, if need be. It was up to him only to judge the proper moment. Takeda shifted slightly and eased a hand grenade from the pouch strapped to the small of his back.

Rather than a flare, the attack signal was to be an exploding grenade. He eased the pin out slowly, held the handle down and squeezed hard to mute the small click as it started against the striker.

He double-checked behind to make certain that his silhouette would be hidden by the dark mass of grass rising towards the volcano and carefully pulled the safety pin and struck the fuse a sharp blow with his hand, got to his knees, drew back his arm and, with the skill developed by hours of baseball at the Naval Academy, hurled it towards the spot where he was certain a machine gun was located.

He heard it bounce once, twice and someone swore. The night flared with the grenade's savage crack and he had the impression of twenty more arcing forward. Explosions shattered the night and they raced forward with fixed bayonets. Surprise was complete and only sporadic rifle fire met them. They dropped into the Australian trenches and killed the dazed survivors.

It was over in seconds. Takeda blew his whistle and sailors streamed from the trenches running awkwardly beneath the burden of a Bren gun and its ammunition chests. Only a few shots were fired directly at them, the rest going wild as tracers scattered the night sky and mortar explosions thumped in every direction.

Takeda had been counting his paces. At five hundred, he blew his whistle again and the platoon went to ground. Swiftly, the Bren was set up and charged. His mortar team opened fire. Silhouettes of charging Australians were seen against the sky and the Bren, coupled with enfilading fire from Tanaka's platoon, cut them down. Every fifth Bren round had been loaded with tracer and Takeda saw the gunner walk the bursts of bullets across the open ground. Shouts and curses reached them and again he blew the recall signal as the first artillery shell screamed down.

Enemy bombers came in low at dawn, while high up in the sun fighters circled waiting to pounce whenever a ground target showed. Takeda smiled. Perhaps we cannot win, he told himself, but we can make them pay dearly.

The bomber stream split in two as it approached the island, one group heading for the area of the old camp where hundreds of fat bulbs skittered from open bomb bays to send great clouds of flame and black smoke rolling skyward.

So that is napalm? he thought. He had read an intelligence report in Sasebo that had described the new weapon as a mixture of gasoline, oil and a resin that caused the mixture to cling wherever it touched and burn with a fierce flame.

The second group of bombers turned west and flew directly over the Australian beachhead. The same kind of napalm bombs began to fall ahead of the Australian defence line across the savannah. Smoke and flame billowed and the dry grass blazed. The trades swept the line of flame generally east and Takeda, from his position on the volcano slope three kilometres to the north, watched the fire burn away the grassy cover. But someone had miscalculated for now the Australians had a burned-out stretch two kilometres wide to cross, under fire from his mortar and machine guns.

At mid-afternoon, the messenger returned with Ueda's report. The Australians had entered the gorge and he had given them a bloody nose at the cost of six dead and five wounded. They had withdrawn, almost to the beach again. There was, Takeda knew, no need to warn Ueda against the return of the enemy bombers. He too would have seen the napalm. Takeda could depend on him to withdraw whenever a bombing seemed imminent and then return to his positions before the Australians resumed the attack.

The bombers returned just at sunset. Takeda was moving the combined platoons towards the site selected for the night's ambush when the familiar roar of massed engines filtered through the trees. The ground vibrated and he guessed that bombs were falling, probably along the line of the gorge to ferret out Ueda's troops. None were diverted towards the savannah this time.

Surprisingly, the Australians had not moved from their positions all day, instead sending out small patrols in an attempt to locate Takeda's force. Their lack of aggressiveness made him think that the Australians had no more stomach for fighting than had the Americans, or the Dutch. He had given strict instructions that all contact was to be avoided and had carefully kept his force out of their path. Only a few scouts had been left in the vicinity, well-hidden in spider holes.

The man on Takeda's left hissed and pointed. Across the shallow watercourse, a figure moved forward in the moonlight. Takeda raised the flare pistol as more figures emerged cautiously from the grass. When the majority were in the sandy bed, he fired. The flare rocketed across the open space to burst against a rock and a withering blast of rifle fire hammered the Australians while the 7.7 millimetre machine gun and the .303 calibre Bren concentrated on the chest-high grass.

The Australians fell back and Takeda poised the whistle. Concussion punched his ears. Three more explosions in quick succession and he heard the express train roar of large calibre artillery rounds tear the sky apart.

This time the Australians had anticipated his ambush – his shouts could not be heard above the exploding shells and he ran down the line, kicking men up and shoving them into motion as the area in advance of the ravine became an inferno of exploding steel. To his left, he saw that Tanaka's position was under bombardment as well.

Dawn found them in rocks midway up the volcano's southwestern slope. Takeda watched the Australians moving forward in an extended skirmish line, tiny figures gliding through the grass. From this vantage point, he could even see the destroyer and the beachhead. The ship lay on the dark sea like a toy yacht and he cursed the Australians, but at the same time admired their tactics and perception. They were a far different breed from the Americans or the Dutch.

They had not waited behind their defensive line out of fear, but only long enough to concentrate sufficient forces and establish their artillery. And they had read his dispositions and planned accordingly. A hint of movement on the right of the line caught his attention and he focussed his glasses carefully. One of his riflemen raised himself above the level of the grass and fired. An Australian soldier twisted and disappeared. The rifleman bent low and trotted away at a sharp angle as nearby Australian troops poured fire into the area he had just vacated. The sniper covering force began to fall back when it was clear the Australians would not be drawn.

His squad and Tanaka's combined had numbered 125 men when they moved down to the beach two nights before. They had suffered four killed in the first attack and twenty-three missing after last night's artillery barrage. Ueda now commanded a total of fifty-four, plus the badly wounded on the volcano. Since dawn, Takeda had kept two ten-man patrols pacing the Australian lines to harass them with sniper fire and they had slowed the enemy somewhat, but not enough to prevent their steady progress. They would cross the five kilometre-wide savannah by noon. And he could see reinforcements moving out of the beachhead.

Takeda felt his confidence ebbing. The Australians now outnumbered them three-to-one and had plenty of food and ammunition, while he had to make do with the few rations that remained to them, supplemented by meagre caches of dried goat's meat and fish. Twice more since the Australian landing, he had radioed for the promised food and supplies and both times, excuses had been given. His ammunition was running low and the last of the Brens had been fired that morning.

At 1000 hours, the destroyer opened fire again. The 4.7 inch guns ranged the slope below them according to a pattern he could not detect, then shifted south and west to concentrate on the gorge which Ueda was holding. No bombers today? Were the Australians beginning to feel the strain of supporting a battalion-sized operation for so small an objective?

At noon, he moved his force higher up the slope and into the trees, then headed diagonally towards a shoulder of rock that gave way to a small valley that led into the island's interior. Takeda called a halt at 1500 hours and as soon as the guard was set he spread a blanket beneath a tree. He hadn't managed more than a snatched hour or so of sleep since the enemy landing and he was dizzy with fatigue. He closed his eyes and shielded them with his field cap. The quiet rustle of the sailors settling down, the occasional clink of a rifle barrel and muttered oaths at the rocky ground soon gave way to silence.

The hot sun burned through the forest canopy and enfolded him in a red haze in which it was impossible to know whether he was asleep or awake, alive or dead. But as tired as he was, his mind refused to give way, summoning up instead a hazy memory of Mariko's features which he could not bring into focus. Strangely enough, everything that had happened to him before the island had receded behind that same gauzy haze. It was simply a matter of hunger and exhaustion, he told himself, and not important. But it was and tonight Mariko would broadcast. He wanted so badly to hear her voice again that a wave of homesickness swept him.

Would he ever marry Mariko now, he wondered, or see his father again? How strange that an entire life could be dispensed with so easily. The things that mattered to him would end when he was dead. Those who knew him would continue their lives. They would honour his memory, perhaps daily at first, then on special days and, finally, he would be forgotten for months or years at a time.

Takeda was not an introspective man. Military training did not encourage such a useless pursuit and, because of that, the thoughts revolving in his head were all the more frightening. Certainly, he had faced the possibility of death many times before, if never with such certainty. But those moments had occurred in battle or in training exercises when there was no time to think of the consequences. All his training, for nearly twenty-five years, had taught him that to die for the Emperor was the soldier's most noble act. He had never questioned that concept and did not now. What he did do was to think about death and its ultimate effect – the cessation of consciousness and participation. He suddenly realised that whenever he had thought about death, it had been a mental exercise, truly idle speculation during which he had avoided too close an exploration for fear of what he might find within himself. He was not inclined to do so now but his mind would not let go. If only I could sleep, he thought with longing approaching despair.

Beyond the self-evident acknowledgement of the Emperor's divinity, Takeda was not a religious man. Tao, which in the strict sense was not a religion but a philosophy, told him to 'Empty yourself of everything. Let the mind rest at peace.' If only he could . . .

Someone touched his shoulder and he opened his eyes to darkness, then sat up in astonishment. He had dozed away the afternoon, dreaming that endless monologue!

'Commander Takeda . . . ?' It was too dark to see the sailor's face.

'Commander Takeda,' he repeated. 'I am Superior Private Wantanabee. I have come to report that the enemy has taken the main camp.'

Takeda jumped to his feet, struggling to throw off the confusion of sleep. 'When?' he demanded.

'At mid-afternoon. The enemy destroyer shelled the cliffs. We took cover as usual to wait for the barrage to stop and while we did so, the enemy attacked us from the flanks. Warrant Officer Ueda sent me to report. I do not think there were any other survivors.'

Takeda strove to keep his expression calm, to contain the horror within himself. Ueda and all his men gone in one afternoon? He could not believe it. Fifty-six men? How seriously he had underestimated the Australians whose next move was now inevitable – they would divide their forces in three; one to hold the beachhead, one to occupy Takeda's camp to deny it to him and the rest to hunt them through the jungle-clad slopes and valleys in relays so that they could never rest.

They moved down into the valley twenty minutes later, carrying only essential food, ammunition, weapons, water bottles and a minimum of clothing. Low in the southwest Takeda heard the rumble of thunder and knew the monsoon rains were only days away. It remained to be seen whether the rains would help or hinder them.

They left all the damaged goods behind in the temporary camp on the volcano's slope, including the man from Ueda's command who had lost too much blood to go on. Those who could walk watched them go, then turned and trudged back to the caves and rocks from which they would make their final stand.

Each man knew they would die before noon and each had voluntarily given up his food ration so that the others could continue to fight. Before marching out, they had assembled and solemnly saluted the doomed men. Their memories, Takeda had promised them, would be revered in Japan as long as the Empire endured.

The sun burned through the morning overcast quickly to torture the line of men weighted with packs of forty kilograms or more as they stumbled and slid across the scree slope. The only noise they made came from laboured grunting and boots striking the stony, hard-packed earth.

Takeda's pack had been improvised from a duffle bag and rifle slings and it dragged painfully against his shoulders. The narrow leather straps cut into the flesh between shoulder and collar bone to produce an exquisite pain made worse because there was no way to bind the duffle bag tight enough against his back to keep it from shifting. Sweat poured into his eyes nearly blinding him and he could only stumble along in a haze of overpowering light, pain and heat.

They marched throughout the endless, breathless day, wrapped in oppressive humidity, pausing once an hour for five minutes' rest. As the sun moved towards mid-afternoon, it burned through the sparse canopy and par-boiled them in the wet air. At this altitude, water was scarce and they were forced to ration themselves, which only added to their misery.

The distant sound of the single fighter aircraft hunting them was obscured by the drone of bombers and they stopped to listen. The aircraft were behind and high up and the trees hid them in any event. At least a dozen, Takeda thought as the first explosions became one long rumble and even at this distance the ground quivered beneath their feet, gently, like the first tremors of an earthquake.

For a moment, Takeda was reminded of the great earthquake of 1924 which had nearly destroyed Tokyo. In Kadoma, his father had soothed away his fears with tales of a gentle, sleeping giant who snored loudly.

Only later had he learned how devastating the gentle giant had been.

He turned to face the slope which they had just crossed. The damned Australians had called in bombers to ferret out the fifty or more wounded soldiers in shallow caves and holes. He closed his eyes, but only for a moment. It was the duty of soldiers to die in battle, he reminded himself. By doing so those men had delayed the enemy force long enough to allow the remainder of the company to escape. The circumstances of death made little difference as long as it was accompanied by honour. His wounded sailors were certainly dying with honour.

They crossed the high ridge that separated the southern half of the island from the more rugged north and began the long descent towards the rain forest. As they did so, the trees and undergrowth thinned until by evening they faced a wide strip of grassland.

In some ways this was worse than the jungle-like growth they had encountered on Timor. The grass was chest- to head-high and saw-edged and cut the unwary like a knife. Within a hundred metres they were covered with dozens of shallow cuts that stung like fire. They learned quickly to wrap their hands and forearms with their shirts and use their rifles like a ship's prow to push the grass aside so that the sharp edges faced away. Still, the grass impeded their progress and each stalk seemed home to a thousand ants and other insects and clouds of mosquitoes and flies worried them, trailing each man like miniature storm clouds.

It was essential they reach the cover of the forest that fringed the eastern and northern coasts before dawn when the search aircraft would return. Takeda drove them on during the long, dark night as a new overcast flowed in from the south and obscured the sky with a solid blanket. Even the nearly full moon was hidden, its light reduced to a bare pearlescent glow.

Just at dawn, they left the open grasslands for the gloom of the forest and the first drops of rain spattered tentatively. Takeda glanced up as the others filed past and, like them, his opinion was divided. The rain would hide them from Australian aircraft but at the same time it would increase their misery. He had been suffering alternating bouts of fever-induced shivering and heat since late afternoon and suspected that it was malaria. For the last few hours only sheer determination had kept them going, but Takeda was now at the end of his endurance.

They collapsed where he halted them, some falling asleep instantly, too exhausted to raise their shelter halves. To those who remained awake, Takeda passed permission to drink and eat $_2$ a swallow of water, two pieces of dried goat, a handful of cooked, dried rice.

With his shelter half rigged as a slanting canopy against the rain, Takeda lay against his pack and endured the agony of shoulders reduced to raw meat by the improvised straps, even though he had torn a spare shirt taken from one of the dead into strips for padding. I'm getting old, he told himself and thought about those around him.

Without exception, all were younger than he, although he was in excellent shape and had always disciplined himself in the strictest manner to overcome what he recognised as his essentially lazy nature. He routinely participated in hand-to-hand combat drills and no one in the company had ever bested him at ju-jitsu. And only Warrant Officer Ueda could beat him with a combat knife – had been able to beat him.

Takeda shivered and thought about Ueda. They had been together since he had assumed command of the company in early 1940. Indochina, Manchuko, Bird Island and Timor; Ueda had been there with him as had the majority of the company, many now dead.

Takeda pushed away such useless thoughts. There was no room, and no occasion for nostalgic memories. They had died in the best of all causes, to free Asia from the domination of the white races that had ruled far too long. For four hundred years the whites had raped and pillaged and oppressed, taking the best and deluding themselves and most of the world into believing that it was their birthright.

Wasn't Australia the perfect example; a vast continent of land and resources badly needed by Asians but occupied by a mere handful of Europeans who proclaimed it 'for whites only'? It was obscene that Asians should starve while ninety per cent of Australia remained empty. Malaya was another example; why should Malaya's rubber go to Europe when it was so badly needed in Asia? But changes were taking place and to his great regret, he was only playing a minor – no, less than minor – role.

Takeda awoke at sunset to find his entire body trembling with fever. His eyelids were stuck together with rheum and he had to wet his fingers to soften the crusts and peel them apart. He had never felt so exhausted in his life, nor in so much pain. Rain drummed against the shelter half and the ground had turned soggy beneath his blanket, like a vast sponge, and soaked him to the skin.

He used rain water to soften the clotted blood in the raw sores on his shoulders where the steep path and uneven terrain had shifted the improvised pack until it had smeared skin away like a giant eraser. Then he woke the petty officers and ordered a sparse breakfast of the nauseous goat's meat.

Afterwards, Takeda eased the pack onto his shoulders and grunting with pain, stood up and waited for the shock to raw nerve endings to ease. When it did, he groped blindly for the rope ends he had secured to the bottom of the duffle bag and tied them around his waist. The pack rode higher, easing the pain somewhat and he got them all moving, noticing that he was not the only one shivering.

*

Rifle fire!

Takeda woke instantly. Two more shots in the distance and the sound of running feet. A shout, more shots and silence.

Petty Officer Tanaka loomed up in the dark. 'Enemy scouts, sir. They attacked one of our sentries but we killed them both.'

With what seemed to require a supreme effort of will, Takeda got to his feet, appalled that he had slept the night through thus placing his burden on subordinates. He ordered a scouting party to sweep the area for the main Australian force, although he was certain that they were far ahead of them.

They had eaten the last of the dried goat the night before and so a handful of rice and a piece of dried fish served for breakfast – far too little to maintain their level of exertion much longer.

As dawn began to filter light through the monsoon clouds, he studied his map. At least the rain kept enemy aircraft activity to a minimum and the periodic downpours obscured their trail. They were unable to dry their clothing and equipment now and skin diseases had appeared almost overnight – fungus rots, sores, carbuncles, boils – and more malaria cases by the dozen. All were affected with diarrhoea and dysentery to some degree. Takeda had ordered them all to cut the uppers from their boots to make sandals but it did little good. The macerated soles of their feet made walking excruciatingly painful, yet they marched at least ten kilometres every day to stay ahead of the pursuing Australians.

Takeda's shoulders were healing but so slowly it was hard to notice progress. On the third day of the march when Tanaka had reported the men assembled, he had stifled a groan and reached for his pack only to find it gone. He turned to see it slung over the shoulder of a young private. Surprised, he reached for it but the boy pulled away. Tanaka hurried up.

'The men have distributed the weight among themselves, sir,' he said quickly, fear evident in his voice at this presumption. 'You cannot possibly carry that pack any longer, sir,' he almost whispered. 'Your shoulders . . .'

'Please, sir,' the private interjected, 'let us do this.'

Takeda did not know how to react. His first inclination was anger. Did they think him incapable of carrying his share of the burden? But an inner voice warned him that there was a difference between pride and foolishness, that the Emperor could not possibly be offended if he did not carry the pack today, especially as his shoulders were raw meat. Yet if he allowed it, wasn't he admitting his weakness?

Tanaka sensed his indecision and clinched it, 'If you are incapacitated, sir, who will lead us in our duty?' Takeda hesitated a moment longer, then nodded, ashamed of the relief he felt.

A stifling silence lay over the island, broken only by occasional bird calls, the rattle of insects and the monotonous drip of rain. In late morning, a scout unexpectedly brought in two men, survivors of the fighting at the gorge.

After they were given water and food, one was able to describe what had happened. 'The enemy opened fire with cannon but Warrant Officer Ueda had made us dig deep slit trenches. Then the bombers came and we withdrew as planned while they dropped their gasoline bombs. Only three men in the most forward positions were killed, burned to death in their trenches. When the bombers left, we started to move back into our positions but the enemy struck at us from across the slopes in concert with the naval guns. They caught us in the open and the fighting was hand-to-hand and very fierce. I was struck down from behind and knocked unconscious. When I woke, it was dark. All around me were bodies, our comrades and the enemy as well. I heard voices that I could not understand and saw lights. I was able to crawl away without being seen.

'In the morning I hid in the trees and that night I started for the food cache on the north shore. I was in the party that had placed it and I thought that sooner or later you would come. On the way, I found Private Osano. I think he is mad, but he did as I told him and . . .' The man broke down at this point and could not go on.

The horror of what had happened at the gorge was etched in Private Osano's face and it was clear that he was verging on madness, if not completely insane. His eyes darted continuously from face to face, yet he shrank from the slightest human contact. His lips worked oddly but only incoherent mumbles resulted.

During the next week, the survivors of the Sasebo Sixth Special Naval Landing Force Company lived a furtive existence as the Australians, as hampered by the rain as they, kept the pressure on. They moved constantly from dawn to dusk, growing weaker and weaker as their food supply dwindled. One day, Private Osano disappeared. They were better off, Takeda knew. Osano had taken to singing at the top of his lungs day and night as the spirit moved him, and more than once they had had to tie and gag him.

Takeda did not dare attempt another ambush, especially after the loss of twelve more men, four who simply died in their sleep and the others from a combination of starvation, disease and exhaustion. Then too, the retreat seemed to have settled into a routine that provided a precarious sense of stability, however treacherous, which he dared not destroy.

They marched from dawn to midday with three thirty-minute breaks, then again until an hour before dark. He had issued orders for everyone to keep a sharp eye open for edible plants and they had found a few yams and some breadfruit trees, part of a garden perhaps, planted by natives from New Guinea before the war.

Takeda resumed their weather reporting schedule in spite of the danger that the Australians might fix their position exactly. The broadcasts gave them a sense of purpose and their constant movement minimised the risk of pinpointing their location. Twice they were able to send coded reports of enemy aircraft and ship movements in Milne Bay. They had been forced to abandon the heavy voice transmitter and loudspeakers, and Takeda found it especially hard to end that connection with home, and Mariko.

At the end of the second week of monsoon rains, the radio operator's gaunt face split in a wide grin. He wrote furiously, translating the code groups from memory, batted the key to acknowledge the transmission and triumphantly handed Takeda the message. A submarine would attempt to bring supplies and remove the sick the following night. Takeda made the announcement with care, not wanting to raise hopes in case the mission failed. Then, in accordance with instructions, they made their way to the coast and mounted a lookout above the shallow cove that had been given as the rendezvous point. In spite of Takeda's desperate pessimism, the submarine surfaced only three hours behind schedule. For once it was not raining and the sky had partly cleared, allowing thin moonlight through.

Takeda made the proper signal with a torch and ten minutes later a rubber dinghy breasted the low breakers and two sailors vaulted out to drag it onto the beach. A young officer in white dress uniform stepped out and Takeda went forward to meet him, conscious that he was barefoot in tattered trousers hacked off with a knife and a filthy, damp shirt. The young officer and the two sailors with him looked indecently healthy when they shone their electric torches around.

The officer introduced himself as Lieutenant Tamura, first officer of the submarine I-15. 'We have brought presents from Rabaul,' he grinned and motioned for the sailors to unload the dinghy. Takeda's sailors crowded forward, eager to help while Tamura ticked off the items.

'Canned and fresh vegetables but mostly rations. Water purification tablets and medicine for diarrhoea, fungus disease and malaria. I apologise that there are no boots or uniforms but they would have taken up too much space. We have also brought ammunition for rifles and your machine guns.'

'Please keep the machine gun ammunition,' Takeda told him. 'We had to bury our last one several days ago. We will survive now only by avoiding the enemy.'

Takeda was desperate for news and pumped Tamura mercilessly and, while the twenty-eight sickest men were ferried out to I-15, they squatted on the beach and talked.

'Our forces have been beaten back from the attack on Port Moresby,' Tamura told him, 'with heavy casualties. The Kokoda Trail was worse than anyone expected and it was impossible to provide sufficient supplies. The enemy have completely surrounded our forces at Buna who are holding a defensive line along the Kumusi River. For how much longer, no one knows.'

Tamura was silent a moment as if gauging Takeda's capacity for bad news. 'The Army has violated every principle of sensible warfare with the Buna operation,' he went on. 'They knew from the beginning that simultaneous air cover for operations at Buna and Port Moresby was impossible.'

Takeda remembered the bitterness expressed during his briefing in Tokyo when the question of air cover in New Guinea and the Solomon Islands was raised.

'Heavy reinforcements from the Seventeenth Army were landed on Guadalcanal at the beginning of September to attack the airfield there, and it should fall soon. I am to tell you that all Guadalcanal operations will take priority over those on New Guinea and so you will be withdrawn.'

Takeda felt relief course through him. He took a deep, shuddering breath. So, he would have his chance to fight for the Empire again, to accomplish something useful after all.

'When?' But he sensed rather than saw Tamura's shrug.

'Soon I would expect. There are rumours that all forces available in the area will be sent to Guadalcanal. Apparently, Imperial Headquarters is annoyed at the army's delay. I have heard that the Americans have only three or four thousand men on the island but of course, possession of the airfield enables them to maintain local air superiority. The rumours say that the Americans have driven tanks across some of our soldiers to execute them,' Tamura said bitterly. 'They are savages . . .

'Once Guadalcanal is captured,' he went on after taking a deep breath, 'our own aircraft will use the island to chase the Americans completely out of the Solomons as we should have done in the beginning. Then we can turn our full attention back to the New Guinea operations.' Tamura dismissed the problems of land combat as only a sea-going naval officer could.

But Takeda, as both a naval and land officer, was not as sanguine about the outcome on Guadalcanal. The key to island fighting, he had discovered was airpower, particularly land based air power which could strike at will. Japanese bombers could reach Guadalcanal and bomb American positions, but without fighter cover they were easy targets for American fighters based on the island.

He questioned Tamura assiduously and learned that naval units based on Bougainville and in the Shortlands, were attempting to run reinforcements and supplies into the Seventeenth Army on Guadalcanal. But they had to operate at night as the Americans maintained a carrier task force in the area. Tamura described how I-15 had escorted one convoy the week before.

'We sailed from Bougainville at 1700 hours and ran at full speed for Guadalcanal. At 2200 hours we received word that a large American warship had been spotted south of Savo Island. We approached on the surface and fired two torpedoes, both of which struck. It was an American cruiser and she sank the next day.' He showed Takeda a dog-eared photograph. The photo was blurry in detail but the burning American ship, a light cruiser Takeda guessed, could be seen in silhouette, listing heavily.

The sick were all aboard I-15 an hour before dawn and Tamura clasped Takeda's hand, then stepped back, bowed and Takeda watched as the dinghy was swallowed up by darkness. Ten minutes later he heard the dull throb of a diesel engine and saw a brief flash of white spume. He had never felt so alone.

In the days following the submarine's departure, no new orders came for them, even though they monitored their assigned frequency every night. Takeda was able to interpret enough of the cryptic, coded signals to other units in the Solomons or on New Guinea to guess that the Americans had forced a stalemate in the area. It seemed to him that as land fighting died down on New Guinea, naval action increased throughout the Solomons. The rations I-15 brought had heartened them all but the debilitating fever and the constant shivering attendant on malaria, which persisted in spite of the quinine, were the greatest morale-destroyers Takeda had ever encountered.

As day followed day and the Australian troops increased the pressure and their supplies ran low again, Takeda realised they were coming to the end of their endurance. The enemy had discovered their last food cache and they had almost walked into an ambush. As it was, Takeda lost seven more men and four badly wounded. His command was now reduced to fifty-six effectives out of the 297 who had sailed from Rabaul.

Although the quinine kept the worst effects of the malaria at bay, two thirds of the other medical supplies brought by the submarine had proven to be common aspirin that had been mislabelled. He repeatedly requested an air drop but they were again being ignored by Eight Fleet Headquarters and Takeda concluded that Tokyo had written them off. He himself was barely able to function now. His feet were so macerated that he could barely hobble. The skin was puffy, wrinkled and black and, in spite of the quinine, he shivered with fever most of the time.

They found a cave high up on the volcano's northeast slope which provided a clear view of the grasslands sweeping down to the beach and the heavy forest to the north. For the first time since the rains began, they were able to build fires and dry their clothes. Takeda, naked and warm, was almost insensible with the sheer luxury of their position. The cave was small and smelled of must and animal droppings and other litter, but that was a small price to pay for warmth and shelter against monsoon rains which fell eighteen hours out of every twenty-four.

They had crossed a swollen river to reach the slope and been forced to wade through a kilometre of swamp. It had taken a long time to tease the last of the leeches from his legs and torso with the smouldering end of a twig and the annoying pain of their bite was just beginning to bother him.

The radio operator had run his antenna wire up to the tree that screened the cave mouth and was sitting hunched before the fire with headphones pressed against his ears. Takeda's head nodded and he jerked himself awake. He didn't dare sleep before the food was served out or he would lose his share.

The radio operator sat bolt upright, then began to scribble a message in the dirt of the cave floor. He listened again, pulled the earphones away and Takeda saw that his face was transfigured with shock and astonishment. Tears ran down his cheeks and his mouth worked without producing coherent sound.

He got himself under control and spoke hoarsely. 'Commander Takeda, the cruiser *Tenryu* will stand in tomorrow night to take us off. We are being withdrawn!'

At first Takeda could not understand what he was saying. The men began to gather around, faces expressing disbelief and shock. Then someone cheered as the message penetrated and the cave resounded to their shouts and laughter. The *Tenryu*. What a coincidence! They knew her well as she had protected them off Bird Island.

'They wish us to acknowledge,' the radio operator made himself heard over the din. 'They want to know how many survivors there will be and if we will need medical assistance.'

Takeda took a deep and shaky breath. 'Tell them,' he whispered, 'tell them fifty-six survivors, all with malaria, starvation, skin diseases . . .' He swallowed against tears, trying to control his relief and happiness. 'Also, transmit our daily weather report.' That would show them in Rabaul, he thought, that they were still the Sixth Naval Landing Force and they could do their duty no matter how difficult the circumstances. Yet, he remained conscious of a heavy sense of failure.

They moved to the designated area on the coast the following evening. Their elation after the announcement had burned itself out quickly, leaving them all weaker and more exhausted than ever. As they prepared for the final march, one sailor had curled into a foetal position. Takeda had seen this happen too many times before and knew the man had simply given up. He swallowed his contempt. How cowardly, he thought.

Takeda was very near the end himself. For endless weeks he had striven to keep up their morale, to outdo them all in endurance, to bully and hector and keep them going, knowing that if he allowed them to rest too long in one place they would never rise again. Every day at morning prayers, he harangued them on their duty to the Empire, knowing they had nothing else to live for.

Although he had long sensed the terrible toll of that burden, he had never thought to reach the point where it would be easier to die than live. Even though he had dedicated his life to the service of the Emperor, he had come to think of death as something desirable, a state that would bring an end to exhaustion, pain and despair. But honour dictated that he continue to struggle to the bitter end and honour was duty and duty was the glue that held the Japanese nation together.

He stumbled and half fell, catching himself barely in time. He staggered on a few steps before the edge of panic sliced into his mind. He had no idea where he was! They had re-entered the forest, jungle was a more appropriate description, and he was lost. In the half light of early evening, dark growth pressed in on him. Rain dripped incessantly from the trees far above his head and soaked them once again and set them to shivering in spite of the moist heat that suffused the atmosphere.

They were sloshing through a shallow swamp created by the monsoon rains. The sandals he had made by cutting away his boots were nearly worn and rotted through. A bootlace he had used to tie them on so long ago that he could no longer remember, broke for the final time and he left one behind. He had neither the strength to search for it or to fashion a new thong.

Takeda fumbled his compass open and struggled to make sense of the erratically swinging needle in the poor light. Then the confusion disappeared as abruptly as it had come the moment he oriented himself. They were, he discovered, marching away from the beach. It was growing so difficult to concentrate... his mind tended to wander away at the slightest provocation...

The beach, when they broke through, was welcome after the dank, tangled recesses of the forest, even though the rain, coupled with a hard wind blowing off the sea, chilled them terribly. Takeda stood to one side and counted the men as they emerged from the trees.

Like him, all were worse than scarecrows, but every man still carried his weapon. In the waning light, he saw protruding ribs and shoulder blades. Uniforms were nonexistent and most, like him, wore only a loin cloth to preserve a bit of modesty. He had made his from his shirt after it had split up the back and the sleeves had rotted under the arms.

He had discarded his trousers when they too had rotted away. The sores on his shoulders and chest, caused by the makeshift pack so many weeks before, had never healed and had festered badly. At times, he thought he could smell the rot and wondered if they had not become gangrenous. But some of the men were much worse off than he in that respect and others were completely naked.

Anything made of leather had turned green with mould and rifle slings had rotted. Cartridge pouches had been thrown away and the cartridges carried in pockets or cloth bags, because in the stifling heat and humidity the brass cases reacted with tannic acid in the leather and formed copper sulphate, or verdigris. Unless the sticky substance was cleaned off before the cartridge was fired, it baked to a hard deposit and welded the cartridge case into the rifle chamber. When the bolt was opened to extract the case, the head tore off leaving a hollow tube jammed solidly into the breech, rendering the rifle useless.

All were feverish with malaria. One man, out of his head, had for two days alternated the coarsest obscenities with Christian hymns. His staggering gait, uncontrolled salivation and mad gestures caused Takeda to suspect that he was dying of brain fever.

He came to the end of his count – fifty-three – two more of the wounded missing. Had they stopped to rest and been unable to get up again? There was nothing he could do about them and Takeda summoned up his last reserves of willpower and staggered on.

His feet hurt so badly he could no longer walk. They were stumps, masses of blisters, blood clots and macerated flesh. He focused on the pain as he had been taught so many years before, and had done so often in the past month, focused it into a ball and squeezed it tighter and tighter until he formed it into a hard nut in the centre of his mind which he could then isolate from his physical being.

The rain stopped after midnight and the cloud broke apart to allow the full moon to shine. There had been a full moon the night the Australians had landed, he remembered. The silvery light skirled the sand and waves lapped softly at the water's edge. Takeda sat half in, half out of the warmish water, allowing the sea to cleanse his legs and body and cool his fever. He had studied the sea with his binoculars, the only piece of equipment he retained other than his pistol. One lens was cracked and mould had grown inside the tube, but the other side was usable. There was not a sign of the *Tenryu*, nor had there been for two hours.

Takeda was not prepared for the wave of disappointment that crushed him. Yet he should have been, he told himself. Nothing had happened as planned from the very beginning. A thousand things could have gone wrong; enemy action that required its presence elsewhere, patrolling enemy aircraft or ships that had delayed or cancelled its attempt. Yet he could not help the despair that clutched at him. His years of training, from primary school through naval college and the years of shipboard duty, no longer had the power to stiffen his resolve.

He touched the waterproof pouch tied to his waist to make certain the two sheets of paper were still there. They had been folded and unfolded so often they were almost in tatters but they were supremely important. On them he had recorded the name of every man who had died or gone missing, and the location of his grave or the place where he had last been seen. He had lost his pencil and the final names were scratched on the tattered sheets with a scorched twig. He ought to add the names of those who had disappeared tonight, he thought. But he hadn't the strength now, nor the means to light a fire. If the list were ever found the names would be checked against the company roster at Sasebo and that would provide the names of the missing.

He would die now. The Emperor could be satisfied that his honour had been upheld. Mariko and his family could be proud...

He must have fallen asleep again, Takeda thought. He had awakened with a start at the grate of wood on sand and pebbles and the sound of voices. He could not understand the words. The Australians have come and it is time to die, he thought. Takeda tried to reach the pistol in his pack but he hadn't the strength.

Strong hands lifted him and he tried to struggle, tried at best to curse. He heard a laugh and a hand brushed his long hair away from his eyes. He felt a canteen rim pressed against his lips and was suddenly conscious of a raging thirst. Then he was placed on a hard, canvas stretcher that jostled when someone pushed against the side. He smelled the rough odour of engine oil and the gentler one of tobacco and suddenly his body raged for a cigarette.

A motor roared and he tried to sit up, to look back. 'My men,' he croaked. 'I cannot leave them.'

The boat rocked as it turned. A face bent close to his but the noise of the engine drowned the words. He was being captured! Takeda struggled to sit up, to reach the side of the boat. He must not be taken alive. The disgrace! If he could only reach the side, he could drown himself in the sea. The rain began again, gentle, persistent. Someone was holding him back. He wasn't a European, or an American, to abandon his duty and surrender or allow himself to be captured. He was an officer, he had taken an oath to the Emperor...

The engine throttled back and all of a sudden the voice speaking so urgently to him was understandable. It was telling him to lie still, that everything was all right. That they had all been taken off the beach and were going out to the *Tenryu*. The voice was Japanese! The ship had come for them and in that instant, Takeda was bereft of the last vestiges of strength. He fell back on the stretcher close to total physical collapse, confused, uncertain, half suspecting a trick and unable to think coherently. Then far away he heard the soft chiming of ships' bells sounding the change of watch. Japanese bells!

It was true, he thought. They had been rescued. Now he could let go of this terrible burden he had carried for so long.

Paris November 1942

The war had brought prosperity to Sturmbannfuehrer Rolle Taubmann. Long gone was the semi-gaunt, perpetually-worried, minor German civil servant, struggling to support a family in Berlin, that he had once known. Torsten Fredriksson remembered very well how they had first met in 1931. Taubmann then had been just another poorly-paid and overworked detective on the force of the Prussian State Police and he a young reporter on his first foreign assignment – the murder of a prominent Swedish businessman robbed and stabbed to death in the Potsdamerstrasse, the most infamous of Berlin's red-light districts.

The Berlin police commissioner had, for some unknown reason, clamped on an unofficial but strict news blackout. Other reporters sent by Swedish papers, old professionals that they were, agreed to share what meagre information they obtained, but he was not yet part of the club and so was left out in the cold.

The thrill of being in a strange country, of dealing with cheating taxi drivers trying to go kilometres out of his way, head waiters inclined to place him at the worst tables, desk clerks who had to be bribed to produce proper rooms and telephone privileges – and information – not usually extended to guests, had given him a taste for foreign reporting and he was determined to make good. He had even concluded a deal the night before with the floor porter for the services of a clean and pretty young lady, his first foreign prostitute.

No, he thought, he had been determined to do whatever was necessary to continue on foreign assignment. Which simply put meant he had to produce results.

The commissioner finally permitted a press briefing three days after the murder. Standing to one side, ignored except when an errand needed doing, was Assistant Inspector Taubmann, shabby in an ill-pressed, ill-fitting suit with worn cuffs and a greyish-white shirt. His face was covered with a thin sheen of perspiration, and an expression of cringing respect.

The briefing was a joke. No real information was provided. It was merely a platform for self-serving oratory by the commissioner. Fredriksson left before it was over and took up watch in a small café across from police headquarters. Finally, at a little after five when the evening traffic and the heat of the summer day were at their worst, Taubmann shuffled out.

The Number 29 Tram which Taubmann caught, with Fredriksson following at the intersection of Friedrikstrasse and Neu Konigstrasse, took him northwest across the city to a run-down residential area bounded by the Gas Anhalt and the Nord Hafen. When Taubmann descended at Boyenstrasse and walked towards a block of cheap flats, Fredriksson knew his instincts were correct. He could even picture the exhausted wife preparing a dinner of boiled cabbage and sausage, her sallow skin flushed with heat. There would be several fretful children . . . He had strolled confidently after the police detective, calling, 'Herr Inspector Taubmann, wait!'

He had introduced himself and interrupted Taubmann's protest. 'Herr Inspector,' again he intentionally addressed him by a superior title, 'I have been most discreet. We have not been followed and whatever you tell me will never be attributed to you.'

Taubmann shook his head and mounted the steps. 'No, I have nothing to say to you. You must speak to the commissioner's office.'

'My paper is willing to pay five hundred Swedish crowns for information about the investigation, Inspector Taubmann. Five hundred Swedish *krona*.'

Taubmann, one hand on the door latch, turned. His surprise quickly gave way to consideration as he calculated the exchange rate and Fredriksson knew he had him. Taubmann glanced up at a third-floor window, then grasped Fredriksson's arm and hurried him along the street and around the corner to a small bar.

Over schnapps, they quickly concluded an agreement. The shambling ordinariness disappeared as the unexpected money galvanised Taubmann's brain to fierce activity. His damp skin glistened with heat and Fredriksson handed over the money with some trepidation. His editor did not like him and had only sent him to Berlin because there was no one else available. Both he and the cashier, a severe little woman rumoured to have once been the mistress of the publisher, had lectured him at length on the necessity for paring his expenses to the bone. Now, here he was, gambling *five hundred krona*! Taubmann described the investigation to date and Fredriksson understood why the police commissioner had wanted it kept quiet.

It seemed that the well-known Swedish businessman had been making the rounds of Berlin's cabarets and other entertainment spots in the company of a high government official from the Chancellor's office and the First Secretary of the Austrian Embassy. There was the question of bribery, of course, but much worse, the three had got drunk and proceeded to beat up the three girls who had accompanied them from a house on Steglitzerstrasse. A group of lorry drivers from Munich had seen the beatings and intervened. In the excitement, the Austrian First Secretary drew a pistol and fired two warning shots. The infuriated drivers then beat up the three men and somehow, during the mêlée, the Swede was stabbed to death. No knife was found among the lorry drivers and the blade used was long and slim, like a stiletto – not a blade a man would carry. The police were inclined to believe the killer was one of the prostitutes seeking revenge, but they had disappeared by the time the police arrived and the two survivors were too drunk to remember who they were or just which address they had come from.

Fredriksson was elated. He thanked Taubmann who then proposed that they stay in touch. 'In my position, I can provide you with a good bit of information,' he winked. 'The political situation in Germany is not good and getting worse, Herr Fredriksson. There are surprising events under development.'

Fredriksson was so happy about the story he would have agreed to anything. Taubmann refused to take his card but memorised his address and telephone number and Fredriksson caught the night train to Hamburg, changed for Lubeck where he raced across the bridge and up the Lagerhaus Quay to catch the last ferry for Stockholm. He sat up all night on the ferry and the train, writing the story on his portable typewriter, and dropped it on the editor's desk an hour before press time. The publisher was so delighted that he was given an instant pay rise and transferred to the international section of the paper.

A month later, Taubmann wrote asking him to come to Berlin. They met in the same dingy bar. Taubmann's new story had a political tinge and concerned strong-arm tactics being used by Adolph Hitler's fascist brownshirts to rig the coming national elections. In spite of his protests to the contrary, Taubmann had seen a document signed by Hitler himself, giving his SA bullies permission to use whatever violence was necessary.

Taubmann admitted that he had become a party member and was a confirmed believer in National Socialism. 'But, Herr Fredriksson, business is business and politics is politics.' This time he demanded one thousand *krona,* five hundred converted to German marks and the balance deposited in a numbered bank account in Switzerland. Clearly Herr Taubmann was learning his business as fast as Fredriksson was learning his.

As late as 1939, Taubmann remained to outward appearances an overworked, underpaid policeman, although at long last promoted to the rank of Inspector. Fredriksson suspected that his secret bank account was swollen not only with his money but that of a number of other benefactors as well. Then in September of that year, Taubmann came to the attention of the *Geheime Staatspolizei*, the Secret State Police – Gestapo. Not for nothing had he spent years working among Berlin's criminal element and he was promoted and put to work rooting out black-market crime. At this he was quite successful, was promoted to Sturmbannfuehrer and in August 1940, was transferred to Paris – the Gestapo's plummiest assignment, under the aegis of Walter Schellenberg's foreign division.

Whenever Fredriksson came to Paris he always made it a point to visit with his 'old friend', Herr Rolle Taubmann at his office in Gestapo headquarters in the Hotel Matignon. Fredriksson insisted on calling Taubmann by his pre-war police title of Inspector, rather than his SS rank of Sturmbannfuehrer, to Taubmann's mild annoyance. He no longer needed to extract money from Fredriksson for bits of news and rumour, preferring instead little presents, such as a kilo of coffee or a pound of beef steak or a few pairs of silk stockings, all still available in neutral Sweden. In exchange, Taubmann was helpful in his search for Jeanette Rodale. Today, however, he was seeing Taubmann on a matter of business, a Ministry of Propaganda-arranged interview regarding resistance activities in France.

Taubmann's well-fed and tailored appearance was due only in part to a share of the black market he had curbed in Paris – a euphemism to conceal the fact that the Gestapo now operated it – as Fredriksson had learned from other sources. Taubmann was now attached to a department concerned with the resettlement of Jews and he must play the old game well, Fredriksson thought, as the inspector stretched a manicured hand across the desk for the telephone receiver.

His sources had given him the details.

The victim, always a rich Jew, would be warned by a Gestapo agent that his family was shortly to be resettled in Poland, or the Government General as the Germans now referred to it. The victim would be told that this was an unofficial warning and that by paying a 'fine', special consideration might be given to his case. The victim, desperate to avoid resettlement, gladly paid the 'fine' which went directly into the pockets of the Gestapo. Finally, the Jew and his family were arrested and they disappeared.

Taubmann was a power in Paris, executing his assignments – and no doubt his victims – with surprising ease and Fredriksson knew that, in addition to the Jewish problem, he also advised the French police on security matters. Fredriksson had no doubt that 'advising' was another euphemism for 'controlling'.

In spite of German propaganda claims to the contrary, the majority of the French had never resigned themselves to either the Vichy or the Occupation Government. Vichy was a standing joke and no one took seriously their claims of pursuing a policy of independence.

One had only to drive about the countryside to see the extent of the

German presence, whether in Vichy or Occupied France. And as well as he stood with the German authorities, even Fredriksson was not allowed, after January 1942, to travel freely in the Channel and Atlantic coastal areas. Strangely enough, there were no restrictions on him regarding the Mediterranean coast. The Riviera had a busy, pre-war flavour until one noticed that the occupants of its beaches were primarily Germans – German soldiers and officials with their wives and girl friends, a sprinkling of French, probably Vichy officials, and quite a few French women who had resigned themselves to the Occupation.

In the cities, the sight of the familiar kepi and cloak of the French policeman was reassuring until one noticed the watchful man in a black leather coat standing nearby. And if the Gestapo agent wasn't to be seen, a German soldier in high jack boots and steel helmet, Mauser rifle or Schmeisser machine pistol slung ready, was.

The other difference that set the German occupiers and Vichy officials apart was, of course, their well-fed appearance which contrasted sharply with the pinched, shivering, threadbare look of the average French citizen. Rumours that the Germans were systematically looting France and other occupied countries abounded. Great quantities of food and goods, it was said, were being shipped east to feed the German civilian and military population. Twice now, while travelling from Berlin to Paris, Fredriksson had seen immense goods trains parked on sidings, wagon doors sealed and heavily-armed troops protecting them. He had already written a column on hunger in France, comparing it to the disastrous famine in Bengal during the past summer, which the British had done so little to alleviate.

Germans like Taubmann had all the food, drink and goods they needed. Frau Taubmann and her brood of five children, five little soldiers so disciplined they seemed unnatural, had grown as sleek and fat as Herr Taubmann in their magnificent flat on the Rue Balang d'Avricourt, near the Arc de Triomphe. Their larders must be overflowing with food as even the Czechoslavakian girl who slaved for them had gained weight.

So, Fredriksson thought, if things were going so well for the Nazis in France, why was Gestapo headquarters in a perpetual state of alarm? His present visit was intended to measure the extent of resistance activities in the Occupied Countries, a subject the propaganda ministry had not been happy about. Still, they had given him carte-blanche, depending, he guessed, on the common sense and self-interest of local German and Vichy officials to conceal the true state of affairs. For the last hour, Taubmann had smugly maintained that resistance activities, despite BBC claims to the contrary, were next to nil. As had similar Gestapo officers in Amsterdam, Oslo, Copenhagen and Brussels. What Taubmann or the Gestapo might suspect, but did not know for certain, was that Fredriksson had already made contact with officials of two underground organisations, Le Gueux in Holland, named after a sixteenth century resistance to Spanish rule, and Milorg in Norway.

'The French are too clever to allow such activities,' Taubmann said. 'They know where their best interests lie. You know the old story, "the Frenchman looks after himself first, his family second and his country sometimes".'

'Are you suggesting that reprisals might be taken for resistance activities?'

Taubmann looked pained at the suggestion. 'Of course not. Are we barbarians? Like the Russians? We prefer to show that cooperation is far more productive than resistance. Oh,' he waved a hand, 'I certainly would be foolish if I said there has been no resistance. But organised? On the scale that British conceit suggests? Of course not!'

He smiled at Fredriksson and sipped his coffee. Fredriksson did likewise and had difficulty restraining a grimace at the bitter chicory taste. With all their power, he thought, even here in Paris the Germans could not obtain real coffee.

'Come, my old friend, the entire world knows of Lidice. Herr Goebbels himself announced that action. And Televaag, in Norway?'

Taubmann smiled comfortably. 'Certainly. And why not? We made no secret of either. Both were reprisals for terrorist actions. The Fuehrer's directive concerning the immediate execution of terrorists agents of any nation, uniformed or not, along with anyone who provides them aid is certainly no secret. Such people are murderers and war criminals and are not protected by the Geneva Convention which the German Armed Forces observe most assiduously. Strict punishment minimises such outrageous crimes.

'This village of Lidice that you mentioned was allowed by the local people to be used as a staging area for a British-controlled terrorist gang, two of whom murdered Reichsprotector Reinhard Heydrich as he was driving peacefully about his business in Prague. Televaag was a reprisal for the murders of two Gestapo agents, also going about their lawful business in Norway. All actions were carried out in strict compliance with the laws of the Reich.'

Fredriksson snorted. 'How are lives saved by such reprisal killings?'

'Very simply, if somewhat cold-bloodedly. Consider. If we ignore provocative terrorist acts by misguided individuals led astray by Allied propaganda, their outrages will escalate. By extracting harsh reprisals for every one of their terror actions, we deprive the terrorist of future support from the local population whom he is misleading. If the terrorist persists in his activities, then the local people will betray him to avoid further punishment. So you see, we are simply acting in the people's own best interests.'

The last was too much for Fredriksson and he switched the

conversation to Jeanette. He hesitated to bring up the subject now but his time in Paris was limited and it was difficult to obtain an appointment with Taubmann these days.

'Ah yes,' Taubmann frowned and sorted through a pile of brown folders on his desk. 'I thought we might get around to that subject.' He smiled, found the correct one and sat back in the leather chair to read it. Fredriksson glanced around, impressed with the new office. The last time he had visited Taubmann he had occupied only a single room. Now he possessed a suite in which luxurious Persian rugs covered the floor, magnificent paintings adorned the walls, paintings he was certain had come from the Louvre and he made a mental note to check the catalogue when he returned to Stockholm.

'My investigating staff has been unable to find a single trace of your friend since she disappeared in July 1940. Strangely enough, she does not seem to have left France, at least in a legal manner.' Taubmann frowned.

Fredriksson spread his hands in an unconscious Gallic gesture. 'But why should she wish to do that? She has no criminal record. She was not politically troublesome? She had no reason to fear the Occupation authorities or the Vichy government?'

Taubmann matched his shrug. 'Who knows what women get up to,' he laughed, very man of the world. 'She was a socialist, you know, and we have records listing large sums of money given to various socialist causes. Perhaps she feared for this reason?'

Fredriksson snorted. 'My dear Rolle, I know Jeanette far too well to believe that. She was typically French when it came to money and she could stretch a sou until it did the work of a franc. The chance of her giving any appreciable amount of money to any political party is as remote as the far side of the moon.' He shook his head. 'As for the socialist convictions, they were crackpot to say the least. She had no ties to any of the mainstream parties.'

'Well, my dear Torsten, I will of course keep looking.' Taubmann hesitated. 'You do realise that not only is such an investigation expensive but that sooner or later my superiors are going to demand an explanation?'

Ah, Fredriksson thought. Here it comes. Aloud, 'I'm not certain what you mean?'

'You came to Paris for a story about the resistance? I suspect to make us look foolish.' He laughed and held up a hand to forestall Fredriksson's protests.

'Please, spare me old friend. I am well aware of your ideas concerning journalistic integrity. After all,' he smiled nastily, 'we've worked together for a long time.' Taubmann closed the folder briskly. 'I will tell you something that perhaps I shouldn't, a breach of Reich security in fact, but I will rely on your discretion. We now have reason to believe that your little Jeanette has disappeared into the Resistance.'

Fredriksson laughed. 'I have to tell you, Rolle, that I find the notion absurd.'

Taubmann shrugged. 'Perhaps her leanings were rather more to the left than you thought. She was a communist, my friend.'

Fredriksson laughed. 'Come Rolle, how can anyone that rich be a communist?'

'Ah, but that is no matter. There are plenty of left-wing groups in France, in all of Europe for that matter, more than willing to flatter a rich, pretty lady with artistic pretensions. Of course, we must not rule out the possibility of kidnapping. During the first days after the surrender, France *was* in turmoil.'

Fredriksson had thought of that possibility and had instituted inquiries from Sweden in the summer of 1940, using friends and contacts in the Swedish Social Democratic and Communist parties who had connections to the international socialist and communist movements. All had produced nothing.

When he told Taubmann this, he nodded. 'I see. But I am afraid your inquiries would have been meaningless. There may be a so-called communist resistance conspiracy, but it is very small, quite isolated and powerless to do more than scatter ill-printed and ungrammatical leaflets about. And the socialists, being socialists and all talk, have evaporated as if they had never existed. There is no support in France for socialism, communism or any other resistance activities.'

Taubmann was aware of Fredriksson's privately-held socialist leanings and delighted in twigging him about them. When the National Socialist Movement first came to power in Germany, Taubmann had been an enthusiastic socialist – until he realised that the socialism in the National Socialist Party was meaningless.

'Rolle, is there something you aren't telling me?'

Taubmann stared at Fredriksson a moment. 'Yes, my friend, I am afraid there is. I now suspect that your Jeanette Rodale is involved with a communist underground organisation. But whether her participation is voluntary or forced, I do not yet know.'

It suddenly occurred to Fredriksson that Taubmann was not referring to the Gestapo, but to himself. Was he up to the same old game he played with the Jews?

'You see, I now know that very large sums of money from her bank accounts in France and Belgium and from certain holdings in other foreign countries were moved through Colonial French banks to London between twenty-fifth May and twelfth June 1940, well before the surrender of France. The sum amounted to fifteen million francs, a great deal of money, I am certain you will agree?'

*

Fredriksson watched from his hotel window as a heavy German lorry full of troops trundled past below. It was raining harder now. A meagre fire burned in the grate and he was grateful for its warmth on this dreary autumn day. Only those foreign visitors the Occupation Government wished to impress were given an extra ration of coal. All others were told they were being allowed to share the common condition – for which they could thank the Allied blockades.

The German lorry passed from view and he turned away from the window. Taubmann had played with him, dropping hints of his efficient investigation up to the moment that he had unleashed his surprise. And the astonishing news that Jeanette had moved fifteen million francs to England had only served to confirm that she was involved in some way with the resistance. Why else; she surely was not in England? Contacts at MI5 counterintelligence had confirmed that. And what had rendered him absolutely speechless was the fact that she had done so in advance of the French surrender, as if she understood what the government had not. Perhaps her political perceptions were not as vague as he thought.

Taubmann. Why had he told him this? Certainly not out of friendship? The very concept was alien to the man. Did he expect a bribe for Jeanette's safe return? But that was ridiculous. Taubmann would certainly know that Fredriksson did not have the kind of money that would make such a risk worthwhile. Did he expect him to persuade Jeanette to reward him? How? The Occupation Government had confiscated everything she possessed.

Or did Taubmann expect him to lead the Gestapo to Jeanette? Ridiculous! After all, he had gone to the Gestapo for help because he had been unable to find any trace of her on his own. All of her friends who might have known her whereabouts had disappeared and on his last two trips to Paris, he had been unable to locate a single one. A sudden thought chilled him.

Had Taubmann suspected Jeanette of resistance activities from the beginning? My God, had Taubmann had him watched all this time, used him to locate her friends and contacts? How else could they have all disappeared without a trace?

He snatched up the phone and started to ask for Taubmann's private number when he realised what he was doing and replaced the handset. 'For God's sake, get hold of yourself,' he muttered.

If Taubmann had indeed used him, the worst thing he could do was to admit knowing. While they might not dare to arrest him, they could make it difficult, if not impossible, for him to continue to work in Occupied Europe and Germany. He went back to the window, lit a cigarette and tried to think.

Paris had always been one of his favourite cities and it made him angry to see her in such a state, like an aging beauty who no longer cared. Several vehicles passed, all German. His suite of rooms was at an angle to the rest of the building, permitting a view of the courtyard below. A large Mercedes Benz stopped and a doorman hurrying to open the rear door was rudely thrust aside by the SS chauffeur. A middle-aged, overweight general stepped out, followed by a pretty, young woman in a fine fur coat. Her hair was piled high in the latest mode with a pillbox hat above. He wished that woman could have been Jeanette; even in company with a Nazi general was preferable to the other forms of entertainment the SS was said to provide. The idea of Jeanette beaten and tortured in a Gestapo cell almost made him physically sick.

Fredriksson knew what had to be done then. It was no use remaining in Paris any longer; if he hadn't been watched before, he would be now. No, the proper approach would be through the British and Free French intelligence services and this time he would not be put off with vague assertions and promises. If Jeanette was involved with the resistance movement, he was certain he could winkle the information from them. He would go back to London as soon as he returned from Germany.

Hamburg January 1943

The snow-covered landscape drifted past the window of the crowded troop train. The flat lands and frozen marshes of the Ukraine were slowly giving way to the rolling lands of Poland.

Major Friedrich Prager had been travelling for seven days by train from his battalion's winter quarters east of Rostov. The thirty days leave that he had been granted, his first since the eastern war began, had already dwindled by twenty-three per cent and he had yet to see Germany's borders.

The ulcer that had made his life miserable since mid-summer was due he knew, despite the doctors pronouncements, to simple exhaustion. My God, he had been continuously in action since 22 June 1941 - eighteen months. He had lost more than ninety per cent of his battalion in the first ten months of the war and of the seven hundred men originally in his reconstituted battalion, less than twenty remained, the rest having been killed, wounded or disappeared during the long summer campaign in the Caucasus.

He had hoped to obtain leave and rest in the spring of 1942 after they were withdrawn from the cauldron at Slavets. Instead, he had been sent to Lodz with the survivors to rebuild the battalion and the work involved was nearly as exhausting, he found, as the long winter spent staving off persistent Russian attacks with little ammunition, less food and no winter gear.

At the staff conference in Kharkov, where the broad outlines of the summer offensive were outlined, he found his battalion had been attached to List's First Panzer Army, Army Group A. While Army Group B drove east towards the Don and the Volga, Army Group A plunged south towards Rostov which occupied a vital position at the confluence of the Don River and the Sea of Azov.

With the battalion at strength once more, they had been hurled into the summer offensive which carried them across the Don basin below Stalingrad, through Poletarskaya, Stavrapol, Pyatigorsk and as far as Ordzhonikdze. They fought one small anti-guerrilla action after another as the Russians retreated and bled them white with hit-and-run-attacks and suicide stands at nameless river crossings and crossroads. When the battalion's casualties were so great he could no longer field an effective fighting force, they were withdrawn for rest and refit. And yet again, Prager was forced to devote flagging energies to fighting the familiar but no less exhausting battle for spare parts, replacements and new tanks.

In addition, there had been all the problems associated with the complete reorganisation of the army which had taken place the previous winter. While increasing its size on paper, every unit from division down to rifle squad was actually decreased. New weapons were supposed to make up the difference in increased firepower, but somehow there were never enough to bring them up to paper strength.

Prager had spent more than enough time in staff positions to recognise that the army needed streamlining, as well as additional divisions. It was a debate that had raged *sotto voce* for years and now it appeared as if the Fuehrer had stepped in with a solution that pleased no one and failed to solve the problem.

When the reorganisation was completed and the summer campaign had actually begun, Prager, among thousands of other officers, discovered that his effectives were nearly a third less than on 22 June 1941!

But in spite of all-too familiar problems with fuel shortages, lack of spares, lack of rations and artillery or aerial support and the fierce resistance by the Russians, he had begun to believe that the Soviet Government really was on the verge of extinction. In the far north, Leningrad was starving to death. In the Moscow region, it appeared that Stalin had thrown every reserve he could scrape up into the line to protect Moscow and abandoned the rest of the country. Nowhere did either Army Group meet serious large-scale resistance.

The Sixth Army crossed the Don and drove south and east, destroying whole Russian armies as they stormed towards the industrial and rail centre of Stalingrad, a city not considered by the General Staff in June as vital to the German offensive. At best, it would serve to secure the northern flank of Army Group B in the Caucasus. Then, unexpectedly, a battle developed and, overnight, the city became a key defence position in the Soviet line – and a major German objective.

Perhaps Stalin and his minions had realised that if Stalingrad fell, there was nothing to stop Army Group B's Fourth Panzer Army from turning south to join Army Group A in the Caucasus. Prager could imagine the panic at the thought of overwhelming German armour loose in the Caspian oilfields.

As late as October, Prager had expected to sit out the winter in comfortable quarters at Rostov, well behind the lines. Instead, in mid-November, the Russians counterattacked at Stalingrad with forces far greater than anyone had anticipated. It was later determined that nine Soviet armies – the Fifth Tank, the Twenty-first, Sixty-fifth, Twenty-fourth, Sixty-sixth, Sixty-second, Sixty-fourth, Fifty-seventh and Fifty-first armies – had smashed through and trapped von Paulus' Sixth and part of the Fourth Panzer Army in the Don bend.

General von Manstein's Army Group Don attempted to relieve the trapped forces but were stopped by two more Russian armies, the Second Guards and the Fifth Shock, and driven back on Christmas Eve. The Fuehrer, against the recommendations of the General Staff, issued strict orders that the Sixth Army was to remain where they stood, not even allowed to withdraw to more defensible positions. He had been assured, so rumour had it, by fat Goering that the Luftwaffe would supply the Sixth Army by air. Prager was not an airman but he knew enough to know that the winter weather alone rendered that promise idiotic. Suitable flying weather between 1 November and 30 April occurred only ten per cent of the time.

Hungarian and Rumanian positions on either end of the Sixth Army line had collapsed at the first Russian blows, but he had heard nothing of the Italian units further north along the Don. Perhaps they had escaped the worst of the Soviet pounding?

The ulcer attack that felled him in December should have sent him to the hospital. But medical facilities were so limited that he received only antacid tablets and spurious advice to avoid tension. When the second bleeding episode occurred a week later, the overworked surgeon recommended he return to Germany for surgery. Prager and his regimental commander had a good laugh. And so he was flabbergasted when the recommendation was approved and his travel documents delivered.

He had not seen Sonja since leaving Hamburg in May 1941, so he did not question the orders and persuaded the regimental commander not to do so either. He knew that he would probably lose his battalion but that seemed of little consequence against seeing Sonja again. They had spent less than two weeks together in nineteen months of marriage.

As the train slowed once more, a collective groan went up. The freezing compartment was crowded, mostly with stretcher cases, but Prager had secured a window seat the first day by virtue of his rank, and kept it. He discovered that not only were there no more than a dozen other officers aboard, but that he was senior to all, including the train commander, an elderly captain called out of retirement, who kept to his compartment suffering with chilblains.

They were plagued with delay after delay and often the train stood for hours in sidings, only to move off again without explanation. Sometimes they were allowed to get down and stretch their legs, but mostly they remained confined to the carriages.

The train was stopping this time in the middle of a vast white desert over which a thin overcast stretched. Several of the men turned to him and, with a sigh, he went to investigate.

One of the dozen of the security detachment aboard, shrouded in thick winter furs and wearing pairs of Russian *valenki* boots, gave him a sketchy salute as he stuck his head out of a window.

'Well, what is it this time?' Prager asked.

'I don't know, Major. The track is clear in both directions.'

Prager heaved the door open and jumped down. He judged the temperature to be thirty degrees below frost as he tramped towards the front of the train. Two winters in Russia had made him adept at such measurements.

A stand of pines, low scrubby things half-buried in snow, edged the tracks a kilometre or so ahead – the source of the engine drivers' nervousness. Prager examined the area carefully as the security detachment stumped up behind him, grumbling about the cold and the uselessness of it all. The sergeant saluted as he passed and Prager watched them trudge along the tracks, ten metres between one man and the next. Prager had watched them before; they knew their business.

They were, as best he could determine, some two hundred kilometres east of the Bug River. He had noticed this morning that they were leaving the frozen marshes of the Pripet behind, at last. The land here was flat and as empty as the moon but, of course, appearances were deceiving. The occasional huts or farms along the railway line had either been burned-out or taken over by security detachments because even here, on the extreme western edge of the Ukraine, almost to the border of the Government General, Soviet partisans were active.

Ahead, west, the snow-covered land ran into the grey afternoon until it blended into sky. A sharp wind sliced his face; a thoroughly inhospitable land in winter, he thought. The engine snorted once and the afternoon was silent again.

He climbed back into the train and made his way to the commander's quarters in the end carriage, shrugging off questions as he went. The captain was a querulous old man, an armoured train officer in the Great War who had been called back to active duty from his job as a stock clerk in a large Nuremberg department store. He was bundled into two heavy sweaters under his tunic, which sported captain's shoulder straps piped in the light blue of Supply and Transport and his legs were wrapped in a down comforter. He barely concealed his dismay when Prager knocked and entered.

'Ah, Major Prager,' he muttered. 'Do come in. Have the security detachment finished their investigation of the woods yet?'

Prager did not mind the question, although the captain should have known the answer, should in fact have been leading the detachment. The carriages, a number of them goods wagons converted for human cargo, were heated only by wood stoves. Because there were eighty men to carriages that had been designed for forty, there was little room to store firewood and they were forced to replenish their supply along the way. Which meant stopping the train to cut wood. But the train commander was more afraid of delays than the cold and resisted all attempts to stop. As a consequence, every carriage but his went unheated during the day and barely warmed at night.

Twice now, Prager had argued the man into allowing him to form a wood cutting detail from the unwounded and this time it took a stubborn fifteen minutes, and the implied threat of an official complaint to the military railway authorities, to persuade him.

As Prager went back through the compartments, he chose fifty ambulatory patients who could handle the work. All agreed enthusiastically; anything to gain release from the everlasting boredom of cards, shivering, desultory conversation and more shivering.

The wind had increased, lowering the apparent temperature that much more, and they hurried down the line, anxious to warm themselves with work. Prager waved to the returning security detachment and signalled them to form a skirmish line in advance of the wood cutters, then smiled at the invective he knew would be turning the air blue.

The wood cutters concentrated on the medium-sized trees and with two men to each, managed to fell, trim and cut up sixty-two trees. It took another hour to carry and load sufficient wood to last them to Berlin, by which time anxiety had driven the train commander outside to jump about and signal continuously for Prager to hurry. Prager pretended not to see him.

That night, he overheard muttered complaints that the cars were too hot.

Dresden, the first major city in Germany, was a madhouse of conflicting official demands, long queues and grim SS troops, whose contempt for the Wehrmacht was quickly made evident. The train drew into the East Station well after midnight and SS troops stormed through the carriages, shouting the men awake and ordering them out onto the platform in loud, rough voices, backed by rifle butts and boots. An SS trooper slammed back the door to Prager's compartment and roared at the eight men to get their asses outside. Startled from a sound sleep, the man had disappeared before Prager realised what was happening. Wearily, he followed the others as they shuffled outside. There were medical orderlies to assist the stretcher cases, but that was the only concession.

The cavernous departure hall was open to the weather and a fierce wind whistled from end to end. Two other trains on adjoining platforms were loading or debarking passengers, mostly civilians who received only a perfunctory check. Around him, exhausted men awakened abruptly, shuffled forward, some dropping out to sit beside the line, unattended.

The stretcher cases were laid in rows along the train, subject to the dirt and steam and worst of all, the cold wind, and the medical orderlies had disappeared. Angered at this callous treatment of wounded and sick soldiers, Prager stalked to the head of the train, pulling his coat off so that his rank was plainly visible. He found the barrier manned by SS *Ordnungspolizei*. No one paid him any attention and so he grabbed the arm of a Dresden policeman standing to one side.

'You,' he ordered. 'There are wounded men on this platform. Make arrangements to take care of them, now!'

The policeman stared at him in surprise, then glanced furtively at an SS officer who turned at Prager's demand.

'What is the trouble, Major?' he asked smoothly. Several SS guards shifted position, one going so far as to lift the muzzle of his machine pistol towards Prager.

'Captain, you will tell that fool that if he moves that weapon once more, I'll shoot him where he stands.'

The soldier looked startled at Prager's threat and the SS police captain waved him back. 'Now then, Major, what is the problem?' This time his voice was not quite so smooth.

'You heard me,' Prager snapped. 'There are wounded men in this queue. They have been on this train for seven days with little heat, less food and practically no rest or medical treatment. All were wounded on the Russian front while the likes of you sit home fat and happy with nothing to do but harass real soldiers. If you insist on continuing this charade, you will arrange to have them taken to a heated room, provide them with food and a place to rest and you will do so now.'

The SS officer laughed at him. 'Get back into line, Major, before I have you arrested.'

'Then do so! It will be interesting to see how you explain the arrest of a convalescent Panzer officer and a holder of the Knight's Cross with Oak Leaves and Swords. I think when the story gets out I can expect to see you at the Eastern Front.'

The SS captain glanced at the angry soldiers, many of whom still carried their service rifles and who, hearing what Prager had said, had begun to push forward. Discretion overruled his arrogance. 'But you see, Major,' he argued smoothly, 'that there are rules to be observed, procedures to be followed.'

Sensing that a face-saving gesture would be far more productive, Prager broke in smoothly. 'Of course there are Captain, and I would be the last to argue with the need for security. Perhaps it was because this train was not designated as an ambulance that you did not realise the condition of its passengers. Surely, neither of us wants a riot? Our superiors would certainly not thank us for that.'

The SS officer relented. 'You are right, Major, I was not aware of the wounded.' He snarled orders to the guards, some to clear the main hall below, others to assist wounded men. One guard was detailed to find the orderlies again and another to procure hot food.

The wounded were helped down the stairs and as Prager followed, he heard the train commander protesting as SS police hurried away with blankets taken from the carriages. The restaurant was opened and a harassed cook wheeled out a trolley with steaming containers of tea and ersatz coffee. The processing went quickly after that and when the last man cleared the barrier, Prager stepped up and slapped his paybook and orders on the desk for inspection.

'I wish to thank you for your courtesy, Captain. You may be certain that I will bring it to the attention of your superiors.'

The SS officer waved the two soldiers checking documents out of earshot. 'I should have you arrested,' he snarled, 'and shot for your interference in a security matter.'

Prager smiled at him. 'Go right ahead, Captain. If you think you can.'

There had been four hours to wait in Berlin before the train left for Hamburg, and so Prager had walked about the city he had known so well before the war and found it changed almost beyond recognition. The area near the Zoo remained relatively untouched, except for the anti-aircraft gun emplacements and the flak towers thrusting up like swollen mediaeval battlements, but the industrial area about the Lehrte Bannhof was becoming a wasteland. Bomb damage, he found, extended in long swathes from the city centre to the suburbs. Berliners continued about their daily business, to all appearances unconcerned, but when he looked closer, he saw the strain.

Berliners were traditionally polite, but no longer. And shops which in the spring of 1941 had been crammed with goods, were now sparsely filled and prices for everything had risen drastically. However, city services – street sweeping, traffic direction, gardening – were still being carried out and the worst of the bomb damage was cleared away quickly.

Rationing may have been introduced, but Prager was outraged to see civilian ski garments on clothing shop racks while troops at the front still struggled for winter clothing even in this second winter of the Russian war.

It had stopped raining by the time the train reached Hamburg. Traces of dirty snow were visible in the gutters or banked against buildings. They halted half a kilometre short and passengers trudged through mud and slush with their baggage to the bombed-out ruin of the Central Station where, once again, Prager endured an SS check hardly more polite than at Dresden.

Unlike the capital, there were no taxis and tram service was sporadic. But in spite of the devastation, the docks were in operation, factories belched fat columns of smoke and people swarmed as busily as ever in this ancient Hanseatic city. Prager waited an hour for a tram. Air-raid sirens went the moment it arrived but people boarded and exited without apparent concern and he followed their example. The tram rattled off fully loaded. The distant rumble of bombs caught them up a few minutes later. On the western side of the city, around Altoona, he decided.

The sky had partly cleared off by the time the tram reached the end of the line on Zoll Strasse. He trudged the path leading to the river walk through the familiar neighbourhood of shops and detached houses, all of which appeared deserted and run-down. But he sensed that he was being watched and wondered if the gossips cloistered behind lace curtains recognised him.

The pounding rumble of exploding bombs could be felt as much as heard, even at this distance. In Russia, there had been rumours that the Americans were experimenting with daylight bombing raids and apparently it was true.

The house was locked and empty. Sonja must be at work he thought, but still the locked door surprised him. It had never been necessary to lock doors or windows in the past. His key had, of course, long since disappeared and he stood in the yard, debating. Perhaps Sonja had left a key with the neighbours. The nearest was two hundred metres away and as he approached the house – which had once belonged to father's old friend, Jacob Meyer – he saw it was tightly shuttered and no one answered his knock.

Prager went back and prised up the kitchen window. Inside, he leaned against the wall for a moment and let the familiar sights and odours of childhood comfort him. Never until he returned did he realise how much this crumbling old house meant to him. For some reason, it remained his anchor, his *home*. He could almost smell his mother's baking, the polishing wax she used and the enamel paint with which she had painted the parlour.

He went through to the parlour and found the stove cold and the ash box empty. Sonja must have cleaned it recently, he thought. Good. It was a job he hated and he grinned at himself. Ten days ago he had been struggling to obtain fuel filters for Mark IV Panzers and ammunition for 7.92 machine guns. Two minutes at home and he was worried about the ash box.

The old house was dingy, yet spotless; even the worn brass spigots in the sink had been polished. But an air of damp and neglect was present and the house was so much smaller, as if it had shrunk, and he laughed at himself. It had also seemed that way on his first holiday from military school.

In the pantry he found a single dish with a strange-looking scrap of meat covered by a damp cloth and a bit of cheese. Prager frowned; was this shopping day? He ate the cheese and ignored the meat. He had eaten worse than that in the past eighteen months but he was home now. He found a bit of tea left in the canister and, disturbed at the scarcity of food, he rummaged through his duffle bag and found the paper and string parcel of real coffee, tea and sugar he had traded for in Russia. The woodbox was empty. In the shed, he found a few sticks of firewood left and swore as he cut more. Hadn't he made arrangements with a neighbour's boy to keep plenty of firewood cut for Sonja? Apparently the boy was not dependable.

He lit a fire in the kitchen stove and while he waited for the kettle to boil, went back out to the shed and found the saw leaning against the wall, rusty and very dull. Still muttering, he sharpened it with a file and cut another arm-load of wood from the pile jumbled against the wall.

Prager drank a cup of tea but it failed to restore him and weary beyond belief, he climbed the narrow stairs to the cold, but welcoming bedroom and lay down on the bed still wearing his greatcoat. He remembered tugging the down quilt over him and nothing more.

A gasp of fear woke him. Prager sat up quickly, fighting the encumbering folds of quilt and clawed at his holster. Sonja screamed when he pointed the pistol at her before he remembered where he was.

'Who . . . who . . . are you?' she quavered.

It took a moment to realise that his face was in shadow and that Sonja could not see him clearly. He leaned forward, laughing.

'It's me, Friedrich. Don't you remember your own husband?"

Darkness had come long ago and Sonja lit a small oil lantern with shaking fingers. As the light flared across his face, her fear gave way to recognition, surprise, relief and joy in turn, and she flew into his arms.

*

Sonja lifted the bucket of boiling water from the stove and poured it into the wash tub, then added two of cold drawn from the spigot. As she started to fill a third, Prager laughed. 'Leave it hot. I haven't had a real bath since August!'

The kitchen, softly lit by a paraffin lamp because the electricity was off, seemed homely, particularly as the stove had warmed the house and banished the smell of damp. Sonja watched in surprise and revulsion while he stripped away clothing which he had not removed in months, not even in the doctor's examination room. His long underwear, what remained of it since it was so full of holes, she kicked away and uttered a small cry of disgust as he peeled the shreds of woollen stockings away from filthy, slug-white feet.

'I'll burn everything,' he told her and tossed his trousers after the underwear.

'Of course you won't,' Sonja protested and scooped them up. 'These need only a good . . .' She screamed. 'Lice!'

Prager laughed. 'Lice are an unavoidable part of war, I'm afraid.' He gathered up the filthy clothing and the can of paraffin and, naked, walked out to the yard. Shivering in the damp cold, he stood on the clothing and poured paraffin onto his head, sluiced it under his armpits and crotch, gasping at the sting of raw spirits on abrased skin. He scrubbed vigorously to kill the lice and hurried back inside.

Sonja went out to throw a match on the clothes and then made him sit beside the stove while she clipped his hair very short, almost to stubble then worked diligently with a comb to remove the stubbornest lice. Giggles overcame her disgust as she trimmed the hair on his chest, beneath his arms and at his crotch and he fended off her teasing hands.

She washed him thoroughly in the hot soapy water and when she finished, the water was muddy.

'A winter's . . . dirt.' He had almost said 'Russian dirt' but caught himself in time.

Sonja used a large towel she had warmed on the stove to dry him and he began to feel human once more. He rubbed the stubble on his head, then at his crotch and caught his reflection in the mirror. 'I look like a hard-boiled egg,' he laughed. 'But a clean hard-boiled egg.' Sonja screamed again as he scooped her up and carried her to the bedroom.

Their lovemaking had not been a success; he had been unable to achieve a strong erection and when he entered her he ejaculated almost at once. Ashamed, he tried to turn away but she clung fiercely, soothing him, stroking his body until he relaxed.

'Later,' she whispered. 'We will try again and it will be better.'

Sonja lay snuggled into his arms. Her body was unbelievably soft and smelled of warmth and comfort. The mixture of paraffin and coarse soap on his own body assaulted his nostrils but when he remarked on it, she only cuddled closer.

'It has been so long since you have been here to hold me that I do not care. Anyway, I am afraid they sell nothing else in the shops now. The last French soaps went in the autumn. I've tried to make a better soap but there isn't enough fat. The children come to collect it twice a week for explosives production.'

Prager was satisfied just to listen as she murmured about the difficulties of civilian life, most of which surprised him. They heard little of this at the front, presumably because of heavy mail censorship.

'The bombers come at odd times, whenever there is good weather. They fly mostly at night but sometimes the Americans bomb by day. The food shortages began last summer but they are not too bad. Clothing is very hard to get, and floor waxes and underwear and . . .'

A steady rain began and he was reminded of the night that Sonja had admitted to being a member of the Soviet communist party. He had been so afraid that it would prevent their marriage and he was glad now that he had persuaded her to conceal the party affiliation in her application for Reich citizenship. No one would ever find out. All such records would surely have been destroyed either by the communists or in the fighting that had raged at her birthplace in Smolensk.

Sonja had drifted off to sleep and he eased out of bed and padded to the window. The night was pitch dark and the blackout had eliminated even the river navigation lights that were usually visible from the house. When he slipped back into bed, Sonja woke and came into his arms, warm and soft with sleep and when he kissed her, she responded fiercely and proved that she was right, that it was much better the second time.

Prager reported the next morning to Tenth Corp Military headquarters and was referred to a military hospital in the northern suburbs. He had a deep distrust of army doctors and facilities and reasoned they would only be worse in wartime. But the memory of the agonising pain in his gut that at times nearly paralysed him forced him to go.

He had put off thinking about surgery for weeks now and so he experienced a sense of unreality as he travelled towards what he saw, rather more dramatically than it warranted, as a fateful rendezvous. The sense of unreality was heightened by the appalling amount of bomb damage that had been done in two and a half years of war. In the dock and industrial areas, it seemed that hardly a block had escaped untouched and his beloved Hamburg reminded him of all too many Russian cities he had seen.

The hospital was jammed beyond capacity with military casualties and beds and cots lined both sides of every hall. A constant din of shouted orders, conversations, cries of sick and wounded, the clatter of crockery and a thousand other sounds reverberated through the corridors and he wondered how in the name of God anyone ever got any rest.

Prager waited all morning in a small room filled to capacity with wounded *Feldgrau*. He identified decorations and awards from every front, but the majority of medals were from the eastern campaign – the *Winterschlacht im Osten* for service the previous winter, or else the green, white and red African ribbon. Most of the African campaigners still wore their lighter-weight khaki desert uniforms. There were also two airmen wearing the insignia of a Luftflotte stationed in Norway and one sailor with a Narvik ribbon.

All but he wore bandages, were on stretchers or hobbled about on crutches, their faces bearing the unmistakable imprint of pain. One man lying on a stretcher seemed barely alive. His bruised face was bloodless and almost as white as the bandages that swathed his head. A young woman sat on the floor beside him, legs drawn under her, one hand resting on the stretcher. Occasionally she wiped his face with a damp cloth, but otherwise sat patiently. Prager had seen far more than his share of badly-wounded men in the past few years and knew that as death approached, the skin took on a waxy sheen. If the wound was bad enough or if he had been given sufficient morphine, a man often drew inward, as if the world no longer held interest for him. He saw these signs in the young soldier; did the young wife know? Women seemed so much more sensitive to the nuances of death, he thought. Was it because they had so much to do with bringing life?

After a while, he began to feel self-conscious about his lack of visible wounds and it was with relief that he was admitted to see a doctor. In the cramped office that contained only a hard chair, a bookcase overflowing with files and a battered desk, he found an elderly gentleman in unpressed tweed trousers, a dingy office coat and old-fashioned pince-nez. His face was lined with fatigue and Prager had the impression he was fighting to remain awake as he read through the army doctor's diagnosis. He had not been asked to undress and the doctor did not bother with an examination.

'Does your stomach bother you now?'

'No sir.'

'When did the pains stop?'

'A few days ago.'

'After you left Russia?'

'Yes sir.'

'Well then, there you are. Your ulcer may or may not be real but the pain is. Induced, I would say, as much by anxiety as by an open sore in your stomach.'

'Anxiety,' he protested in anger. 'You mean fear, don't you?'

The doctor snorted in exasperation. 'Of course I do. And why not. Can you truthfully tell me that you are not afraid when someone shoots at you with a damned great gun? It says here you are a Panzer officer, so unless you are very stupid, riding about in a steel contraption waiting for a shell to strike and broil you alive is bound to induce a certain amount of apprehension, if that word pleases you better.'

'Now . . .' Prager began in confusion.

'We are very busy here,' the doctor said in a weary voice. 'I have no time for bedside manners. There is an entry in your file to the effect that you suffered from exhaustion in 1940.' At Prager's reluctant nod, he slapped the cover closed and pushed it across the desk to him.

'Do you think you are made of iron? The human body is a machine and like any machine can only take a certain amount of abuse. A constant state of fear induces tension which you might liken to over-revving an engine. Prolong the condition and the motor will break down.'

He rubbed his eyes and mumbled, 'The body has many ways of dealing with prolonged fear, or tension, or anxiety; call it what you will. Some slip into a condition which in the last war we referred to as shell-shock. Others into a state bordering on catatonia. Still others break out in skin rashes, become accident-prone or develop nervous tics, or even ulcers. All are warning signs that your body is attempting more than it should. Your body has chosen an ulcer as the way to slow you down. Be thankful; you could be babbling away in a padded cell.'

He was not convinced and it was so obvious the doctor sighed. 'What can be done about my ulcer?' Prager asked.

'Done? We could operate and close the ulcer. Instead, I will order several – I think four or five – months rest and antacid tablet treatment while your body heals itself.' He picked up a pen and began to write.

'But the army doctor said surgery was the only . . .'

The doctor snorted. 'Major Prager, do you seriously think we schedule surgery for a simple ulcer these days? Do you know how many wounded men we have here, how many are being admitted every day; men with serious wounds? Men who will die unless treated immediately?'

'But I can't take four months leave,' he protested. 'I must return to my command. The army doctor did not say anything about convalescent leave . . .'

'You won't die from an ulcer, Major. At least not right away. And if we did operate you would still require two or three months convalescence. If you take my advice, you will go on medical leave for four months and achieve the same end.' The doctor slid the note across to him. 'Here, Major. Take it or not as you wish. But stop wasting my time.'

Somehow, Sonja managed to obtain four days leave from the hospital and they spent every moment together, just walking through the frozen countryside or sitting quietly in the parlour and talking about the years to come after the war. Except for the muted rumble of bombs one afternoon and the occasional drone of engines overhead, the war might not have existed.

They slept late each morning, a novelty for Prager who could not recall the last time he had slept past 0400 hours – four o'clock in the morning, he amended. And they made love often. After his dismal performance the first night, Prager had been afraid it would happen again but Sonja's inherent good humour and common sense, as well as their mutual need for one another, solved the problem neatly enough.

But by the end of the fourth day, the first strains had begun to appear. They had both lived apart too long for one partner to subordinate her or himself to the other's requirements completely and Sonja's insistence that she return to the hospital instead of asking for more leave, angered him.

'Damn it, Sonja, you are only a nurse's aide. Certainly, they can do without you for a few more days!'

Her stiff reply and refusal made him all the angrier because he was honest enough to admit that his request had really come from his own guilt at 'shirking' now that he had decided to accept medical convalescence rather than insist on the operation. A major factor in his decision was the fact that it would allow him more time with Sonja.

Additionally, since his return to Germany he had begun to realise the true proportions of the horror he had endured in Russia these past eighteen months and he did not want to go back, ever. After a few months, it might be possible, he thought, to obtain a posting to France or Belgium, or even Norway, anywhere but Russia. After all, he still had a few contacts in Berlin.

He realised that Sonja's assertion that she was needed at the hospital did not stem from patriotism to her adopted country. She was apolitical and hated war for any reason. Even so, Prager found it difficult to understand that it did not trouble her to nurse the very men who had killed her countrymen. But then, as he had discovered, national divisions seemed to have little meaning for Sonja. She did not bother about the rights and wrongs of a situation; people were hurt and must be tended, nothing else mattered to her. She reacted with the same compassion to the wounded soldier as she would to the victim of a traffic accident.

And it was that perhaps which strained their relationship the most – at least from Prager's standpoint. The war was the central fact of his life. Since September 1939 he had endured and administered horror and he needed someone to relieve him of that burden. Yet, he could not in all sensitivity speak to Sonja of what he had seen in Russia – the agony on the executed Russian girl's face as she choked to death in the hangman's noose, the battered body of the murdered village woman, the civilians massacred in a crossfire between his and Soviet tanks, or the ones he had turned out of the village to be shot down by their own countrymen, or even the murderous partisans he had hanged on his own authority during the past summer in the Caucasus.

These memories were boiling inside him, tearing at him and yet Sonja avoided any mention of the war, anything that might provide him an opening. It was a barrier between them and as it grew, so did his resentment of her.

He walked with her to the tram stop in the half-twilight of dawn. It had snowed lightly during the night and hard frost lay over everything. A cold wind blew along the river and Sonja shivered in her cloth coat. They spoke little during the long walk. Prager smoked a Russian cigarette and fancied that Sonja turned so that the wind brought the odour to her, a reminder of home. This also increased his resentment.

A woman neighbour whom he remembered from childhood joined them at the tram stop. He knew she recognised him but when Sonja wished her a polite good morning, they received only a distant nod. The tram clattered to a stop at that moment, already filled with workers. Sonja kissed him quickly, her lips icy, and Prager promised to meet her in the evening and the tram rattled off.

The sun was breaking through the low overcast on the horizon and the chill seemed less. The fresh snow sparkled as he walked back and unaccountably, he felt alive and full of energy for the first time in months. The grass had frozen to slender spicules during the night and crunched beneath his boots as he crossed the strip of untended park between path and river.

Prager lit a cigarette and watched the river flow past. Its black waters were oily with cold and full of eddies that formed and disappeared in miniature whirlpools along the banks. The river was empty, deserted; the barges that had covered its surface in pre-war days now confined their movements to night, he supposed.

He studied the sky and wondered if American bombers would come today? If it continued to clear off, the weather would be perfect, the kind dreaded at the front – *Stormovik* weather they called it, after the Russian attack planes nicknamed 'Black Death'. The sky was turning from dawn-red to ice-blue and the overcast was breaking up rapidly. He worried about Sonja.

The fire had died and the house was cold but he did not build another. When he had complained about the undependability of the boy he had paid to cut firewood for her, Sonja told him that he had been conscripted the previous winter and had been killed somewhere in the Balkans. Fuel was growing scarce, she told him. Good coal was difficult to obtain and even the poor quality soft French coal was in short supply as the railways were occupied with moving troops and equipment.

They had listened to the radio the night before and Goebbels had boasted of the coming victory at Stalingrad. What a fool the man was if he believed that, Prager had almost said aloud. But Sonja's expressionless face had stopped him.

Goebbels had claimed the war would end in the spring as a great new offensive smashed Moscow and drove the tattered Soviet Armies beyond the Urals. It was the same nonsense they heard at the front. The utter foolishness of that prediction had elicited an involuntary snort from him and Sonja quickly turned the radio off and slipped onto his lap to distract him.

Now that he was alone, he was at a loose end. There was plenty to do, loose shingles to refasten, the shed to be repaired, the plumbing to be cleaned, all things that Sonja did not or could not do and which it was impossible to have done, even if there had been the money. He had been astounded at how prices had inflated, despite rationing and government controls.

Restlessly, he went outside. Perhaps because he lived so much in the open he felt better away from roofs and walls. He found them vaguely claustrophobic and there had been times in the past few nights when he awakened, gasping for breath in the tiny bedroom. Only Sonja's soft warmth calmed him and made it endurable.

The axe was beside the woodpile and he cursed himself for his carelessness in leaving it out. He started to put it away, then decided to cut more wood. He hammered in a new wedge, sharpened it on the grindstone and honed the edge. It and the bucksaw went into his old hand cart and he set out for the patch of forest a kilometre upriver.

Walking along the footpath with the rusted cart bumping behind, he grinned at the picture he must make. He hadn't thought about the cart in years yet it had been his constant companion as a boy. In it he had carried groceries home for his mother, delivered papers in the evening, ran errands and hauled countless cords of wood.

The day had warmed considerably by the time he reached the forest. The sparse snow cover had begun to melt and rivulets of sparkling water streaked the muddy earth. A clean, sharp smell infused the forest and Prager drew it into his lungs. The air held the scent of spring although he knew it was far distant. Pushing into the forest, he saw signs that others had been there before him. Only one man from the surrounding neighbourhood had ever cut wood or hunted here that he could remember. The forest had belonged to a wealthy shipping merchant, a Jew, who employed a gamekeeper to prevent poaching and woodcutting and each spring he hired two or three men to clear brush, weeds, and trees felled by winter storms. Looking at the overgrown paths and the tangled thickets, Prager knew that it had been some while since a gamekeeper had patrolled this forest.

One large oak was badly scarred where some fool had used an axe in a futile attempt to cut it down. How stupid, he thought. Even if they had succeeded, the wood would have been far too green to burn.

A hundred metres on, a tree had fallen across the path. A few of its branches had been trimmed and left in an untidy pile. He examined the tree and decided the wood was dry enough.

Prager shed the old jacket which Sonja had washed to eliminate the smell of mothballs, and began to trim branches away from the trunk. Stiff muscles protested at first but, as the morning warmed, the stiffness worked out and he even began to whistle between his teeth as the axe flashed and bit.

Twice he stopped to hone the edge and admire the growing pile of firewood. The oak, if properly cut and stacked, would provide Sonja with all the firewood she would need for several months. He went back to work, revelling in this simple job so far removed from the business of the battalion with its hundreds of men and vehicles and thousands of headaches and death.

When he had cut a cart load, Prager tied the wood in place and dragged it along the thawing track. The going was easier after he gained the road and by the time he had reached the house and stacked the wood he found it was nearly noon and that he was ravenously hungry.

He ate a woodman's lunch of bread and cheese washed down with cold water in lieu of beer. As he ate, it occurred to him that food supplies were being managed in a strange fashion. Certain staples were plentiful enough, turnips and potatoes – white vegetables. But green cabbage and kale, beans and peas and the like were practically nonexistent in the shops. And of course meat was rationed and scarce, except for the cheapest sausages, which according to Sonja were readily available on the black market.

Sonja looked so thin, so peaked and he knew that she probably was not eating enough. She needed meat, fresh meat if possible with all the vitamins or whatever it was that made fresh meat so nourishing. There had been plenty of deer tracks in the woods. With all the hunters away at war they must be flourishing, even to the point of overgrazing.

Prager went up into the attic and tugged a brass-bound chest into the light from a dormer window. He lifted out the tray that contained his father's military papers, citations and decorations and paused a moment to open the blue box that held the Iron Cross First Class, the South-West Africa medal and the Iron Cross with the white and red ribbon of the city of Hamburg. The old woollen uniforms reeking of camphor followed and he pulled out the wooden crate that Meyer had built for his father's Mauser service rifle all those years ago.

Prager unwrapped the oiled cloth and carried the rifle, an old GEW 98, and a carton of fifteen rounds of ammunition down to the kitchen. The rifle, so much longer than the short Kar 98 he was used to, seemed awkward and unwieldy. Before the kitchen window, he stripped and cleaned the weapon, admiring the fine high polish and the brilliant bluing that signified pre-war manufacture, when craftsmanship was still an important feature even of military weapons. The breech was marked DMW for *Deutches Machinen Fabriken* and dated 1911. His father had carried this rifle in his years on the first eastern front from Tannenberg to Galicia and the stock, although well-oiled, bore the numerous nicks and marks of active service. He pressed five shiny brass cartridges into the magazine, closed the bolt and turned the safety on and went out to the cart and returned to the forest.

Prager spent three more hours cutting and loading wood, until the afternoon ended abruptly and a chill breeze chased lengthening shadows. The sunlight had faded so gradually that he hadn't noticed. Winter returns, he thought.

He decided that he had cut enough wood for one day and worked quickly to pile and tie a load onto the cart and by the time he hauled it over the rough trail to the road, his watch read shortly before 1600 hours – two hours or so until he must meet Sonja's tram.

Prager unlashed the rifle and walked back into the forest to where he had seen the deer tracks leading down to the river that morning. They would have gone there to drink before lying up for the night, he thought. While Prager was not an enthusiastic hunter, as a young boy he had accompanied old Meyer several times and always been rewarded with a share. He laughed quietly at the way his mouth watered at the memory of fresh venison. My God, how long had it been since he had eaten fresh meat?

He found the place where he had seen the tracks, a narrow, almost invisible trace through the trees, and followed it quietly. The track bent to skirt a large oak and he saw the river glimmering fifty metres or so distant through the bare branches.

The quiet forest and the chill air made him remember the heavy-bodied old Jew who moved so silently, a technique learned on the Eastern Front in the First War where he had served with Prager's father. They had rarely failed to get a deer, Meyer and he.

Prager checked the direction of the wind and moved up trail away from his own scent and found a stand of young trees. He broke away several small branches to give himself a field of fire, chambered a round in the old rifle, made certain the safety was on and settled into as comfortable a position as possible.

Dusk drew in quickly and the cold intensified, striking through the metal heel and toe pieces of his boots. He would have to remove them, he thought, as they had done at Slavets last winter. Ah, the Russian cold; this was nothing! Here in Germany, there was food, warmth, a bed, a wife!

A cramp wormed into his stomach as if to remind him and he gasped and bent forward slightly to ease the pain. Acid rose in his throat and he gagged, then leant back and took a deep breath, willing it to subside. He hadn't had an attack in three weeks... why now?

Christ in heaven, the pain was bad and he hadn't thought to bring antacid tablets. He stifled a groan and waited, knowing that eventually it would subside to a bearable ache.

He rested against the tree and mopped icy sweat from his face. The white hot needles had given way to the burning sensation that he knew would persist until he took an antacid tablet. He reached for the bolt handle to lift it and empty the magazine when a sound froze him to absolute stillness. Every sense snapped alert; fear coursed through him and he struggled to master it and turn it to useful purpose as he had done a thousand times before.

A darkish bulk moved and he heard a soft snort and saw a file of animals passing through the trees. He counted eight doe and one stag, well spaced. In the rear a doe hesitated. She raised her head, searching – for him? He sighted the rifle, the pain forgotten and as he did so the stag paused. Prager fixed his eye on the doe and let instinct guide the rifle... it was too dark to see the sights.

Prager heard the stag cough a warning and had the impression that the doe was gathering to leap as he squeezed the trigger.

The muzzle flash dazzled him and the forest exploded into phantom motion as the deer swept off, hooves drumming the hardening surface of the trail. Prager pressed his eyes and turned his head, looking to the side to clear the dazzle as he walked to the fallen deer.

It was an excellent shot; the heavy 7.92 millimetre bullet had struck the animal in the forequarter, penetrating the lungs and probably the heart, killing instantly. Prager knelt beside the warm animal, conscious of a sudden loss as well as a feeling of revulsion. Why, he wondered? It was just an animal with no intellectual consciousness, no emotions beyond those crude ones engendered by instinct and necessary for survival. The doe was certainly less threatened and far less helpless than the thousands, perhaps millions of innocent civilians killed or maimed in the war. God alone knew how many people he had killed. This deer was needed for a practical purpose, to feed his wife. Didn't the religious of the world teach that the earth and all it contained were for man's use?

The twilight was all but gone and the wind was growing colder. Prager shivered and slung the rifle across his back. He used a length of cord to tie the front legs together and decided to gut and clean the animal at home.

For a moment, he was reluctant to touch the soft and still warm body. The tension of life had gone, taking with it the animal's superb muscle tone and leaving only a flabby mass of cooling tissue.

*

Sonja smiled as she descended from the tram and kissed him soundly as it clanged away. With her arm in his, they walked along the river path. She spoke briefly about a young soldier who had been discharged from the hospital today, a special concern of hers as he had been blinded in Norway by a Resistance bomb. Prager told her about the woodcutting and the deer he had shot.

Sonja stooped suddenly. 'You killed a deer... why?'

'For the meat, of course,' he answered in surprise. 'Why else. Meat is so hard to get, you said so yourself, and you really need...'

'But to kill an animal...' she cried. 'Why... there was no need. How could...?' She turned suddenly and hurried down the path. Prager stared after her in astonishment, then followed, wondering if the work at the hospital hadn't become too much for her. Every evening the lines about her mouth seemed harsher, the shadows beneath her eyes deeper.

Sonja was busily preparing a meal of bread and potatoes fried in cottonseed oil when he came in. He hung up his jacket and without a word put dishes and two cups on the table, poured boiling water into the teapot and added the tea. Sonja served the food and they ate in silence. He watched her but she avoided his eyes and afterwards, she washed the dishes, wished him good night and went up to bed. Baffled at her reaction, Prager went out to the shed and lit the lantern.

He looped a rope over a sturdy rafter and hoisted the deer by the hindlegs, then kicked worn straw under the animal. He found and washed a bucket and bled the deer, then gutted the body with a long cut and raked the intestines out and set them aside in a tub filled with water to clean in the morning – a messy, disagreeable job that he did not look forward to, but the less tender portions of meat, ground and mixed with fat, blood and spices would produce sausage. He had considered a deal with a butcher but, as he did not wish to share the meat, decided against it. Nor had he a licence to hunt. He wasn't certain what the hunting laws were these days but trust the Government to complicate it all out of proportion.

He removed the skin, scraped it clean, then scattered salt on the inside, rubbing it in well before rolling it up with the vague idea of selling it to a leather shop. He butchered the deer as he remembered Meyer doing and was disappointed to realise only forty kilos of meat. Storage posed a problem. There wouldn't be time to smoke the meat but then he remembered the old wood bin on the north side of the shed. He wrapped the meat in old cloths and stacked it inside. It would freeze by morning. When he had done all that he could that night, he washed carefully in a bucket of cold water and went inside.

When he slid into bed beside Sonja and touched her shoulder, she shivered at his cold fingers and moved away.

'Sonja?' his voice was puzzled.

She asked without turning, 'Is the rifle registered with the police?'

The question surprised him. 'I don't . . . no, it isn't come to think of it. I had forgotten about it until this morning. Look Sonja, I'm sorry if I've distressed you. But you must eat and I must eat and that is what animals are for. Even when you buy meat from the butcher shop it began as an animal? Now, come here and let me . . .'

'Not tonight, Friedrich, please. I am not feeling well.'

Prager fell back onto his side of the bed and Sonja moved slightly so that they were not touching. He struggled to control his anger. Why ask about the damned rifle of all things? When the Nazis came to power in 1933 almost the first law they passed had decreed that all weapons be registered, but what did that matter? Those laws were for Jews and gypsies. There were thousands of such rifles, and hand guns as well – Lugers and Mausers – all brought back from the First War and lying forgotten in the attics and closets of good Germans everywhere.

Prager made the sausage the following morning and spent the rest of the week cutting more wood than he had planned. But growing frustration and boredom left him with little else to do.

A sudden influx of new wounded from Tunisia and the East meant that Sonja came home exhausted each night. She still refused to discuss the deer and when Prager cooked two steaks the following evening she refused to touch hers. Prager ate both out of spite. Later, feeling guilty at his childishness, he apologised. The deer, he thought, was becoming a barrier between them. Or did it go deeper than that?

The new wounded had a depressing effect on Prager. The magnitude of two growing disasters could no longer be disguised, although Goebbels tried hard to do so on the evening radio broadcasts. His news bulletins and speeches attempted to put the best face on things, but it was clear that German and Italian forces were being squeezed into the Tunisian pocket by the converging British and American armies. There was no talk of withdrawal and the conviction that the Afrika Korps would be abandoned grew in Prager. Why, he wondered were they not allowed to withdraw to Sicily or Corsica?

The Sixth Army was in the same fix, surrounded and cut off and not allowed to break out of the Stalingrad cauldron because it was not politically expedient. Someone might think that the German Army was not invincible after all. But was the abandonment of two badly-needed armies and the deaths or imprisonment of thousands of men sufficient justification for maintaining a myth that political meddling had destroyed?

A letter from a friend spoke by reference to a bar where they had shared a drink once that he was in Mariupol, rather than Rostov, indicating just how far back Army Group A had been forced. The letter made it clear without saying so that there was heavy fighting in the area. But then the

Russians did all their best fighting, and often their only real fighting, in the winter.

He continued to accompany Sonja to and from the tram stop, despite her half-hearted protests that it wasn't necessary. They had entered a period of truce, it seemed. A bit of her previous animation returned and in spite of her obvious exhaustion each evening, she no longer denied him sex. Even so, it seemed to Prager that something was lacking, that her previous enthusiasm had died. But then he wondered if his hadn't as well. What was the old proverb about a wealthy man and a diet of larks' tongues?

Twice more they encountered neighbours at the tram stop and each time they were ignored. One night he broached the subject. 'The neighbours don't talk to you?'

'I am a foreigner, a Russian, and to them the enemy.' Sonja shrugged. 'They leave me alone, and I am polite to them.'

Despite Sonja's lack of concern, it was what he had always feared. She was being treated as his French mother had been, for the moment snubs and ugly glances; later would come outright hostility. Damn these people and their peasant mentalities! If you were even vaguely different, that was enough to make you an outcast.

'Perhaps you should go to Berlin,' he suggested. 'It's a much more cosmopolitan city and no one will care who you are there. I have friends who can help you find a good job and the anti-aircraft defences are better.'

Sonja shook her head. 'Believe me, Friedrich, it would be no different in Berlin. It does not bother me and I have my work at the hospital where they do not care about my nationality. My work proves that I am a good German citizen. None of the neighbours do such work and while they do not like me, they must respect me because I am the wife of an army officer, a major,' she smiled at him, 'serving at the front.'

Prager was learning that it did no good to argue with Sonja. In the time they had been apart, she had matured dramatically. But why should that surprise him, he wondered? Sonja had lived with her parents until she was twenty-three but when he asked her to marry, she had immediately informed her parents that not only would she become his wife, but a German citizen as well. She had then resisted every obstacle and blandishment they could think to employ to change her mind. It was only natural that her independent spirit, caged for so long, should blossom in his absence.

He supposed that part of the problem was his own clumsiness. For too many years he had issued orders or received them and forgotten how to be diplomatic. He sensed that what he saw as the idyllic first days of their marriage had gone forever and he now had to learn to accept her as an individual.

They only needed time to adjust to one another, he told himself. He sensed the depths of her loneliness and, in spite of her brave words, knew that Sonja was frightened in this strange land. Her own home was denied her and she must know that Smolensk had been overrun in the first weeks of the war. She would miss her parents, of course. But did she know about the Commissar Order, Hitler's decree that all members of the Communist Party were to be executed immediately after interrogation? As it was a classified military matter, he doubted it.

Prager wanted to tell her that he understood, that he did not blame her for her reaction to the deer, that he even understood her fears which were evident in the way she had ordered her home against them and walled out anything that reminded her of the war, except her volunteer work in the military hospital, which also reinforced her claim to Reich citizenship. His pay was enough to provide even an occasional luxury. There were no payments on the house to be made, no rent and this far from the city she was safe, even from accidental bombing. With sudden insight, he realised that it was not the killing of the deer that had threatened her, but the existence of the rifle. It reminded her of what he really was, a soldier whose business was killing.

The following afternoon, he walked to Gartenstadt and traded the venison to a butcher for an equal weight of sausage. As he trudged back, the week-long spell of fine weather ended and it began to snow. It was a long walk and he timed it to arrive at the tram stop to meet Sonja. But the tram was thirty minutes late and he was nearly frozen through before it appeared. Sonja explained as they trudged along the invisible path that a bomb had damaged the line that afternoon and the tram passengers had to walk almost a kilometre and wait for another tram car. Other than that, they did not speak much.

If she was curious about the heavy package he carried, she said nothing and in a perverse mood, he did not bring it up. Sonja built a fire in the stove and he unwrapped the meat on the sideboard. The sausage was an unappetising grey colour, with an off-odour and he compared it angrily to the fresh venison and sausage he had traded the surprised butcher.

God knew what was in this mess, or even how old it was. He cut two links for their supper, rewrapped the rest and took it out to the wood bin. He stayed to smoke a cigarette, sheltering in the shed doorway, and watched the pale snow drift past. There must be a full moon above the clouds, he thought as the sky gleamed with a barely discernible opalescence. He knew he was staying outside out of frustration. All his complicated analyses and good intentions of the afternoon had evaporated in the face of her coolness. Again he wondered if she was frightened of, or just tired of him? How could she be so ungrateful for what he had done for her? If he hadn't married her, against his better judgement, she would probably be dead by now. His stomach began to burn and he crushed the cigarette in anger.

The contrast between Sonja and his mother was striking, he thought. His mother had always been attentive to his father's every wish, often anticipating him. He never recalled a harsh word or an argument between them until the pain overwhelmed the old man. But the French were as different from the Russians as night from day, he thought. French women were trained to think of their men before themselves whereas Russian women were taught that they were equal to men and other Bolshevik nonsense.

That evening, while she mended one of his uniforms, he occupied himself with newspapers and a copy of *Signal*, the magazine published for the home front, which he had purchased in Gartenstadt. The paper was filled with war news but Prager wondered which war it was they were reporting.

Great gains were still being made at Stalingrad and in North Africa, or so the magazine said, where the Allied invasion was being pushed into the sea. The U-boat war was going better than ever and England was on the verge of starvation. There were four different pictures of Field Marshall von Paulus in a dress uniform, all taken long before Stalingrad, Prager thought, as in the photo, he wore only the shoulder straps and collar patches of a colonel-general.

Signal was also chock-full of the good life German citizens were enjoying. Dozens of photographs showed the streets of Berlin, Hamburg, Cologne and Munich filled with happy people shopping and relaxing in the sunshine. Not a trace of bomb damage was visible in any photograph and pages were filled with advertisements for Agfa film, Hensoldt prismatic glasses, Voightlander and Olympic cameras and it was all nonsense. When he showed them to Sonja she smiled and nodded but otherwise made no comment.

On Tuesday, the postman delivered a bombshell, a telegram denying his request for sick leave. Travel orders were brought that same afternoon by special messenger for the evening train to Berlin the following day. With the decision now out of his hands, Prager found he was somewhat relieved and made preparations with few regrets. Perhaps, he thought, while in Berlin he could obtain a posting to France, using his ulcer as an excuse.

Dinner was a silent affair that evening. Try as he might, he could not find the words nor the way to broach the subject of their differences and sensed that Sonja could not either. But then, perhaps that was enough for now; to know that the other cared and was concerned. It would be easier by letter.

After dinner, as he smoked a cigarette and watched Sonja wash up the dishes, he discovered that he was actually beginning to look forward to returning to the front. At least there choices were clear cut. It was surprising how in three short weeks, he had grown weary of the sporadic devastation, of the shortages and petty rules and the overweening arrogance of officialdom. He was disgusted with the fact that men fighting and dying at Stalingrad and in North Africa were first being honoured, then abandoned with stirring admonitions to fight to the last man. Civilian life had grown too complicated to suit him.

He missed his command and the comradeship of men who believed in loyalty, honour and duty as he did. He wanted the straightforward, uncomplicated life of a soldier again. Strange, he thought. I had to leave hell to discover how much I miss it.

Sonja arranged to take the afternoon off and Prager met her at the hospital after leaving his duffle bag at the railway station. They walked along the familiar streets, ignoring the bomb damage. The sun was bright on the Alster Bassin but the wind ice-cold, as it had been that day two years before when they had met her parents here to confirm that they were to be married. Both were conscious of the changes since.

Little bomb damage was visible from the lakeside, and watching the people enjoying the winter sunshine, Prager experienced a feeling identical to that of a few days past when he had gone out to cut wood. Then, too, everything had seemed too normal for a great war to be in progress. Only the plethora of military uniforms gave it away; and the pretty girls who had once worn the latest fashions to offices now wore dungarees and turbans to factories and shipyards.

Prager had selected the Atlantic Hotel where Joachim Brenner had given them breakfast the morning of their wedding. The Ander Alster had been hit by bombs recently and a battery of eighty-eight millimetre anti-aircraft guns squatted directly across from the hotel in place of a razed building. Prager's rank, wound badge and Knight's Cross finally gained them a table in the back after a thirty-minute wait. The restaurant was thronged with well-dressed businessmen accompanied by pretty young women, SS officers and party-functionaries in uniforms adorned with a bewildering array of badges and ranks.

Prager's was the only army uniform present. Not far away, four SS officers were drinking coffee and smoking, deliberately holding a table while the queue at the maître d's desk grew longer and his expression more harried. One SS officer noticed Prager looking at them and raised an eyebrow, then leaned forward to say something to the others.

Five minutes later, when they stood to leave, two of the SS officers pushed through the crush and stopped beside his table. Prager had already noticed that none wore higher rank than Haupsturmbannfuehrer, equivalent to Captain. It was cold in the restaurant and his coat across his shoulders concealed his own rank, but not the Knight's Cross.

The two bowed to Sonja and smiled at Prager. 'Home on leave? Perhaps you would be good enough to show us your authorisation,' one said with a supercilious grin. Prager finished lighting his cigarette before looking up. Both wore the insignia of the RSHA, the security service of the SS and, theoretically, were within their rights to demand his identification papers and orders. But SS and the Wehrmacht had long ago agreed to extend normal courtesies of military usage to each other and by those standards the demand of two junior officers, clearly not under specific orders, was boorish. Especially so when one of them leaned down to whisper something to Sonja and she ducked away from his alcoholic breath.

Prager stood quickly, clutched the man's shoulder and dragged him upright. 'I see that your manners are those of a pig, Lieutenant,' Prager said in a tight voice. 'Apparently the SS has given up the attempt to teach civilised behaviour to its recruits, so an apology from you would be meaningless.' He glanced at the other two SS officers who had started across the room. 'Which of you is senior?' he barked. Those diners who hadn't seen what was happening now turned to look.

One nodded. 'Captain Emile Grob at your service.' Instead of coming to attention, Grob clasped his hands behind his back, spread his feet and stared at Prager's throat where the Knight's Cross hung, with a bored air.

'Stand to attention, Captain Grob,' Prager's voice whipped, 'when you address a superior officer.' He slipped his coat off.

Four pairs of heels clicked when they saw the major's insignia. 'Captain Grob, I find your demeanour and that of your companions to be an insult to my wife, to myself and to the German army. Your behaviour is that of spoiled children, not officers of the Third Reich. You sir, will immediately conduct these two men to your headquarters where all of you will report your behaviour to the officer-of-the-day. Proceed!'

Grob's face had stiffened at the public rebuke and now went red as Prager turned away abruptly and sat down. Grob took a deep breath, seemed about to say something but saluted instead. Prager made him hold the salute before returning it and waved them away. There were at least a half-dozen other SS officers of higher rank in the room but none intervened. An embarrassed silence settled and it was several minutes before the buzz of conversation returned to normal levels.

'So it is true,' Sonja whispered in a shaky voice. 'There is no love lost between the army and the SS?'

Prager snorted. 'None! Johnny-come-lately political upstarts who cause us more problems in the occupied territories than they are worth. Once, I saw . . .' He stopped, abruptly.

The luncheon was not a success. In addition to the strain introduced by the ill-mannered SS officers, the food was of poor quality and the prices exorbitant. Afterwards, as they walked to the railway station, Sonja pressed his arm in hers. 'Friedrich, please, what were you going to say about the SS?'

He glanced at her upturned face and read accurately the mixture of fear and apprehension. Had she heard rumours of what was happening to Russia? he wondered.

'A boring story, my dearest. A fight provoked by SS guards and some of the men of my battalion,' he lied. How could he tell her about the SS execution squad he had seen marching Russian civilians into a wood outside Olets one summer's day. He knew that Jews were major victims of such 'special actions', but all communists and captured partisans were also killed – and anyone else who incurred the displeasure of the SS. More than once he had heard it said that the SS intended to completely eradicate all Jews and Slavs, but he doubted that such rumours were true. For one thing, it would be counterproductive to the terrible need for labour. Most such *special actions* that he was aware of were isolated excesses.

Sonja nodded and turned away and Prager felt the pressure on his arm slacken. Before he could assure her that there was nothing to worry about, they turned a corner and saw barricades across the street and a long line of traffic and pedestrians shivering in the bitter wind. Uniformed Hamburg city policemen marshalled the line but several men in black-leather overcoats and civilian clothing checked all documents.

They had no choice but to join the shuffling queue. Prager pulled Sonja against him to shield her from the wind but she resisted and he let her go with a silent curse. Be stubborn and freeze, he thought.

When they reached the head of the line, a middle-aged man with a bad complexion and worse teeth smiled as he accepted their documents. 'I apologise for the inconvenience, Major and madame.'

'What is the trouble?' Prager demanded but the man shrugged. 'A report of smugglers. A moment's inconvenience, sir.'

Prager was inclined to tell him to go to hell and perhaps if Sonja had not been with him, he might have. Instead, 'Your authority, please.'

The man smiled again and removed a small leather folder from his overcoat pocket. A Gestapo identification tag was displayed below a card with the man's photograph.

'I see.' He nodded and the man smiled again. As a Gestapo agent, he needed no other authority.

'I am sorry for the need to make a veteran of the Eastern Front and his beautiful companion,' he bowed slightly to Sonja, 'stand about in the cold.' He studied Prager's papers. 'Home on leave?' he inquired.

'Yes.'

'Ah, you are very lucky. My two sons are away in service. You were perhaps at Stalingrad?'

Prager's lips drew thin. 'You know very well that such information is classified.'

'Of course, how stupid of me.' He handed back the papers and opened Sonja's and his smile faded. 'You are a foreigner?' he inquired in a harsh voice. 'A citizen of the Soviet Union?'

Prager snapped, 'The lady is a German citizen, by marriage, and my wife.'

'I see,' he answered in a voice as cold as the wind and snapped the booklet shut. 'Your papers are in order, Frau Prager. You may go.' He motioned to a policeman and the barrier was shifted. Prager urged Sonja forward, fuming. 'What were they really looking for?' he muttered, half to himself.

'Jews, black marketeers, deserters, what have you,' Sonja answered.

'Jews? Still? I wouldn't have thought there were any left in Germany.'

'There may not be,' Sonja replied. 'But they still provide the excuse for such searches.'

The sections of the Main Station not roped off because of bomb damage were jammed and the waiting hall was a madhouse. Prager retrieved his duffle bag, managed to get two small paper cups of tea from the canteen and found Sonja again in the crush. They drank the lukewarm liquid that was tea in colour only. It was impossible to understand the echoing tannoy system in the damaged hall filled with the shouts, cries, screams, sobs and laughter of a thousand people and the clash and bang of steam engines and the screech of whistles, but Prager was not worried. He had twenty minutes to boarding time.

Sonja took his hand, surprising him. She held it, saying nothing and, wisely, he kept his mouth shut. He shifted position to ease a cramped leg and saw that her cheeks were wet with tears.

Of a sudden, all the animosity he had felt for her in the past weeks evaporated. He cursed himself for an ass and pulled her closer. 'Sonja, you must not worry about the Gestapo. I'm a major in the army and you are my wife, a German citizen. The Gestapo cannot touch you... why...?'

She shook her head and pressed her face against his shoulder. When she finally spoke, he had trouble hearing her in the din. 'I am not afraid for myself. I am afraid for you. I am so afraid that something will happen to you and I will never know. I see the men who have come back with missing limbs, blinded, insane. Every day I am afraid to go into the wards for fear that I might find you there. Yet I go in the hope that I *will* see you because even that is preferable to knowing you are dead, or worse, not knowing. Russia is so big and so many things can happen that I would...'

Prager held her tightly and cursed himself for his cold, unbending attitude towards her in the past week. How could he have been so stupid?

That was the reason she had taken such a terrible job, one she must loathe with all her being. My God, he marvelled, how much love she has for me!

'There is no need to worry on that account,' he said softly and kissed her hair. 'I am the most careful soldier in the world. If there is shooting anywhere within twenty kilometres, I refuse to stick my head outside my tank. The Turtle, they call me.'

Sonja shook her head violently. 'Do not joke about it. I know what can happen. I see it all the time. Do you know how often soldiers have said to me, "I never thought it would happen to me . . . I just knew it wouldn't . . . I was always so careful"? Do you know how many times I have seen those same soldiers die? Sometimes even as I held them and pretended to be a mother or a wife or a girl-friend?'

Prager turned her so that he could hold her face between his hands and kissed her cold lips. 'I will not pretend with you, Sonja, It is bad. But you listen to me now. I love you very deeply. And as long as I know you are waiting here for me, then I am coming back. Not wounded, or in a box. But on my own two feet. The war cannot last forever. We have underestimated the enemy twice now. We shall not do so again. Stalin is at the end of his reserves. Losses are far more terrible for him than they are for us. He has lost entire armies – dozens of them and we have lost only one.'

Sonja shook her head. 'Two, Friedrich, North Africa is lost. The soldiers tell me such things. The Afrika Korps is finished. Only a few patients have come from there in the past few days.'

Prager nodded as Sonja confirmed what he had suspected. 'But that makes no difference to me,' he said slowly. 'If you are here, I will always come back.'

Sonja held him tightly and they drew comfort from one another until it was time to board the train.

The return journey was by far the worst. The carriages were crowded to capacity as far as Berlin where more orders awaited, redirecting him to Kiev immediately. At Dresden, the SS took over twelve of the train's eighteen carriages and commandeered most of the rations and fuel. Twice, Prager tried to do something about it but an army general bound for Kiev had boarded in Berlin and he was frightened to death of the SS and so forbade anyone to interfere.

Prager could not understand this new-found arrogance. Until his medical leave, all his dealings had been with the Waffen SS, the fighting units of the Nazi Party. They too had displayed an unbearable superiority towards regular military but they were at least soldiers themselves. These others were not; most were simply greedy, intolerable, party hacks, useless for anything but garrison and police duties behind the lines.

Something was happening to Germany and the Army. Somehow,

somewhere, both had lost a measure of self-confidence at Stalingrad. The Nazi Party had always been careful to see that the mass of the German people were behind them. Now they acted as if their position were unassailable and, judging from the frightened reaction of the army general, a man decorated and promoted twice since 1940, perhaps they were.

The train rattled across the Czech Protectorate and into the Ukraine and he saw SS uniforms everywhere, many with unfamiliar unit markings. At a stop in the city of Kovel, he overheard two uniformed SS men talking in what sounded suspiciously like Ukrainian. When he spoke to them in German, they shrugged and an SS officer hurried up demanding to know what he wanted. Prager eyed him coldly until he saluted. The officer told him the two SS men were Ukrainians, part of a division of SS troops raised in the Occupied Territories for police work. Prager laughed in disbelief and the officer went white with anger and embarrassment.

'I was under the impression that the SS maintained strict Aryan racial standards?' Prager asked innocently. 'Yet now the *untermenschen*, the Slavs whom you once derided as a mongrel race, are let into your ranks.'

The SS officer was so furious that he could only salute and storm away.

As the train was to be delayed for at least two days, Prager walked through the marshalling yards and obtained a ride into the city in an army lorry. The young Labour Corps driver was close-mouthed about conditions in the city, as he properly should have been, and Prager lapsed into silence and watched the traffic shuttling along the snow-banked road. Other than the number of troops and tanks parked at intersections, there was little evidence of war. Kovel looked like any other Central European city in winter, except that its buildings and people were shabbier.

He obtained a room at the Savoy Hotel, a nineteenth-century structure used as a transit army officers' hostel. Strange, he thought as he followed an orderly to his room, that the Bolsheviks hadn't changed that name which was a tribute to British imperial capitalism.

At dinner in the main saloon, he found himself seated with a Luftwaffe lieutenant colonel wearing the red collar tabs of an anti-aircraft division, a major from the quartermaster's department, a cavalry Rittmeister and an army doctor, a mild little man uncomfortable in uniform who, he confessed, had been a gynaecologist in civilian life. This last occasioned a great number of crude jokes at his expense, which the doctor endured in good part.

The cavalry captain told them in mournful tones that after two years of faithful service at the front, his cavalry unit was losing its horses. 'They claim we are no longer efficient. So I have been reassigned to something called a tank destroyer unit and they are sending me back to Germany for training. I don't want to lose my horses and I don't want to go back to Germany.'

'Why ever not?' the doctor demanded.

'Well, it's like this. Before the war, I was seeing this girl. Her name was Lotte and she was a very generous girl, if you take my meaning. On my last night, in a fit of stupidity, I promised to marry her when I next came home. My mother, whose mouth is as big as a barn door, told Lotte that I was coming and they have already arranged the wedding!' He shook his head, downed his vodka and pounded the table for more.

'Ever since the letter from my mother, I've prayed for the train to be attacked by partisans. Being dead is far preferable to being married to Lotte.' He clapped a hand to his forehead and moaned. 'Three and four times a night was fine for a fling, but she's insatiable. She will kill me the first week!'

They all got royally drunk at the captain's invitation, to help take his mind off his terrible fate. In the morning when they woke on the bar floor, they found that he had gone, and left them with the mess bill.

In Kiev, four days later, Prager was re-examined by a medical commission who found him fit for duty in spite of his ulcer. He was given a large supply of antacid tablets and the following day found himself assigned to Army Group Centre and the Ninth Panzer Army. He was given command of a regiment to be assembled from units shifted east from France and the Low Countries. The mood in Kiev was grim and it was here that he discovered for the first time just how great was the disaster at Stalingrad ... the *Rattenkrieg*, War of the Rats – and in the Caucasus.

At Stalingrad, the entire Sixth Army had been lost with 166,000 killed and another 120,000 taken prisoner. Prager found it difficult to imagine how the General Staff could possibly have allowed it to happen. The propaganda people told them over and over again that the Sixth Army had sacrificed itself so that the First Panzer and the Seventeenth Armies could escape from the Caucasus; as if saying it often enough would make it so.

But Prager had been in the Caucasus with the First Panzer Army and knew better. If they had been allowed to stand fast in late November, they could have held their positions against Budënny's forces indefinitely. Instead, the orders had come one after the other demanding they advance, advance, advance, regardless of lengthening supply lines and weakening flanks.

That afternoon, a rare, fine winter day in the Ukraine, Prager strolled down Kreshchatik Boulevard to a park bordering the Dnieper. The sun shone warm for a few hours and the walks were slushy underfoot. The chestnut trees had been stripped bare of branches as high as a man could reach – gathered for firewood, he thought – and many had already been cut down. Concrete pillars that had once held iron railings or chains long since taken for the war effort – Soviet or German – stood in forlorn isolation.

The river was a level plain of snow-covered ice where children played hockey and their excited shouts sounded almost normal. Three aircraft in formation passed across the city, Me110s he noted absently as the racketing of their desynchronised engines faded in the distance.

Already, he missed Sonja. He had finally stopped flogging himself for treating her as he had. After all, he excused himself, he was a soldier. What did he know about love?

He had seen and experienced far too much since September 1939, and perhaps that was the difference between the front-line soldier and all those who remained at home. The stay-behinds could not imagine the horrors endured while the front-line soldier could not imagine that everyone was not affected the same way as he.

And those differences were accelerated by the way in which Germany had changed in the past two years. She was becoming a nation of party hacks, shirkers and chisellers like the butcher who had hinted that he would report him to the authorities for shooting a deer without a permit unless he agreed to a lower price; or the flint-hearted neighbours who treated Sonja like dirt because she was different; or the impatient tram conductor who should have been at the front; or the supercilious maître d' in the restaurant whose connections kept him out of the army.

Far too many complained about a bit of bombing when they had shelters to run to, while the front-line soldier had only a hole scraped from the frozen ground – if he was lucky. Civilians complained of margarine, coffee and meat rationing while, to the front-line soldiers, these were the greatest luxuries.

Had they, the good Germans, filled the armed forces and left the trash behind – the bully boys in the SS, the hacks in the party and the shirkers in the civil service – while they fought and died on the frontiers to protect the nation? How many other times in history had that happened? Hadn't Persia, Greece, Rome, Byzantium and even Tsarist Russia also exiled those of ability to the frontiers while the trash took over behind?

Prager paused on the arching bridge and stared at the snow-laden ice. Perhaps such trash were in for a surprise this time. Russia was a huge land, a place of opportunity, an undeveloped country like Africa at the beginning of the nineteenth century.

Oil in the Caucasus, wheat in the Ukraine, minerals in the Urals, the potential of the steppe barely realised and God alone knew what in Siberia. Prager was beginning to suspect that he would not return to Germany when the war ended. Let the party and the SS run the fatherland. Here on the new frontier, an entire generation of the best and fittest would grow to maturity. The frontier, like all frontiers would absorb the talent of the parent nation and give back a stronger, more intelligent and determined offspring who would discard the trash.

He wanted to be a part of that creation, he thought, and Sonja would as well. She could return to her homeland as the wife of a victor and a pioneer, leaving behind the sneers of the ignorant.

Perhaps the defeat at Stalingrad and the setback in the Caucasus would wake the General Staff and stiffen their backbones sufficiently to stand up to the politicians. Surely even the most fanatical must see the harm that political interference in military matters had done? Whenever the Army was not allowed to conduct its affairs according to sound military doctrine, Ivan beat them soundly.

For a moment, sight had been lost of the German army's main strength – swift, concentrated movement. But Prager's essential faith in the army remained. Already, it was gathering itself for a war of manoeuvre in the spring. The slavish Russians had expended their last reserves at Stalingrad and in the Caucasus. The time had come to smash her once and for all. And it was the front-line soldier who would do it, not whining civilians and fault-finding party hacks, or an arrogant and useless SS.

Perhaps there was a fellowship of soldiers after all, if not one that transcended national boundaries. He had felt the tug at home in Hamburg and could feel it again beside the Dnieper River and knew it was strengthened by shared hardship, horror, triumph and defeat. It was not something that the Labour Service lorry driver, or an SS officer or even the staff general on the train could experience. But he did share it with that German soldier limping towards him, the one with the bandaged face and his arm in a sling.

In his mood of euphoric optimism, Prager saluted him first. The startled boy flubbed his own in return.

Epilogue

Macedonia March 1948

Torsten Fredriksson climbed after the grizzled major. The terrain was steep and the rocks sharp-edged near the Yugoslav border. It was raining, more drizzle than rain, but cold and damnably uncomfortable. He had torn a hole in the plastic waterproof he had bought in London the week before and his parka and trousers were wet through. He longed to stop and rest and brew a hot cup of tea, but the major was in a hurry and besides, they hadn't any language in common.

They clawed up the last few metres to stand on a knife-edged ridge. The mountain fell away to a valley floor, through which a thread of a river ran, less than two kilometres wide before rising again towards another line of hills that marked the Yugoslav border. He had been here once before – in almost this very spot, in fact – with a group of Greek communist partisans, in 1944. Then the communists had been the allies of this angry, middle-aged major whom, they had told him, had fought with the British after Crete all across the Western desert and halfway up the Italian Peninsula before returning to his own country. Now his fellow countrymen, those who professed to be communists, were his mortal enemies and he wanted only to kill as many of them as possible before they retreated into the sanctuary of Yugoslavia.

I do not really need to be here, Fredriksson told himself. I could just as well have written this piece at home in Sweden. I remember it all too damned well; the grey skies that are either raining or snowing, the harsh lunar-like landscape to which generation after generation has clung with such murderous consistency for five thousand years. I remember the hatred in every eye for the stranger, the feuds that refuse to end and change, only the face of the enemy from Persian to Mesopotamian to Roman to Turk to communist.

But I had to come, Fredriksson told himself, in spite of, and because of, the manuscript of the second volume on his desk at home. World War II could wait. It had had its day and done its damage and now its aftershocks had to be dealt with. And there was no doubt in his mind that this present civil war in Greece was one of those aftershocks. Like so many other civil wars, insurrections and rebellions currently in progress, it was the direct result of the Nazi attack on the Soviet Union only six short years ago – six years that might have been a century, so profoundly had the world altered.

A battery of artillery near the river was pounding the ridge across the valley and Fredriksson could see the shell bursts in the dying afternoon light. He tapped the major on the shoulder and pointed. 'Yugoslavia?'

The major examined the ridge opposite through binoculars and his chapped lips split in a brief grin as he nodded. Fredriksson shook his head. The Nazi legacy – national boundaries had become meaningless; only the strongest guns counted.

Surprisingly, the major indicated that they would rest here. Fredriksson sat down with gratitude and rummaged in his knapsack for the primus stove. When the water was boiling properly, Fredriksson poured enough tea for two into his canteen cup and added the water. The major unwrapped a square of wax paper and offered pieces of strong fetta cheese and flinty bread. Since they could not talk to one another, they ate in companionable silence.

The methodical thump of the guns – British 105s, he thought – drifted up to them. He watched for a flash and began to count. He got to thirty-one before he heard the sound; 3,100 metres, three kilometres plus to go before they could dry out at battalion headquarters.

At times like this, he thought, it seemed the war had never ended. In 1944, it had been the Nazis who had chased the Greek partisan band he had been with into Yugoslavia, for shelter with Tito's partisans – no time for tea then. Today, it was Greek chasing Greek. In 1944, it had seemed worthwhile to risk his life for such a story. Now it only seemed foolish.

But there was more to it than that, or so he kept telling himself. The world was being reshaped. The colonial empires were dying in India, Southeast Asia and in Africa. In Europe and the Middle East, the old values like the old regimes were collapsing. The communists were leading the vanguard and some said they were only continuing what they had begun in 1941, freeing enslaved people. Others claimed they were merely substituting a new form of slavery for old. His own faith in the essential goodness and perfectability of human nature had been so shaken by the events of 1939–1945 that at times he felt as foolish as Voltaire's Candide when he tried to hang on to the last vestiges of his liberal values.

The second volume of his chronicle of World War II and the seven men he had known at its outset were the only things that seemed worthwhile to him any longer, and it demanded more and more of his attention so that he resented even the least interruption by the demands of his world-wide syndicated column, *From Across the World.*

The major stood up and motioned to him. Reluctantly, Fredriksson stowed away the primus stove, emptied his cup and followed him down the stony path towards the valley floor. There was another war to be reported, and another after that and God alone knew how many more stretching into the limitless future.